BITTEN POINT

4 Book Bundle

EVE LANGLAIS

eBook ISBN: 978-1-77384-005-5

Print ISBN: 978-1-77384-022-2

Produced in Canada

Published by Eve Langlais

http://www.EveLanglais.com

Croc's Return

Welcome to Bitten Point, where the swamp doesn't just keep its secrets, it sometimes eats them.

Take one deadly bite and, bam, a man's life is changed forever, or so Caleb discovers when a loss of control leads to him joining the military and leaving everything behind. Now that he's back, making amends is harder than expected.

His ex-girlfriend, Renny, is not interested in excuses. Caleb might have returned, but her plan is to keep him at arm's length. Only she can't. Her son deserves a chance to get to know his father, but that doesn't mean Renny is letting Caleb back into her heart. Now if only her heart would cooperate.

Things get dangerous when a mysterious being starts stalking the residents of Bitten Point. When the monster threatens his son, Caleb knows it's time to unleash his dark inner beast so he can snap at danger, and take a bite out of life.

Chapter 1

I CAN'T BELIEVE the dog gets the front seat in the truck.

Indeed, the big-eyed canine—who barely consisted of a mouthful at five and a half pounds—that his brother called Princess, held the seat of pride *inside* the truck while Caleb merited the box at the back.

Forget logic. Caleb had tried to argue at the train station where his brother awaited him, leaning against the blue body of his Ford pickup truck.

"Hey, Connie," Caleb had said to his bro upon spotting him, which was the first thing he did wrong, closely followed by his second, "Packed on a few pounds while I was gone, I see."

It wasn't just women who took offense at weight jokes.

By the time Caleb stated, "Can you get this rat out of the front seat?" things had evolved from awkward to someone was gonna get hurt.

The frost in his brother's expression would have made a more easily intimidated man shiver.

"That is not a rat. That is a long-haired Chihuahua," his brother informed him coldly. "And my name, since you seem to have forgotten, is Constantine."

Caleb might have argued about it a bit more, but given he was trying to make amends with his family—and this particular branch of his family had grown quite a bit since he'd left—he didn't push the point. He'd wait until later, after a few beers.

Or we could set the tone for how things are gonna go right now. Caleb's time in the military had given him a boldness that resulted in more than a few scraps—his version of stress relief. "That is not a dog." A comment that was met with a low growl and a lifted lip from the fresh appetizer in the front seat.

A dog? Snort. *More like a snack.* The snap of a hungry jaw jarred Caleb, and he pushed back against the dark thought.

No eating Connie's pet. There were some lines even he wouldn't cross. Antagonizing his brother wasn't one of them. "Dude, whatever that funny looking hairball is, it's in the way."

"No, *she* is not. That's Princess's spot." Constantine reached in and stroked the tiny creature.

"Princess?" His level of incredulity rose a few more notches and teetered in the I-must-be hallucinating zone. *And yet I didn't snack on any mushrooms.*

"It's Princess Leia to be exact."

Bigger snort.

His brother shot him a look before turning back to his rat, crooning, "Ignore him, Princess. He doesn't understand your cuteness."

Cute? Had his brother been punched in the face one too many times? "Are you feeling all right?"

"Fine. Why?" His brother glanced his way while still continuing to pet the hairy rat.

"I have to ask because I don't understand why a grown man would want to own something that wouldn't even double as a proper snack."

"Eat my dog and I will skin you and make you into boots." Judging by the hard flint in his brother's eyes, he meant it.

Caleb almost hugged him in thanks. Nice to see some things

hadn't changed, such as their love of bodily-harm threats. Question was, would Constantine follow through?

Caleb should have let the matter go at that point. After all, loving a poor excuse for a dog wasn't the worse thing his brother could have done during Caleb's absence—*at least he didn't fuck up like I did*—but the fact that Caleb ranked lower than a pet stung. "It's a dog. Shouldn't it ride in the back?"

"No. And unless you'd rather walk, I'd suggest you get your ass on board. I've got better things to do than hang around here arguing with an a-hole."

Caleb's spine straightened, and he faced his brother, unable to hide the flatness in his eyes. "That wasn't very nice."

"Neither was what you did."

That stung, even if it was true. "I had my reasons."

"And I have mine. So choose."

Nice choice. Either tell his brother to fuck off and find his own ride, which would really set a tone. Beat the piss out of him and remind him that he was still the oldest? Or let his brother enjoy his petty revenge?

Doing the right thing really wasn't any fun.

I came back to make amends, not make things worse. So Caleb rode in the back while Princess got the passenger seat, perched pleased as punch in her basket that hung off straps wrapped around the headrest. When Caleb asked what the heck that was, Constantine replied, "It's a booster for Princess so she can see out the window."

My brother's dog has a car seat. Meanwhile, Caleb didn't, but at least he had a ride, plus, on the bonus side, he and his brother had not yet come to blows, although it had been close.

I expect before the week is out, we'll exchange a few punches.

Constantine harbored a lot of anger and resentment. When Caleb had left home, his brother was just finishing high school, and given there were a few years between them, they hadn't really hung out much. It hadn't occurred to Caleb that the skinny runt—who'd packed on a good hundred pounds and a few inches since then—would resent his departure so much.

If sitting in the back of Constantine's truck was part of Caleb's punishment, then so be it. It wouldn't be the worst ride Caleb had ever gotten. At least this one didn't have gritty sand stinging at his eyes or snipers taking potshots.

As a matter of fact, he quite enjoyed the view and humid air until they hit the highway, whereupon Constantine made sure he hit the gas pedal hard. The truck shot forward with a burst of speed. No problem. Caleb leaned against the cab of the truck and crossed his arms. He could handle a little wind.

The rut in the road, however, almost sent him flying out of the bed of the pickup truck. He landed hard on his ass and couldn't help his irritation.

"Bloody hell, Constantine." Caleb banged on the window partition on the cab. "Take it fucking easy, would you?"

To which his little brother—who, at two hundred and eighty pounds of mean muscle, outweighed him—replied with an eloquent middle finger.

A laugh shook Caleb, a rusty sound that took him by surprise. It had been a while since he'd found something worth chuckling about. *It's good to be home.*

Coming home, to be specific, the prodigal son who'd strutted off to war, brash and full of himself, and now returned, a wounded veteran who—

"Is getting no goddamned respect!" he yelled as his brother plowed the truck through a puddle on the shoulder. On purpose. *Little bastard.*

He smiled.

The muddy water coating his skin and worn T-shirt couldn't diminish his contentment. Even out here, still practically in the city, the smells of the swamp surrounded him. Moist and thick, the humidity in the air revived him.

Since his departure from home, Caleb had spent years serving his country overseas in barren wastelands, where the gritty sand got in everything and the heat sucked the moisture from your skin, leaving it tougher than a croc's hide.

But he'd left the desert behind months ago. Spent some time up north in Alaska, a shifter-friendly town known as Kodiak Point, as a matter of fact. While hiding out there, he'd scrubbed and scrubbed at his skin until he could pretend the stink of smoke and burning flesh didn't cling to him. Some stains never came out, but they faded to the point where he now felt that he could face the world—scarred in both body and soul. Time to complete his return to the real world and come home, a home that was the same and yet different.

A familiar pink billboard caught his eye. Look at that, Maisy's gift shop still did business on the edge of the highway. The next familiar ad was for Bayou's Bite, where a person could eat the best crab cakes in town. *They also used to make the best deep-fried shrimp and served the coldest beer.* He looked forward to seeing if that was still the case.

What he didn't enjoy seeing, as they headed toward his hometown, was the appearance of several subdivisions that had popped up along a few miles stretch of the highway. Ugh to progress. Not more cookie-cutter houses and townhomes.

Who the hell would want to live in one of those?

Not the folks from his town, that was for sure.

Welcome to Bitten Point, Florida. A tiny town hugging the Everglades and home to a shifter population that spanned a gamut of species, unlike the city groups that tended to cater to one breed and ran all others out.

Rumor had it, the wolves controlled New York and some other big cities out west while the lions owned Texas and Arizona. As for Montana and Colorado, that was bear country.

But down here, where the land was wet and the climate warm to scorching, shifters lived more or less in harmony. Except for that odd flock of Canadian Snow Geese. They spent half their years down south but kept to themselves.

But ignoring those birdbrains—which, rumor held, tasted best when basted with butter sauce—the rest of the shifters lived in peace. And if they didn't, then Big Jim, the mayor of their town, took them out to the swamp for a talking-to. Sometimes, he came back alone.

In the shifter world, justice was swift, and often without mercy. A secret like theirs couldn't be risked. Even though some humans knew of the existence of shifters, such as the higher levels in the military and government, the general populace remained ignorant.

And everyone worked to keep it that way.

A swerve of the truck had him gripping the sides as Constantine veered off the highway to take the main road into Bitten Point.

Getting closer...

His heart thumped a little bit faster, and his fingers tightened to the point that his knuckles turned white.

Don't panic now.

He'd done so well up to this point. Taking deep breaths, Caleb pushed the crippling anxiety back into its little box, a box that also contained a rather large reptile that wasn't too happy with Caleb right now.

Too fucking bad. His beast couldn't be counted on to behave, so it was best to keep him leashed.

For distraction, Caleb watched the side of the road. They should be coming across it soon... There it was.

The welcome sign to town loomed.

Bitten Point.

The image on the massive billboard consisted of a large gator head with its jaws wide open saying, "Welcome, won't you stay for a bite?" The colors had faded since he'd last seen it, and the population on it had moved from seven hundred and sixty-five to seven hundred and ninety-six.

Life had flourished while he was gone.

Just past the billboard, he couldn't help but note that the Itty Bitty Club had gotten a new sign, a neon monstrosity that showed the silhouette of a woman wearing a tiny bikini. An itty-bitty bikini.

For as much as the more puritan-minded tried to get it shut down, the strip club remained, offering visual entertainment, expensive beer, and jobs to those who didn't mind baring a bit of skin.

Main Street remained much the same with the town hall and post office sharing the same building. The grocery store had gotten a facelift, as a chain one had apparently moved in.

There was the pharmacy, right next door to the vet, whose practice had flourished evidently, given they'd also taken over the video emporium that used to fill the space alongside.

As soon as they left the main road, a rapid right turn that sent his ass skidding, signs of civilization, at least the modern kind, faded. Out here, this close to the Everglades, greenery took on a life of its own, determined to thwart progress's encroachment of its territory.

They were in bayou land now and, even better, shifter land.

In the movies and books, humans always feared the shifters living in the city, using the paved streets and alleys as their hunting ground. In reality, with the exception of a few groups, most shifters preferred to remain close to nature, to have quick and easy access to acres of wilderness so, when the beast needed to emerge, they didn't need to fear discovery—or bullets.

Even then, though, they had to be careful. Being a rather large crocodile in bayou country wasn't always a safe thing. Caleb didn't have the scars to prove it—only silver truly ever left a permanent mark, silver and fire to be specific—but he did remember the pain of getting shot.

Damn Wes and his not-so-funny pranks.

The truck turned suddenly, but having expected it, Caleb held on to the sides and let out a triumphant yell. "Missed!" A taunt that almost had him biting his tongue as his brother steered into a deep rut. "Bastard!" He yelled it with laughter, a humor that faded with each mile they got closer to his childhood home—and Ma.

There came that fluttery feeling again. But this was a normal trepidation, not the gut-wrenching fear when he heard the crackle of flame devouring tinder.

Would his mother be happy to see him?

Ma certainly hadn't been too pleased when he'd left, and they'd not talked since. His fault. He cut off everyone in his life. *Everyone...*

So how would Ma react to her son coming home?

He still remembered her parting words...

"That's it, leave, just like your father did. He didn't come back, and neither will you." She might have thrown the words at him with vehemence, but her voice had also choked with tears.

It was true his dad had joined the military, just like Caleb, except his dad hadn't come back alive.

The flag they presented his mother did not make up for the loss of the man who'd taught Caleb to fish and spit but who hadn't been around to teach him how to control the beast.

Not having a father as the reptile within matured, flooding Caleb with its cold views and voracious hungers, meant Caleb didn't have a mentor to teach him the tricks to remaining in control.

No one to teach him how to let the beast out safely.

Could he have asked for help from someone else? Yes. Did he? No.

Instead, I lost control.

Took a bite.

A bite that changed the course of his life. A fatal bite that forced him to leave the small town he'd grown up in, abandoning his family and deserting the one girl—

He punched himself in the leg, the hard blow veering his attention because he was not going there. For years he'd forced himself to not allow thoughts of *her*.

Don't start now. Renny is better off without me.

Chances were she'd gone on with her life. Settled down with someone. Someone who could treat her right and make her happy.

Who made that growling sound? Apparently it wasn't just the croc in his mind rising from his mental prison to snap its teeth that had a problem with Renny being with someone else.

Time hadn't diminished some things, such as his jealousy issues.

He'd always had a she's-mine problem where Renny was concerned. Prettiest girl he'd ever seen and she'd chosen him.

But they couldn't tell anyone about it, not with her dad crazier than batshit, especially after a drinking binge, and his ma determined that he go to college and make something of himself instead of "*Settling down too young and missing out on life.*"

At the time, all the reasons not to be together had made them only more determined.

Nothing better than sneaking out to her place and giving her a hand—on account he was such a gentleman—so she could climb out the window. The memory of those hours they spent under the starlight still had the power to arouse.

People often resorted to pills or toys or weird fantasies to bring excitement to sex, but Caleb still thought the hottest kind of fuck was the type where you were afraid of getting caught by someone's father. A man who kept a loaded shotgun by the door.

The tame sex he'd enjoyed later on, in a bed, just never could compare.

Or was it because no one could compare to Renny?

Don't go there. He gave himself a mental slap, and yet, no matter how many times he told himself to forget Renny, his thoughts always seemed to stray back.

The truck rolled to a stop, the crunch of gravel louder for a moment than the singing of the frogs and crickets.

Shit, I'm home.

For a moment, his breathing quickened, his pulse raced, and it wasn't the humidity that dampened his skin.

Don't panic. Breathe, dammit. Breathe.

Spots danced in front of his eyes, and he felt himself losing his grip. The croc swam to the surface, veering for the weakness and looking to escape.

No. I mustn't lose control.

Stupid anxiety attack. He'd hoped he was done with those. It had been weeks since his last good one.

This simmering bout proved all wasn't well yet in his mental landscape. But he could handle it. The doctor in Kodiak Point had taught him tricks to calm himself. And when all else failed, there were the heavy-duty pills.

But he couldn't just pop a few blue sleeping agents and drop off into a coma for a few hours. He needed to man up.

Step one. Take a deep breath.

Step two. Scratch his balls to remind himself he wasn't a prissy fucking princess.

Step three—

"What the hell are you doing?" Constantine said, snapping him back to the here and now.

Doing? Why having a panic attack, of course, but that wasn't something he was about to admit. "Just taking in all the changes to the place."

And there were plenty to provide distraction. For one, they now actually had a driveway of crushed stone rather than the mud and flattened weeds he recalled. The house that had once sported weathered, gray planks and mismatched shingles was still there, but massively face-lifted with white vinyl siding and a light blue metal roof.

"Are those fucking shutters?" Caleb asked in disbelief, taking in the new windows that had taken the place of the wooden-silled ones. How he'd hated those damned things. When it got truly humid they swelled so tight that they refused to open. When one did open, he'd smashed his fingers in them too many times to count because he didn't get the block of wood wedged under it in time.

"Not just any shutters, but hurricane-grade ones," Constantine replied, his upper body hidden within the truck. When his brother leaned back out, he had his little dog tucked under his arm.

"So that's what you did with my paychecks?" Just because Caleb had left home didn't mean he didn't try and improve his mother's lot in life and, by default, his brother's too.

"Not exactly. Mom used the checks to put me through college."

"Yeah, because you need a college degree to fish for shrimp and crabs," Caleb couldn't help but retort. Full-time college had never been a possibility for him when he finished high school. He'd gone straight to work to support his family and then struggled through the part-time classes at his local college until he quit them to be with Renny.

Constantine saw right through his cruel taunt. "I don't work in the bayou. Haven't since you left, really. Ma wanted to make sure I had a different set of choices when I graduated."

In other words, she didn't want a second son going off to war.

"The place looks good," he grudgingly managed to say.

"Thanks. Come on. We should go inside. Ma's probably got dinner ready for us. She's been cooking all day."

Just ignore the drool, as if he could help it at the thought of one of his ma's home-cooked meals. How long had it been since he'd enjoyed real food?

Stomach leading the way, Caleb vaulted from the truck bed and followed his brother toward the house.

Faced with a front door painted a dark blue, Caleb froze. This wasn't his home anymore. So much had changed. His home. His brother. *Me.*

Caleb wasn't the same guy who'd left years ago. And he never would be again.

I'm damaged goods. Both physically and mentally. He could handle the scars on the outside, even if within he cringed every time someone winced or grimaced at his appearance. What he still had a harder time with was the damned nightmares and panic attacks.

Was he so selfish that he would dump himself, and all his problems, on his brother and mother, who had obviously flourished in his absence?

"You know what. I think I should pop into town first. Maybe grab some groceries. Or flowers. Yeah. I need flowers." Caleb turned on his heel and had his hands on the raised edge for the bed of the truck to climb in when he found himself yanked backwards.

With a firm hand on each of Caleb's shoulders, Constantine frog-marched him to the front door. "Don't be such a pussy. Buy flowers?" Connie snorted. "Ma doesn't need anything but your ugly mug. Why, I don't know."

Neither did Caleb. They'd exchanged such ugly words. Angry ones. Hurtful ones.

Given he couldn't tell her the truth, they'd not spoken since. As a matter of fact, he'd not spoken to anyone in Bitten Point until he called a number he knew by heart and his brother answered.

With his eyes closed and spots dancing behind his lids, Caleb had asked, "Can I come home?"

To his surprise, Constantine said yes.

And now, here he was, shaking like the biggest fucking coward.

Before Constantine could force Caleb to climb the painted porch steps—with an honest-to-god railing—the door opened, and there was his ma.

Unlike the rest of home, she hadn't changed. Sure, there might be a few more gray hairs and a crease or two, but the blue eyes, the trembling smile, and the outstretched arms were—

Caleb took the steps in a single bound and yanked her into his grip.

In a voice choked—with a bug, dammit, never tears—he murmured, "I'm home."

Chapter 2

ONE MORE STOP until I can go home.

Pulling into the driveway of the executive home, Renata Suarez—Renny to her friends—sat for a moment before getting out of her car. Every minute of every day it seemed as if she was rushing somewhere, having to do something. Sometimes she worried she'd get so damned busy she'd forget to breathe.

Heck, I'm lucky if I remember to feed myself sometimes. Good thing Luke was around to remind her that sustenance was required or she might have wasted away.

Yet, somehow, despite all the trials, she was making it. She was providing for her and her son, but at what cost?

I've barely seen him grow up. While the daycares she'd relied on over the years were great at taking pictures and videos, the sad fact was, Renny had missed Luke's first step, the first pee in a potty, and so many other milestones. *But what other choice do I have?*

The bills wouldn't pay themselves.

At least now that she'd returned home, she had Melanie caring for her son before and after school, and at a totally rock-bottom rate. Nothing.

As Melanie explained it, "I'm stuck at home anyways because of my hellions. Might as well have your angelic one here, too. You never know, maybe he'll rub off on my little demons."

How I love that girl. Melanie was the only reason why Renny hadn't left Bitten Point once her dad died. Her best friend was the only thing helping Renny keep her sanity right now, and given all Melanie had done to help, she shouldn't abuse her good will.

Stop lazing around, and go get your son. Exiting the car, she took a few strides to reach the door. Renny walked right into Melanie's house, just in time, too, judging by Melanie's shouted, "I'm going to make you both into rugs if you don't behave."

What were the boys doing now?

Stepping into the living room, Renny caught her best friend since kindergarten with her hands on her hips, hair wisping in curls around her face, and her dark brown gaze focused on two little boys perched on the backrest of the couch.

Those two imps eyed their mother, expressions rife with mischief. Without saying a word, Rory and Tatum leaped.

Melanie screeched, "Demon spawn!" and the boys laughed. The two mini acrobats bounced on the sofa cushions, not at all repentant.

It was hard not to smile, so Renny averted her head, lest the children see her amusement. She sought out her son, Luke, and found that he sat in the corner at the play table, head bent as he scribbled away. She stared at him for a moment, but he never looked up. He ignored her. It was so obvious by the tight set of his shoulders and the furious stroke of his crayon.

Her son was mad at her, and with good reason. She was late. Again.

I won't be winning the mother of the year award. But in her defense, she worked two jobs, and neither of them would cut her slack. *"We're short staffed, which means you need to work later today."* Saying no wasn't an option when she needed that money to survive.

However, she did long for the day that she could tell Benny at the supermarket to take his job as a cashier and shove it in a very nasty spot. As for her nighttime waitressing, despite the late hours, that job she enjoyed, even if some nights her ass was slapped a few too many times for her liking. At least those nights meant good tips.

Renny snuck up behind her best friend, counting on the chortles from the twins to hide her approach.

Then she made Melanie jump. "Having fun again, are we? And yet you're thinking of popping the third?"

Visibly jarred, Melanie whirled. "Dammit, Renny, don't sneak up on me like that. I think I just wet myself."

The twins took that moment to listen to their mother, and their mouths made the roundest O of surprise, but not for long before they went into spasms of giggles, Rory chortling, "Mommy peed her pants." A pause then a yell from Tatum, "Again."

Melanie glared at her brood. "It's a good thing you're cute or else..."

Before anyone could think Melanie was a witch of a mother, it should be noted that she doted on those boys, and while she did mock-threaten them, she was the first to encourage them to explore the world. In other words, climb. Just not the furniture in the house. Her poor curtain rods couldn't handle any more abuse.

"Tickle monster attack!" Melanie yelled before diving at her boys. They scattered, high-pitched squeals along with the thump of bare feet on wood floors. Her friend wiped her arm across her forehead. "Whew. Those two are way too full of piss and vinegar today."

"A little wound up, were they?"

"More like unhinged," Melanie grumbled. "Must mean a storm is coming."

"When isn't a storm coming?"

"Good point. Given the silence, I've only got another minute or two before I need to hunt them down. The last time they disappeared for more than five minutes and were quiet, they slathered hand soap in the hallway and were using it as a slip and slide."

The antics of Rory and Tatum never failed to entertain. Luke didn't tend to such wildness, although, of late, his moods were more erratic. "How was Luke today?" Renny asked before kneeling by her son. He pointedly ignored her, the crayon dropped on the table so that he could thumb his Nintendo DS. He loved that toy, which made the scrimping she'd done to get it for him for Christmas worthwhile. But while he loved the game, it was now also a weapon he used to shut her out.

Ever since he'd begun school, her son had changed. Her shy and cuddly son now no longer wanted her to hold his hand in public, and he no longer crawled into her lap for stories.

He's only four. So young, and yet very much his own person. A little man without the guidance of a father, something he'd only begun to notice.

His immersion in the big wide world of the public school system meant he got to see how the world worked. How other families lived. Not quite five years old, but perceptive for his age, he'd finally asked her not long ago the one question she never wanted to answer.

"Who's my daddy?"

"Why do you want to know?"

Luke had fixed her with a stare. "Other kids have a daddy. Who's mine?"

Did a no-good jerk who'd taken off and never looked back count? What about a guy who couldn't run away fast enough, breaking her heart while, at the same time, leaving her the biggest trial and treasure of all?

A son.

A son who had resorted to the silent treatment when she copped out and said, "I'll tell you when you're older." Weak. So weak.

Parenting fail, and yet telling him the truth now would not change anything.

For all intents and purpose, Luke's daddy was—

"Did you hear? Caleb's back in town."

Crouching didn't prevent the words from shaking her balance. Renny wobbled as she sucked in a sharp breath. Did something of her shock show in her features? Something must have because

Luke finally deigned to look at her and asked, "What's wrong, Mommy?"

Wrong? Nothing. She didn't care what Caleb did. "Nothing is wrong..." She paused before saying baby. Last time she'd used the endearment, Luke was none too pleased. All part and parcel of him growing up. She could remember hating it when her dad called her drools. Only to wish he'd kept calling her that later in life. The time before her mother's death, before the drinking and the finding of God, were the years she tried to remember. Not what Daddy became after.

Renny realized her son was staring at her, having noticed she'd lost her train of thought. She quickly gathered herself. "I'm hungry, bug, are you? And since I won't have time to really cook supper for us tonight, what do you say we hit Bayou's Bite for a bucket of shrimp and fries before we go home?"

"You just wanna go home so you can leave me with Wanda." His lower lip jutted in a pout.

Way to slather on the guilt. *No need, baby. The guilt's always there.* She pinched her son's chin gently. "Sorry. I know I've been working a lot of hours lately. As soon as they hire some more people, I will have more time to spend with you." The promise she feared breaking only served to increase the guilt that gnawed at her, a nagging self-doubt that Melanie had been playing lately.

Her friend would never say anything in front of the kids, but Melanie's eyes clearly reminded Renny of the talk they'd had recently, given the bills were arriving bigger and faster than her paychecks. Broken muffler. Then a tire. The stove that died. Clothes and shoes for Luke. He was outgrowing things so quickly.

"You should go after him for child support," Melanie had said to her on the phone just last week. "He owes it to you."

"Caleb made it clear he wanted nothing to do with our baby." The jerk couldn't even be bothered to reply to her letters. She wasn't going to beg him or his family.

"You have to admit that doesn't sound like the Caleb we know."

Yeah, well, the Caleb she knew wouldn't have just decided one day to abandon family, home, and girlfriend to join the army with barely any notice, just a text message saying, *I enlisted. Don't wait for me.*

As breakups went, it had sucked.

And now Mr. Jerky-Pants was back, and she really didn't care. Now, could her foolish heart stop its ridiculous little flutter?

"What are you doing this weekend?" Renny asked as she watched Luke put on his shoes. God forbid she should offer to help. The little boy disdain was so clear, but her heart broke every time he said, "I can do this by myself."

"Doing?" Scrunching her nose, Melanie made a moue of distaste. "Andrew is making me go to some kind of corporate picnic they're having in the Glades behind the institute. As junior VP, he has to be there, which means, as his wife, I have to go. And wear a bra!" The travesty.

"Sounds like fun."

"Don't mock me. You know how I hate the swamp." Melanie's lips turned down. "The humidity kills my hair. An hour spent straightening it so it can turn into a giant fuzzball the moment I set foot in the bayou."

"I like your frizz."

This time, Renny earned the glare. "You shut your mouth, girl with the perfect, straight blonde hair. I swear, you could be outside in a hurricane and you still wouldn't need a brush. I hate you."

Wearing a smirk, Renny flipped her ponytail. "I hate you, too, and yet I'd still trade in a heartbeat. Although, I will warn you that the saying is false. Blondes do not have more fun." She grimaced.

"Only because someone won't get someone to do something so she can have a life and do, you know, other someones." Melanie arched her brow as she referenced things obliquely.

Renny's mature reply was to stick her tongue out.

Having caught the final act, Luke sighed and, with a very put-out voice, said, "Mom. That is so immature."

She blinked at him then looked at Melanie. "Isn't he too young to use that tone with me? And that word? Who taught him a word like immature?"

"I blame YouTube," Melanie said. "It is the root of all evil and that rude fruit show." Renny went to step out, but Melanie leaned out after her and said, "Hey, so you didn't say what you were doing this weekend. If you're bored tomorrow, feel free to come to the picnic. I could use moral support."

"I thought those were called mint juleps."

"No drinking allowed." Melanie rubbed her belly.

"Are you...?"

"Not yet. But we're trying. I just went through my rounds of testing at the institute, and we'll be starting fertility treatments soon."

Opposite breeds in the shifter world had a harder time producing offspring than the same kind. With Melanie's inner animal being a panther, and her husband a bear—even if a poor excuse for one—they needed all the help they could get. However, because they had to keep their secret, just going to a regular doctor was out of the question. Lucky for Melanie, part of Bittech's purpose was to help shifters with medical conditions under the guise of pharmaceutical testing of the natural ingredients found in the bayou.

"Are you sure you're ready for a third one?" Renny asked softly. She knew things weren't exactly great between her best friend and her husband.

A moue twisted Melanie's lips. "I love being a mom. Although, I wish Andrew was more keen on being a dad. Don't get me wrong, though, he loves the boys." Said a touch more brightly than necessary.

Trying to convince Renny or herself?

Now wasn't the time to push. She'd wait until they could spend a few hours together killing a carton of cookie dough ice cream and listing all the faults with men. "Well, I hope you get pregnant, just so I can enjoy the desserts." A pregnant Melanie was a sweets craving and cooking one. As her best friend, Renny got to taste and take home many of the results.

"I'm going for a girl this time. A pair, if we're lucky, to make sure the numbers are even. Get off the kitchen counter. No more cookies!" she bellowed. Turning a sweet smile on Renny, Melanie, who possessed some kind of satanic blood to switch personas so quickly, asked, "So will you come tomorrow as my plus one?"

"I have a pile of laundry to do. And groceries. And..."

"And this is why your life is so boring. Stop being so damned responsible for once and do something fun."

"I'll think about it." Although Renny wasn't sure a company picnic was her type of fun. Besides, Melanie had an ulterior motive. An extra set of legs to hunt her precious imps down.

Speaking of whom...

Matching mischievous faces peeked and waved goodbye from between their mother's legs.

Renny blew them kisses, and they recoiled with harmonized, "Eews!"

To more shouted threats of "Don't you dare lock the bathroom door," Renny left with her son.

While Luke could open the car door and get into his booster himself, even buckle it, she still supervised. Surely this much autonomy for this age was wrong.

With her son safely strapped into his booster, she got behind the wheel of her older model car, something that came off the production line more than ten years ago. As she drove the road home by rote, she reflected. *Maybe I should take Luke to the picnic instead of the laundromat tomorrow.*

The free food at the picnic and the entertainment value might make up for the fact that she'd have to do the laundry one of her free nights the following week. At least for groceries, she could take Luke on Sunday. He liked it when she raced the cart down the aisles and then jerked to a halt before anyone caught them. Every time, he would fiendishly giggle as she emerged from the aisle looking prim and proper.

Or at least he used to. Her son didn't giggle so much anymore.

Not since she'd started working all those extra shifts and ignored the question in his eyes.

Hard to avoid him when you lived in a space that was only a few hundred square feet. Luke had the bedroom while she got to sleep on the couch. But it should be noted it was a damned comfortable couch.

Space wasn't the only issue. The apartment she and Luke called home wasn't exactly awash in amenities—a tiny electric stovetop, but no oven, a small fridge, and a single sink for dishes, but it was theirs, clean, and, best of all, affordable.

Because no way am I asking Caleb for money.

Her pride wouldn't let her beg that way.

However, looking over at Luke's short-cropped brown hair, she had to wonder. *Is my pride more important than my son?*

Chapter 3

THE MUSIC THUMPED, strong enough to vibrate against the skin, a hard bass beat, and that was all that was really needed for the girl up on stage to strut her stuff. Leaning back in his seat, Caleb eyed the dancer's red leather boots. They looked new and still gleamed with that store-bought shine. Genuine pleather, unlike his snakeskin boots. Authentic skin, he might add. One of the few mementos Caleb had brought back from his time overseas.

The woman on stage wore a minimal amount of clothing. Actually, at this point in her routine, all she had left other than her boots was her thong. Less panty than a tiny scrap of fabric just enough to cover her shaven mound. As for her breasts, they shook and shimmied to the beat as she gyrated, still wearing a flirtatious smile.

For a moment, her gaze strayed to Caleb and then locked. He saw her eyes widen in recognition. She shot him a come-hither smile and a quick-winked invitation.

Cute, but not his type, and that was without even knowing who the hell she was.

As Caleb turned away to see what else was happening in the strip club, Daryl nudged him. "Would you believe that's Bobby's little sister?"

"Fuck off. That's Hilary? Damn. Last time I saw her she was wearing braces and Bobby's old football jerseys."

"She grew up while you were gone. Hell, you should see my own sister. She's Miss Melly Homemaker now. She's even talking about popping kiddo number three."

"Damn, she's got kids?" Last time Caleb had seen Melanie, she was in her last year of high school. "Is your sister still with what's-his-name? That dude whose dad owns that big ass company in the area. Some kind of bio-medical research lab."

"Andrew? Yup. He's now a CEO with the company. Making good dough, too. My sister is living in that new swanky subdivision just outside of Bitten Point."

"Your sister is a yuppie housewife?" Caleb snickered. "Never thought I'd see that day." Not given how much of a tomboy Melanie had been growing up.

"Yeah, my mom is so proud. Apparently, owning a house with a dishwasher and more than one bathroom is an indication she's made it." Daryl rolled his eyes. "Apparently, having an in-house toilet and outhouse one just isn't the same."

Yet another smile stretched his lips. Daryl was a bayou man at heart. He'd never get caught dead in a suit or living a cookie-cutter life.

"I see you've managed to evade getting hitched. Whatever happened to Stacy what's-her-name that you were dating?"

A shudder shook his friend. "Stacy was over like a month after you left. She started talking marriage and babies, and I started talking leaving civilization behind and living off the land..." Daryl shrugged as he grinned. "As it turns out, she wasn't wanting the same things in life I was."

Caleb chuckled and shook his head. Nice to see his best friend hadn't changed. He had to admit he'd wondered what Daryl would do when he showed up at his mom's front door right after dinner—a dinner consisting of a droolingly delicious homemade clam chowder with Ma's special cornbread for dipping.

Caleb had no sooner tucked away two platefuls than someone rang the doorbell.

"Since when do we have a fucking doorbell?" Caleb exclaimed.

"Language," his ma chided in the midst of clearing the table.

"We have a doorbell because I spent thirty bucks to get one. Just because we live by the swamp doesn't mean we can't have amenities," Constantine informed him.

A doorbell, shutters, and new laminate flooring in every room. What had happened to the charming shack he'd grown up in? Caleb could no longer see the marks of his past—they'd painted over some of his best penwork!

As Princess took off for the front door, barking and bristling like a rabid squirrel, Caleb followed after, not out of any interest in who was at the door, but more a wonder if the tiny dog would rip whoever dared come to the house into shreds.

She was certainly freaking out enough to make Caleb think she was perhaps part hound of Hell.

Opening the door, he had no trouble recognizing who stood there. Daryl.

Awkward.

Ma and Constantine weren't the only ones Caleb had more or less abandoned without a word. How had his best friend taken his abrupt departure?

Daryl took a hard look at him and said, "You know you're a dick-head, right?"

"Biggest dick around," Caleb retorted.

To which Daryl smirked. "Not according to the ladies." And that was that. His Latino friend sauntered in and hugged his mother.

Now some people might wonder at Melanie and Daryl's very non Hispanic names. Simple. Their mother was convinced that in order to succeed in the world, they needed a proper name. A very English name. Although, as Daryl once confided to Caleb, the name wasn't what slammed doors in his face, but his tanned skin, tattoos, and attitude. Raised on the wrong side of the bayou, it didn't matter what they wore or how they spoke, people judged. But guess what? Caleb didn't give a fuck and neither did his best friend.

Apparently, Daryl had not been a stranger to his home in Caleb's absence. Perhaps that was why his mother told him—after a dessert of homemade peach-flavored ice cream—that they should go out and enjoy themselves.

Whatever the reason for her wanting to get rid of him, Caleb took it, not eager to get into a conversation with his ma that would prod him about things he'd prefer to bury. See, the thing was, despite the need for secrecy, he wasn't sure he could lie to his mother anymore.

But what about Daryl? He'd probably have questions, too, so Caleb warned him. "I don't know if I'm ready to talk about the last few years."

"I'm not a fucking idiot. It's obvious something serious went down. Why else would you have fucked off in the middle of the night without a word hardly to anyone?"

"I had my reasons."

"I'm sure you did, and I'm sure they're valid, but it doesn't mean it wasn't still a dick move. Lucky for you, though, I've been a dick a time or two in my life, so I know it can happen. However, I do insist you buy me a beer. To remind me why you're my friend."

Just knowing Daryl still considered them friends had Caleb buying a pitcher and telling the waitress to keep them coming. And they weren't cheap pitchers, seeing as how they were ordering them in a strip club.

The Itty Bitty Club—featuring the ittiest thongs and most fabulous titties around—resembled every other exotic dancing bar with tables with enough space between them to give a man a bit of room—so the dancers would come by and offer a little more personal time. The place was cleaner than most. The scarred wood surfaces might have seen a cloth before he sat down. No sticky spots or moisture rings to be seen.

Just don't touch under the table.

The chairs all had armrests, for the entertaining ladies' benefit. It gave them something to hold on to as they lap danced for a large bill or two. Panties on and no body parts grinding didn't mean a gal couldn't straddle the chair and air hump.

Not Caleb's thing, in public at least.

Having gone to strips joints more than a couple of times, Caleb knew the best spot was by the bar, chatting up the usually pretty bartender while watching the show on stage in the mirror.

His buddy, however, had other plans.

"Let's get up close," Daryl had said, leading the way to the stage.

"Why? Seen one, seen them all."

Daryl kept walking and found a vacant spot.

Caleb followed and dropped into the open chair across from his bud.

This is as close as you can get.

Sitting in pervert's row meant Caleb had a great glimpse of the action on stage. Daryl quite enjoyed the show, calling out to the girls, apparently knowing most by name. After a while, Caleb realized he knew quite a few of those gals, too.

"Is that so-and-so?" followed by a "yup" formed the bulk of several conversations. Relaxing. No pressure. Some of his tension eased.

I'm safe here.

Or so he thought until Daryl broke the pattern with a muttered, "Shit. She wasn't supposed to be working tonight."

"Who are you talking about?" Caleb no sooner said the words than awareness made him stiffen. A tingle swept across his senses, a familiar, longed-for touch.

Uh-oh. It couldn't be her. No way. No way could he still feel her in that intimate way he used to so many years ago.

I must be wrong. I mean think, idiot, she would never work in a place like this. Renny was always so damned classy. And let's not forget her daddy would never let her.

Wrong.

What he thought he knew had changed, but Renny hadn't.

Holy fuck, she's more beautiful than I remembered.

Long blonde hair swept into a ponytail showing off the long column of her neck. A figure a little more round than before, but utterly sexy. As to her face... A few years of maturing had taken her soft girlish features and sculpted them. *She's a woman now.*

A ridiculously attractive one, and for the first time since they'd entered the strip club, Caleb had to drop his hands into his lap—so he could mash his fist against his daring-to-stir cock.

Stay down.

Seriously. Getting an erection for her was probably perverse. Titties bouncing all over the place, practically in his face, did nothing, but seeing the one woman in the world who probably hated him, and was clothed to boot, turned him on?

At this point, he should note that while Renny did wear clothes, they were exceedingly sexy and skimpy. In his view, they were not appropriate for this bar—or public viewing.

What does she think she's doing strutting around in that tight-fitting crop top? A shirt that molded to her perfect handful of tits. And who thought those itty-bitty jean shorts she wore, that barely covered her full ass, were appropriate work attire?

Doesn't she know how sexy she fucking looks? What a temptation she poses?

Why the hell did he care so much? Agitated, he turned his attention back to the reason he was feeling the tension creeping back in. Daryl had done this.

Caleb growled. "What the fuck is she doing here?"

Hands raised, Daryl shook his head. "Sorry, dude. I honestly didn't know she'd be here. She doesn't usually work here Fridays."

Usually? "Are you saying she works here on a regular basis?"

"Has been since not long after the baby."

He choked on his sip of beer. "Baby?"

"Dude, did you not keep up on any of the news in town?"

"No." Because a part of him didn't want to know.

"Lots of stuff has been happening."

So he kept being reminded. "Who's she hooking up with?" Because he totally wanted to plant his fist in his face. *Rip into him and kill him.*

He ignored the suggestion. He most certainly suffered from a green problem, but it wasn't jealousy.

Daryl shrugged. "No one that I know of lately."

"What about the baby's daddy? Is he still in the picture?"

"Nope. Not that anyone knows who it is. She went off not long after you left to care for an aunt or something. She came back about six months ago with a kiddo."

"And no one knows who the father is?

Daryl shook his head. "She won't say. All my sister will say is that he was a jerk who wasn't ready for the responsibility."

A certain right fist wanted to show an asshole what happened when he ditched his responsibilities. Caleb knew what it was like to grow up fatherless. Despite the fact that Renny probably hated him for leaving, Caleb didn't like knowing she was struggling.

But that still didn't excuse her choice of work.

Caleb stood abruptly, the chair screeching back against the floor. "I need to see her."

Reaching out, Daryl grabbed his arm as he went to walk by. "Dude, don't do it."

"Do what? Say hello to an old friend?"

"You guys were more than friends. Everyone thought you were going to get hitched. And then you left. No warning. Nothing. She was hurting. Bad. You can't blame her for mistakes she might have made."

Mistake? He'd left, and she had a baby by another man.

He should have been happy to know she'd moved on. Instead, he wanted to kill something.

Biting is good.

He ignored the voice. He did that a lot, and he didn't give a shit what that damned shrink said. Some things were better left locked away.

Because some acts couldn't be unseen.

"I don't know why you think I'm going to blame her for anything. I just want to talk to her. Say hi. Let her know I'm back." And that there were many nights he wished he'd never left.

Seeing her again reminded him of the most precious thing he'd lost.

Yet not leaving was never a choice.

Talking to her would prove a cruel form of torture, but he couldn't stop himself, even as Daryl reminded him, "Dude, don't do it. She knows you're back. Trust me, she knows. So sit down and have another beer. Or, even better, let's take off and go to the Bitten Saloon. It's a short stagger to my place then."

"You know I hate Western. And you're worrying for nothing. Better I get this out of the way now. We were bound to run into each other at one point." Caleb had just hoped he'd find himself better armed when he did—like with a gun so he could shoot any asshole who dared to touch his girl.

Or we could eat them.

The cold thought wasn't his own. He paid it no mind, just like he paid Daryl no mind. Gaze narrowed, he made his way across the room. People wisely stepped out of his way. Could it be the intense glower he wore as he watched a certain pert ass—*an ass I groped too many times to count*— sashayed away? He followed.

Renny ducked into the women's washroom. Did she think to escape him? Caleb was a master when it came to getting his prey. It was what had gotten him into this situation.

I'm coming to get you. Given the women's public washroom was in a strip joint, and the employees had their own behind the scenes, Caleb felt pretty safe following.

No screams as he entered, a good sign, but neither did Renny acknowledge his presence. She knew he was there. She could see him approach in the mirror, just like he could see the tight set of her shoulders and the thin press of her lips.

A peeved-looking woman who sounded it, too. "You made a wrong turn. This is the women's washroom."

Ignoring her welcome, he said, "Hello, baby." The familiar nickname purred from him, unbidden, but once spoken, unable to be retrieved.

A long time ago, that endearment might have once curled her lips into the most beautiful smile. Now it just served to make her eyes flash with anger. "Don't you baby me, Caleb. I have no interest in talking to you."

"I get that, and I don't blame you."

"How magnanimous of you," she retorted dryly.

"You look good." Again, he spoke without thinking—or filtering. *I'd better start watching my words, or I'm going to get myself in trouble.*

Too late. He was in trouble the moment he came seeking her.

At his praise, she sucked in a breath, and a slight flush heightened the color in her cheeks. "You look good, too," she said.

At her obvious lie, his lips tightened. "I'm very much aware of how I look. No need to coddle me." The burns had left a scar, not just on his skin but his psyche. Even if she could ignore the one, he couldn't ignore the other.

"Coddle? I can assure you that would be last thing I'd do for you."

Renny always did have that irritating tendency of telling the truth, but even if she didn't find his scars ugly, that changed nothing.

"As you can see, I'm back."

"So everyone keeps telling me," she mumbled. "As if I care. I stopped caring a long time ago."

A lie that hit him hard and low. *She still feels something for me.*

Yeah, lots of anger.

"I know you hate me, and I just wanted to tell you that I'm going to do my best to stay away from you." Even if all he wanted was to stick to her like honey on a bear.

Her brow arched. "So far you're not doing a good job staying away."

"I thought I should talk to you because I figure we'd bump into each other again at some point, and I didn't want it to be awkward."

"Oh, because this isn't awkward at all." Renny rolled her eyes. "You've said hello. I know you're back. I also don't care, so if you don't mind, there's the door. Use it." She turned her back to him.

Oddly enough, though, he didn't want to leave. As a matter of fact, all he really wanted to do was snare her in his arms and squeeze her tight. Tell her how much he'd missed her and wished things could have been different. He wanted to peel that tiny shirt from her and cover her body in his. Surround her in his scent. Claim her and make her off-limits to others.

The time apart hadn't cooled the attraction on his part at all, but he wouldn't act on it.

Mustn't mark her and claim her and keep. She deserves better.

Thing was, he needed to make sure she hated him because, if she softened at all, like she did now with her body trembling slightly, he might not be able to resist. "So do you strip for money on top of waitressing? Or do you just strut your shit for every dick with a few dollars?"

She whirled on him. "Are you seriously insulting me here?"

"Just questioning your choice in careers." Because he knew she was capable of being more than a waitress in a strip club. "Couldn't you find something a little more—"

"More what? Morally sound? More clothed? Perhaps you'd like me to walk two feet behind men and curtsy when they speak to me?"

"Now you're exaggerating. I'm just saying a nice girl like you should have higher aspirations than working in a titty bar."

"There is nothing wrong with working here. And that's a priceless thing to say, given you came here in the first place. If this place is so disgusting, then what are you doing here?"

Getting a beer? But he didn't have time to voice his reason. Renny was still talking, her voice reaching an incredulous pitch.

"You've got a lot of nerve, Caleb Bourdeaux, coming back into town after everything that's happened and acting as if I owe you anything or give a fiddle what you think."

Once again, he just couldn't seem to keep his mouth shut. "Maybe you should give a damn what I think since no one else seems to be. You deserve a job that doesn't require you dressing like this. For fuck's sake, Renny, your shirt is so tight I can see your damned bra."

"Are my bralines bothering you? Let me fix that."

He could only gape in shock as her hands slid under the fabric of her top, and in moments, she'd managed to unsnap her bra and slide her arms through the straps. She tossed the scrap of fabric at him.

It hit him in the chest, but he clasped it before it could fall. The cottony material still held the warmth of her body. Was it him or the beast that lifted it for a sniff?

Vanilla. Delicious. And tempting, just like the buds of her nipples clinging to the material of her shirt that drew his gaze.

I am in so much trouble.

A trouble he couldn't seem to stop from snowballing.

"What are you doing with my bra?" she asked as he stuffed it in his pocket.

"Keeping it."

"For what?"

Nothing could have stopped his slow, lazy smile. "Inspiration."

It took her only a moment to grasp his meaning, and then she blushed. "Give it back right now. I will not have you—um. You know." Renny stumbled instead of saying the words.

"You gave it to me. It's rude to ask for a present back," Caleb chided.

But Renny didn't seem to care about bad manners. "I hate you." She stomped past him, the skin of her arm lightly brushing him, enough for an electric sizzle. Perhaps she felt it, too, because she stopped and whirled. Her brown eyes sparked. Her lips parted. "Actually, you know what, I do owe you something."

She leaned toward him, and he found himself angling toward her, too, already forgetting his promise to stay away. To—

"Ooomph!" Breath burst from him as she slugged him in the gut.

"That was for being an asshat and leaving." She kicked him in the shin. "That's for ignoring me after. And this is because I hate you!" She kneed him in the groin.

It did not feel good at all, but that wasn't the reason he was breathless and in pain. His agony came not from her blows, but because she'd unleashed the full fury of her devastation.

A wave of emotions assailed him, crushing him with their rawness.

He dropped to his knees, burdened by the weight.

Is this how she truly feels?

So betrayed. Forgotten. Unloved. So lonely...

Still breathless, he couldn't say a word, only reach out to her, but she stepped back from his hand.

"Stay away from me, Caleb. Please." Keeping her gaze away from his, but unable to hide the tears glistening in her eyes or mask the roughness of her voice, she whirled once again and stomped away. She slammed through the swinging door.

And the world lost all hint of life and color.

For a moment, Caleb kneeled, staring at the door that had swung shut. Talk about blown away, and stunned, not just by her revelation of her feelings but her actions.

She hit me.

Sweet, gentle Renny had hit him. She'd even raised her voice and used the A word. *She called me an asshat.* Renny never cussed. He should know. Once upon a time he'd made her speak aloud the dirtiest words. How he loved the way she blushed and stammered saying just the word "damn."

But she wasn't just using stronger language, she hadn't been afraid to get physical and confrontational.

A forceful Renny. He didn't know what to think of it. She'd

changed an awful lot. Because of him? Or was it because of this baby she had, the one she was raising on her own?

For some reason, knowing she had no one to help bothered him, and it wasn't just because he'd grown up without a dad.

Something of his trouble must have shown as he slid back into his seat across from Daryl.

"Nice mug. By the look of you, I take it things didn't go well."

"No. They didn't." And, yes, he might have said it rather sulkily. Despite all his protestations that he should stay away from Renny and she was better off without him, apparently a tiny part of him, that had remained hidden until this very moment, had hoped for a different outcome. Optimism fantasized she would fling herself into his arms and sob how much she'd missed him and still loved him.

I hoped that she loved me still.

However, it wasn't just their showdown in the bathroom that shattered that dream, but the fact that she'd birthed a child. A child she created with another man.

It bothered him. Someone else had touched her. Yet what had he expected?

I expected her to wait for me.

Yet, while he might have harbored that foolish fantasy, he'd certainly not abstained from the opposite sex. *I might have sated some needs, but I never loved them.*

Not like he'd love a certain golden-haired girl.

A girl who'd grown into a woman.

A woman determined to ignore him.

If only he could do the same, but he wasn't having the same kind of luck. In his defense, he wasn't the only one checking out the hot chick serving drinks in short shorts, getting her ass slapped and taking it with a smile while he seethed.

"Dude, that is a serious brood you've got going," Daryl said, waving his hand before Caleb's face and breaking his stare.

"I don't brood."

"Fine, glower. Scowl. Whatever. You need to stop. Renny's not interested, dude, so give it a rest."

But Caleb didn't want to give it a rest, which was why, when Daryl insisted on driving him home, he got out a few miles from home and claimed he needed to walk the rest of the way to clear his head.

Caleb wasn't lying completely. He did walk. Just not home.

Chapter 4

STILL SHAKEN after her encounter with Caleb, after the club closed just after one, Renata took her time wiping down the tables and gathering her things.

Being warned Caleb was in town and seeing him in the flesh were two totally different things. For one, she'd not expected the sharp pang of longing when she saw him again.

How can I still want him?

He'd changed so much. Definitely not the same carefree guy she'd known years ago. Yet, for all the cynical hardness in his features, the sneer on his lips, all those signs he bore that showed he'd faced danger and hardships, drew her even more.

It didn't hurt that he had a rocking body.

A fit guy when they dated, he'd passed in shape into superbly toned. His snug T-shirt had hugged his upper body, revealing broad shoulders, a defined set of pecs, a flat stomach, and arms that could squeeze the life from her.

She almost wished he'd try. How long had it been since she'd enjoyed a hug from a male other than her son?

But Caleb was the wrong person to be craving a hug from.

I hate him, remember?

Right. Hated.

Yet craved.

Abhorred.

Yet her senses tingled.

Wanted to kill.

Yet he made her feel alive.

Even now, with him gone for hours, awareness tickled all of her nerves, a hyper-sensitivity that initially let her know where he was at all times when he was in the club. She might not have an inner beast like most folks in town, but that never stopped her from knowing when Caleb was nearby. Melanie used to call it fate.

Now Renny had to wonder if it was a warning?

Whatever the cause, it made it so hard to ignore him. It didn't help that he kept watch on her while she worked. If she happened to turn and peek, there he was, staring at her, hunger lighting his gaze, stark longing drawing lines in his face.

It might have made a weaker woman melt. Not her. He wasn't going to win her back with either his looks or his attention.

Too bad. So sad. This ship has sailed. You had me once and look at what happened.

Caleb had dumped her ass and gone to war. So what if he returned? So what if he'd obviously suffered judging by the scars he bore? Being only human, she wondered what happened to his face. The scar with its distinctive flat shine spoke of a terrible burn, one that went down his cheek, spotted his neck, and disappeared into the collar of his shirt. How far did it extend?

I wonder if he'd let me find out.

For curiosity's sake, of course, not sensual.

Did it still hurt? She had to wonder if it was why he acted so jaded. So prickly.

Is he trying to keep people away from him?

That wasn't the Caleb she knew, who thrived on hugs and snuggles.

Given the direction of her thoughts, she wasn't too surprised when she exited the building to see Caleb leaning against her car.

She halted in the doorway, torn with indecision. *Am I ready to deal with him?* Would she ever be? Caleb was right in one respect. In a town this size, they couldn't avoid each other forever.

Bruno grumbled from his spot by the door, the red tip of his cigarette glowing bright. "Bloody stalkers. Stay put here for a second, Renny, would you? It will only take me a second to chase that bottom feeder away."

Placing a hand on Bruno's arm, Renny stopped him. "It's okay. I know the guy. He won't hurt me." Because he no longer had the power to hurt her. He'd already done his worst.

"Are you sure? I don't mind crunching him up." As a big bull gator, Bruno meant that quite literally.

Living in the bayou meant accepting certain rules. The first one being shifters made their own rules and they were quite often violent.

"If I need you to smash his face in, I'll let you know. Thanks, Bruno."

"Bah." He scoffed. "I'd do it for fun. Anyhow, I'm going to be here for another half hour locking things down. You need me, just holler."

"I will." Renny stepped away from the safety of the hulking bouncer and strode to her car. She tried to appear nonchalant, but inside, her heart raced. What did Caleb want?

When she was close enough not to shout, she asked, "Why are you stalking my car? I thought we'd said all there was to say inside." And she'd also imagined a whole hell of a lot after she realized what Caleb meant to do with her bra. Every time her hand wrapped around a tall glass, she couldn't help but be reminded.

"I didn't like the thought of you being out here all alone at night. Who knows what kind of creeps are lurking?"

"Calling yourself a creep now? That's harsher than what I would have said. More like clingy and unable to let things go." She stopped a few steps from him, head cocked at an angle as she stared at Caleb, trying to read the mysterious workings of his mind. She came up blank.

"I am not clingy."

"Oh, that's right, you're not, or you wouldn't have dumped me."

His lips thinned. "I had my reasons."

"I hope they were damned good ones." Should she mention there wasn't a reason valid enough to justify his actions?

"They were."

"Good enough to justify leaving me and, other than a measly text, never contacting me again?"

"I said I had my—"

"Reasons? Yeah. Whatever. Move away from my car. I need to get home."

"I'm coming with you."

She gaped at him before gathering her wits. "Oh no you aren't. I can drive myself."

Caleb snorted. "I should hope you can drive, seeing as how I've had too many beers."

"You must have if you thought bugging me for a ride after work was a smart idea."

"Actually, I had a ride with Daryl, but I came back."

Curiosity made her ask. "Why?"

"Like I said, to keep an eye on you and make sure no one bothered you."

"People bothering me isn't your business. I'm not your business. And I don't need you waltzing into my work, giving me hell, and then stalking me after just because we used to date."

Caleb leaned toward her. "Come on, baby, you know we did more than date. We made love in every which way possible."

"I was young and gullible."

"We were horny for each other."

Yes, they were. Sometimes, at night when she was alone, she could still feel the heat and sensual thrill of his hands on her skin, the exhilarating rush of climax.

His reminder made her flush, even as she sputtered, "You're gross."

"No, I'm honest."

A bitter laugh erupted as she latched onto the word. "Honest? Really? That's priceless coming from you. Honesty from the man who ditched me with a text message and even now won't tell me why. Was it something I did?"

He didn't even hesitate. "Of course not."

"Were you in love with someone else?"

"Never!" The word burst from him with force.

"Then tell me why you left."

"I can't."

She exploded. "You are unbelievable. And not just with me. Everyone. Your family. Your friends."

He clamped his lips.

"Why won't you even try and defend yourself?"

"It wouldn't matter if I did. You wouldn't believe it, and I won't use it as an excuse. I treated you bad. I treated a lot of people bad, and I guess now I need to see if I can make amends."

The pieces clicked into place. "Oh, I get it now, this whole stalk Renny thing is about you trying to assuage yourself of your guilt. Dumped Renny, let's apologize and make it all better. Because it's so simple." As if words could heal what he'd done. But, if he thought she forgave him, would he leave her alone? "You know what, on second thought, I accept your apology. I forgive you for running off like a coward. You can cross me off your to-do list." *And get out of my life.*

"An apology isn't enough. I want to help you. You shouldn't be working at the Itty Bitty. You're better than that."

She arched a brow. "Too good for a paycheck? I gotta pay my bills like everyone else, Caleb. Some of us have responsibilities."

A frown drew his brows together. "So I hear. But you shouldn't shoulder the burden alone. Maybe you should force a certain asshole father to give you some help so you don't have to degrade yourself working in a place like this." Caleb swept his hand at the bar behind him.

"My dad died, and even if he hadn't, he wouldn't have raised a finger to help me, not after the baby." A Bible-thumping fellow, Dad had stopped talking to her, and even on his deathbed from a vicious fever he'd caught in the bayou, he turned his head away when she went to say her goodbyes.

"I wasn't talking about your dad. I was talking about your baby's father. It takes two to make a kid."

Her gaze narrowed. Hold on a second... "What about Luke's father?"

"Way I hear it, the deadbeat skipped out on you and the child."

"He did." Was he pulling her leg?

"That's not right," Caleb growled.

"No. It isn't." Incredulity built in her. Surely she was wrong.

"You should force him to take responsibility for his actions."

"You really think so?"

He nodded. "Make the asshole pay."

Sweet baby corn, he really didn't know. "Well, I'm glad you think so, Caleb, because given you ignored the letters I sent you, I kind of figured you had washed your hands of us."

He went still and turned pale. "What are you talking about? What was in those letters?"

"First, let me ask you, did you get them?" Judging by the panicked look in his eyes, he had. "Did you even open them?" He didn't have to answer for her to guess. A bitter laugh erupted. "Nope. You didn't bother, did you? Just chucked them in the trash, just like you did me and your son."

Nope, he didn't know, and she wondered if he'd remember seeing as how he hit the ground pretty hard. She didn't stick around to find out.

Chapter 5

YOUR SON.

The words echoed long after the last rumble of her car died off. Caleb lay on the ground as if frozen. And perhaps he was. He certainly didn't feel anything through the numb shield of his shock.

We have a child together.

No, not together. Renny had the child alone. All alone without anyone to rely on. Without telling a soul, not even his brother or mother because she thought he didn't want it.

Thought he didn't want her.

"Awwwww!" His yell echoed in the sky, and yet it did nothing to ease the bursting tension in him. His beast throbbed below the surface. Drawn by the rage. Fighting for control.

No.

No!

He had to keep his inner self caged.

But I have a son!

A son he was kept from by secrets and deals and a past he couldn't escape.

Except hadn't he escaped?

Caleb had retired from the military unit that had used him. He had escaped his servitude under the crooked rhino sergeant who drew him and others into acts of evil. A certain viperous enemy no longer controlled him.

Caleb couldn't help but touch the scar on his cheek. The price of slipping the naga's mesmerizing leash. Escaping the life he'd never wanted had left its mark, but he welcomed it. That scar signified his freedom, but it also reminded him of how it got there.

As if his nightmares would ever let him forget.

A shadow blocked the wan quarter moon struggling to shine in the sky. A blocky figure stood over him. Red slitted eyes flashed. A gator. Big one, too. *Wonder if he's another one of Wes's cousins?* The Mercers bred like bunnies on fertility drugs, popping kids out all over the place.

"There's no parking or sleeping in the lot overnight," the behemoth said.

"I seem to have lost my ride."

Luckily for him, Bruno wasn't a bad sort—even if he was a damned Mercer. He let Caleb borrow his phone, and that was why, less than twenty minutes later, his brother, glowering behind the wheel of his truck, pulled into the empty lot of the club.

Lowering his window, Constantine snapped, "Get in."

To Caleb's surprise, his brother leaned over and opened the passenger door.

"Holy shit, I get to ride in the truck."

His brother didn't crack a smile. "Only because Princess is sleeping in my jacket."

"Thank God because I was wondering what that bulge was in your lap."

His brother didn't say a word as he drove, but Caleb, for some reason, felt a need to spill. "So it turns out I've got a kid."

The truck swerved. "What?"

"His name is Luke. He's mine and Renny's."

The sudden forward momentum meant Caleb braced himself on the dash as the truck slammed to a stop.

"Get out of the truck," his brother ordered.

"Why would I do that?" Caleb asked.

"Why? Do you seriously have to ask? You know, I can handle the fact that you ditched me and Ma. I get it. I was almost eighteen. It wasn't like I needed you around. But to leave Renny and your kid?" Constantine banged his hands off his steering wheel. "I don't fucking know who you are. But you are not my brother. The brother I knew would never have abandoned his kid." Constantine shoved at him, and it was only the fact that the door was shut that Caleb didn't end up sprawled on the gravelly shoulder. As it was, Con's blow to his arm rocked the truck.

"Before you fucking hang me out to dry, I didn't know."

His brother's gaze narrowed. "What do you mean you didn't know? Didn't she tell you?"

Looking his brother in the eye as he admitted his fault proved impossible. "She tried to let me know. She sent letters. I just never read them."

"Just like you never read our letters, wrote back, or called us. You are such a fucking dick. Get out."

Couldn't argue that point. When Caleb would have opened the door, his brother growled, "Close the goddamned door." Constantine threw the truck into gear and, with a spin of the tires on the loose rock, drove them back onto the road. They drove for about a mile in silence before his brother said, "So I'm an uncle. To Luke."

"You've met him?" Caleb asked, suddenly thirsty to know more about his son.

"More like seen him. Once you left, Renny did for a while, too. I guess so that people wouldn't know she was pregnant."

"Kind of hard to hide, given she came back with a kid."

"Except she didn't come back right away. She's only been back in town about six months or so. I guess she felt like she had to on account of her dad. He caught some kind of disease or something, and she returned to care for him."

"Renny never told anyone he was mine?"

"No."

He couldn't help a pang at the knowledge she didn't want people to know Luke was his son.

But I can't really blame her, given she thought I didn't want him.

His brother slammed the wheel of his truck. "Dammit, I can't believe Renny never told me or Ma the baby was yours. We would have helped her if we'd known."

"As would I." Caleb slumped in his seat. "I've so royally fucked up my life."

"Yeah, you have."

"Gee, thanks."

"You didn't coddle me growing up, and I am not going to coddle you. You made mistakes. Suck it up, buttercup."

"You do realize I am supposed to be the older brother?"

"Then act like one. Or at least stop with this fucking woe-is-me routine. Now that the truth is out, you can be a father to a little boy."

A father...

A wave of vertigo gripped Caleb, and he grasped the console of the truck, lest he face plant into it. "Shit, Con, I can't be a dad. I don't know how. Look at me. I'm a bloody mess."

"You're just like every other soldier who's come home after seeing and experiencing bad stuff. You need time to adjust. You're going to have to learn to adapt. And you need to stop feeling sorry for yourself and accept that shit has happened. Move on, bro. Start anew."

"But I don't know how." Even admitting the weakness made him want to cringe. His croc certainly thrashed in its hidden box, rolling and rolling, ashamed that he feared the fight.

"None of us do, which is why we wing it and we make mistakes. That's life, and she's a bitch." An assertion punctuated by a tiny growl within Constantine's coat.

"Easy to say, but what should I do?" For the first time in years,

Caleb didn't have clear orders. He had to make the decisions. What if he made the wrong ones?

"First off, ask yourself what you want to achieve."

"What do you mean?"

Constantine took his gaze off the road for a minute to fix him with a stare. "What do you want to happen here? Set yourself a goal."

"You mean I should establish a mission objective."

"Wow, the military really did brainwash you. Okay, grunt"—Con flashed him a smile— "here's your mission. Assimilate into life at Bitten Point. Within that scope, you are to become involved with your son."

"If Renny lets me." Which was doubtful at the moment.

"Which brings me to the grovel-to-Renny-in-apology aspect. Add in to that make amends to Mother."

"And irritate my little brother." Caleb couldn't help but toss that one in and then laughed at the mock punch thrown by Constantine.

WITH CON'S help in coming up with a clear mission, it occurred to Caleb that he needed allies, and that was why he found himself on Melanie's porch—in cookie-cutter suburbia where his borrowed pickup truck covered in mud looked like it belonged to a gardener not a visitor.

But at least he looked somewhat respectable. He'd managed a comatose night of sleep with the help of pills and had enjoyed a hearty breakfast cooked by his mother before she went off to work.

When Constantine had a buddy from work grab him on his way, leaving Caleb with some wheels, he had no excuse. Time to work on completing the first part of his mission.

Taking a deep breath, telling the nervous butterflies in his tummy to fuck off, Caleb knocked on the front door.

A short and dark-haired woman flung open the portal with gusto and a hollered, "Don't you dare get dirty. We are leaving for the picnic in a minute." Orders given, Melanie turned to face Caleb and uttered an eloquent, "Oh."

"Hey, brat face." The old nickname came easily.

Still unable to find words, Melanie showed him her happiness at seeing him again by throwing her arms around him in a big hug.

"Good grief, are you sure you're not part anaconda?" he joked as she bound him tight.

"No one's too sure what great-great grandpa was, so you never know. But you didn't come here to hash out my ancestral lines, and since I know you already caught up with Daryl,"—Melanie drew herself out of his arms and peered up at him—"that means there's only one reason why you're here. Renny." Melanie hauled off and slugged him in the gut.

It didn't hurt, but it still made him exclaim, "What the hell? What happened to I'm glad to see you?"

"I am, but you also broke my best friend's heart. Do you know how hard she's had to struggle because you're an asshat?"

A cringe pulled his features taut. "I swear I didn't know about the baby. I just found out last night."

"Like fu—udge," Melanie said, stuttering her reply as a commotion at her feet drew her attention.

A pair of tousle-haired, dark-eyed boys stared up at him.

They didn't blink. Or move.

A waft of chocolate rose from one of them. With a sly grin, the slightly smaller of the two licked a sticky finger, not that it helped the brown smear on his hand. The little tyke regarded the cocoa smear, and Melanie growled, "I thought I hid the chocolate syrup."

"Found it," announced the tyke with no small amount of pride.

"More like it found you," she muttered. "Don't you dare wipe it on your pants."

The little guy listened to his mother and found something else to latch his sticky hand onto.

Caleb didn't have time to move back because the child moved so fast. One minute, the kid looked like he would defy his mother, and the next, he flung his arms around Caleb's legs, peeked up, and grinned. "Hi."

"Holy sh—oot," he said, curbing his language at the last second. "How do you resist the cuteness?"

"You don't, which is why they're spoiled monsters. Tatum, let go of Caleb's leg." Tatum required Melanie leaning forward to pry him loose, but the damage was done. Caleb's jeans were smeared in chocolate. Melanie eyed the sticky spots. "Sorry about that. Terrible twos are nothing compared to the Terrifying threes."

"So these are your boys?" Caleb didn't wait for an answer to his obvious question. He crouched down and studied the faces.

Identical twins in all ways from the messy mop of hair to the solemn stares to the mischief pulling at their lips. If it weren't for the fact that Tatum was slightly smaller than his brother, Caleb didn't know how you'd tell them apart.

The one without chocolate-smeared hands held out his arms and commanded, "Up."

Caleb stood.

The child waved his arms again, and Melanie laughed. "He didn't mean stand up. He meant pick him up. Looks like you've made a friend. That demanding fellow is Rory."

Making friends—even if cute and scary to hold, as the child clung to his upper body like a monkey—wasn't what Caleb came for.

"I need help," he blurted out.

"You're doing fine." Melanie said in a soothing tone. "Don't worry. They're practically impossible to drop now. They've got a grip like their mother. It's when they're babies you gotta watch out. One minute they're diaperless on the change table, peeing in the air while you're diving looking for a towel, and the next they're rolling in opposite directions and hitting the floor. Good thing they're tough, just like their daddy."

Andrew, tough? Caleb vaguely recalled slamming him into a locker a time or two. Which, in retrospect, was a bit of a dick move. But hey, that was high school.

"Yeah, so about that help. I have a son."

"His name is Luke," Melanie announced as she walked away and entered a living room.

Caleb followed, a monkey still on his hip. "You know him?"

"Duh." Melanie rolled her eyes. "I babysit him when Renny's at her day job."

Jackpot. If anyone could help him understand his son, Melanie could, because asking Renny was out of the question. "Perfect. I need pointers on being a dad."

Well, that got her gaping. "You mean you're planning to stay?"

"I think so. Maybe."

Her dark brows drew into a frown. "Maybe? That's not good enough. You are either in one hundred percent or you're out. That boy deserves better than to have his hopes raised, only to have them dashed."

"What if I swore to do my best?"

"What if I swore to hunt you down and geld you if you hurt my best friend and her son again?" So sweetly said, yet he caught the threatening thread underlying it.

"Deal." Because if he disappointed Renny, and now his son, Melanie wouldn't have to hurt him. He'd be dead.

Chapter 6

IN HER SUMMER FROCK–BOUGHT on a clearance rack for a fraction of its price—Renny stood with Luke on the edge of the picnic currently in full swing behind the Bittech Institute.

I shouldn't have come.

She hadn't planned to come, but Melanie—using some kind of alien sixth sense—must have sensed Renny's plan to back out because she called and played Renny the world's tiniest violin.

"But you have to come, or I'm liable to go completely nutso on those uptight human wives of the other executives."

"Have you forgotten? I'm human," Renny retorted. She hadn't inherited her father's shifter gene, but Luke sure had an animal inside. Every now and then, his eyes would flash a vivid green and his irises would slit. What she would do when he shifted into his croc form, she didn't know. She couldn't exactly teach him what to do. The one person who could was the one she wanted to avoid.

A man she couldn't stop thinking about.

After the revelation the night before that Caleb had not even known about Luke, she'd struggled with her emotions. On the one side, she simmered with rage at the knowledge he'd destroyed her letters, and thus ignored their son. But, at the same time, she couldn't help a spurt of hope. Hope because she'd seen the genuine shock in his eyes when he heard of their son.

And admit it, a part of you has already forgiven him because at least now you know he didn't intentionally abandon our child.

Rewind and try to remember, though, that he did abandon you.

For that alone, she should never forgive him, and that would probably work a lot better if she could stop obsessing about him.

Her inability to keep him out of her thoughts proved to be the catalyst for her choice. Rather than stay home and deal with all the chores—and let her mind churn over what to do with Caleb—she chose to go to the picnic.

"Get dressed," she'd told Luke. "We are going on a picnic." Thing was, now that she was here, she wasn't sure she'd made the right choice in coming.

While dressed in her nicest, Renny still felt as if she stood out among the other women in their crisp pastel linens with their perfectly coiffed hair. Her flowered summer frock was almost as bad as Melanie's vivid red strapless summer gown with its high waist and frothy skirt.

A tingling awareness only gave her a second to brace herself before she heard a murmured, "Hey, baby."

Before Renny could reply, her son reacted, whirling to face Caleb, his little body bristling as he put himself between them. A soft growl rumbled from Luke, and she couldn't help her mouth rounding into an O of surprise.

"Luke. Stop that." She almost said, *Don't growl at your father.* The sharp nip to her tongue stopped the words in time.

Even if Luke didn't understand who stood before him, Caleb did, and he sucked in a breath. He looked at her instead of their son, his expression torn, eyes full of panic, his breath coming fast. "So this is..."

"My son, Luke." No way was she confirming this was Caleb's son aloud, not with Luke listening. She wondered what Caleb was doing here and what he planned to do next.

Renny certainly never expected him to drop to his haunches and bring himself eye level with their son.

"Hey there, Luke. My name is Caleb." The big, scarred soldier, who outweighed Luke several times over, held out his hand, anxiety making him tense. Was it her or did his body tremble?

If the moment wasn't so emotionally charged, it would have made her smile.

No smiles. No softening. She had to remain strong. "What do you think you are doing?" Renny demanded.

"Introducing myself," Caleb said, never taking his eyes from their boy. The outstretched hand hung out there, and Luke appeared to ponder the offering before slowly slipping his smaller one into the grasp. Caleb shook it as if it was made of spun glass.

That made her laugh. "He's not going to break that easily."

"I'm tough." Luke puffed out his chest. "Because I'm the man of the house."

"You are?" Caleb replied lightly.

Luke nodded. "Mama said so on account I have no daddy. Rory and Tatum do. So do Philip and Cory."

Her son's unexpected talkativeness caused Caleb to blanch, and he might have squeezed a little too tight. Or her son sensed the weird vibe in the air. Either way, Luke yanked his hand away. "I wanna go play."

"Stay in sight," she admonished as Luke ran off and joined Melanie's boys, who were already leading their mother on a merry chase around the tables set with white linen and covered dishes.

"What are you doing here, Caleb? What are you trying to prove?" With Luke out of earshot, Renny didn't feel a need to temper her words.

"I'm not doing anything. Just thought I'd go to a picnic."

"You don't work for Bittech."

"Not currently. But Daryl was saying I should apply, seeing as how they're looking for more guys to beef up their security."

"If you're staying, then I am leaving."

She spun, meaning to grab her son and go, but Caleb stepped in front of her, a brick wall of muscle that once upon a time she would have snuggled.

"Running away, baby?"

She angled her chin. "Merely trying to avoid a scene. What happened to you staying away from me so it wouldn't be awkward?"

"I changed my mind."

Excuse me? "Well, change it back. You were right. This is awkward." And exhilarating. But most of all, it was scary, scary because she didn't really want to go.

He moved closer, and she automatically took a step back.

"Do I make you nervous?" he asked.

Caleb made her feel a lot of things. Nervous was among them, but maybe not for the reason he thought.

"I don't want anything to do with you. Was I not clear enough before?"

"You don't want to be seen with me. Can't say as I blame you. I'm definitely not as pretty as I used to be."

No, he wasn't, but he was definitely sexier, his boyish edge hardened by experience. The scars didn't take away from his attraction, merely showcased his toughness.

"I am not that shallow, Caleb. I really don't give a pickle what you look like, but I won't have you leading Luke on. He's got it tough enough as it is without you confusing matters."

"What's confusing about the fact I'm his father?"

"Not yet you aren't. That title has to be earned." Because she was damned if she was just going to let Caleb into her son's life without him proving he could handle it.

And he had to prove he wouldn't run off again.

Before Caleb could respond, she walked away, making a beeline for Melanie, who wore a plastered smile on her face and had a death grip on her water glass. A trio of wives surrounded Melanie, cutting off all escape.

Being a good friend, Renny plowed right on through with a murmured, "Excuse me, ladies, but I need to borrow my BFF here for a minute. Girl stuff." She yanked her friend away from the gaggle and, once they'd gone a few yards, stopped.

Melanie blew out a breath. "Thanks for saving me. My inner kitty was really pushing me to sharpen my claws. I'm pretty sure the tall one to my left is made of plastic."

"Don't thank me yet. I'm mad at you. How could you tell Caleb I would be here?"

"That jerk. I can't believe he ratted me out," Melanie huffed.

"He didn't."

"You tricked me."

"Telling the truth isn't a trick, and it was easy to figure out since you were the only one who knew I was coming."

"Fine. So I told him where you'd be. What else was I supposed to do? He showed up at my place wearing a woebegone expression." Melanie jutted her lip and batted her eyes.

Renny snorted. "I don't care how sorry he looks. I'm not ready to deal with him yet."

"You never will be, which is why you need to suck it up. If not for your own peace of mind then Luke's."

"Nothing wrong with my mind." Most days.

"Except for the fact you never got over him."

"What are you talking about? I've dated other guys. Slept with a few, too." None that left a lasting impression, though.

"And how many lasted more than a few weeks?"

Try more than a few dates. "It's not my fault I'm picky."

An eloquent roll of her eyes was Melanie's initial reply. "Why not just admit none of them were the right guys?"

"I have no problem admitting it. I'll know it when I find the one."

"Or you'll deny it until you die a spinster of old age. God, you're stubborn."

"What are you implying?" Renny asked, even if she already knew.

"You are the Queen of De-Nile," Melanie said, the old joke not enough to tone down the seriousness of their talk. "I think that the reason you never moved on was because you'd already found the one."

"Are you talking about *Caleb*?" Renny's voice pitched.

"Are you pining after another guy I don't know about? Hell yeah, I'm talking about Caleb. Admit it, he's the one."

"*The one*"—and, yes, Renny finger quoted it as she said it—"left me without so much as a goodbye or a reason. And now he waltzes back into town and thinks he can say he is sorry and suddenly become a part of my life again."

"Hate to break it to you, girlfriend, but he already is a part of your life. He always will be because he's Luke's daddy."

Hard to argue that fact, so Renny went for diversion instead. "Speaking of daddies, there's Andrew with Rory under his arm, and he doesn't look very happy."

"When is he ever happy?" Melanie muttered.

Trouble in suburban paradise. As the best friend, Renny was privy to many secrets, one of them being the fact that things hadn't been right between Melanie and Andrew for a while. But Renny knew Melanie was doing her damnedest to change that. Was that where the plan for another kid came from?

"Want me to go save the boys?" Renny asked. She seriously meant save, too, because while Andrew might have donated sperm, his fathering skills left much to be desired.

"Too late. They got into the donuts." Tatum, lips powdered in white, his small hands, too, clutched at his father's dark slacks. White fingerprints marred the fabric. Melanie sighed. "Dammit. I better get Andrew's spare set of clothes before he has a fit."

"You travel with spares?" Renny asked.

"Spares?" Melanie snorted. "Try triplicates. I have twin demons of mischief. We're lucky if we only need two outfits a day. And Andrew is so finicky when it comes to being clean. I'll be back in a few."

Melanie teetered off in the direction of the parking lot, stopping halfway to slip off her heels.

Renny held back a smile. Her friend might have married upper middle class, but at heart, she was still a bayou girl, and preferred to go about barefoot.

Alone for the moment, Renny let her gaze rove until she located her son, only to discover Luke was being watched by Caleb, watched with a rapier gaze, and she noted how he clenched his fists instead of lunging when Luke tripped chasing Rory around a tree.

Caleb might hesitate to intervene, but she wouldn't. She went to his side, concern creasing her expression. "Are you all right, bug?"

Before Luke could burst into tears and make a drama about the green stain on his knee, a deep, gravelly voice interjected.

"Of course the boy is fine. He's tough. Anyone can tell just by looking at him. Must get it from his mother."

Renny might have chided Wes for his words, except one moment her son went from looking like he'd start wailing to puffing his chest out and boasting, "Didn't hurt at all."

And off went her boy, chasing the twins again.

A moue twisted her lips. "I can't believe that worked."

"He's a boy." Chauvinism, alive and well, and thriving in Wes Mercer.

Standing, Renny stroked her hand down her skirt to make sure it hung where it should before she took in Wes's appearance, a hard guy to miss. Nothing about the guy was small, from his bulging arms to his wide shoulders to the smirk on his lips.

"Something funny?" she asked.

"Other than the way you're mollycoddling your boy?" The dark arch of his brow spoke of his disdain.

"I am not smothering him. Much." Although hadn't Melanie accused her of over parenting? Actually, her exact words had been very similar to Wes's. *"He's a boy. He's supposed to jump off things."*

At least Wes didn't say the other thing Melanie had as well, *"He needs a father."* And Renny was looking for one. Kind of.

She noted Wes staring intently over her shoulder. "What are you looking at?"

A smile stretched his lips, not exactly a nice one. "Your ex-boyfriend is staring daggers at me right now."

"What did you do?"

"Me?" Wes failed at looking innocent. He'd been born bad. Bad genes. Bad upbringing. Bad boy. But sinfully handsome with his dark hair and tanned skin.

"Yes, you. I know how you like to taunt Caleb. You always have."

Wes's smile widened. "Can I help it if that croc snaps so easily?"

"Maybe if you didn't do it on purpose, he wouldn't freak."

"But here's the beauty. I actually wasn't trying to annoy him when I stopped to talk to you. However, I am so glad I did because he is practically bursting out of his skin. If he were a cat or a dog, he'd have already pissed on you to mark his territory."

Renny couldn't help a wrinkle of her nose. "That's just being gross. And you're wrong. I mean nothing to Caleb, so why would he care if another guy is talking to me?"

"Not just any guy. Me." Wes stepped closer, looming in her space, and for a moment, she wondered what was wrong with her.

Wes was hot. Like super attractive. Yet, even though he stood close to her, the scent of him clean and sharp, she wasn't in the least attracted.

It wasn't because she knew of his reputation as the boy to stay away from. Make that the one all the girls wanted.

He's hot. Which was why she couldn't understand, when he turned an intense gaze on her, which was only enhanced by the slight smirk on his lips, she hardly felt a thing. Mild interest at most.

Her lack of attraction made her bold. "Why didn't we ever hook up?" she asked.

She took him off balance—she could see by the widening of his eyes—but he had a ready retort. "Because you were dating Caleb."

"And after?"

"You left."

She rolled her eyes. "And I came back. This is like, what, the third time we've run into each other? Each time you do a little flirt, and yet you've never asked me out."

"I don't like to waste my time. Any idiot can see you're still pining for Caleb."

"I am not."

"Really? Then prove it." The smile that tugged Wes's lips held a challenge no one could resist. Not even her.

Because I have not been pining for Caleb. She could and would date whoever she wanted. Even a Mercer!

"You're on."

Leaning on tiptoe, she heard Wes murmur, "Oh, this is going to create some chaos."

Maybe it would. Maybe it would throw Caleb into a tizzy, but that was okay. It was about time he got some payback for leaving her.

Let him feel something. Let him realize just what he'd lost.

Renny's lips met Wes's, and there was no electrical spark, no kaboom of the senses. It was...nice.

It thankfully didn't last long.

"I hope I'm not interrupting." The right words, but given Caleb spat them out through gritted teeth, not all that pleasant.

Renny pulled away from Wes, only to stiffen at the possessive hand Caleb dared place on the middle of her back. The fabric of her dress prevented skin-to-skin contact, and yet, awareness ignited in her.

Gosh darn it. An actual kiss did nothing, but Caleb thinking he could claim her in public had her wetting her panties.

It wasn't fair. She tried to move away from his touch, sidestepping left then right. Caleb simply followed her, never relinquishing his claim.

His stubbornness didn't endear him to her in the least. "Hands off," she hissed over her shoulder.

Caleb completely ignored her, focusing instead on Wes. "If it isn't my old school chum."

"Chum? I believe the trending word these days is frenemies. How have you been, snaggletooth? Did you run and leave behind a whole other bunch of people before coming here?"

At Wes's audacity, Renny sucked in a breath.

The tension in Caleb rose a notch. His jaw hardened. "I didn't run. I served my time with the military and left with an honorable discharge."

"Ah yes. The military. Can't say as I ever felt the urge. I much preferred to stay behind and enjoy the benefits of home." Renny bit her lip instead of giggling as Wes winked, so obviously baiting Caleb.

Caleb, though, didn't think Wes joked. "Stay away from Renny."

Jealousy. Oh my, there was no denying it. Caleb was jealous. A spurt of warmth curled low in her body. *No. Don't give in.*

Fight the attraction. Fight it with anger. "You can't decide who I see." This time, she managed to completely evade Caleb's touch and stood apart from both men, arms crossed over her chest.

Wes outright laughed. "You've been told. Hope you don't lose too much sleep thinking about how badly you'll fare when she compares me against you."

His smug assurance irritated her, too. "You might be cute, Wes, but I am not interested in dating a sexist thug."

"Thug?" Wes arched a brow. "I haven't had an arrest since I turned eighteen."

"Doesn't mean you're walking the straight and narrow," Caleb pointed out. "Every one knows the Mercers are dirty."

Wes lost his happy smile. "Maybe everyone should pay more attention before casting out insults. Now, while it's been just fucking grand catching up, I'm going to have to ask you what you're doing here."

But Caleb just flipped the query around. "What are you doing here?"

"I'm here as part of the security detail for this party."

Something Renny had known, but she could see how Caleb might not have, especially since Wes was dressed just like one of the guests. Dark slacks, a dark mauve button-up shirt, the material filmy and light, and a dark gray tie.

"You're a guard?" Caleb let loose a derisive snort. "Isn't that kind of like letting the gator into the henhouse? Also, since when does a Mercer have a real job? What, did you run out of contraband to smuggle? Lost the recipe for your grandpa's moonshine?"

Rather than flaring Wes's temper, Caleb's outburst served only to bring back his cool smirk. "I see serving time with the military didn't improve your sense of humor. And being a veteran doesn't give you an automatic invite to this party. I'm going to have to ask you to leave."

"Melanie invited me."

"Ask me if I give a fuck. I'll bet if I ask her husband, he'll tell me to kick your ass out to the curb." Wes sounded quite confident, and Renny had a feeling Andrew wouldn't side with Caleb. One too many swirlies in high school.

"Andrew always was a whiny dick who couldn't do shit for himself."

Renny winced at Caleb's insult, yet couldn't quite disagree. Personally, she'd always thought Melanie could do better. But then again, her friend technically had, seeing as how she was the one married and living in a real house.

But speaking of Andrew drew Renny's attention to something. "Melanie's not back yet with Andrew's change of clothes."

Surely she'd had enough time to get to the parking lot and back. A vague sense of wrongness made Renny gnaw her lower lip.

"She probably got stopped for a chat."

"Maybe. I'm still going to go find her. It's time I grabbed Luke and headed out anyhow."

"I'll walk you to your car," Caleb offered.

Before she could say, "No, thank you," a murmur rose in the crowd. Even before someone held aloft a familiar pair of heels—only Melanie would wear black stilettos to a picnic—Wes was moving, his hand dropping to his side to grab at a two-way radio.

He pressed the button. "Teams A and B, missing female, five-foot-nothing, in a bright red gown..."

The detail Wes conveyed proved quite elaborate. The man had an eye for detail? Or had he just noticed Melanie?

There was a time in high school when Renny wondered if her friend would date him. The bad boy every mother hated. But Melanie had chosen to be more mature about her choice. Andrew was going places. Andrew was a gentleman.

Andrew also bored the heck out of Melanie. But she still chose him.

From the strand of trees yards away to their left, the twins burst forth, wailing. Standing with his mouth gaping, Andrew did nothing to calm them, leaving Renny to run and gather them into her arms in an attempt to calm them.

"Shh. Calm down and tell me what's wrong."

Rory sobbed. "A dinosaur got mama."

"It's probably gonna eat her." Tatum sniffled.

"What is? Did you see something?"

Matching tousled heads nodded. "A monster," they announced in chorus, but that was all they would say. That and a small voice saying, "It was scary."

"You're safe now," Renny murmured, tucking them close. "I promise there are no monsters or dinosaurs roaming around. I'll bet your mom is just fine, you'll see."

Despite her reassurance, the twins' fear proved contagious, and Renny peeked for her son, cursing herself for not having grabbed him, too. What if something did roam in the bayou?

Something stalked all right, but it was on two legs and had a hand on her son's shoulder.

The look that trusting Luke turned on Caleb wrenched something in her, and she couldn't help but shiver, unable to ignore the ominous portent.

For the first time she understood why Wanda liked to say, "Someone's plotting against us. Get the gun."

Chapter 7

THE MOMENT SOMEONE held aloft those shoes, Caleb came to life.

Danger. Stand on guard.

Given the way Caleb suffered from anxiety, you'd think that a whiff of danger would send him into a fit.

Yet, this was the odd thing about Caleb's psyche issues. Danger always seemed to energize him. It drew his scaly beast. The one he fought to keep hidden, except in times like these when alarm bells went off. He needed the predator to assess the situation.

First thing, where were Renny and Luke? She was easy to spot, her arms slipping around Melanie's wailing twins, but Luke wasn't with her. Pivoting around, Caleb didn't have to turn far to find his son.

The small lad, less than half his size, stood right beside him. A little hand slipped into his, and for once, Caleb didn't flinch at the unexpected contact.

His son might not know yet who he was, but he trusted Caleb to protect him.

He trusts me. Even if he had no reason to. Something in Luke recognized Caleb. Understood Caleb provided safety.

"Will you help find Aunt Melanie?" The murmured request took Caleb by surprise.

"There's already people looking for her."

"But not in the right place. They're looking in the building."

"Of course they're checking there first because Melanie probably went to the ladies room or something." Except why drop her shoes on the edge of the pavement, coincidentally just around the curve of the building where no one from the party could see anything? And why would the twins have come running from the woods screaming?

"The thing in the swamp took her."

"Thing? What thing?" Caleb turned a sharp gaze down at his son, who stared off at the vegetation bordering the cleared field.

"A dinosaur."

For a moment, his first impulse was to scoff, and yet for some reason, Caleb instead asked, "What makes you think it was a dinosaur?"

"It was green and scaly."

"So maybe you saw a crocodile or an alligator. They might seem like dinosaurs."

Holy fuck, his son could roll his eyes like a pro. "I know what a croc and gator look like. And they don't walk on two legs."

Not usually, but the time Caleb had spent in the military, away from what he knew and immersed in a world where the mysteries of magic weren't lost, he'd seen things. Impossible things. He'd met impossible shifters. Men who shifted only partially, sporting the heads of jackals. Stallions, with the upper torsos of men, the centaurs of old. Then the scariest thing of all, the naga, a beast thought hunted to extinction. The serpentine monster wasn't dangerous because of its deadly strength, but because of the poisonous nature of their voice. Whatever the naga asked, a person did. He should know. He'd suffered under the influence of one for much too long. His scar tightened. Fire had severed that slave-like bond.

These experiences meant Caleb was well aware the world was much more vast and varied than most people, even shifters, imagined. It meant he kept his mind open to the possibility of a gator or even a croc walking about on two legs.

"Did the thing have two arms as well?" Caleb asked.

A nod of his son's head. "With claws. And its face was weird."

Face, not muzzle or snout. Interesting choice of word.

Caleb kept a hold of Luke's hand as Renny made her way to him, the twins now clinging to their father—who seemed vastly uncomfortable—confronted with his children's hiccupping sobs.

What a useless tool, but not Caleb's problem.

When Renny got close enough, he asked, "Did the boys mention anything to you after they came out of the woods?"

"As a matter of fact, they did. Something about a monster."

"A dinosaur," Luke corrected.

"Yes, one of them said that. Probably a reptile of some kind that scared them, but I can't see Melanie getting taken unawares by one."

He couldn't disagree. As part of the feline Pantherinae family, even in her human form, Melanie had a very developed sense of smell.

"I don't suppose you've heard of a two-legged lizard man roaming in the swamp?"

A brow arched as Renny stared at him. "Is this your way of insulting Wes again? The Mercers aren't at fault for everything. And, besides, he was standing with us when she went missing."

A clamor went up from the far end of the clearing, where a weeping willow draped the shore to the creek in a thick curtain. From between the strands, a man in a purple shirt appeared carrying something crimson.

Renny squinted, but not for long, as Caleb, with his better eyesight, spoke aloud, "It's Wes, and it looks like he's got Melanie."

"Is she all right?" A fair question to ask since her friend was being carried instead of walking.

A moment later, she got her answer as a shrill shriek shot across the field. "How dare you!"

"I wonder what Wes did this time."

"He's a Mercer. Does it matter?" was Caleb's reply as he watched a throng of people descend on Melanie and her rescuer. "You wanna go check on her?"

Before he'd even finished asking, she was striding towards Melanie, she just never made it anywhere close to her side as a cluster of hens, dressed in pastels, swarmed her best friend with a bevy of questions.

"Oh my God, you're alright."

"What happened?"

"Is it true you were abducted by a dinosaur?"

And a lowly murmured, "Attention slut."

While Caleb towered high enough to see what happened, Renny had to rely on peeks in between the milling bodies, not that there was much to see. Melanie was still in Wes's grip, the Bittech guard for some reason not setting her down or passing her off, probably because Andrew was too busy off to the side whispering in his phone.

Asshat. A true mate would be more worried about his wife.

Catching her best friend's eye, Renny pantomimed a phone to her ear and mouthed, "Call me later."

Melanie mouthed back, "Save me."

Eyeing the chatterboxes having a marvelous time practicing their drama, Renny shook her head.

Caleb couldn't help but smirk. "Aren't you going to wade in there and rescue her?"

"No way am I diving between those hens and their moment." Instead of rescuing Melanie, Renny waved and mouthed. "Bye."

No mistaking the lip synching of "Bitch. I hate you."

"I think you peeved her off," Caleb stated.

Renny laughed. "Good. It's payback for that last blind date Melanie sent me on. How she ever thought that visiting scientist who still lived with his mother would appeal, I will never figure out."

Turning around, Renny began to walk in the direction of the parking lot.

Caleb stuck to her side and said, "Are you sure you don't want to stay and talk to Melanie, and make sure she's fine?"

Renny shook her head. "There's too many *people*"—she inclined her head to the human contingent—"for us to really talk. She seems okay now, so I'm just going to take Luke home."

"Let me walk you to your car."

"You don't have—"

Caleb held up hand. "Don't even start. Melanie just went missing. We don't know why. Her boys and Luke claim they saw something. Now is not the time to let your dislike of me prevent you from doing the right thing."

"I can protect Mommy from the dinosaur."

They both looked down at Luke, who, despite his brave words, looked pale.

A sigh escaped Renny. "Fine. You can walk with us, but I warn you, I'm parked at the back of the lot. Fashionably late means terrible parking."

"I know. I'm by the dumpster." Caleb shuddered. "I forgot to hold my breath when I got out of the truck."

Luke giggled.

They both peeked down, and Caleb saw Luke staring at him. "You're funny," the little boy said. No mistaking the shine of hero worship.

It didn't take a genius for Caleb to understand the scowl Renny sent his way. He shrugged. It wasn't as if he'd done it on purpose to make his son like him.

And he damn sure wouldn't take it back.

As Luke skipped only a few paces ahead, confident in the fact that he had someone watching his back, Caleb muttered in a low tone, "Why so pissed?"

"You're on the scene like, what, twenty minutes, and he's looking at you like you're some kind of demi-god."

"The boy isn't doing this to hurt your feelings."

"I know that, but it doesn't mean it's fair, or not hurtful. I do everything for him and have to fight for even a smile these days. He hands it to you for doing nothing but existing and telling a dumb joke." Her lower lip jutted.

"So you're mad because our son likes me?"

Judging by the scowl she turned his way, yes.

"Do you know I am not even allowed to kiss him on the cheek anymore when I drop him off at school?" She clamped her lips as Luke skipped back and tucked his hand into Caleb's.

"There's our car," the boy announced.

Which meant there wasn't much time left.

Caleb couldn't just let her drive off. Could he? So many things crowded the air between them, and perhaps she sensed it because she handed Luke her car keys. "Bug, can you do Mommy a favor and open the windows so we don't die of the heat?"

With a high-pitched, "Yes," his son zipped off, keys jangling in his fist.

"He seems so small," Caleb noted in the sudden silence.

"Funny, because to me he seems so big now. He's healthy and just the right size for his age."

"You've done a good job, Renny. He seems like a great kid."

A heavy sigh left her. "I know. He's the best, but he is missing one thing in his life. Something I can't give him."

"What? Tell me and I'll get it."

"Can you?" She stopped walking and turned to give him a serious expression. "Because what Luke really needs most of all is a father."

"I thought you wanted me to stay away." Not that he thought he could. Now that Caleb had met his son, he was more determined than ever to stick around.

"Apparently, my brilliant plan to hold off on telling Luke about his father was doomed to failure. Even though I haven't said a thing, anyone can see he's drawn to you."

Like knew like.

"So what does that mean?" He didn't dare make any assumptions.

"It means I wish I was a big bad B-word. Because only a big B would keep a son from his father."

He couldn't help but grin. "Is this your cute way of saying bitch?"

She cringed. "You didn't have to say it aloud."

"Sorry, baby."

"And stop with the baby thing, Caleb. We're not a couple anymore. Just because I think you should spend time with Luke—"

"You do?"

"Yes, I do. But that decision doesn't mean I've forgiven you or that things are okay between us."

Yet.

But I'm going to change that, baby.

This was one mission he wouldn't fail.

Arriving at her car, Caleb frowned. While the body was in decent shape, anyone could tell the car was worn. The tires didn't match, and the tread left on them wasn't deep enough to provide real traction. "Please don't tell me you actually drive this thing?"

"I'll have you know this thing gets me where I need to go. Most of the time," she added under her breath.

"It's got roll down windows." Incredulity colored his tone.

"And no air conditioning. Something about no more freezer thingy stuff in the lines. But it's not a big deal."

"You've got duct tape on the seats."

"With pretty little duckies on it. Are you done insulting my car now?"

"No." A smile split Caleb's lips. "But I can save some for later."

"Speaking of later, maybe you'd like to come over later." She slapped a hand over her mouth as soon as she said it.

Before she could retract, he accepted right away. "Sounds like a plan."

Watching, he stood as few yards away as she started the car and reversed it out of the spot. He was close enough to hear her mutter, "What the hell did I just do?"

But even more heartening were his son's words. "I'm going to show him my DS when he comes."

And Caleb would show them he was a man they could rely on. A man who wouldn't run. Never again.

Only once Renny was on her way did Caleb feel some of his tension ease. The woman he never stopped loving and his son were away from the danger.

Yet his beast didn't settle down. On the contrary, it pushed at the bindings that held it. Pushed. And pushed.

Caleb snarled. *Stop fighting. I am not letting you out.*

For distraction, he glanced to see what happened with the picnic. Caleb noted Melanie striding to the Bittech building, her twins clinging to her hands. Her husband walked a few paces ahead of her, busy on his phone. However, Daryl's sister was of less interest than Wes, who stood at the edge of the paved drive and stared into the woods.

What was he looking for? And more importantly, did it threaten Renny and Luke?

"So which of your cousins played a prank on the boss's wife?" he asked, coming up behind Wes.

The other man didn't turn. "It wasn't one of us. My family knows better than to lay a hand on her."

An odd statement to make. Melanie was in no way related to the Mercers, so why would Wes infer Melanie was protected?

Picking on one of the Mercers, especially one of Wes's siblings, meant bringing a shitload of trouble down on your head. Wes took his job as oldest in his family very seriously. He'd started stealing from a young age to help feed all the mouths, especially once his dad got injured and couldn't smuggle drugs through the bayou no more.

But don't feel sorry for the bastard. Wes might have a strong sense of family, but he was a dick. Belonging to the reptile family didn't mean they got along. On the contrary, their rivalry was legend, especially when it came to hunting in the bayou.

Speaking of hunting, nothing he'd ever tracked smelled as odd as the faintly lingering scent emanating from the direction of the woods. "What is that stench? Or is that your cologne?"

"Do you mean your mom's perfume?" Wes smirked. "On the other hand, if you're talking about that funky smell coming from the woods, then I don't know, but whatever it is, Melanie reeked of it."

"Where did you find her anyhow?"

"Under the willow tree, on the other side where no one could see her. Sleeping like a fucking princess."

"That makes no sense. How did she get there?"

"She doesn't know, and all I found was that smell..." Wes trailed off. "But you didn't stick behind to ask me about some kind of bayou creature. What do you want?"

"Just so we're clear, I'm back to stay."

Wes tossed him a hard look. "Is that supposed to be a warning?"

"Luke is my son."

"About time you claimed him."

"You knew?"

Wes shrugged. "Not at first, but when I saw the two of you side by side... No mistaking that giant square head. My condolences to Renny's snatch."

A growl vibrated through him. "Watch your mouth. I'm warning you right now, I don't want you near my son, and stay away from Renny."

"Isn't that up to her?"

"No!" The word burst from him and Wes arched a brow.

"I wonder what she'll say when she finds out. And just so you know, I have no interest in your girl. I just like to jab at your thick hide."

"Well, jab at someone else. I got enough working against me in winning over Renny. I don't need you mucking around fucking shit up."

"You can have Renny."

"How magnanimous of you." Caleb's sarcasm dripped.

"Not really, more like selfish interest. She's got a kid, and that means she needs someone stable. I ain't ready to settle down."

"Now if only more Mercers would think the same way and keep it in their pants."

"Says the guy with a bastard."

The bruised knuckles as Caleb replied to that statement?

Totally worth it.

Chapter 8

WAS the price of her sanity worth letting Caleb into her life? By the time Renny had reached home, she still wasn't sure. Doing the right thing for her son wasn't necessarily the right thing for her. Being near Caleb tested every ounce of her willpower. Did she have the strength to resist?

She feared the answer.

Confused and anxious, she put a call in to Melanie, only to have it go right to voicemail. It made her wonder if perhaps she should have stayed.

Then we could have spent more time with Caleb.

A Caleb who might be coming over later. Eek. What was she thinking?

She waited fifteen minutes before trying Melanie again.

The call was answered with, "Some best friend you are, leaving me to the tender mercy of those harpies."

"I would have stayed, but—"

"Instead preferred traipsing off with a long-lost soldier. That's fine, ditch your best friend for a hot guy. I get it. Did you finally give him a proper welcome home?"

Heat invaded Renny's cheeks and made her sputter. "I did not sleep with him."

"Yet."

"Never." Okay, that was a lie. It was more like yet, but only if he managed to wear down her resistance. Renny didn't want to get involved. Now if she could just convince the rest of her body to listen. "And why would you think I slept with him?"

"I saw you heading off with him and Luke."

"As protection. With the boys claiming they saw a dinosaur and you disappearing, he was just being cautious. He didn't want to see his son getting hurt."

"Sure he was."

"Fine. Don't believe me. But who cares about me? What in blue blazes happened to you?"

"Renny, such language." Melanie snickered into the phone. "As to what the fuck happened, your guess is as good as mine. One minute I'm walking to the car to get some pants, the next, bam, nothing."

Renny paced her small kitchen, keeping her voice low so that Luke wouldn't hear her. However, keeping it quiet proved hard, given Melanie's story. "What do you mean you don't remember anything after walking away from me? Surely you saw someone or something?"

"Nothing, just a great big blank until Wes planted one on me."

Shock stopped her nervous movement. "He kissed you while you were passed out?"

"That's what I call it, but he claims it was mouth to mouth."

"Do you believe him?" Renny asked.

"Of course not. He's a Mercer."

"Snob." Renny snickered. "Gosh, who would have expected you to ever become one."

"Shut up. I am not a snob. Merely discerning," Melanie declared in her snootiest voice.

Arching a brow, Renny snorted. "Is that what you're going with?"

"Fine. I'm a bitch. But let's look at facts. Apart from Wes, name one other Mercer with a real job?"

"Bruno."

"He's only a third cousin. He doesn't count."

"So did you?"

"Did I what?" Melanie asked.

"Kiss him back, of course," Renny asked.

"Renny! How could you ask that?"

"Because once upon a time you had the hots for each other in high school."

"And then I smartened up."

Yeah, her best friend had chosen stable and boring over sexy. Then again, who was Renny to criticize? She'd gone after the sexy bad boy and look where it had gotten her. "So are you telling me you didn't smooch him back at all?"

"It was totally one-sided. I'm a married woman."

"Who has to schedule sex with her husband."

"It's not Andrew's fault stress at work is killing his mojo. No matter how hot Wes is, I won't betray my vows. Now drop the subject, or I am going to start grilling you about Caleb."

"Nothing to talk about."

"Liar. Spill."

"Okay, so you'll be ecstatic to know that I'm going to tell Luke Caleb's his dad."

"You haven't done that yet?" Melanie screeched.

Renny winced. "I'm working on it. It's not easy to announce to your kid, hey, Daddy's back in town and says he wants to get to know you."

"He does?"

At the little voice from behind her, Renny's eyes widened. She whirled, but sure enough, her son was no longer in the other room watching television from like ten inches away from the screen.

Nope. He'd ghosted to a spot behind her and heard...how much?

"Melanie, I gotta go. Crisis to handle over here." Renny hung up her phone as her son studied her.

"Hi, bug. How much did you hear?" In other words, could she chicken out of the truth for a while longer?

Nope.

"Caleb's my daddy," Luke announced. "I heard you say so to Auntie Mel."

She could only nod.

"Cool. I'm gonna show him my room, too, when he comes over."

And with that, her son turned around and wandered back to his spot just inches from the screen.

He sat still, legs in a lotus position, elbows on his knees, totally focused on the cartoons.

"Um, did you want to ask me any questions?" she asked.

For some reason, she expected the silent treatment, maybe a few accusations, but little boys handled things differently from adults. Luke turned to her and said, "What's for supper?"

With those words, she felt a flutter of panic. She'd invited Caleb over, but never specified a time.

Or given him an address, but that he could find easily enough. Her traitor of a friend had probably programmed it into his GPS.

He could show up anytime, and given he was a guy, he'd want food. Heck, she wanted food. What a pity her kitchen held none.

Dragging a complaining Luke, she fled to the grocery store. She dawdled up and down the aisles, taking way too much time to decide what she wanted. Her budget could only stretch so far, but she didn't want Caleb to think she'd invited him over to guilt him on how they lived.

She eyed the packages of meat in the refrigerated display. So expensive, but she couldn't exactly expect him to be content with a salad and hot dog.

Steak it was, a big, thick one that cost more than she usually spent in a week on meat, and figuring what the hell, she grabbed a smaller one for herself and Luke to share. By the time she'd gathered some fresh vegetables and splurged on a premade dessert, it was almost five o'clock and closing time.

Small towns didn't keep the same hours as the city. Out here, once the sun started to go down, which was fairly early in the late fall, businesses closed, traffic slowed, and people hid in their homes—so the animals could come out and play.

Bitten Point was a shifter friendly town. Sure, it had its fair share of humans—they were after all the dominant race on the planet—however, those that chose to live there knew the secret. And if they didn't, they didn't stay long. There were ways to convince people it was best to move on.

Having grown up among the shifters, Renny certainly didn't fear them, even when they wore their animal shape. A shifter crocodile or bear was no more likely to attack than when they sported their human guise. Only nature's unenlightened hunted, those who walked on two legs, and that was rare. Most wild creatures preferred to go after easy prey.

So when her son said, "Mama, there's something hiding at the edge of the woods," she didn't pay too much mind. Children had vivid imaginations. Heck, Melanie took the doors off her sons' closet so that the boogieman would stop hiding in there at night. As for Luke, Renny got him a bed with built-in drawers underneath so the monster under the bed wouldn't grab him.

Just outside of town, the grocery store with its heavy discounts and clearance bins, bordered the swamplands. While quieter this cool time of the year, the area, with its lush vegetation, still hummed with life, some of it probably intimidating for a little boy.

She tossed the groceries in her trunk and slammed it shut. Only once she slid in her car and spoke to an empty back seat, "Are you buckled in, buddy?" did she realize Luke wasn't in the car. Out she jumped, heart hammering. "Luke? Luke? Where are you?"

"I see something." The faint reply had her scanning the area until she spotted her son standing on the crumbling concrete curb meant to hold the bayou back.

The little bug had wandered. "Come back here. Right this instant."

"Do I have to?" Luke turned with a sulk on his face. "I want to see."

Time to go into mommy mode. Renny planted her hands on her hips. "Now."

"Fine." As he huffed the word, he took two steps, and Renny felt all her breath whoosh as something dark swung from the shadows behind him, just missing his little body.

"Luke! Run!" She screamed the words as she darted toward him, but someone else was faster. A big body barreled past her and scooped a frantic-eyed Luke.

Renny pounded toward Caleb and her son, eyes darting between them and the shadows that no longer moved.

"What was that?" she asked, holding her arms out for her son, and while he clung for a moment to Caleb, in the end, Luke reached for her.

For the moment, Mommy still came first.

She hugged him close to her, eyes closed, trying to calm her racing heart.

"I didn't see anything. I heard your scream and came bolting around the corner."

"I thought I saw something in the woods." An admission that had her eyeing the shadows, and seeing nothing. Had she imagined it?

"Thought you saw...?"

"It was another one of the dinosaurs," Luke confided in a soft whisper. "They escaped."

"What are you talking about? Dinosaurs don't exist." Renny said it, and yet, it didn't emerge very convincing, especially given how pensive Caleb appeared.

"Even if they did, I don't want you to worry about any dinosaurs when I'm around, big guy. I was in the army, and we soldiers know how to take care of overgrown lizards."

"Says the biggest lizard of all," she muttered under her breath.

"The biggest, baby." The low growl of his reply tingled her skin with awareness. She tossed her head, still determined to keep him at arm's length.

But she couldn't do the same for Luke, who wiggled free from her grip. Setting him on the ground, she couldn't help a twinge as her heart swelled and at the same time shrank at her son's instinctive move to stand by his father's side.

Already he's feeling that bond to his father. It shouldn't have hurt, but it did.

"What are you doing here?" she asked. Either Caleb had uncanny timing, or he was stalking her. Funny how neither option bothered her, not like the fear of losing her son did.

"I wasn't sure what time you wanted me over, so I thought I'd grab some food before popping in on you. But..." He shot a look at the store and grimaced. "I arrived too late."

She would have said just in time. What if the thing she'd seen had not run off at Caleb's arrival? Would it have snatched her son like it had nabbed Melanie?

If it's even the same thing, you ninny.

Still, what were the chances of two occurrences of supposed dinosaurs happening in the same day?

"I've got food in my trunk. If you want to follow me," she offered.

"I don't suppose I could ask for a ride. My brother dropped me off because he needed his truck tonight."

"Sure." She could handle the short ride from here to her place. This was a chance to prove Caleb's proximity didn't bother her. She could handle it.

Liar.

As soon as she slid behind the wheel, she noted her hands were shaking. Caleb noticed, too. "Are you sure you're okay?"

"Fine. Just fine." She sighed. "No. No, I'm not. Do you mind driving?"

He didn't question her shakiness. Probably blamed it on her recent fright, and yet the truth was, she felt like a teenager all over again around him. Tongue-tied, hyper aware, and high-strung. She didn't know if she'd scream if he touched her or would melt into a puddle.

Either way, was it perverse to want to find out?

As she switched sides, she peeked in to see Luke buckled in his booster seat, his gaze intent on Caleb.

Apparently, her son's little mind had been churning with questions because one popped free. "Are you really a soldier?"

"I was." Caleb glanced into the rearview mirror to look at their son. "I left Bitten Point a long time ago and fought in a war overseas."

"Did you kill people?"

"Luke! That is not an appropriate question." While Renny didn't mind a healthy curiosity, she drew the line at morbid.

Caleb placed a hand on her knee, an intimate gesture that sucked away any further protest, especially once she realized Caleb wasn't bothered. "I don't mind answering. I did kill some people. It's what soldiers do. We go to war and do what we're told." So grimly said.

"Is the war how you got hurt?"

Renny could have moaned in embarrassment. "Luke, you shouldn't pry like that." Even if he asked some of the questions she'd wondered.

"It happened during my last mission. I got burned in a fire, a big one in a place where I was held prisoner."

"Someone captured you?" It was her turn to blurt out a query.

For a moment, she thought he wouldn't answer. His jaw locked, and his fingers gripped the wheel of her steering column so tightly his knuckles turned white. "Yes. I was a slave for a while to a..." Caleb trailed off as his eyes noted Luke's intent gaze in the mirror. "A really bad person."

"Did you kill them?"

"No." Stark. Flat. "But fear not, that person won't be bothering anyone else ever again. The good guys won the day."

The building Renny called home loomed, and she derailed the serious talk by pointing and saying, "This is our place." She waited for his derision, but Caleb simply pulled to the curb and turned off the motor.

Luke led the way up the outside steps to the apartment they had over the store.

Renny was empty-handed but for her keys, Caleb having insisted on bringing the groceries in. How domestic of him.

As a matter of fact, the next few hours were a surreal vision of what kind of life they could have had if he'd not abruptly left her.

While not a cook—unless catching a bass and spitting it over a fire in the bayou counted—Caleb was helpful in chopping up vegetables while answering questions from Luke, who it seemed had suddenly turned into a chatterbox.

"What's your favorite color?"

"Black."

"Mine is blue. What's your favorite chip? I like ketchup."

"Barbecue."

And on it went. Nothing as intense as the questions in the car, and a good thing, too, because Renny was having a hard enough time keeping her balance without getting caught up in Caleb's past.

Sitting at the small table as they ate almost choked her. *This is what families do, eat together, talk, laugh.*

She kept having to remind herself this wasn't real. Not permanent. Caleb might be there for the moment, but there was no guarantee he would stay.

As the hour drew late, Luke couldn't hide a yawn. Renny said, "Time for bed. Say goodnight to Caleb."

Her son shook his head. "Don't want to go. Wanna stay talking to my daddy."

The moment froze. Renny couldn't have said who was more stunned by Luke's use of the word daddy. Actually, given the fact that Caleb's eyes looked bright—*is he crying?*—she knew who.

It wasn't easy—a part of her screamed, *No, he's mine, how can you waltz in and steal him from me?*—but this wasn't about her.

"Caleb, why don't you tuck Luke into bed? Make sure he brushes his teeth first, though."

"I wanna story, too," Luke demanded. Another ritual passed on to the newcomer. But it was only one night, and could she blame her son for wanting this time with his father?

Yes. I raised him. And she was raising him right, which was why Renny pointed to her cheek. "Caleb can read to you, but I'm gonna need my goodnight kiss now then."

Luke ran to her and threw out his arms. She swept him into her embrace and plastered him with noisy kisses until he screeched and squirmed. "Mommy!"

Setting him down, she watched as Luke then crossed to Caleb and snagged his hand. "Come see my room." As their son tugged him away, Caleb tossed her a look over his shoulder and mouthed, "Thank you."

She turned away, lest he see the tears in her eyes. Not tears of anger that her son had chosen Caleb over her, but over what could have been.

While a part of her desperately wanted to spy on them, she let them have their alone time. If, and that was a big if, Caleb was serious about becoming a part of Luke's life, there would be plenty of opportunities to share bedtime and other things.

Supper dishes cleared away, she had time to sit on the couch before Caleb emerged from the bedroom. "He fell asleep before I was done with the story. I guess I was boring."

"He always does when I read, too."

"He called me daddy." Caleb said it, not able to hide his stunned tone.

"Because you are."

"But I don't know how to be one. What if I fuck up?" No mistaking the fear in those words.

"Welcome to the parenting club. You can read all the books you like and listen to all kinds of advice, but what it comes down to is just plain winging it."

That startled a laugh out of him. "Winging it?"

"It's worked for me so far, so don't be so quick to knock it." A silence fell between them, and she couldn't hold his gaze. "I guess you're going to head out now." Because Luke wasn't there to act as buffer anymore. It was just him and her—and some excitable hormones screaming, *"Do something."*

"Do you want me to leave?"

A question fraught with undertones and, in her mind, a cop-out. "Yes." She didn't miss the flash of hurt in his eyes, which was why she sighed and added, "No. How's that for a clear answer?"

A smile creased his lips, a smile meant just for her. It affected her more than it should have. Warmth curled in her belly.

Caleb still had yet to move from in front of the bedroom door. He cast a glance around, and a frown creased his brow.

"Where's your bedroom?"

"You're standing in it."

"But there's no bed."

"Brilliant powers of observation." Sarcasm slid from her lips but without malice. Most people displayed the same shock when they found out her living situation. "Luke needed a bedroom with a door since he goes to sleep earlier, and this way his toys aren't all over the place."

"You guys could use a bigger place."

"A bigger place means more dollars." Then Renny hastened to add before he thought she was looking for a handout, "We're doing just fine here."

Caleb's lips pressed into a tight line. "Would you stop doing that?"

"Doing what?"

"Getting all prickly anytime I say anything about your life."

"Maybe I'm prickly because you seem awfully critical for a guy who just walked back into it. I'm doing the best I can." To her horror, her voice cracked.

Before she could realize what had happened, Caleb had leapt

over the couch and drawn her into his arms. For a moment, she allowed him to hold her, savoring the feel of his body against hers, reveling in the touch of a man. This man.

Fire licked her senses, rousing them, and raising her temperature.

It would be so easy to tilt her face and find his lips.

So easy to succumb...

Yet so hard to recover if he hurt her again.

There was only one thing to do to destroy the intimacy building between them. She swiped her wet eyes and cheeks from side to side on his shirt and then, for good measure, honked her nose in it.

Chapter 9

SHE DIDN'T JUST DO that.

Oh, but Renny had. She'd blown her tear-stuffed nose on him and then pulled back, a tiny smirk of triumph hovering at the corners of her lips.

Why would she do that? Renny was a lady, albeit a tough one given her upbringing, but still not one to be gross...unless she had an ulterior motive?

She moved away from him, heading for the box of tissues on the counter.

By the time she'd turned around, he was leaning against the back of her couch, arms outstretched, shirtless.

She gaped. "What do you think you're doing?"

"You used my shirt as a Kleenex. I assumed you did that as a hint I should take it off."

"That is not why I did it."

"So you admit to doing on purpose?"

Clamping her lips, she glared at him.

He couldn't help but laugh. "Come on, baby. Relax. Come have a seat beside me. I promise to only bite the spots that turn you on."

No mistaking the sudden inhalation of breath or the way he could practically feel the heat flushing her skin.

Nice to see she remembers...

"I think it's time you left. Luke's in bed now, so there's no reason for you to stay."

"And I say there are too many to list. We need to talk, Renny."

"Talk about what? Luke? I told you that you could see him. He knows you're his father. What else do you want from me?"

"You." The single word slipped from him, and he might as well have slapped her given how she recoiled.

"I can't do this, Caleb. Not again."

The utter pain in those words hurt worse than the scars on his body. He also couldn't leave them hovering in the air between them unchallenged. In a flash, he was standing before her.

"Baby." The soft word left his lips as his arms went around her. She held herself stiffly in his embrace at first. Then sighed.

"I promised myself I'd resist you," she murmured.

He brushed his knuckles against the silky skin of her cheek. "I made the same promise to myself."

She lifted her gaze to him. "You suck at keeping promises."

He knew she meant it in jest, but it made him angry. Not angry at her for speaking the truth, but at himself. "I never meant to leave you."

"Then why did you go? Why, Caleb?"

She asked him for an answer, and he wanted to tell her, wanted so desperately for her to understand it wasn't her—it was him. More specifically the monster inside. The cold-blooded beast he couldn't always control.

Since he couldn't find words, none that would express what he felt, he let instinct guide him. Problem was the survival instinct didn't lead him out the door like he would have expected, but had him dipping his head for a kiss.

She turned her head away, so his lips missed hers but hit the soft skin of her cheek. Undaunted, especially since she didn't move away from his embrace, he let his mouth trail to her ear. She always did love it when he nibbled the lobe.

That hadn't changed. So much hadn't, such as how she made him feel...

A soft sigh escaped her as he tugged at her flesh. Her body softened, and she stepped closer to him, closing the small gap between them.

Coming home. The whispered thought echoed along with a sense of rightness.

Renny fit so perfectly in his arms, her lush body a complement to his hardness. The scent of her, the essence that never failed to enflame the fire simmering within. A fire that burned only for her.

With her melting response to his touch, her body pliant and lush in his arms, he moved his mouth back to hers, and this time, she didn't turn away. Rather, she met him in a sensual embrace, a slow exploration that ignited every single one of his senses. Touch—so silky. Sound—a breathless inhalation. Her taste—more potent than ambrosia. How his entire spirit and soul rejoiced at the joining.

Mine.

And he didn't mean in the owning sense but in the conviction that Renny was the only woman who could ever complete him body, mind, and soul.

The knowledge that she held so much power over him should have made him tremble. He'd been prisoner to a woman before and suffered, but Renny's control wasn't forced. She didn't compel him to act. It wasn't her fault that her mere presence seduced him and had him forgetting all his promises.

How could he even think to stop when he recollected, all too easily, the fiery nature of her passion? Anticipation kept him from pulling away. Desire had him craving more.

Somehow, he ended up sitting on the couch with her draped in his lap. A good thing, too, since a weakness pervaded his limbs, a fine trembling that permeated every fiber of his being as past and present collided in that moment, striking hard at not only his body, but also his heart.

How could I have ever left her?

Why had it taken him so long to find his way back?

He wrapped his fingers in the silken skein of her hair where it tumbled about her shoulders, pulling her head back that he might trace the fine line of her throat with his lips.

The rapid flutter of her pulse teased him, taunted the beast that wanted to bite, but he pushed back against this urge. He didn't want to hurt Renny. In this, the man part of him would have its way.

The tip of his tongue traced patterns on her skin. His lips tugged soon after. However, he wasn't content with just nibbling at her throat.

I have an urge for something juicier.

Ripe peaches were there for the cupping, and he did, palming the full weight of her breast in his hand while thumbing over the peak. Even through the fabric of her shirt and bra, her nipple reacted, tightening into a bud that protruded. A shudder went through her, and a quick peek at her face meant he caught her licking her lips. He rubbed his thumb lightly over a tip.

Another shiver struck her body, and a soft sigh slipped from her lips.

Enticing didn't come close to describing her.

How could he resist?

Caleb dipped his head and teased the tip of her breast, closing his mouth over it and sucking, the fabric dampening as her breath shortened.

"Caleb." She moaned his name.

My name.

She knew it was him making love to her. Accepted and craved his touch. Emboldened by this knowledge, he pushed at the hem of her shirt, lifting it over the swell of her breasts and revealing her ripe peaches cupped in a plain white bra. She didn't need lace or wires to present her breasts. They were perfect.

Fuller than before, he discovered when he unsnapped the clasp at the back, and yet still high, rounded, and...

"Your nipples are darker." He made the observation aloud and could have kicked himself when she went to cover herself with her hands as if shy or embarrassed.

"That happened during the pregnancy."

The reminder made his lips tighten, and he almost pulled away at the reminder he'd failed. But he held back.

If he left now, would she wonder if it was because he'd said something about her body? He never wanted Renny to feel anything less than perfect, and right now, given she bit her lower lip and still covered herself, he could see she wondered if he still found her attractive.

If you only knew how gorgeous I find you, baby, and how many times you saved me from falling forever into darkness.

He pried her hands away so he could stare at those delicious tits—and they were yummy, enough that his mouth watered. He glanced at her and made sure to catch her gaze. "You're beautiful."

She made a noise. "You're just saying that. I know that I'm heavier than I used to be, and I've got stretch marks."

The extra curve to her frame looked better than fine to him. A man liked a little cushion for the pushing. As to the marks she bore... "You have stretch marks, and I have scars. What of it?" He shrugged. "Life sucks. Shit happens. Sometimes it leaves behind a signature to remind you." Like the fire had left its mark, and yet, in the flames, he'd reclaimed his freedom, so it was a reminder he didn't mind. "Some scars you wear as badges of honor." Such as the marks that meant she'd given birth to life. *My son.* How could she think he would dislike the signs left behind? He traced the skin on her belly, the light silvery trails not bothering him one bit.

She ran her hand down his marred cheek, and he shivered as she touched the never fully healed skin. "You've changed."

Yes. And no. Since he'd left the military, he didn't let his other side out. He no longer *changed.* "I won't deny I went through some stuff that affected me, and yet, in some ways, I remain the same. I never stopped caring for you."

"I don't want to talk about that." Her gaze dropped, and a slight tension tightened her frame.

Smooth move, idiot. You ruined the moment.

Caleb expected her to move away, but she surprised him by leaning forward and capturing his mouth, slanting her lips across his and fiercely kissing him, her teeth clashing against his in her frenzy.

If she preferred to act instead of talk, he was good with that. He was starved for her touch, and given how she undulated against him, he wasn't the only one. She lay back against the couch, and he partially covered her, his body on its side that he might still let his hands roam.

Her Capri-style yoga pants were form-fitting, perfect for a hand that wanted to cup her mound. The heat of her scorched through the fabric, and the moisture of her arousal dampened as well.

Her hips rolled as he pressed the heel of his hand against her, and her breath came in pants. While he rubbed, his lips kept busy pulling and nipping at the nipples that he'd exposed.

Her fingers dug into his scalp, holding him to her breast, her soft mewls of encouragement driving him on.

The heat of her flesh taunted him through her pants. He needed to touch her. Now.

He slid his hand under the waistband and then under the elastic band of her panties. He slid his fingers through downy curls and heard her suck in a breath.

Farther he explored, the tip of his finger touching the damp edge of her nether lips. He parted them before inserting a digit.

Hot. Wet. Tight.

Oh fuck.

He pushed his finger into her, wishing it was his throbbing cock instead, but he didn't want to rush things. Didn't want to ruin this moment.

His mission—give her pleasure. He wanted to hear her cry his name. To feel her climax on his fingers or, even more deliciously, on his tongue.

He inserted a second finger in her, stretching her channel, and as he pumped her sex, he bit down on her nipple while she chanted, "Yes. Yes. Yes."

Her body tensed as she approached the edge. Faster. Faster.

"Yes! Yes!"

The blood-curdling scream didn't come from Renny.

Chapter 10

"MOMMY!" The sharp, shrill scream shattered the moment more effectively than a bucket of cold water.

"Luke!" she cried his name, even as she leaped from the couch. Renny hurriedly tugged down her shirt as she scrambled around the furniture to get to the bedroom.

Caleb took a shortcut, vaulting over the couch and entering the bedroom before she even made it to the door.

Entering, she saw Luke huddled against the headboard while Caleb stood, his entire body bristling, before the window.

The open window.

A cool breeze with hints of bayou filled the room, fluttering the superhero drapes she'd fabricated out of discarded sheets. The moist swamp was a familiar smell, but underlying it was something else, a more pungent scent she couldn't figure out.

"What is that smell?" she asked as she crossed the room and held out her arms to her son. Luke dove into them, seeking their safety.

Remaining staring at the window, Caleb answered her. "I don't know what that is. It's a mixture of a few things, none that make any sense."

Well, that was vague. "Did you leave the window open when you tucked him in?"

Judging by the tight set of his shoulders and the shake of his head, no. Despite the ambient temperature, a shiver went through her.

Who opened the window? And more disturbing, why?

"I saw something," Luke sobbed, fear making him a little boy again who clung to his mother.

"What did you see, bug?" She bounced him in her arms, a familiar motion begun when he was just little and needed soothing from a tummy ache or a new tooth.

"The dinosaur found me. It wants to eat me!"

"It was just a bad dream, bug. Dinosaurs don't exist."

The right words for a situation like this, and yet she couldn't deny something had happened. Someone or something had opened that window and left behind a smell that unpleasantly lingered.

Caleb stuck his head and part of his upper body out the window, which she realized, on top of being open, was missing its screen. Could Luke sense the fear in her because he clung tighter, his body seized in terror? He obviously believed something had tried to get in and, more worrisome, given Caleb's actions, he did too.

Who, though, would come after her son?

The same thing that scared the twins and did something to Melanie. Was something dangerous hiding in the bayou? It wouldn't be the first time.

"What's going on, Caleb?" she asked in a voice that sounded too high-pitched, but she couldn't help it. She held her son's head cradled to her as she bounced him on her hip.

Turning from the window, Caleb met her gaze. His big shoulders rolled in a shrug. "I don't know what the hell is going on, but I don't like it. Something tried to get in here."

At his words, Luke whimpered and buried his head deeper into her shoulder.

A growl rumbled, and Renny couldn't help but take a step back as Caleb's eyes glinted feral green, his inner beast rising for a moment.

She couldn't help but be frightened—and fascinated. While she knew Caleb was a shifter, she'd never actually gotten to see his other side, almost as if he was ashamed of it.

Or frightened.

Others had no problem letting their beast out to stretch. It wasn't unusual to see them sometimes roaming at night, although Daryl's black panther was hard to truly see.

However, Caleb didn't revel in his otherness like others did. He kept it tucked away, except during times of intense emotion. Then, and only then, did he sometimes slip enough for the croc to rise.

A brief glimpse was all she got before Caleb slammed the door closed and his eyes turned normal again, but his body still bristled.

"You can't stay here." Flatly said.

She didn't disagree, but there was one problem with his assessment. "I have nowhere else to go." Not entirely true. She could probably crash at Melanie's place, but given the twins' fright that afternoon, did she dare dump her own troubles and fear on them?

Determination straightened Caleb's spine, and his eyes glinted, almost as if he prepared for battle.

Which means I probably won't like his suggestion.

"You have somewhere to go where I can keep you safe. My place."

He was right. She didn't like it at all.

But when it came to the safety of her son, she didn't have a choice.

Chapter 11

IT SURPRISED Caleb that Renny didn't protest much when he told her she was coming with him back to his place. More actually his mother's home, but he didn't think Ma would protest, not when he knew she was dying to meet her grandson.

"Give me a minute to grab some things," was what she murmured instead. Even more amazing, when he held out his arms to take his son, Luke dove at him, arms and legs winding as far as they could go around his body.

It took Renny but a few minutes to pack a bag while Luke lay nestled against Caleb's chest, the trust his son had in him almost enough to bring a grown man to tears.

A quick scratch of his groin took care of that urge.

Loving his family was all well and good, but he couldn't let debilitating emotions cloud his senses. *I need to be alert and ready because danger lurks.*

Something threatened his family, and he had to protect them.

Funny how in less than one day, he'd gone from wondering if he'd ever fit in, from promising to stay away from Renny, to almost sleeping with her, instantly bonding with his son, and now pledging to take care of them both.

Guess I'm sticking around.

And he'd kill anyone who tried to make him leave again.

Bite them good.

Slam that door shut. He didn't need help from that part of himself.

When it came time to leave the apartment, Caleb had to hand Luke to his mother since he wanted his hands free just in case whatever tried to come in had lingered. However, his son refused to be carried.

"I'm not a baby," Luke announced with a jut of his lower lip.

"Of course you're not," Caleb said when he saw the hurt look on Renny's face. "But do me a favor, would you, big guy? Can you hold onto your mother's hand? She looks kind of scared. It's your job to keep her safe until we get to the car."

Slim chest swelling in pride, in pajamas sporting—groan—smiling alligators, Luke gripped his mother's hand.

With Caleb leading the way, emerging on the outside landing and checking for signs of danger, they descended the steps to the sidewalk and quickly moved to the car.

Nothing marred the serenity of the evening. Not even a breeze. And forget the hum of crickets.

There was nothing but the noise they made as their feet hit the sidewalk.

Caleb didn't trust the quiet one bit. "Get in the car," he ordered.

As Renny opened the rear passenger door, Caleb scanned the shadows. There were too many, and forget sifting scents. Whatever tried to climb through the window had left a lingering stench that permeated the air in all directions.

What the fuck is it?

The answer tickled on the edge of his senses, a part of him taunting him with the feeling of familiarity, but at the same time, there was an alien quality to the scent, a sensation of wrongness that made his skin prickle and the croc in his head snap its teeth.

Bite the enemy.

Stop with all the biting. Behave.

The last thing Caleb needed was to lose control of his beast in front of Luke and Renny. He would frighten them for sure. But even worse, what if he couldn't control the reptile he shared a body with? What if *it* happened again?

Once he'd seen Renny and Luke safely into their seats, Caleb made his way to the driver's spot that Renny had left for him.

Sliding behind the wheel, he stared at the push button lock on the door. "You don't even have automatic locks?"

With a spark in her eyes, Renny slammed her hand down on her lock and was immediately copied by Luke. "Is that auto enough for you?"

Yeah, things would have to change around here, starting with the standard of living. Damned if Caleb was going to have his child growing up wanting for shit like he had.

Don't mistake him. His mom had done her best, but one working parent of two busy boys—who went through pants and shoes like no one's business—meant her paychecks had to stretch, and they went without a lot.

But not my kid.

His kid would have the best of everything, even if he had to swallow his pride to get a job. A job, he'd worry about that in the morning. First, he had to get everyone to safety.

The drive to his mom's place was done in silence, the radio in her car not managing more than the occasional spurts of music in between static. He didn't have the breath to sigh anymore when she offered an apologetic, "Antenna snapped off."

It didn't take long to get to his place, but it was long enough for one tired little guy to almost fall asleep.

Renny didn't protest when Caleb was the one to scoop their son from the backseat and carry him into the house.

Oddly, Princess, the rabid squirrel that seemed to think the house was her fortress, didn't erupt into a cacophony of barking. First time since he'd arrived, and Caleb was thankful for it. He swore the dog took sadistic pleasure in lying in wait just out of sight so she could dart at him with sharp barks and a flash of teeth meant to suck a man's balls into his stomach.

A quick glance to his left, across the kitchen, showed his mother's bedroom door was closed and no light showed in the seams. Years of early work shifts meant Ma went to bed by nine p.m. However, Constantine was still up, his furry rat nestled in his lap, one beady eyed trained on Caleb. She didn't bark, but Caleb saw the glint in her gaze and the lift of her lip that said, *I'm watching you.*

His brother raised a brow in his direction, probably wondering at the sleepy child Caleb held and the fact that Renny entered at his heels.

It only took a silent shake of Caleb's head to stem the questions he could see brimming in Constantine's eyes.

As Caleb went down the hall to his room, he only paused a moment to point out the open door that led into the bathroom. Given the secretive nature of his relationship with Renny before, they'd never really hung out at his place. They'd spent most of their moments in the bayou, the soft moss their fragrant bower, the cloud-dappled sky their cover.

Entering his room, which had remained surprisingly untouched during his absence, Caleb pulled back the neatly tucked cover—some military training didn't fade so easily—and lay Luke on the sheet.

Renny came alongside him and pulled up the thick blanket before placing a soft kiss on Luke's forehead, but when she would have left, Luke made a sound.

"Don't be scared, bug, Mommy's not going anywhere." Without a glance or word at Caleb, Renny slid into the other side of the bed and snuggled their child close.

Was it weird to want to climb in, too?

He would have liked to wrap his arms around them both and reassure them he would keep them safe.

I won't let you down again.

Perhaps she sensed this newest vow, a vow he could keep to his death. Whatever the reason, when Renny peeked at him, he was glad of the silence because he wasn't sure he could have spoken in that moment. In her eyes he saw trust.

After all I did...she trusts me to protect them.

Before he could embarrass himself and beg to climb in bed with them—and probably collapse the damned frame—Caleb left, shutting the door softly behind him.

For a moment, he stood in the hall, head bowed, simply trying to breathe. The panic, held at bay the entire time, rushed over him in a wave. Sucking in gasping breaths, he sank to his haunches, dizzy, while his legs lacked the strength to hold him.

How can I keep them safe?

He couldn't even keep himself safe.

I can't let them down.

Not again.

Never again.

So man the fuck up!

Stop the fucking pity party and take charge. He wasn't a coward. He wasn't a weakling.

Taking deep breaths, he pushed the panic back. He forced strength into his limbs and stood. He took the steps needed to get away from the door that separated him from the two most important things in his world and practically staggered into the living room.

"I need a beer." But he wouldn't have one. Not when he needed his senses clear.

"I would have said more like a head check," Constantine remarked from his spot on the couch. "Is it me, or did you just bring a kid and his mother over for a sleepover?"

"I did." A sleepover he wasn't quite invited to.

"I'm a little confused, though. How are you supposed to bang Renny with a kid around?"

Caleb wasn't even aware he'd moved, and he also didn't care just how big his little brother was. He hauled him by the shirt off the couch and snarled, "Don't you fucking disrespect her."

"I think I've got a long ways to go before I catch up to your act, *big brother,*" Constantine said with a sneer. "Do you even know the meaning of respect?"

"I know enough to tell you that I won't have you bad-mouthing Renny."

"Don't worry. I wasn't planning to say shit about her. But you on the other hand…I will mock you anytime I like. Especially when I have a problem with your screwing up Renny and the boy's life again."

"Who says I'm going to screw them?"

"You did once before. I hear it's easier the second time."

Easier? Was Constantine nuts? "Nothing about leaving here and her was ever easy. I regretted it every fucking day."

"And yet you still went. Stayed away for years, not giving a damn about anyone else. Now you come back and you say these pretty words about staying and making up for shit. Can you blame me if I don't believe you?"

"No. I guess you'll have to give me time to prove myself."

"Problem with time is you get a chance to hurt Renny and her boy again."

"What I do with them is none of your business."

"I disagree. This is my house, and I've got a right to know what the hell is going on. That is my nephew down that hall." Constantine stabbed a finger in that direction. "And I'll be damned if I'm going to sit back and let you fuck with him. He doesn't deserve that, and neither does she."

"First of all, how many fucking times do I have to say I'm sorry?" It wasn't easy keeping his voice low and under control, but Caleb tried. The walls of his house weren't thick, and while the air conditioners in the windows provided a quelling hum, he didn't need Renny and his son being disturbed by his still prickly relationship with his brother. "I fucked up. Okay? I fucked up large, and I know it's going to take a lot of apologizing and shit to make people forgive me for it. But I'm trying, dammit."

"By dragging Renny and her boy out in the middle of the night?" his brother asked with incredulity.

"You would have done the same. Twice now, something's come after my son." Caleb quickly brought his brother up to speed. By the time he'd told him about the incident at the picnic, the grocery store, and the latest mishap at Renny's place, Constantine had a pensive look.

"It's happening again."

Well, that wasn't what Caleb expected to hear. "What's happening again? What the hell are you talking about?"

Constantine met his gaze. "I keep forgetting you didn't keep up with the local news. Or at least the shifter news from our town. It first started a few years back."

"Hold on to that train of thought." Caleb held up a hand. "Don't tell me yet. Let's go outside and you can explain what you mean while I check the perimeter of the property."

Because while they'd driven several miles out of town, that thing, whatever it was stalking his child, had obviously no problem traveling or tracking.

Outside the house, the hum of the window cooling units was louder, but despite that, Caleb could hear the comforting sound of crickets and other bayou noises. Nothing out of the ordinary approached, but still, it never hurt to be sure.

As Caleb set off to walk around the house, eyes on the ground watching for prints, Constantine launched into a recap of some of the weird shit plaguing Bitten Point.

"So about two years or so after you left, we had a rash of disappearances. No men, just a few women and children. All shifters."

"Abductions or murders?"

His brother shrugged. "We never really did find out. A few of those who went missing turned back up with no memory of what had happened while others..." He trailed off.

"Never came back?"

"Nope. They vanished as if into thin air."

Or as if swallowed by the bayou. The swamps knew how to keep a secret—and a body.

"How long did this go on for?"

"Not too long. Two-three weeks at most. But at the time it was happening, there was talk among some of the children that they'd seen a monster."

"That looked like a dinosaur?" Caleb asked.

"Actually, no, the rumors I heard said it was a wolfman, all fur and big teeth and claws."

"A Lycan, in the bayou?" An incredulous note entered Caleb's voice.

"No, as in a wolfman that walked on two legs, which we know is impossible."

"Not really." Caleb's discoveries outside the bayou shattered many long-held beliefs.

"What do you mean not really?"

"It means that some of the things we grew up thinking were absolute aren't. Shifters can walk on two legs, or four, or even eight." Shudder. That one still gave him nightmares. "While the ability to shapeshift into a hybrid form is rare, it does exist. I've seen it."

For a moment, his brother simply blinked at him. "Well, hot damn. Can you do it?"

He couldn't lie. "Yes, but I don't recommend it." The mix of man and croc at once made for a strange mental process, but it was better than leaving the croc in utter control.

"Don't recommend it? But why?" His brother's face lit up. "I could be snakeman!"

For a moment, the Goliath that was his brother reminded him of the little boy Caleb used to have following him around, hero worship in his eyes.

"Snakeman?" Caleb couldn't help a teasing lilt. "Leaving a slimy trail everywhere he slithers."

While Caleb took after their dead father and became a crocodile, Constantine, took after their mother, a python. Given his bulk now, Caleb had to wonder just how big his snake had gotten. He wasn't sure if he wanted to find out.

"Snakes don't leave gooey trails." Constantine drew himself straight and adopted a haughty sneer. "Try more like crushing his enemy in his mighty grip."

"Hugging is not a fighting technique."

"Neither are nibbles, crockie."

"I've been trained to fight."

"I guess they threw in the asshole lessons for free."

The rebuke was tossed without any real malice, making it even more effective. "Sorry."

"Whatever. I think from now on, instead of saying sorry, we should start a jar. Twenty bucks every time you say it. I figure within a week, I'll be able to afford a whole new set of tires for my truck."

The fist slugged his brother's arm before Caleb could think twice. It was a habit from his military days when he and the boys shot the shit. For a moment, he could only gape at his brother, wondering how Constantine would take it.

He grinned. "Didn't hurt."

At those familiar words, Caleb did laugh. How many times had they used that phrase growing up, trying to prove who was toughest?

As far as he recalled, Caleb had been in the lead from the time he got shot with buckshot in the ass and grinned—over gritted teeth—while Ma yanked the pellets out with tweezers.

As their laughter died down, Caleb heard a rustle to his left. He zeroed his gaze in, staring at the shadows bordering the yard, the dense foliage providing so many possible hiding spots.

If his years in the military had taught Caleb anything, it was to never underestimate the enemy. Where there was a will, there was a way, and he still had trouble even months after leaving the war overseas in looking at the world with a less than jaundiced eye.

What of the heavy boughs weighed down by lush leaves? Ambush could await the unwary in the treetops. Anyone or thing could lie under the mud and weeds, ready to rise. The enemy could be inside his own mind, waiting to burst free from its bodily prison and rampage.

Let me out. I can scout.

Indeed, his reptile half could, but would the cold creature stop at just that? And what really could his croc self do that the man couldn't?

I know danger is lurking. It can be anywhere.

Knowing this, Caleb would stand on guard, as a man, to stop it.

Since nothing seemed to be disturbing the nightlife—the bayou sounds rolled over his skin—Caleb questioned his brother further about this supposed wolfman haunting the bayou years ago. "I take it they never caught the guy, or wolf, or whatever that was abducting folks?"

Constantine shook his head. "Nope. One day, a kid riding his bike got snatched, the next he was found sitting in the park, no idea how he got there. And that was the last time it happened. Until now."

"So today marks the first incidents?"

"Maybe."

"What do you mean, maybe?" Caleb narrowed his gaze at his brother.

"We got a call into the station"—the fire station where Constantine worked as a firefighter—"that something might have taken up residence in the pond by the park. A bunch of kids claimed they saw something, and since we didn't want any of them getting eaten in case a croc or gator did make its way there, we took a truck out and met up with some of the boys in blue. We dragged the pond and came up empty."

"But?" Caleb prodded, fixing his brother with a stare.

"There was this smell. A weird one."

"Kind of reptile like, but not quite, with a hint of something wrong," Caleb said.

"I would have said more like alien, but yeah. And as for tracks, nothing that made sense."

"What do you mean?"

"I mean did you ever see something that walked with one human foot and one clawed and webbed one?"

No, Caleb hadn't, which was why he slept on the couch that night with a gun under his pillow, one eye open, and an ear cocked to see if the pop-can trap he'd strung outside all the windows rattled.

But the best intentions didn't keep the nightmares at bay.

THE FLAMES SLITHERED CLOSER, dancing bright devils eager to taste anything they could lick. Caleb tugged at his tethers. However, the rope bound him tight.

A prisoner waiting for punishment because he'd dared disobey.

Begging wasn't an option.

Not only would he never stoop so low, there was no one left to hear his pleas.

And still the torrid fire burned closer.

Let me out.

His beast pulsed, demanding exit.

Again, he pulled at the thick twine crisscrossing his wrists. He'd managed to somewhat fray them against the rough stone surface of the wall, but not enough to snap himself free.

There is no choice. Let me out.

The heat pulsed against his skin, crisping his hairs, tightening pores already dry. He didn't want to let the beast out. He could hear the screams of battle. Scent the blood...

Yummy.

The thought repulsed him. The thought made him hunger.

It wasn't right. He shouldn't revel in the wild nature of his croc. Shouldn't crave the same things.

I am a man.

You are also a predator.

He was also on fire. The flames licked at his skin, attracted to the scraps of clothes he still wore, singeing the rope holding him prisoner. But he didn't have time to wait for the flames to free him, not when his skin bubbled.

He screamed, not with pain, but out of frustration. How ironic that the reason he found himself tied was what would save him. He wouldn't unleash his beast for the enemy, but he would have to in order to survive.

His croc snapped in glee.

The change came on fast and vicious, his skin hardening into scales, the shape of his face, his hands, his whole body contorting, reshaping, becoming...a crocodile.

Not a friendly one. Nor a small one.

Last time they measured him, he was over twelve feet from snout to tail. How he managed to expand to that size, he never could figure out. He did know that he and others of his kind took heavier than he looked to a whole new level.

Unleashing his beast didn't stop the flames from kissing his skin. Flesh sizzled.

Smells good.

He would have gagged if he wasn't just a passenger on the reptile train bent on escape—and destruction.

In a frenzy from being cooped away, in pain, and pissed when someone dared shoot at him, Caleb could do nothing to stop his vicious side from lunging at the guy with the gun.

The crunch of bone, the coppery taste of blood, the exultation, his personal horror that he enjoyed it.

No.

No!

Hands touched him. Soft hands. Along with a faint murmur.

"It's all right, Caleb. It's just a dream. Wake up."

Renny! In a flash, his eyes opened, and he saw Renny leaning over him, too close, too tempting.

Let's taste.

Since he didn't know if it was man or beast talking, he barked, "Stay away from me."

She recoiled, as if slapped. "Well, excuse me for waking you up."

He rubbed a hand over his face. "I'm sorry. I don't always react well when woken." He'd punched bigger men than her for daring to lay a hand on him when resting.

"Good to know. Next time you have a nightmare, I'll throw things at you from afar."

Next time?

She seemed to realize her faux pas at the same time he did. He couldn't help a smile. "Does this mean you're sticking around?"

"I think that's a better question to ask you," she retorted.

It came to his notice it was pitch-black outside, and a quick peek over at the DVD player showed a neon-lit time of three twenty-three a.m. "Why are you up? Did you hear something?" He swung his legs so he sat on the couch.

Blonde hair flew as Renny shook her head. "I had to use the bathroom and, on the way back, heard you mumbling in your sleep. Do you have nightmares often?"

A lie would preserve his dignity. He went with the truth. "Every night unless I take the pills the doctor gave me."

"You didn't take them before bed?"

"Of course not. I can't protect you if I'm passed out cold."

"Oh, Caleb." She breathed his name and took a step toward him, a moving shadow that didn't rouse the panic. Another thing rose in its stead. "Are the nightmares from the fire?"

"Yes and no. The fire is almost always part of it." Yet it was the chaos after, where he fought to escape, that plagued his dreams the most.

Renny seated herself gingerly on the couch beside him. "I'm sorry."

He couldn't help a rusty laugh. "You're sorry? You are the person who needs to least apologize."

"Then what do you want me to feel? Pity? I doubt you'd appreciate that."

"There's only one thing I want from you."

Her eyes met his in the darkness, and he could read the longing in their gaze, but also the fear. "And that's the one thing I don't know if I can ever give."

With those words, Renny fled. A good thing, too, else he might have taken his croc's advice.

Claim her. Because there was one thing becoming crystal clear. He needed Renny in his life. But if he moved too quickly, she might run. And he couldn't lose her again.

Chapter 12

RUN. Run.

Renny's chest heaved as she struggled for breath running through the bayou, the thick air cloying in her lungs. Mud squelched between her bare toes, the suctioning pull slowing her pace while rapier weeds whipped at her bared legs. Her nightgown ended mid-thigh and provided no protection.

Just like the moon taunted her, refusing to hide in shadow and help her blend into the darkness.

Splash.

The sudden spray of water as her foot slammed into a puddle drew a short cry from her. Way to pinpoint her location even more. She paused for a moment, unable to hide her ragged pants for air.

Nothing marred the silence but her harsh breathing. Not a sound.

But she knew it was there. Hunting. Chasing. Hungering...

Frantically, Renny cast about looking for a spot to hide. Anywhere.

The swaying fronds and the glitter of water mocked her until she looked to her left. There, not so far from her, was a hill.

It wouldn't hide her from the monster that wanted her, but the man sitting atop the knoll would protect her.

He cast his gaze down and caught hers. A vivid green flare flashed in his eyes.

Caleb.

Caleb was here. He would keep her safe.

Energized, she ran toward him, and he saw her coming. She knew he did. But the beast came as well.

Who would arrive first?

Arms outstretched, she reached for him, even as the fetid breath of the monster washed over her back.

"Caleb! Help me. Caleb." She said his name on a plea.

Surely he heard her, and yet he turned away.

And the jaws of the beast—

With a choked cry, Renny sat upright in bed, her skin clammy, her heart racing—and remarkably uneaten.

Thank God. I'm alive.

But alone.

Oh no! Where was Luke?

Casting back the covers, Renny searched under them in case they hid Luke's small body, but he wasn't there, nor was he anywhere in the room.

Braless, but at least decently clothed in a T-shirt and her yoga pants—because she'd not had the energy to change into something else, not with all that happened—Renny felt no qualms about exiting the room to hunt down her son. She made it to the end of the hall before she halted.

Frozen, she barely dared breathe as she watched—and tried not to cry.

Still wearing his pajamas, Luke stood on the edge of the kitchen watching as Claire bustled around making a pot of coffee, softly humming.

"Are you my grandma?"

The scream Claire let out could have woken the dead. She

whirled, one hand clutching her chest, her wide eyes staring at Luke, who tilted his head quizzically.

"Sweet mother of God. How did you get here?"

"Daddy brought me on account of the dinosaur."

To her credit, Claire didn't react to the interesting excuse as to his presence. "Yes, those dinos can be annoying. Why don't you have a seat, and I'll make you some breakfast. Would you like some pancakes?"

"Yes please, Grandma."

Claire turned around to putter in the cabinets and fire on the stove, but not before Renny caught the glimmer of tears, tears that also filled her own eyes.

What have I done?

When she'd realized Caleb didn't want her or their child, Renny had floundered. She hadn't grown up with an extended family. Her dad, an ornery bear in real life, cut all ties with his family out west when he moved to Florida to be with Renny's mother, a human and an orphan. As a result, Renny didn't grow up with grandparents.

When Renny found out about her pregnancy, her first inclination was to make sure Caleb knew first. Except Caleb never replied, and given he didn't show an interest, she hesitated telling Caleb's mom out of fear she'd get the same reaction that she'd gotten from her father.

"Whore. Spreading your legs for that no account reptile. Your mother would be so ashamed."

Indeed, Mother would have hung her head, just not for the reason her father thought. Poor Daddy had changed so much.

Still, though, her father's words gave her pause. In her naïve logic, she assumed since Caleb knew about her pregnancy, he would tell his mother. What she'd not counted on was Caleb never finding out, which meant Claire never knew she had a grandson.

Four years lost because of foolish choices.

Say it like it is. Pride kept you from saying anything.

It didn't feel good to realize that she'd made a major error. Renny had been so mad at Caleb, so mad at the injustice of the world in general, that she had ended up hurting someone who would have dearly loved her son.

But I have a chance to start making things right.

And if she could make amends, didn't that mean Caleb had that right, too?

Speak of the devil... She felt him before she heard him. "I thought I heard a scream."

"Our son introduced himself to your mother."

Caleb sniffed. "Judging by the smell of bacon and pancakes, they're getting along."

His light tone did not assuage the heaviness crushing her chest. "I'm so sorry, Caleb. I feel utterly wretched about not bringing Luke over to meet your mom. I never meant to hurt anyone."

"I know how that works, baby. Best we can do is move forward and try to not repeat our mistakes."

Turning, she took in not only his serious mien but also his clean-shaven jaw, button-up shirt, and slick, wet hair. Utterly handsome and obviously planning an outing. "Going somewhere?"

"Well, it is Sunday." At her rounded O of surprise, he laughed. "Before you think I've turned to religion, I've got a job interview."

"You do?" She blinked in surprise. This was the first she'd heard of it.

"Yeah, I do. I'm already getting a check from the military, apparently my service and scars are worth something to them, but it's not going to be enough for us to get a decent place."

"Get us a what?" She took a step back from him, trying to decipher his words. "Are you talking about us moving in together?"

"After last night—"

She held up a hand to stop him. "What happened last night was..."

"Special."

"I was going to say rash. You just got back in to town, and I feel like things are moving too fast."

"Then I'll slow down."

"What if I want you to stop?" She didn't, but at the same time, Renny felt as if she wasn't thinking clearly. Caleb touched her, and she just melted. She forgot all the reasons for keeping him at arm's length.

He bowed his head, a big man humbled and defeated in front of her. "If that's what you truly want."

No. She didn't want him to go away. She wanted more of his kisses and hugs and...him. But could she handle the heartbreak if Caleb betrayed her again? "I can't be with you. Not like that." Even if just saying it made her feel as if her heart was shattering into a thousand pieces.

His shoulders slumped as her words hit him. But only for a moment. "Too bad because I'm not giving up." His head snapped up, and his eyes blazed, one hundred percent human, but determined. "I lost you once because I didn't fight hard enough, and I'll be damned if I lose you again. This might not be what you want to hear, baby, but the fact of the matter is, I'm here to stay. I will be a father to my son, and"—he lowered his voice—"we will share a bed." Even if he had to handcuff himself at night so he could sleep beside her without worry.

"Caleb—"

He didn't give her a chance to finish her reply, simply slanted his mouth over hers in a hard kiss that lasted but a second. Then he was walking past her and out into the kitchen, where he ruffled Luke's hair, gave his mother a loud smooch on the cheek, and stole a piece of bacon all before heading out the door with a casually tossed, "I'll be back in a few hours. Don't leave the house until I return."

Of course she couldn't leave, she thought with bemusement. He'd taken her car to go to his interview, leaving her to face the consequences of her actions. Alone.

Face your actions.

Taking a deep breath, she walked into the kitchen with a, "Good morning, Claire."

Renny couldn't deny she deserved the hard look Caleb's mother shot her. "Renny. Why don't you park yourself on a stool while I wrangle some breakfast on a plate for you? Then, I want to hear everything about my grandson."

It took a while to tell Claire everything. Some parts were harder than others. It involved a few tears, which Claire shared with her, a comrade spirit when it came to raising a child on her own. By the time it was done—an eye-rolling Constantine having stolen Luke long before so he wouldn't start craving dolls and a tea set—Renny knew, no matter what happened with Caleb, she wasn't alone.

"You and Luke are family," which, as Claire explained with a wave in the direction of the sink, meant Renny got to do the dishes. Blech.

Chapter 13

BEGGARS CAN'T BE CHOOSERS.

That mantra did little to ease Caleb's irritation when he realized the interview he'd set up the previous night by email was going to be with Wes Mercer, who predictably smirked when Caleb arrived at the Bittech building for his ten a.m. appointment.

"Well, look at what dragged itself into my office." If by office, a windowless room loaded with monitors counted.

Pride made Caleb want to spin on his heel and say fuck it. Pride also made him stay because he had people depending on him. "I like this about as much as you do, which means not fucking much."

"Pretty stupid thing to say considering you're here looking for a job." Wes leaned back in his seat and steepled his fingers, a smirk on his lips.

Caleb set his jaw and held his fists tight at his sides, resisting the temptation to wipe the smirk off Wes's face. "Not stupid, honest. I'm not going to pretend I suddenly like you. Nor am I going to shove my nose up your ass for a job."

"Keep going, although I should mention that, so far, you're not really winning me over. As a matter of fact, I'm thinking you should probably just turn right around and *do* let the door smack you on the way out."

"I am royally fucking this up." Caleb sighed. "Listen, I need this position." He really did. He'd asked around, and unless he was willing to bag groceries, wash dishes, or go bayou fishing, which would put him out of reach if Renny or Luke needed him, then, "This job is the best choice in town."

Bittech didn't just offer a decent wage, as his brother had explained, it provided benefits to an employee and his dependents.

And fuck me. I've got dependents now.

Wes spun away from him and drummed his fingers on the countertop bolted to the wall. The laminate surface formed a ring around the room under the monitors. Atop it sat a half-dozen keyboards and wireless mice. "You do realize that, by coming to work here, you'd be taking orders from me."

Something that still surprised Caleb considering Wes was his age and seemed rather young for the position of head of security.

"I know how to take orders." Too well, as a matter of fact. Except, this time, Caleb would do it by choice, not compulsion.

"What about breaking the rules?" The question emerged oddly, and Caleb noted Wes watching him intently.

"I'm not a rule breaker." His mother had raised him poor, but right.

"What if you had to in order to keep people safe?"

Caleb's brow knit into a frown. "What are you saying?"

"I'm wondering if I can trust you."

"Depends. Trust me to hold your beer while you jump off a cliff, probably. Trust me to not call you a dickhead behind your back, probably not."

Wes snickered. "You know, if you weren't such an asshole, I could almost like you."

"Dude, don't say shit like that. It's creepy."

"What's creepy is the fact I'm even thinking of telling you what's happening."

"Tell me what?"

For a moment, Wes didn't reply. Then he blew out a hard breath. "Fuck it. You haven't been around so you probably don't know and aren't involved."

"Involved in what? Stop acting all mysterious like and spit it out."

"I'm talking about the testing going on here."

Baffled, Caleb blurted out, "What fucking testing?"

"I mean the testing happening right here in the Bittech labs."

"Rewind for a minute so I can understand because I must be missing something. You're saying Bittech is testing folks. Isn't that what a lab is supposed to do?"

"Yes, and on the surface, that's fine. What's not fine is the fact they're not just taking samples from those volunteering. They're bringing in samples from folks who have no idea."

"How can people not know? I mean, I'm pretty sure I'd notice if someone was sticking me with a needle and drawing blood."

"In some cases, they're stealing it from employers, like the fire station, which is mandated to drug test its guys every so often. And the vet, who sends Bittech samples to check for disease and viruses."

Again, not a huge deal, given shifter blood samples could only go to those in on the secret, like Bittech. "So they're keeping samples sent to them. I'm not seeing the big deal yet."

"Because there are other samples they've gotten that weren't freely given. My Uncle Bob, who hasn't seen a doctor since the summer of eighty-seven when he tangled with that nest of vipers, has a file. As does Kerry, my cousin, even though she just moved into town three months ago. There are lots of others, too. Seems like they're documenting everyone in town."

"But why?" Caleb asked.

At that query, Wes shrugged. "Fucked if I know. Initially, the lab was started back in the seventies so that our scientists could study our condition. It then evolved into the doctors helping the hybrid couples get pregnant"—because mixed species didn't procreate easily—"and they've also been working on fabricating our own form of medicine for those rare diseases our shapeshifting genes can't combat. When it comes to cases such as those, I can understand why they kept stuff on file. But the samples I saw numbered in the hundreds. Your brother is in there. Your mother, too. What the hell do they need those samples for?"

A valid question, but it raised others. "How do you know about all this?"

Wes smiled. "As head of security, I see lots of stuff, even things I'm not supposed to. Things that don't make sense, like the number of humans now working here."

"Humans?" Caleb couldn't help an incredulous note. "I could have sworn my brother said most of the people working here are either one of us or in on the secret."

"They used to be. A few months ago, the institute went on a hiring spree. Humans mostly. Humans who don't start out knowing what we are but are told once they pass a few tests. The company has been giving them samples of our blood and hair to play with."

A chill went through Caleb. Hadn't he heard rumors while in the military of scientists messing around with their blood? The whispers at the time were frightening if true. *They're creating an army of monsters.*

And, yes, he meant create. While birth could result in the creation of new shifters, it wasn't always the case. Look at Renny, whose ursine-based father produced an unenhanced daughter.

I don't know that I'd call her unenhanced. Renny might not turn into something with claws, but she was definitely special.

So special that even her father's attempt to have her *changed* didn't take root. See, people could *become* shifters as well. But it wasn't simple. Nothing so easy as a scratch or a bite like the movies portrayed. The creation of a new shifter required the exchange of fluids, lots of fluids, blood being the vehicle of choice, siphoned out of a host and filtered into a human. Not that hard to do with today's technology, but it didn't always work. Most bodies rejected the shifter gene. Some theorized it made sure they didn't overpopulate. Probably a good thing, given the animal within didn't always play nice with others.

"What are the scientists looking for?" Caleb asked.

"That's what I wanted to know, so I asked Andrew."

"And?"

"The little prick told me to mind my fucking business. That all work conducted was being done with the full knowledge of the High Council, and that if I knew what was good for me, I'd keep my mouth shut."

"The little prick actually threatened you? And you didn't kill him?"

Nothing changed outwardly. Wes still wore his human guise, yet when he smiled, white teeth gleaming, it was all gator. "It was close."

"Andrew doesn't want you blabbing, yet here you are telling me this."

"Sometimes a man needs allies."

"Since when are we on the same team?"

"Since something doesn't smell right, and as much as I dislike you, I don't think you'd stand by and watch this town get fucked."

No, he wouldn't, but he also wasn't sure what his plans were yet. "I just got back into town and already you're trying to drag me into something. I came back for a fresh start, not to get involved in some kind of conspiracy theory. I mean, come on, so far, other than letting humans in on the secret, your evidence is pretty slim. I mean, if the High Council is backing it..." Caleb shrugged.

"That doesn't mean jack shit, and you know it. You don't think it's kind of fishy that here's a medical lab, screwing with shifter DNA, and suddenly we're getting messed-up reports of giant lizards running amok?" Paranoia was a shifter's best friend.

"It could still be a coincidence." Said even if Caleb didn't believe it. "Have you talked to anyone else about it?"

"Like who? Most folks in town are in Bittech's back pocket, and those that aren't ain't interested in rocking the boat."

Didn't that sound familiar? Not so long ago, Caleb had been part of a group that knew something was fishy with their military unit. Everyone seemed to know something hinky was going on, and yet, they did nothing about it. And once they confirmed what was happening, it was too late.

I am not sitting back and watching anymore. I will take control of my destiny and like fuck am I letting anyone use me or the people I know.

"If I'm understanding you correctly, you think they're doing more than research. You think they're experimenting." Making monsters.

Wes shrugged. "Damned if I know. Maybe I am just being a paranoid freak. Maybe they're looking for a cure to the swamp fever. Or some kind of hair growth product for humans that they'll sell for a fortune in the marketplace."

"I still don't get why you're telling me. Of all the people to trust..." Caleb spread his hands. "Excuse me if I'm still a touch skeptical."

The other man leaned forward and fixed him with a gaze, his mien serious. "Be skeptical, but be vigilant. Be informed, because what if I'm right? What if this is the start of something that could hurt us all?"

"Don't tell me you've gone heroic?" The swamp would freeze over the day a Mercer turned into a knight for fairness, morality, and justice.

A moue twisted Wes's lips. "Perish the fucking thought. This decision to figure out what the hell is happening is totally selfish because, if shit hits the fan, then my life might get difficult. I'd rather spend my life doing an easy job, going home to drink beer and banging pretty girls than constantly looking over my shoulder waiting for a silver bullet because someone outed us to the world."

A valid fear they all shared. Since as far back as Caleb could remember, the anxiety of the humans finding out they existed was huge. No one seemed to doubt that the revelation of their secret would result in humans loading up on silver ammo and blood-thirsty outrage.

Yeah, that didn't put a lot of faith in mankind. However, to test the theory, they'd have to admit werewolves and other creatures lived among them. No one was willing to risk possibly starting a genocide.

Which meant that, if Wes was on to something, then Caleb couldn't walk away.

"What do you want me to do?" Caleb asked.

"First off, I want someone other than me to know."

"Worried about getting taken out?"

"I don't plan on rolling belly up in the bayou yet, but it never hurts to have someone else in on the secret. Second, start watching."

"Watching what?"

"Bittech. The town. Anything really. I'm going to hire you so you can move around the institute legitimately. Something weird is going on, something that has my gator senses tingling. We've got to find out what's happening and put a stop to it."

"Sounds easy enough so long as we have the understanding that this does not mean we're friends."

Dark brows drew together as Wes frowned. "Never. Once this is over, we shall return to status quo."

Excellent. Caleb did so have fun screwing with Wes. He'd learned some awesome pranks in the military.

"So are you in?" Wes asked.

"I'm in. *Boss.*" Caleb couldn't hide the smirk as he said it.

"Actually, you will address me as Mr. Mercer." Even bigger smirk volleyed back.

The things Caleb had to do... Funny thing was, a job working for Wes while investigating the gator's gut feeling had an uplifting effect. *I'm employed.* Which was good for his new family. And he had a mystery to solve, which made him want to hum the theme from *Scooby Doo*—and eat a giant sandwich.

Damn that stupid pill he took to calm his nerves and halt any panic attacks. It totally fucked with his thought processes—and made him hungry, just like a certain weed he smoked in high school.

"When do I start?"

"Tonight. But not as a company man. I want us to do a sweep of the bayou by town."

"What's the swamp got to do with the stuff happening at the lab?" His eyes widened. "Are we looking for bodies?" *I hope not.* Nothing worse than coming across a corpse and having his croc go yum. Shudder.

"Looking for some of the missing folks is part of the reason. The other is that whatever screwed with Melanie is still out there. After dusk, I'll start from my place on the west side and move toward you."

"You want us to see if we can pinch that thing hiding out there."

"Or find a trace. I've done some patrols on my own, but I could use a second set of eyes."

"I can't believe we're going dinosaur hunting. Want me to keep an eye open for the wolfman, too?"

Wes didn't even crack a smile when he said, "I see you've gotten a bit of a recap of what's been sighted."

"A story about a wolfman kidnapping folks? Yeah. I heard it from my brother. But I'm less worried about the guy with a hair problem than I am of this dino thing people keep talking about. It went after my son last night." It still made Caleb's blood boil and run cold at the same time, given how close Luke had come to being snatched.

"That fucking lizard bastard gets around."

"You make it sound like you've encountered it before."

"In a sense." Swiveling in his seat, Wes turned to face a bank of monitors. "About a week ago, some of the institute's smokers said they saw something in the bayou. I'll be honest, since they were human"—because most shifters tended to shy from anything with flame and smoke—"I thought maybe they'd sniffed some swamp gasses. I mean, a walking lizard man? Sounds fucking crazy, except turns out it's true. Check out what I spotted on one of the surveillance cameras."

With a few rapid taps on a keyboard, a screen, showing a very boring white hallway, changed to another view. Given the greenish cast to the surroundings, it was easy to surmise the video was filmed at night. As to the setting, the empty concrete bay of a loading dock.

"This is so fascinating," Caleb couldn't resist saying.

"Fuck off and watch." The time stamp zoomed ahead, and suddenly something lurched into view. Human eyes in an alien face stared into the camera a quick moment only before it loped away.

Dropped jaw, meet floor. Caleb couldn't say a thing as Wes mumbled.

"Shit, I went too far. Hold on a second." Wes rewound, and Caleb leaned forward, intent on confirming what he thought he'd seen.

Bare pavement, illuminated by a light above the bay door. A barren spot circled by darkness, a darkness that birthed motion.

At the edge of the circle of light, a body lumbered into view. Two legs, one thicker than the other, the skinny one pale and shod in a shoe, while the other was bare and definitely not sporting piggly little toes. The creature had a long torso, dark in color with two arms. A misshapen figure that loped close to the loading dock and paused for a moment to peek up, big eyes, human eyes, staring at the lens taping it.

Human eyes in a monstrous face.

"Holy fucking hell, it is a lizard man."

Or to a child, a dinosaur since it walked upright and kept its arms tight to its sides.

Slowing the video, Wes took it frame by frame to the moment the ghastly visage stared at the camera. No mistaking the baleful glare in the eyes.

The frame froze.

"What the hell is that?" Caleb asked.

"A hybrid of some sort."

"Well, duh. I get that, but how?" While the species could interbreed, with the exception of some big cat species, hybrid crosses just didn't happen.

A bear and a wolf mated, the child was one or the other. A gator took up with a feline, the child, again, was one or the other. But this thing on the screen...

"It's got a beak. And I think that this here"—Wes leaned forward and traced the outline of a shape over its shoulder—"is a wing."

"Are you implying it's a bloody dragon?" Caleb couldn't help it, he laughed.

Wes scowled. "I don't know what the fuck it is. Just like I don't know where the fuck it lives. But I do know it's screwing with the people in town."

That was a sobering reminder. "Haven't you been able to track it? It's got a pretty distinctive scent."

"A scent that disappears into thin air in the middle of the swamp. Not a tree in sight. Nothing. Not even a footprint in the mud."

Caleb's turn to frown. From a young age, everyone recognized the Mercers as some of the best trackers around. People whispered they had to know how to hunt in order to feed all those bastard mouths.

But even if they didn't do it by necessity, the skill was inherent, and one that Caleb respected. Unlike the canine or feline breeds, reptiles like Wes and himself were at a disadvantage on land. While their eyesight and hearing were quite excellent, their sense of smell wasn't as developed as, say, a wolf's.

However, what the nose couldn't smell, the eyes could see, and if Wes said the tracks stopped dead, Caleb had no reason to disbelieve him, even if it seemed farfetched.

"That's why you want me to help you tonight. But surely you could have asked someone else."

"I did."

"And?" Caleb prodded.

"It didn't end up well." No mistaking the flash of pain in Wes's eyes, a quick glimpse that transformed into anger.

This was personal for Wes. "Who else has gone looking for it?"

"A few of us. We've been keeping the news on the down low so we don't scare people."

"Who's us?"

"Me, my brother. Daryl. There are a few others, but like I said, we've been keeping it on the down low."

"Which seems like a stupid idea. I mean, if there's something out there targeting shifters, shouldn't we be letting the whole town know and forming a posse to go after it?"

"You'd think that would be a good plan." A wry smile twisted Wes's lips. "Except the fellow who tried to organize a town meeting went missing."

"And you let that stop you?"

"No. I stopped when the second guy, my brother, went missing, too."

"Your brother? Which one?"

"Gary."

"He was two grades behind us, right?"

"Yeah. He disappeared on his way into town on his motorcycle. Hasn't been seen since."

"I'm sorry, dude." Caleb truly was. No matter his issues with Wes, he wouldn't wish that kind of loss on anyone.

"Yeah, well, Ma and my sisters took it hardest. I think the worst part is not knowing if he fucked off and said screw the town and its problems. Or if something happened to him."

"What's your gut say?"

"That he's alive and in trouble."

"If you think his disappearance is related to the shit happening, why not scream it from the rooftops? Why stay quiet?"

"Because I won't risk my sisters or mother. If the town council is in on the disappearances, then I don't want to tip my hand. As far as they know, I dropped the whole thing. Only me, your brother, and Daryl really know shit. And a few cousins, but they won't say shit and report only to me."

"And lucky me, I got invited to the party." Caleb couldn't help but chuckle. "Well, don't I feel warm and fuzzy. Hoping the town's dino monster will get me, too?"

"I was hoping you'd get taken by crotch rot, but no such luck. But more seriously, I need your help. Anything that can take out my brother is dangerous to us all. More disturbing is the fact that, whatever is going on, someone is willing to go to extremes to keep it secret."

Which meant it was up to them to figure it out.

And stop it.

Chapter 14

IT WAS ridiculous to be so excited about seeing Caleb pull into the front yard with her battered car. Chiding herself, though, didn't stop the giddy thrill that made her pulse speed up as she focused her gaze on him.

Unlike Renny, Luke didn't worry about appearing too eager to see Caleb. With his little legs pumping, he ran at Caleb, who swept him into his arms and flung him in the air.

Renny squeaked. Luke squealed. Caleb laughed.

"Got ya!" Caleb exclaimed, catching their son with ease. Never mind that Renny might have lost a few years off her life.

Get used to it. Daddies don't do things the same as mommies.

With Luke secured on his hip, instead of at the mercy of gravity, Caleb approached.

Her pulse fluttered. Excited. Scared.

She couldn't make up her mind.

Uncertainty still prevailed when it came to how she felt about the ease and speed Luke had taken to his father. The resentment she'd long harbored at Caleb's apparent abandonment seemed to be having a hard time taking root. Anger, much like fine sand, slipped through her grasp. Its departure left a hole quickly filled by anticipation.

And let's not forget heat.

Each time Renny ran into Caleb, the more difficult it became to remember the loneliness of life before he returned. He brought color into her world. Other than Luke, what did she have that made her want to smile for the simple joy of it?

He makes me happy.

Enjoying his presence, though, didn't mean she took to orders very well, and she could see by the frown knitting his brow they were about to have words about it. Good. Because it was time he learned the ground rules. Her rules.

Rule number one, she wasn't going to bow meekly.

Stopping a few feet from her, Caleb took in her appearance. Slightly grubby, given she'd spent the afternoon weeding the gardens while Luke played.

"Hi." She went for cheerful. Maybe it would temper his glower.

"Don't you hi me. What are you doing outside?" he demanded.

"Getting fresh air and exercise." She bent a knee and did a lunge. She might be a few pounds heavy, but she remained limber.

He didn't seem impressed. "I told you to stay in the house with Luke."

Nothing could have stopped her snort. "I'd like to see you entertain an active four-year-old penned in a house with no toys or kids' movies on a sunny day."

"You're his mother. You should have ordered it."

Caleb had a lot to learn when it came to parenthood. She laughed. "I'd like to see you try, and then enforce it. It is rather funny, too, coming from you, given you're the guy who barely spent time indoors. Weren't you like a master at escape?" She'd once overheard Caleb's mother at school lamenting to another parent that, short of duct taping them to a wall or gluing their feet to the floor, the boys just wouldn't stay still.

Apparently a reminder that Luke took after Caleb wasn't a good enough excuse. He clamped his lips tight. "This isn't funny. I told you to stay inside in order to keep you guys safe. Do you realize what could have happened if that thing came back and I wasn't here to protect you?"

"No, I don't know what might have happened because we have no idea what we came across yesterday. It could have been a monkey, fresh from a swamp mud bath, on the loose from the zoo. Maybe he wanted to come inside for a bath." The silly example saw a little chuckle slip from Luke.

"Or it could have been some sick predator that wouldn't be scared off by conventional means. You could have been hurt!" His body shook, and not with anger, she noted, but...fear?

Caleb truly was scared for them.

She might have given him some slack, except he did the unforgivable. He scared Luke.

A tremble went through their son. Her turn to glare. "You stop that naysaying right now, Caleb. You're scaring Luke. And I won't have it. What happened last night was a fluke. Probably some bayou animal looking for food scraps."

"Because you know a lot of animals who can open windows," he drawled with the utmost sarcasm.

No, but she wouldn't back down now. "Raccoons are pretty wily." And hey, the monkey idea wasn't that farfetched. It could happen. Right?

"Except that wasn't a coon trying to get in his room last night."

Luke popped his head from Caleb's shoulder to utter, "The dinosaur was coming for me. But he didn't come here. Grandma said he wouldn't, and if he did, she'd—"

"Fill its snout with salt rock," Claire announced with a thump of her shotgun on the front porch. "So stop harassing the girl, Caleb. The boy needed air. He was never in any danger. I was watching along with Princess."

The dog, upon hearing its name, sprang from the clump of

marigolds in the flowerbed with a bark that startled Caleb into taking a step back, and that made Luke laugh.

The struggle on Caleb's face was funny. Hard to frown in annoyance at getting surprised by a teeny tiny dog when it so evidently pleased their son.

With the tension broken, time to change the subject.

"How did the interview go?" Renny asked.

"I was hired. I start tomorrow as a security guard." He made a face.

"That's great. I hear the dental benefits are wicked."

"Nothing wrong with my bite, baby." A quick wink and a sexy smile brought heat to her cheeks.

"I've got a ten o'clock shift at the grocery store tomorrow. Do you need a ride into work? I can probably drop you off on the way to Luke's school. But we'll have to leave early."

The crossed arms over his chest didn't bode well. Welcome to fight number two. "You are not going to work."

"Oh, yes I am."

It didn't take the tension in his jaw for her to know things were going to get ugly. Apparently, Claire noted it, too.

"Luke, sweetie, why don't you come inside with me and test drive the cookies that just came out of the oven. I've got a cold glass of milk made for dipping."

With a wiggle that saw Caleb setting Luke down, her son went scampering off, leaving Renny alone with a seriously bristling male.

So very hot. But sexy or not, she was not about to back down. "I am going to work tomorrow, Caleb, whether you like it or not. The bills won't pay themselves."

"I know, which is why I got a job."

"Well la-de-da for you. But just so you know, I am not a charity case, and I'm not about to beg you for money."

"No one said you had to beg. I'm just doing what's right. A man is supposed to support his family."

"I'm sure your mother will appreciate that."

"Renny!" He barked her name as his agitation increased, but that was fine because she was getting agitated, too. "Why must you be so difficult?"

"Because I'd like to know who gave you permission to start making decisions for me."

"I'm just trying to do what's right."

"Awesome. Do it, but while you're at it, keep in mind I make my own decisions. You're not the boss of me." Which sounded kind of juvenile when spoken aloud.

"You're being stubborn."

"I'm being a woman."

He glared.

Planting a hand on her hip, Renny glared right back. "Go ahead. Have your hissy fit. Get it out of your system."

"Hissy fit? Is that what you call my effort to try and protect you and Luke?"

"You're right. It's more like a dictatorship. And I'm rebelling. Letting you back into my life doesn't mean you're suddenly in charge. I am."

"What about Luke? Don't I get a say?"

"Yes. But for the moment, the final choices are mine. I might eventually be able to forgive, but it might take longer to forget." Because some things, like betrayal, haunted a girl forever—and the remembrance of a kiss never went away.

She would have expected maybe an explosion about now. Frustration that she wouldn't just fall into his arms and obey without question.

Instead, Caleb chuckled, a low, rumbling sound that tickled her senses.

"What's so funny?" she asked.

"You. Us fighting. The girl I remembered would have never yelled at me."

"The girl you remembered learned to toughen up." Best he knew that now before things went further.

"I like it."

Well, that wasn't the answer she'd expected, and her surprise might have been what led to her being pulled without a protest into his arms.

Oh, just admit it. She wanted to be in his arms. Wanted his lips on hers caressing with that sensual languor only he provided.

His hands spanned her waist, and he lifted her with ease, giving her better and deeper access to his mouth.

Delicious.

The sensual slide of his tongue over hers sent shivers up and down her body.

She slid her arms around his shoulders, digging her fingers into his short hair, keeping him close.

One of his hands slid from her waist to cup a buttock. He might have made small growling sound against her lips. She nipped him in the hopes he'd do it again.

A small voice asked, "Why is Daddy grabbing Mommy's bum?"

Why indeed?

How about because she liked it?

Problem was, there wasn't any privacy to pursue it.

Ugh.

Chapter 15

WE REALLY NEED *a place of our own.*

The thought started when Luke caught them making out in the front yard that resulted in Renny pulling away—with reluctance.

Noooo. I don't want to stop.

But he had to. Now wasn't the time to drag her off to bed or to grope her in the front yard. He was a father now, and while he might not have had one for long, he did know proper parents didn't make out in front of their kid—unless he wanted to scar them for life. Caleb still remembered his horror when his mom got pregnant with Constantine and he realized it meant his mother had—ugh—sex.

But Luke wasn't the only reason he couldn't just toss his woman over his shoulder and indulge in an afternoon of fun between the sheets. His mother and brother were also in the house, and while sneaking around as teenagers to have nookie was fun—and almost a sport—he was a man now. And this man wanted a bed and some privacy.

We need to get a place of our own. This mantra persistently repeated itself throughout the afternoon, hours spent learning how to properly play cars in the dirt—while making *vroom* noises. An educational day for someone who'd never been around children much.

The first thing he learned was they were bloody inexhaustible. When Luke began to ask questions, they never ended, and after the seventh "Why?" in a row, he shot Renny a rescue-me look, only to have her giggle and walk away.

"I'll get you for that," he mock-threatened.

"I can't wait," was her saucy reply.

When his son ran off at one point to find some juice—Caleb having sent Luke to his mom—Caleb stalked Renny down. He found her lounging in a chair at the back of the house, protected from insects by the screened porch, reading a paperback.

"You'd make an awful soldier," he said as he cast a shadow over her.

She grinned up at him. "Why?"

"You left me behind under fire," he growled. "I barely made it through the barrage of questions."

"Just teaching you how to swim the same way my daddy did. Lucky for you, you didn't sink."

"So you think I did okay?" *Shoot me now.* He sounded like such a wuss for even asking. Given he needed to reassert his manliness, he sat on the end of her lounge chair, resulting in the other end flipping up and sending her tumbling into him.

"Caleb!" she squealed.

"That's what I like to hear," he said, shifting his weight so that the chair balanced out. He also kept her on his lap, where she belonged. "Although, if you're going to scream my name like that, the least you could do is get naked first."

"We can't get naked. Someone—"

"Might see," he finished with a sigh. "Being an adult blows."

"And so do I," she said with a wink. "What a shame you'll have to wait for a sample."

Mind blown. The increased heart rate and heat flushing his skin?

Pure fucking arousal. "You are being intentionally cruel. You do realize that, right?"

The smile on her lips turned, if possible, even naughtier. "Who, me? Would I punish you?"

"I hope so." He cupped the back of her head, his fingers digging into the soft mass of her hair. "Because I need to be punished. So I can kiss you for forgiveness."

She inhaled sharply a moment before his lips covered hers, sliding slow and sensually over them, hushing any retort she might have had.

But Renny didn't seem interested in denying him. She kissed him right back, more cruel punishment because he couldn't help but imagine those plush, pliant lips wrapped around a certain part of him. A hard part...

His erection pressed against his jeans, and he felt the seam of her shorts rubbing as she wiggled atop him.

A softly sighed sound was his ticket to deepen the kiss, the slick slide of his tongue along hers sending a shiver through her frame.

Her sensual responsive nature to his touch was another form of torturous tease. Her fingers dug into his back and her arms wound around him, folding him in her embrace. His own hands slid down and cupped her rounded buttocks. A perfect handful that he massaged.

The snap of her head breaking their kiss made him growl. "Get back here."

"We should stop," she panted.

"That's just being cruel." Since she wouldn't give him her lips, he dove in for a nibble at her throat.

Her fingers threaded his hair, tight, almost painful. He couldn't tell if she wanted him to stop his sensual nips or needed more...

More, of course.

He sucked at her skin, and she moaned, "You're playing dirty."

"And loving it. So are you." He could tell. She couldn't hide her arousal from him.

"But someone might see."

And those who might spy were family, and that meant he couldn't kill them.

Yet stopping...*I don't want to stop touching her.*

He rumbled against her skin.

"Caleb!" Said in a way that let him know he had to rein back his passion.

Pulling back from her, he let out a breath, a long, heavy sound. "When did I get old and worried about doing the right fucking thing?"

She smiled. "You matured. And just so you know"—she leaned close to whisper—"it's really, really sexy." She gave him one last lingering and sweet kiss that left him sitting there with eyes closed long after she fled. How emasculating was it to want to relive that moment in perpetuity?

For the first time in what seemed like forever, he felt complete. He'd found what was missing in his life, the last piece—no, not a piece, a person who could make him whole.

Make me happy.

Sappy shit. *I'd be happier if I had a bedroom with a lock.*

But that would come. He couldn't let his impatience rush things. He'd waited years to see Renny again. He could wait a few days longer. Besides, he knew one important thing now.

She still wants me.

Hesitation arising from the past might still come between them, but she was thawing, perhaps even forgiving him. Hope was a hot furnace to a body he thought ran cold-blooded.

"Why is Daddy sleeping while sitting up?"

Not sleeping but dreaming. With his eyes wide open about a future.

The rest of that day, the best Caleb could manage was a stolen kiss here and there that left Renny's cheeks flushed and her eyes bright.

The occasional touch kept his blood boiling while, at the same time, the inability to take things further frustrated him.

He couldn't even take them back to her place, not given he'd promised to meet Wes tonight. He didn't want her being alone, not until they knew this strange monster business was taken care of.

Keep them safe.

The mantra repeated itself over and over. He blamed it for the tremors that hit when he was away from Renny.

Separation? Bad.

He couldn't explain why, but he felt whole when with Renny. In control. Being with her gave him a purpose that had no room for panic.

He did what had to be done. He protected. He provided. He kissed...

Okay, that was less for her than it was for him.

The feel of her lips against his, her hands grasping at his nape, her skin feverish for his touch, the signs she wanted him were there. They bolstered him. Made him strong again.

Strong enough to tolerate the hunter in him wanting to rise for a peek.

I don't know if I want to let you out.

He spoke to his other side, knowing the croc already was aware of his trepidation. Whenever his reptile came out to play, blood ran.

Because that is the nature of the beast.

Something he heard over and over, but it didn't change how he felt. He could handle violence, but his croc self took it to a scary level, dragging him along for the ride, willing or not.

Practice makes perfect.

Did that really apply when dealing with another personality? Every time he let the croc out, he feared losing another part of himself. Of returning less human than before.

Yet, containing the beast didn't work. It still lurked in his head, tossing its own thoughts and emotions into everything Caleb did.

Remember what happened the last few times you tried to cage the beast?

Practice makes perfect. The expression repeated itself.

Stop whining about your split personality problem and get shifting. Full dusk had fallen, and Wes was expecting him, not as a man, but as a crocodile.

Fuck fear. Fear never helped a situation. *I will make fear my bitch.* Time to throw on the scales and do something that would make people, like his family, safe.

But before he did so, Caleb made sure his brother would stand guard in his stead. It involved a conversation that might have made more than a few humans blanch.

"I gotta go on the prowl and see what I can find out about that lizard thing lurking around," Caleb told Constantine after having tucked Luke in and saying goodnight to Renny—which involved more kissing and even bluer balls.

"You want me to curtail my evening of alcoholic debauchery to babysit?"

"Yeah."

Constantine shrugged. "Okay. But I'm telling you right now, if something pays us a visit, I'm not holding Princess back."

Casting a glance at the rat, who wore a pink bow today in her fine hair, Caleb smirked. "Sure, let the hound of hell loose. I'm sure your hairball will do a fine job hobbling any attackers with a rabid gnaw of their Achilles tendon."

"Laugh all you want, but she actually goes for the ankles so she can get her prey to bend over and present their jugular. Princess believes in going for the killing shot." Said with such pride.

Grrr. A tiny lip pulled back, a murderous glare entered those giant eyes, and her ears pointed in aggressive fury.

"There is something seriously deviant about that dog," Caleb said as he glanced again at Princess.

"I know." Constantine beamed. "Pure perfection."

At the words, Princess yipped, but Con missed the canine smirk on her tiny muzzle.

Much as I hate to admit it, that's one fucking smart appetizer.

With that kind of protection left behind for his family, Caleb stripped and walked naked to the edge of the bayou. He dipped a toe in the brackish water, delaying the inevitable. The water was fine. The humming mosquitoes didn't bother him. Not even the mud.

It was the *other* he dreaded.

So long since he'd allowed his feral side to rise. Months since he'd felt the gnawing ache of the hunger, the thrill of the beast as it pursued its prey. The chomp of—

He clamped his eyes shut. But for once, he couldn't stop the feelings. The alien thought process of his beast merged with his consciousness.

Remember what the shrink said.

Don't fight your animal side.

Don't equate what you do while shifted with who you are.

We are hunters. And hunters don't just chase their prey. Sometimes they eat them, too. It's the nature of life.

A life Caleb had tried to deny, worried that there was something wrong with him, that his monster took too much pleasure in the death of others.

But other than that first mistake, had he truly ever lost absolute control? The rest had all deserved what he dished.

Still, it only took one major mistake to fuck me over.

How much worse if the next fuckup happened to Renny or Luke?

But he couldn't think that way. Not now when he needed his senses sharp.

Tonight we hunt.

The lukewarm water bathed his scaled skin, and if a croc could sigh, his did. How he'd missed the smooth glide of his powerful body through the silky swamp. Vegetation tickled his underbelly, the waving fronds not impeding his progress. His sensory spots along his jaw fed him further information—temperature, current, the fact that this water lacked salt.

Maybe once this was over, he'd take his family to the beach. A day spent soaking in the sun and briny water, with Renny in a bikini.

His pleasant fantasy didn't stop him from doing his task.

Tail swishing, Caleb zigzagged across the submerged parts of the wetland. When he had to, he did a belly run across the ground, startling the smaller rodents into hiding.

Thankfully, his reptile did not feel a need to stop for a snack. He'd made sure to have a large dinner so his snaggletoothed side wouldn't be tempted.

With that fear quelled, he found a lot more enjoyment in the bayou search. He spent hours crisscrossing the marshy acres between his house and the Bittech Institute. Nothing. Nothing. *Ooh, fresh turtle eggs*. Nothing.

He was just about to call it quits when he detected it. Another large predator.

Inching up onto the muddy shore, Caleb stayed low, his belly brushing the ground as he took in the situation. He crept forward, frame held high enough to not drag and alert his target. He slitted his eyes, filtering the ambient starlight to guide his steps.

Silently, he moved, the predator facing away from him, upwind, providing a tempting target. Caleb opened his mouth wide, his long, extended snout ridged with sharp teeth. He snapped it shut with a *clack*.

Wes didn't even jump. "Dude, you are seriously loud. Like my brother"—a bull gator—"in a china shop. Did you really think I wouldn't hear you coming?"

It took but a moment to shift shapes, a gasping process that he didn't really enjoy. The youngsters always asked as they approached those puberty years, "Does it hurt?"

Hell yeah, but you got used to it. And if you didn't, you lied so you wouldn't look like a pussy.

Straightening from his crouch, Caleb replied. "I take it you didn't find anything." A few strides brought Caleb to a different fallen trunk to sit on because while nudity might be acceptable among shifters, getting into someone's naked space, unless you were banging them, was considered rude.

"A faint scent trace. But it was old and didn't lead anywhere."

"Are we sure that thing is hiding in the swamp?"

"Where else would it be?" Wes asked. "It's not as if it can rent a room in town."

"So I guess we keep looking."

"Not tonight we aren't. You have a job to get to tomorrow morning."

Caleb rolled his eyes. "I guess I wouldn't want to piss off the boss the first day."

"You got that straight."

For a moment, they sat in silence and let the sounds of the bayou roll over them. The soft plop of water as something surfaced for a bite. The hum of insects out for a night of drinking blood and procreating before the dawn saw them dying. The chorus of frogs, their symphony interrupted every now and then as one of their number went from entertainment to dinner.

"Fucking hell, I gotta ask. Why did you leave?"

Wes's question startled Caleb, and he shot the other man a look. "Why do you care?"

"I don't. I was just surprised is all. Especially given how hot and heavy you were with Renny."

"Something happened, and I kind of had no choice."

"I know what you did that summer." Wes smirked.

Caleb froze. "What are you talking about?" The words emerged from a dry mouth. Caleb had been alone when it happened. And he still wasn't sure what had happened. A blank spot resided in his mind. One minute he was walking home from Renny's, and then, in what felt like a blink, he regained awareness as his jaws were ripping apart a man.

"Considering you left not even twelve hours after you were dumped in the marsh with that dead guy—"

"Stop. What do you mean dumped with a dead guy? What the hell did you see?"

The hard look Wes shot him held a glint of red, the beast he held within but seemed to share his life with in harmony.

"I mean that a couple of guys dragged your scaly sleeping ass out of a big truck and dropped you in the water and then dumped a body in front of you. Some guy wearing army scrubs with a syringe stuck you and ran away. He and the others took off in the truck before you woke up."

Woke up hungry, dazed, and angry. He'd smelled something in front of him and snapped. Chewed. *I killed and ate a human.*

He'd later retched most of it up on shore when he staggered from the marsh, naked and dirty. But the military truck, with its blazing lights and barking soldiers, seemed to know what he was, and what he was guilty of.

Of course they did because... "I was framed." Caleb couldn't help a note of incredulity. "Those fucking assholes framed me. They made me think I'd lost control. They told me I killed a man." The cry he let loose held frustrated fury. All those years he'd blamed himself. Feared himself. Done despicable things because they said he had to. "It was all a fucking lie. And I believed it." Instead of trusting himself.

"I would have told you what I saw back then, but before I could get to you, you were gone. You and a few other boys. You're the only one that came back."

Because shifters were the expendable soldiers, the ones sent into the most dangerous of situations because they were the most likely to survive. "Lucky me."

"Oh, stop it with the pity-me, I'm-so-screwed routine. At least you came back. Can those other guys say the same?"

"No." He'd lost too many friends to count. "But it's hard to forget."

"You don't have to forget. But you can choose to live in the now and create new memories, good ones to remember."

"This is getting way too Kumbaya for me," Caleb growled.

"Don't worry, I was going to mock your dick size in a second."

"And there is so much to mock. I tell you, it's hard carrying that kind of weight around, but the ladies love it."

Wes burst out laughing. "Asshole."

"And I'm a fucking brain-addled tool obviously because, crazily enough, I missed this."

"Missed hunting possibly murderous dinos in the swamp?"

A snicker left Caleb. "Actually, I'm liking this new game." So long as he won in the end. "But more, I missed home. The swamp. A place I can let my croc out that has nothing to do with the war or taking out the enemy."

"They really did a number on you."

"And then some."

But he was healing and, even better, falling in love all over again, which came with a new set of anxieties.

Was his family safe while he was gone?

His chat with Wes over, Caleb took a direct route back to his house, anxious to check on them. What if the creature they hunted had circled back and gone after Luke again?

What if...

Curse it, now he was the one who couldn't stop questioning.

Body undulating, he moved and grooved his way home only to pause at the muddy edge.

Someone is watching.

He almost stayed hidden in the weeds, willing them to go, but that smacked of cowardice.

Striding from the brackish water, he immediately scented the air, but it remained clear of alien odors.

In other good news, the house remained secure. The traps he'd strung along the window intact, the doors closed, and he assumed locked. Nothing seemed out of place.

Everything looked and smelled right except for him. The swamp's perfume clung to his skin, a miasma he would never dare bring into the house. A wooden spoon named Spanky had taught him that lesson young.

Besides, he didn't need to go inside to get clean, not when they had an outdoor shower that drew from their well. It wasn't hot water, but it was fresh, and the bar of soap kept in a dish, lemon scented.

It didn't take long to rinse the bayou from his skin, but even once clean, he didn't move. He remained standing under the spray, face lifted to it, and tried not to react as she drew near.

Renny.

From the moment he'd risen from the waters, he'd sensed her presence and tried not to let on. It wasn't easy, not when he knew she watched.

She sees my beast.

A part of him had wanted to submerge under the murky surface of the swamp. To hide who he was. What he was.

More secrets.

He couldn't do it. If he wanted a life with Renny, they needed to start with honesty, starting with his croc.

This is who I am. Whom he'd never dared reveal back when they were dating. Would she run away?

He might have held his breath when he rose from the weeds and mud, scaled skin rippling and sliding as the magic of the change drew his reptilian features back to the spot hidden within. Smooth flesh, strands of hair, and a face that could pass for human took their place. He walked as a man, straight, proud, and naked.

Did he forget to mention aroused? Knowing she watched, and didn't flee, brought a boil to his blood. He could suntan himself under the heat of her gaze.

But he pretended to not know. *Don't push her.* Let her come to him.

Please let her come to me.

Feeling her stare the entire time he showered did nothing to help his erection. How hard it was—so very, very hard—to not stroke himself to completion. But he didn't dare.

She watched. What would she think if he came without her?

Would she know that he thought of her? Would it disgust her? What if it didn't? What if he spent himself and she needed him?

Pretending nonchalance was so difficult and remembering to breathe as she approached with soft footsteps even harder.

"You can stop faking it. I know that you know I'm here."

He turned to face her, unable to stop a smile. "Say that fast five times."

"I've better ideas if you're in the mood for tongue twisting." Despite the droplets of water hitting her from the spray, she remained close to him. Very close.

The tank top she wore molded the curves of her breasts, outlining their weighted roundness and delineating nipples that shriveled into points as he stared at them.

Tiny shorts hugged her shapely hips, and a hint of rounded belly peeked at him between those skimpy bottoms and top.

"What are you doing outside?"

"Waiting for you."

At his growled "baby," she stepped closer and put a finger on his lips. "Don't get mad. I didn't do anything stupid. I watched from the window until I was sure it was you."

"Just because you see a croc doesn't mean it's me."

"Princess didn't bark."

"But I might."

She slid closer, getting wet in the lukewarm water jetting from the wide rain showerhead. "While I appreciate the intent behind the bark, I think I prefer"—she leaned up on tiptoe to rub her lips against his—"the bite."

He met her partway and was rewarded with the edge of her teeth grasping his lower lip and tugging.

Because he was apparently an idiot, he had to ask, "What are you doing?"

"What does it look like I'm doing?" she whispered with a soft laugh against his lips.

"It looks like you're seducing me."

"Only looks like?" she teased with another nibble of his mouth.

"Feels like, too." He slid his arms around her, drawing her tight to him and deepening the kiss.

For a moment, their hot breaths mingled, their bodies pressed.

Then he groaned and pulled away. He grasped her hands and held them away from him, ignoring her sounds of protest.

"Stop, baby."

"Stop? Why? I want this. Heck, you want this." She punctuated her words with a grind of her hips against him.

His resolved wavered, and he forced himself to breathe as he looked her in the face.

Her perfect face.

How did I get so lucky to have a chance to start over? A chance to have a new life, a true life, with the woman he loved. But, if he ever had any hope of making it work, he needed to start it with honesty.

"You need to know the truth. About why I left."

And that quickly, the soft smile on her lips faded and her body tensed. "What happened to you can't tell?"

"I can't. At least I'm not supposed to. But..." Caleb sighed as he leaned back against the post that held the plumbing for the shower. He shrugged and smiled. "I never claimed I was a good boy. Sometimes, rules need to be broken."

"Will you get in trouble?" She touched his cheek. "You don't have to tell me if it might harm you."

"The people I swore to, they're not around anymore. And even if they were, they already did their worst when they took me from you. Fucking bastards, using me and lying to me, they never gave a damn about me, only what I could do for them." He caught her gaze. "But you gave a damn. You loved me, and instead of respecting that, I chose to keep a promise to some asshats who probably wouldn't piss on me if I was on fire." On the contrary, after the embarrassment of their mission overseas, most would have preferred he died, keeping their secrets intact.

She traced a finger down the scar until the tip of her digit ran across his lower lip. He nipped it. As if he could resist. "You don't have to tell anymore. I know you, Caleb. I might have been angry, but deep down, a part of me knew you wouldn't have left unless you had a damned good reason."

"I did. I murdered someone. Or thought I had."

He waited for it. The recoil, the horror, the quizzical...

"And?"

And? He blinked at her. "And I said I killed someone. Or at least I thought my croc had."

"Thought? Is there doubt about what happened?"

"More like a revelation." He explained quickly what he thought had happened and then Wes's version. All the while he got them out of the shower. He procured two towels from the weather-proof chest beside it.

Wrapping Renny first, he carried her to the picnic table and seated her on its top. He didn't move far away, but rather paced in short strides in front of her.

He couldn't explain the relief that she was listening instead of running. He'd expected several reactions from her, hell, he'd experienced many himself as he lived the past few years, but Renny took his tale without flinching.

When he finished, she tilted her head to look at him. "Sounds like it was a rough time."

"Very."

"But I have a question for you. How could you have thought you killed a man for no cause? I know you, Caleb. You would have never done something like that."

"Wouldn't I? Every time I let the croc out, it feeds. On live things. From the moment I met you, I was afraid I'd scare you off, that the beast would repulse you."

"It's part of who you are."

"A part I always struggled with."

"Why didn't you tell anyone?"

He shrugged. "Tell who? My mom? She already had enough stress without me whining about being weirded out by my croc's antics."

"What about your friends? Their fathers?"

"In case you've forgotten, I'm a guy. Asking for help is like asking for directions. We just don't do it. Especially back then. I was an arrogant little fucker. I didn't want to ask anyone because I didn't want to look weak."

"Nobody would have thought that. Actually, I take that back. Wes would have mocked you, probably Daryl, too, but they were your peers. They would have teased, but they would have helped."

"Wes was never my peer." Rival, yes, and one Caleb never admired, even if he bought the same studded leather coat within a day of hearing about the gator's.

"Whatever you want to call those guys, they would have had your back."

"I know that now." Hindsight was more than twenty-twenty. It was a bitch that taunted.

Renny wasn't done. Her brow knitted into lines as she thought aloud. "According to Wes, it was a setup, and I'll be honest, a pretty obvious one, it seems. I mean, didn't you think it was weird that those guys who stopped you knew so much about you and what happened?"

"Well, yeah, it seemed strange, but things went so fast." He'd also still been reeling at the time, from the shock and, he now realized, lingering effects from drugs making his thought process murky. "They said they knew what I'd done. They threatened to arrest me. To expose me, as a matter of fact." *You're a monster that should pay for his crimes.* "Unless I would agree to a deal."

"A deal that involved you fighting for them."

"Obey. Fight. Kill. The choice was join the military and depart immediately for a mission or have not just myself exposed, but my family, too."

Caleb had stopped to stand in front of her. It was simple for her to lean forward so she might cup his face with both hands. "Oh, Caleb." Moisture brightened her gaze, and he could feel his throat tighten.

"I—" He swallowed. "I was a coward and agreed. Instead of being willing to face what I'd done, I agreed to their terms and left."

He dropped his eyes to stare down, but she wouldn't let him escape. She ducked under and forced him to see her expression.

"You had no choice."

"I could have said no and taken what I deserved."

"You protected your family. This town."

"I deserted you."

"To do the right thing. The hard thing." She brushed her lips across his as she whispered, "I forgive you."

Had someone shot him? Had an axe severed his legs? What else could explain the slump of his knees? The rough seating at the picnic table pressed against his joints. Head bowed, he leaned forward and pressed his face against Renny's belly as he wrapped his arms around her legs.

His body shook. Not quite with tears, more like relief. His heart swelled with love. Hope blossomed in his soul. So many feelings assailed him. Emotions long pent up, thought dead, pressed him in all directions, and yet, in some respects, he felt lighter.

He'd told the truth, and the chains it bound him with no longer held him down.

"Caleb." Softly spoken. She lifted his chin and let him see the love in her gaze. "Kiss me."

He rose to his feet and, in a smooth motion, clasped her to him. Dipping his head, he claimed her lips, trying to show how he felt.

But the taste of her wasn't enough... He wanted all of her.

He pulled away and groaned.

"Where are you going?"

"I need a cold shower."

"Whatever for?"

He spun to face her. "Because if I don't, then I'm going to strip that towel from you and lick every goddamned inch of your luscious body."

"What's stopping you?"

"In case you haven't noticed, we still don't have a bloody room." Who would have ever thought he'd pray for privacy?

"It's almost one a.m. No one is awake but you and me." She leaned back on her elbows and let her knees fall open, the motion undoing the simple tuck of the towel. As its edges peeled away, it revealed the swell of her breasts, the sharp tips of her nipples, and the shadowy cleft between her thighs.

He might have been punched to the head one too many times, but that didn't make him stupid. Caleb didn't wait for another invitation.

He dove on the offering, his hands spanning her waist, an hourglass indent made for holding. His mouth claimed hers, but it didn't remain long, not with the luscious temptations waiting below.

The swirl of his tongue around a brazen peak drew forth a cry from her. And another when he let the flat edge of his teeth tug. He sucked her breasts into his mouth, enjoying the pull on her flesh, the scrabble of her nails on his shoulders and how her heels dug into the base of his spine as she tried to draw him nearer.

He held firm—and he meant *firm*—and kept his teasing play of her nipples, switching back and forth until she just moaned continuously.

Then he blazed a trail down her rib cage to the round softness of her belly. He rubbed his bristled jaw against her skin and felt the shiver that went through her.

He wasn't done with his journey.

Farther his lips stroked, their feathery path leading to one plump thigh. He couldn't help but nibble.

Yummy.

But something even tastier beckoned.

"Open for me," he whispered against her mound. Her legs were parted, but he wanted more. He wanted to see the source of her musky honey.

She lay right back against the picnic tabletop, golden hair spread around her, chest rising and falling as she panted her arousal. She drew her legs farther apart, bringing her heels to rest and grip the edge of the table. She offered herself to him, and he trembled.

She is so damned beautiful. How could I possibly think I deserve her?

He didn't. But he would do his damnedest to do right by her.

Caleb leaned forward and blew hotly on her cleft. The petals to her sex shivered. The heady scent of her arousal surrounded him. The taste of her burst upon his tongue with only one lap.

Sweet ambrosia. He licked her sex with a rumbling enjoyment, an enjoyment she shared and expressed with her moaned, "Caleb."

He parted her nether lips, stabbing his tongue into her heat, feeling the erotic tension permeating her body. He wanted her to come.

Fingers replaced his tongue, a pair to stretch her tight channel while his tongue flicked at her hooded clitoris, causing it to swell so that each stroke made her gasp.

Her pussy tightened around his fingers.

He grabbed her clit with his lips.

Her hips arched off the table.

Pumping fingers and teasing lips followed. She drew in a sharp breath. Her body bowed, she could only gasp, no real sound escaping her.

The final, hard clamp of her channel made him gasp and then exult as her pussy convulsed in climactic waves for him. Yet still, he pushed his fingers in her, drawing it out and then rebuilding it as he found her sweet spot. And stroked it.

Stroked her sensitive G-spot until she was panting and squirming again. But this time, he wasn't content with just fingers. His cock bobbed, hard and ready.

The tip of it butted against her plump lips, slid between them, and then he slammed into her as she wrapped her legs around his flanks and drew him in.

His turn to cry out. "Aah." The sensation of molten heat engulfing him was too much for him to resist.

When she would have grabbed at him, he manacled her wrists in his hands and drew them over her head, stretching her on the table. He held her pinned as he stroked into her.

Long.

Hard.

Deep.

She shuddered even as he retreated.

Then slammed back in, making her cry out.

Pull back. Then in.

Caleb thrust into Renny, his body rigid as he controlled his pleasure. But he wouldn't be able to hold it for long. She was just too exquisite.

Even though he held her hands prisoner, she still managed to drive him wild, arching her hips to take him deep, the walls of her sex squeezing so tight.

He kept moving firmly, trying to remain conscious of the fact that she lay on a table, not a bed. He had to be gentle with her.

But their passion wasn't cooperating.

Without conscious volition, Caleb quickened his pace. He wrapped an arm around her waist and pulled her to a seated position with her ass still on the towel. His strokes got shorter but harder. They banged deep within her sheath.

She clenched around him. Her body pulsed with heat and energy. She buried her face in the crook of his neck and shoulder. The moment before she climaxed, she said the most incredible thing, "You're mine," and then she did the most mind-blowing thing.

She bit him and, for all intents and purposes, made him hers.

Chapter 16

THE PICNIC TABLE wasn't the most comfortable bed, but when they finished making love, neither was ready to separate. Problem was a light rain made it unpleasant to stay outside. So she'd entered the house and cuddled Caleb on the couch. Just for a little while.

Or so she'd thought until she heard the little voice saying, "Mommy, why are lying on top of Daddy?" On the list of awkward questions, that one ranked pretty high, along with "Why are you wearing Daddy's shirt?"

Somehow, explaining that she'd lost hers because she'd gone out to seduce Caleb didn't seem appropriate. She stammered out a white lie. "Mine got wet."

"Very wet," Caleb added, completely deadpan.

"Oh. Okay." And with that, her son wandered away and was soon making truck noises.

She, on the other hand, was making embarrassed groaning ones.

Caleb rubbed her back. "Now, now, baby, it's not that bad. At least we were wearing clothes."

He laughed harder when she elbowed him. Rolling off, she

tugged down his shirt, which came to a respectable mid-thigh, and then marched off toward the bathroom.

It didn't take a peek over her shoulder to know Caleb admired the view, and must have been pretty blatant about it because Luke asked, "Why are you so happy, Daddy?"

"Because I have you and your mom."

She might have stumbled. Stupid ledge between the bathroom floor and the hall.

That morning, Caleb was treated to the hustle and bustle of a family that needed to get ready to get out the door, on time. Luke had to be at school before nine, and then it was time to drop Caleb off with a kiss, then on to her own boring job at the grocery store.

Ho hum.

Until that night when she and Caleb snuck out for a tryst in his brother's truck. They steamed the windows that night.

Broke the picnic table the next.

Made use of the outdoor shower...

Each morning she woke to Luke's grin and Caleb's hug.

It was wonderful.

So the week went, and despite the lack of privacy, and the glower on Caleb's face each time she went to work, she was happy.

On Thursday about mid-afternoon, a familiar tingle let her know Caleb was there. She turned around to find him standing at the bottom end of her checkout aisle.

He wore the official Bittech uniform, and it suited him. She especially wanted to strip it from him.

I will...later.

"What are you doing here so early?" she asked. "I'm not due to finish for another hour."

"Wes let me off early so I could show you a surprise."

"It will have to wait. My boss will never let me leave early." She made a face. "But in other news, I'm not working tonight."

"How come?"

"The club is shut down on account of a burst water pipe in the bathroom."

"I don't suppose it could stay shut forever," he grumbled.

But that was all he was doing. Grumbling. He might not like her job at the Itty Bitty Club, but they'd come to an understanding. While Claire and Constantine—with his sly Chihuahua—watched Luke at night, Caleb kept an eye on Renny at work. Just not in the club and it wasn't because Caleb had an inability to, as he stated it, "Watch guys hit on my girl." Nope, he stayed outside because she requested it.

In a funny twist, Renny found herself really uncomfortable with mostly naked women strutting around him. Not that they dared try anything.

The dancers learned, after the first time he popped in for a beer, to keep their hands off. Whoever thought human women were meek never saw Renny grab a girl by the hair and growl, "Keep your paws off my man, Tina, or I will make your furry ass into a rug."

Because where Caleb was concerned, now that he was back, he was hers. And nothing, *nothing* would keep her away from him.

Although some idiots seemed intent on trying, like her boss at the supermarket who barked, "Suarez, why aren't you working?"

Renny rolled her eyes before facing her manager, some guy sent down by head office to maximize the store's revenue. "Work doing what?" She swept a hand toward her empty aisle. "There's no one here, Benny." Indeed, the few shoppers in the store had yet to finish and need a check out.

"Maybe there's no one on account someone is too high and mighty to do her job because she's too busy yapping."

She clamped her lips tight. There wasn't much she could say to placate Benny.

But Caleb didn't know that. "It's my fault. I was the one who came in and talked to her."

If Caleb thought to diffuse the situation, he was wrong because the manager of the store didn't care. Benny also didn't realize when he took a step forward and aimed his florid face and vitriol at Caleb just who he was dealing with.

"Listen, you scarred freak. I don't need your type coming in here and scaring off my clients."

Renny might take a lot of flack at the hands of this miserable excuse for humanity, but like heck would she let him berate Caleb.

"Don't you dare talk to him like that." She came around the counter and stood before Caleb, who appeared surprised.

"It's okay, Renny. I'm gonna have to get used to hearing shit like that."

"No, it is not okay. You got those scars serving your country, and now this moron thinks he can insult you. Not happening."

"Watch your mouth or you'll be looking for another job." Benny tried to look intimidating, but a human had nothing on the real predators she'd grown up with.

"Are you threatening to fire me? No need." She fumbled at the buttons holding her red vest closed. Renny balled the fabric and tossed it at Benny. "I quit." Turning to Caleb, she smiled. "Looks like I'm finished early after all. Let's go see that surprise."

"You can't quit," Benny hollered after her.

Renny stuck up a certain finger over her shoulder.

"Did you just tell him to fuck off in sign language?" Caleb asked. "That is so freaking sexy."

"Weirdo."

"Your weirdo, baby. Now are you ready?"

"For what?"

"You'll see," was his enigmatic reply.

What she saw was an overgrown front lawn and a tiny house whose wooden shingles were grayed from the weather and, in places, green from humidity. But the windows were intact if bare of curtains.

Inside, the wide plank floor had lost its varnish, but it was swept clean. Renny peeked around the space. The open living room with its sliding glass door to the backyard of the house. The kitchen with its white tile countertops and painted cabinets.

"Why are we here?" she asked, already guessing.

"Say hello to our home."

"Our?" she asked as she spun with an arched brow. "Kind of presumptuous, don't you think?"

He looked crestfallen. "Yes, ours. I mean, after the week we've spent, and—"

She placed a finger on his lips and laughed. "I'm sorry. I shouldn't tease you like that. Of course I want to be here with you."

"Luke, too."

A snicker escaped her. "Well, duh. We're kind of a package deal."

He made a face. "I am so bad at this relationship stuff."

She draped her arms around his neck and smiled. "Oh, I don't know about that. So far you're doing pretty damned good. So good, I think we should test out this place before we grab our son and move in with our stuff."

They made love that afternoon on the countertop. In the shower. And were now curled together with naked limbs in a nest on the floor.

For once, there was no rush to be anywhere. Not even to pick up Luke because Caleb had already made arrangements with Melanie. Since her best friend had to go see Bittech for her fertility test results, she'd drop Luke off on her way home after grabbing a bite for dinner, giving Renny and Caleb some alone time.

From the direction of her purse, her phone jangled, a catchy ditty titled, "I'm Going Bananas," an old Madonna song she'd bought and used as a ringtone for Melanie

Rolling away from Caleb, Renny said over her shoulder on her way to grab it, "She's probably looking for details."

"I thought women weren't supposed to gossip about their sex lives," he said, rolling to his back and lacing his hands under his head. It pulled at his flesh and defined some of his muscles. The scar that twisted down his side did nothing to mar his perfection. Rather it drew her eye more to the beauty of his shape.

It also distracted. She fished the phone out of her purse just as it went to voicemail. Before she could redial, it was ringing again.

She answered with a laugh. "Holy having a cow, Melanie, are you that impatient to hear the details?"

"Renny, he's gone." Said in a voice tight with fear.

The world stopped spinning, and Renny's whole bearing froze as she made sense of the words.

As if from a distance, she heard herself say, "What do you mean he's gone?"

"Luke. He's missing. The twins say the dinosaur got him."

"No." Renny whispered the word through numb lips. All of her went limp, including her fingers, which released the phone. Her knees decided to no longer support her, dumping her to the floor, where she hit hard. But the pain of impact was nothing compared to that gripping her heart.

Chapter 17

AS SOON AS RENNY SAID, "What do you mean he's gone?" Caleb was moving, yet his fastest speed wasn't fast enough to catch her before she collapsed. He dropped to the floor beside Renny, drawing her into his lap even as he dove for the phone.

He tucked it to his ear as he held a sobbing Renny close. "Tell me what's happened."

It didn't take long. Through hiccupping sobs, Melanie let him know what had happened. In a nutshell, Luke was gone.

Taken.

Because I wasn't there to protect him.

It didn't take any kind of medical degree in psychology to see Renny blamed herself for Luke's disappearance. There was plenty of blame to go around, starting with his own.

Damn me for not remaining more vigilant. He'd let his guard down after a week of no sightings. He, Wes, and even Daryl had done some more patrols, but found nothing. Not a single whiff of its unique aroma, not a peep from anyone in town. They'd wondered if the creature had moved on or was dead. Or perhaps it hadn't posed a threat at all.

In his cocoon of happiness, he'd allowed himself to relax, and now, because of his mistake, his son had paid the price.

Unfair!

Caleb slammed the steering wheel as he was forced to stop for a red light. He might have run it, but he somehow doubted the car would win in the battle for space against the rather large dump truck.

"This is all my fault." He growled. "I should have waited until later to show you the place and gone to grab Luke. The blame for this is on me. If I had been there for him, this wouldn't have happened."

"You don't know that."

Yeah, he did, because if he had been the one watching Luke and the twins, he would have never let those boys out of his sight. However, it hadn't been fucking Caleb on guard but Andrew. A man with no predator sense, an idiot who would probably die quickly if he had to survive in the wild. *Because I'd kill him.*

The weak bastard didn't pay attention to those he guarded. Andrew let himself be distracted.

Like I was distracted. Point the finger in the right place.

"This isn't your fault," Renny said, linking her fingers through his where they rested on the car's stick shift.

"Feels like it is."

"We might be worrying for nothing. Maybe Luke just wandered a little too far into the swamp while playing a game of hide-and-seek."

Since she didn't seem to believe her own reassurance, he chose to drive faster and soon drew the car up to the front of the Bittech building.

On the patterned cement outside the main doors, Melanie, with her hands latched to the twins, paced.

Relinquishing her grip on his hand, Renny barely waited for the car to stop before she was tumbling out. "What happened?"

"Andrew was around back with the boys. He says his phone rang, and he turned around to talk to whoever it was for only a second. Which is a second too long," Melanie grumbled. "He knows how quick the boys are. The next thing Andrew knew, the twins came screaming out of the woods, talking about the dino again."

"I might have to kill your husband," Caleb announced.

"Get in line." A scowl marred Melanie's features. "I already told him I'd yank his guts out if anything happens to Luke."

"I'll hold him down for you," Caleb offered.

"No need, Wes already offered."

"Where is Wes?" Renny asked, looking from side to side.

"Looking for Luke, of course."

"Andrew, too?"

Disdain wouldn't allow itself to be contained. Caleb snorted. "Doubtful."

Melanie's lips turned even lower. "He's inside calling some people to get a search party going."

"He's a bear. He should have been able to sniff out his trail." Renny took the words right out of his mouth.

If Caleb hadn't once seen Andrew's puny brown bear, he might have accused him of being a koala. Then again, that was insulting vicious koalas everywhere.

"Where was Luke last seen?" Caleb asked.

"By the willow tree that—Renny," Melanie yelled. "Get your ass back here. You can't go rushing into the swamp like that. You're human. You won't be able to defend yourself."

The truth hit hard, and Renny stumbled to a halt. She whirled, tears streaming down her cheeks. The pure anguish she displayed was something Caleb well understood. Pain was a close companion, but he couldn't give in to his pain right now. Yes, he was chilled to the bone by what might be happening to his son. He was devastated he'd not protected Renny from this. But he was also calm and clear-headed. Not a single shake in his hands, his breathing regular.

Panic had no place right now. The man he used to be stood straight as Renny cried, "I don't care if I don't have a weapon. That's my son in there, and he needs me."

And Renny needed him. Caleb strode to her, making every effort to appear non-threatening, as he did not want her to bolt. Melanie was right. The swamp wouldn't prove kind to his delicate woman. Only the foolish—or desperate—went off into the swamp without a weapon or a plan.

Sensing she was ready to flee, he resorted to words since he wasn't in reach. "What happened to your theory that said he might be playing hide and go seek?"

"I lied. Something's wrong. I feel it, feel it in here." Renny thumped her stomach.

Funny how she pinpointed the spot he felt a twinge, too. The gut always knew.

"You're probably right. Things don't look too good,"—*Great pep talk so far. Why not make her face blanch further?*—"but I will promise you one thing." As he got close to her, he reached out to grasp her hand, giving it a squeeze. "I'll find him." *Fucking right I'll find him, even it's the last thing I do.*

"We'll find him."

He shook his head. "I can't risk you getting hurt. Melanie's right. How would you defend yourself? Make a slingshot out of your bra?" He forced a wan smile, but Renny simply stared at him. Eyes brimming, lips trembling.

Heartbreaking. *Fix this.*

With one last press of fingers, he let her go and went to walk past Renny. As if she'd let him go.

She grabbed his arm and held him until he faced her. "I have to go with you. He needs me."

"Duh, he needs you," Melanie said with a roll of her eyes. As they'd talked, she'd marched herself and the boys over. "You should go, but take this with you."

This being a gleaming gun, redolent with fresh oil, that Melanie pulled out of an oversized purse.

What was more disturbing? The fact that Melanie carried a loaded weapon along with a sealed container of green grapes or that Renny grabbed it, popped it open to take a peek at how it was loaded, then armed it. *Click.*

There went his argument and his resolve.

"Let's go," Renny said.

He might have argued, but Renny was armed with a gun and looked ready to use it. Was it worth wasting a breath asking her to stay with Melanie while he looked? Nope. She'd never listen, not with Luke in danger.

Just like he would never hold back.

"Try and keep up, baby." Caleb ran for the rear of the building, outpacing Renny. His fingers—perfectly steady and adept—slipped buttons from loops and loosed his belt so that, when he hit the edge of the swamp, he could shed that fabric layer and, in the moment before he ducked under the concealing fronds of the weeping willow, take his other shape.

No hesitation. Not this time.

A hunter was needed. A killer, too, because not only was Caleb planning to return with his son, he was also making sure the threat was eliminated once and for all.

Skin stretched, limbs reshaped, and during the process, he heard Renny's jogging steps, but he didn't spare her a thought. Other things preoccupied his mind.

As his claws dug into moist dirt, he opened all his senses. His sensory spots absorbed and sifted the very flavor of the air.

A vivid tableau comprised of scents was painted. So many definite elements, layered and interwoven among each other. Amongst the fetid stench of the beast was the purer innocence of his son. He smelled fear, the sharp acrid tang of a child frightened.

The oddity, though, was how the smell of the creature suddenly appeared. Caleb found no tracks to show how it got there. Could locate no trail to follow, and yet, the beast had been here, been here, and had taken his son.

Maybe he'd missed something. He inhaled deep, as deep as he could, and then sifted the results.

The odors of the swamp permeated the air, nothing strange about that. However, he did note another reptilian scent, a predator. Wes.

They went this way.

Not far, though. He could see where the footprints stopped. At the murky edge of the water.

Water that Renny shouldn't swim in, but she was beyond reason.

Intent on her goal—save Luke—she brushed past him and slogged in the liquid, arms above her head to keep the pistol dry, but vulnerable to anything that hid in the murky depths, and what about when they hit deeper water? How would she stay afloat or defend herself?

Yet he knew she'd never stay behind—not unless she was bound tight—and there wasn't a boat or anything she could use as a...

What of a raft?

He was horrified at the idea his croc projected, and had he been in charge, he might have vetoed it, but his beast was driving at the moment. His reptile floated alongside Renny, back straight and partially out of the water.

No way will my croc let Renny ride him. Nor should she. Forget the indignity, what if my beast gets hungry and thinks she'd make a nice treat?

The disgust his reptile radiated actually managed to shame him. In that one emotional outburst from his other half, Caleb had a shining moment where he understood something truly important. *My beast cares for them, too.*

Renny was *their* mate. Luke was *their* son.

Even cold-blooded predators didn't eat family. Okay, so maybe some did, but apparently no one ever proved that leaked cookbook belonged to the Mercers and that Aunt Tanya's rump roast was anything more than it seemed.

While Caleb grasped his croc's intent, Renny needed a minute or so to figure it out. It took a few bumps of his snout to snag her attention.

"What do you want?" she asked, looking quite cross.

The big reptile moved ahead then across, blocking her with his body.

"What are you doing, Cal?" She cocked her head while asking.

Cal? Had she finally chosen a nickname for him? Ugh, his croc grunted as a spurt of warmth made Caleb mentally grin.

Pay attention, his croc snapped.

His beast was right. He should exult in it later. Speed was of the essence, which meant Renny needed to get her ass on his back so he could get moving. By now, the thing that had taken his son could be anywhere.

But there is nowhere that can hide him.

I will find my son.

Another head butt against Renny and she thankfully grasped his plan. Reaching over him, she grabbed hold and heaved herself on. With one hand doing its best to grip, the other he assumed holding the gun since he could still smell the oil used to lubricate the metal, he set off on a glide.

Which direction, though?

The scent of the creature had disappeared at the water's edge. Had it dove? Fuck no, not with Luke in its grasp.

And it wasn't just fatherly hope that prayed against that scenario. The evidence wasn't there. The rushes of weeds springing upward showed only one disturbance, and that one belonged exclusively to Wes, the lingering scent and disturbance of the fronds a message relayed to the sensory spots along his jaw.

Wes came through here, but the creature and Luke didn't.

But the footsteps ended at the water's edge. A body of water that held no trace of them. So where had they gone? There were no trees for them to climb, no signs of a boat or other floating device. A crazier man might wonder if they'd taken to the air. Impossible for a lizard.

Even one with possible wings? He couldn't help but recall that disturbing video.

If it can fly, though, then it could be anywhere. How could he track something that could take to the air currents and bypass all of the obstacles? Perhaps leave the swamp entirely.

"Where did it take Luke?" Renny murmured from his back. "How will we find him?"

The hopelessness in her tone crushed his heart.

I know where to go.

The man might wonder where to look, but his beast instinctively seemed to know.

Our son.

Did a link truly exist between him and Luke? Was that tickle he felt in his heart more than just trepidation?

Stop yapping or I'll eat something squishy. His croc threatened a mental image Caleb could have done without.

Powerful body undulating in the water, his croc made toward the horizon, where an amber-red sun set. Funny how once his beast had chosen a direction, Caleb noted it was where the tug in his gut led.

It took his reptile and Renny over deep water, his large presence scattering those who feared becoming dinner.

Later. His croc grinned in the water, and Caleb groaned.

Must you do that?

I'm hungry was the snarky reply.

However much his beast side teased, he didn't delay and made a beeline—or should that be crocoline?—toward a rocky hillock, a bramble-covered thumb sticking out of the water.

Thorny Point, a place long avoided by children and adults alike because of the wicked barbed bushes. It had also been ignored by him and Wes during their search because it lacked the right kind of scent.

No scent usually meant no prey, so they never went ashore. But if the creature could fly? A glance upwards didn't reveal anything, but he still had to stop and take a look.

We might be wasting time.

But what if this is the place?

What if it's not?

He swam around the thrusting rocks, wondering if his gut led him astray. A good thing he stuck around, too, because what the senses didn't smell, the ears heard.

A whimper. A little boy whimper.

Luke!

An urgent need to get to the top of the islet imbued him, but first he had to dump a passenger. He maneuvered himself alongside a rock large enough for her to climb on. He didn't think she'd heard Luke—human hearing not being as developed—but she had a motherly instinct that sent her looking for handholds on the rocks and a path through the bushes.

Wait for me. A thought she didn't hear, and that meant he needed to quickly follow. Scrambling through the bramble in his bulky body would make too much noise, and climbing was easier when sporting fingers, which was why he took a moment to return to his human guise. And just in time, too, if he wanted to catch Renny, who'd scurried ahead of him.

At least she wore clothes. Caleb bit back curses as the thorns and prickly branches tore fine scratches along his skin while the moss-covered rocks slathered his skin in goo. But he didn't care about the minor irritations. Razor-sharp blades could have lined his path, and he would have still forged ahead.

His recklessness gave him speed, and he passed Renny, who'd finally paused to tuck the gun in the waistband of her pants. Hard to climb one-handed.

Reaching the top first, Caleb took a second to scan the area. He found himself in a small clearing, the ground hard and knotted, the bushes having been torn out, leaving behind uneven lumps. Within the created space, the reek of the creature permeated. Given the only tunnel in the brambled mess was the one Caleb had created, Caleb really believed his crazy theory that it might have flown had more weight.

During his quick evaluation of the area, a panting Renny had arrived and placed herself at his side. She didn't spare the spot more than a cursory glance. Upon spotting the shadowy crevice at the base of the jumble of rocks in the clearing, she immediately took a step toward it

Snagging her arm, Caleb halted her and shook his head. Putting a finger to his lips, he took the lead, ensuring his body provided a shield in the off chance something came rushing from the darkness of the cave.

After a few steps into the stony crevice, the sounds of the bayou faded, and the only things he could hear were the rasp of their feet on the ground and their breathing.

Noisy, but silence at this point wouldn't completely hide them. Air was being sucked into this cave, and as the current rushed past them, it pulled their scent with it. Surprise was out of the question, but he still tried to remain as stealthy as possible.

The military had taught him well when it came to stalking, a teaching forgotten at the whimpered, "Daddy?" It took Renny grasping his arm to prevent him from bolting ahead.

Only fools rushed in.

Or crazy fucking crocodiles. Snap. His reptile wiggled around inside, but Caleb paid him no mind as he reassessed.

Think with your head, not your heart. Because his head would hopefully keep them all alive.

The tremulous query came from around the bend, a bend he could see because of a faint orange illumination. As he slid around the curve, blind to whatever hid behind it, he held himself ready, still in his human guise. This confined space wasn't made for a croc to fight.

Put him in the water and he would clamp his jaws, grab with claws, and roll with the bastard. On dry land, even worse in a tight cave, his beast would be at a disadvantage.

Good thing he had more skills than just a pair of powerful jaws for snapping. He clenched his fists, and as he fully came around the rocky bend, instinct ensured he was just in time to block the blow aimed at his face.

A fetid whiff of the creature enveloped him.

Found you.

And the monster wasn't happy about that. The impact of the punch against Caleb's forearm forced a grunt from him.

The fucker is strong.

And by strong, he meant a seven-footish, hulking green lizard man with linebacker-wide-plus-some shoulders and a vile smile distorted by the teeth-filled beak.

"Well, aren't you a cute specimen? Not," Caleb taunted as he braced against another blow then jabbed out. His shot connected... with a slab-like chin.

Ouch.

"Is your face made of bloody rock?"

The thing hissed at him and jabbed its tongue. Caleb tilted his head to the side, but didn't quite escape the wet drool.

"Gross, dude." More than disgusting, poisonous.

Caleb would have cursed his stupidity in not suspecting it except he felt himself fading fast. While shifters had a stronger-than-human ability to process drugs, it sometimes took several exposures to build an immunity.

Having never been licked by a mutant lizard before, Caleb proved quite susceptible. And he saw rainbows, but that might have been an old concussion talking as a fist took him in the jaw.

Reeling on his feet, blinking past the rainbows, Caleb sought to regain control.

Must take out this threat before passing out. Caleb swung, but his movements were sluggish. Laughable even.

A granite fist caught him again on the jaw. A jab smacked him in the stomach.

Damn his uncooperative limbs!

Within the space of a blink, Caleb found himself on his knees.

Little hands grabbed at him, and he saw the wavering shape of his son's face.

"Daddy!"

"Caleb."

Two voices yelling for him and he couldn't make his thick tongue answer. All Caleb could do was look up at the reptilian creature that had taken him down with mere spit.

The indignity of it.

The shame... His croc rolled and rolled in a deathly parody in his head.

Asshole.

Who will save our woman and son?

Who, indeed, if Caleb was taken out?

You are not alone.

He didn't have to be a hero today. The important thing was that they survived. And with that thought, he managed to focus enough to blurt out the words, "Shoot it, baby."

Chapter 18

SHOOT IT?

Big blue eyes stared at Renny. Human eyes in the face of a monster.

The gun trembled in her hand, her outstretched arms, feeling the pressure to remain steady, to keep her aim true.

Renny knew how to fire a pistol, smaller pistols than the one she held, but same concept. Aim. Shoot. But this wasn't a paper target or a pop can. *It's alive.* Could she really kill the creature in front of her? *Is it even a creature? I would swear it's a shifter of some kind.* One with too many different parts.

As if sensing her wavering resolve, the lizard beast reached out a hand, misshapen with some fingers and claws, a mash-up of human and reptile. "Nnnnno."

The word shocked her, reaffirming the belief that this was more than just a creature. Was this thing before her the result of a shift gone wrong?

To the side of the upright reptile, where Caleb lay still, his eyes shuttered, Luke crouched. A gaze filled with moisture, he said in a tremulous voice, "Mommy. I'm scared."

So was she, dammit, but could she shoot the thing with human eyes in front of her? What if this was a misunderstanding?

She tried reason first. "Listen, I don't know who you are"—or what—"but I don't want to hurt you. I just want my son back."

The thing cocked its head. It made an odd sound, a cross between a cluck and a purr.

"I can tell there's someone in there." Perhaps not a sane person, given the flat chill in the eyes. "And I'm sure you have a reason why you took Luke. Perhaps you thought you were protecting him."

"He's bad, Mommy," Luke cried out.

This outburst agitated the creature, and it whipped its head sideways to emit a baleful hiss. It also flicked its sinuous, scale-covered tail.

The tip of it swept across the floor in its agitation, knocking something loose from an alcove in the wall. A rock rolled and bounced, stopping at Renny's feet.

Except it wasn't a rock.

A perfect little skull stared up at her. A child's skull.

This isn't a human. It's a monster. Now Renny was the one with cold running through her veins as she steadied her arm. The creature read her intent and lunged as she fired—*Bang!*—and managed to miss! Unused to a gun of this caliber, Renny didn't expect the recoil that threw off her aim. It proved a costly mistake.

The lizard thing hit her and took her to the ground hard.

"Ah!" Renny managed a short scream and stared in wide-eyed horror at the reptilian face above hers, the jaws cracked open wide, the venom dripping from its fangs.

Struggling with the body pinning her did nothing. It outweighed her too much to even rock it.

"Let go of my mommy!" Luke cried.

Oh God, her little boy. Even as her hands scrambled to hold back the nightmare visage, she screamed, "Run, Luke. Run and find help!"

The strength of the creature was frightening. It barely seemed to make an effort, and yet it pushed toward her face as if she didn't hold it back at all. Fetid breath washed over her. Those big blue eyes didn't bother to hide their malevolence.

She closed her eyes tight lest she witness her own death.

Only death didn't come. Rescue did.

"Like fuck. Get your slimy green ass off my baby!" Caleb roared.

Opening her eyes, Renny was just in time to see the body of the creature get plucked and tossed.

The lizard hit the wall hard, but that didn't stop it. Hitting the ground, it sprang to its feet, its forked tongue flicking.

"Food plays? Fun." The grotesque words emerged on a sibilant hiss.

"It's a shifter," Renny breathed, unable to hide her horror.

"It's an abomination," Caleb growled, standing between Renny and the beast.

Just in time, too, as the monster dove at Caleb, and the next thing she knew, they were wrestling, the muscles in Caleb's biceps bulging as he fought to hold the fury of the creature back.

"Get out of here, baby," he grunted, his words so reminiscent of what she'd told Luke. But just like Luke had lingered, so would she. Caleb had made a vow to never let her down, to always protect her, and she loved him enough to do the same.

Since Luke had tucked himself out of sight around the corner, she didn't waste time looking for him. She hit the ground on hands and knees, the faint illumination from an electrical lantern causing more shadows than revelations. She looked for the gun she'd lost as grunts and thuds sounded, the battle between man and lizard happening in earnest.

But a man couldn't hope to hold against a monster.

"Argh."

She turned her head in time to see the injury. A swipe of a claw across Caleb's shoulder saw blood streaming, bright red against his skin, the coppery tang filling the air.

The monster gurgled in triumph, and Caleb stumbled back, head shaking as if dazed. “Don’t let is scratch you,” he warned, his words slurred. “Poison on its claws and saliva.”

Dropping to his knees, Caleb blinked as he tried to fight the effects of the drug. The creature let out a warble, took a step forward, and lifted its arm, claws extended, ready to swipe.

“Caleb!” she cried. No. This couldn’t be happening. They’d just found each other again.

I can’t lose him.

Cold metal met her fingers, and she spared a quick glance down to see Luke had found the gun and placed it in her hand. She didn’t need his solemn gaze to know what had to be done.

“Die!” Renny screamed the word as she fired the weapon, this time holding it with both hands, but even then, the recoil screwed with her, and she hit the lizard in the shoulder. Missed. Fire again. Hit. The lower belly.

Then it was on her, and it was all she could do to avoid its wide-open jaws. Luckily, it wasn’t drooling hard enough to poison her. On the contrary, it seemed to be most careful that she remained conscious for its pleasure.

“Eat you alive.” The sibilant words brought her level of terror to a whole new level.

Renny heard screaming—hers, Luke’s, hers again. And then she went silent, her cry lost at the sight of Caleb, but a Caleb like she’d never seen. Half-man, half-croc, big, muscled and oh so very pissed. Caleb loomed, and in this hybrid shape, in fury and size, he was more than a match for the monster.

With webbed fingers, tipped in claws, Caleb grabbed the thing and lifted it. Tossed it. It hit the wall and rose, just like before. However, this time, her half-shifted lover was there to greet it.

“Don’t. Hurt. My Family!” Caleb managed to spit the words out of a less-than-human mouth filled with teeth as he grappled the thing into submission.

He wrapped a thickly muscled forearm around its neck and

squeezed. Squeezed tight enough that those blue eyes widened. The mouth, lined with venomous teeth, gaped as it gasped for air.

But Caleb didn't relent. He kept applying pressure until the light in those uncanny blue eyes faded. The body went limp. He held on a while longer, but there wasn't a single twitch.

Caleb released the creature, but when Renny would have run to him, he held up a scaled hand and said, "Don't. I'm not myself. I don't want to hurt you." While more guttural than usual, she had no problem understanding his words. She just didn't agree with them.

What a load of... "Bullshit." Renny said the word and smiled at the shock in his eyes. No matter what shape he wore, she knew those eyes. Just like she knew him. "You would never hurt me. Never hurt us," she amended as Luke threw himself at Caleb.

Still in his half-shape, Caleb caught the little body and held his son gently against him.

Renny approached and placed a hand on his chest, not caring if it was covered in scales. Not caring if, right now, Caleb was caught between two worlds, man and beast. This was who he was, and he needed to know that.

"I love you, Caleb."

"Me, too!" Luke piped in. "Daddy killed the dinosaur."

Or not. Renny screamed as a hand closed around her ankle, the sharp points of the claws digging into her boots.

Bang.

"Stubborn fucker. Heal from that," Wes snapped. Turning his gaze on Caleb, Wes smirked. "Dude, put some fucking clothes on. No one needs to see your shriveled green lizard."

Caleb glared, and Renny probably didn't help the situation by bursting into giggles.

Chapter 19

THE BURNING SCOWL Caleb turned Wes's way didn't deter the other man from giving a sneered, "You're welcome. Looks like I got here just in time."

"I had things under control," Caleb managed to say through his strangely shaped jaw. Weird didn't begin to describe his partial shift, a shift he was losing his hold on as his adrenaline dissipated.

Renny stepped away, Luke cradled in her arms, a situation his son was not happy about it.

"Put me down. I'm not a baby," Luke protested.

If his jaw wasn't in the process of realigning itself, Caleb might have laughed at her indignant look.

Ignoring them all, Wes knelt by the monster's corpse. "Well, this is fucking interesting," Wes muttered as Caleb's last joint popped back into its human shape.

"What did you find?" Renny asked, crouching down to look at what held Wes's interest.

The other man held up the mottled arm of the dead creature. Even through the scaling and discoloration, Caleb noted the tattoo.

"Recognize it?" Caleb asked.

"No, but then again, I don't go around cataloguing people's tats."

"Hold on a second," Renny said with a frown. "I thought shifters couldn't do tattoos, something about your skin rejecting the ink."

"Natural-born shifters can't have them, but someone who was turned with one already..." Wes shrugged. "Possible, I guess. I don't know too many converts, though, so I couldn't say for sure."

"If this guy was intentionally changed, who did it? And what?" Even with all Caleb had seen, he'd never come across anything like it. "I've never heard or seen anything like it."

"Me either. And it doesn't smell right," Wes mumbled, reiterating the problem Caleb had since their first encounter with the thing.

"It's like a mishmash of stuff I know, with something else thrown into the mix."

Wes looked up at him. "Yup. And look at this." This time, their attention was drawn to the neck of the creature, where singed flesh formed a ring.

"What the hell would do that?"

"Makes me think of a shock collar," Renny observed.

Which only served to deepen the mystery.

What also proved complicated? Getting them all back to dry land. Lucky for them, Wes had a weatherproof bag he'd brought along on the hunt—*"A must have for all swamp predators so they don't get caught out in the open with no underwear."* He also had a phone.

It wasn't long before they were back on dry land, Bittech property to be exact, inside one of the docking bays, shifters of all castes called in for the search and eventual rescue gathered around the corpse of the lizard thing.

While everyone stared, eyes wide with confusion and shock, only a few whispers were uttered.

"Who was it?" No one seemed to recognize the body or the tattoo.

"What is it?" The hybrid mix was not something anyone ever recalled seeing or hearing about.

"Who did this?" The question that haunted them most of all.

Who would do such a thing? And why?

Bittech claimed no knowledge of the creature, and despite Wes's suspicions, Caleb had seen Andrew's face. Either the man was an excellent actor or he'd never seen the monster before. No one could fake the revulsion on his face.

Yet, the fact remained, this thing wasn't naturally born. It had been made.

A mystery that would require solving, but not tonight. Tonight, Caleb took his family home. Not the new one with its bare rooms, but his childhood home, where he knew they would all feel safe.

Constantine, who it turned out had done his fair share of searching but in another direction of the swamp, had arrived before them. He sat on the couch, freshly showered, with his dog sleeping on his lap. Or not.

Princess opened a single eye, just a slit, and the corner of her mouth lifted. Her canine version of hello or the one he suspected of meaning, "I've got my eye on you."

As Renny bathed Luke, Caleb hit the outdoor shower unit to sluice the bayou from his skin. Rinsing it, though, didn't help him from reliving the moment in the cave when he'd thought the creature would kill Renny.

This finally brought on the shakes. He dropped to his knees as the realization he could have lost Renny and Luke truly hit him.

So close, so close to losing to that monster.

He'd known he couldn't fight the beast as a man, and his croc knew that it wasn't the right weapon either, but when they decided to partner together... Together they formed an incredible duo. For the first time, they'd truly shared everything—body and mind.

And he hadn't eaten anybody. *Score!* Except now he was kind of hungry.

Feed me. Lots of fish in the bayou. Crunch. Crunch.

Sometimes I'm really tempted to see you made into a purse.

But their banter wasn't acerbic in nature. Caleb finally understood his croc's cold sense of humor, and he now knew he could trust it.

Trust himself.

To placate them both, he made himself the thickest roast beef sandwich ever using the reddest parts he could find.

Compromise, the key to living in harmony with himself.

A clean Luke was spat out from the bathroom, dressed in clean pajamas with dogs on them—sigh—and wet hair. "Watch him, would you, while I shower?"

Seemed simple enough. Caleb swung his son into his arms and carried him to his room. He tucked him in bed, worried at how quiet his boy was, but at a loss as to what to do. He pulled a book from the nightstand, something with a happy title and happy cartoon faces, but he hesitated.

He put the book aside and paced. "Your mom should be out of the shower any second now." She would know what to do. The right thing to say. *But I'm his father. I should know how to handle this.*

"Do you need anything?"

Luke gave a slow shake of his head, then his mini me peered up at him, and the surge of love for this child—*my son*—took Caleb to his knees so he could meet Luke's gaze without making him crane.

"Are you all right?" Caleb asked, knowing all too well how some events could mark a man and weaken him. Except...he'd not caved to weakness or anxiety. Not this time. As a matter of fact, Caleb realized he'd not felt that debilitating panic hardly at all in the last week. And since Renny had slept with him, he'd not needed his pills because being with her held the nightmares at bay.

She's better than any head shrink or drug.

"I was scared," his son admitted, his chin drooping. "I'm sorry."

"Don't you dare apologize," Caleb admonished. "Fear is normal. Hell, don't tell anyone"—he lowered his voice—"but I was pretty scared, too. That was one scary dude."

"He's gone though, right?" Uncertainty wavered in his son's eyes.

Yes, but the mystery remained of where it had come from.

However, he wasn't about to worry his son further. Caleb gave him the reassurance he needed. "That monster isn't coming back."

"Even if it did," Renny said, stepping into the bedroom, "Daddy would take care of it."

At her certainty, his chest swelled. "Always," he promised. "I will always be there for you." He whispered those words to Luke as he kissed him on the forehead, tucking him in for the night. Nothing could ever tear him from those who needed him. Who loved him.

As Caleb rose and readied to leave, Renny hesitated. "Maybe I should stay with him."

And maybe Caleb needed to put a bell on a certain mutt because Princess suddenly scooted through his legs, startling the fuck out of him before she hopped onto the bed, did a circle, and lay down, tucked against Luke. His son reached out a hand to stroke the dog.

"Go, Mommy. I'm not a baby. 'Sides, Princess is here, and she's a good guard dog."

Freaky dog more like it, given he could have sworn Princess winked.

Shutting the door, he and Renny made their way to the living room, only to notice Constantine still hogged the couch.

"I can't wait to move into the new place," Caleb said with a sigh.

His brother snorted. "That makes two of us then. But until that happens, which is tomorrow, by the way, because I've taken the day off to move your shit, you guys can borrow my room. You know, so you can have some privacy."

"Really?" Caleb couldn't help his surprised query.

"Yeah, really. You might still be an asshole, but you're my brother, and you've had a rough night. You both have, so take my room for the night, but you'd better strip those sheets in the morning," Constantine muttered as Caleb, not wasting any time, grabbed Renny around the waist and carted her back down the hall.

She giggled as he closed the door and leaned on it. "That was kind of rude."

"No, rude would have been kicking him off the couch to make out with you."

"And is that what we're going to do? Make out?"

"For starters," he said with a grin.

Her teasing lilt faded as she asked, "Do you think it's over?"

He hoped so. "Unless there's another one of those mutants running about, then yeah."

"Who would create such a thing, and why?"

He shrugged. "I don't know. Maybe we're wrong. We can't know for sure anyone made it." Something he didn't entirely believe, but he sensed she needed reassurance. Hell, so did he. "The world is a big fucking place with lots of secrets."

"Except between us." She caught his gaze. "I saw you tonight, Caleb. Saw you. Saw your croc. Saw what you could do."

As she spoke, his body tensed, fear coiling in him. Was this where she finally realized she couldn't handle him?

"You took care of me, and our son. I know you were scared of letting the beast out, but..." She took a step toward him and cupped his face. "Even when you change, you're still you. Still my Caleb."

"A man capable of killing."

"A man who will protect us with everything he's got." She leaned close and kissed him. "A man I love." In a flash, he bound her so tightly she laughed even as she gasped. "Caleb!"

He loosened his grip, just a little, and buried his face in her hair. "I love you, too, baby. So fucking much it scares me. I lost you once to the croc inside me—"

She shook her head. "No, you lost me once because people wanted to use the beast inside you. But we're smarter now. We won't ever let that happen again."

"Never." A promise he sealed with a kiss, a kiss that started out soft and sweet.

However, Renny didn't want gentle, or so he surmised as her teeth nipped at his lower lip. Her mouth left his mouth to travel the length of his stubbled jaw, moving down the column of his throat and pausing over his pulse. She sucked at it, a seemingly innocent gesture that meant a lot to his kind. Letting someone close to a jugular was the ultimate trust.

She kept sucking as her hands tugged at his shirt. He helped her to strip it from his body. He couldn't help but lean against the wall as her lips continued their exploration, burning-hot touches across his upper body. A bite of his nipples. A raking of her nails down his chest to the waistband of his athletic pants.

As she knelt, she yanked at them, baring his erect shaft and pulling a, "What are you doing?" question from him.

The smile that curved her lips went well with the teasing glint in her eye. "Take a guess."

Why guess when she showed him?

"Baby..." He whispered the word as she drew him into her mouth and proceeded to blow him. Literally.

Chapter 20

FUNNY HOW SURVIVING what seemed like certain death left a woman feeling more alive than ever. Or was it the man standing before her that had brought her back to life?

They'd both gone through so much. Pain, betrayal, heartache. But now that the secrets were exposed, apologies made, and love rekindled, there was nothing keeping them apart.

Nothing to stop her from showing Caleb her love—and affection.

There was also nothing stopping her from showing him how much she appreciated him, loved him.

She took him into her mouth, the velvety skin of his shaft a sensory delight to explore. While thick, she could accommodate him by stretching her mouth wide. Even then, her teeth grazed him, a sensation he enjoyed if his shivers were anything to judge by.

She dug her fingers into his hips, giving herself leverage to bob her head back and forth along the length of him, savoring every hard inch. Loving how he pulsed and even twitched in her mouth.

The soft moans let her know he was lost in the moment, but she wanted more than that. She wanted him to lose control. To lose himself in her.

She worked him with her mouth, her tongue dancing patterns on his skin, her lips suctioning his plump head. She suctioned hard, willing him to come, but Caleb had other ideas.

"You're driving me wild," he growled as he pulled her to her feet. But she didn't remain on her feet long. In a whirl of bodies, he had her pinned against the wall, suspended by the sheer strength in his hands.

"I love you," she murmured. Loved his strength, all of him.

"And I," he whispered back as the tip of him entered her, "have always." Thrust. "Loved." Deep grind. "You." With that last word, he claimed her mouth, even as his cock claimed her pussy.

He pounded into her, stretching her with his size, reaching deep within and touching more than her G-spot. He touched her soul.

Together, they panted and thrust in and against each other, together racing for the pinnacle of bliss.

When she would have cried out, he caught her lips, not only swallowing her expression of pleasure, but she reveled in every single quiver of his body, and then his own unrestrained cry as he orgasmed and brought her with him.

Together, they rode the wild storm of their love and emerged from it breathless, dewy, and smiling.

But she did have to wonder, "Why are you laughing?"

"Because for the first time since I got back, we had access to a perfectly fine bed, and yet we didn't even come close to using it."

She smiled. "Seems a shame to waste it, unless you're too tired."

Her teasing dare bore fruit. And later on, nestled in his arms, she couldn't help but murmur, "I'm glad you returned."

"So am I. And I'm never leaving again."

But they would be investing in a lock, given Luke's exclamation the following morning of, "Mommy, you forgot to put on pajamas!"

Epilogue

THE DINOSAUR SIGHTINGS stopped the night they killed the monster, as did the disappearances, but the bodies of those missing were never found. Five in all and none of them the remains left behind in the cave.

Actually, the Bittech lab tests showed the skeletons found, eight that they could be sure of, were all several years old. It closed a few cold cases and made many wonder just how long the dino creature had lived there undetected.

As no one could come up with answers, the curious went back to their lives, even Wes, because no matter how much he and Caleb, along with the others, searched, they could find no wrongdoing by Bittech or any of its employees. Their paranoia proved groundless, but Wes refused to give up.

"I'm telling you there's something fishy going on."

Caleb didn't disagree, but without a trail, or any clues, there wasn't much he could do other than promise his aid should Wes discover something. In the meantime, while they waited to see if life would stay normal, he had a family that needed him.

Although it had been only a few weeks since Caleb's return, life had changed drastically. All for the better.

With the house Caleb had scored meeting approval from Renny and Luke, she'd given her notice to the guy she rented her apartment from, and they were already moved in. Even better, with Caleb's mom quitting her job to become a full-time grandmother and babysitter for her grandson, it meant Renny could stick to one job, part-time. He wasn't crazy about her choice of remaining as a waitress for the Itty Bitty Club, but she was working the day shift now and home before dark. While he might not like her job, his best friend Daryl loved it because Renny made sure he got the employee discount on drinks, which meant more tips for everyone since Daryl spent most of his lunches there.

Goddamned perv. But Caleb loved the guy, so he tolerated it.

Life was fucking sweet. He was in love. Had a son. A job.

As for his croc, since their recent understanding, Caleb found he didn't resent it, but then again, he also made sure to let it out as often as he could. In return, his reptile slumbered more peacefully in his mind, and while it didn't give up hunting entirely, at least Caleb could content himself that the prey they hunted wasn't human.

And he felt more human than he had in years.

Except when the football hit him in the head, and Daryl laughed. Then he chased the damned cat, who was nimble no matter his form, up a tree while his son cheered him on and Renny clapped.

Life was fucking grand—*and we'll eat anyone who tries to mess it up.*

Snap.

WELL, this didn't bode well. Finding oneself tied to a chair, fully clothed and alone, was never a good sign. Naked and with a lady friend? Totally another thing.

But nope, no hottie in a latex suit. No feathers for tickling. Yet Daryl was definitely bound and a prisoner.

There was a light somewhere behind him, probably a lamp, given it didn't come from overhead. It provided enough illumination to see his odd situation. Seated in a straight-back, metal-framed chair with a plastic bucket to cradle his large frame. The kind of chair you saw in cafeterias and, judging by the wobble when he swished his hips, not too solid.

That's method number one to escape.

Two was snapping the tape that bound him to the chair. A simple twist of his large upper body should do it.

Onto the third item, what of his hands? Those were, surprisingly enough, taped in front of him.

By whom, fucking amateurs? Don't they know how dangerous I am?

Who the hell secured a dangerous predator with their hands in front of them? Because, seriously, if there was anyone dangerous, it was Daryl.

Not conceit, simple fact.

Daryl tested the tape binding his wrists together. He didn't break it right away. Never act too hasty, not if one wanted the element of surprise. But he almost forgot his own rule when he noted the duct tape was patterned with ducks.

What the hell?

He peered down, and sure enough, more of the happy yellow rubber duckies swam across his chest across the tape layered there.

Mmm...duck. His feline did so enjoy a well-roasted one.

Apart from feeling a little peckish, Daryl was wondering if this was a joke. After all, this was the least intimidating abduction he'd ever heard of. When he recounted this story to his buds, he'd have to make sure he changed the ducks to sharks. Because at least they had big teeth. Or maybe he'd tell them he'd broken out of chains.

Yeah, big silver chains. That would impress them.

The dim light barely illuminated the place. Probably a good

thing, given he was pretty sure the pink carpet, worn smooth in spots, was a relic from the nineties while the television, in its big hulking case, should have collapsed the dresser.

A classy motel, probably on the side of the highway somewhere, used as a quick pit stop by truckers and those looking for a place to wash and rest on a journey to somewhere.

But how did I get here?

That was the question because last he recalled, he was chatting with that lovely cocoa-skinned woman—and he meant *woman,* with curves that would spill over his palms, luscious lips that would look perfect about waist-height, and dark curly hair that spilled over her shoulders.

Hair that I wanted to pull, which was why I asked her if she wanted to go somewhere quieter.

To his surprise, she'd readily agreed, and they went outside. Whereupon she fucking stabbed him with a needle!

So was it any wonder when she walked in, not even two seconds after his recollection, that he blurted out, "You're the bitch who drugged me." And despite what she'd done, he still found her freaking hot, even if she did have a gun pointed at his face.

"Keep talking, darlin'. You're making my finger awfully twitchy." She canted her head to the side and smiled.

"I've got something that will fix that." And, yes, he made sure she got what he meant with a wink.

What he didn't expect was that she would laugh and say, "Oh, darlin', you wish you were man enough to handle me."

A dare? How he loved a challenge. His inner kitty twitched its tail in excitement. "You probably shouldn't have said that." He held her gaze and smiled as he snapped the tape holding his hands. His lips quirked as he stood with the chair and flexed, freeing himself and sending it crashing to the floor.

His sexy kidnapper slowly backed away, the gun never wavering, a touch of fear finally sparking in her eyes. But not enough to worry him, not when he could sense her skin heating as well.

"I'll give you a five-second head start," he offered.

Because his cat did so love a chase.

Growrrr.

Instead of bolting, though, she pulled the trigger at almost point-blank range.

Up next: Panther's Claim

Panther's Claim

Hitting on the wrong woman finds Daryl regaining consciousness in a motel taped to a chair. Things were looking up—and not just below the belt.

A sexy, cocoa-complexioned veterinarian—with killer curves—wants answers, and he's only too happy to give them to her, for a price—say a kiss, or something more, from those luscious lips.

The problem is Cynthia isn't the type to fall for flirty words and panty-dropping smiles. She tempts Daryl into helping her. Teases him into acting. Claims his heart without even trying.

But that was okay because...*She's mine*...and someone was trying to hurt her.

Hell no.

This kitty isn't afraid to unleash his claws and rescue the woman he wants.

An intriguing, hot woman, a mystery, and danger? Sounds like fun, and Daryl is ready to play. He'll do *anything* to claim Cynthia as his mate.

Chapter 1

Mom: *Hey, baby girl, what did you do today?*
Cynthia: *Oh, I just shot a guy full of tranquilizers, kidnapped him, and brought him to my motel room. He's currently duct taped to a chair, completely at my mercy.*
Mom: *So can we expect you to bring your new beau to dinner next Sunday?*

AND, no, Cynthia wasn't exaggerating. Now that she had reached the ripe old age of twenty-six, apparently her eggs were in dire need of fertilization.

"You're not getting any younger," said her mother.

"Time you popped some cubs and settled down with a nice boy. Have you met Henrietta's nephew?" That from her Aunt Sonya.

"I'll kill any man who dares think he's good enough for my baby girl." Growled by her father.

God but she loved that man. Bragging about her pops was something Cynthia had no problem with. A big man, a grizzly bear married to a she-wolf, he always did spoil her, driving her mother absolutely wild.

"She's got you wrapped around her little finger," her mother railed when he fed her ice cream just before dinner.

"Yup."

Unabashed at getting caught, which always made her mother smile. Mom might grumble, but she loved their close bond.

Mom would smile a heck of a lot more if I settled down.

Ever since Cynthia had turned twenty-five, one would think she'd crossed some kind of line that counted down the fact that she was wasting her most fertile years. Totally incorrect. Being a veterinarian and medically inclined meant Cynthia knew she had at least another ten-fifteen good years to squeeze out a kid or two, if she wanted.

If.

Right now, she just wanted to find out what the guy taped to the chair knew.

The guy she'd kidnapped.

Oh my God, I'm a felon now.

It proved more frightening and thrilling than expected.

Daryl—a name her victim provided after buying her a very blue cocktail—had proven a little more difficult to maneuver than expected. Huffing and puffing truly wasn't attractive—"Ladies don't sweat!" she could just hear her mother lamenting—but a little exertion and perspiration were unavoidable as she heaved his limp, and heavy, body from the car. Okay, less heaved than allowed gravity to help. Once she unbelted him from the passenger seat, where he snored after she'd drugged him hard, he'd more or less tumbled out of the car to the ground.

Thunk.

Oops. That might leave a mark.

A less-prepared woman would have had to drag his sweet ass—and, yes, her super villainous self noted his fine glutes—to the door.

But Cynthia remembered something her dad taught her. *Work smart, not hard.* Smart was grabbing the foldable dolly and some bungee cords from her trunk. And, no, it wasn't strange she traveled with those.

As part of her job as a vet, she carried a whole bunch of things to make her life easier. She dealt with animals on a daily basis—the furry household, not the six-foot-something male kind. Given limp bodies were a pain to move—*mental note to self: next time I kidnap a guy, choose a lighter one*—a folding dolly with stretchy cords was a smart business expense. And what did you know? It wasn't just perfect for securing and carting around animals patients. It worked well with unconscious men, too.

I still can't believe I drugged him.

Then again, the plan was hastily hatched during the drive to Bitten Point. A good thing she had nefariously plotted given the second drink she shared with her target made it harder to remember why she should watch herself around the hunk. His voice charmed from his first uttered, "Hi, my name is Daryl." Given his practically irresistible charm, she was very glad she'd come prepared with needles strapped to the inside of each arm and hidden by her long sleeves. Still, she wondered if she would have the nerve to stick him with a needle and drug him.

And just how did a nice girl get the kind of drugs needed to take down a fairly large man?

Cynthia couldn't speak for all vets, but she carried around readied needles at all times.

Never know when I might need to tranq a rabid coon, or a seductive hunk.

She really needed to stop thinking of him that way. Attractive on the outside didn't mean he was hot on the inside.

But he sure seemed nice when we were chatting...and even nicer when we were dancing. His hips rubbing against her, his hands around her waist, his essence swirling around her in a heady mix.

Stop thinking that way. Daryl wasn't a nice man.

As she taped his hands, she hesitated to put a strip over his lips. She had no desire to silence him. Not with tape at any rate.

Kissing is much more effective.

And dangerous. So dangerous because with one kiss from those lips, she'd almost forgotten why she'd lured him out to her car.

Quick, don't think about what happened next.

Stick to the plan, she reminded herself as she wound the sticky stuff around his hands. To those who wondered at the duct tape, it should be noted she never left home without it. Duct tape would one day save the world. It certainly had saved her cheeks as a child when she used it to secure a quickly scribbled drawing to her wall, over another drawing *on* the wall.

A woman who believed in being prepared, Cynthia possessed a perfect storm of items in her trunk, items that begged her to go through with her plot to abduct.

Yanking on the handle of the dolly, she wheeled Daryl to the motel room door. Last one on the block, and since she could park out front, it gave her a decent chance of not being seen. Not something she'd actually planned, but a coincidence that now came in handy.

Fumbling her key before sliding it in and unlocking her door, she didn't waste time wheeling Daryl into the room quickly and then shutting the door.

She darted to the wide window gaping onto the parking lot and yanked the dusty curtains shut. Pitch black descended except for the red numbers on a clock.

Dammit.

I suck at this whole subterfuge thing. Parting the curtains for some of the outside ambient light, she located a lamp and clicked the switch. A feeble light illuminated the tawdry room. She darted back to the window and slammed the curtains shut again.

"Gunh."

At the sound, Cynthia's gaze darted over to Daryl. She'd strapped him upright to the dolly, and while his head lolled forward, she noticed the finger on his hand twitching.

He's waking again?

She couldn't help but curse. *Stupid, giant-bodied, very healthy, super healing, well-endowed... Oh, don't think about his endowment.* Hard to forget since she'd felt it press against her when they slow danced.

I can't believe he's waking up already. She fumbled in her purse for yet another needle of the tranquilizer. She was starting to run low.

How many is he going to take?

She'd already given him way more than she would have expected. *Good thing I had more than a few.*

The miscalculation wasn't entirely her fault. Shifters metabolized drugs so much faster than normal animals. "You're a strong kitty," she muttered, her lips clamped around the plastic lid for the needle. With a yank of her head, she uncapped it, jabbed at his shoulder, and pushed the plunger.

His body gave a twitch then relaxed again, but for how long?

Get him into position before he wakes up.

Heaving his dead weight into a chair proved interesting. It took more grunting and cursing and sweat than she liked. She might have wolf blood in her veins, but that didn't make her as strong as say a bear, and Daryl was one big pussycat. She just wasn't sure what kind. Growing up, she didn't meet many shifters, she and her parents kind of being outcasts and all—darn those closed-minded clans and packs. But not having a developed catalogue of shifter scents didn't mean she could mistake the distinct feline scent.

How he smells doesn't matter. It's his weight that I should worry about.

His heavy body couldn't curb her determination. She managed to get him on the damned chair—*Victory!*—and bungeed him around the waist before placing another around his ankles. But what of his hands, and the rest of him?

No way would those stretchy cords hold him.

The duct tape came to the rescue. What she didn't count on was using almost the entire roll.

Damn but he's big. His chest wide, his arms thick, his...

Focus. She made sure he was properly secured, ready for interrogation when he woke up, which would happen in the next ten to fifteen minutes given how quickly his body metabolized the drugs.

Shifters had a much more developed system for processing foreign agents, such as drugs or diseases, that entered their bloodstream. Their power for recuperation was remarkable. The way they could heal without a scar from all but the most grievous wounds was astonishing. Silver and fire were the only sure ways of truly hurting them. But only humans or the most depraved of shifters usually resorted to those kinds of torturous methods.

Speaking of torture...he was definitely at her mercy.

I could do anything I liked. Her body would have liked to rub a bit more against him, and her lips yearned for another taste.

The situation might not be the norm for Cynthia, but that didn't mean her lustier side didn't take note of the handsome fellow, and there was a lot to note.

She'd already dealt with his great size. She also knew that his bulk was muscle, not fat. Lean, nicely toned muscle that she couldn't help but feel as she lugged his unconscious butt around—*and when we danced. Remember how nice it felt to be snuggled in his arms?*

Yeah, she did, but she also remembered who he was. A possibly very bad kitty. A bad kitty who needed to give her some answers.

And this was the only way you could think of getting them?

Most people would have just asked. Cynthia had certainly meant to, but when she saw him sitting at the bar, her heart had skipped a beat. When he smiled at her, damned if her panties didn't get wet.

She couldn't say no to the drink. She answered all his flirty questions. Asked him flirty ones back. Yet Cynthia couldn't force the words out that she really needed an answer to. Couldn't bring herself to make that accusation.

Chance after chance arose to grill him—during their drink then that intimate dance, a slow grind that heightened all her senses. Every inch of her had tingled.

Under his erotic spell, she fell without a fight. The next thing she knew, they were in her car, making out. He kissed her, kissed her with a hungry passion she matched.

"Why don't we go somewhere?" he whispered in her ear as he nibbled the lobe.

And it was those words, those innocuous—or not—words that brought her back to reality.

Did he say those same words to Aria?

Cynthia palmed a syringe in each hand and timed it perfectly. In a double swoop, she stabbed him with the needles and released the tranquilizer. He recoiled, eyes wide with disbelief. Then anger. "Why you..."

The chemical cocktail she used was good. He never finished his sentence, and she implemented her quickly concocted plan.

Now, here they were. A first time kidnapper and her victim.

When he wakes up, he's not going to be happy. Nope, which was why she needed the gun.

Darn it, the gun. She'd left it out in the car.

Best she grab it. She might need its daunting presence to make the man talk.

Look at me, acting all gangster. Her mother would have a fit.

Chapter 2

Daryl's T-shirt of the day: *"When I'm good, I'm really good. When I'm bad, I'm better."*

AS OMENS WENT, finding himself bound to a chair, fully clothed, didn't bode well. Not that Daryl had anything against bondage. It should be noted that were he naked and with a lady friend, he would totally be *up* for it.

Alas, he wasn't being prepped for an erotic experience by a hottie in a latex suit. *So if I'm not tied up for sex, then why am I a prisoner?*

There was a light somewhere behind him, probably a lamp given it didn't come from overhead. It provided enough illumination to see his odd situation. He was seated in a straight-back, metal-framed chair with a plastic bucket to cradle his large frame. The kind of chair most often seen in cafeterias and, judging by the wobble when he swished his hips, not too solid.

That's method number one to escape.

Two was snapping the tape that bound him to the chair. A simple twist of his large upper body should do it.

Onto the third item, what of his hands? Those were, surprisingly enough, taped in front of him.

By who, fucking amateurs? Don't they know how dangerous I am?

Who the hell secured a deadly predator with their hands in their lap? It wasn't conceit to think of himself as perilous, just fact.

Daryl tested the tape binding his wrists together, only a few strips thick. Too easy, yet, he didn't break it right away. Never act too hasty, not if he wanted the element of surprise and more information. But he almost forgot his own rule when he noted the duct tape was patterned with...ducks?

What the heck?

He peered down and, sure enough, more of the happy yellow rubber duckies swam across his chest on the tape layered there.

Mmm... Duck. His feline did so enjoy a well-roasted one.

Apart from feeling a little peckish, Daryl was wondering if this was a joke. After all, this was the least intimidating abduction he'd ever heard of. When he recounted this story to his buds, he'd have to make sure he changed the ducks to sharks because at least they had big teeth. Or maybe he'd tell them he broke out of chains.

Yeah, big silver chains. That would impress his friends.

The dim light barely illuminated the place. Probably a good thing given he was pretty sure the pink carpet, worn smooth in spots, was a relic from the nineties while the television, in its hulking, plastic case should have collapsed the dresser.

A classy motel, probably on the side of the highway somewhere, used as a quick pit stop by truckers and those looking for a place to wash and rest on a journey to somewhere.

But how did I get here?

That was the question because last he recalled, he was chatting with that lovely cocoa-skinned woman—and he meant *woman,* with curves that fill his palms, luscious lips that would look perfect about waist height, and dark, curly hair that spilled over her shoulders.

Hair that I wanted to pull, which was why I asked her if she wanted to go somewhere quieter.

To his surprise, she'd readily agreed, and they'd gone outside. Whereupon she fucking stabbed him with a needle!

So wasn't it any wonder when she walked in, not even two seconds after his recollection, he blurted out, "You're the bitch that drugged me." And despite what she'd done, he still found her freaking hot, even if she did have a gun pointed at his face.

"There's no need for nasty names."

"Says the woman who drugged and kidnapped me."

"This is your fault. You left me no choice."

"No choice but to accost me?" How dare she attack him with her lips and sensual nature!

"What else could I do? You shouldn't have tried to get me drunk and force me to make out with you."

Forced? The pliant lips beneath his and the hot pants were anything but. "You could have said no."

"That's the problem. I couldn't, which is totally your fault and why I had to abduct you."

The logic went right over his head. He blinked. It still made no sense, especially the fact that she appeared irritated with him for being...too attractive? "I think this is the first time in my life I've been tempted to throttle a woman." And then kiss her.

The gun waved in the air. "You go ahead and try it, darlin'. But I warn you. I can feel my finger getting twitchy." She canted her head to the side and smiled as she threatened. Spoken with confidence, yet he caught how she licked her lower lip, and her breathing was a little fast.

"I have something to cure that twitch and a whole lot of other things." And, yes, he made sure she got what he meant with a wink.

What he didn't expect was that she would laugh and say, "You wish you were man enough to handle me."

A dare? How he loved a challenge, just like he enjoyed this repartee. If he'd found her appealing in the bar when they flirted, now she was downright scrumptious. "You probably shouldn't have said that."

Time to up the stakes and show her who truly was in control. He smiled as he snapped the tape holding his hands. Let his lips quirk as he stood, with the chair stuck to him, and flexed, sending it crashing to the floor.

She slowly backed away, the gun never wavering, a touch of fear finally sparking in her eyes, but not enough to worry him, not when he could sense her skin heating as well.

What game did she play? Was this a prank? Something concocted by his buddies? Did they wait nearby, ready to mock him for having been taken down by a woman?

He didn't really care.

Wanna play. And it wasn't just his inner kitty that thought it.

"I'll give you a five-second head start," he offered.

Because this cat did so love a chase.

Growrrr.

Instead of bolting, though, she pulled the trigger at almost point-blank range.

Chapter 3

Cynthia: *So I shot a guy in the face.*
Mom: *Will he recover in time for Sunday night dinner?*

PROBABLY. She might not, on the other hand.

The look on Daryl's face when the paintball hit him in the forehead and then spattered? Incredulous, and funny, which was why she laughed.

As for his not-so-human roar? Yeah, that got him shot a second time, in the gut.

"Would you stop doing that?" he snapped.

The yellow paint running down his cheeks made his irritated expression more clownish than scary.

Since she'd apparently miscalculated—something that didn't happen often, given she was good with numbers—she thought, *what the hell*. She shot him again.

An expression of disgust crossed his face. "Oh, now you're gonna get it."

Click. Click. The stupid thing jammed, and she was out of ideas.

Tossing the gun at him, Cynthia squeaked as she dove to the side. She wasn't quite sure where she thought she was going, but Daryl caught her easily enough and bound her tightly in his arms. They proved a lot more effective than her tape.

This situation probably wasn't good, so could her body stop tingling in excitement because he held her clamped to his chest?

But we like this chest. Her inner wolf liked it so much it thought she should lick Daryl and mark him as off-limits.

Um no. More because she did kind of worry that licking might lead to other things, fun things they'd probably both enjoy, if he didn't kill her first.

"Who are you, and what are you doing?" He gave her a slight shake.

Was he seriously trying to steal the whole give-me-answers scenario from her? "Oh, heck no, darlin'. This is my kidnapping, which means I'm in charge and I ask the questions."

Twisting her in his arms, he perused her.

She stared right back.

He fluttered sinfully long, dark lashes at her, which only served to give the paint clumping his lashes a chance to cling together. He squinted at her, and she bit her lip as she tried to hide her mirth and failed. She burst out laughing.

"This is not funny." Spat out through gritted teeth.

"Yeah it is. I mean, you should see yourself."

He scowled. "You did this to me, and I still don't know why. Why waste time with this pathetic excuse for a kidnapping? Is this some practical joke?"

"No joke." Not even close. "I told you. I need answers from you."

"So instead of asking me"—he waved a hand around the room—"you came up with this brilliant plan." He didn't bother to hide his mocking.

"I had to improvise." Had to because she'd not expected the level of attraction and confusion she'd encountered when she met him. Not expected the certainty that came from her gut, a gut that she trusted, claiming he was innocent. Yet, how could she believe he was not to blame when she'd not asked him a single thing?

And did I neglect to ask because I didn't want the answer?

Or didn't ask because she knew he wasn't the nefarious person she'd feared? And, no, she didn't fear. Hence why she'd gone through with her crazy plan, a plan doomed to failure because Daryl was right. She sucked at the whole kidnapping and intimidation shtick. *How did I ever think this would work?*

The problem of living mostly among humans and not shifters? Underestimating what they could do.

"Honey, you really screwed up."

She had. Still caught in his grip, she tensed. *Did I misread him? Is this where he turns into a raving lunatic and kills me?* She wouldn't die without a fight. Now, if only she knew how to protect herself. Her mother said ladies fought their battles with words, and when that didn't work, Daddy stepped in.

Unfortunately, words seemed to be getting her in more trouble and Daddy wasn't here to save her. *Uh-oh.* Her breathing shortened as the extent of her error was made clear.

A frown creased his brow. "Are you seriously scared of me?" He set her away from him and crossed his arms. It did nothing to lessen his intimidation factor.

But Daddy did it better, and her mom had taught her that it wasn't size or strength that counted, but attitude. While Cynthia found herself still a touch scared, his attitude did somewhat reassure, and some of her confidence was restored.

She snorted "Scared, of you? Ha. You wish. More like cautious. Never know what you crazy feline types might do."

"Do?" Daryl arched a brow with clear incredulity. "Isn't that the whole pot calling a kettle something? I mean, let's take stock here. You committed at least three major crimes, maybe more, to talk to me, so I have to wonder, what exactly is it you're accusing me of being capable of?"

"You know."

"No, I don't, so you'd better tell me."

"Or you'll what?" she challenged, which probably wasn't the brightest thing she could have done, but her inner wolf still insisted they had nothing to fear.

Good kitty.

Which totally went against what she thought. *He's a bad kitty. Sexy kitty.* Trying-to-suck-her-under-his-spell-again kitty.

A sensual smile tugged his lips. "If you don't start telling me what this is about, I am going to put you over my knee and warm that sweet ass of yours with the palm of my hand. Naked."

She sucked in a breath. "You wouldn't."

"Try me." And then, as if to addle her further, he stripped off his shirt, revealing a torso thick with muscle, but also showing a few scars. Round ones.

Had someone shot him?

It should have made him seem scary—her mother warned her away from bad boys who ran with people who owned guns—but as he mopped his face with his shirt, wiping the paint clear, she couldn't help but stare at him, riveted.

The man proved more of a temptation than expensive Godiva chocolate. It made a girl want to clamp her lips tight and not give him what he wanted, so she could get what her body craved. Him touching her.

Sweet heaven. How good would that feel? But this so wasn't the right time and place. She just wished she didn't have to keep reminding herself.

Think of Aria. Aria was the reason Cynthia was doing this. Thoughts of Aria centered her.

"I'm looking for my friend."

He arched a brow. "And? That's not telling me much. What friend? Why? What makes you think I know them?"

"You know her."

"If you're that certain, then why not just ask me? Why go through with this?" He swept a hand at the chair and its flopping strands of tape. "Come on, honey. You're gonna have to give me more than that."

Why did those words sound so dirty when he said them?

"I'm looking for Aria."

Blank look.

"You know her. Petite"—Cynthia held up a hand to about her chin—"skinny girl. Short brown hair. Nice smile."

The more she spoke, the harder Daryl shook his head until he interrupted her with, "Honey, you're going to have to do better than that. I don't know any Aria. And you've described any number of girls I know. Why are you looking for her anyhow? Why can't you just call her? You're not planning to kidnap her, too, are you? Am I your practice run?"

The questions he tossed her way in rapid succession almost crossed her eyes. This wasn't going how it was supposed to.

Oops, I think I said that out loud.

"And how did you expect this to go?" Daryl flopped onto her bed and tucked his hands behind his head. She stared at him.

The devil smiled.

She wished she had her gun so she could shoot him in the crotch.

"I expected you to wake up properly frightened. Because you were my prisoner and I had a gun," she stated, still miffed he'd not taken her kidnapping and intimidation seriously.

"You had a gun with a red tip."

"And? What's the matter with that? It makes it easier for you to see that the barrel is pointed at you. You should have been scared."

He snickered. "I guess no one ever told you that a red tip means it's not a real gun."

Way to suck all the wind out of her sails. Her jaw snapped as she clamped her lips. No, she'd not known about the red-tip thing.

Cynthia knew very little about guns in general, other than pulling the trigger seemed to work.

Which begged the question, how did she procure the gun in her trunk? Simple, she'd confiscated the toy from some boys who thought it was funny to shoot the squirrels in the park. She taught them otherwise with a harangue that would have reduced her mother to proud tears. "So you knew all along you weren't in danger?"

"Anyone using rubber duckie duct tape isn't someone to fear."

She couldn't help an annoyed mutter. "I knew I should have used the skull head one." But she was saving that particular roll for Halloween.

"I still don't get all the drama. Wouldn't it have been easier to ask me at the bar if I'd seen your friend?"

She squirmed. "Probably. But I kind of suffer from a syndrome. I get it from my mother."

"And what syndrome is that?"

"Acting without thinking. Usually on account I'm panicking."

"Do you always kidnap people and threaten them with death by rainbow paint when stressed?"

"You're my first."

"And last."

Was it her, or did those words emerge a little growly? "So did you see her?"

"I can't answer that if I don't know who this Aria girl is. Don't you have a picture? Something?"

As a matter of fact, she did. The last image Aria synced from her phone to her social media profile. Cynthia located it in the gallery on her phone and loaded it.

As she showed Daryl, she saw his expression turn from curiosity to surprise. "That's your friend?"

"Yes, that's Aria. She's missing, and according to this picture, you were the last person to see her alive."

Chapter 4

Daryl's permanent marker tattoo on his arm in the tenth grade: *Mom inscribed in a heart.*

AS DARYL STUDIED THE IMAGE, he couldn't deny that was him in the pic, smiling brightly beside a cute girl he vaguely recalled. When had he seen her—two nights, maybe three, ago? She'd been a little tipsy at the bar, but he couldn't resist her request to, "Take a pic so I can totally make my friend jealous because you are so her type."

Was this mocha honey the friend? And if so, was he her type?

Why not ask? "I don't suppose you molested me while I was all tied up?"

That out-of-the-blue query had her mouth hanging open, and she blinked. "Are you for real?"

"Totally. Want to touch me again and see?"

"No." Lie. He heard her suck in a breath before answering. "I'm beginning to wish I'd kept you asleep for longer."

"So you could touch me." He winked, wondering if it would drive her nuts.

It did.

"No," she snapped. "There will be no touching."

"But there already was. And kissing."

"Which won't be happening again," she said with her chin tilted stubbornly. Was it wrong that, amidst all this weird drama, he still wanted to taste those lips?

Where was the anger that she'd drugged and kidnapped him? Where was the indignation that she thought he'd done something to her friend?

Fuck it. She's cute. "Anyone ever tell you that you're hot when you're angry?"

Even hotter when she combined livid with aroused. "I really should have left you in the parking lot instead of lugging your fat butt inside."

Daryl frowned. "My ass is not fat."

"If you say so."

"I know so. And just so you know, even if you'd ditched me on the side of the road, I would have still come and found you."

"You wouldn't have found me."

"It wouldn't have mattered where you went. I still would have tracked you down." Funny how seriously he said that.

"Why?"

Because she's mine.

He ignored the determined thought. "Do you really have to ask why? To finish what we started, of course." Because he still hadn't forgotten the sweet taste of her lips.

He took a step forward, and she took one back, then another, until she had placed the bed between them.

She shook a finger at him, a finger he wanted to pounce and nibble. "There you go distracting me again, and you wonder why I drugged you. I'm beginning to think you don't want to answer about Aria. This picture says you know her, and I demand to know where she is now." The wagging finger stabbed the screen of her phone.

"Demand all you want. I didn't really know the girl. Like I said, she wanted her pic taken with me, but that was it. As soon as she had it, she was back partying with a group of people."

"Her last tweet said she was off to bed."

"And you thought she meant to bed with me?"

"Well, you were the last image she uploaded."

"I slept alone that night."

"Says you," she said, trying to cling to her suspicion.

He laughed. "Says my buddy who left with me."

"So you don't know where she is?" Her shoulders slumped, and he wanted to spring from the bed, gather her in his arms, and tell her not to worry.

Wait a second. What the hell just happened?

He didn't just think about promising aid; he did it. In a blink of an eye, he found himself hugging the crazy she-wolf and murmuring, "Don't you worry, honey. I'll help you."

"My name is Cynthia. But my friends call me Thea."

"Thea is a name for a good girl, not a seductive kidnapper," Daryl said, leaning back far enough that he could wipe the tears streaking her cheeks. "I think Cyn suits you better." Because he'd wager she was sinfully delicious. "And I want you to stop worrying, right now. We'll find your friend. I promise." He'd find this Aria chick and bring a smile to Cyn's lips and earn a juicy thank-you kiss.

And claim her, added his panther.

Uh no, we're not, was his reply.

We'll see, his cat taunted.

We're screwed. Yeah, they both thought it, but for different reasons. Me-fucking-ow.

Chapter 5

Mom: *Why didn't you answer your phone? I tried calling.*
Cynthia: *I know. I was ignoring it because I spent the night with a guy last night. (Pause.) Mom? Aren't you going to say something?*
Mom: *Sorry, baby girl, just updating your social media status to "in a relationship."*

SIGH. Perhaps Cynthia should specify that she'd spent the night with Daryl but didn't actually do the horizontal tango.

She still wasn't even sure how the whole sleepover thing had happened. Actually, she did.

It's his fault. Daryl insisted on remaining with her because, "There's two beds. Seems a waste of time for me to go home when I could just sleep here and make sure we get an early start on looking for your friend in the morning."

"What about your job?"

"It's the weekend, Cyn. You'll have me all to yourself."

Shiver. Did he have to make that sound so wicked? "Fine. Whatever. Just stick to your bed. No funny business."

"Would you like to tie me up again to make sure I behave?" He winked at the suggestion, a flirty act that, in turn, did wicked things to her body.

She told her treacherous libido to behave. Then she told her wolf to stop with her antics, too, since her inner lupine wouldn't shut up with the whole lick—or pee on—Daryl thing.

I am not urinating on him. For any reason. So what if her Aunt Noelle swore by it? There would be no marking of males, at least not today. Bondage, however... "The next time I tie you up, I'll be using chains. Great big ones."

"I like the fact you think there'll be a next time."

A rumbly growl poured from her, a mixture of exasperation and too much interest. How could she both want to throttle and kiss him at the same time?

Probably because getting close enough to throttle him means putting hands on him and having him in the right place for another one of his delicious kisses.

No more kisses. He would like it too much. She just hoped the whine her wolf let out wasn't also out loud.

Flicking the light off, she snuggled under her covers, back turned to him, her attempt to tune him out.

She heard fabric rustling then nothing.

"Do you always sleep in your clothes?" he asked, almost startling a scream from her.

"No. But then again, I don't usually sleep with virtual strangers."

"Strangers? After all we've already been through since meeting? I'm wounded, Cyn. What a low blow. Wanna kiss it better?"

Yes. "No."

Sigh. "A man can hope. And I was serious. You really shouldn't sleep in jeans or a bra. You'll chafe that sexy skin of yours."

"Skin isn't sexy."

"No, but the curves it's covering are. Would you prefer I said you were tasty?"

She'd prefer he *tasted* her. Ugh. Would her mind please stay out of the gutter? It hadn't been that long since her last boyfriend, and she had a fresh set of batteries at home in her rocket that kept her from getting too physically wound.

His concern with her clothes made her ask, "What are you wearing to bed?"

"If I said nothing, would that convince you to join me?"

No, but it certainly played havoc with her body. Heat flushed her skin as she tried to not think of him naked with the rough cotton sheets rubbing against his skin, his muscled body unfettered by any constraining fabric.

Could extreme sexual teasing make a girl lose her mind?

"Are you ignoring me?" he asked, derailing her thoughts.

"I'm trying to, but someone keeps yapping. Mind shutting up for a bit? I need to get some sleep so I can be clear-headed for tomorrow."

"Good plan. We wouldn't want you coming up with any more half-witted plans."

"I resent that." While her plan might have run into a few bumps, in the end it had proven fruitful. Cynthia knew more about Aria's last moments, and she now had an ally in her search. About time because the cops certainly hadn't proven useful.

The human deputy behind the desk at the cop station in Cynthia and Aria's hometown certainly wasn't interested in helping.

"You said it yourself. Your friend's on a road trip across the country. She probably lost her phone or is camping out somewhere where there's no signal."

"I'm telling you she's missing. We need to file a report."

"And I'm telling you that, until you have more evidence, there's no point."

The deputy wouldn't be budged, and Cynthia left the police station frustrated.

Wasn't the fact that Aria hadn't been seen or heard from since that fated image taken in the Bitten Pint bar enough? And what the heck was it with this town and its obsession with using bitten? Yes, the place was called Bitten Point and, yes, a lot of its residents were carnivores, hence the whole chomping thing proving apt, but still, just about every business played on that word.

Who cared about a town with no originality? Aria was missing, and no one was looking for her. No one was worried.

Am I wrong or overreacting? Could it be that Aria is just partying somewhere?

If it were anyone else, maybe, but Aria wasn't the type to not keep in touch. She and her bestie never went a day without talking, and it had now been at least three. Cynthia didn't care what the cop said. Her gut insisted something was wrong. Aria had encountered some sort of trouble, and Cynthia was going to find her. She just hadn't let her parents know. Mother would have forbidden it as too unladylike and dangerous, and Daddy would have locked her up and said he'd take a look. Which, bless him, he would, but Daddy was hobbled by a broken leg. A mishap at work that would keep him immobilized for days as it healed, then weeks as he fooled the humans who didn't know how quickly shifters could heal.

With no one else to turn to, Cynthia had to set out on a search. Anything for the best friend she'd met during her teen years when the wolf began to emerge and Cynthia realized her human friends would never fully understand her.

But Aria did. Aria came along in grade seven, wearing black, with several piercings in her ears and a tough exterior to protect a fragile heart.

Aria was a product of the foster system. Found abandoned in the woods at a young age, she'd come into her eagle younger than Cynthia, and with no one to guide her. But the day she transferred to the group home down the street, they'd met, mostly because Aria dove onto Cynthia, slammed her into a tree, and, with wild eyes, said, "You smell different. You're like me. Except more doggyish."

A rather rough introduction, but Cynthia and Aria, from that moment, became the best of friends. The very best, even after the group home spit Aria out into the world at eighteen. But Aria wasn't alone. She had Cynthia.

And now Cynthia had Daryl. Between the two of them, maybe they could find her friend, if Daryl was telling the truth. Did he truly have nothing to do with Aria's disappearance? Or had he done something to her friend?

The kitty is good, her wolf promised.

Yeah, but according to his wrecked T-shirt, when he's bad, he's even better.

And it was with that thought warming her that she fell into a restless sleep.

THE ATTACK, when it came, arrived on silent hinges, yet she still woke.

Uh-oh. In the excitement of shooting Daryl and everything else, she might have forgotten to lock the door.

Who cares? Move, howled the wolf in her head. Trusting the instincts of her beast, Cynthia rolled and fell off the bed. She hit the floor with a thud and huddled as she tried to make sense of what had happened.

Someone is in the room.

Someone or something? The scent tickling her nose also had her wrinkling it. Ugh. *What is that nasty stench?* It seemed kind of familiar, like wet fur after a run in the rain, but with a strong mildew undertone mixed with rancid animal musk.

Whatever shared the room with her stank and wasn't here to play nice, or so she surmised from the sounds. Snarl, growl, and a heroically stated, "I've got this."

While Cynthia might have chosen to hit the floor for cover, Daryl went after the intruder.

Grunt. Thud. A muttered, "Stand still, you hairy fucker."

Such language! Then again, the situation might warrant it. With Daryl keeping the person or thing occupied, Cynthia dared to peek over the edge of her mattress wishing she wasn't such a wuss. But alas, while she might have an inner wolf, hers was perfectly content to stay on the lower rungs of pack hierarchy.

Fingers clutching the bedspread, she looked. Forget seeing anything in the pitch black. Only the red glow of the clock was visible, displaying the ungodly hour of four-thirty a.m.

The longer she stared in the direction of the tussle, the more she began to discern. Murky shadows coalesced into two shapes. One, naked but for a pair of briefs, the other... What the hell was that other thing? It stood like a man. It had the right number of limbs, and yet... there was something off about it.

Enemy. Her wolf snarled inside her head.

Well, duh, the weird dude was a bad guy, but what was he?

Since Daryl seemed to be having some luck keeping the intruder distracted, she scurried over her bed for the lamp, fingers fumbling for the switch and lighting the room.

Something let out a nasty snarl. Something with lots of hair, she noted, as she finally saw their nocturnal guest.

"Good grief, what is that?" she said, her voice low with repulsed wonder.

"It's a bad..." Daryl grunted as he struggled to get his arm around its neck. "Bad dog."

"Is it a shifter?" Albeit a kind she'd never seen. It seemed to possess many wolf characteristics, yet this hybrid shape wasn't something she'd ever heard her mother talk about. Animals didn't walk on two legs, for starters, or have such human eyes.

"Who cares what the hell it is? Give me a hand." Because despite Daryl's bulging muscles, he was straining to keep the slobbery jaws from snapping on anything vital.

"I don't know what to do!" Panic increased her heart rate. Pitter. Patter. Double time, and faster still, as the wolfman managed to turn them and slammed Daryl into the wall.

He let out a grunt. "Do anything! Zap it with one of your needles."

The sedatives, yes, good plan. Better than the one she had that involved her whistling to snare the thing's attention, tossing a stick, and seeing if it would fetch. At least Daryl's plan might work. Hers lacked a stick.

Diving to the table, she riffled through her bag, spotting two more needles loaded with drugs. She grabbed them and flicked the caps off.

Holding them shoulder height, she couldn't help watching with wide eyes as Daryl and the wolfbeast wrestled for control.

When Daryl hit the wall again, she knew she had to act. With a shriek of, "Hello. My name is Cynthia Montego. You might have hurt my friend Aria. Prepare to sleep," she attacked, and by attack, she meant that she jabbed the creature in its hairy butt, which, not surprisingly, did not go over well.

It howled in fury, she squeaked like a purse-sized Yorkie, and Daryl snorted, "Did you seriously just parody *The Princess Bride*?"

"And now I'm channeling Jamie Lee Curtis from *Prom Night*." Cynthia shrieked as the wolfman turned baleful eyes her way and swung hairy paws tipped in claws, narrowly missing her as she danced back.

"Oh no you don't. The only guy touching that sweet skin is me," Daryl—clad only in black briefs—snapped. He wrapped a thick forearm around the beast's head. He yanked it to him. "Drug it again. With the adrenaline he's got going, two ain't enough."

"I have no more," she cried, wringing her hands together. What to do? She still hadn't found a stick.

"Bonk it on the head."

Goodness but Daryl was good at thinking of logical stuff under pressure. Grabbing the lamp, she ran at the monster, only to jolt as the cord didn't release right away. Once it did come whipping from behind the nightstand, it stung her in the buttocks.

Worse than that, though, the room was plunged into darkness.

The pitch black didn't mean she couldn't hear them struggling and grunting.

But how could she aim if she couldn't see? A yank of fabric pulled the curtains open, letting in the feeble light from the flashing neon sign—Nap Bites.

It proved enough illumination for her to see, take aim, yell, "Hi-ya!" and bring down the lamp hard.

With a crack, the hairy intruder went limp. Daryl dumped him on the floor and wiped his bloody lower lip.

"That is one smelly fucking dog."

Cynthia might have taken more offense at his derogatory term if she hadn't agreed. Besides, he might be right.

"What are you doing?" Daryl asked. "Checking it for a name tag?"

Having dropped to her knees beside the hybrid creature, she could understand his curiosity. "I'm checking it out. Look at this. It's wearing a collar." A thick metal ring that hummed uncomfortably against her skin when she touched it with her fingertips. But that wasn't the only thing interesting about their sleeping intruder. "I don't know how it's possible, but I think this thing is part German Shepherd."

"Excuse me? I think I must have fucking misheard you."

She didn't immediately reply as she sniffed, gagged at the unwashed smell, then sifted the scents. "I'm not sure how it happened, but I've treated enough German Shepherds"—because her uncle had helped her get the contract with the local K9 units—"to say with certainty that we are looking at a canine shifter, not a wolf one, and in some kind of hybrid shape."

"It's a half shift," Daryl remarked. "Not easy to achieve. And odd that it's holding even with it currently unconscious. It takes a lot of concentration to hold that shape."

Daryl was proving an interesting fount of information.

"I didn't even know that was possible."

"Because not many can do it."

"What about the dog thing? Do you have many of them living in Bitten Point?"

He shook his head. "This is the first time I've ever encountered one."

"So he's not from around here?" Cynthia regarded the slumped body and chewed at her lower lip. "I wonder if he's somehow connected to Aria's disappearance."

Daryl never had a chance to answer because a shadow blotted the light coming from the window. Before Cynthia could turn her head to see, round two of chaos erupted.

The glass shattered in a tinkling display of glinting shards that sprayed into the room. Via the gaping hole, a figure dove through, and it didn't seem to care or worry that it might get cut by the lingering spikes of glass.

Then again, anyone with head-to-toe scales probably wasn't that concerned about scratches.

Cynthia might have spent a moment longer than necessary staring. Way more than six feet tall, possibly closer to eight, a two-legged dinoman spread leathery wings in their motel room and hissed.

"What is that?" she gasped.

"Whatever it is, I doubt it's friendly. Distract it for a second, would you, while I change."

It took her a second to realize he didn't mean clothes. While the previous fight hadn't left time to shapeshift, it seemed Daryl wanted something more than human fists to face the lizardman.

What of his request to distract it? She didn't have any live mice to dangle, just herself, a juicy chocolate morsel. Gulp.

"Here, lizard, lizard," she crooned. A forked tongue flicked in her direction. She recoiled with a disgusted, "Ew." Being a vet hadn't cured her of the dislike of being licked.

Although she might make an exception for Daryl, but only if they lived, which, given dinoman sported great big claws and bigger teeth, didn't seem likely.

Apparently, Daryl was determined to change those odds. A sleek black shape launched itself at the monster.

Only to find itself batted aside.

That pissed off the kitty. It yowled in challenge, but before Daryl could attack again, their first furry intruder woke up, and he was not a happy puppy.

With a snarl, he dove on Daryl, which left her alone to deal with the lizard. It turned a cold, dark gaze in her direction.

Eep.

She grabbed for something, anything, and tossed it.

The fluffy pillow hit the thing on the arm, and even she couldn't pretend to not see its disbelieving expression.

In full-blown panic, she grabbed another pillow and held it before her, an utterly useless shield. "Don't you take another step," she threatened, or else she might just pee her pants.

Think. There's got to be something I can do to avoid becoming this lizard's midnight snack.

She needed a better weapon. Or...

Her eyes alighted on her purse still on the table. It didn't have any more needles, but she did have some outside in her car.

Question was, could she make it and grab them in time?

No time like the present to find out.

The reptilian thing, tired of toying with her, lunged. She screamed as she dove out of its reach, her nimbleness coming in handy. She hit the table with her hip, but ignored that bruising pain as she dove for the still-open door.

At any moment, she expected claws to tear at her back, but instead, she heard a snarl. Daryl to the rescue.

What must he think with her looking like she fled? To a car that was locked. Oh shoot.

She banged on the trunk and let out a yell of frustration. A whisper of sound and a puff of air were all the warnings she had.

Move.

Throwing herself sideways, she made it out of the way of the wrestling pair, the four-legged panther of before now a two-legged beast able to grapple for domination.

What was going on? Two-legged dog men, a giant lizard with wings, and now Daryl, some kind of two-legged catman? Had she entered some surreal comic book adventure?

Bang.

The lizard thing was slammed into the trunk of her car. Then the roles were reversed, and Daryl hit it.

Off they rolled, to thud against the pavement, but Cynthia was more fascinated by her blind luck. In their struggle atop her car, they'd popped the trunk. She wasted no time diving in and grabbing what she needed. Shaking hands filled the biggest needle she owned. She didn't have time to fill a second because the dogman came bounding out of her hotel room with a vicious snarl.

"Good doggie?" she asked, pressing against her car.

Snarl.

"I've got treats."

A step forward with an evil glare.

"Fetch." She tossed the rubber cap to the needle, but its gaze never wavered. She trembled and held the syringe in front of her like a puny sword. While bigger than the last two she'd used, would she be able to use it in time to save herself?

The wolfman launched himself. She closed her eyes and... remained untouched.

Once again, a furry feline had slammed into the hairy impossibility and taken it to the ground.

Daryl had saved her again.

Or not.

From the shadows limped the big lizard thing, and it looked pissed.

Cynthia feinted left then right. It didn't fall for it, its intent gaze never moving from her.

She might have let out a whimper, but she remained still, watching it approach. Leathery fingers tipped in claws grabbed at her arm. They pierced skin, but so did she, the giant needle finding flesh. She depressed the plunger, shooting it full of drugs.

"Night night, gecko man," she slurred. Funny thing, she was the one getting tired. Sleepy. Eyes fluttering shut as she slumped to her knees and...

Chapter 6

Daryl's T-shirt: *"Poke me and die."*

WHEN CYN'S lashes fluttered and she opened her eyes, he made sure she saw him first thing. Not his best idea.

"Eeeeeeeeeek!"

He stuck a finger in his ear and wiggled it. "Must you shriek so loud?"

"Where am I? How did I get here?"

"You're in my apartment. I brought you here after the attack."

Far from reassuring her, his reply widened her eyes. "Oh no, did you drug me and then kidnap me? Did you take liberties with my person while I was sleeping?" Her gaze narrowed in suspicion.

"I didn't touch you." But not because he didn't want to. Cyn posed quite the temptation, but he'd resisted. Barely. "Exactly what do you remember?"

She blinked as she nibbled her lower lip, an endearing habit he wanted to try—on her. He'd nibble that lower lip anytime.

"Last I remember, I was sticking the giant lizard with a needle. Did we win?" Her expression brightened with hope.

"Not exactly." To his shame, the sudden appearance of lights in other motel rooms, plus heads poking out, had sent the two creatures fleeing. One by air, the other on foot—er paw. Daryl could have probably at least tracked the one, however, sluggish from the narcotic in the lizard thing's claws, and not wanting to leave an unconscious Cyn alone, he'd opted to let his friends take up the chase.

While Wes, Constantine, and Caleb scoured the woods for the dogman, Daryl tucked Cynthia's luscious cocoa body in the car, out of harm and curiosity's way, and then dealt with the cops when they arrived.

It wasn't as if he could hide the broken window or the smears of blood on the pavement or in the motel room. Daryl stuck to the truth, and no, he didn't end up in a special hospital for people who claimed to see walking lizard men and dogs.

Instead, Pete, Bitten Point's sheriff, called in, on their secret frequency channel, all available personnel to track the assailants.

"What do you think they were after?" Pete asked.

"Damned if I know." But Daryl had to wonder, was the attack targeted? Were those two monsters after him or Cynthia? And more worrisome, would they try again?

Because of his reluctance to leave Cyn without defense and the fact that he still sought to stay ahead of the drugs in his system, he took her home, to his bed.

Was it wrong he admired how good she looked against his royal blue sheets? He managed to remain a gentleman—albeit reluctantly. He left her dressed, and untouched. While he did think of binding her, with silk scarves to his bedposts, he didn't. Why resort to props when he could hold her down himself?

"What are you doing on top of me?" she asked, quite breathless.

Pulling her arms over her head, he pinned them so she couldn't fight. "I am making sure you don't go anywhere."

"I was just trying to sit up."

Why? He liked her flat on her back, with him pressing against her. "Why were those things after you?"

"Me?" Either she didn't know, or she had some kick-ass acting skills. "Who says it wasn't just a random attack?"

His gut did. "I think you were targeted."

"But why? And for what? Do you think this has to do with Aria?"

Did it? Either those things were after Cynthia because she was poking around, asking about her friend, or the disappearances were happening again.

Was Aria a victim? Had Cynthia almost become one, too?

If I'd not decided to spend the night to drive her nuts, she would have gone missing, too, I'll bet. Missing or dead?

Either possibility blew. And it wasn't that he suddenly cared about Cynthia or anything. Nope. The woman was just a curiosity, something his cat wanted to check out.

Naked.

Then mark.

Permanently.

Uh, no.

Daryl shook his head, meaning to chastise his inner feline, but Cynthia caught the gesture.

"Why does it look like you're arguing with yourself?"

"What would make you think that?" he asked.

"Because I often argue with my wolf, too." She smiled, an impish and, at the same time, sheepish grin that hit him below the belt, and she noticed. Her eyes widened.

Before she could remark on his rather impressive hard-on—because his girth made it difficult to miss—fact, not arrogance—he asked quickly, "Why the hell didn't you shift into your wolf during the fight? It would have probably been better than the pillow you used as a deadly missile."

He didn't miss the heat suddenly flushing her cheeks. "Um, my Lycan side doesn't like to come out in front of strangers."

"We were in a life-and-death situation. Surely she could have made an exception."

"No, and I don't know why you're making a big deal about it, seeing as how we prevailed."

"Barely."

"Is that why you drugged me? Because you were mad?"

He leaned forward until their noses touched. "I did not drug you. The lizard thing did, but given you're awake, it seems the effect is wearing off."

"Then why do I feel so lethargic?"

Should he explain it wasn't lethargy but smoldering interest that stole her strength? "That's not the drugs, Cyn. That's all me." He smiled, a slow, sensual curve of his lips. "I'm game to stay in bed if you are."

"We can't."

"Why not?"

"Because we don't even know each other."

"Hi, my name is Daryl, and I think you're fucking crazy, but hot." More than hot, she totally made his inner kitty wish it could purr.

"You should get off me."

"No."

"What do you mean no?" She pulled at the hands tethering her, and she bucked under the weight of his body, not that either dislodged him.

"That's it, honey. Keep squirming. That feels *good*." He showed her how good and ground his hips against her.

"Oh." She gasped, but before she could say more, his lips slanted across hers with a firm claim.

He'd wondered, in the time since their last kiss, if perhaps alcohol or something else had turned their first embrace into something more. How could an almost stranger ignite his blood and have him throbbing so quickly and so hard?

He wasn't drunk now.

He couldn't blame the drugs.

Touching her lips proved even more electric than the first time, the taste of her exquisite, the feel of her under him...dangerous.

Dangerous because it made him forget he needed answers.

I think I might understand why she felt the need to act so rash. She wasn't the only one who couldn't stay focused.

Rolling off her, he tried to ignore her soft sigh of loss. *I wish we had more time to play, too, honey.*

"I'm going to need to know everything you can tell me about your friend," he said, his back turned to her lest he lose control once more.

Don't mock his lack of restraint. It had happened once already when he'd stepped back to admire her on his bed then found himself covering her as soon as she twitched a muscle.

"What do you want to know?"

"Everything." It took about fifteen minutes for him to fish all the relevant info from Cynthia, such as Aria's appearance, itinerary, all the images she'd posted before her disappearance, and the facts that Cyn liked to gesticulate with her hands as she spoke and she had the most delightful lips.

"...and that's how I ended up at Bitten Pint bar last night looking for you."

He interrupted her. "Do you have a boyfriend?"

"No, and neither did Aria. I highly doubt it's her ex trying to get back with her. He's moved on with some other chick. Last I heard they were getting married."

"So no special someone back home?" And no, he couldn't believe he asked either. Shoot him now.

"Nope, Aria is single."

"I was asking about you. Do you have anyone special back home?"

"No, and I don't know why you're asking. I'm not the one missing."

"A man likes to know if a woman is spoken for before he makes a play. I'd hate to have to hurt someone."

He was really starting to enjoy the way he could startle her. Now if only she wouldn't keep startling him back.

"Well, given you've already made a few moves, I'd say it's kind of late to ask. Just like it's probably a little too late to tell you that I have jealousy issues. So, since you seem intent on trying to seduce me, I should warn you. I don't share."

"I thought sharing was caring."

"That goes for desserts, not boyfriends."

"I didn't realize we'd jumped from me putting the moves on you to us dating."

"We aren't dating."

He smirked. "And yet we've already spent the night together."

"Because you promised to help me find Aria. I don't even think you're my type."

"Got a thing against Latino men?" It wouldn't be the first time he encountered some unwarranted hostility.

"No, I have a thing against guys who are too hot for their own good."

He couldn't help a surge of warmth. "You think I'm hot?"

"No." A blatant lie given the blush and heat radiating from her body.

"I think you're hot, too." Even if her hair was a fluffy halo around her head. She'd lost the elastic that held it back. He hoped she never found it again because she was damned cute.

And that's a nice handful for pulling.

Rowr.

"I know I'm hot." She rolled her eyes as if it was obvious, and he laughed. "But hands off, Casanova. I am here on serious business."

"So does this mean no hooking up?"

She snorted. "Will you stop trying if I say no?"

"No." Said with an unrepentant grin.

"Then expect to get shot down. Now, if you can direct a bit of blood from your groin to your head, can we get back to finding Aria?"

A knock at his apartment door saved him from the fabulous

insanity that was Cyn. He left the bedroom and headed to the door. He didn't need to peek to know who was there. He flung open the portal to find Constantine and Wes standing on the stoop. A peek behind them showed no one else. "Where's Caleb?" Daryl asked.

"Gone home to check on Renny and his kid. If there's another lizard thing running—"

"—flying."

"—around, then we'll need to be vigilant."

"You mean you've seen that thing before?" said the woman he should have tied to the bed.

Cynthia, thankfully dressed, despite his best attempts to get her to shed clothes at bedtime, appeared by his side.

What possessed him to curl a possessive arm around her waist?

It didn't go unnoted.

"Is this the chick those things were after?" Wes asked with an arch of his brow.

"This chick is called Cynthia," she remarked, but at the same time, she didn't move away from his loose embrace.

A bite of Daryl's tongue prevented him from saying, *Mine.*

Cyn didn't belong to him. And she never would. Daryl must really need to get some sleep, or those drugs were still affecting him, because his inner feline was acting awfully weird. Daryl wasn't into anything long term or serious, even if Cyn was a babe.

Seeing a girl a few times, no strings, that was cool. Anything that involved a toothbrush in his bathroom, half his closet gone, and boxes of feminine unmentionables in his hall closet? Never. Not happening.

He'd grown up with a mom and sister. He loved them both, but damn, those crazy women drove him mental.

What idiot would volunteer for that? No sex was that good.

It seemed extreme, and while he didn't mind trying his hand at many a daring sport, the whole relationship thing wasn't his scene.

And I usually move on when a girl shoots me down. Not to mention, he shouldn't even like Cyn, especially considering what she'd done. Drugged a guy. *Made out with me.* Kidnapped him. *Put her hands all over my body.* Restrained him. *Bondage!* Shot him. *Which so deserved a spanking.* His hand on her—

"Dude! Pay attention." Constantine snapped his fingers in front of him.

"What?" Daryl asked.

"What should we do next since we didn't find anything? The freaking trail stops by the main road, not even a half-click from the motel. Looks like someone gave our thing a ride."

"A monster with a human buddy?" A crease pulled at Daryl's brow.

"The thing did wear a collar," Cyn added. "And it had this odd buzzy feeling to it. Could someone be controlling it?"

"Even better question, what is it?" Wes leaned against the wall, jeaned leg bent, his boots unlaced and scuffed. The T-shirt he wore rivaled Daryl's with its vintage KISS logo. "I ain't never smelled anything like them before. And everyone else I've talked to says the same."

Cyn waved her hands. "One of them is part canine. How does that happen? Is it a shifter or something else?"

"You mean like the Sasquatch in Canada?" Those big, hairy things were big, hairy things. They didn't magically shrink into humans that could easily hide. Instead, they lived scattered on plots of land that spanned acres. People might mock Bigfoots, but they were really fun to drink with.

Shaking his head, Constantine tapped his nose. "I don't think they're proper shifters. They don't smell right."

"They do have a certain alien quality, and their ability to hold that hybrid shape means that might be their natural form."

"So calling it dogman and dinoman is accurate?" Wes snorted. "Can't we change it to something a little less cartoonish sounding?"

"It is what it is," Constantine said.

"At least now we've got a little more evidence than before. Blood samples were taken from the scene and sent to Bittech for analysis."

"When will we get the results?" Daryl asked.

Wes shrugged. "We'll start getting data in a few hours, but the full battery will take a few days to process. In the meantime, I think enough people saw something tonight that we can maybe stir some shit up about it."

"You're not afraid someone will go missing again?"

The last time one of their group had tried to call a town meeting with their suspicions that there was something wrong in Bitten Point, that person had disappeared. Wes said he'd given up hope on finding his missing brother, yet Daryl knew Wes still looked, every free moment he had, convinced his sibling was out there somewhere in the bayou.

It happened every so often that a person morphed into their animal and didn't come back. Ever. Those shifters were called wildlings. A cute name to describe a horrible state that meant the animal took over and the human part of the mind was trapped. It mostly happened among the emotionally wounded. But had Wes's brother, Brandon, gone wild, or had something more nefarious happened? Something related to that dinoman and furball?

When his buddies left, promising to catch up again in the morning, Daryl locked the door and turned to Cyn.

"We should go to bed." Daryl let his lips quirk as he said it.

Cyn backed away from him. "No thanks. I'm wide awake. We should start looking."

Shaking his head, he shot down her idea. "It's after one in the morning."

Her brows shot high. "How is that possible? Those monsters attacked us at like four a.m."

"They did, and then you napped the day away. We both did." He locked all the doors and finally collapsed. "At this point, dawn is only a few hours away. Businesses we need to visit are closed. Exactly where will you look?"

Now some women might have proven stubborn at this point and continued to refute simple logic. Man logic. The right kind of logic.

A logic she grasped?

"You're right." She smiled and stretched, back arching, breasts thrusting forward. "We should go to bed." She turned and presented that sweet booty of hers. An ass a man could totally sink his teeth into.

And he would. He caught up to her and reached to grab Cyn, except she scooted out of the way.

"What do you think you're doing, kitty-cat?" She tossed him a look over her shoulder.

"Kitty-cat? That's not exactly a very masculine name. Couldn't we go with something else?"

"Prefer Casanova, do you?"

He froze and frowned. "No."

"I like Kitty-cat. It's cute."

Usually, being called cute would work for him, but he got the impression she didn't mean it in the most complimentary way. Why would she insult him? The realization made him smile. "I see the game you're playing." Hard to get.

"Good." She turned, framed in the doorway to the bedroom. "We can play some more in the morning. Night."

When she would have shut the door—with him on the outside!—he interjected his foot. "What are you doing?"

She peeked through the crack, eyes dancing with mirth, lips a sensual smile of teasing. "I am going to bed. In your bed. Alone. Wearing this." She dangled a T-shirt—"Poke me and die." Surely she didn't mean it.

She kicked his foot and wedged the door shut. Locked it.

Then...giggled.

Oh, it was on.

Chapter 7

Mom: *Is that a man's shirt in your laundry?*
Cynthia: *Yeah. It's from the night I took Daryl's bed and made him sleep on the couch.*
Mom: *I thought I taught you to share.*

BLINKING OPEN HEAVY LIDS, the first thing Cynthia noted was the dark eyes above hers, staring intently. Then, the familiar smirk.

Too late, she'd already let loose a shriek.

"Nice to see you, too, honeybuns."

She wrinkled her nose. "I am not a donut."

"Honeybuns aren't either, but you're both sweet."

The cheesy line made her groan, and she closed her eyes, only to snap them open as she exclaimed, "How did you get in here? I distinctly remember locking the door."

Disgust creased his features. "I learned to bypass those simple bedroom locks by the time I was in grade three. All you need is a butter knife."

If it was so simple, then why had he waited so long to enter?

Such a bad thought. She should be happy he'd not pushed the issue and insisted on joining her in bed. She'd have set him straight at the first amorous attempt.

Snicker. It wasn't just her wolf that mocked her.

A part of her had hoped he'd not let a locked door stand in his way the previous night. Hoped he'd slide into bed with her and...

"What are you doing?" she asked as he yanked the covers back. Clutching at the blanket to keep herself covered, she gave him the eye.

An expression he took as invitation, given he put a leg on the mattress with a muttered, "Move your sweet ass over."

Does he really think he's joining me in bed?

Forget thinking. He was, probably because she scooched over. The mattress dipped under his weight as he stretched out. Given he possessed quite a few pounds of thick, tanned flesh, encased in a lickable body, she found herself smooshed against him. She could think of worse places to be.

Or we could stay like this for a while. She could try and deny her attraction to Daryl all she wanted. Denial didn't make it true. She found him highly intriguing, sexy, and, let her not forget, arousing because, when he tried to kiss her, she melted like a piece of chocolate in the sun.

Lick me, head to toe.

Oh dear. Not exactly the right kind of thought to have when pressed against the object of her lust. He was a feline. Chances were he could smell it.

It might have proven more embarrassing if he was not sporting a huge boner, and, no, she didn't see it. She accidentally felt it.

With hot cheeks, she moved her hand away and wondered if he thought she'd groped him on purpose.

No wonder he's confused. She was sending out very mixed signals. Heck, she wasn't even sure what she felt herself.

"What time is it?" she asked. An innocuous question, something to focus on instead of how nice it felt when he placed his arm across her pillow and nudged her head onto it.

This was nice.

Must resist.

But how could she? The man was freaking cuddling! She'd never felt so blissfully relaxed and content.

And then he had to be a guy.

"I think it's time my luscious Cyn peeled the clothes from her body." Daryl ran a hand down the side of her body, tickling across her ribs. He left a trail of awareness in his wake and then had her holding her breath as he reached the hem of the shirt she'd borrowed. Fingers with callused tips brushed the tops of her bare thighs. Where would they go next?

"You want me to strip?" she muttered, her voice low and husky.

"Totally." The full width of his hand palmed her leg, branding her. "Then I want you to stretch that gorgeous body. I want you awake and ready because..." His lips brushed her forehead. She shivered. "You need to take a shower, honey. You reek of dog and lizard. Like badly. So badly, in fact, I'm going to have to wash these sheets."

With that, he rolled off the bed so quickly she couldn't help but fall face-first onto the mattress—where she stayed, utterly mortified.

Rejected because I stink. Her wolf whined with her head tucked between paws.

Good thing one of them was feisty and wouldn't stand for it.

Oh heck no. He'll pay for that comment, she thought as she pushed herself onto her elbows. The fact that he was right didn't enter the equation. No man should ever tell a woman she needed to bathe.

And probably brush her hair, she gauged by the ginger pat of her hand on out-of-control hair. Her carefully brushed and sprayed curly do was a tad in disarray. Okay, a fuzz ball atop her head. But there were chemicals for that...which she didn't have. Rats.

"Do you have any kind of oil? Moroccan oil is best, but cooking will do as well."

He might have been talking before she interrupted, but he certainly wasn't now. Now he gaped at her with his jaw dropped. Such a cute jaw, too, with that little goatee thing he had going, the short kind that covered just the bottom, front edge of his face with a little line bisecting up to his lower lip. So sexy.

Want-to-kiss-it sexy.

"What do you need oil for?"

"Taming my curls."

For a second, he froze. He might have let out some kind of sad meow sound before he turned enough to see her. He stared. She stared right back, but her gaze did narrow when he burst out laughing. "You're talking about the hair on your head."

"Of course I am. What other curls did you think I was talking about?" At his arched brow, she got it and blushed. "That's gross. Why would I grease myself down there?"

He snickered. "Should I really answer that?"

The heat in her cheeks went up a few more degrees. "Can we stop talking about the situation down below?"

"I'd rather not. This is one of the best morning conversations I've ever had. So, do you shave?"

She pushed herself up on elbow and gaped at him. "You did not seriously just ask that?"

"Why not? Can't a man be interested in the trimming?"

"No, because it's none of your business."

"Oh, it's my business all right," he practically purred. "I'm making it my business. But on second thought, don't tell me how you garden. I am going to totally enjoy finding out myself when I pay a visit down there. With my lips."

She sucked in a breath and wanted to hold her tongue, but how could she when his words ignited her? A part of her hoped he meant it—*I want his lips to touch me*—and yet, she couldn't help but deny it. Or should she say dare him? "There will be no lips placed on my body, especially not down there."

He rolled his eyes and gave her a mocking grin. "Well duh. You need to shower and brush your teeth first."

Oh, he did not just do that. Again. "You think I stink?"

She thought he stank. Actually more like he tortured. What was the female equivalent of blue balls? Because she might have it. Parts of her certainly wouldn't stop tingling and, even at times, throbbing. He was to blame. Him and all his sexy parts.

And what did he want from her? One moment, he was seducing her with words and touches, and the next, he practically, on purpose, pushed her away.

Pushed. Her. Away.

Was he as freaked out by their mutual attraction? Did he perhaps suffer the same doubts?

Was it possible to torture him back?

Let's find out.

The plan formed in less than a second, which meant it would be a good one, one that moved so fast she didn't even know what was happening until she stood there naked.

In the blink of an eye, she'd jumped from the bed and pulled off the shirt. His shirt. The scent of him surrounded her, even marked her skin. The loss of clothing should have given her a chill, yet who could feel cold when bathed in the heat coming from Daryl's watching eyes?

Let's see just how uninterested you are, darlin'.

She looked down at her breasts. She'd not worn a bra to bed. Sleeping unfettered was so much better, and her breasts were happy to show the love by having her nipples harden into points. Naughty suckers.

Mmm. Lips. Pulling and tugging.

Must not get distracted, even if he was. Poor Daryl. He stared without so much as blinking. His body stood poised, rigid with attention. That wasn't the only rigid thing about him.

He wants me.

It was heady knowledge. It brought out the imp in her. Since he admired her plump handfuls, she cupped them. "I see you're admiring these. Nice, aren't they? And real, too." She squeezed. He might have made a noise. "I'd let you touch, but you know"—she lowered her voice and leaned closer—"I'm such a dirty, dirty girl."

Yeah, he definitely made a pained sound that time.

She held in her smirk until she'd made it past him out of the bedroom into the main living area. From there, she noted an open doorway through which she could see tile.

Before she'd made it over the sill, she squeaked.

The slap on her ass was sharp. Crisp. Titillating and frustrating, seeing as how Daryl didn't follow through. "Don't forget to use lots of soap, Cyn. And by the way, I like the way you tend your garden. I'll be by for a picnic later."

Later? There wouldn't be a later if she killed him because, seriously, the man was begging for a maiming—or mauling, naked.

It was cat versus dog, and for every minor victory she claimed over him, he stole one right back from her.

It should have annulled her attraction for him. Ha. Everything served to make him only more appealing. So why resist? Why say no?

Because he keeps teasing and not putting out.

Then again, so was she.

A conundrum she'd solve after she made herself smell pretty.

Then see if you can resist me, darlin'.

The shower proved refreshing, his razor sharp enough. His shampoo was some kind of inexpensive two-in-one that did little to help her hair. While the towels in the cupboard over the toilet proved clean, they held the unmistakable scent of him.

Throw it on the ground, and we'll roll in it.

Her sometimes-timid wolf didn't have a problem insisting. Cynthia settled for wrapping the terry fabric around her body, sarong style.

Wiping her arm across the misted mirror, she grimaced at her hazy face. *I look the same.*

A round face, her cheeks often called apples, and big lips that could use a dab of pink moisturizing balm. Her eyes seemed bright, perhaps more than usual. Her hair...yeah, she wouldn't talk about the hair.

She looked fine. Given what had happened, she might have expected to see some sign of her ordeal. Dark shadows under her eyes. A haunted look in her gaze. A hickey on her neck.

Okay, that was wishful thinking, and she could just hear her mother if she went home sporting one. *"Branding should be done in discreet places. But in case it happens, wear a scarf."*

Please tell me Mother has a drawer full because she loves wearing them. Any other reason didn't bear thinking of.

Needing distraction from the fact that her parents might have, indeed, once in their lives, done something traumatizing in order to beget their only child, she dug around Daryl's vanity looking for some basics. The deodorant she found in the drawer, when sniffed, did not prove powdery fresh, but at least it gave her something to scent her skin.

Something that touched his.

She really enjoyed the application of the stuff a little too much and shoved it back in the drawer. Another drawer revealed a few toothbrushes in wrappers. She grabbed one and brushed her teeth, trying not to think of the fact that he had so many because he was a player.

Not my problem or business. He can be whatever he likes. He's not my boyfriend.

No, he was worse than that. The more time she spent with him, the more she wondered if he was her mate.

The shifter population was torn on the whole fated-mate concept. Depending on who a person spoke to, some were convinced all shifters had one perfect mate somewhere for them. Some claimed you knew the moment you met. The shock was like no other.

But then again, others scoffed at the idea of it. Mate at first sight? Never—simply animal attraction.

Cynthia often wondered if those who didn't believe had just never encountered it themselves.

Which begged the question, what did she think?

Do I essentially believe in love at first sight? At fate drawing together two people who were meant to be together?

Or was it simply lust, and one compounded by her anxiety over her friend?

She wished for a clear answer.

Instead, she caught another glimpse of her hair.

That was at least something she could fix. She sleeked it back as best she could, and then, when she couldn't find an elastic of some sort, she ripped a facecloth until she had a few strips, which she wove together to make a tieback. It would prevent a full-on pouf.

Since she'd entered naked, she had nothing to change into, not that she would have donned any of her dirty clothes. She had to rely on her towel to cover her.

Or strut by Daryl in the buff and see what happens now that I'm clean.

Less is sometimes better. Something her mother always said.

She ensured the towel covered all her parts—parts he'd seen, but that didn't matter. It was all about presentation. She emerged from the bathroom, the aircraft carrier roar of the fan following her, only to squeak, "There's people here!"

Indeed, Daryl had an apartment full, one of which was the big fellow they'd met the night before, who held tucked under his arm like a precious football a small dog, which she recognized as a long-haired Chihuahua with a pink bow in her hair. Pet or snack?

Beside the dog-toting guy, there was that big gator dude she also recalled. He didn't have a pet in his arms, but he did bring a smirk.

She replied with a frown as she quickly took in the rest of the strangers—a blonde-haired woman, a little boy, and another big guy with a scar on his face.

"There you are, Cyn." Daryl, leaning against the breakfast bar to his kitchen, smiled at her. "I was beginning to wonder if I needed to rescue you from drowning. I'm always ready to practice my mouth-to-mouth."

"And I love opportunities to keep my knee's aim in shape. So you might want to wear a cup."

It wasn't just Daryl that laughed. "Isn't she just Cyn-fully insane?"

"Enough of your screwing around. What is going on? Who are these people, and why are they here?" And why was she meeting them in a towel?

"It's a gathering of the minds, and muscle," Daryl said with a grin.

"In Daryl's case, it's the idiot," grumbled the scarred fellow. "I don't know if you remember meeting us last night. The first time, you were drooling all over the back seat."

"I do not drool."

"Really?" Daryl interjected. "A shame. But don't worry, there's lube for that." As if he'd not said something outrageously provocative, Daryl began the introductions. "You met Wes, he of the no-smile, last night. That freak over there holding this afternoon's snack..." *Yip!* "Okay, fine, we won't eat Princess today, but mostly on account of the fact that Constantine is bigger than me and likes that little furball."

"Touch my dog and I will digest you slowly." A threat not made with much heat, and one she'd wager got tossed around often given Daryl simply laughed.

She wasn't close enough to truly scent him properly, but the apartment wasn't big enough for her to avoid it entirely. It tickled at her, reptilian in feel, but nothing like the gators she'd worked with when she interned at the zoo. "What are you?" she asked. Probably not the most polite query, but it wasn't just cats who were curious.

Constantine didn't take offense. "I'm a python."

"He wishes," snickered the last guy in the room. "I mean, have you seen the size of his dog?"

Grrr. The bite sized mutt took offense at the remark.

"Don't make me sic Princess on you," said the big snake, but it was the tiny, curled lip of the dog that proved most fascinating.

Would the little thing truly attack something fifty times or more her size?

Daryl clapped his hands. "No letting Princess loose in here. Too many ankles standing on my carpet. Blood is a pain in the ass to rinse." Daryl brought his attention back to her. "That guy bugging his little brother, who isn't so little anymore, is the dead man formerly known as Caleb."

"He's also an idiot, but we like him anyway." The blonde who'd spoken waved. "Hi, my name is Renata, but my friends call me Renny. This is my son, Luke. Say hi, Luke."

The little boy never looked up from his tablet as he uttered, "Hi. Nice to meet you." Of course, it sounded more like hinicetomeetyou, but Cynthia got the gist.

"Nice to meet you, too?" She couldn't help the high note at the end. Surreal didn't cover meeting and conversing with strangers while wearing a towel and nothing else.

Shifters might have more free concepts when it came to the wearing of clothes, but they still didn't openly entertain naked. At least not the people she knew. She'd heard out west things were different, and a lot more naked.

"I brought clothes," the blonde woman called Renny said, holding up a bag. "Daryl said you needed some, what with your motel room busted up last night and the cops having cordoned it off."

So much for her suitcase and other stuff. What would she do without a wallet?

As if Daryl read her mind, he said, "I managed to sneak out your purse, but your clothes kind of got wrecked in the fight. But no worries. I'll understand if you need to wander around naked until you have a chance to go shopping."

She might have answered, but others beat her to it.

"Daryl!" Renny exclaimed.

"Yeah, Daryl," Wes mocked. "Stop thinking with your little brain and let the woman get some clothes on so we can turn our attention on the big picture here."

The big picture not including outrageous flirting with a bad kitty.

With a smile of thanks, Cynthia snatched the bag of clothes Renny offered and dove into the privacy of Daryl's room. She hurriedly dressed, and when she exited, she heard them in the midst of discussing the attack.

"By all appearances, they're back."

"Not exactly," Caleb interjected. "The dino creature can't be the same one. The lizard thing we killed a while ago is still dead. His parts are being examined at Bittech."

"What lizard thing?" Cynthia asked as she exited the bedroom.

It was Daryl who told her. "A few weeks ago, we actually ran into another one of those lizard things. It tried to kidnap my sister, Melanie, and then went after Caleb's boy." He waved to the child playing.

Caleb took over. "We had to track it down and, even then, only found the thing by luck. It was hiding out atop an almost impassable rocky spire in the swamp. At the time, we didn't know it could fly."

"Can it?" Her brow furrowed. She knew enough about shifter structure to know how exact the physique for an avian shifter had to be. Because of the huge mass involved, and strength, only those who truly kept off the weight and worked hard built the muscle needed to make it all work.

Aria could do it, but she admitted it was tough, and exhilarating. Cynthia preferred her two feet on the ground, yet her preference didn't mean that lizard thing stuck to walking.

"Flying is the only logical explanation for how this thing keeps popping up out of the blue."

"It would also explain the way the scent trails start and stop. It can simply swoop in, grab the person it wants, and fly out without triggering any alarms."

"That's all well and good," Renny said, "except lizards can't fly."

"Some dinosaurs can," said Luke, showing he was listening more than it appeared.

"Dragons can, too." Several pairs of eyes focused on Cynthia, and she squirmed. "What? Just because we have never met a dragon doesn't mean they don't exist. I mean, look at all the stories that have them. They had to have some basis."

"Unproven fears that are given shape," Constantine said with disdain. "Dragons aren't real."

"They're making them."

This time, the eyes swung to Luke, who kept tapping at his screen, boomeranging some Angry Birds at mocking green pigs.

"Hey, little bug." Renny crouched alongside her son. "What makes you say that?"

"I heard it."

Judging by Renny's clenched jaw, Cynthia wasn't the only one chafing at the speed of the revelations.

"Heard it where, bug?" Renny asked.

Luke finally turned his gaze toward his mother. "I can't say." He turned back to his game.

Caleb knelt beside his son. "Listen here, big man, if you know something about this lizard thing, then you need to tell us."

"Why are we asking a kid?" Wes asked aloud. "Kids know nothing. He is probably thinking of some baby cartoon he watched."

Cynthia saw Caleb ready to retort, except Renny placed her hand on his arm and shook her head.

"Wasn't a cartoon." With a knot on his forehead, Luke glared. "I heard Tatum and Rory's daddy talking about how the dinosaur was a poor 'scuse for a dragon."

"Andrew? Andrew knows about these things? Why that no-good bastard." Daryl bristled as he pushed away from the counter he leaned on.

Constantine blocked his path to the door, placing a hand on Daryl's chest to prevent him from leaving. "Slow down. You can't go after Andrew based on what one little boy says. Don't forget, Andrew is the CEO over at Bittech. For all we know, what Luke overhead was part of a conversation about some of the research done on the one they've got in the labs for testing."

"Yeah, not likely," Wes volunteered. "They stopped testing."

"What do you mean? I thought they were supposed to run a gamut of blood work and tissue samples from the one we killed." Caleb frowned.

"Funny thing that. The initial results returned inconclusive. So they did them again. Lo and behold, they claim the corpse we brought them was not a lizard man but a caiman."

"That was no croc. Look at the body."

"There is no body. In order to hide it from curious human scientists working there, they had it cut into pieces and made sure none of them appeared like actual body parts. Those parts were accidentally incinerated with the other waste."

"So, there's still the pictures that were taken. Refute those."

"What pics?" Wes's smile held no trace of amusement. "They're gone. That entire folder dedicated to the creature, locked behind a secure firewall, deleted. Vanished. It doesn't even show on the backup."

"All of it's gone?" An incredulous note hued Renny's query.

"This is bull—" Caleb slid a glance over to his son. "Brown gooey stuff. The guys over at Bittech are covering it up. Someone's trying to get rid of the evidence because that was no croc. Not even a hybrid one. It kept its half-shape after death."

"Is that important?" Cynthia asked. She knew some things about shifters, but was really more knowledgeable when it came to animals.

Caleb rubbed his face, looking tired. "Half-shapes aren't something everyone can do. You have to really have a handle on the beast if you want to be able to balance equal power in the body and mind. It's not easy to do and, because it involves having a foot in each world, not meant to be. So if someone dies in the midst of it, the control slips and the body snaps back to its natural form, which is human."

"Except the dinoman stayed a dinoman."

"Did he? We now have scientists saying otherwise." Wes pushed away from the wall. "The body was destroyed, and the samples swapped for a reason. Someone is trying to prevent us from getting at the truth. The question is, who?"

Funny how a knock at the door, a firm, no-nonsense knock at such a serious moment, could result in utter silence.

Everyone looked at each other, but no one said a word as the knock came again, this time even more insistent.

Cynthia found it odd the dog didn't bark, but a glance showed Princess was well aware there was something trying to obtain entry. Her tiny ears were pricked, her eyes intent on the door, and her muzzle drawn back over pointed teeth.

"Are you going to get that?" Constantine whispered.

Daryl jolted. "Shit. I guess I should." With a predatory grace, Daryl strode to the door and peeked through the hole. "Who is it?"

"Pete."

Who is Pete?

A question she apparently uttered aloud because Renny answered. "He's the sheriff for the town."

Daryl quickly opened the door, and a big fellow, dressed in a dark uniform loomed in the opening, filling it with his bulk. The man's jowly cheeks sported a prickly shadow that matched the short spikes atop his head. Pete gave everyone a nod and said in a low voice to Daryl, "I need to speak with you outside."

"Whatever it is you've got to tell me, might as well come in and tell us all."

"This message is just for you."

"I have no secrets."

"That's just it. You need to start keeping some," Pete snapped.

At the numerous inquiring looks, the portly sheriff sighed. "Fuck me, I need to retire. I don't need this political fucking shit complicating my life."

"What shit? What the hell is going on, Pete?" Daryl demanded.

"I don't know what the fuck is happening. All I know is I've been told to drop the investigation on that attack at the hotel, to burn my personal notes based on what Daryl told me at the scene, and I was ordered to tell Daryl to keep his mouth shut, or else."

"Or else what?" Cynthia said.

"Doesn't matter." Daryl scoffed. "I am not going to keep quiet about this. There is something seriously wrong happening here. Mutant shifters or animals or something. And they're dangerous. We need to warn the people. Tell the council and get them involved. To..." Daryl trailed off, probably because Pete kept shaking his head.

"Don't you get it yet? Who the hell do you think has the clout to call me and tell me what to do? Did you really think I'd roll over and bare my belly to just anyone?"

It was Wes who got it first. "The fucking council knows about those creatures."

"Impossible," Cynthia exclaimed. "If they knew, then they'd be wanting us to do something about it, not zip our mouths."

"And yet that's exactly where my coded orders came from," said Pete with a shrug. "I don't know who sent them, or why, but there was no mistaking the council's seal."

Most shifter groups tended to rule themselves, usually under the leadership of an alpha, or someone elected—often by battle—to keep their secret society running smoother. But while groups had a certain autonomy, it was only because the shifter high council allowed it.

The SHC, as Cynthia had been taught, had been around for centuries, setting shifter policies in order to help prevent the spread of their secret. They acted in cases where some of their kind got out of line or brought too much attention to themselves.

Judge and executioner, without a trial. The wild nature of most shifters meant a need for speed in such matters and a swift resolution. Often that resulted in a very final outcome.

So if the council was involved in this mess and had demanded Daryl and all the others abstain, then the choice was clear. They'd have to drop the investigation.

Aria would remain lost, and those monsters would continue to roam.

Lost in her depressing thoughts, Cynthia barely noticed when Pete left. It took Daryl's clapped hands and, "Okay, now that he's gone, let's assign some tasks," for her to realize the group had not given up.

"You're going to keep looking? But what about the SHC?" she asked.

"The SHC is asking for a tribal accounting if they think we're going to sit back while some monsters prey on our town," Constantine said with a hint of a sneer.

"While those monsters roam, my family is at risk," was Caleb's reply.

"They took my brother."

"And we need to find your friend," Daryl said, finishing off the reasons.

In that moment, Bitten Point started growing on Cynthia, and a lot more pleasantly than that fungus that had claimed her razor in the motel shower.

Chapter 8

Daryl's Bumper Sticker: *"If you can read this, you better have brought the lube."*

IN DOWNTOWN BITTEN POINT *later that day…*

"Why did we get stuck with the library research as our task?" Cynthia grumbled. "Shouldn't that smart Constantine fellow and his little dog be here? I hate reading."

Not true. She liked reading interesting stuff. Sifting through boring newspaper articles for mentions of weird shit happening was time consuming—and didn't feature bare-chested Vikings sweeping damsels off their feet for ravishment.

Who needs a Viking when I have Daryl?

Stupid, yummy Daryl, who looked good in anything he wore, which, at the moment, was comprised of well-worn yet snug jeans, a T-shirt that claimed he was a Bikini Inspector, and flip-flops.

The man had his own sense of style, and damned if it didn't work for him.

"Constantine would be the one best suited for this task if he wasn't working."

"What does he work as anyhow?" Atlas? The big dude who held the world up on his shoulders?

"Fireman. He's on the roster and can't just take a day off on a whim."

"I would hardly call tracking murderous lizardmen and dogs a whim," Cynthia hissed as she followed Daryl through the winding stacks of metal shelving that bore the weight of books.

"And I'm sure if he told the fire chief what we were about, he'd agree, but given we were just warned by Pete to not say a word, we thought it best we not be too blatant with our flaunting. So Constantine went to work as if everything was normal, but meanwhile, he'll be milking the boys at the station to see if anyone knows anything."

"How is that being discreet? Won't he get in trouble if he's caught?"

"Constantine knows how to keep it on the down low."

"You must be able to if you've kept the secret of shifter existence in Bitten Point so long. Is everyone in this town one of us?" Cyn asked as they passed a petite woman, her red hair caught in a loose bun. "And was that really a fox?" She craned to look over her shoulder. "My dad said they were killed off by the British in the hunts overseas." She knew the smell because she'd treated a few mundane ones during her time interning at the zoo.

"A few vixens and their mates survived. They managed to make it across the ocean and settled here. They are, however, very rare. As to your other question, no, not everyone in town is a shifter. At last count, there were about a thousand residents, not counting transients and visitors. Only about half are shifters. We're too close to the Everglades and too big of a town to get completely bypassed by the humans."

"I noticed Renny's human, and she knows our secret."

"Of course she does. Not only is she mated to Caleb, but she's also a dormant descendent."

Dormant, a term often used to describe those who held the shifter gene in their body yet never managed to touch their animal. While a few youngsters manifested young, most shifters didn't fully change until their teens. Puberty was rough and hairy for those who managed to find their inner beast.

But not all could get that line of communication going. Some found their other side remained dormant. Yet, even for their inability, they were still capable of possibly passing on the gene, which screwed with those who'd chosen science as a profession and studied them because, for all intents and purposes, dormants were human.

"I can understand why Renny knows, but I've seen other humans in town, people who don't act like they know." Ignorance wasn't just a bliss. It was a smell.

"They act that way because they probably don't. I'd say almost half the humans roaming our streets have no idea." Amazing how most folks would explain away strange things just so they didn't have to face the possibility that maybe their world wasn't what it seemed.

"Isn't it dangerous to have them around?"

"It would draw more attention to push them away. In order to maintain a façade of normalcy, Bitten Point can't reject people. We just encourage them not to stay."

"How?"

"Shitty service and food are a good start."

"But what of those you want to stay? How do you seduce them?" Innocuous words, and yet, was that a teasing smile on her lips?

"How's this for a reason?" Daryl dragged her to him and mashed his mouth against hers, catching her startled gasp, feeling the pliant softness of her lips against his.

The fire that simmered on low whenever she was around ignited. She opened her mouth and let the tip of her tongue touch his. A bold strike. A sensual one.

Flames raced through his veins and heated his skin as he sipped from her.

"Ahem." The cleared throat had them separating, but instead of showing embarrassment, Cyn's cheeks dimpled as she smiled. "I'm sorry. Are we in your way?" She threw herself on Daryl, pressing him against the book stack. "There you go, plenty of room to go around. Or did you want to stay and watch?"

It wasn't the invitation to linger that intrigued him, but the hint they weren't done.

The older woman pressed her lips tight in disapproval. "Hussy." She flounced off with a sniff of disdain.

Cyn giggled. "Wow, talk about uptight. Then again, she is a cat."

"Hey!" he protested.

With another giggle, and no repentance, she moved away from him. A shame.

"Are you going to deny felines think they're better than everyone else?" she queried.

"Why would I deny the truth?" His turn to grin.

"Such a bad kitty." She shook her head, but smiled. "This town is a mish-mash of castes."

"The bayou is just one of those places where all kinds of life flourishes, but it is also every man, cat, canine, or reptile for himself."

"I've never run into so many different flavors of shifters. Actually, I've never been in a place where the humans are outnumbered."

"Really? Where did you grow up?"

"In Atlanta."

"I thought that was big lion country?" He couldn't help his disdain for the snobby fellows enamored with their manes.

"It is, but they allowed us to live there when my mom's family objected to her marrying Daddy."

Nothing could have stopped him from asking, "Why did they object?"

"He's a bear. A loner bear, with not even one sleuth to call his own. When he met my mom, he was renting a bedroom and all his stuff fit in a duffel bag. My grandparents apparently thought he was beneath them. They forbid them from dating."

"I take it that didn't go over well."

"My parents decided to risk it all and eloped. They never went back."

"Did she regret it?" An answer Daryl really wanted to know because his own parents had followed a similar path, except, in their case, Dad was the one from the well-to-do family. His mother was considered the trash from the wrong side of the tracks. The lack of amenities and the hardness of their life eventually led to his dad leaving.

"Regret?" She laughed. "Never."

"You were lucky."

"I guess. Why do I think your story doesn't have the same happy ending?"

"Let's just say my dad missed the benefits of money and prestige. We became an embarrassing mistake of his youth."

"I'm sorry."

"Don't be. My mother said, if he wasn't smart enough to know what a good thing he had, then we were better off without him."

"So you never see him?"

"Oh, every so often he'd pop in with his fancy car and expensive gifts. He stopped, though, after we gave him crabs."

"You infected your father with a disease?"

"Not those kinds of crabs." He rolled his eyes. "We filled his expensive BMW with real ones. Turns out they're rough on leather."

How he loved the sound of her laughter.

"So you have a sister?"

"Melanie. Yeah. She's married to Andrew, who runs Bittech Industries. They've got boys known as Terror 1 and Terror 2."

"I'm going to guess they take after you."

He adopted the most innocent expression he could. "Are you implying I'm bad?"

"Yes." She didn't even attempt to lie.

"You already know me so well, Cyn." And he wanted to know more about her, but as they'd talked, they'd reached the door to the microfiche room, to which he held the key. "It occurs to me that I never asked if your friend was a shifter."

"Aria is a bird. An eagle to be exact. But she's not bald."

He whistled. "An avian caste. We don't see many of those. I think Bitten Point currently has two that I know of. Used to be three, but one of them disappeared a few years back when we first spotted signs of trouble."

Cyn fingered the machine instead of him. Lucky hunk of metal. "And that's what we're looking for? News about old attacks? Shouldn't we be using the Internet?"

He slapped the microfiche box on the table. "Not if we want shifter news. Ol' Gary, who has to be close to a hundred, because tortoises tend to be long-lived, has been running a periodical for our kind for years now. Paper only. Limited copies. And much like some *Mission Impossible* episode, the copies are burned after being read. Except for..." He flourished his hand over the boxed film.

"And this is considered safer than having it scanned and uploaded to a Dropbox or closed online forum?" she grumbled as she pulled out the first strip and squinted at it.

"Not everyone trusts the Internet. Especially not with all those hackers who do their best to steal and dump info. The library is managed by our kind. Only a shifter can ask to see these."

"And what if a human accidentally gets their hands on them and tells the world?"

"Who's going to take this seriously?" he said, gesturing to the screen.

A picture of George Mercer, in his massive gator shape, lurking in the water, eyeballs peeking. The headline? *Bayou Hunters Target Gators and Crocs.* The gist of the article was how to play safe.

But not everything was a help piece. It talked about births, deaths —not all of them natural. Poachers were a worry for many of their kind.

Problem was, when someone disappeared, the reason wasn't always clear. Were they caught by a hunter? Did they run into trouble or find a bigger predator? Did they move on? Turn wild? Or was there something more nefarious at work?

With Cyn perched in a chair beside him, they fed the machine a page of film and scrolled through the images, each square a page from the periodical. They began with an issue starting a few years ago when the first batch of trouble cropped up.

Chili cook-off. Swamp Bite Races. Street sale. Mundane items that he quickly skipped through.

As soon as he finished one slide, Cyn had the next ready.

"This doesn't make sense," she muttered as she held a microfiche page in the air. She peered at it. "It looks like there're items missing."

"What do you mean missing? Maybe someone put the slides in out of order." He glanced over at her.

"You're misunderstanding." She pulled several microfiche sheets out and placed them in a row. Jabbing her finger at them she said, "Look." Each sheet had about twenty squares of film. The tops of them were labeled with the date the paper came out.

"The dates all line up. I don't see any missing."

"No, because the info they were trying to hide was wiped."

It was then he focused more on the individual film sheets and noted what she had. To be sure, he fed one into the machine. He quickly scrolled through the Bitten Point family picnic article. The garage sale with lots of baby stuff. Then a smear. The next page was fine. Then another smear and another. Then the rest of the paper, fine.

He swapped it for another, the week after. Same thing. Some of the film blocks were too damaged to see.

"It's like someone wiped them," Cyn said, jabbing at the screen. "You can see it used to be an image."

"Wiped on purpose, or was it an accident?"

"Well, it seems kind of suspicious. I mean, those are the dates you wanted to peek at, yet look." She pulled out some later ones, ones for the fall, after the first round of troubles died down. "See? These ones are completely intact. As are the early ones." She showed him a few of those, too. "But all of the ones over this two-month period have the wiped spots."

"It still could be an accident."

"If someone spilled something, it would smear across a few of them, not specific boxes. Someone got to these before us."

But who? The librarian seemed surprised when they told her what they'd found. According to her, no one had asked to see them recently, and they didn't keep a log.

"We need to find out what was in those missing spots," Daryl said as they left the library and emerged to mid-afternoon sunshine.

"But how can we find out? You said it yourself, the papers are destroyed."

"Unless you're a hoarder. Come on, I'm going to take you to meet Gary."

They needed answers, as more and more it looked as if a giant cover-up was in effect. Someone didn't want people digging or finding answers.

Too bad. This curious cat wasn't giving up.

Chapter 9

Cynthia: *So I'm on the trail of a major cover-up and could be in danger.*

Mom: *This better not be an excuse to skip Sunday dinner.*

THERE WERE times in a person's life when they met someone they just immediately felt connected to. Someone you trusted and couldn't get enough of.

Growing up, Cynthia had found Aria. They had that connection, but as they'd gotten older, they moved on to new opportunities—and discovered boys.

Cynthia went to vet school and found a career. Aria went through a series of odd jobs before her most recent departure on a quest to find out what she wanted in life.

Despite the fact that they led two completely different lives, when Aria went missing, Cynthia didn't hesitate to go looking for her and, in the process, found Daryl. A man with whom she felt a strengthening connection, especially now that she was pretty sure he was one of the good guys. He and his friends certainly seemed determined to dig at what happened in Bitten Point. They were doing things, investigating, just like real PIs.

She was pretty sure that was even cooler than being a kidnapping gangster. The less exciting part was realizing there could be danger.

"Daryl?" She said his name softly and waited for him to reply. He currently thumped his hands on the steering wheel to some classic AC/DC song.

"I love it when you say my name like that, Cyn. What's up, hot stuff?"

The man had the ability to make her heart go wild with just some huskily spoken words.

"Are we in danger?"

"What makes you ask?"

"Those things that attacked my motel room the other night, they could have killed us."

"Yes, but we prevailed."

But had they? "Those two creatures were kick ass. I mean, maybe you might have done all right with them, but let's admit it." She peeked down at her curves in their snug black yoga pants and her hip-length, cowl-necked, coral pink T-shirt. "This body was made for things other than fighting."

I don't know about that. I do like wrestling. Wrestling wasn't fighting if done naked.

"You were quick on your feet."

"I threw a pillow at it." And tried to play fetch with a dogman, but she didn't mention that failure. *Because it might have worked with a real stick.* She totally believed that.

"The sheer shock of that bought you a few seconds."

"If by shock you mean mocking. But seriously, the point I'm making is those things should have been able to take me out."

"You think they were trying to incapacitate us, not kill us."

"Yes and no. I think our visitor, dogman, was trying to kill us. He came in quiet and he went after us, but that lizard thing didn't."

"It smashed through the window. It fought me."

"You dove on it. You guys didn't fight long before dogman was back."

"Then it came after you."

A totally pee-her-pants moment, but even she had to admit, "It was coming after me slowly."

"So he likes to tease his prey. Not unusual for a predator. Sometimes we like to play with our food."

"You're a cocky guy."

"More than you can imagine, Cyn."

How he made her shiver when he said her name in that tone.

"So this guy we're going to see, he's a—"

Wham!

The impact of something big hitting the car rattled her entire body. The world fragmented into a loud crash. Screaming metal. Vivid cursing. Her head snapped to the side, and her breath whooshed from her.

Cynthia flailed her hands, not that it did a thing to help as their vehicle went screeching across pavement because something shoved them.

A glance to the side showed Daryl's jaw taut and his eyes intent. "Fuck! Hold on, honey. I'll get us out of this."

Exactly how was he planning to do anything?

Their car, shoved across the asphalt, hit the other side and then teetered along the ditch.

"Unbuckle," Daryl yelled over the noise.

"Why?"

"Unbuckle now," he shouted again.

As her fingers jumped to obey, the car tilted, enough that she could feel herself falling toward Daryl.

This wasn't good. With a click she barely heard over the crunching of metal, the seatbelt unclipped, and she lost that restraining strap. She barely had time to catch herself before the car went over almost completely. It hit the angle of the ditch on the other side, her window facing the sky.

A thump rocked the car, and it didn't take a genius to realize something had landed on the car, especially since, a moment later, a face leered at her through her unbroken window.

Crack. The window spiderwebbed as it was struck by a meaty fist.

She shrieked.

"Let me past you," Daryl demanded. He was crouched under her somehow, but with her wedged in the way, he was unable to stand or go any further.

"You want the psycho outside, you take him." To those who said she was chicken, she said try smart. Strength came from making the right decision. Foolish pride had no place here, so she let the person most capable take care of the situation.

Someone shattering the window and shoving a hand in with a gun? *More of a Daryl problem,* she thought from her spot in the back. She'd managed a quick wiggle and just in time, too, because, when that fist holding the gun dropped in through the broken window, Daryl lunged and yanked.

She preferred to not think what the cracking sound meant. Still, it didn't stop her wince at the bellow of a man in pain, a man pissed and wanting to do very vile things to Daryl.

I don't think many of his ideas are physically possible.

Undaunted by the promise of pain, Daryl laughed as the arm was withdrawn. "I'd like to see you try."

With those daring words, Daryl gripped the side of the window and, limber as a gymnast, lifted himself through.

Dude had some serious muscle.

Alone, she had to decide what to do. Only a coward would stay inside the car, and much as it appealed to hide, she had to do something.

She grabbed the front seats and poked her head through, only to squeak and yank back as a body fell atop the broken passenger side window. The head of a stranger, the hair short and almost platinum, dangled, blocking her escape...at least from the front. Here in the back, she had other options, and she rapidly took stock of them

She stood in the back, her feet on the window of the other door. She had access to a door, but she already knew if she tried to open it, gravity would work against her. Not to mention if there was another guy atop there, and he stood on it, she'd never get it open enough. But that wasn't the only way out.

I have to break this window. But how? She had no weapon, and her shoes were floppy.

But your fist is solid.

Her wolf recoiled. Ow.

Yeah, ow, but she couldn't stay in here when she could hear something happening outside.

She pulled back her fist, and her wolf snapped in her head, *Wrap it first.*

Protect it. She didn't think twice of yanking off her shirt. She wore the bra she'd salvaged from her previous outfit and yoga pants.

The fabric of her top wound around her knuckles. She pulled back and let loose, and lost her balance as her fist hit nothing.

"Eep," she squeaked, falling face first into the seat. Better than gravel. She peered at the open doorway.

Daryl stood framed in it with his feet braced on the car's body. He let out a low whistle. "Is that for me?"

A shy girl might have crossed her arms over her boobs. A saucy one would push her breasts out.

A smart woman would hold up her arms and say, "Get me out of here. I smell gas."

A stream of curse words left Daryl's lips as he reached in to grab her wrists. He yanked her from the wreck just as they both registered the sound of screeching tires.

Standing on top of the wrecked car, she had a moment to see a black SUV scream to a stop. A body limped to it and opened the rear passenger door. The driver's window lowered, but the angle of the sun made it impossible to see inside.

Click. Flicker. A flame danced atop the lighter held in the other vehicle's window.

Surely they wouldn't dare toss it. After all, their groaning comrade was on the wreck with them.

The flame on the butane lighter didn't waver, the lit wick able to handle a little toss, a perfectly arched throw that her eyes tracked to where it landed in the bed of the pickup truck pinning them in the ditch. A pickup truck loaded with barrels of fertilizer.

Uh-oh.

Before Cynthia could scream, she was hurtling off the car, mostly because Daryl was yanking her. The landing on the ground proved jarring, but that wasn't what made her whoosh her breath. Daryl landed atop her, covering her with his body.

But the worst had yet to come.

Boom!

The world exploded.

Chapter 10

Daryl's borrowed T-shirt from Constantine: *"I heart Chihuahuas."*

IF DARYL IGNORED the T-shirt that he'd borrowed from Constantine to replace his shredded one, Daryl wasn't doing all that bad.

The ringing in his ears from the explosion had mostly stopped. The singed hair would grow back. Cyn was spared it all because he'd shielded her, and he'd lost his T-shirt only because they needed it to stop the blood.

He'd not emerged unscathed from the incident.

When he'd first rolled off Cyn, the intense heat and smoke making him hack—and, no, he did not need any hairball remedies—he'd known some shrapnel from the exploded car and truck had hit him.

However, he was less worried about that than the inferno only yards away. The intense flames and billowing smoke saw him reaching down to drag Cyn to her feet and limp off into the farmer's field. They crushed the burgeoning stalks in their stagger until Daryl deemed them far enough to take a break.

He dropped to a crouch, facing back where they came, while Cyn sank down beside him.

"Are we safe here?" she asked.

Boom. The explosion shook the ground, but nothing rained down on them.

"I'd say yes so long as the fire doesn't start moving our way."

Given the direction of the breeze, it seemed unlikely, but with one of mother nature's deadly weapons, you never knew.

He spotted her shivering as shock set in.

"Those people were trying to kill us."

"Yes, and might not be done trying, so try and stay low. I don't know how well they can see through all that smoke, but I'd rather not let them know right yet that we made it out alive."

"You think they'll try again?" She practically squeaked the words.

He hoped not because, given their recent hardcore attempt, he might not be enough to keep Cyn safe.

A smart guy knew when he needed allies. He yanked his phone from his pocket and hit speed dial. Wes answered on the first ring.

"What is it?" Wes snapped. "I was kind of busy."

Daryl kept it to the point. "Attacked on fourteenth line just past the giant culvert. Call the fire department. And I'm gonna need a first aid kit."

"Are you all right?" Wes said in one ear while Cyn muttered, "I don't need any Band- Aids."

"A few bruises and cuts, no biggie."

"Daryl! What is sticking out of your back?" Cyn's shriek made his features pull, mostly because Wes snickered.

"See you in a few. Hope you survive."

That was in question and not because of his shrapnel hit, but because Cyn's shrieking panic might lead the killers to them.

"Why didn't you say something?"

"It's no big deal."

She gaped at him. "No big deal? There's a chunk of metal sticking out of your back."

"That might explain why it hurts a little. Pull it out, would you, and press your hands on it. It will slow down the flow of blood."

"Are you insane?"

"Impaled. They don't sound anything alike."

"I can't believe you want me to yank that thing out. You need a hospital."

"Why, when I have a vet?"

"Being a vet doesn't mean I know how to fix you in this shape." She gestured to his body.

"I'll admit there's only one long and hard shape I really want you to fix, but if that's going to happen, then first, you need to pull this piece of metal out of me. It smarts."

"Smarts?"

"Hurts like fucking hell. Now would you pull it?"

As she'd antagonized him, she'd actually been checking out the wound. He wondered if she was doing it on purpose to distract him. Did she think he was a pussy?

Nothing wrong with a majestic cat, his panther sniffed.

"Good news. The chunk isn't thick. Think sheet metal rather than spiked. And I don't think it went too deep."

He wondered if she was biting that lower lip as she gently palpated his skin. "Pull it."

"Should I count?" she asked.

"Pull it."

"Are you sure? I mean, what if—" Yank, and then another tug.

He bellowed as fabric jammed against him. "What the hell?"

"I pulled it out like you wanted."

"You could have warned me."

"I thought you didn't want me to count."

"That was before I knew you were yanking out two pieces."

"Don't be such a baby."

Was she chiding him? "I'm not crying."

"Whining is just as unattractive."

"I don't whine," he sulked.

"Sure you don't," she teased, kneeling by his side. It was then he truly noted what she wore. Or didn't.

The bra could barely contain those ripe peaches. Those pants hugged her curves.

I wanna hug those curves. And lick 'em.

An open field was maybe not the ideal seduction spot, but a man took what he had. Of course, it helped if she saw things his way.

"I don't suppose you're into kissing booboos better?" he inquired with a hopeful lilt.

"Daryl! This isn't the time or place."

"Does that mean that's a yes for somewhere else?"

"No. I mean, maybe. I mean—we're over here!" she shouted over his shoulder, having spotted the tall strides of Wes.

And there went their alone moment. It became an hour or more of sirens, along with people in official uniforms with questions. More questions. During that time, he acquired a new T-shirt and Cyn's boobs were covered—in another man's shirt. Another male's scent.

Grrr.

No amount of rubbing himself against Cyn could erase Wes's scent from it, and the jerk knew it by his smirk.

As to their story for the authorities?

Chalked down to an unfortunate accident. The pickup truck came out of the side road, not seeing them, and plowed into their vehicle. The burnt body found wedged through the window of the car was written off as a Good Samaritan thinking they were still in there and coming to their aid.

The fact that the same Good Samaritan had a gun was glossed over. Just like the fact that Daryl was injured didn't make it onto the report.

If no one human knew about his injuries, then in a few days, when he was healed, no one would take note.

As the chaos died down, he and Cyn leaned against Wes's well-kept Bronco. A fireman in yellow pants held by suspenders and wearing a heavy jacket strode toward them, pulling his helmet off as he approached.

Constantine tossed his hat onto the fire truck before continuing their way, unsnapping his jacket as he came. "Fucking thing is hot."

"But keeps your skin baby soft," Wes snorted. "What's the word on the fire?"

"Officially, the guy driving the pickup, high on fumes from the leaking fertilizer in his truck, slammed into your car and took you into the ditch. Not realizing you were gone, he was checking inside your car when the plant shit ignited, kaboom."

"And, unofficially, we just learned that there is a connection between what happened a few years ago and now." Because there was no denying a correlation now. Too many coincidences meant something was fishy.

"I don't get what they're worried about us finding. I mean, they seemed to wipe their tracks pretty good." Cyn's two cents.

"Good or not, they were worried enough to send some guys to take us out." It still chilled Daryl to know how close Cyn had come to peril.

"If it's intentional, then doesn't that mean they knew where we were going?" Cyn pointed out. "And if they were that determined to stop us, what about that Gary we were on our way to see?

A sudden silence descended, broken by the abrupt crackle on a police scanner.

"Code 10-80. 139 Weeping Willow Lane."

"Isn't that Gary's house?" Wes asked.

Indeed it was Gary's house, on fire, with Gary in it. The old man lived, but only because he managed to crawl outside, where he passed out on the grass.

An ambulance had taken him away to the town's clinic. His age made his injuries grievous, but the stubborn coot would survive. He was too tough not to.

Gary's house, unfortunately, didn't fare so well. Amazing how an old home, with original timber frame and siding, filled with books and magazines and newspapers, burned. It burned to the ground. Not a shred of paper left. Ashes for clues and a dead end in their investigation.

With it being close to happy hour, they hit a bar where they figured there was little chance of being questioned. The only place in town where everyone minded their business. The Itty Bitty.

Of course, Cynthia didn't see the logic in their choice. She stood in shock, eyes wide as she took in the sights, before exclaiming, "You brought me to a titty bar?"

Chapter 11

Cynthia: *So I went to my very first strip joint and am thinking of trying pole dancing.*

Mom: *I hear that's how all the super models keep their figures trim.*

Cynthia: *Men threw money at me.*

Mom: *I hope you invested it into a 401. It's never too early to start.*

PERHAPS SHOUTING titty bar wasn't the best thing to do when surrounded by scantily-clad women who turned an evil eye their way.

Daryl brought his lips to her ear. "Careful, Cyn. It's just a bar like any other."

"With women who take off their clothes for a few bucks," she hissed back.

"A few bucks?" Wes snorted over his shoulder as he led the way, wending his way through the tables. "I've spent way too much of my paychecks here. Hell, I've probably singlehandedly put a bunch of the dancers through college."

"Me, too," Daryl added. At Cyn's dark look, he smirked. "Just doing my best to support my community."

Surely it wasn't jealousy making her dig her nails into her palms? "Isn't there another tavern in town? One that serves food?"

"The Itty Bitty has food, too."

"Is any of it not made in a deep fryer?" she queried.

The guys exchanged a look. "I think the peanuts aren't."

In other words, nothing healthy after the day she'd had. Perfect. "I'm in." She was starved. She felt herself shrinking...*shrinking*... She needed food. Stat!

Her revival began with a nice iced tea—touched with a little something extra—served by none other than Renny.

"You work here?" Cynthia couldn't help but blurt out.

"Tuesday through Friday until supper time. The money's decent and the tips are amazing."

"Beyond amazing," Caleb grumbled as he slid an arm around his woman and laid a kiss on her tilted lips. "Much as I might have initially disliked it, the fact is it's a decent place to work. They treat the girls here a hell of a lot better than other places."

"That's because Bobby knows happy dancers means happy clients, and happy clients keep coming back for overpriced beer."

"I come for the beer-battered onion rings," Daryl admitted as he took a seat against the wall then growled at Wes when he would have taken the other. Daryl shot Cyn a look and patted the seat beside him.

Wes and Caleb took a seat on either side while Renny leaned a hip against the end of the table.

"So what the heck happened?" Renny asked. "You guys look and smell awful."

"Car crash."

"Attempted murder."

"Trouble."

The various blurted answers all pointed to the last.

"I'm going to go out on a limb here," Wes announced, "and say that the SHC knows we're still looking into what happened."

"You think they're the ones that came after us today?" Cynthia squeaked.

"They wouldn't have resorted to hired thugs. Why would they do something so messy when they would have just sent the SHC Private Guard to pick us up?"

"Wes is right. They wouldn't have to be subtle. If they claimed we were imperiling our secret, they could have just snagged us. No, whoever came after us today was looking to make a statement."

"A pretty fucking loud one," Caleb rumbled.

"An attempt that failed, raising the question, will they try again? After all, they now know we're digging into the past. Or were. With Gary's house destroyed and the microfiche useless, have they eliminated all the sources we can search? If they have wiped all evidence, do we have to worry about them coming after us again?"

"Are we sure they eliminated everything?" As eyes zeroed in on Cynthia, she explained. "So far we've been looking for written-down accounts. Internet searches. Police reports. Reported news. You are all assuming that something was written down. But what if people were threatened back then, too? Told to keep their mouths shut?"

"Then there wouldn't be a record," Caleb said slowly. "However, the people would still know, even if they've kept silent all this time."

"If we find them and talk to them, let them know there's other people involved now, maybe they'll tell us what they saw or know."

"One big problem," Wes interjected. "How do we figure out who knows what?"

That was a problem none of them had a solution to. And they were still pondering it when the food began to arrive, served by a buxom blonde in pigtails, wearing a skirt that might have once been a bandeau in another life and a bikini top that was environmentally friendly with its lack of fabric.

Cynthia disliked her instantly, and it had nothing to do with the fact that the overly exposed woman flashed her hussy smile at Daryl and squealed. "Sweetie, it's been a few days since I saw you. I thought you'd forgotten all about me."

"Of course he did because I'm his favorite barmaid now," announced a freckled redhead with a big round tray bearing drinks and wearing tiny shorts that were smaller than most of Cynthia's underwear.

The gong show part occurred when the third and fourth woman appeared at their table to wave and giggle at Daryl while exclaiming they were his favorite.

"You're not just a bad kitty. You're a tom kitty," Cynthia exclaimed. "You're a regular here."

"Because of the employee discount," Daryl explained.

"You don't work here, do you? Don't tell me you're a stripper?" The idea shocked and titillated. She'd never gone to see any male strippers before, but if Daryl was the one taking it off...

"The only stripping I do is in private—"

"Or drunk," Caleb volunteered.

"Renny's the one letting me use her discount on the food. Their rings really are yummy. Try one." Daryl shoved the crispy tidbit at her lips, and it was automatic to open them and take a bite.

Crunch. Salty, and sweet and... "Those are freaking good." She snatched the rest of the onion ring from his hand and popped it in her mouth then took a sip of her beer.

Perhaps there was merit in coming for the food, but the flash of boobs on the stage as different girls came out every few songs proved distracting. To his credit, Daryl didn't seem to pay attention. None of the guys did.

On the contrary, Daryl showed he was most aware of her presence by the hand he laid heavily on her thigh, his occasional squeeze and gentle rub keeping her in a constant state of awareness.

Still, though, the man brought her to a strip joint. That didn't exactly scream romantic to her.

And is that what you want? Romance?

What she wanted was for those tarts to stop parading their half-naked bodies by their table and blowing kisses. It made her a touch irritable, so she let the object of her ire feel it.

"You know this whole search thing wouldn't be so complicated if you'd managed to snag one of those things the other night," she accused, noticing that her first beer seemed to have been replaced with a fresh one. She gulped another sip, the liquid courage warming her.

"What can I say? Those monsters got away."

"And you didn't go after them." She shook her head.

"Of course I didn't. I stayed with you to make sure you were alright."

"You lost our only lead." A tiny part of her felt naughty for baiting him, but just then, another perky pair went bouncing by.

Daryl didn't seem to notice. He stared at Cynthia—the winner with clothes on! "Did you escape a mental institution?

"No."

"Are you taking any drugs? Were you dropped on your head as a child?"

"No and no. Why?"

"Because only an idiot would give me shit for sticking around to take care of an unconscious woman who was just attacked."

Caleb groaned as he leaned over. "Dude. You did not just go there. Stop now."

"Stop what, poking holes in her craziness?"

She straightened after guzzling the last of her beer. "I'm not crazy. Just impulsive."

"Impulsive means you do wild, spontaneous things. Crazy means you're not firing all your mental cylinders."

"I am too impulsive."

"Really?" Daryl's eyes glinted with challenge. "Prove it. I dare you. Let's see how impulsive and sinful you really are."

"You can't just put me on the spot like that," she sputtered.

"A truly impulsive girl wouldn't have a problem."

"You want proof?" Cynthia shoved her chair back and stood. "I'm going to go on that stage and shake my booty. Is that impulsive enough?"

He leaned back in his seat and crossed his arms. "Go right ahead."

"I will." She didn't move.

He smirked. "I knew you wouldn't do it."

"It occurs to me that your dare is probably meant to distract me from the fact you screwed up and let those two thugs go free."

"I did not screw up. I was taking care of you."

"Sure you were."

The sound he let loose reminded her of the frustrated one she'd managed to get her parents to utter more than a few times.

She tried the trick that worked on her daddy. She batted her eyelashes.

"Got something in your eye?"

"Nope, but I'll give you something to eyeball," she muttered.

Welcome to logical plan number...okay, she didn't keep count, but she knew there was a good reason why she was marching for that stage—other than the beer circulating in her system—and crawling onto the platform because it didn't have any stairs she could see.

The stage was in between acts, but music still blasted, a certain recent song coming to an end leading into another one, a retro one that was rather dirty.

So dirty.

So perfect.

And not as scary as expected. Now that Cynthia stood in the spotlight, she couldn't see the crowd or the tables, just vague shadows, not that she looked for long. Cynthia always danced with her eyes closed. Gaze shuttered, arms held out to her sides, and hips rolling, she began to dance as she let the beat of "Touch Me" by Samantha Fox thrum through her body.

Her shoulders moved, rolling into her torso then down to her waist. Her ass jiggled too. This wasn't so hard.

Until someone reminded her where she was. "Take it off!"

Strip? Someone actually wanted her to strip?

Isn't that why we're up here?

Take it off. A body was a beautiful and natural thing. It wasn't something she tended to show off, but with her inhibitions lowered and her skin prickling with awareness—because Daryl watched—she found the hem to her shirt and pulled it over her head.

It got caught for a second on her messy bun of hair, but not for long.

With a triumphant grin, she whirled it around her head and let it loose.

Someone caught it because she heard someone exclaim, "Smells smoky."

Yeah, because I'm on fire. And not literally this time unlike the incident with the barbecue.

Her hips undulated, along with her arms, in a body wave that brought whistles from the audience.

Funny how being the object of attention could prove flattering, but not as flattering as the man who'd pushed his way to the edge of the stage.

Daryl's gaze smoldered with heat. She shook her hips and waggled her shoulders and felt a spurt of triumph—oh, yes, and heat—when a tic formed by his eye. He liked what he watched.

He wanted...

She wanted, too. Cynthia dropped to the floor and crawled to him, knowing her breasts hung heavy in her bra. The tips of them ached they'd drawn so tight. She stopped mere inches from the edge, less than a foot between her and Daryl. She could practically see the electric awareness sparking between them. She smiled and arched as she threw her head back, exposing the smooth column of her neck to him. Open invitation.

"Get down," he growled, or did she just read his lips? Did it matter? His intent was clear. He wanted her to get down? Her smile curled into something utterly wicked and mischievous as she obliged, dipping her hips to the stage and then letting a wave of sensual motion roll through her body, projecting her breasts outward. The erect nubs of her nipples poking through the fabric of her bra led the way.

The tic became more pronounced as his lips went into a straight line, but she knew it was only partly in anger. She had only to peek below his waist to see he was affected in another way.

He wants me. Much as he might blow hot and cold, that one fact remained.

But what would it take to make him finally break?

Let's find out. She pressed herself against the stage again, her hips flush with the floor, and she licked her lips as she moved in time to the music.

It was utterly decadent. Even if she still wore her yoga pants and her brassiere, she was moving in ways that left nothing to the imagination.

But some people needed visual help, hence the yelled, "Take off your top. Let's see those titties!" The request came with a shower of bills, a green paper rainfall that managed to break the intense stare between her and Daryl. It disintegrated the erotic spell they were under.

Before she could react to the request, the money, and the sudden realization of what she was doing—*in public!*—Daryl turned and grabbed the guy who'd suggested she strip further. Her very irate seeming kitty held the bulky man off the ground, and she could only watch in shock as Daryl's fist met the guy's face with a snarled, "Don't talk to my woman that way."

My woman. Did he just say that? Had he just defended her honor? Swoon because she'd never seen or heard anything hotter in her life.

Chapter 12

Daryl's other bumper sticker: *"Get a little closer. My fist wants to talk to your face."*

HE HAD NEVER SEEN anything hotter than Cyn on that stage, and while Daryl would have enjoyed watching more of her sensual tease, the whole punching a patron in the face didn't go over well with management, even if he was a good tipper.

With a little protest—*"Buddy was totally asking for it."*—Daryl was escorted from the premises, but he didn't fight his ejection because, to his relief, Cynthia was right behind him.

With a pat on his back, Bruno, Itty Bitty's bouncer, told him to, "Stay out of trouble and see you in a few days."

Stay out of trouble? Where was the fun in that? And speaking of trouble, what was Cynthia thinking when she got on that stage and titillated those pervs?

You dared her, his panther reminded.

Maybe, but he never expected her to do it. Never expected the ridiculous heat that came from watching her.

Fuck, when she'd stripped off that shirt, he'd practically leaped across the room to toss a tablecloth at her. Only by the thinnest thread of control did he walk, not run, to the stage, and once there, he got caught in her mesmerizing erotic web.

A woman with smoke streaks on her face, her hair in a messy and wild bun, looking as if she'd escaped an apocalypse, shouldn't have ignited every single atom in his body. None of that mattered. He just about combusted. He almost dragged her off that stage so he could toss her over a shoulder and take off with her somewhere. Anywhere. He wanted, make that needed, to touch her.

Needed. Her. *Mine.*

"Are you okay?" Her soft query startled him from his pensive thoughts, and he whirled to face her, only to teeter as he caught sight of her shirtless, wearing only a bra. It was enough to make him want to yowl at the sky and then curse. "Bloody fucking hell. Where's your top?"

She shrugged. "I don't know. Somebody in the crowd caught it."

Way to remind him that someone else had it and was probably doing unmentionable things to the shirt. Wes's shirt, snicker.

"Put this on." He went to pull off his own shirt, but she put a hand on his arm.

"Don't be ridiculous. I'm perfectly fine with what I'm wearing. Heck, I've got a bikini top with less material than this."

She did? *Drooling is not acceptable.* Cats did not slobber like a common beast. They took action. Just one problem. There weren't many actions he could take in a freaking parking lot, in which none of the vehicles belonged to him.

"We have to get out of here, but we don't have any wheels," Daryl grumbled.

"No shit, Sherlock. It's your lucky day, though, because I've got you covered," said Wes, who stepped out of the bar and immediately lit a cigarette. A new habit? And not one often seen with shifters who, like most animals, had a healthy dislike of flames and a respect for their body. But who cared if Wes was a smoky gator? He tossed Daryl his keys. "Take my truck since your car is wrecked. I'll catch a ride with my cousin, Bruno." The same bouncer who had just escorted Daryl out.

Daryl caught the keys. "Thanks, dude. Are we going to meet up in the morning and plan our next move?" Because, despite the attack today, they couldn't give up. As a matter of fact, the deadly actions served only to demonstrate they needed to get to the bottom of what was happening in Bitten Point.

Wes took a long drag and shook his head. With smoke curling from his nostrils, he said, "I gotta go into work so you'll have to go it mostly alone. But I'll have my phone on me, so call if you and Cynthia find anything."

"Will do." Those were the last words said for a while. In silence, Daryl and Cyn got into the truck, the rumble of the motor and the static-laden western song crooning from the stereo the only sounds. He eased them out of the parking lot, driving on autopilot, the only thing he was capable of at the moment.

Today, they'd faced death, a mind-blowing deal on its own, but that wasn't what had him so fucking frazzled.

Blood simmered through his veins. Arousal heated every inch of him. The evil cause sat beside him, her hands primly folded in her lap.

As if anything about her was prim. She'd disproven that a short time ago when she practically dry humped that stage.

How wrong was it to be jealous of that worn platform?

Cyn was the first to break the silence. "Hey, if I need to stick around Bitten Point for a while, I'll have to make some cash. Think the owner of the Itty Bitty would let me do a few shifts here and there?"

"No."

"Why not? I thought I did pretty good."

She did. Much too well. "You are not working there." He growled the command.

"Why not? It's a good place to make money. Renny says the management is great with the staff."

He knew he shouldn't say it, but that didn't stop him. "You are not taking clothes off for strange men."

"Why not?"

He swerved to the side of the road, slamming the truck into park so he could face her. "Why not? Because you are only taking them off for me."

Who said that? Since when did he care if a woman stripped for a living? Since when did he demand exclusivity?

Since I met Cyn.

Seeing her lips—those lusciously teasing lips—parting in rebuttal, he did the only sure thing to keep her quiet. He kissed her.

Kissed her with the passion that she inspired with just a tilt of her lips.

Embraced her with the fervor of a man pushed to the edge.

He claimed that mouth as his and his alone, and knew she'd succumbed when she uttered the softest mewl of pleasure and wrapped her arms around his neck.

The front seat of a truck wasn't the best place to make out. Daryl didn't care. He wasn't about to stop, not when he had Cyn right where he wanted her, in his arms.

A sinuous slide of his tongue was met by the sweeter touch of hers. He sucked at it as his hands roamed her bare skin, impeded only by the strap of her bra.

What strap? Deft fingers unhooked it, and it was simple enough to peel the offending material from her.

Her head tilted back as his lips moved in a slow glide down her taut neck. He paused over the flutter of her pulse. Rapid. Erratic. Excited. All of her was excited. The heat of her skin and the musky scent of her arousal said so.

He let his lips trail over the roundness of her breast, nipping and tasting the skin before reaching his goal.

One puckered berry. Yum.

"Daryl!" She gasped his name as he clamped his mouth over that tempting tip, inhaling it into his mouth and then sucking it, each tug making her cry out and dig her fingers deeper into him.

How her erotic response spurred him on. His erection was a throbbing ache in his pants, but he couldn't stop. *Wouldn't* stop.

He lavished attention on her other nipple, savoring the feel of it in his mouth, loving how heavy her full breasts felt cupped in his hands. He squeezed them, pushing them together so he could rapidly flick his tongue between her erect nubs.

She panted. She moaned. She even squirmed in her seat. But that wasn't enough for this curious cat. He wanted her screaming *his* name as she came on his fingers.

"Lean back against the window."

Already half turned, she complied, and for once, she didn't ask questions, just leaned against the fogged glass, her eyes shuttered, her lips ripe from kissing.

Naughty thing that she was, she cupped her breasts, even brushed a thumb over the moist peaks.

Tempting. So tempting, but he had another goal. He worked her yoga pants down, enjoying how she wiggled her hips and lifted her ass so he could pull them off enough to bare her teeny tiny panties to him. And he meant tiny.

"If I'd known you were hiding those under there..." he growled.

"What would you have done?" she asked in a voice husky with desire.

"This." He leaned down and tugged at the only thing keeping him from tasting her. The fabric stretched as he tugged, making their removal with teeth impossible. And unacceptable.

He felt no qualms about tearing the offending things from her. She was bared to him.

Much better.

Despite the cramped front seat, and the console in the way, he still leaned over to bury his face between her thighs. He nuzzled her exposed mound, humming against it, the vibration making her gasp as she clutched at his hair. Her hips wiggled, but she couldn't really spread them. Her pants, while lowered, still kept her legs tethered, giving him only a few scant inches to work with.

He'd manage. His tongue found her clitoris, already swollen. He gave it a test lick then delved farther and found the lips of her sex slick with cream.

Yum.

He lapped at her as best he could, but the space was tight, just like she was tight, he noted when he let his tongue return to her clit so his fingers could take its place.

He slid one into the heat that was all Cyn. All wet. So wonderful.

As he flicked his tongue against her pleasure button, he slipped a second finger into her, feeling the walls of her sex squeeze and pulse around them.

Tight. Oh so fucking tight.

He pumped her with his fingers as he licked and nibbled, loving how her nails dug into his scalp and she uttered soft cries. Faster he worked her, loving her erratic heart rate, heated skin, and gyrating body.

When her climax hit, she screamed his name. "Daryl!" Oh yeah! And still he kept thrusting and licking, addicted to the feel of her quivering on his fingers.

The scent of her surrounded him and drove him a little crazy. It was the only thing to explain what happened next, and no, he wasn't talking about the embarrassing fact that he almost came in his pants like some fucking virgin. He meant the other thing he did.

The bite. The mating bite. Oh hell.

Chapter 13

Cynthia: *So, Mom, a guy bit me today while we were making out. Mom? Mom? Are you listening? I said Daryl left teeth marks on me.*

Mom: *Sorry, baby girl. Just sending in the engagement notice to the local paper.*

HE BIT ME!

Now, in the normal human world, biting happened. It was a passion-induced thing or a turn-on. In the shifter world, nibbling happened, like hello, tons of carnivores here; however, there was biting, and then there was *the bite.* Some called it the claiming mark or the mating bite. Whatever a person labeled it, this one was different. For one, it broke skin, and two, a true bite bonded a pair together.

She might have wondered at that if it hadn't happened to her, the sink of his teeth into her skin triggering a second orgasm, sending her to cloud a gazillion. It was the most amazing thing she'd ever experienced, so it took her a moment to come back down and realize that

Daryl was plastered against his side of the truck, looking as if he'd stuck his finger in a socket.

She would know the look. She'd done it once before, on purpose, too. Not being very old at the time, she'd wanted to see if she could become electric enough to light a bulb. She didn't, and her hair had never been the same since.

This bite was kind of having the same effect. For all intents and purposes, Cynthia hadn't changed, and yet at the same time, it felt as if everything about her had tilted.

Something in her world had shifted, and it was all his fault.

Coming down from an orgasmic high was never easy, but the headlights illuminating the cab of the truck as a vehicle pulled in behind them did help.

Daryl craned and squinted. "Shit, it's the cops. Probably checking to see why we're parked."

The why was obvious, one only had to note the steamy windows to know they were making out.

Cyn giggled. "Think we'll get a ticket for indecent exposure?" She truly was embarking on a life of crime since coming to this town.

"We won't be getting a ticket because you're going to put this on." This being his T-shirt.

She might have said no, but she had no idea where her bra was, and since she heard a door on the police car behind them slam shut, that meant they were about to have company.

Despite her short-lived stage dance, and her random query to Daryl, Cynthia wasn't too sure she was ready to embark on a life that involved showing off her naked booty—although she did enjoy Daryl's jealousy at the thought.

Quickly, she pulled the warm T-shirt over her head and tucked it over her breasts. Shiver. Even the light brush of fabric was too much against nipples, still so sensitive from his oral play. Top part covered, she also wiggled her pants back over her hips and butt, the moistness of her sex soaking the fabric. But she was covered and just in time, too, as a *tap, tap, tap*, came at the window.

Daryl rolled down the window and adopted a casual mien. "Hello, Chet. Nice evening."

"Everything all right?"

"Never better." Even she heard the false brightness in Daryl's tone.

Freckled arms leaned against the window, and a deputy's face, his green eyes dancing, peeked in. "Evening, ma'am. I take it that things are fine with you, too?"

"Yes. Not all of us are big pussies when it comes to certain things." She felt no qualms about the jab. If Daryl was going to act as if he'd committed some unbearable act, then she would totally rub his whiskered face in it.

"You might want to take your *discussion*"—small cough—"somewhere else. It's not safe to be out and about these nights. There are things roaming."

Those words caught Daryl's attention enough to partially snap him from his glowering stupor. "What things? Have you seen something?"

Chet's fingers gripped the window, and he peered down, as if trying to decide what to say. It took him a few moments, but he raised his gaze again. "I'll deny it if anyone asks, but I know you and the lady were attacked, twice now by the sounds of it, so it's not like it's a secret. Stuff has been happening around town. Homes broken into. Women and children scared by what they claim are monsters."

"No men are reporting anything?" Cynthia interjected.

Chet shook his head. "Not that I know of."

"But that means nothing. Guys aren't as likely to run to the cops and tell them that a swamp monster scared them." Daryl shrugged and grinned. "It's a man card rule."

The deputy laughed. "My wife says it's our stupid gene."

Cynthia couldn't help but retort, "She might be right." And when Daryl protested with a "Hey," she stuck out her tongue.

"But seriously, while we've not gotten reports about anyone going missing, there's definitely something out there stalking and scaring folks."

"And taking people," Cynthia added.

"Who?" the deputy queried.

"Aria's missing."

At Chet's blank look, Daryl and Cynthia filled him in, but by the end of it, he was shaking his head. "Never even heard wind of your missing friend."

"I never technically filed a report."

"Still, though, one of our own kind comes to Bitten Point and goes missing, that should have been noticed. Where was she staying?"

At that, Cynthia blinked. "I don't know. She never actually said."

"You might want to see if you can find out if she was staying at a motel in town or if she was camping. And what about her car? Didn't you say she was driving?"

As Chet listed some things they should try and figure out, Cynthia was struck with one question that they'd forgotten to ask. "If you know all this stuff is happening, then why doesn't the town? Why isn't there a warning being issued to keep people safe?"

A grimace creased the deputy's features. "That is one of the things that's bugging a few of us. We've been nagging the sheriff to put out an announcement, even if it's a red herring one to watch for the wild dog and giant gator in the bayou. But we've been told to keep our mouths shut."

"Did the sheriff say why? Or who ordered it?"

"All he'd say was it came from above him, and that, if we didn't want trouble, we'd listen." Chet blew out a breath. "But shit, I mean, if something is coming after the folks in town, people I know... It ain't right."

No, it wasn't right, and the deputy gave them lots to think about, which might have explained Daryl's silence as they drove away. Yet the tension emanating from him was born of more than worry about the situation happening.

I think he's still disturbed by what happened, even though it was totally his fault. He seduced me. And now he clenched the wheel of the truck and stared straight ahead.

Ignore me, will he?

Not likely. He was the one who made her girl parts tingle, who made her see stars, and who'd bitten her. He'd done it, and now he thought to pretend she wasn't there? Well, two could play that game —and play it better.

When Daryl pulled the Bronco into a spot in the alley behind his place, she didn't wait for him before flouncing from the truck.

"Slow down," he snapped as she bounced up the fire escape steps, the same way they'd exited earlier.

"Make me," she sassed.

"Cyn!" He growled the words and then, a second later, cursed.

She wondered why until she breathed in. Weird dinoman smell permeated the air. She froze on the stairs and held her breath as her wolf perked its head and took a whiff.

Above us. The creature waited for them.

She didn't protest when Daryl squeezed past her. Let him face the threat first. She crept behind him, scared, but determined to have his back. Although she wasn't sure what she'd fight with. It wasn't as if her wolf would want to come out and give her a paw.

We can't let him see.

Her wolf didn't like anyone to see. Her mother and father could claim her deformity wasn't a big deal all they wanted, but it was a big deal to Cynthia's wolf. Apparently, her furry side was afraid Daryl would turn from them if he knew.

It's not something we should be ashamed of. Yet, no matter how many times Cynthia tried to reassure, her wolf was too self-conscious.

They couldn't hide their ascent on the stairs, the metal creaking with every step. They reached the metal grate landing for his floor, only the third thank goodness. To her surprise, Daryl didn't stop at his window but kept going up, two more floors, right to the parapet of the roof itself.

More slowly, she followed, partially because that was a lot of damned stairs, but also so she could assess what was happening instead of rushing in. She stayed crouched out of sight, watching as Daryl clambered over the lip of the roof and then strode to the middle of the building. How unafraid he seemed, standing there in just pants and his flip-flops. The muscles of his back were barely visible even without his shirt, the scattered clouds hiding most of the starlight from the sky.

She might have questioned what he saw. After all, the roof appeared deserted, yet, the smell lingered.

"Show yourself. I know you're here," Daryl boldly dared it.

For a moment, nothing happened, and then, as if stepping from the shadows themselves, a figure lumbered out into the open, not close, just enough for them to recognize the towering shape, the tips of wings tucked behind, along with the oddly human and somehow alien shape of the creature.

"If it isn't dinoman. Did you come back for round two?" Daryl rolled his shoulders and cricked his neck, limbering his body.

"Sssstupid cat," the thing hissed. "You are no match for me."

"I don't know. Why not put on your human face and we'll go at it the old-fashioned way."

"I can't."

Not "I won't," but can't. Cynthia wondered at the wording as she crept higher on the ladder to better see the lizard man. While the feeble starlight wasn't much help, she still managed to note a glint of metal around the creature's neck.

"Can't show your face?" Daryl snorted. "Why not? Afraid I'll figure out who you are and come after you?"

"Who I am is not important. The town must be warned."

"Warned of what? That you're terrorizing them?"

"Not me." The thing kept forcing words out, his pronunciation chunky, as if the words were familiar but his tongue wouldn't cooperate.

"Are you going to try and convince me you're different than your buddy who kidnapped my friend's kid? You attacked me and Cyn last night. For all I know, you're the other asshole who rammed our car today."

"Not me," dinoman stated again. "She must leave. All of you must. Terrible things are..."

Before the creature could finish, his body jerked. Even though she stood yards away, a charred smell wafted on the evening breeze.

Probably sensing his chance, Daryl darted forward, hands extending into claws, only to swipe at air. Dinoman was no longer there. The creature dove at the side of the building and threw itself into the air, arms and legs tucked tight to its frame. With a snap of unfolding canvas caught by a stiff breeze, the wings unfurled. Those massive leathery spans flapped, displacing air and keeping the reptile man's body from smashing to the ground below. With a final hissed, "Run while you can," it soared off on air currents that weren't so kind to those with two feet.

"Fuck. He got away." Poor Daryl sounded so disappointed.

Clambering onto the roof, she ran to him, uncaring if he'd been a jerk in the truck. A chill invaded her limbs, and she needed reassuring warmth.

Daryl caught her and tucked his arm around her. "You okay, Cyn?"

"Fine. But I can't help but wonder why he came here."

"To finish what he started last night." Stated as if it was the most obvious thing.

But was it? She shook her head as they walked back to the stairs. "I don't think that creature meant us any harm. I mean, think of it. He could have totally taken us by surprise. He can fly. Why not swoop at us on the stairs when he had the advantage?"

"Maybe because he wanted a bigger area to fight."

Halfway through his window, she stopped to say over her shoulder, "I don't think he wanted to hurt us."

"He's not the good guy, Cyn."

"Are you sure of that?" she questioned, still stuck halfway in the window. "I mean, did you notice he was wearing the same collar as the dogman the other day?" It made her wonder if dinoman also wore one the previous night. Possible. She might not have noticed before on account of the whole trying-to-stay-alive thing.

"So he's someone's pet. That doesn't excuse his actions."

"No, but maybe explains them. What if he doesn't have a choice? What if someone is making him do those things? Just before he took off, I think someone activated his collar."

"I thought I smelled roasted gator. But I don't see what difference that makes. He, and whoever is controlling him, needs to be stopped."

Need. Cynthia needed a few things herself. One, to find a clue as to Aria's whereabouts.

Two, she needed a shower. In a bad way.

And three, she wanted Daryl to stop pretending something utterly wicked and wonderful hadn't just happened in the truck.

She finished climbing into his apartment and had her hands on the hem of her shirt, determined to do something about items one and two, when a cleared throat caught her attention.

Uh-oh. Someone was in there with them. Someone whose scent was so familiar she'd not initially realized they were there. She froze before she could strip her shirt and managed a weak, "Hi, Mommy. Hi, Daddy."

Chapter 14

Daryl's poster behind his couch: *Three kittens playing with yarn. (Don't judge, it was a total chick pleaser—and they were really cute.)*

SO, exactly how was a guy supposed to comport himself when meeting a girl's parents for the first time, shirtless, still smelling of smoke—oh, and let's not forget the musky scent of pussy on his fingers and lips.

Given a certain father glared at him—and he meant glare with pointed daggers, laser beams, and maybe a few bullets—and stood well over seven feet, Daryl was less than keen to get too close.

He could probably crush my head with those hands.

Or swing us by the tail, agreed his feline.

With good reason in either case, seeing as how he'd totally gone to third base with his daughter.

Since Daryl planned to live to a ripe age—with all his body parts intact—he did what any self-respecting guy would do. He managed a gruff, "Excuse me, folks, I really gotta pee," and took off running. He also took the straightest path, and that involved vaulting over the couch so as to not get too close to Cyn's daddy, and dove into the bathroom.

Safety. Ha ha! He'd made it. He shut the door to the facilities and leaned against it.

A rabid bear didn't come charging through. Things were, while not yet looking up, at least not getting worse.

Could things get any worse?

He'd bitten Cyn. Had the most erotic moment in his life. Ran into her father. Seen one possible future, and it was crushing. Literally.

Exactly what direction should he take to stay out of trouble?

Did a safe path even exist?

Since when did he care about safety? This feline lived on the edge. Danger and adventure were practically his middle name. No, seriously, he craved adventure, given his job as a construction worker wasn't all that exciting, but it was great for keeping him tanned.

Can't tan if I'm six feet under. And before anyone went calling him a pussy, the guy towered at least seven freaking feet! Add in he was Cyn's dad, and Daryl was screwed without lube.

"Shit." Realizing he'd said it out loud, he leaned over and turned on the tap. With the rushing sound of water covering his actions, he muttered a few more choice curse words.

What were her parents doing here? How the hell had they gotten into his place? Should he hide in here until they left? That seemed pretty chicken, even if he was fifty percent sure Cyn's father would try and kill him.

You also forgot the part where you abandoned Cyn.

It's her parents.

Even worse.

Fine. He'd have to go back out and save Cyn, but he couldn't go out smelling like he did. Having experience with mornings where he hit the snooze button one too many times, he was well experienced when it came to quick bathing. He stripped and jumped into a shower that started out cool since he didn't wait for it to heat. The bar of soap lathered his skin, leaving it fresh smelling—a shame, he rather enjoyed wearing Cyn's scent on his skin. Maybe he'd rub against her later.

Lick her again.

Great idea.

She is our mate.

Bang. He wondered if anyone heard him rap his forehead off the tile wall. It was hard to war with a lifetime of casual affairs to a ridiculous certainty she belonged to him.

Mine.

Help.

He pretended he didn't whimper that word as he rinsed. The towel hanging on a hook provided a handy dry, but he couldn't go out wearing it. Given his washer and dryer were in the bathroom, hidden behind folding doors, he managed to find some clean clothes. Wrinkled, but who cared? At least he smelled more presentable, not that Cynthia seemed pleased that he'd washed away the evidence of their dalliance.

As he stepped from the bathroom, wisps of steam misting about him, she tossed him a tight-lipped look. *The look.* A look that men all over the world feared.

His mother used that look on him as a child. It still worked, but wow, was it even more frightening on Cyn's face.

"Feeling better?" she snapped as she crossed her arms over her chest. She also cocked her head, sending her untamed hair flying. So much hair. He loved it. Wanted to grab it and pull it and...

Um. Yeah. Not exactly the right time to be thinking about that. Big head, stand down. Little head, use some of that brain matter before he was doubly murdered, probably by Cyn first.

He made an attempt to alleviate the tension. "I feel much better, thank you."

"Awesome, because Daddy has some questions for you."

"He does?" Because it looked more like her daddy had an ass whooping waiting for him.

"I'm sure you won't mind telling him how we hooked up and what we've been doing." He caught the barb she sent his way and could have kissed the smirk teasing her lips. "My turn to strip out of these clothes and get clean," Cyn announced as she skirted her parents for the bathroom. As she brushed past Daryl, she murmured, "Hope you have a few lives left, darlin'."

With those reassuring words, she closed the door and left him alone with *the parents*. Dum-dum-dum. Did anyone else hear ominous music playing?

"You must be Daryl," said the woman. Where her husband was big with a dark complexion, she was short and rotund with pale skin. She also had the wildest honey brown hair, totally at odds with her prim knee-length skirt and perfectly pressed blouse.

"I see where Cyn gets her smile and gorgeous hair from."

A hand reached to pat it. "Thank you. It runs in my family. I prefer to keep it tamed, but Larry likes it like this."

"He doesn't care about your hair, Eleanor. He's trying to kiss ass because he's gotten our baby girl embroiled in something dangerous."

"I have not. It just kind of keeps happening," he added with a shrug.

"How did you meet?" Eleanor asked, her eyes bright with rapier interest.

Should he mention the whole kidnapping thing? Exactly how much did Cyn's parents know about her current quest to find her friend?

"We met over drinks." *And then went back to her motel room and slept together.* He didn't mention that part mostly because that platonic evening with a hot woman would totally ruin his reputation as a bit of a ladies' man. *Rowr.*

"Drinks, eh?" The stare narrowed.

Translation: *You thought you could get my daughter drunk and put the moves on my precious baby girl.*

Was it too late to run for the window and the swamp?

His cat smacked him with a furry mental paw. He could handle this. "Cyn came to the bar looking for people who might have seen her friend. She recognized me from a photo. We talked about it. Once Cyn realized I had nothing to do with Aria's disappearance, she agreed to let me help her."

"And do you help all young naïve girls by having them come stay with you?" A dark brow arched, and teeth were bared.

Even if Cyn's father stood with a leg in a walking cast, Daryl didn't doubt the man could hurt him, hurt him badly, especially since Daryl couldn't, out of respect to Cyn, hurt him back.

Fuck.

"Larry, stop teasing the poor boy. I'm sure he's got nothing but honorable intentions toward our girl. Right?" Eleanor's bright eyes pierced him.

"Um." He knew what the right answer was. It was on the tip of his tongue. It showed on the marking on Cyn's inner thigh. He just couldn't say it aloud. Saying the words "Cyn is my mate" would irrevocably change things.

Yet didn't things change the moment I touched her?

Before Daryl could blurt something that would probably see Larry's granite fist meet his face, a phone rang. More like sang "Hotel California" by The Eagles.

Three sets of eyes went to the smartphone dancing on the counter, a cord dangling from its charging port. It was Cyn's phone, left behind on their excursion today so it could charge its totally dead battery.

Should they answer it? The song seemed to taunt them to do something. But still, none of them moved.

Steam preceded a certain irate mocha hottie as she stalked from the bathroom, wrapped in a towel. "Are none of you capable of answering?"

No, they weren't, since a smiling face and the name Aria lit up the screen.

For a moment, Cyn's face blanched, and then she recovered and snatched at her phone answering with a, "What the hell, Aria? Why haven't you been answering? You scared the poop out of me."

There was an avid listening audience as Cyn turned to lean against the counter, phone held out, the speakerphone activated. She didn't need to put her fingers to her lips for them to know to keep quiet.

"Sorry, Thea. I've been roughing it the last few days. Communing with nature and all. You know how I love to sleep under the stars."

Everything sounded fine so far to Daryl, yet for some reason, Cyn's lips pursed. "Yeah, well, you had me worried. You usually call every day."

"Shit happened. I was just calling to let you know I am fine."

"Where are you now?" Cynthia still bore that crease on her forehead. The tension practically oozed from her.

"Here and there," was Aria's vague reply.

"Are you in Bitten Point?"

Even Daryl, who'd never met Aria, knew that the laugh she uttered was fake. "I'm long gone from that place. Just wandering the road."

"Listen, why don't we hook up? I took some time off from my practice. You know, the stress and all. Why don't I join you? We can have a real Thelma and Louise adventure."

"You can't do that." The most starkly said thing so far. "You should stay home. I'm busy. Real busy."

"Busy doing what? Aria, is everything okay?"

The rustle of a hand covering the receiver was very noticeable, as was the sudden silence as the call was muted on Aria's end.

It didn't take a genius to decipher the agitation in Cyn as she twirled a wet strand of hair on a finger, as if her curls needed any help.

When Aria returned, it was abrupt. "I'm fine. Everything is fine. I've met a guy. A hot guy. He's traveling with me. That's why you can't come. Maybe next time. Listen, I gotta go, Thea. I'll try and call you in a few days, but if I don't, don't worry. I'm having the time of my life."

"Then tell me where you are," Cyn whispered. "Aria—"

Her friend cut her off with a rushed, "Bye." Then the line went dead, and Cyn's knees buckled.

She didn't hit the floor. It took Daryl leaping and diving so he hit the floor first, but better he take the impact than Cyn. Injury averted, he squirmed to a seated position, holding her on his lap.

"Come on, Cyn. No need to freak. At least we know she's alive."

Obviously Aria had managed some kind of covert message because that was the only explanation for Cyn's distress. "You don't understand. That conversation, all of it was fake."

Her father dropped to a knee, the one in the cast outstretched, and touched Cyn's cheek with a ham-sized fist that was rough in texture yet gentle in its touch. "Baby girl. Don't you worry about Aria. Daddy's here, and we'll make sure she's safe."

Eleanor sniffed. "Of course we will. The nerve of keeping her prisoner. Don't they know she's the second daughter of my heart?"

Cyn sniffled. "How will we find her?"

"First thing in the morning, we'll go looking for where she stayed and her car."

"She rides a motorcycle," Cyn said.

"Whatever. Chet's right. We should have been looking for where she was staying. Maybe then we'll find a clue."

"Sounds like a fine idea," Eleanor exclaimed with a clap of her hand. "We'll see you in the morning."

Larry turned his head to address his wife. "What do you mean we'll see them? Thea's coming with us."

"To stay where? Our hotel room only has one bed, silly bear."

"So we rent another room."

"The hotel is full," said Eleanor through gritted teeth. She grabbed her husband's arm. "We should go. Let these two rest. Here. Alone."

Why did Daryl shiver when Eleanor winked at him?

Larry got to his feet and glowered down at his wife. "Go? We did not drive six hours for us to just leave our daughter with this—this—"

"We are leaving *now.*" Spoken with utmost steel at odds with the sweet smile Eleanor turned Daryl's way. "We'll see you two tomorrow morning." Gripping her husband by the arm, they went out the door, leaving them alone but still able to hear Larry's muttered, "I don't like it."

"I know, dear. Get over it. And hand me your phone. I need to post a status update."

Still seated on his lap, Cyn groaned.

Daryl immediately turned his attention to her. "Honey, are you all right?" Had she hurt herself falling against his rock hard body? Fact, not much conceit.

"I'm fine, but not for long, and neither are you. You do realize that my mother is now announcing to the world that we're sleeping together?"

"But we aren't." Yet, which was splitting hairs.

Cyn let out a very unladylike snort. "My mother doesn't care about those kinds of details. She just found me with a guy, in his place, wearing his shirt, looking like we just fooled around in a firepit. You're lucky she didn't start measuring you for a tux."

"So we'll set her straight."

"Good luck with that."

Did Cyn have to giggle when she said it?

To change the subject, which was veering uncomfortably close to the thing he'd done that should not be named, he said, "We should talk about Aria's call. Even I could tell the entire thing was bullshit."

Widening her eyes, Cyn glanced at him. "You didn't buy it either?"

"Not for a second."

"Good because the whole thing was bogus. Aria hates camping, and I mean hates it with a passion. She is a girl who loves a soft mattress with cleans sheets. Also, if she were going to hook up with a guy, she would have told me. In today's world, a girl can't be too safe. There's a lot of freaks and psychos out there, so the first rule of dating is to let someone else know who we're seeing."

"Did you tell anyone about me?" He could have slapped himself for asking because he'd just implied they were involved, which they were. But still. Fuck.

"Of course I did. I told my mom. Who then announced it to the world on Facebook."

Good thing he didn't believe in social media, although it might explain the congratulations he'd gotten on his way into the library with Cyn today.

"Speaking of your folks, why did they show up? Because you sure as hell never mentioned they were coming."

"You'd know why if you'd stuck around instead of running with your tail tucked to have a shower and abandoning me to papa bear and mama wolf," she accused, firing him an intense glare.

"They're your parents," was his cop-out.

"What man leaves a girl he just dragged to a strip joint to get interrogated by my dad?"

"A smart and still living one." There wasn't an ounce of repentance in his reply or grin.

"You are a bad cat."

"The baddest, honey. Feel free to punish me anytime." For a guy determined to try and slow shit down, he kept daring her to touch him.

Yes, touch me.

Instead, she snorted. "You wish. Now that my parents are gone, you're all Mr. Suave and Sexy, but I haven't forgotten your cold shoulder in the truck. What the heck was that about? Did my *garden* not appeal?" She wasn't about to let him off the hook, it seemed.

But how to explain that the fact he'd lost control enough to mark her scared the living fuck out of him? Like seriously scared.

Was he ready for the type of commitment a mating entailed?

One woman, one pussy, one person to go home to for the rest of his life?

Until we have cubs. The reminder did not reassure, but rather than shy away from her and use the opening she gave, he reassured her. "I've never played in a nicer garden." *Argh. Shoot me now.*

"Shooting you would be too kind."

Oops. She wasn't supposed to hear that. "I'm feeling really uncertain right about now."

"And I'm feeling rather uncomfortable in this wet towel."

Was she really? Because he was rather enjoying the fact that they were both still sitting on the floor, him a lap for her to cuddle in.

Wouldn't I enjoy it more, though, if she took off the towel?

Fucking right he would.

Slam on the brakes.

Why couldn't he stay in control for five minutes where Cyn was concerned? *Let me have some semblance of pride or a choice.*

Except it seemed there was no choice. Much as it might terrify, there was something happening between the two of them. Something he couldn't seem to stop, and really, did he even want to?

With Cyn, he came *alive.* What kind of idiot would throw that way?

Chapter 15

Cynthia: *So I slept with Daryl.*
Mom: *Might I remind you that a true lady saves herself for the big day, or at least until she gets a ring?*
Cynthia: *Um, Mom, I saw all the scarves you wore in those pictures when you were dating Dad.*
Mom: *So I hear the local restaurant serves a lovely crab cake.*

I'M SUCH AN IDIOT. Or a masochist. No matter how many times Daryl blew hot and cold at her, Cynthia couldn't help but want him.

At times, she wondered if he suffered the same confusion over what happened between them. Did he also struggle against the undeniable pull drawing them together? She would have thought the bite mark made things clearer, but instead, it had made things worse.

Do I want him?

Yes.

Then why did she still fight it? Why fight what they both wanted?

Why indeed? It wasn't as if they had anything else to do. The hour was now too late to allow for a proper search, and she could admit, to at least herself, that she didn't feel safe outside in the dark. Then again, today proved the daytime was no safer.

She had almost died today in that car crash. Then almost died again when Daryl's dexterity with his hands and tongue brought her an ecstasy that stopped her heart for an eternity or two. She certainly remembered being unable to breathe.

She definitely wanted to do it again. She wondered if the intensity and pleasure were a one-time deal? Could they even come close to replicating what they'd shared a second time?

She wouldn't mind finding out, and since they were in for the night, no time like the present to find out. The questions now was, take the bold or sly approach?

She couldn't have said if it was chance or intention that her towel got snagged when she stood from his lap. Did it matter? She added an extra swing to her hip as she walked away from him to the bedroom.

He might have made a strangled sound. He definitely didn't sound all there when he remarked, "Cyn, you seem to have lost your towel."

She tossed him what she hoped was a coy look over her shoulder. She couldn't be entirely sure of the effect, given she felt her hair drying in a fluffy mane around her head.

Hard to worry about hair, though, when she stood completely naked in front of a guy who'd just jumped to his feet and stalked her, and she meant stalked. Every step measured, his eyes practically glowing and smoldering with erotic intent.

He stopped barely an inch from her body. Head cocked, she met his stare, licked her lips, and threw herself at him when his arms wrapped around her, yanking her off her feet for a kiss.

How he confused her with his mixed signals, but dammit, that didn't mean she resisted his touch.

Their passion was wild, almost violent in its intensity. He might have rammed her against the nearest wall, or she might have dragged him there. Either way, her spine pressed into the firm surface, her legs spread at the insistent push of his thigh. His hands held her pinned, feet not quite touching the ground.

She devoured his lips, loving the taste of him, loving the sizzling passion that never failed to erupt every time they touched. A passion that seemed to grow, not lessen with every new caress.

"You're driving me completely mad, Cyn," he rumbled against her lips.

She nipped him and murmured back, "It's not that bad once you get used to the strange looks."

"I want you so fucking bad it hurts."

"Then why aren't you doing something about it?" She let her lips travel the length of his rough jaw then down the strong column of his neck. She sucked, unable to prevent herself from leaving some kind of mark on his skin.

Marking him as mine.

He didn't seem to mind because, head tilted back, he groaned, even as his leg moved slowly against her, the fabric of his pants a welcome friction against her moist sex.

She let out a small cry of surprise as he lifted her higher, enough that her legs could wrap around his waist. He slipped a hand between their bodies, finding her trembling core and sliding a finger in.

She clenched at him, wanting more. Wanting him. His cock. Inside her. Thrusting. Now!

A sound of frustration left her lips as her questing hands couldn't quite reach far enough to rid him of those annoying pants.

"Need help?"

"I need you." She said the words without even thinking, and he sucked in a sharp breath.

He also acted. The finger left her channel, the whir of a zipper filled the silence, and the hot head of his shaft slapped against her a moment later.

As he rubbed the swollen tip against her nether lips, she couldn't help but shudder. Anticipation made her muscles tighten so that, when he went to slide the head of his dick into her, he had to push, her snug sheath too excited to relax.

While one hand gripped her ass, the other cupped her face, drawing her to him for a kiss. How that man could kiss. Exploring and nibbling and teasing.

She sighed, and he slammed his cock home.

Sweet heavens, yes!

She locked her legs tight around him and snared him as well with her arms, keeping him close, loving the decadence of his T-shirt against the bare skin of her upper body. As he thrust, quicker and quicker, his kisses slowed until, with a groan, he rolled his head back. The cords in his neck bulged. He was holding off, holding off for her.

Not for much longer. She was right there, on the cusp. Each time he buried himself to the hilt, her pleasure edged higher.

She licked the exposed part of his neck, humming against his skin as he pumped her hard and fast. In and out, he slammed his cock, not too rough, but not too gentle either. Hard, fast, and passionate, just the way she wanted him.

"Give it to me." Did she growl it aloud? He certainly took things to the next level, and her sex gripped him, fisted him tight.

And then he changed the angle, just a little bit. He hit that sweet spot within her.

That did it. "Oh my God, I'm coming."

She burst. At least that was how it felt, as if a dam in her had opened, letting pleasure swamp her with wave upon wave. It was too much. Too much. Too...

She bit him, her teeth latching to flesh and holding on as she kept shuddering and groaning. She didn't let go, even though he yelled her name, "Cyn!" and came with hot spurts.

Together they clung to each other, wrung weak by the tsunami of bliss. Shaking with the aftermath. Then sinking to the bed he carried her to, still entwined. As she placed her head against his chest, she smiled as she thought of her next call to her mom.

Cynthia: Yeah, so what should I do if Daryl needs a scarf to hide something?

Mom: Why would you hide it? Let the ladies and tramps know he's off the market.

Chapter 16

A T-shirt a friend ordered for Daryl after meeting Cyn: *"Screwed with a great big silver Philips head."*

WAKING the next morning with a luscious mocha honey against his body? Awesome.

Seeing his neck in the mirror after he took care of business in the bathroom?

"What the fuck? Cyn! Cyn!"

He bellowed her name as he stalked to the bedroom then almost fell over his suddenly ungainly feet because she rolled in his bed, flopping onto her back. The sheet pulled away during her twist, and she'd not dressed after their playtime—*Rowr*! What this meant was a stunning display of breasts. Breasts he knew intimately.

We should go over and say hello again.

No, he had to focus. He needed to have a serious talk with Cyn.

It's too early to talk.

Yeah, and according to his panic, too early to get serious about a girl.

Say that to the bite you left on her thigh.

Excuse him, but they were talking about her lapse in judgment, not his. "Do you know what you did?" The words emerged a tad growly.

"I know, and I enjoyed." She licked her lips and winked. "But I gotta say I thought only roosters crowed at the crack of dawn." Pulling her arms overhead, Cyn stretched as she yawned.

He couldn't help but stare, harden, and desire. Maybe he should get back in bed with her?

Stay strong.

The sheet slipped farther, showing the rounded swell of her belly, the indent of her waist, the top of her garden.

Meowr? Such a pained sound, and it came from him as she flashed him. But he would resist. He'd seen boobies before, and just because hers were splendid was no reason to forget his complaint.

"Don't you try and distract me," he said, wagging a finger. He pointed at his neck. "Look at what you did."

"I see it." She smiled.

Did she not understand the gravity? Perhaps if he explained. "You bit me. Why would you do that?"

"Why wouldn't I?"

"Because you shouldn't have." Weakest reply ever and it wiped the smile from her face.

"Well, that's priceless coming from you, seeing as how you bit me first." She crossed her arms over her chest, but under her breasts, causing them to plump. It also pushed them together, creating a mysterious valley—*that is really begging to get explored, with my tongue.*

Argh. She was doing it again, playing dirty, and the blood fueling his brain fled south, which was why he made the colossal error of saying, "That bite was a mistake."

The narrowing of her eyes almost saw him take a step in retreat.

"A mistake?" She flung back the sheet, spread her thighs—*thighs that were wrapped around my waist last night*—and pointed to the perfect crescent on the inside of her thigh. "Do you often make mistakes like that?"

"No." Because he wasn't even entirely sure it was a mistake. A part of him screamed this was right. She was right. And perfect. Yet... "I'm not ready for this." He could feel the panic clawing at him. Or was that desire because, really, instead of an urge to run from the woman who challenged him, he wanted to dive on her?

Oops. Wait, he did. He yanked her arms over her head and pinned her to the mattress.

"Now what are you doing?" she asked, trying to sound cross, but instead coming across as slightly breathless.

"Saying good morning hopefully without my foot first."

"I really wish you'd make up your mind on what you want."

"You." Yeah, the word slipped out.

Her eyes widened, however she didn't have a chance to reply as his phone chose that moment to ring. He dove on it before he had to deal with his admission. He should have checked the number first.

"Hi, Mama." Practically said on a sigh.

"Don't you hi me, *gatito*."

It was too much to hope Cyn didn't hear. The giggle said it all.

No matter how many times he begged—and pleaded with his biggest eyes—his mother kept calling him *gatito*. Translated: kitten in Spanish. He was a grown man. It just wasn't right.

His mother didn't care if he thought it emasculating, just like she cared too much about his love life. "What is this I hear about you seeing a woman?"

"You know I don't believe in dating."

The hot glare between his shoulder blades practically turned him into ash.

His mother sniffed. "It is only because you have yet to find the right woman, *gatito*. Your sister says you are living with a girl you just met."

"No, I'm not."

A cleared throat as Cyn objected. Damn her acute hearing.

And damn his mother's sharp ears, too. "Are you going to deny a woman has been sleeping at your place the last two nights?"

"Okay, there is a girl staying here. But it's not what you think."

"Two nights. And you've been spending the day with her. Don't deny it. My sources saw you."

"I really wish you wouldn't spy on me."

"What else is a mother to do if she wants to know what her son is up to? A good thing, too, or I wouldn't know you'd gotten serious with this girl."

"Who says it's serious?"

His mother let out a very unladylike snort. "You let her sleep over. Twice."

"You make it sound like I only have one-night-stands," he hissed into the receiver, feeling heat roasting the tips of his ears.

"Those girls you're dating might as well have been. You never brought them to your place."

Because he had this thing about sleeping alone, a rule he'd now broken and didn't regret.

He flashed a glance at Cyn and caught her smiling smugly.

"You're reading too much into this. I'm just helping her out with something."

Cyn snickered before she drawled, "You've been helping me all right." And, yes, the minx did wiggle on the bed and wink.

"Can she cook?"

In the bedroom, totally. But that wasn't what his mother wanted to know. "Listen, Mom. I gotta go. I'll talk to you later."

"Love you, my *gatito*."

"Love you, too, Mama."

A man wore his embarrassment as a badge of honor. He spun to face Cyn, who grinned. "Who's a cute gatito? I would have never pegged you for a mama's boy."

"I am not." Much.

"I won't judge you for it. I'm sure there's no way your mother is as bad as mine."

I wouldn't wager on that.

The phone rang again, a soundtrack from the *Minions* movie. He didn't even have to look at the number when he answered. "Hey, Melanie."

"Who's Melanie?" Cyn mouthed, an irritated look on her face.

"It's my sister," he mouthed back.

The beaming smile proved very distracting, which was why he turned away again, but it didn't stop his sister's whispered, "Is that girl you've been hanging out with there right now?"

Amongst shifters, who possessed rather decent hearing, secrets were hard to keep and conversations were rarely private.

Before Daryl could reply, Cyn did, loudly and with a mischievous glint in her eye.

"Hi, I'm Cynthia. Your brother's been helping me look for my friend Aria."

Daryl held the phone away from his ear as his sister shouted, "You're the girl Renny and Caleb have been helping."

"Along with Constantine and Wes," Cyn added.

"Wes is working with you, too? Not that I care," his sister quickly added.

At this point, he realized who was the third wheel. Daryl held out his phone and, in his most sarcastic tone, said, "I'm sorry. Am I getting in the way of your talking to my sister?"

It wasn't just Cyn who said yes.

He could only gape as his honey grabbed the phone, tucked it to her ear, and began chatting with Melanie.

Blink.

This wasn't happening.

First his mother meddling in his love life, which should be noted wasn't new, but usually his mother tried to fix him up with the daughters of friends, girls Daryl never bothered with. This was the first time his mother had taken an interest in a woman Daryl found on his own.

Actually, she found me. And he'd not been able to stay away from her since.

Shit. How did that happen? How could he not be tired of her yet? Or ready to have some alone time and "me" space?

To the sound of Cyn and his sister talking, he wandered out of his bedroom, utterly bemused. Only a day or so ago, he was a single swinging bachelor. He'd almost earned his own table at the Itty Bitty he enjoyed the entertainment so much.

He had a feeling Cyn might have ruined him when it came to breasts and half-naked women.

Despite how hard he tried, he couldn't remember a single exotic dancer now that Cyn had taken the stage, not only in his memories, but his heart, too.

All he saw when he closed his eyes was her. The recollection of her splayed across his bed, skin a tempting chocolate, lips so berry bright and plump.

We should break the phone and give her a proper good morning. Maybe nibble on that other thigh.

Argh. No. Slow down. Going to her now would admit something, something he was still in denial about. A man needed coffee before dealing with relationship woes.

As he sipped the hot brew—with eight cubes of sugar, cream, and then a cement mixer to stir the sweet sludge—he listened to Cyn chatting and laughing with his sister.

A few minutes later, she wasn't laughing as she strode out of the bedroom, phone in hand, utterly naked. "You never told me you had twin nephews."

"I told you I had nephews."

"Yeah, but you neglected to mention they were twins. Do they run in the family?"

Couldn't they talk about something else, such as her need to put on a nun's outfit? But no, she continued to taunt with her nakedness, and the glint in her eyes said she wanted an answer.

"Twins tend to run on my dad's side."

Cyn frowned. "You could have warned me."

"Warned you? Why would it matter?"

She arched a brow and cocked a hip, which proved rather interesting, given she did it naked. However, his distraction didn't mean he missed her words, but he still made her repeat them.

"I said you didn't use a condom. So unless *you're* on the pill, then babies are a possibility."

A man was entitled a long blink while he processed this. He could even hyperventilate a bit. Babies? No. Oh hell no. Yet, she was correct. They'd skipped protection. Daryl rarely used condoms because his kind proved impervious to most diseases. As for pregnancy... "Aren't you on the pill?" Wasn't every woman nowadays taking it? The hormones in it worked on shifter females. They just needed a much stronger dose.

She shook her head, sending her hair fluttering. "No, I am not. I don't like the way it makes me hairy."

"But... We... That is..." He couldn't say it aloud, let alone contemplate it.

"Had sex. I know. And now I could be pregnant because someone didn't pull out."

He stabbed at his chest. "You're blaming me? You could have told me you weren't taking anything."

"I might have except I was kind of lost in the moment, which, again, is totally your fault. And, besides, what guy doesn't use one until he knows for sure?"

A guy who was also lost in the moment. "It was just one time."

"One time? One time could mean twins in there." Her turn to poke herself in the belly. "I know we've marked each other, but that's a bit quick, kitten."

"Don't call me kitten."

"Why? Does it make you think of your mommy?"

No. Cyn definitely didn't invoke any maternal thoughts, but she sure did ignite carnal ones.

A woman indicating she might be with his child should have sent him fleeing. Running for the swamps to hide.

Not this kitty.

This kitty found himself stalking toward her, drawn despite himself.

As for Cyn? She didn't flee. On the contrary, she also moved, and neither stopped until they were pressed against each other. Since he wore only boxers, nothing could stop the sizzle that arced between their bodies. Their gazes caught.

"I think we can both agree there is something happening between us," she stated.

He nodded in agreement.

"I'm not sure where it's going, but for the moment, I'm going to stop fighting it. Are you?"

"Is that wise?"

She smiled. "Are you seriously asking the crazy girl? No, it might not be wise, but I'll be honest and say I've never experienced anything like being with you."

"Me either."

"So why don't we agree for the moment to just enjoy ourselves, find Aria, and then see how things pan out? Maybe go out a few times, hang out."

"Are you talking about dating?"

"Which sounds kind of backwards, given we've munched on each other's skin and shared a bedroom, but yeah, we should *date*." She winked as she sashayed to the bathroom, her round buttocks tempting.

He couldn't help but stare, and kept staring long after she'd left his side. He visibly startled when she stuck her head out the door and sighed.

"In case you're that oblivious, that was an invitation to get your ass in here. We could both use a shower. I promise I'm very dirty."

He wasn't oblivious, just overwhelmed, but not so much that he didn't get his ass in that bathroom. It was a good thing they had lots of hot water because she got plenty dirty before she got clean.

Just in time, too, as insanity came to plague them again.

Chapter 17

Cynthia: *So thanks for letting Daryl and I have some time alone last night. We managed to get a few things talked out.*
Mom: *So he proposed?*
Cynthia: *No!*
Mom: *Why not?*

IF ONLY CYNTHIA WERE EXAGGERATING. Poor Daryl, she'd given him hell for not warning her about the twins in his family, but then again, she'd not truly fully cautioned him about her parents.

Tit for tat, and something they'd have to deal with if they did stay together. She'd have to live with his genetic disposition that might see any fertilized eggs of hers split. He'd have to learn to put up with her parents. The good news was her folks lived hours away.

The bad news was they had no boundaries where she was concerned.

Towel wrapped snugly about her body, she exited the bathroom in a cloud of steam, having enjoyed a little private time with his razor and her legs. She also made sure her garden was pruned.

She was feeling pretty good until she screamed, "Mom, Dad, what are you doing here?"

"We told you we would be back in the morning," rumbled her father. Dressed in khaki walking shorts and an eye-popping Hawaiian shirt, her father had taken a spot on the couch, his leg in the walking cast stretched before him.

As for Mom, she was dressed in pressed white slacks, a pastel-colored blouse, and hair that defied gravity with its poufy height. "You look a little tired, dear. Long night?"

Given how used to her mother she was, it would take more than a sly innuendo to embarrass Cynthia. "I'm fine, Mother." If by fine she meant sexually sated, kind of seeing a guy, and wondering if she was pregnant with a pair of tadpoles.

Daryl strolled out of the kitchen area, looking way more relaxed than a man should. "About time you got out of there. My mom's been waiting to meet you."

The morning seemed determined to make her blush.

"Your mom? Just let me get dressed and—" Yeah, the universe wasn't going to grant her the kindness of putting on underwear and a bra before meeting Daryl's mother.

There was no denying the woman who emerged from the kitchen was Daryl's mother. It wasn't just the tanned skin that gave it away, but the same dark gaze and straight nose. But where Daryl's chin was distinctly male, his mother's angled into a point, and she was tiny beside her son.

"Cyn, this is my mother, Luisa. Mama, I'd like you to meet Cynthia. She's um"—he paused and sent her an indecipherable look before shrugging and saying—"my girlfriend."

Dear God. Had he just publicly announced their status? Too late to take it back now. Her mother had heard and leaned forward in her seat. Some predators smelled blood in the air. Her mother smelled a wedding dress.

Luisa eyed her. "Does she cook?"

The question might not have been directed at her, but Cynthia answered it anyhow. "Yes. I can cook. Bake. As well as balance a checkbook, plan a dinner party for twelve, and wear heels while doing it." Her mother had insisted Cynthia learn certain skills growing up. Some like culinary creations she did well with. Others that involved needle and thread... Best not spoken of.

"Family is important?"

Her mom got in on the conversation. "Very. My Thea is a good girl. Never any problems with her."

The two women shared a nod, and Cynthia could already feel the tight strings of a corset as her mother plotted to reproduce the nightmare of her sweet sixteen dress shopping, but on a grander scale.

In that moment, Cynthia totally felt like a coyote and was only missing a sign that said "help" as she tumbled off a cliff.

"Excellent. My Daryl needs a good woman to keep him in line. Don't forget, *gatito*, we are having dinner on Thursday. Bring your girlfriend." Daryl's mother paused at the door. "You and your husband should come, too." *You* being Cynthia's mother.

"We'd be delighted." Her mom beamed, a smile that was entirely too wide and happy. "Since I can see you're busy here, baby girl, we'll just take off. Daryl says you're meeting some friends to look for Aria's last whereabouts. But we'll be helping, too. Your father, being a car guy, is going to check out the junkyard just outside of town to see if Aria's motorcycle is there. Don't get into too much trouble."

"How about not any at all," grumbled her dad as he followed her mom out the door.

With the quiet *snick* of the door engaging, they were once again alone.

Blink. A few breaths.

No one came barging in, and Daryl still stood across the room looking entirely too calm.

Not acceptable. He should be as frazzled as her hair.

She dropped the towel. He spat out coffee.

"Could you warn me if you're going to do that?"

"No." She didn't even pretend to think about it. "What was all that about with your mom?" Although she feared she knew. *Looks like my mom isn't the only matchmaker. We are so screwed.*

He shrugged. "Don't look at me. I came out of the bathroom as my mom was frying the bacon."

"There's bacon?" She didn't quite run to the kitchen, but it was close.

"Then while my mother whipped out some pancakes, your parents just walked in like they owned the place."

"Yeah, Daddy's not big on knocking. Or visiting people. He must like you." She beamed at him, a smile somewhat ruined by her chewing on a strip of pure pork heaven.

She plopped herself onto a bar stool and snagged a pancake with a fork from the platter stacked high with them, smothered it in butter and syrup, then moaned as she ate it, interspersing sweet bites with crunchy, salty bacon.

Fingers snapped in front of her nose. "Are you listening to me?"

"Um, can I lie and say yes?" She batted her lashes and wondered if he would get offended if she stole the last piece of bacon.

Screw it. She wanted it. He could spank her for it later.

Instead of the palm of his hand on her ass, she got a rundown of their battle plan. She straightened in her seat.

"Wes and Caleb are going to check some of the nearby campgrounds for signs of Aria."

"But Aria doesn't camp."

"That may be, but just in case, they're going to look."

"And what are we doing?" Although, whatever they did, she doubted it would rival the sex they'd had the previous night.

"We are going to be joined by Constantine to search the three motels in town."

"Why do we need his help? Wouldn't it make more sense to split up?"

"Given the attacks on us, not really."

Good point and a sobering one. While Cynthia was worried about dealing with her matchmaking mother—and now Daryl's, too—she couldn't forget that, despite Aria's call, there was something that smelled in Bitten Point, and it wasn't the swamp gases.

"Will the motels give us information on Aria? I thought there were some privacy laws against that."

"Yeah, but nothing a little nudge or a twenty won't fix, especially if they're shifters. Once they find out it's about a missing girl, they'll cooperate."

Cooperation was all well and good, but that required something for the desk staff to relate. After hitting the three motels within the town to no avail, they even hit a few on the outskirts. Money did exchange hands a few times, but the answer still remained a big fat negative. No one had seen a petite girl on a motorcycle, or if they had, they lied about it.

"It makes no sense," Cynthia grumbled, squished against the passenger door of Constantine's pickup truck because Daryl, for some reason, insisted on taking the middle spot on the bench seat.

Apparently, getting to ride inside the cab was a privilege, as usually the passenger spot was reserved for Princess, Constantine's dog. Not for this trip. His large-eyed furball currently sat in the big man's lap.

Having treated her fair share of Chihuahuas as a vet, Cynthia knew they were extremely loyal with the heart of a lion. Seriously, those pipsqueaks feared nothing, and she'd gotten her fair share of nips when giving needles to know.

"Maybe your friend didn't book a motel for the night but stayed with a friend," Constantine ventured.

Frustrated at their failure to find anything, Cynthia snapped, "Are you calling her a slut?"

"You tell me."

Daryl threw out an arm, and she hit it before she could dive across the seat. When it came to Aria, Cynthia was her fiercest defender. In Constantine's case, he relied on his little dog. Princess peeled back her gums and growled.

Cynthia growled back.

As for Daryl, he tried to turn a chuckle into a cough before saying, "I'm sure that's not what he meant."

The big man at the wheel shot her a brief glance. "No, I wasn't calling her a slut, but asking if Aria might have spent the night with someone is a legitimate question. I mean, we've been concentrating on retracing her last steps and finding out more about those creatures who attacked you and have gotten nowhere. So it's time to change tactics. The best clue we have right now is your missing friend. We need to know more about her time in Bitten Point before that last night in the bar, starting with where the hell she was staying. If none of the hotels and motels remember her, and you're sure she wouldn't camp, then where was she sleeping and showering?"

Constantine's calm logic extinguished the fire in her. Cynthia slumped onto the seat. "Sorry I went all gangster on you. Especially since you're only trying to help. I don't know where she was staying, but it is possible she spent the night with a guy. Aria's a bit of a free spirit." Aria had learned at a young age to have a live-for-the-moment attitude. She took her pleasures when and where she could.

"Except you said she wouldn't have hooked up with a guy without telling you." Daryl grabbed her hand and held it, giving it a comforting squeeze.

"She never has before. But what other explanation is there? She had to stay somewhere." Cynthia could have kicked herself for not knowing. It just never came up in their previous chats, and for some reason, while Aria might have pinged the night at the bar with her phone, she never checked off a hotel or motel. Only foolish single women traveling alone would give out those kinds of details.

"We are fucking idiots," exclaimed Constantine with a snap of his fingers. "What about the bed and breakfast by Sal's place? The one past those orchards."

"Bedbug Bites?" Daryl said. "I thought the broad running that place shut it down."

The skin on Cynthia's body crawled at the thought of nighttime critters munching away. "Hold on, Bedbug Bites? What the heck kind of name is that for a B&B? Who would stay there?"

"Not humans," Daryl replied with a grin. "I told you the town had its methods of keeping them away. But a shifter would know the truth and realize it was a friendly joint for our kind."

"If that's the case, then why didn't we check this place out?" she asked.

"Because it closed down years ago to the public after Mrs. Jones' son went missing during the first round of monster appearances."

"If it's no longer open, then what makes you think Aria might have stayed there?"

"Because it might not be as closed as we thought," Constantine answered. "Veronica, the lady that owns the place, might not be publicly advertising she's open, yet for someone who is supposed to be living there alone, she gets a lot of groceries delivered."

It begged the question of, "And how do you know this?"

"My brother's mate. Renny used to work at the grocery store and was the one bagging the items for delivery. She thought it was weird, but none of her business."

Weird indeed, enough that they had to check it out.

The drive to this last-ditch effort took them down a lonely side road, one with deep ruts that had her bouncing since Cynthia couldn't find the oh-poop handle on the door. Don't mock her strong language. Being gangster didn't mean she could resort to the fouler words others used. Her mother's voice was too strong for that. *"Don't make me get the soap."* Shudder.

The second time she flailed for purchase and accidently squashed Daryl in his manparts, he grunted, but then put a stop to her unintentional damage. He dragged her onto his lap and anchored his arms around her. They still bounced, but now she could claim it was rather fun, given her proximity to a certain hottie.

"Where is this place? The ninth circle of Hell?" she grumbled as she almost bit her tongue when they hit a pothole determined to suck in the truck.

"It's right on the edge of the swamp," Daryl replied. "All this land belongs to Veronica Jones. Her husband's family got it generations ago, over fifty acres, if I remember correctly."

Fifty acres of untamed jungle, given the foliage encroached upon the road. If she heard any banjos, she might start begging to turn around. Damn her ex-boyfriend for making her watch *Deliverance* and *The Hills Have Eyes*.

One moment they were looking lost and about to become meat-fodder in a horror movie and the next they emerged onto a paved, cobblestone drive that wound around a grassy circle with a stone bird bath in the middle.

The chill and uneasiness in Cynthia's bones didn't leave at the sight of the grand plantation home, the likes of which weren't often seen in these parts.

Tall columns graced the front and flanked the wide single step up to the pair of carved wooden front doors.

The pale siding had seen whiter days, the green and black hue of time and mildew doing its best to recolor them. Windows gaped upon the drive, their reflective surface showing the green foliage of the wilderness that surrounded the cultivated parts of this space.

As they stepped from the truck, Daryl doing so with one arm around her waist, holding her aloft as he slid them out, she couldn't help but smell the lushness of the greenery.

And the acrid stench of… "Dogman was here!"

No mistaking the nose-wrinkling smell of wet dog in dire need of a bath. Just like there was no mistaking Aria's bike tucked under a tarp off to the side of the drive.

Cynthia pushed out of Daryl's arms and ran to the familiar black cover with the patches they'd crazy-glued to repair tears. She dropped to her knees and lifted it to peer under. A red frame with hand-painted white daisies met her view. "Aria's here. We found her."

"I wouldn't get too excited yet," Daryl cautioned.

Her excitement plummeted.

"Don't get that look. I'm just saying that her bike being here doesn't mean she is. For all we know, she was taken from here and they left her stuff behind."

Good point, but she still couldn't help a little elation that they'd finally found some clue that Aria was in the area.

The hours for the B&B were posted on an engraved plaque alongside the doors. Registration from one p.m. until nine daily.

That was what the sign said, and here they were, almost five p.m., yet the door would not budge when pulled.

Daryl rapped his fist against it and then stood back to wait. They all waited. However, the only signs of life were in the buzz of insects around them. The bloodthirsty suckers went after the city girl with evil intent. Cynthia needed to get away from them, say like inside a house with doors and windows bearing screens. A problem remained, though. The door was locked, and no one seemed inclined to answer.

"Maybe the front desk person went to the bathroom?" she ventured.

"And locked the door so no guests could get in?" Daryl snorted and shook his head. "The only way this wouldn't be open was if we were mistaken and this place isn't a B&B at all."

"But the sign says—"

"That sign is old and was probably never removed when she shut down."

She couldn't refute Daryl's logic, given the plaque appeared fairly tarnished.

"Something's not right." Constantine uttered the words while looking off in the distance. A frown creased his brow, and his body was tense.

No, something wasn't right, and she didn't mean just the state of her hair in this humidity. The whole place oozed of creepiness. She would know. She'd watched her fair share of horror movies, and the one thing they all taught was don't go into the spooky, abandoned house.

Her inner canine whined. *Danger.* Eyes watched. Menace lurked. She shouldn't let paranoia get the better of her. Or should she listen to common sense?

"Maybe we should leave." She tucked herself tighter to Daryl, and he put a reassuring arm around her, but it couldn't dispel the chill.

"What's wrong?"

"I don't know, but Constantine is right. I don't feel right about this place. Maybe we should call the cops and let them come check things out."

"But what about looking for Aria? She was obviously here."

"You said it. Was. Her bike's been parked there for a while." The intricate spider web in the wheel rim with its desiccated catches said so. "She's obviously not in there."

"Or she is, but can't get out," Daryl countered, playing devil's advocate.

"Hey, guys, do you see Princess?" Constantine asked.

"Not me," she replied.

"Me either."

Constantine craned to look around. "Princess! Where are you? Come to Daddy."

The incongruous appearance of the giant Constantine baby-talking his dog proved hard to ignore, and she bit her lip lest she snicker. It was a battle she didn't fight alone, given Daryl's snort.

A sharp bark lightened the expression on Constantine's face, and he moved quickly around to the side of the house. They found a decent-sized yard with taut vinyl strung from the house for about thirty feet to a tree that served as a post. Laundry flapped from it, some of the fabric hanging by only a single pin.

Bark. The sharp sound drew their attention to Princess. The small dog stood on a wooden stoop, pawing at a door. It had a window set into it, covered in a flower-patterned curtain.

Instead of rapping on the door, Constantine peered in.

"See anything?" Daryl asked.

"Nah. It's just some kind of mudroom with a washer and dryer. I am going to go inside to check it out," Constantine announced.

"Should we? I mean, isn't that breaking and entering?" Cynthia whispered. She couldn't have said why she kept her voice low, maybe to avoid disturbing spirits, or because if conspiring to commit a crime, she probably shouldn't shout about it.

"It's only break and enter if the door is locked." Daryl pointed at the splintered jamb. "Looks like we're not the first ones to want in."

The realization only increased the size of the knot in her stomach.

Don't go in!

Her wolf really, really thought it was a bad idea. Funny, Cynthia did, too, but to not follow meant staying outside. She cast a glance at the bordering swamp vegetation, most of it thick enough to hide any number of threats.

She clasped Daryl's hand tightly. She was sticking to his side and hoping they didn't run into anything dangerous, especially since she no longer had any needles. The supplies she'd brought had gotten toasted in the fire.

That won't be cheap to replace. But considering she'd escaped alive and unscathed, she was still ahead of the game.

Constantine put himself to the side of the door and, with one hand, pushed at it. It remained closed. It took a firm shove to swing it open.

She held her breath, her body tensed... Nothing jumped out.

Princess showed no fear and scampered over the sill. The big guy slid through next, Daryl at his heels, and since she held his hand, Cynthia followed as well, a choice she regretted with her first step into the house.

Ugh, Cynthia thought. *Ooh, dead thing,* was her wolf's addition. Sometimes, having a wild animal with different ideas about good and bad provided an interesting mindset.

While her nose wrinkled at the stench of something wrong, and she didn't mean just wet-dog wrong, her wolf wanted her to follow the smell that made her gag.

Don't puke.

"What is that smell?" she gasped, and why was it so hot? It seemed the air conditioning in the place wasn't working, the indoors just as hot and humid as the outside. Hotter perhaps even.

"AC is off. Actually, I think the whole power to this place is." Constantine flicked the pair of switches by the door, but the overhead light remained dark.

As they slipped from the mudroom into the kitchen, the smell grew stronger. Cynthia filtered some of it by having her T-shirt pulled up over her nose. She glanced around, noting the flies that buzzed around a pile of dirty dishes in the sink. Fruit in a bowl, barely recognizable, made a great science experiment.

It seemed someone had left without cleaning first.

In here there was more evidence something had happened, and not recently, given the fridge, when opened, showed moldy food. The power had obviously been gone for some time.

"Where should we check first?" Daryl asked.

Other than the mudroom, there were two options in the kitchen. One archway led to the dining room, the other to the hall. She could spot the rails on a staircase leading to a second level.

"Let's check the registration desk first."

Cynthia wanted to vote for the dining room. She could tell the stench was stronger out in the hall. She could almost see the miasma of wrongness in the air.

Death, her wolf advised.

Death and decay, and the culprit was the body they located on the floor behind the front desk.

Cynthia slapped a hand over her mouth, but it wasn't enough. While she could handle sewing wounds and minor operations and even blood, what she saw on the floor? That sent her running to puke outside.

Chapter 18

Daryl's T-shirt of the day: *"I'm a ray of fucking sunshine."*

INSTEAD OF CHASING AFTER CYN, who was looking to fertilize nature with her breakfast, he yelled after her. "Don't go far from the house and keep Princess with you."

Cyn wasn't the only delicate lady in need of fresh air. Daryl kind of wanted to join them. However, outside wasn't where the clues were.

As for letting her out of his sight? The dogman scent trace wasn't recent, just like this body. Judging by the lilac-colored pants and matching blouse, the corpse was probably what remained of poor Mrs. Jones.

"Looks like an animal got to her," Constantine observed without touching the body.

"Animal, or one of our new friends?" The stench of decay proved too strong to pinpoint if it was the dogman or dinoman that got to her, yet given he'd not scented anything reptilian, he was going to lean toward the canine.

"We should search the house. See if there are any more victims."

"Think we might find the guy who did this?"

Constantine shook his head. "This wasn't done by no guy. Only a monster could do something like this."

True. "Should we stick together or split up?"

"Want me to hold your hand, too?" Constantine snickered.

"Fuck off," was Daryl's reply. "It's a valid question, given those dudes are tough as nails."

"If you run into one, then let out a scream."

"Excuse me, but don't you mean bellow in a manly fashion?" Daryl retorted.

A snort left Constantine. "I'll check out the main floor." His friend stalked into the living room area.

"I take it I'm checking the bedrooms then," Daryl muttered, not that anyone heard. With a quick peek out the window, and spotting Cyn pacing, her expression pale, Daryl went looking for more bodies —and really hoped he didn't find a particular one.

While Cynthia was holding it together pretty well, given her friend's strange disappearance, he knew finding Aria dead would crush her.

He couldn't allow that to happen. *I care too much about her to see her hurt.*

Gag. And, no, it wasn't because of a hairball. He was thinking and feeling things he'd never imagined for a woman, and it came without effort or even thought. It was all so damned freaky, but he couldn't stop it, nor did he want to.

I want Cyn in my life. Even more, he wanted her happy.

The fact that the decaying smell receded as he tread carefully upstairs proved somewhat reassuring. The line of closed doors? Not so much.

When the first knob he tried wouldn't cooperate, he didn't think twice. He lifted a booted foot and kicked.

Bang!

So much for keeping their presence secret. Nothing came charging out of the other closed doors, although Constantine did yell, "Do you need Princess to save you?"

"I hope she gives you fleas," he hollered back. The joking served to ease some of his tension, but he truly breathed a sigh of relief when he realized the room he'd entered might have feminine belongings scattered, but no body.

But that doesn't mean they're Aria's.

After a quick peek in the closet and attached bathroom—both empty—he headed back into the hall. Three more doors to go.

The next one he kicked proved empty, the bed neatly made, the bathroom empty of toiletries. Not so for the next two. The first one, while tidy, did have a suitcase in the closet and clothes neatly hung. The other room was more of a disaster with men's apparel strewn all over, not out of violence but more a slovenly nature.

With their discovery, he'd go out on a limb and wager the first room belonged to Aria, a guest of this B&B, who wasn't alone in being missing. What happened to the other two occupants?

Utterly strange, yet he didn't pause to check it out further, not when he realized there was still a third floor. The spiral steps at the end of the hall wound upwards, but he couldn't see what lay above him. He emerged onto a small landing lit by a porthole window set in the side of the house. The paneled door didn't impede him. A swift kick took care of it.

The entire third floor, which might have begun as an attic, had been transformed into an apartment. The open area contained a living room with a small kitchen area. On one side, he found a bedroom, the scent of lilacs strong. The faded quilt on the bed reminded him of the one his mother kept in the linen closet because her grandma had made it. The dresser, made of carved wood, held an array of crystal bottles, perfume in some. Others seemed to hold only colored water. Even though he smelled nothing in here that seemed out of place, he checked the closet.

Nothing. So he headed to the other side where the first door yielded a bathroom. Nothing strange there.

But the next room proved sad. Pictures of a boy, awkward-looking with a stiff smile, lined the walls, the progression in age easy to follow. There was a twin-sized bed in here, covered in a navy blue comforter. Figurines—*Star Wars* and wrestlers and other comic book icons—were spread across the dresser and the two shelves hung on the wall.

A bedroom shrine to the son Mrs. Jones had lost.

He backed out and shut the door. No use in stirring up ghosts.

As he strode to the large diamond-shaped window, intent on peeking outside—*oh admit it, you want to check on Cyn*—he peered around Mrs. Jones' living space. Certain details popped out at him such as the fact that it was decked out in posh furniture, the leather on the couches real and buttery soft. Hung on the wall he noted a television to make even the biggest man drool. The carpet underfoot proved thick and lush—no cheap Berber here—just like the appliances gleamed with newness. Daryl had to wonder how big her husband's life insurance policy was because there was no freaking way this remote bed and breakfast brought in the kind of money needed for luxury at this level. If it did, then he was in the wrong business.

Nothing stood out in this space, apart from the largesse, so he returned to the second floor and stepped in the room he'd pegged as Aria's.

Cyn stood at the foot of the brass railed bed, hugging a bright scarf to her chest, her eyes bright with tears. "These are Aria's things."

He moved close enough to wrap an arm around her, pulling her close to his body. "We'll find her."

"But will she be alive or like that—that—" She couldn't say it, and he didn't even want her to think it.

He pressed her face into his shoulder, letting the fabric of his shirt absorb her tears. Soothing noises hummed from him as he stroked her back until, with a sniffle, she lifted her face.

"I'm sorry," she hiccupped.

"Don't be sorry for caring. You've done great so far. I mean, look at everything that's happened to you. First, you're a drugging kidnapper, then a pillow-smashing thug, then a bumper car survivor. And let's not forget femme fatale."

She snorted, the sound watery, but already getting some of her spirit back. "Okay, that was stretching it. And you forgot coward. I totally tossed my cookies downstairs."

"But stopped to rinse your mouth," he noted with a quirk of his lips.

Her nose wrinkled. "I did, and I popped a mint. I saw them in a jar on the counter. Oh God. I just ate a dead person's candy."

Before the tears could start again, he said quickly, "Sniff. Tell me what you get."

"I can't. My nose is stuffy."

However, the excuse gave her a chance to collect herself, and he really wondered how bad he had it for Cyn, given she honked her nose loud and hard, but he thought she was still the cutest damned thing he'd ever seen.

Shoot me now.

It was with their asses in the air, and their snoots to the ground, that Constantine found them.

"Pete and a few deputies are on their way. They're not announcing it on the airwaves because they want to check the scene first in case there's something we need to hide about our kind."

"Of course he's not announcing it," Daryl grumbled, trying not to sneeze at the dust that hadn't seen a vacuum in a while. "Announcing it might let people know there's a killer amongst us." It still bugged him that their own sheriff was going along with the secrecy.

"I don't smell the dog guy in here," Cyn announced, sitting back on her haunches.

Daryl leaned on his heels as well and frowned at the room. "I don't either, yet there's something here. Something that doesn't belong."

"Wasn't this the shirt she was wearing in the picture?" Constantine said, holding aloft a crimson top and touching his nose to it.

Cyn snatched it. "Yes, and there's that chunky pendent she wore with it. So she did come back here that night."

But what happened to her next?

Chapter 19

Cynthia: *So I came across a dead body today.*
Mom: *Need help burying it?*

SINCE DARYL and Constantine seemed determined to investigate every fiber in that B&B bedroom, Cynthia left, but descended via the rear steps. The boys had given the house an all-clear, the dogman stench restricted to the outdoors it seemed, and old at that.

In the distance, she could hear the sound of car engines and doors slamming, the sign chaos would soon descend in the form of cops.

Cops here to investigate the body in the front hall, a body that wasn't Aria's, thank goodness.

But it could have been. Whatever attacked the owner could have easily gone after other guests.

Daryl said it was a good sign they'd not found any signs of violence against Aria. Personally, Cynthia thought that was worse. It meant whatever came for her best friend didn't give her warning or time to defend herself.

According to Aria's phone call, she lived, but for what purpose? She'd heard Daryl and his buddies toss around the idea of shifter experimentation, and with the chief of police insisting the SHC knew what was happening and wished to turn a blind eye, she had to wonder if those suppositions were in fact true.

Was someone taking shifters from Bitten Point and playing God with them?

Shiver.

Surely not. The Shifter High Council would never stand for that. Would they?

The rear staircase led to an open area of sorts at the back of the house. On one side, a hallway stretched, and the faint whiff of decomposition made her tummy clench.

Not going that way.

On the other side was another wide arch leading to a formal dining room, done old-school style with vintage crown molding and white wainscoting, offset by dark and gleaming floor and window trim. The walls above the chair rail wall were hung with rose-patterned wallpaper, somewhat faded, yet a perfect look for a home of this style.

Off the dining area was a room that could only be termed a parlor with its blue velvet-covered chairs held aloft on spindly legs. Wooden curio cabinets with glass shelves were packed with eggs, all kinds of Faberge type eggs, in a rainbow of colors.

She heard a commotion of voices as the cavalry arrived, but she had no interest in answering their questions yet. Leave that to Daryl and Constantine.

The French doors to the garden beckoned, and she stepped out of them, breathing deep of the air, redolent with the smell of fresh flowers with an undertone of bayou. Like many places in Bitten Point, this home's property skirted the edges, the wildness of the swamp vegetation providing an interesting contrast with the more cultured and planned elegance of the garden.

A stone bench by a pond only a few paces from the door beckoned. She sat and let her fingers trail in the water, melancholy tugging at her spirit. To think they'd finally found a clue about Aria's last moments and immediately hit another roadblock when no true path to her friend emerged.

Why couldn't we have found a map or some coordinates that said Aria is here?

Then again, once she found her friend, she'd have no reason to stay.

Ahem.

Okay, so she did have a reason—Daryl, but she still wasn't too sure what he saw in their future.

If our mothers have their way, we'll be married before the end of the next week. But it wasn't up to their parents to decide, although it would help if they could.

It was pretty obvious Daryl had not meant to mark her. Romantic as it was that he'd lost control, she knew they couldn't base a future on a lapse of reason, a moment of passion. She was just as guilty of it as he was.

Lust shouldn't decide whom a person spent the rest of their life with.

Is lust all we have?

What about her enjoyment of his presence? Their love of onion rings. The way he made her feel.

But he doesn't know our secret.

Her wolf was so worried, yet Cynthia could state with a fair measure of confidence that she didn't think Daryl was the type to care about a defect on her part.

"It's not that bad," she muttered aloud.

As if her wolf listened. She seemed perfectly content to hide within.

Some people's inner beast proved aggressive, and strong-minded, insisting on being a part of all the decisions and getting their fair share of time outside the human skin.

Not Cynthia's wolf. Her wolf was more than happy to let

Cynthia stay in charge. Yet Cynthia in charge didn't mean her wolf didn't look out for her.

Danger.

The sudden stillness in the bayou caught her attention. Her head perked, and she was pretty sure her ears did, too, even if they couldn't move in this shape.

The hush that fell was unnatural. The swamp was never quiet, not when its residents always made noise. Yet something had silenced them. A predator walked nearby.

It belatedly occurred to Cynthia that perhaps sitting out here wasn't the wisest course, all alone in a place where murder and other nefarious acts had taken place. Never mind there were cops out front as well as Daryl and Constantine nearby. Could they reach her in time should something attack?

Eep.

Darting glances around her, Cynthia scurried back to the safety of the house, closing the French doors and locking them. Silly, really, given a determined person—or creature—would easily smash through the glass.

Funny how, a few days ago, these types of thoughts would have never crossed her mind. Now, though, she saw danger everywhere. Sometimes in plain sight.

Her mouth opened as she watched the lizard man with the leathery wings step from the shadows of a willow tree on the edge of the property. His gaze locked with hers, and he took a step forward. She took one back.

A part of her wanted to scream. Yell. Do something.

Daryl and so many other people were only steps away, but if she called for help, the lizard thing would take off, and despite his appearance, she wasn't entirely sure he intended to hurt.

Still, a girl couldn't be too careful. She whirled for just a second, eyes scanning the parlor for something to use as a weapon. The brass figurine on the mantel for the fireplace looked as if it might have some weight. She tugged it, but instead of coming free, it bent on a hinge.

But that wasn't the most startling thing.

With only the faintest of creaks, the façade for the fireplace slid to the side. Instant wet-dog smell wafted out, but of more interest, she recognized Aria's worn pink bunny slipper on the inside of the cavity. She hesitated before the opening, the brave part of her insisting she go looking for her friend. The smart part of her consciousness smacked her brain and told her to go get Daryl.

Before she could turn around, something clocked her from behind!

Chapter 20

Constantine's shirt, a present from Daryl:
"If my Chihuahua doesn't like you, then neither will I."

DARYL PEEKED from the bedroom window, watching Cyn in the garden. Her fingers trailed in the pond water covered in a layer of lily pads. A part of him wanted to shout at her to come inside. Something agitated his feline. It paced his mind, insisting she put herself in danger by sitting out there alone.

Then again, walls hadn't saved the old woman who now lay dead behind the counter, nor had it protected Aria, it appeared, or the other occupants whose dusty articles remained scattered and forgotten.

What happened here?

As a guy who'd tracked his fair share of prey in the woods surrounding the bayou, Daryl knew how to piece together what happened from scent.

Certain emotions and acts held a particular flavor to them. Violence had a flavor, sharp and hair-raising. Fear was a sour and acrid stench. Blood, of course, had its own scent, coppery and meaty at the same time.

None of those were in this room, yet Aria must have disappeared from it or nearby because on the dresser was her purse and, inside it, her wallet and some cash.

As Daryl stared from the window, he stroked the short beard on his chin, watching Cyn and wondering if perhaps with the danger floating around he should send her away. Send her somewhere safe, somewhere with no abnormal dogmen or dinomen or attempts to kill or, as Cyn appeared convinced, of things trying to kidnap her.

With her friend missing, though, would Cyn leave? She possessed a delightful stubbornness, along with a love and loyalty for her friend. But the harder they looked, the more dire things became.

And the more convoluted.

Look at the wealth of clues in this B&B alone. Several disappearances, none reported by the owner of the house—*perhaps because she was involved?*

Could knowledge be the reason Mrs. Jones had died? A loose end snipped before it could spill any secrets?

Despite the attempts to wipe their tracks, we're getting closer. Daryl could sense it, almost smell it with that sixth sense predators had when they were closing in on their target. When they did get in sight, he was coiled and ready to pounce.

Something rotten was preying on Bitten Point, going after the unknown and vulnerable. It had to stop. *I will make it stop.*

Movement outside the window grabbed his attention. Cyn rose and moved away from the pond to scurry inside. Had she heard or seen something?

The edges of the bayou lined the cleared yard, the stretching tendrils of the swamp looking to take back what it had lost.

It didn't take Daryl long to spot the lizard creature, stepping from the filmy tendrils of the tree. The thing stood and stared in the direction Cyn had gone. Then it lifted its head and caught Daryl's gaze immediately.

Nothing else was done. No rude gestures or implied body language. The dinoman didn't snarl or howl or blow fucking fire or whatever his weird kind did.

He just stood staring, and in that moment, Daryl wondered at its story. How did it become what it was? Because Daryl was now certain there was something unnatural, something forced or created, to make the two creatures they'd encountered the way they were.

The fading sunlight glinted off metal around the creature's neck, that odd collar that Cyn argued controlled their actions.

The lizard man, as if sensing his curiosity, reached a hand to grasp at the collar. Tugged it. Roared.

Then roared in Daryl's direction before loping into the vegetation bordering the yard. Only then did it occur to Daryl that he should have gone after it or at least told Constantine to while he tried to keep its attention.

The thing was a monster. It needed to be stopped.

The sound of thumping feet announced the arrival of the sheriff and a deputy. He peeked in and sniffed. "Any other bodies up here?"

"Nope, but the girl this room belonged to is missing."

"It happens," Pete replied. "Look at my son. One day, he's working at Bittech, the next he takes off, won't tell me where he's gone, and only calls to say he's doing great."

"At least your son is calling."

"I heard your lady got a call, too. So what makes you think this girl is missing?"

"I'd say the dead body downstairs proves something is going on."

"Looks like a simple robbery to me." Pete tucked his thumbs into his belt loops.

"Wouldn't shit have to be taken for it to be theft?" he pointed out.

"We don't know for sure what's gone yet. Could be they were after the old lady's cash."

"Or someone is trying to cover their traces."

A grimace wrinkled the sheriff's face. "Watch that you don't let paranoia get to you, boy. It's a wily creature that sinks its claws in and looks for ways to feed itself. While conspiracy theories are fun, most times, the simplest answer is the truth."

Daryl might put more stock in Pete's attempts to allay his fears, except he'd now seen too much in the past few days. He'd experienced things that really hit close to home, like when his sister disappeared for a little bit a few weeks back. What about the fact that Cyn almost got killed? He counted himself damned lucky she'd emerged unscathed.

Our mate needs protecting.

Gack. And, no, that wasn't a hairball that just about made him choke. It was the realization that he cared so much about Cyn. Cared.

Oh hell. No matter how many times he wanted to deny it, he was falling for Cyn. The bite wasn't an accident. He wanted her to wear his mark to show the world she was his.

Although, if I wanted it to show, perhaps I should have put it in a different spot. In order for someone to see it, she'd have to take off her pants.

Hell no. The only person she would strip for was him—even if the money was ridiculously good. Daryl wasn't afraid to apply a double standard to his girlfriend. It seemed he had jealousy issues he'd never known existed. Coveting Cyn. It sounded fucking dirty and fucking great.

The mental cursing and somewhat dirty thoughts went a long way to helping him deal with his epiphany and Pete's inane assertions that there was nothing untoward happening.

The sheriff and Constantine had their heads together talking, but mostly about the basics they'd discovered.

"I should go check on Cyn."

Yes, we should. Our mate needs us.

Cool it, he told his inner feline. *Admitting that I want her in my life doesn't mean I'm about to super glue myself to her side. She is a grown woman. I can't smother her all the time.*

We should cover her at night. Naked.

Deal.

Some people might find his mental bargaining with his cat odd, except Daryl was of the mind that sharing a body meant sharing decisions, compromising. Some people let themselves completely control the beast, going so far even as to repress it. His friend Caleb had done that for a long time, fighting his inner crocodile, convinced the cold-blooded reptile inside him was evil.

Caleb learned that balance was needed, something that Daryl had known all along.

With his determination that Cyn would be fine on her own—she was, after all, in a house now crawling with officers of the law, and not only were they all armed, they were shifters as well—he decided to check out those other rooms again, especially once he noted that Constantine and Pete had left the room to explore. He trailed behind, ignoring his panther pacing in his mind. Running downstairs to check on Cyn would wait.

The room a few feet down the hall held the interest of Constantine and Pete. They sifted through the stuff in the room, with the sheriff actually locating a wallet on the nightstand.

"The driver's license is for one Jeffrey Moore. He's from New England, according to this."

"But what was he doing here?" Constantine asked.

It was Daryl who noted the jacket hanging on the back of the chair, but more importantly, the name badge pinned to it.

"He's got a Bittech Employee card." Daryl held it up. "I'll have to call Wes and see what he knows about him."

As head security guard, Wes had access to employee records and had suspected, for a while, the company of underhanded dealings. The CEO, who happened to be Daryl's sister's husband, told Wes that everything they were doing was SHC approved. More and more, Daryl wondered if their blind acceptance of that was foolish. The SHC was only as good as the people ruling it.

"Here's his laptop." Constantine pulled it from a case and put it on the bed.

The laptop booted as soon as the power button was held down. However, the log-in screen stumped them, and less than a minute later, the screen went black as the laptop died.

"I guess Mr. Jeffrey Moore is keeping his secrets."

"For now. I'll take a peek at it," Constantine offered. "I might be able to find something."

Pete scrubbed a hand over his jowls, suddenly looking every one of his fifty-three years. "Do that, but keep it on the down low. Report only to me what you find. We don't want to make you a target."

"What happened to us maybe being paranoid?" Daryl couldn't resist the jibe.

Pete's lips pressed tight together. "I'm still hoping there's a rational explanation for all this."

"Other than the obvious that they were taken?" The snort went well with his arched brow. "I don't know why you keep covering it up."

"I told you, the SHC—"

"Fuck the SHC. There are people disappearing and being murdered. *Murdered.*" Daryl growled as he took a step forward. "So be a man, be an officer of the law, and do your fucking job. Protect the fucking people of this town. Or, if you can't do that, then at least make an attempt to do what's fucking right."

For a moment, Pete's face hardened, and Daryl braced for a punch. Surely the bigger, older man wouldn't let Daryl ream him like that, even if well deserved.

Instead, the lines in Pete's face sagged, along with his shoulders. "I know you're right. There is something wrong. Problem is, being right isn't simple... Or safe."

A voice called out from the hall. "Sir. We've cleared the main floor and swept the grounds."

"Did you find anyone else?"

Chet poked his head in the door, his freckled cheeks pale. The body wasn't something any one of them took lightly. "No more bodies, if that's what you're asking."

"What about suspects?"

"Negative. While we came across a few scents, there is no one but the men we came with and these two on the premises."

"And Cynthia," Daryl added.

Chet frowned. "Is that who's in the main hall? That body is still there."

"Body? I'm not talking about a corpse. I'm talking about Cyn, the girl you caught me with the other night. About chin-high, cocoa skin, and smelling of wolf."

Even before the Chet shook his head, Daryl was moving. He trampled down the stairs, taking them two and three at a time, doing more vaulting than stepping. On the main level, he took a moment to smell the air, paying little attention to the pair of guys taking pictures of the body.

Given they couldn't hide a murder, they treated it like a crime scene, bagging and tagging items while, at the same time, removing or wiping clean any evidence of this being a less-than-human crime. Actually, in this case, they would spin it as a wild animal attack. Yet that weak explanation wouldn't work with the abandoned items found on the second floor.

Hard to hide three disappearances in one place.

Maybe four.

No. Don't think that way. But he couldn't help a spurt of anxiety as he noted Cyn wasn't in the main hall or out front with the cop cars. Nor did he locate her in the kitchen, the comfortable living room, or the dining room. However, in the last, he did at least catch a hint of her scent. He followed it, ignoring its trail to the French doors and, instead, approached the fireplace.

He sniffed long and deep. There was Cyn, still smelling of his soap. Then, another scent he recognized, but didn't. It tickled with familiarity.

It was Constantine who had caught up to Daryl that nailed it for him. "That's the same smell that came from that guy's room."

"But I thought the theory was he was missing. This scent is fresh." It also didn't seem to move from this room.

Following his nose, and trying not to think of that ditty from the Froot Loops commercial, he went to the patio doors, grasping the fabric of the hanging drape and bringing it to his face. "He hid in the curtains. Then"—Daryl dropped the material and pivoted to face the fireplace—"he crept out while Cyn was standing here." Standing before the mantel, Daryl frowned. "And then it's like they both disappeared."

"First we have dinoman and dogman. Don't tell me just found invisi-man."

A frown pulled Daryl's brows together. "This isn't fucking funny, dude. Cyn is missing."

"I wasn't being funny. I mean, come on. Given what we've seen, can you really deny the possibility?"

"Yeah, I will, because invisibility as a trait could happen. All it would take was a very chameleon-like method of blending into the background, but at the same time, background blending wouldn't hide scent."

"Says you. Science can—"

"Kiss my ass," Daryl retorted. "She did not vanish into thin air with some dude." It wasn't even something he could contemplate, and besides, his cat was poking him again, and given it was right about Cyn needing him—*don't you fucking smirk at me, kitty*—he wasn't about to ignore it again.

"Fine then. If you don't think invisi-dude took her, then where did she go?" Constantine gestured to the room. "I might not have your developed sense of smell, but I have eyes, and they don't see her in this room. Or any of the rooms in this house unless she's hiding."

Grr. Ruff.

During their discussion, Princess had entered the room with its impractical chairs and other dainty items. She sniffed at the fireplace, tiny black nose pressed to the floor.

Grr. Ruff. She made noise again and pawed at the wall.

"Do you have to tinkle?" Constantine asked his dog.

If a dog could give a disgusted look, Princess did. Very deliberately, she turned from Constantine and scratched the wall. Then she turned just her head to shoot her owner an expectant look.

"She thinks there's something there." Impossible given the dining room was on the other side of that wall.

Daryl took the few strides needed to peek through the archway. Big wooden table, straight-backed chairs, a chandelier. No Cyn. Just a plain dining room...that was narrower than the room he'd just come from.

A frown pulled at his features. He strode quickly through to the kitchen, a kitchen the same size as the back room.

An idea glimmered, and he returned to the sitting room, more specifically the fireplace. He crouched down to peek at the edges.

Princess gave him her first approving look ever, and it occurred to Daryl that maybe the dog was kind of cute.

"What are you looking for?" Constantine asked.

"Seams. See them?" Daryl traced the line up the jut of stone then across the mantel. His hand brushed a statue, which wobbled.

It didn't fall, but was it him, or did the fireplace tremble?

He knocked the statue over, and it stayed flopped as the fireplace shifted to the side, revealing a dark entrance.

"I'll be damned. Secret passage." Every young boy's dream.

A whiff of mildew and dust wafted but, of more interest was a familiar scent. "Cyn and that fellow went this way."

"It looks like it goes down," Constantine observed, sticking his head in. "I wonder if this links to the tunnels I hear they built."

"What tunnels?"

"My grandfather told me about them when I was a kid. Rumor has it pirate smugglers built tunnels under the bayou, linking them to an oceanside cove."

"Surely they would have caved by now."

Constantine shrugged. "Maybe, except rumor also has it they were used back in the eighties and nineties to move drugs."

"That's insane. How the hell would we not know about tunnels under the town?" Daryl prided himself on being a smart guy, or at least an observant one. It burned he didn't know about this possibility.

"No one knows, for the same reason humans don't know we're right under their nose. A well-crafted lie is sometimes easier to believe than the truth. And let's be honest, we might be half-beast, but even we can't know about everything that's going on. The swamp is too big, and we are too few."

"And not everyone gives a shit." Just like some people could be bought. Greed wasn't just a human failing.

Daryl began to strip out of his clothes just as Constantine turned around. "What the hell, dude?"

"I'm going after Cyn. Since neither of us has a gun, I'd rather be prepared to fight."

"We could ask the cops for help," Constantine suggested.

No way could Daryl have held in his snicker.

Constantine joined him. "Okay, so we don't want to share the fun. I'm cool with that, but unlike you, I am going to keep my clothes on and rely on these two things." A big fist met the palm of his other big hand. When it came to fisticuffs, Constantine proved deadly and very light on his feet, something most of his opponents didn't expect. They had a chance to regret their mistake usually for about two seconds before Constantine knocked them out.

Daryl loved the money he collected on those wagers.

The change from smooth skin and two legs to four tipped in paws with claws wasn't a whoosh and a blink-of-the-eye procedure. It didn't take long—nature's way of ensuring they weren't vulnerable in between shapes—but the rapidity of an entire body changing its cellular structure to a new shape was not exactly pain free.

However, the pain proved fleeting, the excruciating agony in but a few blinks of the eye that was quickly forgotten in the thrill of wearing his other shape.

As his panther, all of his senses were sharper. The world might come to him in a slightly different way, yet there was nothing strange about it. He understood what the different shades he perceived meant, from the air currents to the heat, to the sharpness that allowed him to discern even the faintest of patterns in sifted dust.

As he padded into the hidden entrance, he did not yet bother to lower his nose to smell. No need. The trail practically blazed before him.

With each step, his cold fury grew. Felines might prove disdainful by nature. They might seem like good time tomcats with no cares, but that just hid the cold predator within. Cats were territorial, and if there was one thing Daryl thought of as his, that was Cyn.

She's my mate. And she needed him.

He just hoped he found her in time.

Chapter 21

Cynthia: *So a psychopath knocked me out and chained me to a wall.*

Mom: *Does this mean you're going to be later for dinner?*

REGAINING consciousness with a throbbing head was either a sign she'd had a really, really good time and drank a few too many or, in this case, seeing as how she was chained to a ring hammered into a cement wall, really, really bad.

Cynthia groaned as she pushed herself to a seated position, all she could manage given the circumstances. The metal rattle of the handcuff on her wrist kept her on a short leash. Her captive status also seemed a clear indicator someone wanted her to stay put. Given Cynthia counted herself a normal woman with normal reactions, she didn't take it nicely, or quietly.

"Let me go! Help! Someone, save me. Help!"

Scream as she might, no one came. No matter how she abused

her vocal cords, no one answered. All she could hear was the steady *drip drip drip* of water.

Bummer—and it gave her quite the urge to pee. No urinating would happen until she got loose, though. She tugged at the metal bracelet holding her prisoner, heaving and ho-ing, to no avail. Even propping her feet on the wall and pulling with all her weight didn't budge the ring firmly embedded in the wall. It did, however, dig the metal into her wrists, and in turn, her inability to free herself depressed her.

It's useless.

Breaking free using brute force wouldn't happen. She slumped, with her back resting against the cold, dank wall. Such a barren and icky place. How had she gotten here?

One minute she'd peeked in a secret passage, and the next, she'd woken here with a throbbing head. Where was here, though, and how long had she been unconscious?

Without a watch or a phone, she couldn't tell how much time had passed. This place had no window to gauge the position of the sun. For all she knew, bare minutes or hours could have elapsed. One thing she could probably count on was that the longer she remained here, the more likely it was that whoever chained her would return. It didn't take a refined sense of smell to note the strong stench of a dog left out in the damp.

Even more disturbing was the hint of the same type of meaty decay she smelled at the B&B. *Please don't tell me there's a body in here.* The feeble light from the one dangling bulb didn't exactly illuminate the shadowy corners piled with moldy boxes and crates.

The skitter of tiny feet didn't reassure. Where there scampered one rat, more surely followed.

We have to get out of here! Her wolf's insistence only served to heighten her own anxiety. Surely there must be something she'd missed, some way to escape. She'd already tried brute force and failed. What of a tool, an item she could use to pry at the metal links?

A crowbar would be perfect.

Her rude kidnapper, however, had failed to provide anything she could use within reach, or so she discovered when she visually catalogued every inch of the space. A very strange place.

It resembled a bomb bunker with concrete walls, sturdy shelving bolted to it, and metal cans, rusted on the edges, the labels long since molded into obscurity. The corners held leaning piles of boxes, most of them collapsed and spilling moldy straw. Packing material before those popcorn Styrofoam pieces came along. Whatever the room's use, it seemed as if it had been abandoned a long while ago.

Which really doesn't bode well for rescue.

Clink. Cynthia tugged again at her manacles and then glared at the cuff ringing her wrist. If only she could shrink her hand.

Hold on. She eyed her body—her very human body. There was a way to make her wrist smaller.

Stripping down wasn't easy one-handed and crouched on the floor. It also proved chilly in this dark place, lit by only a single light bulb flickering from the ceiling. How nice of her kidnapper to leave her light. It would have been nicer if he'd left her alone.

With her arm bound, Cynthia could only partially remove her shirt, but with it hanging off her shackled arm, she didn't fear getting caught in the fabric. Nothing more rookie than getting bound in clothes during a shift. It had happened during her teenage years when she found herself self-conscious about stripping down on a full moon for a run with others.

As naked as she was getting, she sucked in a deep breath. *Ready?* She couldn't have said if she aimed the query at herself or her wolf. Teeth gritted tight, she allowed the change to happen. It drew a sharp cry from her. Expecting the pain never made it any easier. However, much like childbirth—or so her mother claimed—the pain soon faded, leaving behind only the unpleasant memory.

In her four-legged form, her wolf took the driver's seat, but Cynthia remained very much aware. The deciphering of things proved a little odd. Her vision wasn't quite the same. The things she found interesting did not grab her wolf's attention at all unless it happened to be a nice pair of leather shoes—mostly because her wolf did enjoy chewing them. But still, a love by them both for fine leather products gave them something in common and a reason to go shopping.

As her wolf, things like scent, the visible evidence of tracks, and other things took precedence. Even better than this different perspective of her situation was the fact that her slimmer paw slid from the manacle with ease. Freedom!

But a freedom to go where, and what shape should she keep? As her wolf, she proved fleet of foot and definitely tougher. Right now, survival trumped her wolf's vanity over their appearance.

Poking her head out the door proved easier than expected, as whoever had left her here didn't latch it all the way. It took a bit of pawing, but she managed to wedge it open, only to find herself in a dark tunnel. The only light came from the bulb in the room. Out here, she noted a hum to the air, a machine-like hum probably from a generator that would explain the electricity to the room.

Lifting her nose, she sniffed. Cement. Dogman. Mold. Somebody else's scent, the same one that she'd vaguely noted in the room with her. Decay also permeated the air, along with something familiar.

Aria?

Her eyes popped open, and she took a step in the direction of Aria's scent. She took another. After a few steps, though, she realized she was going in the opposite direction she'd come from.

I might get lost. She paused, torn between finding her friend and going back for help.

Aria would never turn back. She'd find me. Because Aria was a true gangster with no fear. For her best friend, Cynthia would pretend she was brave, too.

Now just tell that to her racing heart.

On paws that really weren't crazy about the cold and dirty concrete, she tread, passing a few doors, most of them closed and, those that weren't, dark inside. The tunnel had very few lights working, the single bulbs spread few and far between, but at least she could see. Not exactly a good thing in this case.

The farther she went, the more her oh-poop meter waggled and wiggled and begged her to run in the opposite direction. Reminders that Aria needed her, that Cynthia could be brave, bolstered her.

Long gone, though, was the intrepid kidnapper and needle jabber. Things had gotten so dire with the discovery of the body. The adventure Cynthia had boldly gone on had turned sour.

Not entirely sour; we did find Daryl.

And now, even if by accident, she'd found the trail for her friend. The familiar smell teased Cynthia into going on, forcing her to rely on a courage that trembled in fear. Finding a second lone slipper didn't help her shaky confidence.

What if I find her dead body?

Cynthia doubted she could handle that alone. What if she ran in to dogman? She still didn't even have single Scooby Snack. What if she saw a giant rat? There wasn't a single chair to stand on and scream if she did.

The what-ifs piled on top of each other, slowing her pace, until she stood shivering in the dank corridor.

Poop on a stick. What am I doing?

Running off blind again, that was what, and look at how much trouble that got her in most of the time. Perhaps she should do something smart for once, make a mature and informed choice such as going back the way she came and fetching some help.

The dilemma of what to do kept her frozen until she heard the hair-raising howl of something on the hunt. Instinct screamed it came for her.

Eep!

Chapter 22

The shirt Daryl planned to buy for Cyn:

"These tits belong to a jealous boyfriend. Stare at your own risk."

THE TUNNELS that led from the secret fireplace entrance were long and twisty. They also branched off a few times, but they could have branched off a dozen more. Daryl would have still followed her scent.

His four paws ate the tunnel in giant strides, his feline for once not protesting the fact that it got its feet wet or that they didn't explore the interesting scents permeating the place.

Urgency drove him to run faster and faster, probably because, from a side tunnel, the fresh scent of the dogman overlay that of Cyn's. It seemed there was more than just one person using these hidden corridors. The lack of steady lighting, and the twists, made it difficult to predict what lay ahead. It didn't help that, in a few spots, parts of the tunnel had caved. While someone had dug an opening through these spots, they proved tight, especially for Constantine, who, being a rather bulky kind of fellow, couldn't always fit his broad shoulders through with ease. As for Princess, she dashed along not daunted at all, her sideways gait and lolling tongue expressing excitement at the chase.

The biggest dilemma came at a fork in the tunnels. Via one, Daryl could scent Cyn, and yet Princess dashed down the other.

"Princess! Come back to Daddy," Constantine called.

But the little dog was off, barking in the distance.

"Shit," Constantine cussed as he loped off after the dog. He shouted, "Dude, I gotta go after Princess, but you should keep going after Cynthia. I'll catch up."

Constantine would have to because Daryl wasn't about to wait for him, not when he heard the echoing howl from the tunnel holding Cyn's scent.

I know that sound. The hunting call of a predator. He put on a burst of speed, pushing himself harder and faster, almost running past an open doorway that suddenly appeared. He slowed his mad dash, but was still caught by surprise by the hairy body that hurtled from the room.

He'd found his recent nemesis—dogman.

Had Daryl worn his human shape, he might have snapped something witty like, "Hey, dog breath, eaten any shit lately?" But cats were more suave than that, so he settled for a *Meowr* and a snarl as they wrestled for dominance.

This time, he kept his panther form rather than resorting to a half-shift. His teeth were sharper this way, his claws more deadly. When the dog thing tackled him to the ground, he paid for it in blood, as Daryl tore the thing's skin to ribbons.

Unlike a normal creature, dogman didn't cry out in pain. He only got madder.

And more slobbery. *Like, ew, wear a fucking bib.*

Then Daryl felt it, an electric sizzle as if someone had touched him with a lightning bolt, except it came from the creature or, more likely, the creature's metal collar.

Daryl released the monster, who hissed and snarled as its fingers grabbed at the ring around its neck.

"You know that won't work, Harold." The man who stepped into view wasn't a stranger to Daryl. While the guy was a few years older, he recognized him as Sheriff Pete's son, Merrill.

The knowledge went a long way and explained why Pete wasn't keen on people finding out what was happening. His son was involved, and not in a good way, judging by the revolver in one hand and the remote in the other.

Given staying a cat wouldn't get him any answers, Daryl swapped shapes and hoped Merrill wouldn't use that moment to shoot him. Bullets hurt. Having gotten shot at a few times when he was younger and liked to play chicken with hunters, Daryl preferred to not explain to his mother, again, why she had to dig bullets out of his flesh.

Stretching to his full height, Daryl eyed the sheriff's son, sparing only a passing glance at the dogman crouched at his feet.

"What are you up to, Merrill?"

"Just doing my job."

"Does doing your job involve killing people and kidnapping others?"

The guy shook his head. "If this is your attempt to get me to talk and spill my guts, then you might as well stop now. I'm not telling you a damned thing. Why bother, when you'll soon be experiencing it? We need new subjects. Your girlfriend will make a good one, but you'll be even better. We don't have any felines to play with."

"I won't be a lab rat for your sick game."

"It's not a game. Everything I have done is fully sanctioned."

"You can't tell me the council agreed to let you kill people."

Merrill's lips twisted. "A regrettable accident. We've had a few recently. But nothing we can't hide. We've been doing it for years.

And, now, enough chatter. Get on your knees with your hands behind your back."

"Or what, you'll shoot me? I'd rather die than go willingly with you." Actually, he'd rather chew Merrill's face off and then pee on him, the ultimate feline disdain.

"Who says this gun has bullets?" The smile on the other man's face was anything but reassuring. "The lab prefers its subjects uninjured. Hence why this gun is charged with tranquilizers."

Uh-oh. Before Merrill finished talking, Daryl dove to the side, avoiding the first shot. A narrow tunnel, though, didn't give many options for movement. With nothing to lose but his life, Daryl did the only thing he could. He charged Merrill, taking the guy off guard.

They tumbled to the floor, hitting it hard. A metallic clatter let Daryl know Merrill lost his grip on the gun, but he'd kept one on the remote.

"Kill him," Merrill screamed, and Daryl didn't have to hear the low snarl from behind to know dogman—a man who used to be called Harold—rose to the command.

Wrapping his hands around Merrill's throat, he managed one hard tap, two, before instinct had him rolling to the side, and just in time, as Harold pounced.

The impact knocked the remote from Merrill's hand, and Daryl caught a moment of panic flashing in his eyes.

Before he could think on it, Harold jumped on him, hairy paws and claws slashing at him. Daryl caught the fur-covered wrists and held him at bay, barely.

Their struggle pushed him back, the dog-like creature strong, strong enough that Daryl lost ground. His foot stepped on something that crunched. It was enough to make him stumble.

"Fuck. " He grunted the word as he felt himself fall to the floor and then thought it again as he strove to keep Harold from ripping out his throat.

I'm a goner. In that moment, Daryl began mentally saying

goodbye to a few people. His position under Harold definitely placed him at a disadvantage.

The slavering jaws lowered. The wild light in Harold's eyes held not an ounce of humanity, nothing but a killing hunger.

It might have been lights out at that moment if something hadn't hit dogman and knocked him off balance.

Stumbling to his feet, Daryl noted a small wolf facing off against the much bigger Harold.

He could smell the fear radiating from her, see the fright in her eyes, yet she stood there, hackles raised, lip peeled back in a snarl, attempting to defend him.

Ah, how cute.

"Don't you worry, honey. I've got this." Daryl shot the dogman in the back with the tranquilizer gun he'd scooped off the floor. Shot him a second and third time, just to be sure.

Harold snarled, took a staggering step toward Cyn, then slumped to his knees before slamming face-first into the floor. Daryl didn't waste a second longer watching to see if he stayed there. He swung around looking for Merrill, but of the other man, he couldn't find a trace. The bastard had slipped away.

Relief suffused him as he turned back to Cyn and realized she was safe. Safe, yet why did she huddle against the wall, head hanging?

"Are you hurt, honey?" Daryl stepped over Harold and crouched before her. Stretching out his hand, he meant to stroke her, but she swung her head away from him. "What the hell? What's wrong?"

He gave her space as she changed shape, fur getting absorbed by skin, bones cracking and reshaping. A few blinks of an eye, an agonized moan, and then his mocha honey was slumped before him.

He dragged her into his arms, ignoring her squeak. He squished her in a giant hug. "Fuck me, but I'm glad I found you."

"You came looking for me."

"Well of course I did. You didn't really think I'd let you get kidnapped and not do anything, did you?"

She tilted her head and gave him a small smile. "You're the first man, other than my daddy, to ever rescue me."

"Do you often need rescue?"

She shrugged. "I panic."

"Not this time you didn't. You saved me, Cyn."

She ducked her head. "I couldn't exactly let him eat your face. It's kind of cute."

"Only kind of?" He laughed. "Wait, don't answer that. I'm just glad your wolf came along in time. She's a cutie, by the way."

He felt her stiffen. "You don't have to pretend."

"Pretend what?"

"That there was nothing wrong with my wolf. I've come to grips with it."

"Grips with what?" He frowned. "I didn't see anything wrong with your wolf. Four paws. Fur. Ears. Great big teeth."

"A stubby tail."

He snorted. "And? What of it?"

Her turn to frown. "I don't have a proper wolf tail, just a little wee stub of one that the doctor says came from my dad."

While it didn't happen often, sometimes interbreeding of the species mixed up some traits. But Daryl didn't get the big deal. "So what if you've got a bear's ass. I happen to like your ass."

"It doesn't bother you that I'm not perfect?"

Daryl squeezed her tight. "That's where you're wrong, honey. You are perfect. Just the way you are."

"If we weren't in a dark tunnel beside a snoring dog thing, I would so reward you for that remark."

"Don't think we can manage a quickie?"

A shout from up the tunnel. "No, you don't have time. None of us do. We need to find a way out."

Before Daryl could ask why, a rumble shook the tunnel. Then another.

It didn't take a healthy fear of fire for him to realize the smoke he smelled, even if still faint, probably didn't bode well for them.

Constantine appeared, jogging toward them with his little dog tucked under his arm. "Something's happened to the tunnel we came in through. We need to find another way out and fast before the smoke gets any thicker."

"What about him?" Cyn pointed to the slumbering Harold.

Given the trouble dogman had caused, Daryl's first impulse involved leaving him. However, with Merrill having fled, they still needed answers.

"We should bring him."

"I got it." Constantine heaved Harold into a fireman hold and led the way through the tunnel, but not very far, as another rumble shook the tenuous structure. The flickering light overhead went out, and the next one, yards away, didn't provide much illumination.

Water hit Daryl in the face, a stream of it that got thicker as the ceiling overhead spiderwebbed with cracks, cracks he couldn't really see because of the thick gloom, but could easily imagine.

"Run!" Constantine yelled.

Run where?

They took off sprinting, Daryl holding Cyn's hand tight lest he lose her in their mad and dark dash.

A faint light ahead showed one of the few light bulbs hanging from the ceiling. But more important than that, there was a ladder bolted to the wall nearby it.

Constantine dumped Harold and his dog before he scrabbled up the rusty rungs so he could shove at the trapdoor overhead. It didn't want to move at first. Yet, assaulted by Constantine's determined, shoving shoulder, it creaked, it groaned, and finally inched open. Mud slid into the cracks, but Constantine gritted his teeth and pushed again, heaving past the layer of swamp on top of the hatch to reveal a night sky.

Leaping to the floor, Constantine jerked his head at the opening. "You two go first. Then I'll grab this guy and follow."

With the smoke getting thicker, and an almost visible shiver vibrating the tunnel around them, Daryl wasted no time shoving Cyn at the ladder. He also couldn't help but gaze with a bit too much interest at her bare ass as it wiggled up.

A smart man, Constantine looked the other way. Daryl clung to the rungs next, moving quickly and lithely until he emerged in the swamp. He immediately turned and knelt.

"Hand Harold to me," he told Constantine.

"Princess first."

The little dog didn't seem impressed they were handing her around like a football, but at least she didn't try and tear Daryl's arm off.

Next, Constantine bent down to grab the hairy bastard, but it seemed it wasn't just opossums who could play dead.

With a snarl, Harold leaped and swiped at Constantine. The big man managed to avoid a deadly swipe from those paws, but, in so doing, missed a chance to grab Harold before he bolted away down the hall toward the thick smoke.

Constantine took a step, two, after him, and Daryl barked, "Don't even fucking think about it. This place is about to collapse. He's not worth dying over."

With a sigh, Constantine turned and grabbed the ladder just as another tremor shook the place, a tremor that kept going as something in the distance exploded. Smoke suddenly billowed from the hatch.

Without further ado, Constantine emerged from the ground, yelling, "Move away from it before it collapses."

Eyes wide, Cyn scurried to obey, and with Princess once again scooped off the ground, the three of them ran away, feet sloshing through ankle-deep muck, and didn't stop until they reached a copse of trees with thick trunks. Under its boughs, they huddled as the tunnel they'd just escaped gave a final belch of smoke. The hidden structure collapsed, sucking in a pile of water and muck with it.

The swamp took back what belonged to it, but it hadn't fed on Daryl and his friends, not tonight.

Hopefully not ever.

Chapter 23

Cynthia: *So I think I'm going to stick around Bitten Point.*
Mom: (*silence*)
Cynthia: *Mom?*

IT DIDN'T TAKE AS LONG AS expected to make it back to the B&B, especially since they had a bright beacon to follow in the sky. The hardest part was realizing they'd have to appear naked.

However, that fear proved groundless because Daryl sent Constantine ahead, and the big man snagged them some clothes.

Not much was said during that trek. What could they say? Harold had escaped. The tunnels had collapsed, and the only clues they had to where Aria went were gone. But where? And why?

Questions for the moment that would go unanswered, but other things might come to light. With the murder and the fire at the B&B, this time there was no hiding what happened.

According to the cops who'd witnessed the blaze, the fire seemed to start somewhere under the house. Nobody knew how, but the result lit the sky for hours. And everyone in town knew the place burned.

Everyone who could give a hand fighting the flames showed up, but there was no saving the structure.

Luckily, everyone made it out of the house in time, except for Sheriff Pete. No one had seen him since the inferno began. His men surmised he'd gotten caught in the blaze, but Cynthia—who now had a much closer relationship with sin because of Daryl—figured Sheriff Pete had set it to cover his and Merrill's tracks. Then he'd disappeared, just like Harold, the dog guy, disappeared. She'd like to think they all burned to a crisp, caught by the flames, but even she wasn't that naïve. Evil did like to flourish.

According to the fire chief—and Constantine confirmed—it would be days, if not longer, depending on structure damage, before they could venture into the ruins to look for bodies or to even try and venture into the tunnels leading from the house. The chances of it remaining unscathed, or even navigable, were pegged as unlikely. Whatever the tunnels hid below would stay that way, leaving them with more questions than answers, the biggest question being, was Aria still alive?

It annoyed her that they might never know what had happened. The fire obliterated any clues. Ashes to ashes. Secrets to dust.

From the ruins of disaster, though, rose hope. While Cynthia might not know where Aria was, she wouldn't relinquish the belief that her best friend lived and would find her way. *She's been through too much in her life for it to end so soon.* And Cynthia truly believed her friend was around Bitten Point somewhere, which meant Cynthia would stick around, too. But Aria wasn't the only reason to stay.

I am not going anywhere unless Daryl goes with me.

Since the human world couldn't know of their involvement in the fire at the B&B, it was thought best that Daryl, and Cynthia, vacate the area. Despite the cover-up in their presence, she did have to field one frantic call from her mother.

"Thea, baby girl, thank goodness you're alive. When we heard about the fire, your father went grizzly."

"Tell Dad I'm fine." More than fine, she was going home with Daryl. Home, oddly enough, being wherever Daryl took her.

"Ask your parents what hotel they're at." Daryl didn't turn his head as he asked.

A frown creased her brow. "Why?"

"So I can drop you off. You and your folks should leave town."

"Mom, I'll call you tomorrow." She hung up and stared at him. Poor Daryl seemed tense since they'd left the fire. He clenched the wheel of Constantine's truck that had survived the explosions from the propane tank alongside the house with only a few new dents. His friend said he'd catch a ride with one of his firehouse buddies. Daryl didn't argue, but Cynthia did make a mental note for them to score some wheels. With her car destroyed, and Daryl's on loan to Caleb, they would need transportation. "What's wrong with you?"

"Nothing is wrong with me."

"So why are you trying to dump me on my parents? What happened to hanging out to see where things were going?"

"That was before you almost died. Again!" He slammed his hands off the steering wheel, the jolt sending them swerving before he got control again.

"But I didn't die. Neither did you." And neither did Aria, she hoped. "The only people who have come to an early end are the bad guys. And I say good riddance."

"What if they didn't perish? What if they're still out there?"

She gaped at him as she realized the problem. "You're worried about me."

"Of course I'm fucking worried about you."

"Anyone ever tell you that you're adorable, kitten?" She intentionally teased him.

"Don't call me kitten. Or adorable."

"Why, does it make you think of your mommy?"

She could practically hear the air hissing through his clenched teeth. "This isn't amusing, Cyn."

"If you say so. If you're done whining—"

"I am not whining."

"Says the man who needs a baguette and cheese."

"You're driving me insane, Cyn."

"Good," she retorted as he pulled to a stop by his building. She hopped out of the truck and went skipping up the fire escape. He followed close behind.

This time, nobody waited for them outside or inside. She no sooner entered his apartment than the soot-stained shirt she wore went flying and hit the side of the garbage pail in the kitchen. Close enough.

"Cyn, what are you doing?"

"Getting these smelly things off."

"Then you need to get them right back on because, as soon as I grab some cash, I am putting you on a train back to the city."

"Good luck with that. I am not leaving."

"And I say you are. It's too dangerous for you here."

"It's dangerous for our kind everywhere."

Daryl scrubbed a hand through his hair. "Why must you be so stubborn? I don't want you getting hurt. Dammit. When I realized you were gone..."

Ah, how cute. The big, bad kitty was worried about her. Silly guy. Didn't he understand yet that sending her away wouldn't fix the problem? Perhaps she should point that out.

"So you think putting me on a train, by myself, that will drop me at a huge station downtown, again, by myself, is safer than me staying here with you?"

He blinked. Opened his mouth. Shut it. "There are no murdering dogmen or dinos in the city."

"No, there are crazy taxis and gangs and any number of other bad things that could happen to me. Unless this is your way of saying you don't want me." She thumbed the waistband of her pants and eyed him, wondering if she was misreading things. After all, what sane man would want a girl smelling of smoke and muddy swamp, with hair sticking out in crazy directions?

She wiggled her hips, and while her yoga pants did move down a little, it was on her bare, jiggling breasts his gaze focused.

"I'm getting naked," she said, pushing the fabric over the swell of her buttocks.

"I see that." His fists were clenched tight to his sides, his face even tauter. Yet for all his attempts to appear unaffected, he couldn't hide the heat in his eyes. "Why?"

"Because I'm dirty, Daryl. So very"—shimmer—"very"—shiver—"dirty." Her pants landed in a pool of fabric at her feet, and she stepped out of them. "I'm also very, very much in love with someone."

"You are?"

"Very. And I think he loves me, too, which is why he's so freaked out and trying to send me away."

"If he said yes, would you leave?"

She strode toward him, hips swinging, loving how his gaze locked with hers. She stepped right into him, and he laced his arms around her.

"I'm not leaving you, Daryl. I bit you for a reason. Because you're mine."

With those words, she broke free of his embrace and skipped to the shower. She didn't enter the warm spray alone. Daryl was right behind her.

He spun her under the hot water so he could plaster his lips to hers in a searing kiss. His mouth said what he couldn't. His body spoke the words he didn't know how to say. But she was all right with that because actions were what mattered.

As the water sluiced them clean, wiping the traces of their adventure, she molded herself to him. The heated hardness of his erection pressed against her lower belly, pulsing with excitement. Her sex throbbed as well, arousal already running rampant through her. It took only a touch from Daryl to ignite.

"Take me. I need you," Cynthia gasped in between pants.

"What if I want to go slow?" he murmured in between nibbles of her lower lip. "Maybe I want to take my time for once. Explore every inch of your luscious body. I think I need another taste of your cream. Maybe spend some time sucking those hard little berries of yours."

"Great ideas, for later," she growled. She grabbed his hand and pressed it against her mound. "Right now, I need you take care of this."

A groan left him the moment his fingers touched the slick folds of her sex.

"I want you," she whispered into his mouth.

Those words proved his breaking point. Daryl spun her around until she faced the tile wall. She braced her hands against it as he grabbed at her hips to pull her bottom back.

Without being asked, she spread her feet and tilted her butt to tempt him. The hard head of his cock rubbed against her, spreading the petals of her sex, dipping in enough to wet him with her juices.

He was going slow, so slow. She wiggled her bottom, pushing back and not above begging. "Please."

His hands gripped her waist as he pushed himself deeper. She couldn't help clamping down on him, squeezing his cock tight. It seemed to take forever before he was fully seated inside her, and then he paused.

She might have growled. She definitely pushed back against him, wiggling her bottom to seat him more deeply.

His fingers dug into her hips, and she heard him suck in a breath and then lose control. The withdrawal of his cock was only so he could pump her, slam her, thrust into her willing sex fast and hard. The sound of slapping flesh went well with her moans of pleasure.

Then he stopped.

She made a sound of protest, one he swallowed as he turned her around to face him.

"Put your leg around my waist," he ordered, and grabbed her thigh, bringing it up and, at the same time, exposing her.

He slid back into her, his long cock filling her, his lips finding hers under the warm spray of the shower. Everything was slick and wet.

Faster. Faster. His hips pistoned as he drove into her, each hard slap of his body bringing her pleasure higher. His lips trailed from hers along the line of her jaw, nibbling as he continued to thrust.

As her channel squeezed tighter and tighter, on the cusp of ultimate bliss, his lips feathered across the vulnerable skin of her neck.

Her breathing came in frantic pants. His mouth sucked at her skin. As she let out a low moan of bliss, her body trembled then shuddered as she came and came with violent intensity, as not only his cock spurted hotly within her but his teeth clamped down on her skin to mark her.

Claiming me.

And she couldn't be happier.

Only once they were snuggling in bed awhile later, skin still damp from the shower and flushed from lovemaking, did she let her fingers trace her newest mark on her neck.

"You bit me again," she stated.

"Yup."

"Why?"

He rolled her on top of him, anchoring her with his hands on the cheeks of her ass. "Because this time I knew what I was doing, and I wanted everyone to see it."

"What are you saying?"

He groaned. "Are you going to make me explain this out loud?"

Her eyes crinkled as she smirked at him. "I am so that there's no mistake."

"Fine. Think of the chomp as my panther claiming you."

"What of the man?"

His lips stretched. "The man wants to live Cyn-fully ever after with you."

What luck, so did she.

Epilogue

Cynthia: *I love him, Dad.*
Dad: *Harrumph. (Translation: I don't think he's good enough for you, so when he hurts you, I will skin him alive.)*
Cynthia: *Love you, too, Daddy.*

WHIR. Scratch. Scratch.

Cynthia awoke to find her mother leaning over her, measuring tape in hand, and a pencil clenched between her teeth.

Used to her mom's weirdness, she didn't make a peep, but Daryl let out a very unmanly "Eep!"

"Don't mind me. Just taking a few measurements." Her mother let the tape suck back into the reel while she jotted down some notes in a binder she'd placed on the nightstand.

Curbing her amusement took Cynthia biting her lips, but she failed to completely muffle a snicker as Daryl made sure the sheet was tucked higher on his chest.

"Measuring what?" he dared ask.

"Uh-oh," Cynthia muttered. "You shouldn't have gone there."

Mom slotted her pencil above an ear and beamed at him. "I am measuring the surface area of the bed and the surrounding floor. I already calculated the swath of space from the front door of your place to the bedroom. I do assume you will be using the front door and not the window again when you bring her back?"

"Bring her back from where? And what exactly do you need all those measurements for?" Daryl straightened to a seated position in bed, his eyes acquiring the wild look she'd noticed more than once in the early images of her dad taken with her mother. Poor Daryl had the look of a big cat caught in crosshairs. No escape.

"It's for the rose petals, of course. I figured we'd have them flutter on the floor in a straight line from the door leading to the bed. Which I've already ordered new linen for. White, of course, so the petals contrast nicely."

"But I like my sheets," Daryl exclaimed, clutching them tighter to his chest.

Her mother sniffed. "Those are bachelor sheets. Once you're married—"

"Married?"

"We'll also look into upgrading your living arrangements. Maybe we'll do it together." It was almost painful to watch the sudden idea bloom, especially since Daryl didn't know any better and had no time to brace. Cynthia bit her inner cheek as Mother dropped her biggest hit yet. "It's time Larry and I relocated somewhere new. I hear there's some nice housing available in town. Perhaps we can find two on the same street or, even better, side by side."

A sane man might have leaped from the bed—naked parts swinging—and run screaming into the bayou. But Cynthia hadn't fallen for Daryl because of his mental stability.

Her bad kitty got a look Cynthia didn't trust, especially since he smiled. No sane man would smile in the face of her mother's machinations. "That all sounds fantastic. We should have you close for when we start popping out kids."

"Kids?" Her mother breathed the word.

"At least a couple. And given you've got the marriage well in hand, I think Cyn and I should get working on that while you scout the local schools."

"Nothing but the best for my grandbabies," her mother crowed as she dashed from the room. "Wait until I tell Luisa we're going to be grandparents."

Cynthia didn't move until she heard the door slam shut. Then she turned on him and exclaimed, "You just told her we're going to have kids. Are you on catnip?"

"No, I'm in love. With you."

And that was all that really mattered.

Life in Bitten Point sucked Cynthia in, and over the next little while, though they didn't find Aria, her friend managed another phone call, a strange one where Aria said, "Don't look for me. I'm fine."

As for Cynthia, she was more than fine. She was in love, and gangster, especially when she got Renny to draw a permanent marker tattoo of a kitten on her butt.

STUPID SWAMP. It sucked at her limbs when she tried to rest. It coated her in a slimy second skin that reeked. But at least it hid her from the trackers.

She knew they were out there, searching. Hunting...

Hunting for me so they can drag me back to that place.

Never.

She'd been running and hiding for hours, and still, she didn't feel safe.

Knowing what she did, would she ever feel safe again?

An ululating shriek came in the distance, an eerie sound that echoed and froze the breath in her lungs.

They unleashed the hunters. She'd hoped to clear the swamp before that happened. Hell, she'd hoped to make it to a certain safe house before nightfall. However, the bayou hadn't cooperated, and now that nightfall had arrived, the chase was truly on.

As the primal scream came again, she didn't move for a moment, just remained crouched in the mud and weeds, hoping against hope the hunter wouldn't spot her.

For a moment, a shadow appeared against the moon, a rapier-gazed creature aloft on leathery wings.

Did it see her? Would it dive? Would it—

Shrieking in annoyance, it banked and flapped away.

A few dozen heartbeats later, she dared to breathe again and face forward, only to blink at her newest predicament.

Grrr.

The vicious sound came from a beady-eyed creature, muzzle curled back to reveal tiny teeth.

Seriously? She'd eaten squirrels bigger than this for snacks.

But, of more concern was the shadow that rose above them both that said, "Well, well, Princess, what do we have here?"

"Trouble if you don't get out of my way." Aria glared at the big dude through a dirty hank of hair. Even she could admit she lacked an intimidation factor, yet when he dared to laugh, she didn't think twice before acting.

The handful of mud hit the behemoth square in the face with a satisfying splat.

"Did you seriously just do that?" he asked with clear annoyance as he wiped the mud from his face with a hand.

"Get out of my way."

"Or what?"

Perhaps flinging a second handful wasn't the most mature response, but before she could claim he deserved it, Princess attacked.

Up Next: Python's Embrace .

Python's Embrace

Welcome to Bitten Point, where the swamp insects are nuclear-sized and the residents like to bite.

Don't mock Constantine's dog. Princess might weigh only six and a half pounds, but she's tough—so watch your ankles. Be warned, if she doesn't like you, then neither will Constantine.

Except he kind of likes Aria, even though Princess would prefer to bury her in a hole.

Could it be because Aria has secrets? Lots of them, and they all have to do with the danger stalking Bitten Point. People are missing, and some have turned up dead. Monsters are roaming, and not just the swamp at night, but the streets too. At the heart of the mystery is a bite-sized woman, a woman Constantine wants to hug tightly in his coils and...keep forever?

A cold-blooded snake, Constantine can't help but crave the warmth that is Aria, but can he keep her out of mortal danger long enough to make her his mate?

Chapter 1

STUPID SWAMP. The water had long ago leeched all the warmth from her limbs. Worse, though, was the mud. It sucked at Aria's limbs when she tried to rest. It coated her in a slimy second skin that reeked so badly even the bugs didn't dare make a feast out of her. But at least it hid her from the trackers.

Despite the fatigue drugging all her senses, she knew they were out there, searching. Hunting...

Hunting for me so they can drag me back to the institute and silence me forever—or worse.

Never.

Capture wasn't an option. Since her escape, she hadn't stopped running. She'd swum until her arms threatened to fall off. Slogged through thick marsh until her legs filled with heavy lead. She wanted to lie down and take a long nap, but that would mean giving up, and that wasn't an option.

The monsters at Bittech hunted her, and she didn't mean just Merrill and his henchmen. Real monsters existed. Beasts without conscience. They would just as soon find her as kill her. Nowhere was safe, not land, air, or water.

But I refuse to be their next victim. She wouldn't give in without a fight.

An ululating shriek came in the distance, an eerie sound that echoed, silencing the normal creatures that roamed the night. Stillness descended as even the bugs stopped their hum, and her breath froze in her lungs.

They unleashed the aerial hunters. She'd hoped to clear the swamp before that happened. Hell, she'd hoped to make it out of Bitten Point before nightfall. However, the bayou hadn't cooperated, and now that full dark had arrived, the chase was truly on.

As the primal scream filled the dark sky again, she didn't move for a moment, just remained crouched in the mud and weeds, hoping against hope the hunter wouldn't spot her. She couldn't help but crane to peer at the sky overhead, dark yet glittering with thousands of stars.

For a moment, a shadow appeared, spotlighted against the moon, a rapier-gazed creature aloft on leathery wings.

Did it see her? Would it dive? She ducked down lest the whites of her eyes give her away. She lay huddled, still and barely breathing.

Shrieking in annoyance, the hunter banked and flapped away.

A few dozen heartbeats later, she dared to suck in a lungful of air and face forward, only to blink at her newest predicament.

Grrr.

The vicious sound came from a beady-eyed creature, its furry muzzle curled back to reveal tiny pointed teeth.

Grrr.

Did it seriously think to threaten her? She'd eaten squirrels bigger than that for snacks.

But of more concern than the aggressive appetizer was the shadow that rose above them both. A deep voice said, "Well, well, Princess, what do we have here?"

"Trouble if you don't get out of my way." Aria glared at the big dude through a dirty hank of hair. Even she could admit she lacked an intimidation factor, yet when he dared to laugh, she didn't think twice before acting.

The handful of mud hit the behemoth square in the face with a satisfying splat.

"Did you really just do that?" he asked with clear annoyance as he wiped the mud from his face with a hand.

Dumb question seeing as how she had. "Get out of my way."

"Or what?"

Perhaps flinging a second handful wasn't the most mature response. Her excuse? *I'm tired.*

Before she could explain how he deserved it, Princess attacked!

The tiny dog soared over Aria's shoulder, and she swiveled her head to watch as the little runt latched its teeth on the coral snake lying on the rock beside Aria. Princess shook her head viciously, not releasing her latch while the serpent hissed and spat its displeasure.

The incongruous sight made Aria blink, but it didn't change the scene. The tiny dog still held on, and the snake's spastic death thrash slowed.

Aria fluttered her lashes again as a large hand waved in front of her eyes.

"Let me help you out of the mud." The low rumble had her turning to peek up, way up, at the speaker.

In the gloom, she couldn't tell much about the dude other than he was big, really freaking big, and unconcerned that the little dog had viciously taken on a poisonous snake.

"Shouldn't you be helping your mutt?"

He snorted. "Princess would be offended if I butted in. She's more than capable of taking care of herself."

Sounded familiar. Aria also had an independent streak, and that meant she eschewed his offer of a hand to crawl out of the muck—because it was so much more impressive when she slogged through the sucking mud and crawled onto the scrub grass.

But she did it, just like she'd escaped Merrill and Harold and all the others hunting her.

Exhausted, Aria flopped onto her back, probably not her wisest course of action, especially since she didn't know the intentions of the big guy. For all she knew, he was some hillbilly psychopath who'd played a role in the making of the movie *The Hills Have Eyes*—stupid Cynthia making her watch it. Good news, she didn't hear a banjo. And really, how dangerous could a guy be who called a tiny mutt Princess?

Her gut didn't twinge. Her inner eagle didn't caw or flutter her feathers aggressively. Trusting her instincts, Aria remained lying on the ground, giving her tired body a needed moment of respite.

Given the big dude surely didn't see women crawling out of the swamp every day, she expected a barrage of questions. Normal people would ask things like, "What are you doing out here?" or, "How long do you intend to live?" Men with tempers didn't take kindly to women slinging mud in their faces.

The stranger, however, didn't say a word, but he did strip his shirt off and use it to mop his face. The shadows didn't allow her a clear view, but she saw enough to realize his bulk was comprised of muscle, not fat. Lots of muscle.

We should stroke it and soothe his ruffled feathers, her eagle suggested.

There would be no stroking. Aria looked away and noted his dog had finished with the snake. The poisonous serpent lay limp on the rock, and Princess pranced and yipped, celebrating her kill.

"What a good girl. Did Daddy's princess kill the nasty viper?"

Had the big guy seriously just baby-talked to his dog?

Rolling onto an elbow, she gaped at them.

The guy had crouched down to grab his little pet and held her cradled in the crook of one arm. The darned thing was barely a bite, yet the big dude, who smelled slightly reptilian himself, toted Princess as if she were made of fine spun glass while Aria lay in the dirt, looking and smelling like a pile of refuse.

So unfair. Although why she cared she couldn't have said. *What does it matter if he mollycoddles his dog? And who cares if I'm filthy? I'm not looking to impress him.*

We need a bath, her avian side complained. While she could handle a little dirt, her inner eagle cringed at the filth coating them. Birds did not like filming their bodies with mud. It impeded their ability to fly.

Speaking of flying, time to get out of the swamp. She'd already spent too much time lying there and needed to get moving before the hunter made another pass.

Aria sprang to her feet, but moved too fast. Her vision wavered, as did her body. A hand steadied her.

"Careful there. I wouldn't want you to face-plant out here."

"Let me guess, you've got a softer spot for me to plant myself on? Like your bed or the backseat of your car?" She'd heard all the come-on lines, and none of them impressed her.

"Uh, no. What I meant was Princess does her business in this area. It's why we're out here, as a matter of fact. She had to do her business."

Squish. Aria's toes squeezed the warm piece of poop, and she couldn't help the hysterical giggle that bubbled from her. "Shit."

Chapter 2

WHAT TO MAKE of the woman who'd just crawled from the bayou wearing only a bra and panties? In all his years, this was the first time such a thing had happened, at least to Constantine.

As he cradled Princess against his body, he couldn't help but catalogue the enigma standing before him.

What a tiny thing, not even close to his chin, and slim too. A layer of muck covered her. He couldn't smell if she was human or shifter, but by the way she moved, he would have wagered shifter—an animal with grace, given her fluid movements.

Questions brimmed on his lips, the foremost being, *who are you*? Yet, he held off. He sensed a certain skittish quality about her. It wouldn't take much to send her fleeing.

She can't run if we hug her. Squeeze her. Hold her tight.

His inner snake only ever had one solution for everything.

Perhaps instead of crushing her to death, we should try cleaning her up and getting some answers.

Because he'd wager her story had a lot to do with what he, his brother, and friends had been investigating over the past while.

Something hunted the people of Bitten Point. Something screwed with them, and it was past time they screwed back.

Or screwed her.

Bad snake, and he didn't mean his shifter one. A certain part of him showed a little too much interest in the mud-coated woman in front of him. How perverse to lust after a swamp creature, especially one who'd stepped in poop and possessed a very dirty mouth.

Very dirty...

He interrupted her litany of curses. "Listen, my place isn't far from here. I've got an outdoor shower if you'd like to sluice off."

The mud-spattered face peeked at him with suspicion. "I am not getting naked for your entertainment."

"Keep your clothes on then while you shower, see if I care, but you might find them uncomfortable, and it will be harder to rinse your, um, girly bits." Not usually a shy man, Constantine balked at mentioning her more feminine parts, especially since he found himself more interested in them than was normal.

"Don't you worry about my girly bits. As for stripping, exactly what am I supposed to wear after my shower? And if you say you, I will probably hurt you."

The threat drew a chuckle from him. A tiny lady, but feisty. He liked that. "I've got some spare clothes you can borrow so you don't have to parade around in your undergarments or the buff."

Her arms crossed over her chest, hiding her petite assets. "How do I know I can trust you?"

"Lady, I don't know what kinds of guys you associate with, but I can assure you I have no interest in ogling or molesting someone barely bigger than my dog. I prefer my ladies with more meat."

The words were meant as reassuring, yet her eyes flashed. "There is nothing wrong with being petite and fine-boned."

"It is if you want something to chew on." Constantine heard her suck in a breath and could have groaned. *I did not just say that.* But he had. Odd, because he wasn't usually one to talk crude to the ladies.

Given arguing in the swamp wouldn't get them anywhere, he turned on his heel. Despite the darkness, he didn't have any problems finding his way. He'd lived by the bayou for as long as he could remember. And he could remember a long time. Just about the only thing in his life he didn't recall was his daddy. That cold-hearted snake had left as soon as Constantine's mother announced her pregnancy, and the asshole had never come back.

But as his mommy said in his father's defense, it was in a snake's nature to leave once he'd fertilized a female.

Constantine's retort when he got old enough to reply, "Real men don't run from their responsibilities."

Words he meant, and yet, the fear he'd turn out like his father made him shy from relationships. *I don't want to be my father.* Already a python shifter by nature, he didn't want to add "lowdown bastard who ditched those who needed him" to that description.

As he strode from the edge of the marsh, dog tucked under his arm, he didn't bother to peek and see if the woman followed. Princess watched for him. Her little head turned to spy behind, her body tense in his grip.

It took only a few minutes of walking before the porch light appeared, a beacon in the darkness that drew all manners of flying bugs. This close to the Everglades, they saw their fair share of insects, some with enough legs and pinching mandibles to worry him. Princess had delicate skin.

A few more strides and the house he shared with his mother came into view. By most standards, it wasn't much. A compact, three-bedroom bungalow on wooden stilts. Heavy rains sometimes made the house appear as if it floated like an isle.

It chagrined him to realize he wondered what the woman thought of his home. *I'm not ashamed of where I come from.* Not ashamed, and yet, he kept pouring money into renovation projects. He also poured a lot of sweat and curse words.

The result? The house looked a lot more presentable than it used to. It had better seeing as how Constantine had spent plenty of his paychecks since he'd started working to improve the place. New siding, new windows, along with a roof he and Daryl, his older brother's best friend, had replaced themselves.

On the inside, he'd gutted the kitchen and put in new cabinets for his mom. Nothing fancy. He'd grabbed those prebuilt white ones on a clearance at the big box hardware store the next town over. But his mom loved it. Just like she loved the laminate flooring he'd installed throughout.

It might not seem like much, but it was home. *My home. Take it or leave it.*

Again, why he gave a shit, he couldn't have said. Besides, it wasn't as if she would be staying. He'd get her cleaned up and on her way as quickly as he could.

No leaving. Oursssss.

Not ours and, hell yeah, she was leaving. Constantine didn't run a home for muddy waifs. Even feisty ones that intrigued him.

He veered from the house as he hit the yard and headed to the outdoor shower unit. It didn't have much in the way of privacy, consisting of a single pole sticking up from the ground embedded in a concrete slab. The green garden hose, which he'd buried underground from the house to the outdoor unit, was clamped to the post and ended in a rusted showerhead at the top.

"There's the shower if you want to use it. I'll go grab you a towel. Ma keeps a pile of them stacked by the back door." Because, sometimes, Constantine liked to play in the mud, too.

The woman didn't reply. As a matter of fact, she'd not said a word at all. Whatever. He didn't pause to see if she turned on the water. Didn't care either if she stalked off. Less trouble for him if she did.

A squeak of a handle getting cranked and the sound of rushing water let him know she'd stayed, but for how long?

The woman had yet to explain why she'd crawled out of the swamp, and while she didn't seem keen on his presence, she'd not taken off or demanded a phone.

Who was she?

Ourssss.

Despite his inner reptile's certainty, he was sure they had never met her before. Then again, given the coating of muck on her skin, she could have been his next-door neighbor for all he knew. Except old Kenny next door was about two hundred pounds heavier and a guy.

Still tucked under his arm, Princess wiggled, and he put her down on the ground beside him. His faithful companion stuck to his heels as he made his way to the mudroom at the back of the house he shared with his mom. And, no, he wasn't a mama's boy. Much.

However, he saw no reason to move out when his mother owned a perfectly sized house for them to share. He helped out with the bills and the man's work that needed doing while she cooked and washed his clothes. But it should be noted that he did do the dishes.

Within the mudroom, think plywood box on concrete patio stones, which basically acted as a shelter for the clothes washer and dryer, he snagged a clean towel with some vivid pattern. His ma long ago had given up on white linens. He and his brother were too dirty for it.

While in the mudroom, he also pulled open the dryer and scrounged out a long T-shirt, but he didn't bother with pants. He doubted she'd fit in his or his mother's. The woman he found possessed a waist so tiny he was sure both his hands could span it with room left over.

Someone needs to feed her.

I've got something to feed her.

Fuck, what the hell was wrong with him tonight? Ever since the fiasco in the tunnels a day or so ago, he'd found himself on edge. Jumping at shadows. Turning to check out every single noise. However, being vigilant didn't explain his odd interest in the muddy waif. Except she was probably not so muddy now.

I wonder what she looks like.

As he exited the mudroom, his gaze veered her way, and he noted she stood to the side of the outdoor shower, hand outstretched under the gushing torrent.

"It usually works better if you get under the spray," he remarked as he approached.

"It's cold."

"Well, duh. It's an outdoor shower. You didn't really expect us to pipe hot water out here."

The dirty look she tossed him from under a wet hank of hair almost made him smile.

"Hot water would have been nice."

"So would not tossing mud at people you meet for no reason. But I guess we both can't get what we want."

Her lips twitched. "Touché. Hypothermia it is then."

"Once you get the mud off you, then we can get you into some warm stuff."

"What? Aren't you going to offer to warm me up yourself?" An impish tilt of her lips showed pearly white teeth. Teeth that he'd love to have nip him.

No, I don't. "I already told you, lady. You're not my type." Now someone tell that to his libido, which kept making sly remarks in his head.

"Good to know. Then I guess there's no need to tell you to turn your back while I strip off these rags."

The bra was first to go, and before he could avert his gaze, Constantine caught a glimpse of small peaches, tipped with hard buds, barely a mouthful. Yet so very tempting...

He quickly turned his head and heard her soft chuckle. "Prude."

"Most women would call it respect."

She snorted. "Now there's a word I don't hear often. Most men seem to think the fact I have a hole between my legs makes me fair game."

"Then I feel sorry for you because, in my world, women are to be cherished and protected."

"Must be nice."

Was it him, or did her words hold a wistful note? He didn't dare turn around to see, but he wanted to. Wanted to see the water cascading down her body, moisture pearling on the tips of her breasts.

Get a grip. He hung his head and closed his eyes. He clenched his fists, too, as he breathed deeply, wondering at the strange effect she had on him.

Boring thoughts, such as the grass he needed to mow, helped him to somewhat resist her allure. The chatter of her teeth as she sluiced off under the spray also aided to bring him under control.

As soon as the water shut off, he held out the towel that dangled from his fist, still not daring to turn around.

She snagged it from him. "That was f-fucking cold," she stuttered.

I'll warm you up. He thought it, but said, "Are you decent?"

An unladylike sound emerged from her. "Not according to most of the people who know me."

"I meant are you wearing the towel?"

"Yeah, why?"

Pivoting on his heel, Constantine forgot what he meant to say as he saw her face. A face he recognized.

"Holy shit. You're Aria. The girl we've been looking for." The woman they'd combed the town for only to hit dead ends, literally. The body count kept growing.

The irony of her appearing practically at his doorstep would have made him laugh, except his snake chose that moment to hiss.

Finally, we have found the woman we've been waiting for.

Like hell.

Chapter 3

DAMN AND DOUBLE DAMN. How did this guy recognize her?

"No, I'm not," she hastily replied. The last thing she needed was for word to get around that she'd escaped and surfaced. The crooked gang working in the underground lab at Bittech would come after her for sure if they found out. Better to let them think she'd died in the swamp.

As a matter of fact, she shouldn't let anyone know her whereabouts until she'd spoken to her boss and had gotten her ass to the safe house he'd told her to use in case things got hairy—or in this case, leathery.

The big guy snorted in reply to her rebuttal. "Of course it's you. I'm not a fucking idiot. Cynthia showed us enough pictures of you for me to know what you look like, especially now that your face is clean."

"You know Cynthia?"

"Damned straight I do. She hooked up with Daryl as soon as she came to town, and we've all been looking for you."

A moue twisted her lips. "Cynthia was supposed to go home and forget about looking for me." But she should have known her best friend wouldn't accept her disappearance.

"Don't be giving her shit because she cared."

A sigh left her. "I am not giving her hell, but her caring and coming to look for me complicated things. And how do you know Thea anyhow? Who are you?"

"Constantine Xavier Boudreaux."

She blinked. "Wow, that's a mouthful." Only too late did she realize how that sounded, and judging by the grin stretching his lips, so did he.

"More than a mouthful, and handful."

She couldn't help a roll of her eyes. "And there you go proving my point men only have one thought in their little brains."

"I thought we'd just ascertained mine was big." His smile widened.

A piercing shriek broke the staring match between them.

Immediately, she tensed and turned to look at the sky. "We need to get to cover."

"It's just some swamp bird looking for some dinner," the big man said as he leaned down to scoop his dog off the ground.

"I know. That's the problem. I think I might be his dinner." She muttered the last part, but he still heard.

"Don't worry. Whatever that is won't dare mess with us."

"Shows how little you know. And if you're not worried, then why are you picking up your dog?"

"Because she likes to be cuddled." He said it so seriously.

And she almost retorted, *I'd like to be cuddled, too.* Except she didn't. Usually, that was.

Aria didn't like people touching her, but for some reason, she couldn't help but wonder what it would feel like to have this big guy put his hands on her.

Madness. Maybe a result of her time spent as a prisoner. *Am I going mad?*

Before she lost her mind, she needed to talk to her boss. "I need a phone." And a place out of the open. Despite Constantine's assurance that nothing would attack, he didn't know what she did.

The hunters weren't ordinary birds of prey, and while supersized, Constantine wouldn't prove a match for those psycho beasts.

"Why don't you put this on first?" He thrust out a hand in which he gripped dark fabric. "I brought you a shirt."

"Is it a special shirt that I can use to dial someone's number?" was her sarcastic reply. She did, however, snatch it from him and tugged it over her head. Once it covered her, a yank on the towel pulled the damp cotton away from her body. "What should I do with this?" She waggled the wet towel.

"You can drop it in the laundry room."

"Which is where?" she asked.

"This way." Without any warning, he bent and forced her onto a wide shoulder before standing again.

Stung with shock, it took her a moment of dangling down his back before she yelled, "Put me down. What do you think you're doing?" Her shock at his actions explained her racing heart, but what she didn't understand was her eagle's lack of reaction. Where was the outrage? The anger?

A male should show his dominance.

Before she could digest that foreign concept, Constantine explained his illogic. "I am carrying you so your feet don't get muddy. And before you freak out some more, I might add I am doing the same thing with Princess."

"And this is the only way you thought to carry me?" she managed to say, not without a lot of incredulity.

"I only have one hand, lady. What else did you expect?"

"You could have put your dog down and carried me in both your arms."

A snort shook his frame. "Yeah, no. I'm not about to have my hands full and my dog vulnerable to whatever is in the sky."

As if to add weight to his argument, another screech pierced the night, closer this time. Aria couldn't help but shiver. While he might imagine the normal variety of hunter, she knew better. They needed to get out of the open.

She held her tongue, lest he change his mind about letting her use the phone. Another part of her, though, wondered at her blind trust of this behemoth.

This close, she could truly scent his skin. She'd spent enough time around shifters lately to realize he was a reptile of some kind. Kind being the key word.

"What are you?" she blurted out.

He didn't hesitate. "A snake. Python to be exact."

"I've never seen a snake shifter before."

"That's on account we're pretty rare. I got the gene from my dad. And you're one to talk about rare, seeing as how eagle shifters are just about extinct last I heard."

"How do you know what I am? I didn't realize snakes had such a good sense of smell." She answered her own question immediately. "Cynthia." Was there anything her best friend hadn't divulged?

Mental note to self: buy duct tape for her blabber- mouthed bestie.

"Were both your parents eagles?" he asked. A valid question since the same types of breeds had an easier time procreating.

"I don't know. I never knew them." Orphaned at a young age, Aria didn't just have no memories of her parents. She didn't have pictures or even names either. She knew nothing at all about who and what she was.

Coming into her shifter heritage as a teen had proved terrifying. The first burst of pain when she'd morphed for the first time sent her into a blind panic. It was a wonder she'd survived, given she crashed out of her bedroom window and tumbled to the ground, breaking an arm. She got in trouble for that, her foster parents not taking kindly to what they thought was a runaway attempt.

In a sense, they were right. She wanted to run...away from herself. For a few years, she thought herself a freak, a monster, until she met Thea.

Actually, I crashed into her. She'd slammed Thea into a tree and exclaimed, "You smell different. You're like me. Except more doggyish."

Not the most auspicious of intros, and yet, from that moment, they became the best of friends.

It helped Aria to realize she wasn't alone. Thea was just like her, well, not exactly like, given Thea morphed into a wolf, but her friend knew about shifting. With her guidance and the lessons learned from Thea's parents, Aria came to understand what she was. She'd just never discovered who she was.

As they entered the house, another cry pierced the night, closer this time. Constantine shut the back door, shielding her from the eyes of the hunter. Or was that hunters? Merrill and his gang had more than one type of creature at their disposal. Would he dare unleash them all, though, in the hopes they'd bring her in—dead or alive?

Constantine crouched down, but if she thought he meant to put her down, she was mistaken. Only the dog got that privilege.

It seemed Princess didn't like her loss of status.

Yip.

"Sorry, Princess. Daddy's got to get Aria warm before she falls apart from shivering."

"I w-won't break." It might have sounded more convincing if she'd managed to say it without chattering teeth.

"No, but you might get sick. We need to get you warm."

How about you just wrap me in those big arms of yours? He certainly felt awfully warm for a man who was supposedly cold-blooded.

She almost giggled. Then she frowned. What was wrong with her? Aria didn't cuddle. Nor did she want a man to hold her or warm her.

Dizziness assailed her as Constantine flipped her off his shoulder to cradle her in his arms. *Now who's the princess?* She bit her tongue before she could taunt the dog out loud.

"Let's get you to bed."

Bed with the big hunk?

"I'm not sleeping with you," she mumbled, barely managing coherence her shaking got so severe.

"Would you stop it already with assuming I'm going to molest you? I have no interest in you. Other than making sure you don't get sick and die on me."

"I don't get sick." She truly didn't. Shifters had an amazing ability to heal from things.

"You might not get sick from normal things, but you spent quite a bit of time, from the looks of you, in the bayou. There are things out there that will make even the toughest of us ill. Swamp fever isn't something to scoff at."

"I don't have a fever. I'm cold." So cold, right down to the marrow of her thin bones.

"Give me a second and we'll work on that." He dropped her onto a bed with a mattress so hard she didn't make a dent.

"I need a blanket." Forget the phone. Right now, she just wanted to get this numbness out of her limbs.

He yanked a cover over her, a thick one. Still, she trembled.

"I'm cold," she complained in a plaintive voice she didn't recognize.

"I should call a doctor."

At the mention, her eyes opened wide and she uttered a frantic, "No. Don't call anyone. No one can know I'm here."

"What's going on, Aria? Who are you running from?"

"The monsters." She giggled.

"What monsters? What are you talking about?"

"Can't say. It's a secret. Shhh." She muttered the words as her eyes closed. "So cold." The shivering wouldn't stop to the point her bones ached.

A heavy sigh filled the silence before the mattress beside her dipped.

In a flash, she popped open her eyes and regarded Constantine, who lay facing her.

"What are you doing?"

"Warming you up. Roll over."

"But—"

"Must you constantly argue? Roll over so I can warm you and leave."

The tough side she'd cultivated as a veneer against the world wanted to protest his help, even if she needed it. She ignored that voice and obeyed Constantine's deep, rumbled command instead. She tilted onto her side facing away from him.

An arm came around her and yanked her close, tucking her against the massive length of him. The intimacy of the position had her sucking in a breath. Tucked so tightly against him, she could feel the hardness of his frame, but even better, the heat.

He radiated delicious warmth. A soft sigh exhaled from her as her shivering body soaked it in.

A large hand splayed across her belly, spreading warmth of a different kind through her. Her bottom wiggled, inching closer to him. As she felt a certain distinctive hardness, she froze.

"Um, what happened to my not being your type?" she asked as the evidence of a massive erection pressed against her backside.

"You're still not my type, but I am a normal man and you are a woman. Not much I can do to change that. But don't worry. I'm not planning to do anything about it. I am tired, so if you don't mind, can you stop arguing for one minute and go to sleep?"

Not argue? But it was what she did best.

Except, in this instance, she didn't really want to talk him into moving away. In that moment, Aria enjoyed a warmth and peace—*I feel safe*—she'd never enjoyed.

Exhausted from her escape, and safe within the cocoon of his body, Aria fell into a restless slumber.

Chapter 4

NO SLEEP FOR ME TONIGHT.

Constantine, despite his claims to the contrary, found himself much too attracted to Aria to feasibly manage any kind of sleep.

It made no sense. He'd not lied when he told Aria he preferred bigger girls. Taller girls. Women who could handle a man his size.

Aria didn't have an extra ounce of fat on her anywhere. Then again, since she belonged to the avian family of shifters, staying slim wasn't just a necessity, but a fact of life. In order to have the ability to actually fly, bird species needed to remain light.

Everything about her was slim, even her little butt. Little but not unnoticed where it pressed against his groin.

Hisssss.

Talk about pure torture. Never before had an erection of this magnitude plagued him, and without her doing a thing.

What kind of perv lusted after a woman when she was so evidently exhausted and chilled from her ordeal? Sure, he'd climbed into bed with altruistic intentions, but altruism didn't stop the dirty thoughts in his head.

Wrap around her. Squeeze her.

His reptile really didn't see the problem. The man, however, didn't let his baser self dictate his actions.

As warmth returned to her limbs, her body relaxed.

He heard more than saw as Princess hopped onto the bed, a bed with a lower frame so she could make the leap. He opened his eyes and noted his dog's big eyes fixated on Aria's face. Princess let out a small *grr* and *yip*.

"Shh," he hushed. "She's sleeping. Don't wake her."

His tiny dog didn't seem to care. She growled again. Someone didn't like her spot being usurped in his bed.

How cute. His little puppy was jealous. "Come here, baby. Come snuggle with Daddy."

Since he'd gotten Princess a few years ago, rescued actually from a pet store that caught fire, lots of folks eyed their pairing with incredulity. But that was because they just didn't understand. From the moment those huge eyes caught his where she stood in her cage, barking with the ferociousness of a rabid pit bull but the size of a hamster, he'd fallen in love.

His friends mocked his choice in pet only once, unless they had a good dental plan. Some guys loved their cars. Others collected shit. Constantine doted on his dog.

He also pretty much lived by the motto on one of his T-shirts that said, "If my Chihuahua doesn't like you, then neither will I."

As Princess crawled under the blankets and snuggled up against his spine, he couldn't help but wonder if he might have to revise that stance, though, because, while Princess might not like Aria, he quite did.

Attraction, though, didn't mean he ignored the weirdness about her re-appearance. What did she run from? Where had she spent those missing days?

He and his friends had combed the town, yet no one had seen any trace of Aria after her last visit to Bitten Pint, the local bar.

They did eventually find her things in Bedbug Bites, a bed and breakfast thought closed down. Within that B&B they'd discovered not only her abandoned personal items, but also the body of the owner. More importantly, they'd found some old smuggler tunnels under the house.

However, forget any clues or directions to Aria or the culprits terrorizing their town.

A crooked sheriff set fire to the place and left them back at square one.

But they might now finally have an advantage. *I found Aria.* Actually, she'd found him, but either way, he'd bet a lot of the answers were inside her head. Questions that would have to wait until morning when she woke.

Forget her fatigue. *I should wake her up and demand answers.* While she rested, their town was being stalked. Friends and families fought off attacks, and those who failed went missing.

Who was behind it? Dinoman and dogman, mutant creatures, were at the heart of the conflicts, yet they hadn't come out of nowhere. Someone had created them.

The owner of Bittech, a medical institute that did experiments on shifter blood and genes, claimed innocence and that all their work was sanctioned by the SHC—Shifter High Council, the governing body for their kind.

Should the blame go to Sheriff Pete, whose son, Merrill, appeared involved?

Who could they point the finger at? Who could they punish?

Every trail they followed had led to a dead end. Until now. He couldn't help but inhale the scent of Aria and wonder if, in his arms, slept the missing piece of the puzzle.

What had Aria seen? What did she know? And the bigger question, could he protect her from what she ran from?

Like duh. Of course he would. *I'll crush anyone that lays a hand on her*. And, if they were tasty, eat them.

Chapter 5

THE HUNTERS CHASED HER, with raucous calls and murderous intent. Through the woods she sprinted, arms slapping away branches, spitting out the cobwebs that clung to her face as she ran into them.

But she dared not stop or slow down.

They'll kill me if they catch me. Or, worse, they'd do to her what they'd done to countless others. *Make me into a monster.*

She burst free from the foliage and found herself teetering on the edge of a cliff. Arms windmilling, she strove to keep her balance. Down didn't look like an option with its steep incline and sharp rocks. Behind her, a creature bayed, a thing that had once been a man but now was lower than an animal.

I can't go back that way. That left her only one option.

Up.

She flung herself into the air, arms spread, calling forth her eagle. The pain proved excruciating but fleeting. Arms turned into wings. Feet into claws. Her face pulled into a beak while her eyes got razor-sharp vision.

With a mighty pump of her wings, she soared, emitting a

laughing caw as the hunters spilled out onto the cliff she'd just perched on, howling their disappointment into the air.

Ha ha. Miss me, miss me. Now you get to—

The heavy weight slammed into her, shocking the breath from her lungs, and she went plummeting down, down, down, in a deadly spiral. The ground rose to meet her and—

"Wake up."

The shaking of her body and barked words had her eyes springing open. For a moment, disorientation assailed her as she cast her gaze frantically about. "Who are you? Where am I?"

"It's okay, Aria. You're safe. It's me, Constantine, remember me? I helped you after you crawled out of the swamp."

Ah yes, the big snake man with the little dog. She recalled him, just like she recalled she'd yet to put a call in to let anyone know where she was.

She struggled to sit up, but didn't make it all the way before dizziness had her clamping her eyes shut and slumping back down.

"What's wrong with me? Why is it so hot in here?" She managed to thrash her legs and push off the covers.

A chilly hand pressed against her forehead. "You're burning up."

Burning with desire. Through slitted eyes, she regarded Constantine. The man proved quite attractive in daylight. "You're cute."

His brows rose. "Excuse me?"

"And polite. Do you have a girlfriend?" She squirmed on the bed as fire coursed through her veins.

"I really don't see that it's any of your business."

Aria's lips curved as she stretched out. "I hope you don't because she wouldn't like it if she knew I was sleeping in your bed."

"I don't have a girlfriend, so you needn't worry."

"Me, worry?" She giggled, a bubbly sound that went with the floating sensation inside her head. "I'd kick her ass. I don't share."

"I think you're delirious."

"I think you're right," she mumbled. It didn't take his remark for her to realize her thinking seemed off.

"We really should call a doctor."

"No doctor. No one can know where I am. Not even Thea." She flailed her hands and gripped his loose T-shirt. "Promise me you won't tell. Promise."

He blew out a breath. "This is crazy. You need a doctor. You've got the swamp fever."

"So give me some pills. Just swear you won't tell anyone I'm here. You'll be in danger. Everyone is in danger."

"I've got some antibiotics from when I cut myself on the job. I didn't need them, but the emergency room doctor was a normal dude and didn't know that. I'll go grab them. Don't go anywhere. Princess, guard her."

As if Aria could go anywhere. Her limbs felt weighted, concrete filling her bones.

Something blew hotly in her face, and she opened eyes she didn't realize had shut to see a tiny furry face glaring at her.

"What do you want?" she muttered.

Grrr.

"Don't worry, squeaky toy, the feeling is mutual."

And she was obviously more delusional than she realized, seeing as how she conversed with a dog, if something that wouldn't even make a meal could be called a dog.

Something wet and chilly slopped onto her forehead. "Open your mouth." Fingers probed at her lips, and she spread them enough for him to slide some pills into her mouth. The bitter taste had her grimacing and complaining.

"Oh, gross."

"Drink." The stern command came as he lifted her upper body and pressed the rim of a glass against her lips.

She swallowed. She didn't have a choice. It was that or drown.

"You're mean," she muttered.

"Says the girl I've done nothing but help so far."

"I need a phone." While her body seemed determined to melt into a puddle of useless goo, her mind got moments of clarity.

To her surprise, he pulled a cell phone from his pocket. She grabbed it with shaking hands that dropped it.

"Fuck."

"Not now, you're kind of sick," Constantine retorted.

"You are not funny. But you're still cute." Ugh. Someone shoot her. It seemed she couldn't trust her mouth to keep her inner thoughts secret.

"So cute I'll help you dial. What's the number?"

Number? Dammit. She didn't remember her boss's number by heart. It was programmed in her phone, and she no longer had that sucker. Which again sucked because it was only a few months old. It would cost her a fortune to buy out her stupid contract.

Fingers snapped in front of her. "Earth to Aria, come in, Aria."

She turned her gaze back to him, trying to focus but having a hard time. "Would you stop moving?" she complained.

"I'm not. You're sick and need to lie down."

"Not until I call Thea. I need to know she's safe. I worried her the last time I called, and I shouldn't have done that. But I had to. Just in case I didn't come back."

"You are back now. You're safe."

"Safe?" Again, the hysterical laughter burst free. "No one is safe. I have to stay away from her. I should stay away from you, too." She swung her legs over the edge of the bed, only to have them immediately moved back onto the mattress.

"You're not going anywhere."

"You don't understand, they're looking for me."

"Who is?"

"The monsters." She slapped a hand over her mouth. She shouldn't have told him about that.

"I know about the monsters, Aria."

"You do?"

He nodded. "I've been looking for them for a while now, but have not had any luck. Do you know where they are?"

"Yes." They were in cages. A whole row of them.

"Where, Aria?"

She opened her mouth, but instead of spewing words, she spewed water.

In other circumstances, she might have been appalled that she'd tossed the meager contents of her tummy on the man trying to help her, but given her limbs chose that moment to go spastic, she concentrated more on not biting her tongue off.

But uncontrollable spasms didn't mean she didn't utter a very apt, "Fuck!"

Chapter 6

ANOTHER MAN MIGHT HAVE TAKEN offense to the fact that the woman he loaned his bed to barfed on his favorite T-shirt—"I <3 Chihuahuas." However, Constantine wasn't a dick.

As Aria's eyes rolled back in her head and her body convulsed, he acted. He yanked his television remote from the nightstand and wedged it between her teeth. Then he straddled her waist, pinning her body with his own, his hands clamped around her wrists, holding them over her head lest she shake herself right off the bed.

It was at that moment his mother chose to walk in.

"Constantine Xavier Boudreaux. What on earth are you doing to that poor girl?" she yelled.

Uh-oh, she'd used all his names. "Can't you see I'm helping her? She's having a seizure." And a good one, too. It vibrated her whole body.

"I'll call the doctor."

But that is the one thing Aria doesn't want.

Before his mother could pivot and do exactly that, he barked, "Don't. You can't call anyone."

"Are you insane? The woman is obviously sick."

Yes, but if it was the swamp fever, it would pass if he treated it with the pills he had. *But what if it's something else?*

He wasn't a trained medical professional. He couldn't care for her. Yet, he remembered the terror in her eyes, the plea to not let anyone know she was here.

I promised.

The tremors eased. Aria's body went limp, and while she remained pale, her breathing whooshed in and out in an even cadence.

He climbed off her. "It stopped."

"I see that," was his mother's sarcastic reply. "But those spasms could come back."

"If they do, or she gets worse, then I'll call the doc. In the meantime, she asked me to keep her presence quiet."

"Why? What did she do? Is she a criminal? Who is she?"

"This is Aria."

His mother's brows arched. "Isn't that the girl you've been looking for?"

"Yes. I found her by the swamp last night, exhausted and running from someone." Or something.

"Do your friends know you've found her?"

He shook his head, and his mother frowned.

"Don't give me that look. I'm going to let them know, but I thought I'd wait until she could tell them herself." Not a complete cop-out. They'd already know if Aria hadn't gone into convulsions.

"I don't like this." His mother's lips pursed. "There is something rotten in this town."

"There is. But don't worry, Mom, we're going to find it." And crush it.

If only he could crush whatever ailed Aria. He called in ill to work so he could spend the day tending her. Not that there was much to tend. She laid there, still as a corpse, her skin sporting a waxy pallor. The shallow breaths she took seemed barely enough to keep her heart pumping.

As he kept a vigil by her bedside, Princess on his lap helping, he surfed the Web on his phone, searching for symptoms of swamp fever and how to treat it. Except he wasn't sure that she suffered from it.

Sure, she presented many of the symptoms with the fever, the chills, and the vomiting. However, those convulsions weren't typical. They also didn't return. The fever did, though, and he spent that night sponging her on and off with a cold washcloth, battling the extreme heat radiating from her skin.

When it spiked at a hundred and seven, just past dawn the next day, he was ready to call the doctor, except, as he started to dial, Aria came to life.

She sucked in a huge breath. Her eyes opened wide. She sat bolt upright in bed.

He put down his phone and approached her slowly, noting her pupils seemed to track him, just like her nostrils flared as if testing his scent.

While subtle, he noted the fine hairs on her arm rise, and her gaze narrowed. She bore the look of an animal debating fight or flight.

"Where am I?"

"In my bed."

"Where is that? And who are you?" she asked, a hint of impatience in her tone.

A furrow marred his brow as he replied. "We're in my house on the outskirts of Bitten Point. As for who I am, don't you remember me finding you in the swamp?"

"No." Flatly stated. "I don't remember coming to this town. Or you. Or me for that matter." The lines in her forehead deepened, and she whispered her next words. "Who am I?"

Chapter 7

THE PANIC in her threatened to overwhelm. Everywhere she looked, she drew a blank. She didn't recognize a single thing. Not the room with the paneled walls painted a medium gray. Not the scarred wooden dresser with the small stereo on top. She especially didn't remember the big guy towering at the foot of the bed, watching her intently.

Is he my boyfriend?

He was certainly attractive enough with a rugged face complemented by a square jawline, piercing eyes, and a strong nose. The size of him proved impressive. How did he manage to find shirts that wide?

And who the hell wore a shirt that said, "Don't get between a man and his Chihuahua"? She couldn't help an incredulous note as she read it aloud.

A furry rat chose that moment to hop onto the bed and bare its teeth.

Without even pausing to think about it, she leaned forward and growled back. "Don't start that shit with me, Princess."

"You remember the dog's name but not mine?"

How offended he sounded. She shrugged. "Can't remember mine either. Guess we're even."

"You're Aria."

Her nose wrinkled. "That's an awfully girly name."

"Maybe on account you're a girl."

For some reason, that made her snort. "Okay. Whatever. What's your name then?"

"Constantine."

"That name seems familiar. Wasn't he an angel of some kind?"

"I'm hardly angelic."

So he claimed, yet she couldn't help but have the feeling he could easily assume the role of protector.

He keeps me safe.

An odd assertion to have, yet it felt right.

"Are you my boyfriend?" That would explain why she was in his bed wearing a T-shirt and nothing else, a T-shirt that she doubted belonged to her and not just on account of the stupid dog saying on the front. The massive tent of fabric hung on her slim frame.

"No, we are not dating."

Was it her, or did she sense a "yet" in the air? "If we're not dating, then why am I in your bed, wearing your shirt and nothing else?" Not even panties, she suddenly noted. "You fucking pervert. Did you drug me? Is that why I can't remember anything?" Her eyes widened as she accused loudly.

"What? No. Hell no. I wouldn't do such a thing."

"Says you."

"Yeah, says me, and I don't appreciate the fucking accusation, especially seeing as how I took you into my home after finding you half dead in the swamp, gave you my bed, and just spent the last twenty-four hours mopping your sweaty ass and forcing you to guzzle fluids, which, I might add, you barfed on me, trying to keep you from dying."

"If you're so concerned, why didn't you call a doctor?"

He gaped at her. "Why? Because you bloody well begged me not to."

"And you listened to me?"

"I'm wishing I hadn't, believe me, lady."

"I'm no lady." The words came out of her with familiarity, as if she'd said them many a time before.

"You're also not a gracious guest. Gonna claim you forgot your manners with your name?"

"No. I think that part of my delightful personality is all me," she replied with a smirk.

He laughed. "You're definitely very forthright. And I guess you deserve a pass given the situation. But let's get one thing clear. I am only trying to help you. So work with me."

Work with him or just plain work him? Playing with that bod would require some serious climbing skills. But now wasn't the time or place. "Now that we've kind of ascertained you're not a murdering rapist," or so she hoped, "can you tell me a bit more about who I am and how I got here?"

So he did. He told her of some girl called Cynthia who had come looking for Aria when she went missing. How they searched the town for her to no avail. Told her of the attacks by impossible creatures. The missing people. The dead ones, too. And, finally, her arrival the previous night.

When he was done, she whistled. "Damn, angel. That's some crazy story."

"Angel?"

Her lips curved. "From the sounds of it, you played the part of my guardian angel. Saving me from the monsters in the swamp and then watching over me as I fought off whatever bug I caught out there."

"Just doing the right thing. Us shifters have to stick together."

"Shifters?" She wrinkled her nose. "What the heck is that supposed to mean?"

He regarded her with a flat stare. "Shifter? You know, as in you turn into an eagle. I turn into a snake. While we're different species, we still are basically the same kind."

"Hold on there, angel. I listened to your messed up fantasy story of monsters coming after folks because you're cute. But if you think I'm going to believe for one second that you're a..." Her voice trailed off as the man before her rippled. As in his skin undulated and changed, turning from tanned, smooth flesh into something darker, mottled, scaly.

"Fuck!" She screamed the word even as she leaped from the bed. Her feet hit the floor, but her legs wobbled and refused to hold her. Down she went, knees hitting hard, yet that didn't stop her from crawling for the door, scrabbling before that *thing* came after her.

"Sssstop it."

"Or what?"

"Or I'll sssssic my dog on you," was the monster's sibilant reply.

As if summoned, the little dog from hell flew past Aria and braced herself in the doorway. A lip curled back on the muzzle, baring sharp teeth as she uttered a ferocious growl.

Aria pressed her forehead to the floor and muttered, "This isn't fucking happening. I must still be sick. Hallucinating. Out of my freaking mind."

"Or," a deep voice rumbled from behind her, "you could admit that maybe I'm telling the truth."

Given his voice sounded normal again, she canted her head to the side to peek at him. Constantine regarded her with a serious expression. A human expression.

"People aren't supposed to turn into things."

"Humans don't, but we do."

We? Aria might not recall much, not even her own face at the moment, but surely he didn't speak the truth. Wouldn't she know if she was this shifter creature he claimed?

She blinked, and suddenly, the room around her disappeared. She soared, high in a clear blue sky, cold wind rushing past her face.

Another blink and the room returned. But it didn't bring her sanity with it.

Brawny arms wrapped around her upper torso and plucked her from the floor as if she weighed nothing but a feather.

My feathers are lush, and fluffy.

An odd thought to have, yet it felt right. True. But fucked up.

While Constantine might have manhandled her off the floor, he didn't deposit her back in bed. Instead, he headed out of the bedroom into the hall.

"Where are you taking me?"

"You need a shower."

A certain amount of feminine pride raised its head. "Are you saying I stink?"

"Yup."

Perhaps the real her, the one with memories, might have taken offense. This Aria, however, laughed. "Touché. I guess I am pretty rank." The sour smell of sweat permeated not only her skin, but also the shirt she wore.

He set her on her feet in the bathroom, but her legs still wouldn't hold her.

Down she dropped. He moved quicker, slipping to his knees and catching her. For balance, she threw her arms around his neck.

"Nice moves, angel."

"If anyone deserves that name, it's the girl with actual wings."

She snickered. "I might not remember much at the moment, but I'm pretty sure I lost my chance of earning those a long time ago." No way she had wings. Not ever. The idea of her having some eagle inside her that might burst out at any moment? Entirely too crazy. "So if you're not an angel out to save me, then what are you?"

"The snake in the garden, I'm beginning to think." He rose quickly as he muttered the words, setting her upright and propped against the sink.

The comforting strength of his hands left her waist, their loss immediately noted. *I don't want him touching me.* Total lie. She might not feel quite herself at the moment, but she couldn't help but notice Constantine exuded *man.* He moved with a freaky grace and had the most deliciously toned body, if huge. He treated her with kid gloves, yet he dared to challenge with his words—and, yes, even tease her. Tease her senses and skin.

What is wrong with me?

Why did she find herself unable to stop thinking of him? Perhaps if she stopped staring in his direction?

She looked down at her toes—*pink toenails?* Odd, she wouldn't have taken herself as someone who'd choose such a girly color. *Heck, I wouldn't have thought I went for pedicures either.*

But it wasn't her choice.

"You have to get your toes done," Thea said for like the millionth time as she lounged in the ass-pounding massage chair, feet propped in front of her so the attendant could scrub the hell out of them. "I mean, think of it. What if you meet a hunk, and you want to do the naughty tango?"

"First off, it's fucking, not dancing, and second, I still don't get what my toes have to do with this. It's not like I'm going to shove them in his mouth to suck."

Thea grabbed at her perfectly straightened hair—a job that took over two hours of extreme patience. "Toe sucking? Never. That would tickle way too much. I'm talking about having your toes look good for when he's got you flat on your back and your legs are hiked with your feet up around his shoulders. Which reminds me, we're also hitting the wax today, my hairy Sasquatch friend."

A heavy groan left Aria. "Why do you do this to me?"

"Because if you don't look good, I don't look good." Thea grinned as Aria shook her head. "How about because you need to get laid in a bad way."

Yeah, she did, but it wasn't her fault most of the men Aria met were tools, as in guys she'd rather slap than fuck. "Fine. We'll do the legs, but stay away from my girly parts."

"I agree. Leave that bush hairy. The whole seventies retro thing is totally in. You should see how curly mine has gotten."

Slapping her hands over her ears, Aria screeched. "Too much info."

"...doing?"

"Hunh." Aria snapped out of the vivid mental video. She'd just flashed on a memory. That was a good thing. Perhaps this amnesia thing wasn't permanent.

Snap. Constantine clicked his fingers in front of her a second time. "I am wondering if you should go back to bed."

With a little difficulty, she focused her gaze on him. Before she realized it, her fingers brushed the skin of his cheek, a cheek that looked utterly normal right now.

Stillness invaded him, and she could have sworn he even held his breath. She could understand that reaction because she held her breath, too. The moment between them stretched, almost visible, a thing of awareness, curiosity, intimacy. She let him into her space.

Am I usually closed off?

Usually, yes, but now...now she wanted to touch. So she did. The fingers on his cheek pressed against warm flesh. Not monster. Not snake. Soft, supple skin met her feathery exploration of his face.

Her hand moved down, the tips of her digits encountering some bristly roughness.

"You have a five o'clock shadow."

"Yes. Why wouldn't I?"

Her gaze rose to meet his. "You're a snake. I would have imagined you as hairless."

Big fingers clasped hers and drew her hand to the top of his head. The soft hair threaded like silk through her raking fingers. "Does this feel fake to you?"

"It's so fine in texture."

"Yeah, and to give you credit, you're probably not far off the mark when you mention the hairless thing. My chest is pretty bare. But the good news is, so is my back."

She made a moue. "Too much info, angel."

"No, too much info is saying I've got a full bush down there."

No peek down needed when her cheeks brightened at the obviousness of his claim. But his bold words did draw a feisty retort. "Is this your way of saying you've got a snake in the grass?"

Laughter barked from him, loud and genuine. "That was fucking funny. But more seriously, we snakes get a bad rep. Just because people are scared of us doesn't make us inherently bad. I'd like to think I'm a decent guy who just happens to have been born with a cool ability."

"So you are born? Not bitten or..."

"Or what? Did I drink blood? Can I walk in daylight? Is it true my tongue can make you scream?"

"Conceited much?"

He winked. "Not conceit if it's true." He turned away from her and went to the doorway. "I will leave the door open so I can hear you in case you run into trouble."

"You're not going to stay and watch?" She couldn't help but tease.

For a second, she could have sworn his eyes changed just a little. A low, almost yellow glow entered them, the pupils narrowed and slitted.

How dangerous he looked in that moment. Inhuman. She shivered, yet it was not in fear.

Mine.

What a strange idea, and certainly not why she held out her hand and said, "Can you help me get into the shower?"

Okay, she might not know herself too well yet, but she would wager good money that she wasn't the type to ask for help, from anyone. Especially not some guy. A hot guy.

Oh my God, I think I might be a slut.

Well, that would suck, yet explain why, despite her current mental dilemma, she still found herself hugely attracted to him, attracted and totally flirting with him.

Good thing he knew how to resist.

"I think you'll be fine. I'll leave you alone now. Holler when you're done." He fled from the washroom.

Asshole, she thought with a glare in that direction.

Coward. He had disappeared awfully quick. Unless... Clarity widened her eyes. No normal, single guy would turn down a chance to help a woman get naked and into a shower.

"Holy shit, he's gay," she muttered aloud.

"Am not." Constantine suddenly framed the door.

"How the hell did you hear that? I thought you left."

"I told you I wouldn't go far."

Not far. He must have stood just outside the door. She didn't know if she should call him a perv or preen that he couldn't bring himself to go farther.

"So you like girls then?"

"Yes."

She cocked her head. "What about me?"

Did he look as taken aback as she felt? There was being forthright, and then there was balls out on the table, directly asking.

Shit. *What is wrong with me?*

Blink and the scenery changed. She was in a cell now, a cell whose walls she'd memorized.

"What is wrong with me?" she asked again, not that anyone bothered to answer.

A glance to her side had her gasping.

The needle moved toward her arm steadily, the glass vial attached to it full of an amber liquid with hints of darkness.

Don't touch me with that. *Yet she couldn't move, not a single limb, pull as she might. The straps on the gurney held her tight.*

They'd tied her down like an animal because they were treating her like an animal. No better than a lab rat.

"This will only hurt a little bit," the man said. He bore a fringe of white around his crown, and his facial skin held the creases of time. He wore the long white coat of a doctor yet didn't wear a stethoscope

around his neck, nor did she like his bedside manner. After all, what kind of doctor tied down their patient?

A mad-scientist type.

"Don't touch me," she growled. "Don't you dare."

Another face came into view, sporting a smirk wide as a barn door and begging for a smack. "This is what happens to little girls who come snooping."

"What are you afraid of me finding?" she challenged.

"Nothing now. You'll have more important things to worry about in a minute than whether or not our operation is on the up and up. Staying alive being the first and foremost."

"You can't do this," she repeated, eyes frozen to the slow descent of the needle. She thrashed as hard as she could, her slight frame twisting, yet not even coming close to loosening her bonds.

No escape. They've grounded me. I'm caged. *Her breathing came fast and furious while her heart pounded.*

"No," she screamed as the sharp tip of the needle pierced her skin.

No one listened.

The plunger depressed, and liquid fire entered her veins.

Chapter 8

STANDING IN THE DOORWAY, a voyeuristic perv, Constantine knew he should go. *I need to go.* And farther than two feet from the door this time so Aria could shower. He truly meant to leave her alone, except her eyes glazed over and he knew her mind went wandering again, leaving nobody home to pilot the body.

Already in motion, he caught the way her body tensed then relaxed all at once, letting gravity yank at her.

Once again, Aria fell, and once again, he caught her, but only because he slid under her baseball style so she landed in his arms and lap.

He prevented her from getting hurt yet... *She wouldn't be fainting in the bathroom, though, if I hadn't pushed for her to shower.* What she really needed more than a bath was more rest and some food.

"That's it, little birdie, back to bed you go."

"Little birdie as a name is utterly offensive," she snapped with a touch of heat.

"Says the lady calling me angel."

"Would you prefer I call you little birdie?" And, yes, the brat did aim her gaze downward.

"Ain't nothing little about me, *chickadee*."

Her gaze narrowed. "Are you seriously trying to antagonize me?"

"I would never do that, *starling*." He did have to bite the inside of his cheek at that one.

Exasperation blew between her lips. "Stop it."

"Or what?" he challenged.

A sly look entered her gaze. "I see what you're doing. If you want to kiss me, just get it over with," she dared back. "I know you want to."

Damn her, he did. "I don't," he lied.

"Why am I so utterly certain you're lying about that?" she mused aloud.

"Your animal instinct is guiding you, even if you don't recognize it."

"It should guide me to some water and soap. I reek."

"No water. Bed."

"I am totally taking a shower," she stubbornly insisted as she pushed at his chest and struggled to get off his lap.

"Like hell. You just about face-planted again."

"At least this time there's no poop."

"You remember meeting me?"

She grinned. "I guess I do. So see, I'm fine. Getting stronger every minute. I got faint because I remembered something."

"Are you sure it's a memory?"

"Pretty sure, that or I have a sick imagination." As she told him what she recalled, his eyes widened.

"They injected you with something. Now we really need to get you to a doctor."

Short hair flew and whipped her cheeks as she shook her head. "No." She pushed hard enough to get to her feet. "We can't tell anyone."

"We have to tell someone," he argued. "Cynthia and my friends are still looking for you."

"Fine. We'll call her and let her know I'm alive and to stop looking. But we're calling after my shower."

She did seem much steadier. Also, he knew the reviving effect of a shower after a strenuous night. Firemen often came home exhausted, dirty, and needing a moment to clear their mind and wash the world from their skin.

"As my *dove* commands." Rising also to his feet, Constantine leaned over and peeled the vinyl shower curtain back, revealing the smooth, seamless plastic shield he'd installed during a long weekend after he tore out the cracked and stained tile.

"I am going to peck your eyes out," she grumbled as she brushed past him, lifting a foot to step into the tub.

"I've got something better you can pet."

Constantine didn't usually resort to bawdy flirting. Where these dirty innuendos came from he couldn't have said. Probably Daryl's bad influence. Yet, he'd known Daryl for years and never used them before, so why now? Why her?

Most women would have retorted with shock at his bold words. Rejection was possible, too.

What he didn't expect was Aria, with a mischievous glint in her eyes, to pop a pearly-toothed grin. "You're the man with all the bold words. Well, let's see how you stack up when under pressure." Aria stepped fully into the shower and lifted her arms. "Take the shirt off. I dare you."

She didn't just do that.

She had.

I dare you. Those three words were the downfall of many a man. Constantine would like to say he held the strength to resist. He didn't. See, he believed in the man club, the one with a double-standard, fucked-up sense of rules. The membership card might only exist in the minds and thoughts of men, but that didn't make it any less real or potent. And he knew his damned card would get shredded for sure if he didn't strip the shirt off the sexy woman in the shower.

I must do this for the sake of mankind.

Gulp.

Be strong.

While his T-shirt hung loose on Aria's frame, it didn't dangle much past her hips. He could practically see the vee at the top of her thighs.

I never did see if she trims or not.

Personally, he liked a girl who went natural. Something to nuzzle.

Water from the shower began to spray the white cotton she wore, making it cling, especially around her chest.

How could he have thought before her breasts were too small? Never. He gladly admitted his mistake. They were perfect. Two perfect round domes with protruding peaks begging for his mouth.

"Are you going to do it, *angel*?" Her words teased huskily over his skin.

Do. Her.

No, wait. She meant something else. The shirt. The shirt had to come off.

On stiff legs, he clambered into the shower, placing himself across from her. Given the tight fit, it put him close to her.

She peeked at him. "Not leaving yourself much room to take the shirt off, big guy."

He leaned down until his mouth hovered just over hers. "I need to be close to do this."

Rip.

Chapter 9

OKAY, this might really make her a whore, but holy fucking hot. When Constantine gripped that shirt and tore it in two as the last of his words brushed her lips with hot air, it was like seriously off the charts, sexy, hot.

"Challenge met," he murmured, brushing his mouth ever so lightly over hers. "Now shower, my smelly duck."

Before she could screech at him, he fled, leaving only his soft chuckle floating behind.

He also left behind one really aroused woman, one who wanted to chase him down for vengeance, the naked kind, but also a woman who found herself laughing at his deviousness. "A point for the snake."

And a thank-you. Things got pretty intense between them for a moment. Events might have gone from "help me" to "fuck me" with just a single kiss. Even if she'd been a slut in her previous life, it didn't mean she had to be one now. Time to get her head out of her pussy and back onto what happened around her.

As she stood under the spray, its reviving heat stimulating every part of her body, she reviewed a few key facts from what Constantine explained to her.

One. *I am in danger*. In and running from it by the sounds of it.

Two. Someone had done something to her. Injected her with a foreign drug. As such, she couldn't necessarily rely on her instincts or even her rationality. Did the fluid they inject her with cause any kind of mental impairment or an as-yet-unknown physical one?

As she lifted her face into the hot water, she wondered if her amnesia was related to the injection.

It didn't take long to clean herself. She didn't want to waste time. Now that she seemed recovered, at least bodily wise, she had to find some answers.

Such as, what do I look like?

So far in her visions, she'd seen other people. Oddly enough, while she had a sense of self, she had no visual image to go with it.

Stepping from the shower, she grabbed a towel and wrapped it around her moist body. She tucked the corner between her small breasts, cinching it.

Over the vanity, she spotted a mirror. She stood before it, hands braced on the vinyl top that held a pink, seashell-shaped ceramic sink. Very retro.

I'm stalling.

The steam from the shower clouded the mirror, and she leaned forward to wipe at it with her hand. It didn't take long to clear a swath and see herself.

This is *me.* While she didn't recall seeing her image before, it still seemed familiar. Aria stood pretty short, which she already knew. She noted other facts, such as the fine bone structure, the pointed chin. The finely arched brows. The long, sloping nose. The thin lips with the slightest indent on the top. Her hair, shoulder length and bobbed. With a...

"Aaaaah!"

Her shrill scream brought Constantine running. He skidded into the bathroom. "What is it? What's wrong?"

"My hair," she gasped.

"What about it?" he replied. "It's clean. Wet, though, but there's a dryer under the sink if you need one. No big emergency."

"Not that, you idiot," she grumbled. "Look at this." She yanked a hank of it in the air for him to inspect.

"Yeah?" He blinked at her.

She explained slowly, as if to a moron. It was that or smack him. "It's white."

"Yeah."

"Don't you get it?" she exclaimed.

"No."

Such a man. They never noticed what was right in front of them. "It's not supposed to be white."

"How do you know that? Did you remember something else?"

"No, but that doesn't mean I don't remember that *this* isn't supposed to be white." She shook the offensive chunk.

"Are you sure about that? Because you had it when I first met you."

His reply took her aback. "What do you mean it was already there?"

"I didn't see it when you first crawled out of the muck on account you were so dirty."

She scowled at his reminder.

"But after you rinsed, I saw it. And you've had it ever since. Although"—he reached out a hand to touch the white band—"it does seem wider than before."

"This is great. Just great. First I'm apparently being chased by something in the swamp after being missing for a while. Then I find out I've been injected with some weird sort of mutant virus."

"We don't know that for sure."

She glared at him for his interruption. "Oh please, you don't believe that for a minute. And now, look at this, white hair. It's wrong, I tell you. So wrong. I'm only twenty-four."

"You remembered your age?"

She blinked as he took her completely off topic. "I did. Damn. That's weird how stuff keeps filtering its way back in."

"And you'll remember more, I'm sure, once you eat."

"Food?" At the mere query, her stomach rumbled. "Yes, food. I could totally go for some fried calamari right now."

"Seafood? Did I say you were an eagle? More like a seagull. Get dressed and we'll go get some."

She shook her head. "Impossible. I don't dare go out until I remember more. And, besides, you said I had to call Thea."

"Calling Cynthia will only take a few minutes. Then we can pop out."

"I have no clothes."

"Actually, I found some of Renny's stuff in the dryer. My mom has this habit of stealing hers and Caleb's and my nephew's laundry and doing it."

"That's a weird habit."

"She's got a laundry fetish. It's harmless. Now stop stalling."

At his gentle tug, she followed him from the bathroom back to his bedroom, where Princess lay on his bed, glaring at Aria.

"I left you a pile of clothes..." He trailed off. "That's odd. I could have sworn I left them on the bed."

"Are you talking about those?" Aria pointed to a puddle of fabric on the floor.

"Princess. Did you drag those clothes onto the floor?" He gave her a stern voice, one meant to chastise.

His dog rolled onto her back, four paws in the air, and gave him puppy eyes.

It was stupidly cute. So cute. Aria steeled herself against it. However, Constantine melted like a marshmallow over a hot flame. "Who needs a belly rub? Does Daddy's sweet girl need one?"

Aria sighed before she muttered, "That is seriously pathetic."

"I think someone is jealous you're getting a belly rub, Princess," the jerk smugly retorted, fingers tickling someone other than Aria.

Oh hell no. He's mine. He's...

The jealousy came on fast and furious. She needed to counter it. Needed him to go away—and stop scratching that damned dog.

"I am not asking you for a belly rub." She whipped the towel off and flung it to the floor. "But I do have a magic button that likes getting stroked." She arched a brow at him, and she could have laughed when he fled the room with a shouted, "You play dirty."

I might, but damn, it's fun. It would be even more fun if he stayed instead of running.

Quickly, she dressed, the clothes he'd found loose on her, but at least they covered all the important bits.

With a tentative tread, she exited the bedroom and made her way down the hall. Just out of her sight, she could hear a cupboard slamming shut along with a drawer.

The home didn't have an open floor plan, so she went from a hall right into a simple kitchen and found Constantine. He had his back partially turned from her as he poured them hot water from a kettle into mugs.

"I don't drink tea." She preferred coffee. Black. And strong enough to make her feathers protrude like quills. Another fact about herself.

"Me either. I'm not big on caffeine, but chocolate, on the other hand"—he handed her a mug—"is the beverage of champions."

Hot cocoa? She raised the cup to her lips and breathed deep of the rich cocoa scent. "Nice." Actually heavenly. She plopped onto a stool, closed her eyes, and inhaled again, triggering another mental movie.

Her finger crooked around the handle of the fine china cup. A peek over its rim showed it held hot cocoa, with little marshmallows bobbing on the surface. Steam rose and tickled her nose with the rich chocolate smell.

Aria raised it to her lips and took a sip, just a tiny one so she didn't burn her tongue. Her taste buds exploded with pleasure at the perfect mix. Sweet, with a hint of bitter to showcase it.

Very yummy and how nice of the lady who ran the bed and break-

fast to make it for her. Even better, the owner of the B&B had delivered it to her door.

Talk about excellent service.

"Pancakes and bacon sound all right, dearie?" the owner of the B&B asked as she set a domed plate on a small table by the window that had a pair of facing chairs.

"Sounds awesome." Aria took another sip of the hot cocoa then a long pull of the liquid. A hearty breakfast sounded like just the thing she needed before she went out and began her research on the town and, more specifically, Bittech. She'd arrived only the day before and had spent the afternoon and evening familiarizing herself with town and the local bar.

Seating herself at the chair, she grinned as the landlady whipped off the cover of the dome and revealed a plate stacked with fluffy pancakes and crisp bacon. She set her cup down, and it was promptly refilled.

"Thank you." Odd how the words came out slowly. Actually, she felt kind of sluggish, maybe because the chocolate didn't have the much-needed morning caffeine jolt. But sugar was a good substitute.

Aria chugged the contents of the cup, only to feel her eyes get heavier, the lids tugging down, trying to shut. The fingers holding the cup relaxed, and it fell, spilling hot cocoa everywhere. The cup wasn't the only thing falling.

The pancakes provided a soft landing for her face.

"They drugged me!" Aria exclaimed as she snapped out of memory lane.

"Who did?" Constantine asked from where he leaned against the counter, both of his big hands wrapped around the super-sized mug.

"The lady at the B&B. What was it called?" She tapped her chin.

"Bedbug Bites," he supplied.

"Yes. That's it. The broad who runs it drugged my cocoa." The nerve. Aria slammed her cup down, sloshing the contents.

He arched a single brow as he took a sip from his mug before saying, "Is this your way of saying you think I'm like her and trying to drug you with cocoa?"

She frowned at him. "Of course not. I trust you." She really did. Odd that. "I'll prove it." She grabbed the mug and chugged the contents before slamming it down again. "Ta da."

"I don't suppose you recall anyone ever telling you that you're crazy as a loon."

"Would you stop with the bird names?"

"No."

"You suck."

"Any time."

She glared. "Not everything is grounds for sexual innuendo."

"That's because you lack man-spective."

"What's that mean? On second thought, I don't want to know." Her tummy rumbled, giving her the out she needed. "What are you making us to eat? I don't suppose you have some bacon?"

"No bacon, but I think we have some leftover chicken wings."

Her nose wrinkled. "Cannibal."

For a moment, a look of horror crossed his face. "I'm sorry—I didn't think—"

She snickered. "I'm kidding. As far as I recall, I eat meat." The innuendo proved too blatant to ignore, so she rolled with it. "I especially love sausage. The long, thick kind." His gaze heated as she leaned forward and whispered, "The longer the better, so I can bite the tip off. Crunch."

He winced. "I guess I deserved that."

A giggle bubbled out of her. "Not entirely your fault. I think we're both to blame for setting the other off. Before we totally make this awkward, where's the phone so I can call Thea?"

"Use my cell." He slid it to her across the counter. She snagged it and dialed. Then paused.

"What's wrong?" he asked.

"How do I know this is the right number?"

"You don't, so hit the call button and find out who's on the other end."

True. The worst that could happen was she dialed a wrong number. The phone rang and rang until a guy answered it.

"Hey, Constantine. What are you doing calling Cyn's phone?"

For a moment, Aria froze at the unfamiliar voice. "Who is this? Where's Thea?" Concern over a girl she barely remembered made her tense.

"This is Daryl, her boyfriend, and I am still trying to figure out—Cyn, hand that back." The phone made a few noises as it got manhandled, but eventually, the static quieted and a perky voice said, "Cynthia here. Who am I speaking to?"

"Thea?"

"Aria! Is that really you?"

"Yes it's me." At least in body. The mind they still had to work on.

"Where have you been? I've been worried sick about you."

"I've been around. Dealing with stuff." Like a giant dude and his vicious dog.

As if sensing her stray thought, Princess barked at her, right by her ankle. Were there any arteries down there she needed to worry about? Just in case, Aria tucked her feet behind the rung on the stool.

"Where are you? I want to see you. Are you with Constantine? Is that why you're calling from his phone?"

"Yes. No. Kind of. But you can't tell anyone. I mean it, Thea. Not a soul can know. I think I'm in trouble." Talking to this woman proved easy, familiar even.

"I think everyone in town is in trouble," Thea said quietly.

"You should leave."

"So everyone keeps telling me. Actually, Daryl is the biggest pain in the ass about it, but I'm not going anywhere. Where Daryl stays, I stay."

"I told you we should have stayed in bed," was his less-than-subtle shout from the background.

"I told you my mom was getting the new one delivered today."

Thea's mom was here? Aria could see her in her mind's eye, buxom and with even wilder hair than Thea, holding out a tray of fresh-baked sesame seed cookies.

Perhaps Constantine was right. Maybe seeing and talking to people would keep jogging the memories.

"Your mom is in Bitten Point?"

"Dad, too."

"Why? What's going on? And since when do you have a boyfriend?" Because, as far as she could recall, Cynthia was single. Or so Aria thought. Kind of hard to tell with the memory thing.

"I do now, and we've kind of shacked up together. It's kind of serious."

Just how many days had Aria lost? "How long has it been?"

"Not long, I know. Totally crazy, but I can't help myself, Aria. I met Daryl, and it was like *boom*."

"More like snore," he interrupted again. "Or aren't you going to explain you drugged me so you could molest me at your leisure?"

"I did not molest you. Much." Giggle. "Sorry, Aria. You don't need to hear that stuff. Because I'm hoping you're doing that stuff with a certain guy we both know. Hint. Hint."

"It's not like that," she hastened to explain. "He's just helping me out." Helping her out of clothes, but then doing nothing about the fire he started. *He's not a very good fireman, obviously.*

"I'm sure he's helping you. Helping you so much that you don't have time to put on some clothes and visit with a friend."

"I'll have you know I am fully dressed."

"For how long?" Thea snickered.

Good question, given just glancing at him made certain parts of her heat. "Anyhow, the reason I called was to say don't look for me. I'm fine."

"Fine and yet you're acting awful weird and secretive."

"I have my reasons. Please, Thea. Trust me on this."

A big sigh came through on the line. "I guess if you're with Constantine, I can stop worrying."

"Please. And also, don't tell anyone you know I'm alive."

"Why? Are you still in trouble?"

"I gotta go. Congrats on the new boyfriend."

Before Thea could ask any more questions, Aria hung up. Her brow furrowed.

"What's up, my little parakeet?"

"I'm trying to remember if I have a boyfriend."

Chapter 10

OKAY, so Constantine's vehement hissing might have been a little over the top. That did not excuse Aria's smirk and taunting, "Someone is jealous."

Indeed, he was, which made no sense. They weren't dating.

Yet.

Ever.

Ha.

Nothing worse than losing an argument to yourself.

"Are you ready to go?" he asked, lest he spend too much time trying to decipher the muddled state of his mind.

"I don't know if leaving right now is a good idea."

"I disagree. Hitting a few places you might have visited could trigger some memories."

"Or bullets. What if someone does want to kill me?"

"Then it will be a first date we'll both remember."

The words hung in the air, yet another clue that things between them weren't behaving like they should. He kept saying and doing things he'd never imagined. He got the impression she did, too. But they both covered it up.

"Come on, don't be a scared budgie. My truck's outside. Within ten minutes, we'll be in town and sitting down to eat." He saw the war of indecision flash on her face. "Come on, you know you want to go. What if you walk into the diner, and bam, you get all your memories back?"

"Exactly what kind of menu do they have?"

"They deep fry most of their seafood and have the best homemade fries and frothy shakes you ever sucked back."

The recommendation tilted the scales.

"Let's go. But I'm telling you right now, if I get killed because you miscalculated, I'm coming back to haunt your ass."

"If it's any consolation, if you do get killed, I'll avenge you."

She wrinkled her nose. "Not reassuring, angel."

But his feisty lady didn't protest any further, which was why they found themselves eating a short time later.

Or at least he ate. She picked at her food like a fussy bird.

"I'm done." She pushed her plate away.

He couldn't help but stare at it. "You only ate half of it."

"I know. I usually eat less than that, but I guess I was so hungry. And it was awfully good. I am so full that, even if I could sprout wings and fly, I doubt I could heave myself off the ground." Aria patted her belly.

"That is not a meal."

"Says the guy who's like twice my size."

"I'm eating it." No way would Constantine let good food go to waste. He couldn't help but notice she watched him, a hint of a smile on her lips.

"What's so funny?" he asked once he'd cleared her plate.

"You are. I don't know why you were complaining about my eating habits when it seems the leftover food was just what you needed."

"A man needs his energy."

"Energy to do what?" she asked with an arch of her brow.

A slow grin pulled at his lips. "All kinds of things." Things a man shouldn't think about doing with a woman he barely knew, who didn't even know herself.

"Let's make one of those things taking a walk downtown to see if something jogs my memory."

Constantine paid the check, but before he could slide himself out of the booth, he noticed Aria stiffen. "What's wrong?"

She leaned forward and lowered her voice. "That guy, the one at the counter. I know him. Or at least I recognize his face."

"Another memory flash?"

She nodded.

"Do you know who he is?"

Her shoulders lifted and dropped. "No idea. I only got a quick glimpse of him swigging a beer."

Constantine's gaze followed the man as he left the restaurant, brown takeout bag in hand. "I've never seen him before." He stood. "Let's go."

"Where?"

"To find out where he's going of course. He could be a clue to unraveling your memories."

They exited Bayou Bites into bright sunlight, just in time to see a bright blue smart car leaving the parking lot.

She couldn't help but shake her head. "Oh hell no would I get in that."

"Why not? I hear they're good on gas."

"I like the things I trust to be bigger."

No way could he stop himself from swelling his chest when she glanced his way. "Big is always better."

She might have snorted, but her cheeks also turned a lovely shade of pink. "In the case of cars maybe. No way am I trusting that tiny tin can to protect me," she noted as she followed him to his truck.

"Says the girl who rode a motorcycle."

"I ride a motorcycle?" she asked as he pulled open his truck door.

He grabbed her around the waist and lifted her inside. "Yup. Nice one, too, 1200 ccs."

"I wonder what it feels like to have all that power between my legs," she mused aloud.

Did she do it on purpose? He felt sucker-punched and slammed her door shut before getting in the other side.

She didn't look at him, simply pointed. "Get moving before we lose him."

"Patience, goose."

She smacked him in the arm. "Idiot."

He laughed.

"So how did you know I rode a bike?" she asked. "Or let me guess. Thea again."

"Actually," he commented as he pulled out of the parking lot and followed the blue car at a distance, "I saw your bike at the B&B before the fire broke out."

"You saw my baby? Where is it?"

"Baby?" he queried with an arched brow.

"You have your dog. I have my machine."

"I take it you flashed on your bike."

"He has a name."

"He?"

"Anything that vibrates my girl bits that well has to be masculine in origin."

"So what do you call him?" he asked.

She fidgeted in her seat. "I don't remember."

Lie. He prodded. "Yes, you do. What is it? Tell me."

"Laugh and I will hurt you," she advised.

"Hurt me anytime you like, oriole."

She rolled her eyes, but he noted the hint of a smile curving the corner of her lip. "It's Fred."

"Fred? Who the hell calls a bike Fred?"

"I do, and I'll have you know it's short for Sir Frederick Full Throttle."

He couldn't help it. He snickered. Snorted. So she punched him, hard as she could in the space of the truck cab. As if it stopped him. He barely felt it. "I've had mosquitoes hurt me more," he teased.

"You want pain, I'll give you pain," she muttered.

She placed a hand on his thigh.

He tensed. And he wasn't talking about his muscles, but rather a certain part of his body with a mind of its own.

She danced her fingers closer to his package, his noticeably bulging package.

"What are you doing?" he asked, switching his gaze between the ass end of the car he trailed and Aria, who sat staring at him, eyes shining bright.

"Hurting you."

Shit, she was going to sack him. Her hand moved, and he might have swerved as he prepared for the pain...of pleasure?

His breath caught as she cupped him, the heat of her palm branding him even through his denim.

Tell her to squeeze it.

This was one time his other half totally had the right idea.

Aria had her own, though. It involved rubbing him, back and forth, a heated friction that made him ache.

"Yessss." Excited, he couldn't stop the sibilant hiss.

She squeezed him. Held him. Drew his breath in fast pants and—

"Don't stop," he exclaimed as her hand moved away. He shot her a glance and noted it primly folded in her lap.

"Oh, I am stopping. But let me ask you, how are your balls?"

Heavy and aching and... He opened his eyes wide. "That was just mean."

"I told you I'd get you back."

Flipping his gaze forward, he set his lips in a line, not amused at all by her laughter. How could he laugh when he might die because his poor balls and cock wouldn't be able to stand the disappointment?

"Are you sulking, angel?"

"No, my toucan."

"My nose is not big."

No, damn her, it wasn't. It was cute and tiny, with a tilt at the end.

"So whatever happened to my bike?" she asked, pretending as if she hadn't almost gotten them killed in a crash by sending all the blood in his brain south.

"I'm not sure. I don't think it got damaged in the blaze, but more than likely, someone towed it. I could find out if you'd like." Although why he offered, given her cruelty, he couldn't have said.

"I would like." She leaned forward. "Hey, where is our dude going?"

The small car turned off the main highway onto a side road. "Looks like he's staying local." Interesting, given Constantine didn't recall ever seeing the guy. The town wasn't huge, but it didn't take long to recognize most people. Then again, as the world got busier, so did their town. It wasn't as if Constantine went out much.

"What's in that direction?"

"Not much. A few houses and Bittech. He could be an employee there."

Except the guy drove past the turnoff for the medical facility and kept going. They followed him several miles out of Bitten Point until he pulled into a roadside motel.

Constantine drove past, not too far, before he turned around. He brought them close to the motel before parking on the shoulder. He debated their next move.

Rat-tat-tat. He drummed his fingers on the steering wheel.

"What are you doing?" Aria asked. "Let's go talk to him."

"If we do, we'll be tipping our hand that you're not just alive, but hunting down clues to your disappearance."

"Didn't we tip it when we went to the diner?"

"Yeah, but you gotta admit those deep-fried shrimp were totally worth it."

"I think we should go and talk to him. Even if I don't flash a memory, maybe he can tell me where we met."

Valid points, yet Constantine wasn't sure about it.

Given the violent happenings he'd encountered, did he dare risk the recently discovered Aria to possible violence?

Or am I hoping that, by not remembering, she'll stick around for a while?

It irked him to even contemplate he had an ulterior motive in staying back. Aria deserved his help.

"Okay, we'll go talk to him, but stick behind me until we know he's not armed."

Slapping the shifter into drive, Constantine crawled his truck through the parking lot that paralleled each of the motel units. He parked across the back of the small blue car, blocking its escape.

With another firm admonition to stay behind him, Constantine approached the peeling green door for room number seventeen. He knocked.

While he waited, he sniffed the area and frowned at what he found, or more like didn't find. Exhaust fumes, cigarette smoke lingering in the air, oil from a car a few rows down leaking from a blown gasket. He also smelled humans, mostly male, a few perfumed females. What he didn't scent were any animals.

No shifters had come this way, which made their friend inside human.

A curtain beside the door twitched, but the door remained locked. Someone was trying to avoid them.

Bang. Bang. Bang. "Open the door. I know you're in there. Don't make me open it for you." The flimsy portal wouldn't stop a determined boot.

"What do you want? I don't know you. Go away."

Aria, tucked behind, actually listening to his instructions, whispered, "Just kick in the door, would you?"

"And have the cops called on me?" he muttered back. "He'll open it." He stated it with more confidence than he felt. Louder, "I just want to ask you a few questions. About a girl you might have met at a bar a few days ago."

"Are you a cop?"

"Nope. Just a friend looking for some answers."

To his surprise, the door opened, only a few inches, the security chain pulling taut as the fellow put his face in the crack. "Why do you think I know anything? I'm just in town doing some work for a lab. I don't really know anyone."

Before Constantine could stop her, Aria inserted herself in front of him. "Do you know me?"

"You! Oh hell." The door slammed shut.

"I think that answers the question," Constantine dryly remarked.

Bang. Bang. Bang.

"Go away. I want nothing to do with her. Because of her, I got into so much trouble. I was lucky I didn't lose my job."

"What did I do?" she exclaimed.

The door pried open again as a single eyeball glared out. "As if you don't know."

"She doesn't." And Constantine was tired of the dude screwing with them.

Boom. While he might not want the attention kicking a door in might cause, snapping a feeble chain? No problem.

He shoved at the portal, sending the guy blocking it stumbling as he advanced into the shabby yet clean room.

"What's your name? How do you know Aria? Who are you working for?"

"I don't have to tell you nothing," the stubborn guy insisted. "I'm calling the cops."

A finger stabbed in the dude's direction. "I remember you now!" Aria exclaimed. "You're the guy I kissed outside the bar."

Wham. Constantine's fist stopped the guy from dialing 911—and he also wouldn't be doing any more damned kissing any time soon either.

Chapter 11

ARIA COULDN'T HELP a bemused blink as Constantine laid Jeffrey —*that's his name*—out cold.

"What did you do that for?" she snapped, perusing the unconscious body with her hands on her hips. "Now how's he supposed to answer our questions?"

"He was going to call the cops."

"And it didn't occur to you to just take the phone away from him?"

"No, because I was too busy wondering why you were kissing a twerp like him."

She gaped at him. "Are you jealous?"

His nostrils flared. "Yessss." The word hissed from him. "But I don't know why."

Just like she didn't know why his jealousy pleased her. Another aspect of the crazy attraction between them. An attraction she needed to deny—at least for the moment. "His name is Jeffrey. He's a lab technician at Bittech."

"You remember him?"

"A bit. We didn't really talk much."

"Too busy doing other things?" Constantine growled.

"No, because I'd just gotten into town that day and was doing my best to chat with everyone at the bar. Jeffrey was there with a few guys from Bittech, having some beers."

"So how did you end up kissing?"

Given she doubted Jeffrey was her type, she hoped it wasn't her dreaded slut side making do with whatever was close at hand. "I flirted with him. Nothing serious. I flirted and chatted with everyone there." Or so she vaguely recalled. The bartender made a mean martini. "I got him talking about his job, and when I found out he just worked there as a lowly tech, I was going to move on. Except..."

Jeffrey saw his chance to impress a girl fleeing, so he blurted out, "I know about the secret levels."

"What secret levels?" Constantine asked.

Aria visibly startled, not having realized she'd spoken aloud. "I don't know. I'm just repeating the parts I remember from the memory flash. He also said, 'there's weird shit happening at Bittech, and I'm not just talking about the lousy cafeteria food.'"

"Wes Mercer, who works there as a guard, is convinced they're up to no good as well, but we've never managed to find anything concrete. But Wes is still convinced. If there are secret levels, then that might explain Wes's conviction that things happen out of sight."

"Things done out of sight and secretively are usually a sign folks are up to no good. I recall being excited about this news. I don't know why, though. Why would I care what they're doing at a medical research facility?" Her nose wrinkled.

"Are you a news reporter?"

She shook her head. "I don't think so. And according to Cynthia"—who had called during lunch despite being told not to—"I'm kind of vague on what I do for a job."

"Maybe you're a secret agent spy."

He said it in jest, yet something about his words rang a bell. It just didn't trigger a memory. "I wish I knew why I was so interested in Bittech."

"It could be because they're a medical institute for shifters. The humans think they're researching the effects of bayou plants on human cells, but in reality, they're supposed to be researching the shifter genome, and they also provide fertilization for infertile shifter couples. But I say supposed to because we've begun to suspect it's not just research happening, but experimentation, too."

"You think they're the ones who jabbed me? But why? Why me?"

"Perhaps they thought you'd be an easy mark. Cynthia did mention you were orphaned. Perhaps they assumed no one would come looking for you."

How sad that she didn't have a family to care. *I have Cynthia and her folks.* The thought and certainty did warm her.

As Aria paced the motel room, she noted the door remained ajar. She kicked it shut lest someone walking by wonder at the strange tableaux. In order to clarify the memory, she recited it in point form aloud. "So, I met Jeffrey at the bar, where he bragged about his super access. For some reason, I needed to know more. I remember wanting into the institute, so I stole his access card."

Much like a femme fatale on screen, Aria had lured the slightly tipsy fellow into the parking lot. Once there, she feigned a sudden passion for him that involved a lot of slobber, on his part, as he mashed his mouth against hers. Shudder.

The poor sod thought he was getting lucky. In reality, Aria groped him so she could steal his employee keycard. Once she'd switched the card to her own pocket, while keeping her lips clamped tight lest a stray tongue visit, she pushed away from Jeffrey and, with a high-pitched laugh, said, "Goodness, but that was hot. You make a girl want to forget she's saving herself for marriage."

While he stood there bemused, she'd hopped onto her motorcycle and sped off.

"Did you go to Bittech that night?"

Her lips twisted along with her forehead as she strove to remember anything past getting on her bike. "I don't know. Everything after me leaving the bar is a blank." Not entirely—she remembered also wiping her arm across her mouth to wipe Jeffrey's slobber. "Ugh."

"Why ugh?"

"Why is it that the only kiss I remember is an awful one?" As a former slut, shouldn't she have tons of hot-kiss memories?

"We can't have that."

Before she could ask what he meant, Constantine drew her into his arms and kissed her.

Kissed sounded so trite, though. This melding of their lips, the electrical spark that arced, and the languorous heat invading her limbs was far more than just a kiss. It was an explosion of her senses. A knee-buckling and breathtaking foray into passion.

As his mouth caressed hers, she couldn't help but moan and part her lips. The access led to his tongue sliding into her mouth sinuously so that it could twine with hers.

She couldn't have said when her arms wound around his neck or when his hands cupped her ass. Hell, she wasn't sure of her own name at that moment and not because of the amnesia. The passionate inferno licking at her nerve endings made only one thought possible.

More.

Her body pressed firmly against his, yet she still wanted closer. How would it feel to press against him, skin to skin? Clothing separated their flesh. Wretched fabric. His height impeded her as well from rubbing against him as she desired.

A mewl of frustration left her, but he understood it, or he felt the same thing because he lifted her high enough that her legs could wrap around his waist, pulling her heated core against him. How decadent, the feel of her sensitive sex rubbing and glorying in the hardness of his erection.

Her back hit the wall, and he took a turn grinding against her. Her breathing stuttered as he applied pressure with his body against the part of her that longed for his touch.

And then Constantine was gone. One moment he held her, pleasured her, brought her to the edge of longing, and the next he set her down so she leaned against the wall.

Why?

She blinked open eyes heavy with passion to note the door to the motel hung open. Sunlight streamed in and showed her completely alone.

"Shit!" Where was Jeffrey? Probably trying to stay ahead of a chasing Constantine.

Flying to the door, she peeked out in time to note Constantine's hard pounding on the pavement had him almost within arm's reach of a sprinting Jeffrey, who ran full-out, screaming, "Help! Help!"

Help came from the most unexpected place. From the sky swooped a lizard, or at least that was how it seemed. The body had a serpentine feel to it, even with its two arms and legs. The skin appeared green and scaly, every inch of it thick with muscle. The leathery wings spanned wider than she would have thought possible outside a fairytale with dragons.

The flying lizard dipped, clawed hands outstretched. It shrieked an ululating cry.

Jeffrey happened to peek upwards, and she saw him blanch. He stumbled as he lifted his arms to cover his head.

The clawed fingers of the flying monster clasped Jeffrey's arms.

"Argh!" The blood-curdling scream brought a few people to peek out of doors. What must they think to see the thrashing legs of the man as he was lifted into the air by a creature that shouldn't exist, a creature that stole their clue and taunted them with a raucous caw of triumph?

While Aria didn't remember the beast, the sound triggered a deep shiver. And she could have sworn a voice whispered in her head, *Hide.*

She ignored the suggestion as she clambered into Constantine's truck. He jumped in a moment later and gunned the engine. "Let's get out of here before the cops show up and ask us questions."

"Not keen on explaining how a flying lizard stole the guy we knocked out?"

"With this many witnesses all claiming it, they'll be hard-pressed not to listen. And that's a problem. This brazen act is going to bring attention."

"Not our fault."

"It's someone's, though. Did you see the collar around that thing's neck?"

She shook her head. Addled by the kiss and stunned by the creature, she'd not noticed much.

"I've heard of those collars before. Daryl and Cynthia said the pair of hybrids they dealt with wore some. We think they're some kind of device to control the monsters."

"You think someone is making those creatures do these things. But why? I mean, why kidnap Jeffrey in plain sight?"

"Perhaps because they thought he'd become a liability."

She clasped her fingers together. "Am I a liability? Will it come after me next?"

"No."

"You don't know that." She couldn't shake a sense of trepidation.

"You're right, I don't, but I don't plan to let you out of my sight, so if it does try, it's going to have to go through me."

The declaration warmed, even as it sent chills. *I don't want him to get hurt.* "I'm putting you in danger."

He took his glance from the road to shoot her a hard stare. "You're not doing anything to me. I chose to help you. I still plan to. A little danger isn't going to make me run away."

"This is more than a little danger."

"What can I say? I do everything big." He tossed her a wink.

She bit back a smile. "So I'm beginning to see. Where to now?"

"I think you've had enough excitement for one day. We're going home. Princess needs me."

Princess wasn't the only one.

Chapter 12

AS CONSTANTINE PULLED into the crushed gravel drive in front of his house, he noticed not only his mother's car, but his brother's, too. Odd because Caleb usually worked during the day. What had brought him out for a visit?

Exiting his truck, Constantine had no sooner slammed the door shut when his mother, her rotund figure still dressed in her scrub outfit that she wore for her work at the seniors' residence, came flying out of the house.

"I killed it!"

"Killed what?" he asked as he rounded the hood of his truck to give Aria a hand, except she didn't need one, having already nimbly jumped to the ground.

"I killed a monster. Come see. He's in the yard."

Grabbing Aria's hand, Constantine followed his mother's excited wobble around the house until they entered the backyard.

An alien scent assailed him. Reptile, with a hint of wrong. Sickness, with a sweet, rotted tinge. And death in the form of blood, a giant puddle of it under a winged creature, but not the same one they'd seen at the motel.

This one was smaller. Much smaller. The slight frame was covered in downy gray fur, no scales, yet the reptile scent pervaded.

"What is that thing?" Constantine asked as he approached his brother, who knelt by the corpse.

Princess took that moment to let out an excited yip and left her post beside the body to fly at him in a sideways gait that looked awkward but adorable.

Letting go of Aria's hand, he swept his dog into his arms. "How's my little princess?" he asked, giving her wiggly body a nice scratch.

Yip. He snuggled her to his face, his affection for his dog not something he hid.

"I'd mock you and your bonding moment, but I have to say your dog is growing on me," Caleb announced. "She's a damned good watch dog and the reason why Ma even knew this thing was here."

"Was my little princess a brave puppy?" he cooed, and she almost expired of happiness.

"More than brave," his mother replied. "I let Princess out when I got home from work. Next thing I know, she's barking like mad, and I look out to see this *thing*"—a moue of distaste aimed at it—"trying to catch our valiant guard dog. So I grabbed the shotgun and took it down."

Indeed she had taken it down with a fist-sized hole through its upper body. His mother didn't mess around when it came to ammo for her weapon. As she explained, "If I gotta protect myself from something big and stupid enough to mess with me, then I am making sure it ain't getting back up."

"Who's a good girl? Who is she?" Constantine sang as he tickled his dog under her chin.

Wiggle. Waggle. Princess loved the praise. Aria, however, seemed less than impressed with his dog's impressive skills. She rolled her eyes before walking toward the carcass. He gave her credit for not flinching or throwing up. The thing sat on the bottom rung of the pretty scale. Limbs somewhat misshapen, its face a freakish meld of human and a few things, it seemed. Monkey and something else. The fingers were tipped in claws, much like the hooks of a rapier-type bird.

"It kind of looks like a flying monkey," Aria remarked as she tilted her head to the side to contemplate it. "You know, like the one in that *Wizard of Oz* movie."

"Again, you remember an old classic but not your life?" Constantine couldn't help but tease.

She grinned. "What can I say? I'm being selective about what I recall. Weird thing, I'm having trouble with my memories from about a half-hour ago." And, yes, she did wink.

It threw him for a loop. *Is she implying she wants another kiss to remember?*

"I've never seen anything like this thing before," Caleb remarked. "Whatever it is, I'm going to wager it's not natural. See its wings?" His brother stretched one out, the membrane unfolding and stretching taut. The wing appeared covered in leather skin, not feathers or fur. "The wings are just like those of that dino creature we killed a while back. The one that took Luke."

A scary time. The fear they'd all gone through when the little boy was kidnapped by the monster wasn't something Constantine wanted to relive. Thankfully, his nephew had emerged unscathed and the culprit was dead. However, they'd celebrated too quickly, given the abomination wasn't alone.

"Similar and yet not. As I recall, that thing had scales, not fur, and it was at least twice the size of this one."

"That's because I think this one is a child. A teen, actually."

At Aria's soft-spoken words, all eyes turned to her.

"What makes you say that?" he asked.

"Because I've seen it before."

Chapter 13

THE MEMORY TOOK her by storm.

The shove in her back propelled her forward, and she stumbled, her hand flailing out and grasping the metal rods of a cell door. Actually, she noted as she peered around, they were cages. Not very big ones either, just deep enough for the occupant to sleep stretched out.

Between the cages were spaces wide enough that, despite the arms stretching through, they couldn't touch anyone else.

The scrabble of claws drew her frantic gaze to the cage she clutched.

Fingers, half flesh toned, half pale gray furry tufts, clung at the bars. Big eyes, blue and wide with fear and panic, peered at her. The mouth, protruding from the face, rounded in an O, and the most horrible sound emerged from the mouth.

More horrifying than its appearance was the realization it was a child, a teen she'd wager, given the skateboarding T-shirt and surfer board shorts it wore.

"You are looking upon the next generation," a voice whispered by her ear. "And you'll get to be a part of it, too."

Unfortunately, she couldn't tell them any more than that. The scene unfolded itself in a blink within her mind, leaving her with the memory of the eyes, so sad behind the bars caging it. That creature still had some humanity left to it, but barely. This thing, lying dead on the ground? All monster.

It was decided to keep the body a secret for the moment, and not because they feared trouble if they brought it to the right authorities. Any creature attacking was fair game. In the shifter world, if someone had gone wild and posed a danger to others, especially humans and their love of discovery, then swift measures had to be taken. Usually permanent measures. Justice arrived on swift wings.

She blinked as the knowledge became available.

"I say we keep it to ourselves for now. Daryl's got a friend who might be able to look at it," Caleb told them.

"Do it. I mean, giving it to the friend can't be any worse than the one we stashed at Bittech. Maybe this time it won't disappear, and we won't get bullshit reports that what we found was a regular animal.

Bittech. Bittech. Bittech. Once Caleb left with the carcass, his mother in tow to stay with Renny and Luke, Aria found herself alone with Constantine. And his dog, a chaperoning Princess.

Chastity belts had nothing on that dog. Every time Aria got anywhere close to Constantine, the mutt wedged her way between them.

Being a man, he was oblivious to the game his dog played, but Aria recognized it, and she wouldn't let it get in her way.

Way of what?

Claiming Constantine.

What? She refused to think upon it. Not when she needed to assert herself.

The maturity level in the room when her big angel left to use the washroom dropped considerably when Aria got down on her knees to growl at Princess. In her defense, the dog started it.

When he returned, it was to find Aria perched on a stool, looking perfectly prim and behaved.

"Did I hear Princess growling at something?"

Her lip twitched. "I think she saw a squirrel."

He eyed her askance, but didn't push it. Meanwhile, Princess shot her a glance, one that Aria thought said, *Thanks for not ratting me out.*

As if she would. Constantine would probably take his dog's side if she did.

"Want a cup of cocoa?"

"Sure."

As Constantine busied himself putting a pot of water on to boil, she leaned on the counter, steepling her arms so she could rest her chin in her hands. She watched Constantine move in the kitchen, light on his feet for a man his size.

She mused aloud. "So, I was thinking."

"Why do I feel that should come with a warning?"

"I'm not Cynthia. You're safe." The certainty that her friend was the one with crazy ideas stuck. As did the belief that Aria always went along and sometimes embellished those wild plans.

"I highly doubt I'm safe," he muttered, his back to her as he spooned the hot cocoa into cups.

What was that supposed to mean? "If you want out because of the danger, just say the word and I'll leave."

He whirled. "Don't you dare go."

"Okay, I won't. But you just said you don't feel safe around me. And you're right. It's not. It seems everything connected to me leads to monsters."

"I can handle the monsters. What I'm less sure about is how to handle you." Piece spoken, he whirled back to the mugs, pulling the whistling kettle from the stovetop.

She blinked a few times as she digested his words. What did he mean by handle her? Since she wasn't sure she wanted the answer, she brought their conversation back on track. "I'm noticing a common theme among my memories and the monsters. Have you noticed that everything keeps pointing back to Bittech?"

"I do, which is why I'm having a hard time believing it."

"Occam's razor."

"I know the term, but not what it means," he said, stirring the brew in the cups with a spoon.

"Simplest answer wins. In other words, don't try and complicate the truth. Maybe things keep pointing back to Bittech because they got complacent and, in turn, lazy about covering their tracks."

"It just seems too easy," he said as he slid a mug in front of her. "Think about it for a second. Considering how long these things have been happening, even if they were getting sloppy, I find it pretty odd that all of a sudden events are escalating to the point they're not even trying to stay hidden. Monsters out in daylight. Dead bodies. People missing left and right. And wouldn't you know all the blame seems to be centering on the one company authorized to do legitimate research on shifters."

"I think it's a great cover. I mean, they have access to medical supplies, personnel, even blood work and other tissue samples. Is it so farfetched to think that underneath the veneer of legal activities, nefarious ones are also occurring?"

Hands wrapped around his mug, he nodded. "True. I mean, who would suspect a shifter-run installation of being so crooked? I guess I just don't want to believe that a company with our folk working at it would do something like that. I mean, for fuck's sake, Daryl's brother-in-law is the CEO's son."

"Has Daryl talked to him about it?"

"Yeah. And so did Wes, the guard who works there. Andrew claims they're not doing anything that hasn't been sanctioned by the SHC."

"Sanctioned?" She frowned. Something about that niggled. "Are you sure they've given their approval and just what that approval is for?"

The question should have proven an easy one, yet Constantine opened his mouth then shut it, taking a moment to think. "You know what, I don't know that anyone ever truly asked them. I mean, Pete told us they wanted us to back off, but then again, turns out Pete's son was involved, so his info is now suspect. As for the rest, other than Andrew's claim, my sources all got this second and third hand."

She swallowed the rich, sugary brew before replying. "So shouldn't we call someone on the SHC council?" Her mind blinked, and she saw herself in a hallway, the carpeting dark blue and almost new, the walls a muted gray. An older fellow grasped her arm to pull her aside and whispered, "Remember, tell no one. Trust no one. Report only to me."

Who is he?

Constantine shot a frown in her direction. "One does not just call up the SHC and question them."

"Maybe someone should."

Setting his cup down, he scrubbed a hand through his short bristles. "The last time someone did, they went missing. Wes's brother tried to do something about the shit happening, and he vanished into thin air."

"People don't just vanish."

"They do sometimes in the bayou," was his ominous reply.

His phone rang, a shrill old-styled ring that filled the ominous silence his words had wrought.

He glanced at the lit display. "I gotta answer this."

She took another sip of the cocoa as she peeked out the window. Constantine paced away from her and spoke in low tones to whoever called.

The sensation of something just out of reach plagued her. Something that she'd learned niggled. The answer seemed close, so close. If only she could find and pull the thread that would unravel the mystery in her mind.

"I gotta go out for a bit."

She returned to the present. "Where do you have to go? Who was that calling?"

"The fire station where I work. A body was found in a tree in the swamp. Since it might be shifter-related, I got called in."

"What am I supposed to do while you're gone?" Aria would

never admit it aloud, but the thought of staying alone in his house, with the swamp that hid so many dangers nearby, did frighten her. She wasn't sure what her strengths were in a fight.

Poison.

What?

This odd, disembodied voice talking to her every so often really freaked her out.

"Angel, is it normal to hear voices in your head?"

Her out-of-the-blue question narrowed his eyes. "Depends on how many of them are telling you to kill someone."

Her lips pursed, and she glared. "You are not amusing, dickwad."

"Is it wrong to like that name better than the emasculating name of angel?"

"You'll be my cutie patootie angel in front of your buddies if you don't answer me. Do you hear voices?"

"Me? When did it become a question about me?" As she leaned toward him, practically snarling, he laughed. "Yes, I hear *a* voice. Emphasis on the single entity who feels a need to chat me up sometimes."

"So your snake does talk to you." Winner for strangest conversation of the year.

"Talks, thinks. When our animal side is taking a backseat, they're more or less dormant. They will awaken for extreme emotions or because of a sixth sense when it comes to danger. They also like to meddle and throw in their two cents."

"By they, I mean it, or is that he?" Her brow furrowed. "Whatever the fuck is inside you, it doesn't make you kill things?"

Constantine might have joked before, but now he looked utterly serious. He braced both palms on the kitchen counter and angled closer. His intent stare locked her eyes on him.

"Aria, is something telling you to kill things?"

"Not exactly. A voice just told me I use poison."

"Told, but you didn't see yourself actually doing it?"

"No."

"That's not exactly solid evidence of anything then, is it?"

"Except it sounded true. Felt true. I poison things." She slumped. "And here I was hoping I secretly had some cool judo moves I could use in case someone came to attack me."

"You won't need cool moves because I'm dropping you off somewhere safe while I check things out."

Somewhere safe being with Cynthia and Daryl.

Chapter 14

AS CONSTANTINE DROVE AWAY, leaving Aria at the tender mercy of her best friend, who clutched Aria to her bosom swearing she'd never let her out of her sight, he couldn't help but chuckle remembering the words Aria threatened.

"I will poison your beer."

What could a man reply to such a dire threat?

"If I can't drink, then I'll need to do something with my lips. See you later, my little peacock." Wink.

And then he fled. He'd probably pay for that later. He could see Aria getting even for leaving him with Cynthia, who exclaimed, "Have you put your toes around his ears?"

Not yet, but he hoped his little bird would soon. Damned woman turned his world topsy-turvy. She made him want to be the man his father wasn't, a man she could count on.

Crazy thinking. The kind of crazy you got from sniffing gas for too long.

He barely knew Aria. A man didn't suddenly want a commitment with a girl he'd just met, who didn't even remember who she was.

Don't forget Princess hates her.

Then again, Princess hated almost everyone. She tolerated his friends. She kept trying to get between him and Aria, though.

Should he take it as a sign?

Thing was he didn't want to keep his distance. Couldn't. Even now, dumping Aria off to go to work irked him.

He wanted to spend more time with her. Getting her to talk, he enjoyed discovering piece by piece the different fragments that comprised Aria.

The more he saw, the more he liked. Yet, that like kept distracting him.

I almost got her killed today.

An exaggeration, but a possibility given what happened to Jeffery. What if the winged beast had grabbed Aria instead? What if that furry flying monkey at his house today had done more than piss off his dog because it wouldn't land for a proper terrorizing?

Ma killed it. But, as he'd seen today with the flying thing, whoever they stalked had more than one creature at its command. They were also getting more brazen about using them.

Once the monster comes out from the closet, can you really shove it back in?

The answer terrified him in a way nothing else in his life ever had.

What if the human world found out about them? Scholars in the shifter world had long theorized that humanity might accept them, but even if the majority did, there would always be a faction who didn't trust *the animals.*

A mob usually started with only one cajoling voice. Just like it took only one bullet to end a shifter life.

Dark thoughts that led to carnal.

How? Because if their very existence hovered on a precipice where tomorrow could see them exposed and hunted for extermination, then he should seize the day. *I should seize Aria.*

Take her. Hug her. Squeeze her.

Or he could destroy the monsters and find the one controlling them. Take that danger out of Aria's life so he could take his time with her.

Snort.

Why not do both? Help save his town, save his ladybird, and maybe attempt something his father never did—a happily ever after.

He'd think on it. First he had work to do.

The trip out to the murder site didn't take long since he went there direct. He joined several others of his shifter brethren who also worked with the fire department for Bitten Point.

Luckily, only a few humans, which they couldn't avoid hiring due to labor law, also worked with them. In cases such as these, with a suspicious dead body, they were conveniently left out of the rotation.

People thought it odd the fire department showed on so many scenes that didn't even have a trace of smoke. People tended to think of them only in terms of fire. Except firemen, especially in smaller communities, played a larger role.

They also had the tallest ladders.

As Constantine braced the ladder for his buddy, Mick, he peeked around. The scene where he found himself was actually not quite in the swamp, the land firm and dry under his feet. The copse of trees growing wildly here sat on federal land and wasn't open to anyone but game officials.

So how had someone spotted the body?

"No Trespassing" signs proved the irresistible lure for teenagers. Dragging a girl by the hand, and saying they'd protect them from crocs and snakes, many a teenage boy got lucky in these woods.

Not poor Boyd. Poor Boyd had been lying atop Steph, doing his best to score a home run when his date started screaming—and it wasn't because of his technique.

As it turned out, opening her eyes while he nibbled on her neck and shoved a hand up her shirt wasn't enough to stop poor Steph from noticing a dead body hung in the branches of the tree overhanging them.

It put a damper on the date, for Boyd at any rate. Steph, just a few steps out of high school, was twirling her hair and chatting to the young policeman who showed up on the scene wearing an impressive badge and a gun.

Mick clambered up the ladder and muttered his findings, not too loudly, as he knew Constantine would hear him.

"It's male."

"Dead or alive?" While pretty sure it was the former, it never hurt to be sure.

"Definitely dead, but not for long. The blood is still fresh. No sign of rigor yet either. Poor bastard, I hope he died quick after whatever got him tore his face off."

No way could Constantine suppress a wince. That had to hurt. "Any identifying marks? Do we know who the victim is?"

"Fingers are gone. Chewed off it looks like. Damn, whatever did this to him, it's almost like they didn't want us to identify him."

Except once Mick untangled the body and eased it down to Constantine, he realized he knew who it was. He recognized the shirt.

Jeffrey. Last seen in the claws of a winged lizard. Now dead. Fuck.

Once the body left the branches of the tree, it was up to the cops and other crime scene dudes to take over—taking evidence and suppressing it in case it raised too many flags.

Since his services were no longer needed, Constantine didn't stick around. *I have somewhere else I should be.*

And as much as his python wanted that to be by Aria's side, that wasn't his destination.

If he assumed the winged creature had targeted Jeffrey specifically, then that meant the dead Bittech employee knew something.

I had him in my grasp. Dammit. If only I'd not let him escape.

If only he'd not kissed—nah. He wouldn't regret the embrace with Aria. Hell, if he'd known ahead of time Jeffrey would get snatched, he might never have stopped.

Thinking of Jeffrey proved sobering, though. The man was dead. Killed. But why? What did the guy know, and of more interest, did he perhaps write something down? Could there be a clue in his things?

I need to search his room before the cops identify the body and get to it.

Despite breaking a few speed limits, Constantine made it too late to the motel.

"Fuck." He couldn't help but mutter an expletive as he noted the billowing smoke obscuring a twilight sky.

Given cop cars blocked the road, along with fire and news trucks, he parked on the shoulder and walked the rest of the way. He couldn't get too close to the scene of the fire—they had the area cordoned off—but he stood amongst the crowd, a spectator that watched the hypnotic leap of bright flames.

The motel burned, and to his trained eye, he could already tell there would be no saving anything.

"Any idea how it started?" he asked a fellow beside him.

"Started in room seventeen. I should know, I was right beside the damned thing when the alarms went off. Weird thing, though, was the room was empty on account the guy staying in it got grabbed by some kind of giant bat."

Bat? Had to love how the humans wedged the truth into whatever box fit it best.

Since this wasn't his jurisdiction, Constantine got to watch as others put out the fire. He probably shouldn't have spent that much time getting hypnotized by the destruction, yet he couldn't help himself.

For one, it was warm and his snake did so like the heat.

Second, he needed the heat because the very act of arson made his blood run cold. Things were snowballing, and he feared how far they would go. And who else would die.

This violent act only served to reaffirm his conviction that time drew short. At the rate the blatant acts happened, and in front of witnesses, discovery seemed imminent. Death and injury were becoming commonplace. His time and window with Aria could find itself limited.

He should go to her and continue that kiss they began. Bring it to its rightful conclusion.

He choked—ironic really, given as his python usually choked others. But the thought of taking things to the next level terrified him.

What if I'm just like my dad?

Aria was an orphan. Could he give her a family only to yank it away because his snake got bored?

You never left Ma.

True, yet with Ma there was no pretense or expectation. She'd love him no matter what. He could do no wrong—unless he accidentally left the seat up and she fell in the toilet in the middle of the night. He paid for that with starched laundry.

You would never abandon Princess.

Of course he wouldn't because she loved and relied on him. He had a duty to protect, care, and adore her in return.

Couldn't you do the same thing with Aria?

Why not? Constantine usually took his duties seriously. Just because his dad had left didn't mean he would be the same. He'd proven himself reliable so far. Why would he suddenly change?

I am not making a decision about Aria and the future yet.

He had better things to do, such as make a pit stop to see Wes, his brother's frenemy. Personally, Constantine didn't have a beef with the guy. He seemed nice enough. Not his fault Wes bore that bad luck name—Mercer.

Everyone knew the Mercers, the family whose name was usually spoken with a condescending sneer. In some respects, they deserved it. A good number of Mercers tended to skirt the law or outright flaunt it.

Yet others, like Wes and Bruno and a few other Mercers, did try to live the straight and narrow. Not that it mattered in the grand scheme of things. Born a Mercer, always a Mercer.

Constantine felt kind of bad for Wes. The guy got a bad rap because of his birth, not his actions, kind of like his snake.

But becoming bosom buddies wasn't why he popped in to see Wes. He wanted to update him on the newest aspects of the case. A phone call might have proven quicker, but paranoia had him wondering now if those were safe to use.

Someone seemed awfully well informed about their movements. Did someone spy on them? The movies certainly made it seem like it was easy.

Ironically enough, he went looking for Wes at his place of work, Bittech. Despite more or less running the entire security division, Wes still liked to rotate his shifts around, supposedly to keep a feel for staff and goings on.

As Constantine pulled into the front of the mirror-glass-plated building, he shut off the engine. He wanted to hear if anything approached.

The bright security lights proved harsh, their fluorescent glow bathing things and giving them a stark, dead appearance. Wes, however, didn't stand under its bright glare. Gators were nocturnal creatures for the most part. Nasty bastards, too, if riled. The big guy, a rival for Constantine's own bulk, leaned against the building, the red tip of his cigarette pinpointing his presence.

Nasty habit and one Constantine didn't get. Fire and smoke were a shifter's worse enemy—other than discovery. Why would anyone intentionally inhale the shit?

"What was so important you couldn't talk to me on the phone?" Wes asked, grinding out the butt under the heel of his dull black combat boots. They should have looked out of place with his pressed slacks and dress shirt, but then again, that dress shirt had two buttons undone, the tie hung loosely, and Wes, no matter how much gel he put in his unruly hair, would never look quite respectable. None of the Mercers ever did.

"I saw one of our friends today."

The slouch disappeared as Wes straightened and fixed him with his dark gaze. "Which one?"

"The flying dino. I saw it clear as day when it swooped out of the sky. It attacked some dude I'd gone to visit."

"It actually attacked?" Wes's voice pitched almost as high as his brows.

"I didn't see the attack part, more like the kidnapping. Damned thing plucked him off the ground and took off with him like he was some kind of mouse. Some kids found the body in a tree. It wasn't pretty."

"Who was he?" Wes asked sharply.

"One of your Bittech fellows by the name of Jeffrey."

Wes's brows drew together. "Former employee. He was canned almost a week ago for compromising the institute's security."

"Lost a key card, did he?"

"How the fuck did you know that?"

Explaining Aria would take too long so he summarized with, "A little birdie told me. Anyhow, the flying lizard thing didn't just take off with Jeffrey. He tore off his face and fingerprints, too. I only recognized him because of his clothes."

"The monster has gotten a taste of blood. That's not a good thing," Wes noted.

"No kidding. I also don't like the fact that it's hunting in daylight."

"I wonder where it's holing up in between sightings."

"No idea. He seems to poof in and out of thin air. Without tracks, he's impossible to follow. Lizard thing wasn't the only weird monster spotted today. Another one visited my house. Ma killed it." He couldn't help the pride in his words.

"Another lizard creature?" Wes barked.

"No. This one was more like a mutant flying monkey. Weirdest fucking thing I ever saw. Covered in fur, not scales. This one had quite the tail, too. A long, whip-like appendage with a barbed end."

Wes struck a match and lit another cigarette. He took a long pull before asking, "Did you bury it? Or feed it to the gators?"

"Neither yet."

"Good plan. We need to study it for clues. We can use it as proof to the SHC that there's shit going on."

"I think there's more than enough proof at this point for us to admit that the High Shifter Council doesn't give a rat's ass."

"Are you saying you're just going to give up?" Wes blew the question out as casually as the rings of smoke.

A snort escaped Constantine. "Like fuck. I can't. There's still at least one more lizard creature out there, murdering folks. We still don't know for sure dogman is dead." He shook his head. "I can't stop. Not until I know we've taken care of all the people, or things, involved. I need to keep Aria and my family safe."

Wes paused, hand suspended in air, the glow of his cigarette jutting from between his fingers. "Keep Aria safe? I thought that was the girl Cynthia said was missing."

"I found her. More like she found me. Anyhow, I'm kind of keeping an eye on her on account she lost her memory and she can't remember if anyone is out to get her."

A dark brow kept rising until Wes finally said, "Have you been sniffing swamp gases? Or has the group been keeping shit from me? No one told me she'd been found."

"Things were kind of hectic, and Aria was really adamant I not tell anyone about her."

"Too late now."

Very true, so Constantine laid the whole thing out for Wes, except for the kiss. That he kept private.

At the end of it, Wes lit yet another cigarette.

This time, Constantine felt a need to say something. "Are you trying to make yourself into smoked gator meat?"

Acrid smoke blew into his face. "We'll all die someday. Some of us sooner than others."

"Whatever, dude. Anyway, I should head back to Daryl's and grab Aria and Princess."

"You staying at your place?"

"I don't know. I was thinking of getting a room in town. The house is pretty isolated, and while Princess is pretty tough, she is small."

"What of the woman?"

"She's pretty tough and small, too, but she knows how to hold her own." And for the things she couldn't handle, he'd be there to help.

"Don't tell me she's got you whipped already?"

"Nothing wrong with a guy getting serious about a girl."

"Until that girl leaves you because you're not good enough. Women are trouble. It's best to steer clear."

Constantine had to wonder as he drove away just who had crushed Wes's emotions to the point he sounded so bitter. The only girl he'd ever really seen the guy serious about was Melanie, but it had been years and years since their breakup. Hell, they'd both been kids in high school still.

As Constantine drove, he broke a few laws regarding speed and texting while driving. Yet, it was worth it, given the enthusiastic way with which Aria flung herself out the door, Princess at her heels, waving a hand over her head while Cynthia yelled from the door, "If those toes go anywhere near his ears, I'll expect details."

As Constantine came around the front of the truck, his heart rate accelerated. Enjoyment at seeing her inflated him with warmth. It didn't help that she smiled as if pleased to see him.

Ours. We should hug her and squeeze her.

Or he could take the cowardly route, drop to one knee, open his arms wide, and exclaim, "Where's Daddy's sweet baby girl?"

Mock him and die.

The babbled words were totally worth the sight of his dog careening at him with her lopsided gait, tongue lolling as she emitted happy yips.

"You hate the name angel, yet you don't think that display is emasculating?" Aria couldn't hide her sarcastic lilt.

"Nothing wrong with a man's love for his dog. Jealous?"

He peeked at her as he scooped his dog into his arms.

She might have spat, "No." But this close to her, he could hear the patter of her heart, a rapid thump. Even odder, he could swear he felt her disappointment.

Perhaps he had sniffed swamp gases because, in the next second, he stood and pressed his lips against hers, a fleeting kiss before pulling away, and with a grin, he said, "How's my fluffy-wuffy little swan?"

Instead of taking offense, she stepped into him and, reaching on tiptoe, nipped the tip of his chin, and growled, "Hungry."

Unfortunately, she meant for food. Real food.

And where could a guy take his gal late at night with his little dog where they served great food and didn't ask questions?

The Itty Bitty, of course.

Chapter 15

NOTHING LIKE TAKING a girl who barely needed a bra to a strip joint, with giant, bouncy boobs all over the place. It made Aria feel somewhat inadequate in the chest area. She took her irritation out on Constantine.

"I can't believe you brought me here." Seriously, he didn't seem like the type who went to the nudie bar.

"I know how it looks," he muttered, his fingers laced through hers as he weaved her between the tables. "But trust me when I say the food here is excellent, the discretion top-notch, and besides, Renny works here, so I get a discount."

Was the food the only thing he got a discount on?

Shoving the irrational jealousy away, she tried to keep an open mind. After all, Aria knew stripping could provide a decent income.

How do I know that?

Shit, don't tell me I'm a stripper?

She really wished she could remember what her job entailed before coming to Bitten Point on her supposed road trip. Thinking about her past, though, resulted in a shushing sound, as if her own mind forced her to forget.

"Let's grab this booth at the back." Constantine gestured to the U-shaped seating area, which, to his credit, sat farthest from the stage.

Before Aria slid in, she couldn't help but ask, "I am not going to stick to it, am I?" Nothing worse that getting glued to a foreign piece of furniture by unidentifiable globs. She refused to even entertain the thought of what those globs could be in a strip joint.

"This place is cleaner than most bars, actually. Much like snakes, exotic dancers and their places of work get a bad rap."

His words definitely put Aria in her place and also reminded her that she wasn't one to stick her nose in the air. She wasn't any better than anyone in here. From the bits and pieces she recalled, she'd done things she shouldn't take pride in. Funny how some of those same things people disapproved of were acts she still remembered with fondness.

"What are you ordering? I'm starved."

He cocked a brow at her. "I don't think they serve three chicken wings and seven and a half fries."

"Ha. Ha. What a funny guy. See if I share any of my leftovers with you now."

"Ah, come one. You gotta let me have them. You can't let good food go to waste." Then the big, dumb idiot batted his lashes and grinned.

He looked so bloody stupid and absolutely gorgeous at the same time. "You're whacked."

"Only with you. Most of my friends think I'm kind of dry with the humor."

"Or they don't understand it. That happens to me a lot."

Reaching out, he snagged her hand. "This is going to sound dorky, but I'll blame it on hunger. I kind of like you"—his lips stretched—"bluebird."

"I'm wearing pink. And I like you, too." In what was the most awkward conversation ever. Since when did a guy hold her hand and try to look in her eyes as he claimed affection? Or was there another reason why he was acting so sappy?

"Are you stoned?"

He frowned. "No, why."

"Because this is weird, angel. Guys don't profess emotions in a strip joint."

Turning his head from side to side, Constantine surveyed the room. "What's location got to do with it?"

Aria couldn't help but giggle. Sincerity rang in his words. He truly didn't grasp the oddity. But she let it pass. Until he said, "So, I feel I should tell you right up front that, if we do take things further, I can't promise anything more than a casual thing. We snakes don't have a good track record with sticking around."

"So you're asking me out and breaking up with me all at once? How does that work?"

"I wasn't breaking up with you. And, I, um, didn't realize we were dating."

"Just because I might have been a slut in my other life doesn't mean I am going to be in this one. So if we're going to be making out on a regular basis, then I should at least be your girlfriend." Because then she wouldn't be a whore. She'd just be doing what she had to in order to keep her man happy.

He blinked. "That was confusing, but from what I think I understood, you're my girlfriend."

"Well, I thought I was, but then you broke up with me by saying snakes leave."

"We do. At least my dad did. It's something genetic about our kind. So even though I kind of really like you, it could be that some switch in my head turns off at one point and I'll just pack my things and go."

"Go where?"

Again, he regarded her for an instant. "What do you mean go where? Somewhere. I don't know exactly. Just that it might happen."

"Why?"

"Why what?"

"Why are you going to leave me?" As she asked, a woman dressed in black yoga shorts that hugged her every contour with a tight T-shirt and a large tray arrived at their table.

"Hey, Renny," Constantine said, relinquishing his grip on her hand.

"If it isn't my favorite brother-in-law," she teased as she placed some plates in front of them. Several plates. "I ordered your favorites with a little extra for your lady friend." A curious gaze turned her way, and the woman waited.

"Shit. Sorry. Aria, this is Renny, Caleb's wife. This is Aria," he told the other woman, who, done serving them food and drink, tucked the tray under her arm.

Brown eyes perused her. "So you're the girl that they were looking for. Glad they found you. I know when the lizard man took Luke, I was scared out of my mind for him."

"I don't know what took me." As Aria blinked, she faded out into a new scene.

Through woozy eyes, she could see a ceiling. White plaster with a few hairline cracks and one stain. Whose ceiling did she admire?

A turn of her head showed a wallpapered wall, the pattern faded.

A blink, and when she reopened her eyes, she noted legs. Strangely shaped legs in dire need of a shave. More like a lawnmower, given how thick the hair grew.

What the fuck? She turned her head and peeked upwards. She noted the towering shape of a dog on two legs. A fucking humanoid dog. It glanced down at her, but it didn't loll its tongue in a happy greeting.

The muzzle drew back over black gums, revealing pointed canines. A low, rumbling growl came from it. Ominous. Deadly.

Fly away.

She flung herself to the side, in an attempt to get on her hands and knees. She needed to move away from the weird monster.

She didn't go more than a few inches before a hooked foot sent her tumbling, and she only barely missed smacking her face off the floor.

Before she could recover, she noted she was face to shoe, as in leather loafer.

"And where do you think you're going?" a voice asked.

"Help me." The words emerged weak, trembling, just like her body.

"Help, oh I plan to. You scared her, Harold, with that hairy mug of yours. Or is it your breath? Perhaps you should stop snubbing your nose at the milk bones I offer."

It took her slow mind a moment to grasp the man in the leather shoes spoke to the dog creature.

A rumbling sound filled the air. It held menace, and it drew a shiver of fear. It cut off abruptly with a sharp yelp.

"Tsk. Tsk. Bad doggie."

The acrid stench of burning hair revived her a bit more, but while her mind woke, her body remained sluggish.

"Would you open the fireplace already? We need to get the girl out of here before your mother notices she's gone. I had the devil of a time trying to get the sleeping agent in the cocoa. Last thing I need is for us to be caught. Although, if your mother does stick her nose in our affairs, then you know what will happen."

Grrrr.

Aria pushed to her knees, but wavered, the drugs still coursing through her system, her every movement weighted and laborious.

"Grab the girl."

The hairy thing called Harold hoisted Aria by the armpits, none too gently either.

"Lemme go," she slurred.

"Not today. Today you get to help us make history. Or you'll die."

Snap.

The fingers clicked in front of her eyes, and Constantine's worried voice said, "Aria, earth to Aria, come in, Aria."

"Sorry. I kind of wandered there."

"What did you remember?" he asked.

"Them taking me into some kind of secret tunnel through a fireplace."

"Who did? Who took you? Do you remember?"

She did, but did she want to admit what she recalled? It seemed so farfetched now.

"There was a shifter and a man."

Constantine leaned on the table, and even Renny crouched down to get in closer. "Do you remember their names?"

"Harold and..." Her brow wrinkled. "I never heard another name."

"Was Harold by any chance a dogman?"

She gaped at him. "Yes. How did you know?"

"He's the same one we talked about before."

"You didn't give him a name."

"Because I have a hard time equating a name like Harold to whatever that thing is."

She shuddered. "There is something very unnatural about him."

"What about the other man?" Renny prodded. "Can you remember any details about him?"

"He's an ass."

A snort blew past Renny's lip. "That describes too many men."

"Tall, but really gangly."

"Smell?"

Aria's nose wrinkled. "I don't know. I was so fuzzy at the time on account of the stuff they laced my cocoa with."

"Any other details?"

"Reddish blond. He wasn't dark-haired. But not much else. I mostly saw his shoes." Finely cut, buttery looking, hand-stitched shoes. She'd recognize them again if she saw them.

Hunger took over at that point. Renny left to take care of other clients, and they dug in, Constantine having three bites for every one of hers. But she savored those bites, closing her eyes in delight at the crisp crunch of the home-style fries and the tang of the lemon pepper on the wings, sweetened by a light lemon sauce. Then there were the corn tortillas with a cheese and spinach dip. She ate a whopping eight of those.

Constantine ate the rest—well, almost all the rest. He did sneak tidbits to Princess, who sat beside him in the booth.

"If I keep eating like this, I'm gonna be too heavy to fly," she said with a pat to her belly. She froze. "Holy shit. I said I could fly."

"Now you sound like Peter Pan. You always could fly. It's just that your subconscious is revealing these tidbits a little at a time."

"I prefer that to the in-living-color movies." Those took her out of the moment and proved jarring, but not as jarring as the floorshow.

A shrill scream erupted from across the room. In a flash, Constantine slid from the booth and stood before her, scanning the room.

Another scream, louder this time as a girl dressed in a plaid skirt and tied-off white blouse came running from the curtains at the back of the stage. She wasn't alone in making an appearance on the runway.

The fabric, hanging as a red velvet shield, came tearing down. A grand entrance for Harold, the dogman from her most recent recollection.

Holy shit, he is real.

And when his baleful glare turned her way, she swallowed hard because she knew to the depth of her being, *He's coming for me.*

Chapter 16

WHILE HE MIGHT NOT MIND a little fur, Constantine had to admit tonight's floorshow pushed that limit.

The hairy beast loped onto the runway, not even wearing a thong or pasties while the red and blue and white lights streaked and swerved, giving the creature a surreal appearance.

Dogman—because he just couldn't think of him as Harold—let out a howl when he glanced their way. Freakish paws/hands pounded its chest.

"What is he, part gorilla?" he mused aloud.

"Does it matter?" hissed Aria. "We need to get out of here."

"Why?" He didn't turn to peek at her, but he did ask the question.

"Because he's coming for us," she yelled as she ducked under the table.

A good place to hide if she didn't have him and Princess—his valiant dog who stood atop the table barking and bristling—to protect her.

Constantine braced his feet on the floor, spread his arms away from his body, and waited, timing his next move carefully. He grabbed dogman mid-leap and used the momentum to swing him away.

Crash. The loose table on the floor couldn't handle the force of the body landing and it skidded before collapsing. The impact didn't stop the beast.

Harold, still wearing his collar and looking more rabid than a certain dog in a movie, sprang to his feet, ignoring the scattering patrons as they bolted for the exit.

Harold had eyes for only Constantine.

Good. Let the monster focus on him instead of the others. He flexed his fingers. He could use a bit of exercise.

With a sweep of his arm, Harold cleared a table laden with beer bottles. The tinkling breakage of glass brought a few stray screams from those still within the room. They, like Aria, chose to dive for cover instead of running.

Princess loved a challenge, and Constantine could only watch with bemusement as his dog bolted to within a few feet of Harold, where she proceeded to prance and bark madly.

Grawr.

As if that intimidated his dog. Princess squatted, peed, and then turned her back with a disdainful diss.

GRAWR! "Schnackk," Harold lisped.

The dogman spoke, and Constantine bared a smile. "No one's eating anyone today." Unless Aria was on the menu—a menu for him alone. "Forget about my brave Princess. What do you say you and I play, Harold? Does the big, ugly doggy who needs a bath want to play fetch?"

"That sounds like something Cynthia would say," Aria muttered from behind him.

Compared to a girl. His ego might never recover. As Harold ran at Constantine again, he revised his plan. Hand-to-hand with the rabid beast might not prove his best course of action. He didn't have the claws or slavering jaws the monster did.

Yet he wasn't one to swap into his snake without good cause, especially since there were still witnesses around. Snakes freaked people out. Didn't matter if he was the good guy here. People would see his python and scream, or try to kill him.

But he was less worried about that than the opinion of a certain woman.

Did he want to scare Aria?

That would solve the problem of me possibly walking away. Get her to leave first.

What a cowardly way of dealing with his fears.

As Harold once again leaped, front paws tipped in claws extended, he ducked and let Harold soar over his head to crash into the table behind him.

Aria squeaked, but scuttled out from under the table.

"Run," he advised. "Get outside if you can, into my truck." Where he hoped nobody waited for them.

Flipping around to face the really pissed-off dog thing, Constantine stripped off his shirt and put his hands to the button of his pants.

"Why the fuck are you stripping right now?" Aria yelled, not having run away as he told her to.

"Gonna unleash my mighty snake."

"That better not be a reference to your dick."

No, but he should note his cock was mighty, too.

As Harold scrambled from his awkward wedge between the banquet seating and the table, Constantine shed his clothes. *Yessss, rid yourself of that unneeded, unnatural skin.*

His head lifted and his eyes closed as he mentally called his python.

While his cold-blooded beast didn't often talk to him, not like wolves and cats that had noisy partners, they did communicate through feelings.

So he felt the cold satisfaction as his body rippled. Every molecule undulated, and moving in a wave, they gathered and reformed. Reformed into something different.

One limb. One slick and smooth body.

"Holy fuck!" his delicate lark yelled.

It might have to do with his impressive size. Long, so very long, with a defined pattern on his skin.

I am attractive. It was only right the female admired his traits.

But the mating would come after the battle.

The enemy was almost upon them. He held his serpentine body upright as his jaw unhinged, opening extra wide. He hissed, the sharp points of his fangs projecting.

The smelly-thing hit him, and he whipped backwards, the enemy atop him. Claws went to rip at his flesh, but got caught in the thick leather of his skin. Still, it did sting.

He sank his teeth into the creature, wishing his had poison like some of his cousins. But he had something almost as good.

His tail, often possessed of a mind of its own, rose from the floor and moved with purpose. It slithered across the back of the hairy thing then tucked around its chest, back around again.

The dog let out a rancid, hot puff of air. Definitely not dinner material, but good for a squeeze.

The coils of his body tightened around the dog thing. Clawed fingers dug at him, some piercing the skin. The pain served to only tighten him further, a crushing vise around the unnatural thing until it exhaled one final time and went limp.

Since there was no point in keeping the body trapped, the length of him uncoiled from it, letting the limp meat sack fall onto the floor.

Movement from the corner of his eye caught his attention. His head pivoted as his body rose higher, a tall stalk towering to give him a vantage point.

The female observed him. *His* female. She did not exude fear, not much at any rate. He slithered closer, bobbing down to peruse her. Her breath caught, but she did not flinch.

Not prey.

Not this one.

He circled around her, around and around until she stood amidst a loose mound of coils.

A fluttery touch against his skin as her hands came to rest on him.

"You're hurt," she said.

Words he understood but couldn't reply to. The tip of his forked tongue flicked forth, and now she did lean back ever so slightly.

That did not prevent him from tasting her skin. He would know her flavor.

Voices yelled from afar. Others appeared to approach.

She pivoted in her ring and regarded him. "Angel, you have to come back now. There're people coming."

Perhaps they would provide a cleaner repast than the foul one on the floor.

"You have to change. We can't know who's coming. You know your kind get a bad rap. I don't want them to shoot."

Bullets. Ripping, tearing holes. No. Those did not appeal. And it was cold in here. Time for a nap.

Constantine threw his head back and heaved a deep breath as he came back to himself.

Of course, there was no hiding a six-foot-plus naked man on the floor standing a little too close to the naked dog thing.

Thinking quickly, Aria doused him with beer from an intact bottle.

When questioned, he stuck to his guns with a slurred, "I don't know."

Chapter 17

ARIA COULDN'T HELP but laugh at Constantine as he drove them to his house. Princess sat on his lap, one eye cocked, watching for trouble—in other words, making sure Aria didn't put the moves on her daddy.

As for Constantine, he kept his gaze trained on the road while sporting a stern countenance.

"Oh, come on, it's not that bad."

He snorted. "Not that bad? I think neutering would have been preferable to you telling the cops I was stripping for you."

"I only said it to explain your nakedness." Because poor Constantine didn't have time to pull on his pants before the cavalry arrived.

"Men don't striptease."

"They do out in Vegas." She had a vague recollection of a very drunk Cynthia dragging her to a show where the men wore G-strings, leather chaps, and nothing else by the end of the show. Made her want to ride a cowboy at the time.

"They can do whatever they like out west. I don't strip."

"Why not?"

"It's weird."

He sounded so discomfited she couldn't help but tease. "Some guys make good money at it. You've got a good body and some serious moves. I think you could make a killing taking it off and shaking that snake."

"Snake?"

"I'm sorry. Should I have said your python?"

This time, he couldn't hide the quirk of his lips, although he tried to remain serious. "I am not stripping for money."

"How about for free?"

"How about not at all?"

She needled him because it was fun. So often he seemed to send her off balance. About time she returned the favor. "You know that's not technically true, given you just did it in public, in front of not just me."

"Only because I had to shapeshift. My legs can't fuse together properly if I'm wearing pants."

"Ever thought of wearing a dress?"

"No."

"What if I suggested you wore a kilt?"

"I am not letting my junk hang loose under a skirt. I'll keep it in my pants, thank you."

"Speaking of junk..." She snapped her fingers. "You just reminded me of something I wanted to ask, but you were kind of busy at the time. Where does your worm go when you're in like snakeman mode?"

"Worm?" He shot her a glance.

"Would you prefer the term willy?"

"I'd prefer it if we dropped the topic. Or if you're that obsessed with my dick then, by all means, grab a handful. Or mouthful. I'm not picky."

She knew he expected his words to shut her up. Except it was more fun to say, "Maybe I will suck on it."

Nothing more empowering than being able to tease she might blow him and have him almost crash the truck into a ditch.

"You are a tease," he growled.

"Only if I don't put out."

He did better at controlling his swerve this time, but that didn't stop her laughter. "So why are we going back to the house? I thought you said it would be too dangerous," she mentioned as she took note of the familiar landmarks.

"We just got rid of one of their main players. We got rid of another this afternoon. At this point, we've weakened them and shown we'll fight back. And we've proven we can win. Whoever it is behind the attacks will want to regroup before striking again."

"You mean gather his troops so they can stack the odds when they come after us again. That's not exactly reassuring." She wrinkled her nose.

"If you wanted reassuring, you would have left town by now. But you, my brave hawk, crave a bit of excitement."

She thought she had until the attack in the bar. "I highly doubt that, seeing as how my first instinct was to hide under a table." In retrospect, her cowardice burned. But what could she have done?

Lit your drink on fire and tossed it at dog boy, Molotov style.

Hindsight sucked. Aria had gotten used to the voice talking in her head. What she had a bigger problem with was the violence it usually encouraged.

I thought we liked to poison.

Among other things.

It was the other things that worried her. As did the fact they were getting closer to the bayou, which meant closer to his house, a bed, and then seeing what would happen.

Since the explosive kiss they'd shared, he'd admitted to liking her, but also the fear he'd leave her. Honest, if not easy to hear.

Meanwhile, she could admit she also liked him and feared him leaving her. A fine dilemma.

But is that really any different from anyone else when they first start dating?

Everyone suffered doubt. Everyone entered relationships with the best of intentions. Sometimes, love grew stronger over time, or so the romance books claimed. In other cases, the bloom of lust wore off and the little things nagged until couples split.

She'd seen it happen before. While Aria might not have a family of her own, she'd grown quite talented at observing the families of others.

Funny the things she remembered. Most of her early life seemed okay to access. It was the more recent stuff she had problems with still. The biggest problem of all being what to do with Constantine.

I haven't known the guy long enough to really be thinking about this seriously.

Yet she couldn't help it. Which begged the question, why? Other guys scratched an itch. She didn't worry about getting involved with them or taking advantage of their bodies. With Constantine, though, she worried.

This is a man who could hurt me. Not physically, but because he made her want to stick around for a while. Maybe give that whole, "hey, you're cool, let's hang for a while" thing a go.

Commitment. Not something she knew too much about. Not something she felt comfortable with.

For some reason, she just couldn't think of Constantine in terms of only once. With him, it would be all or nothing.

She'd nicely circled back to her main dilemma again, the one where she feared to jump because she might fall flat.

But if I don't take that leap, I cannot spread my wings to fly. Faith that she would stay aloft. Could she give that faith to Constantine? Did she dare take a chance, grasp what she could, and give what simmered between them a chance to fly?

Nothing ventured, nothing gained—a motto never more apt than now.

The headlights of his truck illuminated his house, their stark brightness reflecting off the dark windows.

He shut down the engine, and they both sat in the truck for a moment, listening to the sounds of the night. The steady chirp of crickets. The hum of mosquitoes. The ticking of a hot engine cooling.

The sounds of normalcy.

"What are we waiting for?" she whispered.

"The weird part is, if I say flying monkeys, it's actually the truth."

"I hope there's no more of them." Shudder. She definitely wouldn't watch the movie about Oz without remembering the mutant version.

"I hope so, too, and yet I keep wondering what other monsters might be out there that we haven't seen yet."

"You think there's more?"

"Yeah. And for all I know, they're waiting in the shadows." He drummed his fingers on the dash of his truck.

"That seems unlikely given the nightlife seems pretty noisy and active." The distant croak of a toad punctuated her belief.

"Or they've been lying in wait so long that no one is taking note anymore."

"Are you scared?" she asked.

It wasn't just Constantine who snorted. His dog did, too.

"I'm not scared for me, but I am worried about you. Maybe coming back here wasn't such a good idea. I mean, we're pretty isolated. If they attack en masse, I might not be able to defend you."

"I thought you said you didn't think they'd try anything until they regrouped."

"I've reassessed that belief."

She rolled her eyes. "Stop second-guessing yourself. They're either here or they're not. And going somewhere else doesn't mean they won't follow. The best way to know for sure if something lurks is for one of us to go outside as bait." No sooner did she say it when Aria swung open her door, but before she could hop out of the truck, Princess scooted across her lap, onto the running board, then leaped to the ground.

"Just had to one-up me again, didn't you?" she muttered as

Constantine flung himself from the truck with a cried, "Princess, stay where Daddy can see you."

While he might show concern for his dog, he also showed some for Aria as he loped around the truck. He arrived in time to grab her and swing her to the ground.

She didn't move away, and he didn't remove his hands. They stood for a moment, bodies close yet not quite touching, staring at each other.

"I don't hear any monsters."

"I don't smell any either," he replied, his gaze unwavering. The air between them sparkled with electricity. His hands on her waist were firm. Dare she even say possessive?

He drew her closer.

Yip.

With a sharp bark of annoyance, Princess broke the stalemate, yet she couldn't break the anticipatory tension humming between them. Nothing could, short of an attack. But nothing lurched from the darkness to eat them. Nothing swooped from the sky to snatch them. They made it into the house, not far, before their lips met with a hard clash of teeth.

Given Constantine's height, she needed help to reach. His hands spanned her waist and hoisted her so that their mouths could meet.

Meet sounded so trite, though. It was more an explosion of hot breath, wet tongues, and frantic need.

She cupped his face, loving the feel of his skin as she sucked at his lower lip.

"I want you." The words rumbled against her mouth.

They made her shiver and only served to increase the heat invading her.

"I want you, too." The soft admission made him groan, and she found her back pressed against the wall as his mouth continued to devour. Or did she devour him?

Did it matter?

There was nothing stopping them now. Nothing to prevent her

clothes from being ripped from her body. She was just as violent with his clothing, her hands pulling at his T-shirt until he yanked it over his head, baring his skin.

The flesh-to-flesh contact of their upper bodies had her sucking in a breath. Could skin sizzle?

It felt like hers did.

With a strength she admired, and a body she longed to worship—with her tongue—Constantine pinned her to the wall. A good thing he held her aloft because arousal liquefied her limbs. She trembled, boneless at his touch, her body aware of every sensation.

The unshaven edge of his jaw scraped across her tender skin, abrading and awakening it as he kissed his way over to her ear.

He nibbled it. *Oh my*. He sucked on the lobe, and she moaned. It seemed she had an erotic spot, and he exploited it with hot breath, tugs, and sucks until she panted and clutched at his shoulders.

Then he left the tender shell of her ear, his lips trailing down the column of her neck. He leaned back, using his lower body to keep her pinned as he kissed his way down to the valley between her breasts.

Keeping one arm anchored around her waist, he let his other hand roam. Slightly callused fingers cupped a breast, his thumb rubbing against the protruding tip. Her nipple tightened to an even sharper point.

It took some adjusting, him hoisting her higher on the wall, but the new height meant he could latch his lips around her aching peak.

She made a noise as she clutched at his head, with pants and moans urging him on.

Take it deeper into your mouth.

He did. He sucked her breast in, the heat of his touch exploding in her.

Gasping and squirming didn't mean he hurried. Oh no. He took his time torturing her poor nipples, first one then the other. The nubs tugged with his lips, his teeth nipping at them while his tongue swirled around them.

He drove her absolutely crazy with desire, enough that she gasped, "Stop teasing me and fuck me already, would you?"

"But I'm having fun," was his rumbled reply, the words quivering on her skin.

"And I want to come." She didn't need to say on his cock. He understood, and it was his turn to shudder.

He still wore his pants, and he took a few fumbling, precious seconds to push them down. Then it was her turn to lose her bottoms, his hands rough in their removal, but titillating as proof of his excitement.

Once he bared her to his touch, he repositioned her against the wall, his hands cupping her ass cheeks while his lips scorched hers in a passionate kiss. It rendered her quite breathless. His shaft throbbed against her belly, hot and *alive*.

As arousal ran like liquid fire through her veins, she sucked at his lower lip, her entire being thrumming with excitement.

I need him so badly.

"I need you."

He echoed her thoughts as he drew his hips back and let the hard length of him bob up from where he'd trapped it under her body. He angled his hips far enough back that the tip of him teased.

He might have his hands full, but she didn't. She kept her legs loosely coiled around his waist as she reached down. She gripped his cock firmly, and he sucked in a breath. Stroke. Stroke.

She slid her hand on him, keeping the head of his mushroomed shaft rubbing against her core.

Her arousal moistened the tip of him, covering him in a glistening sheen that made the rub against her clitoris even more moan-worthy.

"If you don't stop, I am going to come before I get inside you," he growled, his fingers digging into her cheeks.

"Oh no you don't," she muttered. She pulled at him, inserting the head of his cock into her sex, but then couldn't get him any farther.

He locked his body, and she growled. "What are you doing?"

"You're tight."

"And you're big."

"Exactly."

He worried about hurting her? She took her gaze from their bodies and their intimate joining to see he held himself rigid, the cords in his neck tense and shaking.

"Don't worry about me, angel. I can handle a little thickness, and I don't mind a bit of rough." With those words, she grabbed him by the cheeks and drew him close that she might kiss him. As he relaxed, she tightened her thighs and, with a chuckle of excitement, thrust with her hips, sheathing him.

"Fuck!" The word burst from him and was swallowed, much like her sex swallowed him.

She nibbled the tip of his chin. "I think fucking is a good idea."

His reply was a steady, groaning rumble as he began to move his hips. He moved them slowly, too slowly for her level of arousal. In, slow and languorously, letting her feel every inch, then out, a slick retreat that had her sex clutching at him.

No, don't go.

Back in, the slick friction making her tremble. She clung to him, digging her fingers into his flesh, making a high-pitched, breathless noise.

"So fucking tight and sweet. Hold me tight. I'm going to increase the pace."

Did he know telling her would just heighten her excitement?

Her legs locked him against her, and since he couldn't pull out as far, he thrust deeper, butting against her sweet spot. Then he rotated his hips. Swirl, thrust, push, rub. The intensity against her sweet spot put her on the brink. She practically sobbed the pleasure of it.

How perfectly they fit together. A man with size, strength, and, best of all, the ability to use his rigid shaft and stretch her oh so nicely.

"Fill me. Fuck me." She managed to suck in a breath to huskily beg.

He groaned, the low rumble vibrating her being.

Faster he moved, the thrust of his hips grinding his cock into her.

He was so hard. So thick. So fucking thick.

Even as she came, he remained thick, perfect. Her body exploded against and around him. Waves of utter bliss stormed through her, shaking every atom of her being and then returning to run over her again. And again.

Endless ecstasy as he kept grinding and pushing and...

He came. Fiery hot, he jetted into her, bathing her womb with his seed. Leaving his mark.

The moment proved so utterly perfect, especially when he leaned his forehead against hers, his breathing hot and ragged. She understood the need to recover.

Explosive didn't even come close to describing the cataclysm of the orgasm. She should note she did remember sex. And that was all it was. Sex. Not this intensely passionate and intimate joining of not just their bodies but, dammit, their souls.

I thought I didn't believe in that kind of sentimental shit.

Not anymore.

He's mine.

Her words. No one else's.

But not everyone agreed.

Chapter 18

THE LOW, grumbling growl drew Constantine's attention away from the glorious after-sex lassitude he indulged in.

Making sweet love to Aria had proved even more incredible than he imagined.

How could any man want to walk away from this?

The question was a good one, but took a backseat to his dog growling. What had his Princess on alert? He didn't sense any danger. His sixth snake sense didn't tingle, yet his pup didn't sound happy.

"What's wrong, Princess?" As he asked, he firmed his grip around Aria and carried her to the washroom, where a shower sounded like an awesome plan.

A shower with soap, rubbing, and naked skin. Hell, yeah.

Grrr. Ruff.

Princess still didn't seem happy. Something perturbed her. Constantine stopped short of the bathroom and looked around, checking for signs of danger. Not sensing anything amiss, he peeked down at his dog, who sat at his feet, big eyes staring right at him.

"What is it, baby girl? Tell Daddy what's wrong."

"She's jealous, angel. I don't think your Princess likes to share. And do you know what?" Her lips nuzzled the skin at his neck. "Neither do I." Chomp.

Aria bit down hard on his skin, so hard he gasped, his cock hardened, and his dog lost her shit barking.

He fell against the bathroom wall with a heavy thud.

"What the hell was that for?"

"Just proving a point. Princess thinks I'm dangerous and wants to take me out," she whispered with warm breath against his throbbing skin.

"I think Princess is right. You are dangerous. But then again, so am I." And his dog would have to learn to share him because he wasn't ditching Aria. "Princess, Daddy needs to take a shower to get clean."

"Oh no, it will be dirty," Aria promised.

Fuck. He couldn't stop his cock from swelling at her words. "Go guard the house. Be a good girl."

Yip. With a woebegone look in his direction, Princess slunk out the door, and he might have felt guiltier if he hadn't caught the dirty look his dog aimed at Aria, but he could understand the glare, given Aria murmured, "I win."

"No, I win, because now that I've got you wrapped in my arms, you can't escape."

"Why would I want to?" she asked.

"Because I'm going to do such bad, bad things to you."

She shivered. "Please do."

He would. As soon as he got some hot water to sluice them off.

Keeping her tucked against him, where she belonged—*hug her, squeeze her, never let her go*—he turned on the taps. The hot water tank was just behind the shower, not far, so that meant it didn't take long for the jetting droplets to warm.

He stood in the tub, putting her back into the hot spray.

She sighed and leaned back into it, exposing the smooth column of her throat, a gesture of trust among predators.

He nuzzled the skin, tempted to leave a mark of his own. But the moment wasn't quite right.

But I can make it perfect.

He leaned her back, forcing her back to arch, pushing her sweet tits into the air.

Absolutely mouthwatering. He freed one hand that he might run a finger around her breasts, tracing them.

She muttered a husky, "What are you doing?"

"Admiring the view."

She snorted. "You don't have to lie."

"What makes you think I'm lying? Does this feel like I'm lying?" He slid her far enough that she could feel the hard jut of his cock, already raring to go.

Her eyes opened then shut as the shower water got into them. "Ugh," she exclaimed.

He laughed and turned her, putting her sideways so her head could lean against the tub liner.

It didn't impede his view. It actually made it easier for him to lean down and grab a tip with his lips.

She gasped, and her fingers clutched at his scalp. "I don't have big breasts."

"And?" He bit down on the nipple, causing her to dig her nails in for a delicious bite of pain to offset his mounting need.

"Just saying I don't have big boobs. Or much of an ass."

"And again, I say what about it? From my perspective"—suck—"they're"—squeeze of those cheeks—"perfect."

And mine.

All mine.

A concept that really was growing on him. Just like she grew on him. Usually, snakes shed unwanted epidermal layers, but this was one time he wanted to wear someone else like a skin. He wanted Aria to wrap herself around him. He also wanted to taste her.

Now.

Like this very instant.

"Brace yourself," he warned. He set her feet down on the bottom of the tub and made sure she leaned against it. He dropped to his knees before her, letting the weak spray of water hit his shoulders and roll down his back.

As he brought his face level with her mound, he parted her thighs.

A rapidly sucked-in breath drew his attention upward. He noted her watching him, biting her lower lip.

He didn't need to see her face, though, to smell her arousal. This close to her sex, he could scent it. It tempted him.

He brushed her inner thighs with the rough edge of his beard, scraping the bristles over tender flesh.

A shudder went through her. Another when he nosed at her, rubbing his face against her pubes, inhaling her scent. Her essence.

He imprinted her so that he would never forget.

I'll never forget. How could he when she smelled so deliciously woman? So decadent.

He lapped at her, a long, wet swipe of his tongue across her clit.

That brought the grasping fingers to tear at his hair.

Another long lick and she made the most beautiful mewling sound. But her clit was only one treasure to discover.

It took only a swipe of his tongue for her plump, pink lips to part for him. Her honey coated his tongue, drugged him with her arousal. How sweet she tasted. He needed more.

Lapping at her, he probed and teased her sex for a moment before returning to her clit and sucking it.

Captured by the pleasure he lavished upon her, Aria dug her fingers in harder. She clutched him so tight.

Yes, tight. So good.

He wanted to get crushed by her. The more pleasure he gave, the tighter she got.

She also got wild, a little rough, her hips bucking and thrashing.

I like it.

And she liked it when he gripped her hips in his hands, his outdoor-tanned skin against her white flesh a pleasing contrast.

Mine.

Holding her fast, he lashed her with his tongue, and with her ability to buck gone, Aria moaned, loud and often.

When her body began to quiver, he knew he'd taken her as far as he could. She was ready for him.

In a swift motion, he stood. He caught her lips with his, sucking at the moaning passion, swallowing the sound of her pleasure.

His finger probed at the swollen entrance to her sex, thrusting into her, a finger fuck that had them both swaying their hips.

"Turn around for me," he ordered.

She did better than just that. She turned to face away from him, braced her palms against the wall, and thrust out her little ass.

And he ran into a dilemma. She was too fucking short to do it like that.

Fuck.

She peeked over her shoulder. "What are you waiting for?"

"A step stool to magically appear." He growled in frustration.

It took her less than a second to grasp the problem, and the minx laughed. "Poor angel. I guess we'll have to get innovative."

Apparently, her idea of innovative involved her streaking wet and naked out of the bathroom, leaving laughter and wet drops as a trail.

He followed, his cock leading the way, right to his bedroom, where she had placed herself on hands and knees, legs partially spread, exposed and ready for him.

She tossed him a coy look over her shoulder. "Is this better?"

Since he doubted he could speak coherently at the moment, he simply nodded. With her so temptingly laid out before him, he couldn't stem his impatience. He knelt on the bed behind her and rubbed the head of his cock against her wet lips. He parted them with his swollen head, watching how her pink core trembled as he kept his cock just out of reach.

He pushed just the head in. The very tip.

A shudder went through her.

"More?" he queried. Despite her claims earlier, he didn't want to overwhelm her.

"You talk too much," she grumbled as she thrust backwards. It served to impale him within her sex.

Slick, vise-like heat.

He threw his head back. Feeling the pleasure of being within her. Trying to hold on for just a moment longer but struggling because she felt so gloriously wonderful.

But I can't come without her.

His hips ground against her, slow swirls of pressure, while his finger sought and found her swollen pleasure button.

He rubbed, and thrust, and rubbed, and thrust. And...

She screamed as she came, fisting him tight with her orgasm, drawing forth his own climax with the strength of hers.

He bellowed her name, and he coiled his body around her. He claimed her with his seed and perhaps even his fucking soul.

How could he not? The second time proved maybe even more glorious than the first. Without the impatience of their earlier need, he truly got to savor her. Taste her. Feel her.

She's like a drug. Addictive. He already wanted another hit.

It made him want to sing his feelings aloud. Thing was the song he chose—"Hit Me Baby One More Time" by Britney Spears—made Aria giggle hysterically when he finally gave in and crooned it.

But that laughter only brought them closer. And in his bed that night, they did manage to hit it two times.

Yesssss.

Chapter 19

THE NOXIOUS SMELL WOKE HER. She opened her eyes and let out a screech as Princess waggled her butt inches from Aria's nose and let a second fart rip.

"Why you mangy, smelly bitch!" Before she could throttle the little neck with two fingers, Constantine strode into the bedroom.

"What's going on in here? What's all the yelling about?"

"You tell me!" Aria glared at Princess, who sat smugly on the foot of the bed.

"Why are you in such a foul mood?"

"Your dog farted in my face."

His lips quirked. "I highly doubt that."

"I'm telling you she just did."

"How is that even possible? She's sitting on the end of the bed. Besides, Princess is a lady. She doesn't get gassy."

Aria stabbed a finger in the direction of the pooch. "That thing did too fart and on purpose. She doesn't like me."

Constantine scooped his little pooch from the end of the bed, and Aria waited for the chastising to begin.

"Poor Princess. Is that lady being mean to you? And in your own room."

Her jaw dropped.

"Come with Daddy and I'll give you a nice treat."

Pivoting, he went to stroll out the bedroom door.

"Are you fucking kidding me? You're rewarding that thing?"

He turned back and glared. "That *thing* is my dog, and I don't appreciate you insulting her."

With that, he spun around and marched out, and she could have sworn that damned dog wore a smug smirk of satisfaction.

It shouldn't have irked her that Constantine preferred his dog over her. It shouldn't have, but it did. And like fuck was she going to accept it.

Flinging the covers back, she stalked after him.

Stark naked.

"Come back here, angel. I am not done talking to you," she yodeled.

As she entered the kitchen area, he turned around from the front door, which shut with a click.

"Thanks for giving me a chance to get Princess outside and playing along."

She blinked at him as she dumbly said, "What?"

"Princess is having a hard time accepting her daddy has finally brought a mommy into her life."

"Mommy?" The word emerged on a faint squeak.

"We're going to have to be very careful about her feelings while we work on getting her to accept you."

"Hold on." She held up a hand. "You mean that entire 'hey, Aria, woman I fucked like a zillion times last night, is a mean lady, Daddy loves you' was a bullshit cover story to spare your dog's feelings?"

He beamed. "Yes. I'm so glad you understand."

"I don't, but your complete insanity still hasn't deterred me from liking you. A little."

"Don't you mean big?" The smile widened.

"Was it?" She arched a brow. "I don't recall. Maybe you should show me again, angel."

"Any time, my pink-nippled warbler."

Her nose wrinkled even as she laughed. "Okay, that was really not sexy."

"Oh, come on, I thought it was a clever play on words."

She laughed. "No, an awesome play on words is me going woodpecker on you."

His eyes widened. "Okay, you might be right. That sounds totally awesome."

"Then why are you wearing so many clothes?"

Knock. Knock. Knock.

The hard taps at the door stopped Constantine from shoving down his track pants. He frowned. "I wonder why Princess isn't barking."

"Someone you know maybe."

"Princess barks at just about everyone except my nephew. She loves him. Get your sweet ass to the bedroom while I see who it is. Grab the shotgun from the linen closet in the hall, too, would you, just in case."

Shotgun? With the towels and bedding?

Welcome to swamp country.

"What about you? What are you going to use?"

He shot her an incredulous look. "What do you think I'm going to use as intimidation? Me, of course." He let his muscles ripple, and he winked.

She doubted he heard her snort over the next firm knock.

"Go before I give whoever is standing there an eyeful."

"I'm going." But not because she wasn't curious. Constantine did get one thing right. Her buff situation was not exactly conducive for greeting people.

Skipping the shotgun in the hall, because firearms weren't her thing, she hurried to his bedroom and glanced around for something to wear. She could have rummaged through his drawers, yet she found a large T-shirt hanging over a chair. By the looks of it, Constantine had worn it but not deemed it dirty enough yet for the hamper.

She shrugged it on, enjoying the fact it held his scent, all the while listening through the closed door to the soft murmurs of two men. One had to be Constantine, but who was the other?

It must be someone he knows. Although even she had to admit it seemed strange they'd yet to hear a peep out of Princess. The only time the rodent kept quiet was when she stalked and hunted something. When that dog went on the prowl, she became eerily ghostlike.

Aria had noted the interesting technique when she visited with Cynthia. Princess had a thing for Cynthia's new boyfriend. She enjoyed silently slinking and then lunging with barks and snarls at Daryl's ankle. She never actually bit the man, and yet each time, Daryl screamed, "No blood on the rug."

With the continued silence, she had to wonder, *Is Princess hunting?*

She moved to the window overlooking the backyard. Scanning the area, she didn't see the furball with her pink and rhinestone collar. About to turn away, she noted movement in the foliage at the far end of the yard. She froze and stared as a creature strode from the bayou. A lizard man much like she'd seen before, but she would have sworn the one staring at the house wasn't the same one that had taken Jeffrey. This one stood taller, straighter, with a gaze more piercing, and still human.

I know him.

The flashback hit her hard and fast, and she slumped to Constantine's bed, her mind gripped by the recollection.

She woke in a cage. A freaking cage! The one thing all birds hated.

As Aria jumped to her feet, she noted they were bare and that she still wore her workout clothes—even if she never made it outside after breakfast for a jog. Damned cocoa.

She couldn't help a wrinkle of her nose as the most unpleasant aroma met it. The fabric she wore reeked strongly, the putrid scent of unwashed dog that had rolled in a pile of manure.

But at least she wore clothes, unlike others. Peeking around, she noted other cages, cages with occupants. She couldn't say people. Not quite, even if some still bore human characteristics. But two arms and two legs—and in some cases, human faces—couldn't hide the fur, feathers, and extra limbs some of them sported. It also couldn't mask the madness emanating from them.

What horrific nightmare had she woken to?

Where am I?

A sudden cacophony of sound—grunts, screams, moans, and even a few muttered words—filled the air. "Kill me" and "Kill him" being foremost.

Kill who? The steady thump of feet had her gripping the bars and craning to peek. Someone approached. Someone the other prisoners hated—and feared—with such vehemence.

He soon came into sight. A man, not even an impressive one. The same man who'd loomed over her drugged body.

The bastard who put me in a cage.

He came to a stop in front of her cell. On either side of him, standing as sentinels, monsters.

On the left, she recognized Harold, the dog-like thing that played a part in her abduction and whose stench permeated her clothes and skin.

Someone needs to give him a flea bath and some dental dog cookies for his smell.

The other creature flanking the guy with the fine-stitched loafers appeared humanoid in shape, but that was where all resemblance to humanity ended. Over seven feet, leather-skinned, with giant bat-like wings, he stood with a stoic countenance. His alien features, consisting of a flattened nose, sharp cheekbones, and a ridge atop his head, made his appearance frightening, but it was made more so by his still human eyes.

The man in the loafers chuckled, but she didn't find it reassuring. "I see you're admiring Ace. At least that's what I call him. My ace in the hole when it comes to getting shit done. And our first true success story. Ace used to be a patient here."

"Patient or prisoner?" she retorted.

"The distinction is irrelevant at this point. Ace is one of our greatest accomplishments. A meld of species in order to create the perfect hybrid."

Perfection must lie in the eye of the beholder.

She pointed at Harold. "So if Ace is a success, what do you call that one?"

The smile did not diminish. "Are you talking of Harold? Yes, he didn't quite turn out as expected, and yet, he has his qualities, hence why I keep him. Every genius should have a loyal pet."

"You're a sick bastard."

"Name calling? How rude. Then again, we never were formally introduced. I'm Merrill, the head of this project."

"Project? This is a crime. An abomination."

"Only some of our results can be called that. I will admit, since we started live trials, we've had a few cases that have gone wrong. We keep them here for study. Science learns from its mistakes."

"I've heard rumors of your mistakes making it out in public. They're killing machines."

"Indeed they are, which is why, every so often, we have to let them out or they go quite crazy. The darned things are always hungry, and sometimes only freshly hunted meat will do. I find them useful for taking care of people who might otherwise cause problems."

"This is insane."

"You just don't understand progress. You'll thank me after we improve you."

She recoiled, shaking her head. "Don't you dare even think of it. I won't stay here and be your guinea pig. You can't keep me here."

"Do you really think I'm going to let you leave?" Merrill stepped closer to the bars, the better to smirk at her.

"Let me go! You can't keep me here." Panic and fear raised her pulse rate. Her heart fluttered madly in her chest, beating to get free.

"I'm afraid you're not going anywhere, my fine, rare eagle. Not now. Maybe not ever." Merrill's grin widened. "I've got so many uses for a girl with your kind of DNA."

"You can't do this. I work for the SHC. I'm here on their behalf."

"I know. Who do you think warned me you were coming? I've even gotten permission from them to work on you."

"You lie," she claimed. "The SHC would never agree to that. Just like they would never agree to the experiments you've been performing."

"They didn't just agree. They've provided some test subjects. Like you. A nice healthy female in her prime. We're about to start phase two of our project. Interbreeding. Your hips are a little narrower than I would have liked, but C-sections are all the craze nowadays to keep those pussies tight."

The blood in her veins turned to ice as his words filtered. "You're going to inseminate me?"

"Maybe. Or perhaps we'll try it the old-fashioned way first. Harold would like that, wouldn't you, Harold? I hope you don't mind doggy style. As you can imagine, it's Harold's favorite position."

The lolling tongue on a certain dogman dripped. She might have vomited a little in her mouth.

"You're sick."

"Not anymore. No one has to be. I can cure everyone."

"Making people into monsters isn't a cure."

"Tell that to my bank account."

"I won't let you do this."

"You can't stop me."

During this entire conversation, Ace watched, but said nothing. He said nothing as they brought her for preliminary testing and blood samples. He said nothing when they forced her to call Cynthia and falsely claim everything was peachy keen. Yet, she couldn't entirely hate him. It was because of him she escaped. He'd left the cage unlocked after bringing her back from a session. Not by accident either. She saw him pretend to lock the door to her cell. Saw his pointed stare at her.

She took advantage and ran, ran fast and hard until she ran into a certain snake and his faithful pup.

The thought of them snapped her back to the present. She had to tell Constantine what she remembered. But of more importance at the moment was the fact that Ace had disappeared from the yard. *Where is he now?*

Not knowing meant she should arm herself before joining Constantine. *I should get the gun he mentioned from the linen closet.* Except she didn't have the skill to fire it. The last shotgun she'd tried to shoot had sent her flying a few feet, to land hard on her ass.

She needed a weapon more her size. Something she could hit an opponent with. But what?

She scanned the room and didn't spot a baseball bat or lacrosse stick. Not even a lamp to whack someone with. In that split second while she scanned her options, her gaze landed on the perfect item. She grabbed a sock from the floor and, while in motion, snagged keys and a small trophy of a dog that said, "1st in show." She stuffed the items into the sock and wound the open end in her hand.

As she opened the door of his bedroom, the sounds of a scuffle, along with vicious snarls and barks by Princess, came to her. She paused, gripped by indecision.

What should she do? She could hear the thumps and grunts of a fight. Would one puny sock really make a difference?

Perhaps she should, instead, run for help.

I'm not a coward.

And she wouldn't let him face whatever threat she drew to him by himself. The sock in her hand began to swing.

Stepping into the living room, she stopped dead instead of throwing herself into the fight. Her stillness didn't stop her cotton weapon from moving back and forth like a pendulum.

Shock at the visitors reminded her of something Merrill had said, that crucial tidbit about the SHC warning him of her arrival. Except only one person had known she was coming.

Parker.

My boss. The guy who sent me here and set me up.

Chapter 20

OPENING THE DOOR, a ready greeting on his lips, Constantine froze as he beheld a stranger. Not too tall, probably just shy of five-foot-ten, the man sported silver hair with only a few hints of darker gray. The fine suit he wore hung on his slender frame.

"Can I help you?" he asked.

Dry lips stretched in a vulpine smile. "Well, if it isn't the snake's son. I'm surprised you stuck around here. As I recall, your father couldn't wait to leave."

At the mention of his father, Constantine froze. "You know my dad?"

"Knew. He worked under me for years. As a matter of fact, he was one of the men I trusted to help start Bittech. Took him months to get all the permits and such sorted. Busy fellow, and I don't just mean on the job site. I'd heard he'd knocked up a local before he returned to our home office."

"You mean my dad never intended to stay?"

"Why would he when he had a perfectly fine family back home?"

Breath whooshed from Constantine, the casual statement a firm emotional punch.

"You lie."

"Why would I? Your father was only in Bitten Point temporarily. Didn't your mother tell you about the way he vanished every weekend? It was because he returned home every Saturday and Sunday to see his real family." The man smiled. "You have two half-brothers, by the way. They work for me, but lack the skills I prized your father for."

The shocking admission shattered long-held beliefs. *My dad didn't leave because he was afraid of commitment. He left because he already had a family elsewhere.* The truth, while painful and twisted, in a sense set him free.

Dear old dad was a two-timing shit who got my mother pregnant and then walked out on her. But from the sounds of it, while he'd abandoned one family, he did care for another.

If Constantine ignored the bastard, cheating part, it gave him hope that maybe he could have something long-term with Aria. If he survived. Because he didn't need his python's warning hiss to recognize the danger the man before him posed.

"Who are you? And what do you want?" Because holy moly, his oh-shit meter was going crazy. His snake writhed in his mind, begging to get out.

Strike first. Squeeze hard.

An extreme reaction, given the older man in front of him, while a wolf in a suit, would prove no match for his mighty coils.

"Is that any way to address an esteemed member of the Shifter High Council?"

"You're a councilor?" Don't scoff at his ignorance. Constantine didn't pay much mind to shifter politics. He lived his life, in his town, and followed the rules.

He should also note not many could recognize the council members, given the only time people dealt with the SHC was if they'd broken some kind of hardcore law. And even then, local justice tended to be swift.

"Indeed I am, which gives me a lot of power, son."

"I'm not your son."

"Ah, but you could have been. Your mother was a little free with her affections back in the day. Alas, I couldn't stay to oversee things, and your father got to her first."

Constantine couldn't stop his fist from flying, but to his shock, the older man grabbed it—and held it!

"Why are you here?" Constantine growled. He pushed against the man who held him, managing movement only because of his weight. A victory short-lived, as the other guy braced his feet and pushed back.

How is he so freakishly strong?

"I am here because you won't stop asking questions and sticking your nose where you shouldn't. I was willing to let your actions slide out of respect for your father, but then you just had to go and help that stupid bird."

This guy knew about Aria? Shit. "Bird? What bird? The only poultry we have in this house is the chicken in the freezer."

A fierce scowl crossed the man's face. "Don't lie. I know about the woman staying here."

"No idea who you're talking about. There's no one else here."

Tsk. Tsk. The man shook his head, even as a smile stretched his lips. "You should know better than to try and bullshit me. I've got my men watching the house as we speak. They've reported she's in here. And you're going to tell her to come out."

"Like fuck."

"I thought you might say that, which was why I brought some incentive to obey."

Constantine's blood ran cold as a leathery hand appeared above the councilman's head, the knuckles bristling with coarse fur. Hanging from its grip, one shivering little dog.

"Princess." He couldn't help but breathe her name.

Big eyes lifted to meet his, not in defeat but rather embarrassment. He knew his dog well enough to understand she took the sneaking in on her territory, and worse, getting caught, very personally.

Bad move. Now you've pissed my dog off. And the man. And the snake.

But how to escape from this with everyone intact?

If he didn't call for Aria, they would kill his little princess. *I can't allow that.*

He opened his mouth, but before he could speak, his dog acted. From limp and faking defeat to snarling dynamo with gnashing, sharp teeth. His dog wiggled in the grip holding her prisoner, twisting enough that she managed to sink her canines deep into flesh.

The hairy thing—part gorilla, part fucking nightmare—bellowed and flung his arm outward. Princess let go of her prey and came flying—right at Constantine!

I have to catch her.

He stomped his foot down on the councilor's instep then kicked at a knee. The blow didn't connect. However, it forced the guy to release him. Just in time, too.

Lunging to the side, Constantine caught his dog. However, he couldn't stop his momentum, nor did he want to. He charged forward, but his aim wasn't for either danger posed by the wolf or his henchman, but the umbrella stand by the door.

His fingers curled around the wooden stock of the shotgun his ma kept in case of nighttime critters—or, as she liked to call them, tomorrow night's dinner.

As he yanked it from its spot, he took quick aim, raising the stock of the gun to chest level. He had a moment to look in the eyes—the very human, if crazy eyes—of the hybrid. He hesitated, only a fraction of a second, as he braced the gun against his hip.

Not human, his inner snake hissed.

He applied pressure to the trigger.

BOOM!

The millisecond pause gave the beast the time he needed to dive out the door. A shame. The elephant-sized slug would have probably taken him out.

The loud noise certainly made the old guy eye him with more wariness. The sound also served to hide Aria's arrival, swinging...a sock?

Of more interest than her choice in weapon was her expression. The shock on her face proved unmistakable. Her face turned pale, and her jaw dropped. While whispered, Constantine still caught her words, "Parker? You're behind this. You set me up. How could you?"

Even Constantine paused to hear the reply.

"Because you're a nosy pain in my ass who wouldn't stop harping in my ear about the strange shit happening in Bitten Point." The councilor flung his hands in the air. "I know shit is happening because I'm the one behind it."

"But you're part of the council. You're supposed to protect our kind from discovery and becoming lab rats."

"Times change. The world has changed. It's time we changed with it. I'm tired of cowering for weak humans. We are stronger than them. Better. It is we who should walk with our heads held high."

"You're a monster."

"No, you're looking at one of the successes." Parker flexed an arm. "The strength of a bull, literally. But without the bone-headedness. I've also got the stamina." The wink brought the shotgun in Constantine's grip to bear.

"You've got balls to be flirting with my chick in front of me," Constantine growled.

"The biggest balls, son. I've also got the upper hand. Submit and maybe I won't hurt you. Why, you might even become one of our success stories."

"I won't let you experiment on me."

"Who said you had a choice? Either come with me quietly or die. The choice is yours."

"Neither," Aria exclaimed. The swinging sock went flying, whipping out and hitting Parker with a solid thunk. The older man staggered, a hand pressed to his face, the gush of blood from his broken nose seeping through his fingers.

"Bitch! You'll pay for that. Bruno, attack!" The injured man screamed the word, and through the open door rushed a thick body, arms tucked tight so that it could fit through the frame.

Constantine didn't have time to turn and shoot before the hairy thing hit him. His arms went wide, and Princess, whom he'd not put down on the floor, went for her second flight that day.

Shit.

He had a moment to note Aria catching his dog before he hit the floor with a thump hard enough to rattle the house.

As he braced his hands against the jaw of the beast trying to bite his face off—a truly ugly blend of monster—he saw the streak of Aria's bare legs as she ran past.

Run. Hide. Her best course of action, given he found himself a little preoccupied with staying alive.

"If you can't subdue him, then kill him," Parker ordered as he strode past. "Be sure to bring his body to the lab when you're done. Even if he's dead, I can use his DNA."

The man who'd dared attack Constantine, in his own home, left. Not much he could do about it, given he wrestled with a monster.

The rabid creature had a thing for digging in its claws. Constantine could have handled a few puncture wounds. It was the lethargy that stole his strength that proved his undoing.

Poison? Shit. That brought a new level of danger to this fight. But he did have one advantage. It wasn't his first time getting drugged by venom. As a boy who'd grown up in the bayou, he'd gotten his fair share of bites over the years, which meant his body knew how to resist it.

He also knew how to fake it.

Sometimes, in order to gain the advantage, a man had to pretend a disadvantage, such as closing his eyes and allowing his body to go limp, hoping that wouldn't result in his throat getting torn out because that Parker dude had a need for him.

The stupid beast bought the act. The heavy weight on his chest moved. Claws scrabbled for purchase on his laminate floor, and Constantine found his arm gripped. He fought hard not to react as the creature dragged him across the floor to the front door. Only once the thing heaved him onto the front step did he jump to his feet with a roar.

Okay, more like a hiss as his snake pushed back the remaining lethargy of the poison and tried to burst free.

The sudden attack caught the monster by surprise, allowing Constantine to grab him by the head and drop to the ground hard.

Crack. A broken neck took care of the rabid Bruno, but Constantine knew there were more. He could smell traces of the flying lizard, a guy currently out of sight, but he proved the less pressing problem because it seemed Parker had brought more allies than expected.

Men, human ones he'd wager by the combat gear they wore and the guns they raised, waited outside a black SUV. Another truck with tinted windows sped away, probably carrying the cowardly Parker. A shame because he so wanted to give the dickwad a hug.

We'll find him later and give him a sssqueeze. First, though, Constantine needed to extricate himself from the current dilemma.

A pair of armed humans held guns trained on him while Princess barked and nipped at their impenetrable boots. If only one of them would lean down so his dog could go for the jugular. Instead, they didn't give Princess a fair chance. They kicked her, sending her little canine body flying.

Princess. No. She landed in a thick bush, a bush that didn't move. A bush that did not bark.

I think they killed my dog.

Unacceptable. And punishable.

With a hiss, part of his snake burst free. For the first time in his life, Constantine managed a half shift. He kept his arms, but his head morphed into a diamond shape, his fangs dropped sharp and curved, and from the top of his tailbone exploded a sinuous tail.

Holy fucking cool. But he'd gloat about his super-duper hybrid shape later.

The tip of his tail lashed at the guy who dared hurt his precious princess. Being humans, at the sight of his majestic serpentine self, they panicked and fired wildly. A few of their darts stuck to his flesh, the tips not managing to penetrate his scaled skin. Puny inconveniences.

He unhinged his jaw and darted at the enemy. They screamed. How human. How useless.

They scattered from his mad dash.

Run fassst. Run far. I will still find you. And hug you. It wasn't just his python that wanted to hug bad guys. He wanted to squeeze them, too, until their eyes popped from their head and they breathed their last.

Cold-blooded excitement fueled his chase, but his prey wasn't as frightened or disorganized as he thought. They broke apart and turned, firing at him. He couldn't avoid both sets of missiles. One of the darts hit the more vulnerable flesh under his arm, stinging and injecting a lethargy-inducing drug into his system.

His adrenaline kept him awake, but for how long? *I've too many things to do before I can sleep.* He needed to find and save Aria, and he didn't know how Princess fared. Losing consciousness now would spell not only his doom, but theirs, too.

I must recover. As his legs refused to carry him with a drunken wobble, his body morphed again, his legs splitting the seams of his pants to fuse together in one long tail. He slithered from the men and their guns, his bottom half undulating on the ground.

It was then he heard the bark. *Princess lives!*

Alive, but not for long if the winged lizard monster leaning over his dog had its way. "Ffffuck offfff," he shouted, rolling the sound on his forked tongue. It was enough to draw the attention of the monster.

It faced him with an evil glare, the madness in its eyes chilling. Not the same creature he'd smelled from before, the one with the human stare. This was the murdering one. The one that, without mercy, had torn Jeffrey's face off.

A true killing machine. But Constantine knew cold-blooded. He lived it every day. And he would live for tomorrow.

His tail whipped from behind and around the body of the lizard thing, but he got him only around the waist before the creature pumped its wings and tried to rise from the ground. Constantine's weight acted like an anchor and kept it grounded. While the thing couldn't fly, it did manage to drag, and Constantine could do nothing to stop it, especially since all his body wanted to do involved finding a nice, warm spot so he could sleep.

The many darts now being fired into him from behind injected him with lethargic poison, more than he could handle.

His strength ebbed, and the thing yanked him to the edge of the yard then onto the outskirts of the bayou. It kept tugging him past the muddy shore so that the water sucked at his body, his oh so heavy body.

In the distance, he could hear Princess barking. He heard the thudding footfalls of the humans approaching, ready to claim their prize.

Too much. Too much for him to handle alone.

He let go of the lizard thing. Let go and let himself sink. Sink in the water and slither down into the darkness that embraced him.

Chapter 21

THINGS HAPPENED SO FAST. One moment Aria flung the sock at Parker to distract him, and the next Constantine grappled on the floor with a monster while she made a miraculous catch of a flying dog.

Even more astonishing, Princess allowed herself to stay nestled in Aria's arms without trying to tear a chunk off. Common ground made them temporary allies. But their truce didn't change facts. With Parker threatening, and Constantine occupied, they needed to fly. Like now.

Aria barreled out the door, Princess tucked under her arm. A part of her cringed that she didn't stay to help Constantine, but Aria knew she couldn't stand against Parker. It wasn't just the henhouse that feared wolves.

Outside proved no safer, though. Men with guns aimed her way, and Ace stood blocking her path.

"Move!" she shouted.

Except her orders couldn't compete with Parker's shouted, "Grab the girl and put her in my car."

No. Ace only mouthed the word, but Parker must have seen it because a moment later, Ace hit the ground on his knees, his face a rictus of pain. As Ace curled his fingers around the collar, the burning stench of his flesh made her tummy churn.

Though under obvious torture, he struggled to get to his feet. To obey his master Parker or to help her? She couldn't know for sure. She couldn't take any chances.

Given Ace knelt in her way, Aria did the only thing she could think of. She ran at him. Princess wiggled in her grip, and as Aria leaned down to scoop a handful of rocks, she let the dog loose. Then she rose again, hands full of debris that she flung at his face.

Despite his obvious pain, Ace saw the dirt coming and turned his head, thus missing her as she bowled into him. For a second, as their skin made contact, it sizzled—in a fried chicken kind of way.

Ouch! Hissing in pain, she pushed away from Ace, but not before booting him in the ribs and kicking him in the head to the excited yips of Princess, who darted in with snapping teeth.

One problem out of the way, she kept moving. As she ran, she noted Princess galloped beside her on stubby legs. Something fluttered in her mouth.

Speaking of flutter, a wild beating pounded in her chest.

Free. Fly free. Let me out.

This time the knowledge of her inner eagle didn't frighten or freak her out. Instead, she welcomed the known presence of her friend and invited her in.

Take us to the skies.

Except she couldn't bring forth her bird. She tried. She pulled. It remained out of reach.

I'm a prisoner! She shared her eagle's horror, yet it wasn't the knowledge that she couldn't shift that made her stumble, but the darts that hit her.

Her tiny frame couldn't handle the injection of so many drugs at once. As she slumped, she heard Parker again. "Grab the girl and bring her. We'll leave the others to clean up the mess."

What mess? The house was clean. Her thoughts whirled in a chaotic circle, her eyes lost focus, but she felt enough to know Ace was the one to scoop her in his arms and toss her in a waiting black truck.

From the backseat, she craned to look, noting as the SUV sped away that the monster that attacked Constantine in the house had dragged his limp body outside.

He's dead. The realization hit her like a hurricane gust, sending her falling, falling, falling into an emotional spiral.

It wasn't the fact that Constantine couldn't help her that traumatized, but more the fact that she'd killed him. She'd brought this danger to his home. And because of her, he was dead.

A chilling realization she didn't get to mull over for long because darkness swallowed her whole, and the next time she woke, she was strapped to a gurney, in a room filled with boxes, packed and ready for shipping.

Where am I? Didn't matter. Wherever she'd found herself didn't bode well.

I'm awake. But for how long? As soon as Parker or any of the other bastards in this place noticed, they'd drug her again. *Drug me and do unspeakable things.*

But they misjudged if they thought their sleep-inducing darts would stop her for long. She'd experimented a lot growing up, drugs of all kinds. She'd batted at butterflies on 'shrooms. Eaten bags and bags of chips while high. She had a bit of a built-in resistance now when it came to illegal substances. It was why she now resorted to tequila. The fiery liquid could be bought cheaper and was less likely to get her arrested.

And if I get out of here, I am buying the biggest bottle I can find and getting properly sloshed.

If she got out. A frantic urge to escape saw her scrabbling at the straps that held her down.

She eased off the table, her feet bare and sticking out from the bottom edge of the plain cotton gown she wore. The latest fashion statement worn by prisoners held by madmen.

Her naked toes curled from the chill in the floor, but that worried her less than the fact that her knees threatened to buckle.

Oh hell no. She couldn't collapse here. Not now. Who knew what would happen to her the next time she passed out.

I don't want to become a monster. Already she felt something different within her. Her eagle was still present, but it couldn't get out. It was stuck within. A temporary glitch in her ability, or a more serious symptom of the last time she'd found herself a prisoner and injected?

She wavered on her two feet as determination pushed back the lingering drugs. Time to take stock of her situation.

Dire.

Kind of obvious, so she took a peek around. The room must have served as one of their examination spots. Counters along two sides. The gurney she'd eschewed for her own unsteady two feet. Nothing remained in the room except for boxes. Someone was packing up their operation and readying to leave. Given she still lived, she'd guess they meant to bring her with them.

Like hell.

Time to blow this joint, this time for good. Putting her ear to the only door in the room, she took a listen. She could hear muffled voices and the odd stray word or phrase—"Hour," "Trucks waiting," "Time for a coffee?"

It was busy out there. Too busy for her to hope to slip out unnoticed.

And she shouldn't leave without a weapon, but what could she use?

No guards had left a loaded gun for her to use. In opening a box labeled medical supplies, she hit the jackpot.

With shaking hands, she filled the syringes she found wrapped in crinkly plastic with the contents of a few bottles, a chemical cocktail that would either induce hallucinogenic butterflies or nightmares. Either worked.

Armed with one in each hand, she couldn't help the rapid flutter of her heart as she heard the scrape of a key in the lock.

They'd come for her. *But they're not taking me.*

She flattened herself against the side of the door. It opened. A guard took a step in and uttered, "What the fuck?" as he noted the empty gurney.

His surprise proved her advantage.

A mere human mercenary dressed in black fatigues, he couldn't move fast enough to avoid the pair of needles she jabbed him with. She managed to depress the plungers before he flung her away.

She hit the wall with a thud, but while it caused her to shake her head, she recovered. The guard, on the other hand, blinked and blinked again as the cocktail coursed through his bloodstream.

With laced fingers, she swung at him. The super fist knocked the guard hard into the wall, where she plowed into him, shoulder first. He slumped to the floor, eyes shut, unconscious. The additional kick to the head—because she recognized Mr. Handsy from her last stay—was for good riddance.

That done, she went to the door and peeked out. The hustle and bustle had died down. A few cautious steps in the hall showed a lack of windows, but several doors. All of them open. All of the rooms empty. Useless. None of them provided an escape.

However, she'd kind of expected that. If she were correct, Parker had brought her back to Bittech, in the hidden subterranean levels.

I escaped from here once before. She just couldn't remember quite how. She did know she wouldn't find any windows to climb out of, which left her only one real choice. The elevator.

From her last stay, she already knew it required a keycard, which she filched from the snoring guard's body. To avoid discovery, she shut the door behind her, engaging the lock.

An invisible clock ticked in her head, urging her to make haste. Any moment, someone might come looking for her.

She dashed to the elevator and slapped the card against the scanner. It took a moment, but the screen turned from a processing flashing red to a green approved. The elevator door slid open, and she couldn't have said who was more shocked, the human wearing a lab coat who peeked up from his tablet, or her.

"You're not an employee. How did you escape confinement? And what do you think you are doing?" he exclaimed.

"Checking myself out," she muttered as she lunged at him. Amazing how many human doctors worked for Parker. While the doctor might not have an animal side to call on, he was still bigger than her. They grappled. Well, mostly she clung to him and tried to stop him from slamming the red alarm button on the wall of the elevator cab.

A rabid fierceness possessed her. She yelled as she wrestled. Grunted. Stomped her bare feet and thrust with her knee until she made contact. Usually, the expression was hit two birds with one stone, but in this case, she hit two balls with one bird knee.

As the man slumped, she shoved him out of the elevator doors. It was only as the doors shut that she noted she'd dropped her stolen keycard. It mocked her on the floor outside.

Too late to grab it. The elevator sealed itself and moved. She just didn't know where. She flattened herself against the back of the cab, hands clammy with sweat, a tremble to her frame, but her fear only strengthened her determination to fight.

The elevator jolted to a stop, and she braced herself as the door slid open.

She gaped as one of her jailors, the lizard thing known as Ace, filled the opening. Despite the fact that he'd helped her escape before, she couldn't ignore the fact he'd dragged her here on Parker's orders. Running into him now didn't bode well.

"Going sssomewhere?" Ace hissed, his forked tongue adding sibilance to his words.

"Well, your hospitality has been great and all, but I really think I should be heading out."

As he leaned in closer, Ace's wings fluttered, the leathery sound alien to her ears. She knew what wings sounded like when ruffled, the soft whisper of feathers. This noise had none of that soothing quality.

"Ssso sssoon? I think that isss a good idea."

"What?" She couldn't help replying, her eyes wide.

"Run hard and fassst," he advised. Ace wrapped a leathery hand around her arm, and he pulled her from the elevator. "Run and don't look back."

"I'm not a mouse to be hunted," she hotly complained, tugging at his iron grip.

Ignoring her feeble attempt, Ace dragged her down the hall to the far end where an EXIT sign mocked her with bright red letters.

It was only as they passed a room with its door open that she noted the slumped body of a guard no longer paying attention to the dozens of monitors.

"What did you do to him?"

"Made sssure he wouldn't pay for my actionsss."

Aria gazed at Ace in askance. What game did he play? He'd just captured her and brought her to Bittech on Parker's orders. Then again, Ace didn't have a choice with the collar around his neck. She'd seen what that collar could do with poor rabid dog, Harold. The smell of burning hair never quite went away.

The controlling collar rested around Ace's neck, a heavy reminder he didn't control his choices or actions.

They've caged him.

A horrible thing to do to anyone, enough to drive many to madness, except Ace didn't exhibit the same rabid fury in his eyes as the other monsters she'd met. As a matter of fact, he showed no emotion at all.

Even now, as he tugged her toward that hope-inspiring EXIT sign, he maintained a placid expression. He didn't seem to care about anything, which made his sudden interest in her all the stranger. *Why does he want me to run?*

Perhaps he toyed with her. Some prey liked to play with their food.

I won't be anyone's dinner.

A door along the hallway opened, and a man in a white lab coat exited. He looked up from his clipboard with a frown. "Where are you taking this subject? And why isn't she in a cage on the truck already with the others?"

"Bite me," was Ace's reply. "I don't answer to you."

The answer seemed to satisfy the guy because he made no move to stop Ace as he tugged her past.

The EXIT sign led to another elevator, one she didn't recall ever seeing, with only one button.

The elevator doors slid shut, enclosing them in the tiny cab. Earlier, she'd travelled without qualm, even if she didn't like the small box. Now, with Ace taking up most of the space, she couldn't help but pant as the confined area closed in on her.

The doors reopened to a cavernous room she'd never seen before. Abandoned skids, empty of cargo, littered the space, as did a few empty cages.

"Where are you taking me?" Aria dug in her heels, but that didn't stop Ace's advance. His grip tightened.

"Ssstop fighting me," he hissed. "I'm trying to help you. It is not sssafe for you here."

"Duh. I think the kidnapping and confinement gave it away. Wait until I tell the SHC."

Ace snorted, a blustery sound. "Who do you think is running this place?"

He confirmed what Parker claimed, and her heart sank. But that didn't mean she didn't pump him for more info. She'd need every bit of evidence she could get if she was going to convince people to do something about the corruption on the council. "Bittech is managed by some dude and his son."

"Who get their orders from sssomeone on the council. And that person wants you out of the way."

"Parker." She growled his name.

"Parker is nothing but a lackey, no matter how big he might think he isss."

Another player involved? Just how high did this travesty go? "Why did he come after me?" Because Parker was the one who'd encouraged her to find out all she could when she expressed an interest in the reports she'd seen.

"Parker goes after everyone who dares come sssnooping."

Snooping? She'd barely even begun asking questions. "People are going to come looking for me, especially if I go missing again."

"At this point, I don't think Parker cares."

"Because he and the rest of the people working for him have gone cuckoo." How else to explain the insanity?

"Parker's unfortunately all too sane, even though he's played with some of the drugs they're developing here. Merrill, on the other hand, is nutsss. Almost as nutsss as the other experiments."

"Are you crazy?"

His steady gaze met and held hers. "I'm a man trapped in a monsssster's body. What do you think?"

She thought he avoided the question. "Where are you taking me?" If he said the kitchen for a dash of salt and pepper, she'd know the answer.

"You have to leave now before it'sss too late. Eventsss are about to escalate. People are going to get hurt."

Matching her short pace to his longer one, Aria frowned as she asked, "Why are you helping me? Why do you care?"

An ugly chuckle rumbled from him. "I don't care. But anything that fucksss with Parker and his sssycophants works for me."

"Why do you stay if you hate them so much?"

At the end of the hall, Ace paused before a closed door without any markings. "Because where would I go? Monsssters don't get to live in the real world."

The door they went through didn't require a keycard. The push bar creaked as Ace shoved it. On the other side, there was no elevator to use, just a long set of stairs that stretched upward. She eyed them with a groan.

"Is this the only way out?"

"The only way you stand a chance. If I take you out the main entrance, you'll never make it out of here alive. Your bessst bet isss to get lossst in the swamp."

The swamp? Again. "Why does that sound familiar?"

"Because that'sss how I helped you essscape lassst time. But then, instead of leaving town, you ssstuck around."

Not her fault she'd lost her memory. She had time to mentally grumble about the prospect of once more crossing the swamp as she trudged up the stairs.

At the top, she huffed a little as Ace waited for her by the door.

Despite his admission, she couldn't help a nervous query. "How do I know you're not setting me up?"

Human eyes in a reptile face glanced at her. "You don't. You want to ssstay inssside, then ssstay." He released her arm and moved away as the door swung open at his shove. "But, if you ssstay, you'll ending up wishing you'd died."

With those final words, Ace turned on his heel and took the stairs down, two by two, the pointed ridge of his wings jutting above his shoulders. She spent a moment staring and realizing, despite his alien appearance, Ace remained a guy, a guy stuck between a rock and an even harder place. He was right. Where could he go that people wouldn't hunt him?

She turned her gaze toward the open door, where the pungent scent of the bayou called.

Freedom? It seemed too easy. She took a step then another, emerging from the hatch set into a hillock, camouflaged from all but the closest inspection.

No strident alarms blared. She took a few more steps, clearing the doorway completely, and felt the cool pre-dusk air on her face.

It seemed she'd spent more time than expected in her cell. The colorful rays of a setting sun painted the horizon. A beam of sunlight crested the treetops, and its warm rays bathed her skin. Much like a blossom, she absorbed it, inhaled deeply of the life and vitality flowing all around her in the swamp.

Stop smelling the freaking flowers and get your ass moving.

A helping hand on getting out by Ace didn't mean she should waste time. Who knew when Parker or Merrill would notice she'd gone? Once they did, the hunt would happen. She knew too much.

A tug on the door and the hydraulics kicked in, sucking the portal into its slot and sealing it shut. The greenery and rock stuck to the surface, and once closed, it blended in.

She wouldn't be going back that way, which meant no going back now. Turning, she surveyed the area.

It seemed she stood on a bit of an island. Nothing really big enough to even mark on a map, but large enough for this secret exit and a ramshackle dock. While the dock boards rotted, the dock still served a purpose as a landing point for the two boats tied there. This deep in the swamp, it was the best way for landlubbers to move around.

Given the swamp was her escape, she didn't want to make it easy for Merrill and his disreputable gang to follow. She quickly unlashed the blue boat, tossing the loose mooring rope into it before giving it a shove. Then she worked on the knot holding the other craft, a camouflage-colored, flat-bottomed fishing craft with a small motor at the back. Just as she tugged the last knot loose, it started.

A siren whirred to life, not loud or outside, but from within the compound itself. Its strident blast made the ground on the hillock hum, and that, in turn, vibrated the dock. Even the water nearby shivered.

It lasted less than a minute before stopping.

Odd. She took it as a sign she should get going.

Before she could step into the bobbing craft, the door in the hill cranked open and Merrill stepped out with a smarmy expression and an overtly cheerful, "Leaving so soon?"

Chapter 22

ONCE THE DRUGS dissipated from his system, Constantine rose from the water, a sea serpent cresting the surface, pissed but alive. For some reason, people seemed to forget that his snake thrived in aquatic conditions. While a python couldn't truly breathe underwater like a fish, he could, however, remained submerged for up to thirty minutes. All the time he needed to let the poison leach from his system and for the assholes who'd attacked him to take off.

How shoddy of his enemy to leave thinking he was dead. Not dead. Not happy. And not going to let them keep his woman. He also wanted vengeance for his dog.

You abandoned Aria and Princess.

The realization burned, then again, had he died in a futile battle, they'd have no one to come to their rescue.

As Constantine slogged from the swamp, his anger burned even hotter as he noted the destruction of his home. The rabid lizard seemed unhappy at the loss of its prey. Not a single window remained intact. The siding lay strewn across the lawn in a ripped and senseless mess. All the work he'd put into the place, all the money, all the love, destroyed because of a power-hungry bastard and his sick pets.

Speaking of pet, a sharp yip drew his gaze down, and he could have wept—manly tears of course—when he noted his little dog loping at him sideways, tongue lolling.

"Princess!" He swept her into his arms and couldn't help but laugh as she lapped his face in excitement. "I'm so glad you're safe."

Yip. Translation: *I am going to pee myself I'm so happy you're back.*

"I don't suppose Aria got away?"

Gruff.

"No, eh?" His lips turned down. "That blows because you know I can't let them keep her. I have to go find her. But how and where?"

In his arms, Princess wiggled, her signal she wanted to be let down. He placed her on the grass and watched her dive toward a bush. She emerged with something in her mouth. She dropped it at his feet and sat, tail quivering, ears perked.

He knelt and whistled. "I'll be damned, Princess. Where did you get a keycard for Bittech from?" Who cared? His dog might have given him the solution to rescuing his woman.

A smart man, the first thing Constantine meant to do before haring off to save his girl was to call for backup. Except his phone lay smashed on the ground, and his ma had long ago gotten rid of their house phone since they both had cells. This meant he had no other means of outside communication.

Fuck.

He could drive to find help, but every minute he wasted was a minute Aria spent in their grasp. Still, storming Bittech on his own was nuts. He'd have to make at least one detour to get the ball of attack rolling. He snagged his keys and headed out to his truck.

It shouldn't have surprised him they'd trashed his vehicle, but it did hurt. He loved that gas-guzzling beast.

Another person might have given up at this point. Not Constantine. There was more than one way to get around the bayou.

"Wanna go for a swamp cruise?" he asked Princess as he stripped.

Yip-yip.

Some people might have found it odd to see a giant snake, slithering through the watery marsh, a canvas sack clutched in its teeth but, strangest of all, would have been the little dog, standing atop the head, keeping her paws dry.

Mock him or his dog and he would hug you to death.

The afternoon waned as he moved, time passing more quickly than he liked given he'd had to take a watery route.

Arriving near the Bittech property, he slithered from the water with Princess leaping off once they hit solid and dry ground.

The change from snake to man took but a moment, the wet wipes in his waterproof sack cleaning most of the bayou from his skin and the clothes he pulled out dry and loose in case he needed to shed them in a hurry.

Somehow, he didn't think slithering into Bittech or striding in naked and covered in mud would get him where he needed to go. The card Princess stole, he tucked into his pants pocket.

With long strides, he approached the building, Princess trotting at his heels. The parking lot was almost empty except for a large moving truck that rumbled as the engine idled.

As he approached, someone slammed down the roll-top door at the rear of it. In moments, the driver, a guy he didn't recognize in a ball cap and visored glasses, got into the vehicle. It rolled off with a groan of a big engine and a puff of diesel smoke.

Ignoring the vehicle, Constantine approached the main building. The sun dipping deep in the west meant this side of the lot found itself bathed in shadow, yet he still saw a form detach itself from the building, the bright red tip of a cigarette marking its trajectory as it fell to the ground.

"Constantine, what the hell are you doing here?" Wes asked as he got closer.

"I'm here for Aria."

"Your girl's not here."

She's here. His snake sense said so. He peeked through the glass doors to the lobby and noted it seemed stripped bare. Even the potted plants were gone.

"What's going on? What was that truck doing here? And where is all the shit you used to have in the lobby?"

"Gone. Sudden orders from above. Some kind of inspection said the building was unsafe. Sinking into the bayou apparently. So they're moving the operation."

A convenient excuse that Constantine didn't let slide. "Moving or going into hiding?"

Wes frowned. "What makes you say that?"

"Because the guys who attacked me at my house today were from here. And, if that's the case, it makes me wonder if you've been bullshitting us all along."

Wes tapped a cigarette out of his pack and slid it between his lips, but didn't light it. "Bullshitting you how? I'm the one who has been saying for a while there's something shitty happening here."

"And yet, you haven't found a clue."

"Because there's nothing to find." Wes swept an arm behind him at the building. "What you see is what you get."

"Is it?"

"Are you calling me a liar? Don't believe me? Then be my guest. The place is wide open, buddy. Go and search it. You'll see your lady friend isn't there."

"Aren't you going to come with me?"

"Need me to hold your hand?"

Honk. The horn prevented Constantine from answering.

Wes turned as a car rounded the building and flashed its lights. "Fuck. I gotta go. That's my boss trying to get my attention."

"I'm going in there," Constantine warned.

"Knock yourself out. You won't find anything on those floors."

I know. He recalled what Aria had said after one of her flashbacks. At the time, he'd scoffed, but now, fingering the keycard in his pocket, he wondered.

They're hiding a whole secret lab under the building, she'd insisted.

A secret lab that didn't seem so farfetched since their discovery of old tunnels used by Merrill and his pet dog to move around without notice.

Upon entering the building, he noted no one was there to pay him any mind. The strip-down operation became truly apparent with only items that were truly bolted down being left behind. Even the chairs in the reception area had vanished.

As Constantine entered the elevator, he peeked at the buttons and found himself stymied by his lack of choices. B, 1, 2, 3. "It would really help if they labeled the dungeon lair," he grumbled to Princess, who sat at his feet.

Despite the handy buttons, Constantine had to wonder if the elevator went anywhere else. He jabbed at the B button. The elevator went down and opened onto a utility area loud with the hum of machinery. He pressed all the buttons one by one. Then together.

He kept seeing the same floors over and over, but not a sign or scent of Aria. Nothing to make him believe there was anything else to Bittech.

Frustrated, he exited into the lobby. Now what?

He exited the building and went around it, noting as he moved, the sun truly dipping. Twilight would soon arrive, making his search even harder.

If I'm even in the right place. The keycard in his pocket seemed to say so.

Hold on a second. He pulled the card from his pocket with the sudden realization he'd not used it once while inside. Of course, all the doors were open, wide open on empty rooms. Still, though, he didn't recall seeing a place to use it.

That in and of itself niggled his suspicious side.

Moving around the building, he arrived at the back. The loading dock area proved empty but for one lone truck. A big, white cube truck with no driver.

Strange, but that wasn't what caught his attention. Upon going around to the back of the vehicle, he sniffed.

I smell an alien.

Let's go give it a hug.

Chapter 23

"FUCK." Vulgar, yet very apt Aria thought as the mad lizard with the bat wings came darting through the hidden door first, his hiss of excitement unmistakable.

After it came a canine creature much like Harold, who scuttled on all fours.

Behind them both strolled Merrill, hand outstretched, a little black remote in it. Of more concern was Ace, who staggered behind and held a tranquilizer gun.

She almost opened her mouth to accuse him of setting her up, except she noted Ace had the fingers of his free hand on his collar. His expression seemed tauter than usual. Even though she stood a few yards away, she smelled burning flesh.

Whatever Ace did now, it wasn't willingly.

I need to fly. She pulled at her inner eagle, willing it to come forth. But as before, her eagle refused to listen.

And Merrill laughed. "What's wrong? Are your wings not working?"

"What did you do to me?"

"Something I do to all new test subjects. Inhibit your ability to change. A neat trick, wouldn't you say?"

No, because it brought forth a fluttery panic and she couldn't help but ask, "How long does it last?"

"Only a few days. I've yet to have my scientists perfect the formula. But never fear, it will last long enough to get you to our new installation where a shiny new cell awaits, along with your next dosage."

She took a step back. "You won't get away with what you're doing. Too many people know about Bittech and the experiments."

"I know. A shame. Packing up and moving is such a pain in the ass. But Parker's promised me an even better location, one where I'll have access to even more shifter genomes. Now be a good girl and come with me."

"Never."

"Ooh, a bad girl. No wonder Harold wanted you so much. A shame he slipped his leash and got impatient. But never fear, my faithful sidekick, Fang here will be more than happy to help me with my next round of experiments. My pet lizard, though, can only watch. He has a tendency of ripping apart his paramours. And you're too precious to lose quite yet."

Ice filled her veins. "I won't let you do this."

"You won't have a choice." Merrill smiled as he said, "Anytime now, Ace."

Ace looked down at the gun, but didn't move otherwise.

Merrill's gloating expression turned sour, and she noted his finger holding down a button on the remote. "I said shoot her, you stupid fucking lizard."

"No." The single syllable was pushed out by the man with leathery skin. The whiff of roasting flesh tickled her nose.

In that moment, she felt sorry for him, and thankful. Despite the pain, he was trying to help her, and what was she doing? Standing around like a fucking idiot.

"Shoot her, goddammit." Merrill blew spittle with his angry command.

"Fuck you."

Not liking that answer, Merrill did something with his remote that drew a sharp gasp from Ace.

Body gripped in a convulsion, Ace couldn't hold on to the gun. Hell, he couldn't even remain upright. He hit the ground twitching.

Leaving Aria truly alone with a madman and his pets. His very, very dangerous pets.

"Grab her, but don't damage her. We need her whole for what I have planned."

"As my masssster commandsss."

Grawr.

"Like hell," she retorted. The camouflage boat she'd untied had drifted a few feet from the dock. It didn't take much of a leap to land in it. She thanked her lightweight, petite frame for it not tipping over. Although it was close. She waved her arms for balance as she adjusted to the sway and made her way to the engine.

She plopped onto the last seat on the boat as Fang came tearing at the dock on all fours, his barely human eyes wild with animal hunger.

She couldn't look at him and start the motor at the same time. Besides, who wanted to look insanity and death in the eye?

A quick glance down and she noted the pull cord. Yank. *Whirrrrr.* Yank harder. *Whirrr.* A third and the motor turned over. *Rrrrr. Rrrr.* She slapped the throttle.

Vroom.

The boat shot forward and just in time. There was a splash in the wake she'd just left as Fang leaped after her.

Hysteria at the situation made her wonder just how bad he'd reek of wet dog when he got out.

On the shore, Merrill stood waving his remote, his face a mottled red. "She's getting away. Fly after her, you overgrown fucking lizard."

The mad one flapped his leathery wings and lifted from shore.

As the boat gathered momentum, drawing her farther from the

hillock, she couldn't help a hysterical laugh and even waved bye-bye to Merrill.

She'd escaped. Fang and his dog paddle would never catch her. Merrill was stuck on shore. And if she could make it to the tree line only yards away, even his flying pet wouldn't be able to catch her.

I'm free. Free to tell everyone in the shifter world what happened beneath the floors of Bittech Institute.

A reckoning would come once she told the shifter world. Merrill and Parker might take off before the hammer came down, but no matter. They could run and hide, but those seeking justice would find them.

And I will help in the hunt. They would pay for what they'd done.

A sudden engine noise had her craning, and she noted that a new man must have emerged from the open door on the hillock. The guard and Fang piled into the boat she'd set adrift. Damn Fang for grabbing it and dragging it back. Stupid dog knew how to fetch.

But she did have a head start and less weight in her vessel. What did chill her to the bones, though, was the shrill cry in the sky. The crazy lizard hunted.

Maybe he'll get distracted by something in the swamp.

A vain wish.

A shadow swept over her. She didn't need to peek upwards to guess what it was. She veered her boat under the concealing fronds of the boughs on a drooping tree and ducked low as she puttered through them, sharply turning a few times. As she guided her craft through almost hidden intersections, she fervently prayed she'd not only lose her tail, but also the eyes in the sky.

When she felt she'd gone far enough, she killed the motor and let it drift as she listened.

The hum of insects filled the air, along with the gentle sucking sound of water lapping at a muddy shore.

Then she heard it, the piercing ululation of a hunter overhead.

Had it spotted her? She craned to look above. However, the heavy foliage screened her view. So where was the hunter?

She kept low with her hand on the pull cord of the motor, yet when a creature finally revealed itself, it surged from under her boat, tipping her into the water!

Chapter 24

THE DISCOVERY of the scent revived him.

Finally a clue. Loping to the back of the truck, he grabbed the lip of the roll down and pushed. It went ratcheting upward, a noisy indication of his presence, which hid his gasp.

Within the truck he found boxes, stacked on top of each other, and a cage. A big, empty cage.

Princess yipped, drawing his attention. Turning, he noticed she seemed very interested in the utility shed at the back end of the loading dock parking area. A pretty big shed, actually, for the amount and size of yard tools this place needed. As he neared it, he realized the shed also hummed.

Perhaps Bittech kept a backup generator outside. Not unheard of, but of more interest was his dog. Parked in front of the closed access door sat Princess. She cocked her head and then pawed at the door.

The realization it required a keycard to open galvanized him. Throughout his search of Bittech, not once had he used the card in his pocket. He'd not needed to because that Bittech was just a front.

Sliding the plastic rectangle free, he popped it into the card slot. The light went from red to green. *Click.*

He pulled the door open and stepped into an empty room. The entire shed was swept clean, not a single lawn tool to be seen. But at the back, dull metal door gleaming, one elevator door—with a card slot.

"What do you think, Princess? Is this the secret lair?"

Yip.

The card once again gave him access. The doors slid open, and he stepped in, the myriad of smells setting off a chain reaction of recognition and repugnance. Alien, lizard, simian... All the flavors were there, along with human. And was it wishful thinking, or did he detect a hint of Aria's sweet scent?

The walls of the elevator didn't prove exciting. Scuffed metal panels with a rail running along the back. No buttons here. Just a screen saying, *Please scan your access card.*

He flashed it and heard a beep. The screen changed and showed several choices. Instead of numbers, the floors possessed names: *Admin, Research, Holding.*

The first option sounded as if it might have folks who would probably recognize he didn't belong. Research would probably involve guys in white coats, if there were any left. It didn't take a genius to realize Parker and his merry band were jumping ship.

Option number three it is. Call it a hunch, but he'd wager that was where they kept their prisoners.

The smooth gait of the elevator didn't let him know how far he sank, but it felt as if he descended a while. It made him wonder how the hell they'd built such a place and without anyone noticing. Then again, shifters were kings when it came to hiding.

As the elevator descended, anticipation churned in his gut. His fists clenched at his sides. What would he find? Aria was so delicate. It wouldn't take much to hurt her. Or was she already gone? Taken away in one of those trucks.

No. He refused to believe he'd arrived too late. The belief didn't dispel the anxiety, which, he might add, didn't mean he was afraid or about to turn yellow-bellied.

Nothing wrong with caring. And if you didn't agree, he'd happily take you out to the swamp for a big hug until you changed your mind.

The doors slid open with only the slightest *whoosh.* Braced, he waited for someone or something to jump at him. But there was nothing to see, just an abandoned counter with a swivel chair on castors and the dusty rectangle left behind to show where a monitor used to sit.

Constantine walked the long hall lined with cages. Empty cages. Mostly. A few held misshapen lumps that emitted a foul stench. Others had blankets strewn in them. One cell even held an abandoned stuffed bear.

The scents stung his nose, the scent of wrongness. Alien. Fear...

At the bars of one cage, he stopped. Sniffed.

Aria was here. This was her cage. The one he'd wager she escaped from before finding him. He spun around, horrified at what it all meant.

His dog whined, and he turned to find her standing before a cage. He ran to her, wondering if she'd found a clue, only to skid to a stop.

It seemed they'd not taken everyone. In the cage, something wrapped in a woolen blanket moved. A head lifted, the face covered by dank and stringy hair.

"Help me," it whispered.

Constantine gripped the bars. "Do you know where they hide the key?"

"Help me." The figure scuttled closer to the cage, remaining on all fours. Princess backed away, a low growl rumbling.

The alien aroma left a bad tang in his nose, but Constantine didn't flee. It wasn't its—or was that a her?—fault she'd become something less human. Something twisted.

He crouched down as she came close to the bars. "How can I help you?"

With a whip of her head, the hair flew back, and mandibles snapped at his gripping fingers. Constantine fell backwards, digits intact, but one of them oozing blood as the tip of her pincer mouth caught him.

The blanket fell away, and he could now see the true horror within the cage. Less woman, more spider, with stunted legs growing from her torso covered in bristled hair. Most horrifying, she maintained some human features, and a voice.

"Help me. Meat. Feed me. Meat. Hungry." She cackled.

He shivered.

The pointed tips of her legs, covered in human flesh, jabbed through the bars, but Constantine, taking a moment to scoop his dog first, was already fleeing. They could take his fucking man card for running. No way was he sticking around this place. Not when Aria wasn't here. He had to find her before they turned the woman he thought of as his into one of those things.

With his dog tucked under his arm, he returned to the elevator and hit the level above. There he found more signs of a rapid departure in the shape of doors left open, a few boxes fallen and a general air of rapid abandonment.

And in one room, Aria's scent and a snoring body. Not hers, but that of a guard.

Aria had been here, and recently, too. Now if only he could follow her scent trail. However, the varied and frenetic mishmash of odors from the mass exodus overpowered her more delicate bouquet. A quick search of the other rooms down the hall didn't find any trace of her, so he went up another level.

He exited to find more chaos. More abandoned offices with open drawers, loose papers, dusty marks of items taken.

But as he went down the hall, he caught a scent. Her scent. He ran toward the red EXIT sign at the far end. He pushed through the door to find another elevator. And then a cavernous room and, at the far end, another door and stairs. All along the way, her scent taunted.

He took the stairs in threes, bolting up them, urgency fueling his speed. At the top, he paused only a moment before slamming open the door and startling a man. A man he knew by face and name.

"You're Merrill."

"How did you get here?"

Constantine smiled, the chill smile of a predator who had cornered his prey. "Does it matter? Where's Aria?"

"Gone. Hopefully dead, the problematic bitch."

At those words, Constantine charged him. And once the man lay dead—*regenerate from that, asshole!*—he went looking for his chick.

Chapter 25

THE BOAT TILTED OVER, and she hit the water with a splash, yet didn't sink. The heavy coils of a sinuous body wrapped around her, but forget panic. She wanted to smile instead.

As her head broke the surface of the water, she sucked in a breath of air, but didn't scream as she came face to face with a python.

"Hello, angel."

A forked tongue flicked, and Constantine hissed.

"I don't think this is the time for tongue." She smirked. "How about later if we make it out alive?"

The serpentine head bobbed in agreement.

A cry shrieked from the sky overhead. Her reptilian lover peeked upward.

"Merrill's pet is looking for me," she explained.

Was it possible for a snake to grin?

Weaving in the water, Constantine carried her, drawing her past the remains of the second boat, Fang and the other occupant nowhere to be seen.

Nessie had nothing on her serpent.

She heard the fierce bark of a certain Princess, and she strained to peek. Only once she saw did she exhort him to, "Hurry before that lizard makes Princess into a snack."

Although, Princess seemed determined to prevail, even against the odds. The valiant dog darted to and fro, avoiding the reaching talons of a flying lizard no longer controlled by a certain remote. Probably on account of Merrill lying on the ground with his head tilted at an unnatural angle.

Before they could hit the shore and rescue her, Princess squealed as the thing scooped her in a clawed hand. It sprang into the air, taking the dog with it.

"Oh, hell no. If anyone gets to eat that thing, it's me," she grumbled. Her feet hit the ground, her wet gown came off, and she strained. Hard as she could. She pulled on the essence of her eagle. Pulled and pulled and...

A caw of success vibrated on her lips as her flesh turned to feathers, arms extended into wings. Pushing with her legs, she sprang into the air and extended her wings. A few mighty flaps and she was airborne. She immediately followed the lizard bastard.

She uttered a challenging cry. It was answered, the lizard thing halting in mid-air and hovering. The creature held Princess aloft, grinned, and then opened its mouth wide.

Intending to eat the dog didn't mean it managed to. Princess turned rabid, twisting her head far enough that she managed to chomp it on the wrist. The leathery skin might be tough, but it proved no match for needle-like, determined teeth.

A screech from the creature and it forgot its plan to eat the furry snack. Of course, Princess's new situation, which involved plummeting to the ground, wasn't any better.

A choice faced Aria; let her mighty eagle take down the enemy in the sky or save one stupid little, annoying dog.

The things I do for the man I care about.

She plummeted, her wings tucked tight to her body. Streamlined, she arrowed through the sky, hurtling after the little furry form. As she neared the point of no return in her dive, she reached out. The hook of her claw caught on the collar Princess wore, and she banked out of her suicide plunge, catching the air currents before they crashed into the ground.

Of the lizard monster, there was no sign. He'd escaped.

For now.

As she hit the ground, she changed until she wore her own body. A body that got crushed against another naked one as a happy Constantine hugged her.

"I'm so glad you're safe."

"Are you talking about me or your dog?" she asked against his bare chest, Princess's furry body squished between them.

"Do I have to answer?"

She snorted. "Probably best if you don't."

Yip. Princess agreed.

As he released her, she took a peek around. "I see you took care of Merrill, but what happened to Ace?"

"Who?"

"The other lizard guy. The one who helped me escape. He was here when I took off in the boat."

Constantine shrugged. "No idea. When I came out on the hill, only Merrill was here. Dumb fuck thought he was tough."

"Proved him wrong?"

"I proved a hug is mightier than the fist." He grinned.

The ground under foot rumbled, enough that she reached out to steady herself using his rock-hard chest. A thick arm curled around her waist.

"What was that?" she asked.

Smoke billowed from the door leading back into the secret installation.

"I think someone just cleaned up some loose ends."

"So how do we get out of here?"

As he glanced at the swamp, she groaned. "Oh, hell no. I am not going back in there."

Luckily, she didn't have to. Her eagle was now hers to call upon again.

With night blanketing Bitten Point, hopefully no one noticed the eagle skimming the swamp, keeping a close watch on a snake, who wore a little dog as a hat.

Landing in the yard behind his house, she shifted back and gasped. "Constantine. Your poor house." She took in the damage and couldn't help the guilt that filled her.

"I don't give a fuck about the house. You and Princess are safe. That's what matters."

As was his mother and brother and sister-in-law and their kid and a whole bunch of other people who poured into the yard from the house all demanding answers and, after some red-cheeked moments, offering them some robes.

The most astonishing part of that evening in the yard wasn't the fact that they lit a firepit and roasted hot dogs and marshmallows over it, or the fact that no one thought it odd Constantine held her perched in his lap with Princess in hers. The weirdest part was how they all acted as if she belonged.

Here. With him.

And the urge to fly, to seek new skies, to drift upon new winds, didn't strike.

Can I make a life here, with him? What of the better question, did Constantine want her to stay?

Chapter 26

IT SEEMED to take forever before everyone left. A man loved that his friends and family cared, but dammit, right now Constantine cared about more important things, such as peeling that robe from Aria, bathing every inch of her body, and then checking her to make sure for himself that she had emerged unscathed from her ordeal.

The house with its wreckage couldn't handle them for the night, so Caleb loaned him some money and dropped him and Aria off at a motel—run by shifters, so no questions were asked about their lack of normal clothing.

Once the motel room door closed, Constantine turned to Aria with a smile. "At last. I've got you alone."

Yip.

Aria snickered. "Better explain that to your dog."

But Princess didn't require explanation. With a look of disgust, his dog jumped onto an armchair and curled into a ball.

Poor jealous baby. She'd come around. He hoped.

"Shower time," he announced.

She arched a brow. "Is that just your way of getting me naked again?"

"Yes."

"Why didn't you just say so?" She laughed, but she also dropped the robe to the floor and led the way into the white-tile washroom. The brat even bent over to turn on the tap.

It was enough to strangle a man.

Hug her.

Good idea. He wrapped her in his arms, hugging her tight to him, closing his eyes as he finally relaxed enough to realize she was safe.

"You're squishing me," she said when she finally realized he wasn't letting go.

"Get used to it," he retorted while manhandling her so she had to face him.

"You like hugging, don't you?"

He couldn't help but smile. "Just a bit."

"I'm good with that." Her arms wound around him and squeezed just as tightly.

Perfection. However, their bodies that closely entwined meant he didn't get to look at her. And he really, *really,* wanted to take a peek.

Lifting her, he climbed into the shower. Only then did he release his grip on her.

With a seductive smile, she leaned back against the tile wall. "So in all the excitement, I don't know if I said thank you for coming to rescue me."

His eyes tracked the finger that drew a line between her breasts and then dipped lower. "If you ask me, you were doing a pretty damned good job of saving yourself."

"Guess I did, but a girl does like to know she can rely on her man." She paused, and she peeked at him, a coy smile curving her lips. "And I think this girl should thank the angel who saved her."

"No need to thank. I'd do anything for you." Never had he spoken truer.

"Really? You'd do anything? Then wash me, would you, because I am so done with smelling like a swamp." She wrinkled her nose, and he laughed.

"Your wish is my command."

The soap sat on the dish inset within the tile wall. He made quick work of its wrapper. The lemon scent filled the shower as he lathered his hands. He rubbed those soapy palms over her breasts, cupping them and watching with hunger as those berries puckered, begging for a bite. He saw no reason to wait. He lowered his face and brushed it across an erect nub, lapped, spat, and rinsed his mouth.

"Too clean?" she teased.

"You're evil to tease a man suffering," he mumbled.

"What are you going to do about it?"

Why tease her right back, of course.

She inhaled sharply as he dipped in for another taste. A bite. Her back arched, and she thrust her breasts at him, begging him to do more than flick his tongue. He ignored her invitation and spent more time circling around the erect tip.

Lithe fingers weaved through his hair, tugging him close, attempting to force his mouth to take her engorged nipple. As if she had the strength to make him do anything.

He chuckled, blowing hotly on her nipples, loving how they tightened further.

"Bite them," she begged.

"Giving me orders?" Hot, but not what he had planned. He stood, forcing her hands to release their grip. Before they could choose a new spot, he clasped them in an iron fist and pushed them over Aria's head.

She arched, thrusting her body at him, the warm water sluicing down her frame.

With his free hand, he gathered the bar of soap. "I don't believe I was done with this." With the slippery soap in hand, he pressed against her mound, rubbing against her downy curls. A shudder went through her.

He could understand how she felt. His whole body hummed, vibrated as if full of electricity. A live wire waiting to zap.

His soapy hand slid between her parted thighs, brushing over the petals of her sex. Her breath caught, and her body went taut, anticipation heavy between them.

With her hands still braced over her head, he kept rubbing against her core while dipping his head for another taste of those nipples.

She cried out. She thrashed. But sweetest of all, she moaned.

Need burned within him. Arousal made him painfully erect.

"I don't think I can wait any longer."

"Then don't," she replied.

Releasing her hands, he palmed her waist and hoisted her, high enough that her legs came around his waist. Her arms wrapped loosely around his neck. He peered between their bodies, admiring the slickness of their skin. The tip of him brushed against her wet curls. By angling his hips, the head of his cock pressed against her sex.

She sucked in a breath as he pushed in, watching his shaft slide into her slick heat. Deeper. Deeper. Fully seated.

And her channel constricted him and hugged him so deliciously tight.

With a gasp of pleasure, he pulled out then slammed back in. Out. In. Her legs squeezed around his shanks, holding him close, burying him within her welcome heat.

He couldn't help but drop his head so that his forehead pressed against hers. The soft pants of her breaths fluttered over his skin as he seesawed in and out of her.

The sharp nails in his shoulders were but a pinch and meant she'd reached her cusp. He thrust deeply, one last time, so deep inside her, then threw his head back and hissed.

Hissed as her channel hugged him tight.

Sucked in a ragged breath as her sex undulated around him.

Held her close knowing he would never, ever let her go.

Oursss.

Epilogue

SNUGGLED against him later in the motel bed, Aria couldn't help but think that, despite everything that had happened, she'd never been more happy or felt more at home.

She sighed with contentment, so utterly blissful...until the dog stuck her cold, wet nose against her spine.

With a scream, she sat upright. "Your dog hates me."

"Love me, love my dog." Rolling onto his back, hands laced behind his head, Constantine smirked.

She glared at Princess. Princess glared back. And then she saw it, the twinkle of mischief in the dog's eye. The slight curl of a lip.

"Your dog is sly."

"Yup."

"Ferocious."

"Yup."

"Kind of cute if you don't mind the fact she could tear out the tendons in your ankle."

"See, I knew she'd grow on you."

"Don't think this means I'm getting one of those stupid

Chihuahua shirts." She'd seen part of his collection. It was enough to make her want to migrate.

"I've got a better idea for a pair of matching ones. Custom designed, I might add. Yours will say, *I hear a voice and it doesn't like you.*"

"What about yours?"

"Mine will say, *Me either.*"

She laughed as she rolled atop him. "I like it, but I feel like I should add that the voice in my head kind of likes you."

"What of the woman?"

"She likes you, too," she murmured, rubbing her nose against his.

"That's good because I like you, too."

And the moment might have gotten really sappy if Princess hadn't taken that moment to gag beside them on the bed.

But Aria didn't mind because, in her python's embrace, she finally found what she'd been searching for—a family. A home. And a bratty dog to call her own.

AT THE CLICK of a key in the lock, Melanie stood from the couch. Ever since she'd gotten the call about the fire at Bittech, she'd wondered, *Was Andrew in there when the bombs went off?*

At least they thought it was explosives. How else to explain the massive boom and rumble? The utter destruction of a building made to withstand hurricanes.

Is my husband dead or alive? And of most interest, had he played a part in the destruction? Once upon a time, she would have claimed no way, not her benign husband. But now that it turned out the rumors of Bittech running an experimental underground installation were true, she realized she didn't know the man she'd been sleeping beside for years.

The bright red door, which she'd painted to stand out from the others in the cookie-cutter neighborhood, swung open, and through it stepped Andrew.

Her husband.

The traitor.

When her best friend, Renny, had called her with the news about Bittech, not just the destruction of it, but what had been discovered before it blew, she'd not wanted to believe it. Believing it meant reevaluating her entire life since high school. It meant admitting she'd made a colossal mistake in marrying Andrew.

Andrew walked in as if he still held the right. Hell no.

She raised the gun in his direction. "Don't take another step."

He barely spared her a glance. He never spared her anything, not his attention or his love. He definitely never let her borrow his nice and shiny BMW. She got stuck with the practical mini van. She enjoyed her petty revenge by sending the boys with their daddy in his pretty car—with slushies.

Tossing his keys on the side table, Andrew dropped his briefcase. He still had yet to acknowledge her or the weapon she aimed.

"I said don't move. Or, even better, get out."

That finally drew his attention. The traitor raised eyes and didn't even bother to hide his disdain. "Or you'll what, Melanie? Shoot me. We both know you don't have the guts. So stop wasting my time and pack a bag. Quickly now. Wake the boys, too, if you intend to bring them. We're leaving here as soon as our transportation arrives."

"I'm not going anywhere with you."

"I'm sorry, did I say you had a choice?" Andrew's hand shot out and grabbed hold of the wrist with the gun. He possessed a stronger, wiry strength than she would have credited. He held her with ease.

"Asshole. Let go of me. I'm not going with you."

She struck at him with her free hand, but the man she thought she knew, the one who couldn't stand the sight of blood, the one who wouldn't even squish a spider, held fast. Held her firmly. With his free hand, he slapped her.

Her head rocked to the side, and she tasted blood as the edge of her teeth cut her lip.

"Don't hit her." The low growl came from behind Andrew.

Usually, running into Wes made her massively uncomfortable, the whole ex-boyfriend thing being a large part of it. Not this time. She'd never been happier to see him.

Despite her throbbing cheek, she still turned a triumphant smile on Andrew. "Yeah, Andrew. Don't hit me."

"You meddle in things that are none of your business, gator," Andrew barked over his shoulder as Wes filled the open doorway.

"Men don't hit women."

"And employees don't back talk to their bosses. So mind your place, gator, or you won't have that cushy job anymore. I called you here to help me, not give me lip."

"Help you?" She uttered the words through frozen lips.

She waited for Wes to refute Andrew's words. To slap her bastard husband upside the head. Instead, Wes tightened his lips.

He's not here to save me. The realization hurt more than it should have.

"How could you?" she whispered.

He said the same thing to her now as he had when they'd broke up, and she'd cried, "why?"

"Because."

But Melanie wasn't a teenage girl anymore, and as she slammed her foot down on Andrew's, forcing him to loosen her gun-wielding hand, she retorted, "Because isn't an answer."

Neither was shooting first, her husband or her ex-boyfriend.

Bang. Bang. But it sure felt damned good.

Up Next: Gator's Challenge .

Gator's Challenge

Welcome to Bitten Point, where the toughest battles happen within the heart.

Once upon a time, a girl loved a boy but married another man. What a mistake, especially since that man has been using her as part of his sick plot to experiment on shifters. And he's got a plan to use their sons.

Over my dead body. But Melanie might need help keeping her boys safe.

Wes is keeping secrets, lots of them, but he doesn't have a choice.

The people he cares about are in danger, and he'll do anything to protect them, but that struggle intensifies when the girl he never stopped loving is drawn into danger.

Can this gator meet the challenge of not only freeing himself from the blackmailing grip of Bittech, but also find a way to be with Melanie, too?

Chapter 1

A LONG TIME AGO, a young girl loved a boy from the wrong side of the swamp. Everyone told her to stay away. *He's bad news.* He was a Mercer, the family everyone talked about with a sneer and contempt.

Good girls shouldn't associate with bad boys. She never claimed to be a good girl, and no one told her what to do. She made her own decisions, and she decided she wanted him.

From the first moment she met Wes in high school—a high school she was late attending since her mother insisted good girls went to Catholic school—she saw right away that the boy with the lanky hair and leather jacket had potential. For one thing, he turned out to be a lot different from what the rumors claimed. Wes wanted better for himself and his family. Wes had goals and dreams, dreams he shared under shaded boughs in between kisses. Back then, she believed they would have a happily ever after. Believed a boy when he said he loved her.

Young, in love, and innocent—until the day he dumped her. For her own good, so he claimed, the icing on a bitter, heartbroken cake—and she meant that quite literally. The jerk broke her heart on Valentine's Day, right after he ate the cupcake she'd made that said "I love you."

"You're better off without me," he said, wisps of smoke curling from his nostrils, as he couldn't help a nervous drag from his cigarette. A nasty habit she planned to cure him of, along with his tendency to wear black shirts with heavy metal bands on them.

"I don't understand. You're breaking up with me?" She couldn't miss the nod of his head. "Why?"

"Because."

"Because isn't an answer."

"It is when you're a Mercer."

"You promised you'd love me forever."

"I lied."

He didn't love her. He'd never loved her. All that they'd shared? A big, fat lie.

Those words smashed her heart into pieces. Such a mournful meow moment. Such an eye opener. It was also the first time she'd truly let her Latina rage overcome her.

Anger led her to cleanse herself of him by burning every single picture and thing he'd given her—even that stupidly adorable stuffed gator wearing the shades. For days, weeks, even years afterward, she claimed to hate him—stupid, rotten jerk. She believed that with all of her being. Yet, her heart still pitter-pattered every time she caught a glimpse or heard Wes's voice. It irked her to no end that she never felt the same kind of pitter-patter for her husband. Poor Andrew, he just didn't inspire that kind of passion.

And she missed the spurt of excitement, that quick rush of her heart and the heat of anticipation. So many times, Melanie couldn't help but long for what could have been.

We could have been so great together if he'd given us a chance.

She forgot all her foolish dreams when she shot him. She should probably add she'd shot her husband, too.

Rewind a few moments, though, to the hour before she pulled the trigger. Picture her as she alternated sitting on the couch and pacing her living room floor, a polished oak that required a little too much wood polish to stay pretty. Imagine her chewing her fingers after promising Daryl, her brother, that she wouldn't do anything foolish. As if anybody who knew her would believe that.

At the click of a key in the lock, Melanie stood from the couch, every atom in her body trembling. Ever since she'd gotten the call about the explosion at Bittech, she'd wondered, *Was Andrew in there when the bombs went off?*

At least they *thought* it was explosives that had taken down the medical institute. How else to explain the massive boom and rumble resulting in the utter destruction of a building made to withstand hurricanes?

Is my husband dead or alive? And if alive, had he played a part in the demolition?

Once upon a time, Melanie would have claimed no way. Her benign husband, with his love of documentaries and a sizzling game of chess, would never stoop to something so heinous. But that was before she and her friends discovered the truth behind rumors of Bittech Institute running an underground installation that experimented on shifters. More sobering, Andrew had to know about the testing, the kidnappings, and the monsters killing innocent folk in and around town. It shocked her to realize, as more and more of the truth unfolded, that she didn't know the man she'd slept beside for years.

Have I truly been so blind?

Told you not to mate him. Her inner feline never had cared for Andrew. As if she'd trust her cat after she'd been so wrong about Wes.

The bright red door, which she'd painted to stand out from the others in the cookie-cutter neighborhood, swung open, and through it stepped Andrew.

Her husband.

Possibly a traitor to all shifter kind.

Even now, she didn't want to believe it. Believing it meant reevaluating her entire life since high school. It meant admitting she'd made a colossal mistake in marrying Andrew.

Being wrong meant listening to her brother's taunting "I told you so." Daryl never had liked her husband.

Andrew walked in as if he still held the right.

I'll be the judge of that.

The gun that she'd removed from the safe felt heavy in her hands. She still raised and steadied it in his direction. Usually, she wouldn't touch the thing. Weapons were for prey. As a panther shifter, she preferred to let her predator take care of problems menacing her. Yet, her cat couldn't ask questions, so she brought out the weapon Andrew had bought a few years ago as protection against neighborhood vandals. The reality that he could shift into a bear and tear the head off any idiot who entered never factored into the equation of whether they should get a weapon. When it came to his wild side, Andrew was woefully lacking.

That's not the only thing he lacks, her kitty slyly reminded.

It wasn't always about size, although, in this case, Melanie had the furry balls to keep the weapon aimed with a threatened, "Don't take another step."

Despite the warning, Andrew didn't listen or even spare her a glance. He never spared her anything, not his attention or his love. He definitely never let her borrow his nice and shiny BMW. She got stuck with the practical mini van. She enjoyed her petty revenge by sending the boys with their daddy in his pretty car—with slushies.

Tossing his keys on the side table, Andrew dropped his briefcase. He still had yet to acknowledge her or the weapon she aimed.

"I said don't move. Or, even better, get out."

Yes, run. So we can chase. Her cat was in dire need of exercise.

Her words finally drew his attention. Andrew raised his gaze to meet hers. No surprise. No trepidation. Only disdain, an expression she'd never seen on him before. "Is that any way to greet me, dear wife?"

"It is when I've been listening to reports all night long about the stuff happening at Bittech."

"Did the town gossips run to tattle on me?" He smirked.

"It's more than gossip."

"You're right. It is." His smile taunted and threw her for a loop. How entirely out of character. Who was this man?

"You're not going to deny it."

"Why would I? It's true? Now, put that thing down." He took a step toward her.

She steadied her hands. "I said don't move."

He didn't bother to hide his amusement. "Or you'll what, Melanie? Shoot me? We both know you don't have the guts. So stop wasting my time. You need to pack a bag. Quickly. Wake the boys, too. We all need to leave."

"I'm not going anywhere with you." And neither were her boys.

"I'm sorry, did I say you had a choice?" Andrew's hand shot out and grabbed hold of the wrist of the hand holding the gun. He possessed a stronger wiry strength than she would have credited. He held her with ease.

In her mind, her cat snarled, not liking this unexpected turn of events.

"Asshole. Let go of me. You can't force me to go anywhere." She struck at him with her free hand, but the man she thought she knew, the one who couldn't stand the sight of blood, the one who wouldn't even squish a spider, held fast. Held her firmly.

When did he become so strong?

"Shut your annoying mouth. I've heard quite enough from you." With his free hand, he slapped her.

Slapped. Me!

Her head rocked to the side. She tasted blood as the edge of her teeth cut her lip. She didn't know what shocked her more, the fact Andrew had hit her or the fact she didn't shift into her cat and rip his face off. Her feline certainly growled inside her mind.

Come on out, kitty. Show him who's more vicious.

Rowr! Which, translated from kitty speak, meant with pleasure.

Except, when she pulled at her inner beast, tried to coax her out... Nothing.

I can't shift!

Fear made her eye Andrew differently, with a reminder of what the rumors claimed. "What did you do to me? My panther can't come out."

"Much as I'd love to play with your pussy," he said with a leer that just looked plain unnatural, "I know what your claws are capable of. So I gave you a little something to keep you in your skin."

"You drugged me!" She screeched, struggling anew, only to reel as he cuffed her again, a stronger blow that made her see little birdies.

Swat at one and let's see how they taste.

Blink.

"Don't hit her." The low, growled warning came from behind Andrew.

Her heart stuttered.

Usually, running into Wes meant trying to hide her discomfort—and resisting an urge to kick him in the manparts. Not this time. She'd never been happier to see the big Mercer.

Andrew's in trouble. She practically sang the words in her head. Despite her throbbing cheek, she still turned a triumphant smile on Andrew. "Yeah, Andrew. Don't hit me." *Or Wes will hit you back harder.*

Meow. Nothing like the prospect of a smackdown to make her feline regain some pride.

"You meddle in things that are none of your business, gator," Andrew barked over his shoulder as Wes filled the open doorway—and she meant filled, considering the width of his shoulders.

"Men don't hit women." A flat statement.

Chauvinistic, but she'd take it.

"And employees don't backtalk to their bosses. So mind your place, gator, or you won't have that cushy job anymore. I brought you along to help me, not give me lip."

"Help you?" Melanie managed to utter the words through frozen lips.

Peeking at Wes, she noted his stony expression as she waited for him to refute Andrew's words. Even better, she hoped Wes would slap her bastard husband upside the head. Instead, Wes tightened his lips.

He's not here to save me. The realization hurt more than it should have.

"How could you?" she whispered. *How could he betray me again?*

He said the same thing to her now that he had when they'd broken up and she'd cried why.

"Because."

But Melanie wasn't a teenage girl anymore, and as she slammed her foot down on Andrew's—*take that, you bastard*—forcing him to loose her gun-wielding hand, she retorted, "Because isn't an answer."

Neither was shooting first her husband or her ex boyfriend —*Bang*! *Bang*!—but it sure felt damned good.

Chapter 2

SHE SHOT ME!

Wes couldn't believe it, and yet, at the same time, he couldn't blame Melanie. How must it look, him showing up on her doorstep, Andrew claiming Wes came to help?

It looks exactly how things are. I work for her husband, and between the pair of us, we're tied for the asshole of the year award. The fact that Wes didn't obey willingly didn't factor. In Melanie's eyes, he had just become the enemy.

And she'd acted.

She shot both him and Andrew.

Another man might have lost his shit at that point. Probably retaliated, too. Andrew sure as hell wasn't happy she had the guts to fire that gun. But Wes? Fuck, he loved that brave side of her. *That Latin fire of hers always was sexy.*

What he hated was seeing the look of frustrated realization in her eyes as Andrew chuckled, the harmless blanks she'd fired leaving merely a bruise on the flesh.

"Stupid, stupid Melanie. Did you really think I'd leave a loaded gun around here, knowing you might use it on me?"

Dawning understanding shaped her visage as she glanced at the useless weapon in her hand. "You filled it with duds. You knew this day would come."

"Of course I did. And it's past time that you grasped I'm not the teddy bear you thought I was." Andrew's malicious smile did not resemble his usual dough-faced demeanor. Beneath the nerd façade lurked a bad man, a man who kept getting worse.

A bad man I have to work for.

Told you we should have eaten him. His gator never had liked the asshole—and that began before Andrew had hooked up with Melanie. But he hated him twice as much after.

"It's all true then, isn't it? You knew about the things happening in our town. The disappearances, the deaths," Melanie stated, taking a slow step back.

"I knew and helped cover them up. Amazing what a lot of money and a few choice threats can do. Did you know most people have a price?"

"What was yours?" she asked Andrew.

"No one paid me to join in. I immediately saw the potential when my father drew me into the secret a few years ago."

"You should have said no. Done the right thing."

"Who are you to say what's right?" Andrew rocked on his heels and held out his hands wide. "We are doing cutting edge things with gene manipulation. Achieving wonders you can't even begin to imagine."

"Wonders like the lizard monster who killed those people? What about Harold? That dog thing you made out of that poor B&B owner's son."

"With success comes some bumps."

"I'd say a psychotic flying lizard who craves human flesh is a little more than a bump."

And she doesn't even know the half of it, Wes thought.

"You are only focusing on the negative. You forgot about the positive."

"I don't see how any of this is positive."

"Because you lack vision. But you'll understand. Soon everyone will see what we've been doing." A zealous light gleamed in Andrew's eyes, the scariest illumination of all.

"They'll see you're a monster."

Andrew's lips tightened. "Enough of the stalling and name calling, dear wife. Gather the boys. We have to go."

Wes could predict the words before she uttered them with a triumphant smile. "The boys aren't here."

With a narrowed gaze, Andrew snapped, "What have you done with them?"

"Kept them safe from you," she spat.

"Perhaps you should have worried about keeping yourself safe. Grab her."

The order Wes dreaded had come. For a moment, he thought about telling Andrew to fucking get her himself—and then smacking him when he did.

However, there were lives at stake, lives he cared about.

We care for Melanie. A warm reminder from the cold part of him. A reminder he ignored as he lunged for her.

But she darted out of reach. She always was fleet of foot, something he counted on.

Turning on her heel, Melanie darted into the bowels of her home, leaving him with a glimpse of hair bouncing and pert ass moving.

Damn, I love that ass.

Loved. He'd lost all rights to that perky butt years ago.

"What the hell are you waiting for?" Andrew yelled. "Go after her. I need her to tell me where the boys are."

Say no. Say fucking no. He bit back the words and did as Andrew ordered. He went after Melanie, perhaps not as quickly as he was capable of, perhaps not even as efficiently. This was one hunt he didn't want to win.

As he turned the corner of the hall, he noted four doors, all shut. Opening door number one, he noted a guest bedroom, done in a soothing pale yellow. The bed bore a flowered comforter and fluffy pillows.

No Melanie.

On to door number two. A pair of matching beds, perfect for twin boys. The beds were empty, the comforters covered in grinning sharks, smooth and untouched. On the walls hung posters of *Transformers*, *Star Wars*, and even one for the *Jungle Book*.

Toys lay scattered on the floor—cars and dinosaurs and building blocks. A room for Melanie and Andrew's boys, boys that could have been Wes's if he'd not fucked up and let her go.

Speaking of letting go, he'd spent enough time in the empty room to know she'd not come this way.

Out in the hall, he inhaled. As a shifter, even in his human form, some of his senses remained enhanced. Take his sense of smell, for example. A myriad bouquet of aromas came to him, but the freshest—and most enticing—belonged to Melanie. Even though he knew she didn't hide behind the next door, he opened it, mostly because he wanted to hear that note of impatience from Andrew as he yelled, "Did you grab her?"

Peeking into the bathroom with its white subway tile, dual sink, and the shower curtain with more sharks on it, he could say with utmost honesty, "Not yet."

One door left at the end of the hall. Her scent led right to it. He paused a moment before gripping the knob and opening the door to the master bedroom. The room where Melanie slept—and had sex with that fucking a-hole Andrew.

Irrational jealousy burned inside him at the view of the king-sized bed with its red and gold comforter and the stack of fluffy pillows.

Tear it to shreds. His inner gator knew what it wanted to do. It had no problem admitting jealousy, a jealousy he no longer had a right to.

Stepping farther into the room, he noted the open window. A slight breeze fluttered the curtains covering it.

As he heard an impatient Andrew finally coming to investigate for himself, Wes moved to the window and leaned out for a peek just as his boss entered the room.

"Did you find her?"

Looking out, he spotted Melanie perched atop the fence separating her yard from the next. His eyes met hers and locked for a moment.

I see you.

I hate you and will tear your guts out if you come near me, hers replied.

He almost grinned.

"No sign of her, boss," he said, holding her gaze. He gave her a slow wink. "Looks like she got away. Do you want me to go outside and see if I can pick up her trail?"

"No. We need to leave before her brother or one of his friends show up. She's not that important in the grand scheme of things."

Maybe not to Andrew, but in Wes's world, she still meant way too much.

And you let her get away.

Chapter 3

PERCHED ATOP THE FENCE, Melanie heard Wes lie to Andrew, and while it didn't forgive his many trespasses, she couldn't help but grudgingly thank him for it. His lie let her escape.

Maybe I'll kill him quickly instead of slowly.

As her feet hit the ground on the other side of the fence, she paused to listen.

Her ears perked as she heard Andrew tell Wes not to bother going after her. Good thing because, with the mood she was in, she might have gone looking for a sharp tool and turned Wes into a purse. Bloodthirsty?

Yes. And she felt no shame. Some people resorted to yoga when pissed. Others gorged on ice cream or hit the gym. When she felt particularly annoyed with Wes—which was every time she caught sight of him—she tended to hit Bayou Bite for deep-fried gator chunks. The un-evolved kind, of course, but that didn't stop her from wishing the juicy morsels in that yummy crunch belonged to Wes. *I'd love to bite him.*

Now if only the bite wasn't somewhere naughty below the belt as he held her hair and moaned encouragement.

Sigh.

So many years gone by and she still couldn't wipe those erotic memories from her mind.

A voice from behind almost made her squeak.

"Are you okay?"

Brother Daryl, here to keep an eye on her while she helped them with the plan.

Oh yes, they had a plan, a plan that had almost gone to hell because of a few factors they'd not imagined.

"Wes is in cahoots with Andrew."

With his lips pulled tight, Daryl uttered a low growl. "I fucking knew it. Knew there was no way he couldn't have seen anything more concrete about Bittech's involvement while he was working there."

"Yeah, well, he knows, and him showing up to act as a henchman almost screwed the plan. Andrew sent him after me."

"Fucking bastard! Good thing you were quick."

"He let me go." Even now, she still didn't get it. Why hadn't he come after her? Wes could have easily caught her, yet he'd winked and lied to Andrew. She didn't understand it, and the confusion about his actions annoyed her. "Did I stall them long enough for you to get the tracking device put onto the car?"

Daryl grinned, his white teeth gleaming in the darkness. "Fucking right I did. Now we sit back, watch, and see where they go."

Because watching was the whole purpose in leaving Melanie in her house. Given everyone now knew about the nefarious deeds Bittech was involved in, everyone wanted to know where they'd packed up and gone to. The new Bittech location needed to be found—and taken apart. The plan was to let Andrew lead them right to it.

"What are you guys gonna do when we find out where they've gone?"

That remained the question no one had an answer to. Usually, in the cases of shifters behaving badly, the Shifter High Council got involved. And, by involved, Melanie meant they usually terminated the misbehaving culprit. Keeping their secret at all costs was the prime rule they all lived by. Break that rule and pay the price.

But what happened when the ones breaking the rules did so at the behest of a corrupt SHC? What recourse was there when those elected to protect them were guilty? The knowledge that Parker, a councilman, was involved and spearheading the experiments on shifters threw them all for a loop. If they couldn't trust the SHC, then who did that leave to save them?

The dilemma plagued her as Daryl drove her back to her Aunt Cecilia's house. Since her aunt had gone west for a few weeks to visit her daughter, it was where Melanie had stashed the boys, along with her mom, to keep them out of harm's way. It still surprised her Andrew had come back to their house. When they'd hatched the plan, a part of her figured, if he was guilty, he'd just run.

He hadn't. Andrew had come looking for her and the boys. A good thing she'd sent them away ahead of time. She'd not expected things to get so crazy so quickly, nor for Andrew to have help. Even her ace in the hole, the gun, hadn't helped since it was loaded with blanks.

He knew this day would come. He'd proved more prepared than her.

It surprised her that Andrew seemed so interested in taking her and the boys with him. He'd never shown much of an interest in his progeny—achieved after several rounds of fertility at Bittech. Mixed shifter castes did not reproduce easily.

I don't care if he's their father. He's not getting his grubby paws on them. The boys would stay with her no matter what happened next with Andrew. She'd have to ask around for a good divorce lawyer.

We could save time and annoyance by simply killing him. Her feline didn't take to their mate's betrayal kindly.

The headlights on Daryl's car lit the small house at the end of the driveway. Not a big place, with weathered green siding, a front yard replete with gnomes and pink flamingoes. Aunt Cecilia loved bright colors and fanciful garden ornaments.

Through the windshield, Melanie could see the aluminum door at the front hanging drunkenly, the thicker wooden one wide open. More terrifying of all was the sight of her mother wailing on the step, a hand held to her head, blood streaking through her fingers.

The hair on Melanie's body hackled.

"Mama!" No sooner had the car skidded to a stop than both she and Daryl spilled out and ran to their mother. She couldn't help but smell the lingering trace of something reptilian. Her heart raced a mile a minute, and she couldn't stop a fluttery panic.

"What happened?" Daryl barked.

"I tried to stop it," her mother wailed. "But the monster thing batted me aside as if I were nothing. Then he licked me." A shudder went through her mother as she grimaced. "And I froze. I couldn't move a muscle as that monster took the bambinos."

"My boys? He took my boys?" Melanie's voice pitched as the horror of what happened hit.

"I am so sorry. I couldn't stop him. The lizard monster came and took them both."

It took everything Melanie had not to shriek. But she couldn't help grabbing her hair in two fists and pulling hard. She needed the pain to focus, anything to not think of what might happen to her precious babies.

Daryl knelt before their mother. "This creature, did he fly away with them? Run off? Do you know which way it went? Perhaps I can pick up its trail."

A shake of her head and their mother explained. "I don't think he did either. I heard an engine. Someone drove that thing here, and he took the bambinos." Fresh tears and wails shook her mother's body, and even though Melanie wanted to shake and curse and scream herself, instead, she wrapped the rotund body in her arms and rocked with her mothers. Tears streamed down her cheeks.

That bastard took my babies.

And she was going to get them back.

She just didn't know how. No one did.

Daryl put in a call to Caleb, who arrived soon after with Renny and Luke and his mother. Given Constantine was holed up in a motel recuperating from his rescue of Aria, they left him out of the loop.

No point in disturbing him until there was something they could do.

"Where did that monster take them?" Since Melanie had asked this question at least a dozen times, no one bothered to reply. Andrew, Wes, the lizard monster, everyone involved with Bittech had vanished without leaving a clue or trace.

The GPS tracker they'd thought would solve all their problems and lead them to Andrew, and all the other asshats involved in the Bittech madness, proved a bust. Somehow, Andrew, or Wes, had figured it out. When Daryl went speeding after it, Melanie balancing the tablet displaying a map and a blinking icon, they found the tracker less than a mile from town on the side of the road.

Seeing it there, along with Rory's teddy, brought to her lips a much-needed scream.

On her knees, she wailed to the sky. Screamed in rage. Fear. Anguish.

Yowled until her brother forced her to move.

So much for Daryl's plan. *My babies are lost.* And she didn't know how to find them.

After that failure, they'd returned to her mother's house. They talked in circles, but nothing, nothing goddammit, brought her babies back!

"I need some air," she mumbled, unable to listen to another word. They could tell her only so many times, "Don't worry. We'll find them," before she got an urge to scream again.

As she went to slip out the front door, her brother grabbed her arm. "You shouldn't go outside alone."

"Why not?" She uttered a mournful laugh. "Maybe if I'm out there, they'll come and take me, too. At least then I'd be with Rory and Tatum."

"We'll find them, sis. I promise."

Except this was one big-brother promise Daryl couldn't keep.

Melanie stepped out of her house, leaving Daryl, Cynthia, Caleb, and Renny to keep hashing out ideas. The moist air of the bayou filled her lungs, and she could have cried.

How she'd missed the smell of home, this home, the one she grew up in. Her cookie-cutter neighborhood, while nice, didn't have a familiar feel and welcoming vibe. She hated living in the 'burbs, even if she did have a three-bedroom house with two and a half baths—a sign, according to her mother, that she'd made it.

She'd have traded her gorgeous ensuite in a heartbeat for a happy marriage.

But at least I have my boys.

Missing boys. Sob.

She sat on the step and drew her knees to her chin. Hugging them, she rocked, the ache inside her hard to bear.

I failed them as a mother. She'd miscalculated so badly. She should have sent them farther. Should have gone with them.

Instead, because she'd misjudged the depravity of her husband, they were gone. But not dead. *Oh, please no.*

Surely she'd know if they'd left this plane of life. And if they had, she might just—

The phone in her back pocket buzzed. Odd for many reasons. One, it was well past midnight. Two, pretty much anyone who would call her this late was in the house at her back.

With shaking hands, she pulled the cell from her pants pocket and, upon seeing the caller ID, answered.

"You bastard, where are the boys?"

"Watch your mouth or you won't ever see them again," Andrew threatened.

"I'm sorry." The apology left a sour taste in her mouth.

"You should be. After all, you were the one who tried to hide them first. Just not very well."

"I want to see them."

"You will, but only if you follow my instructions to a tee. Starting with tell no one I've called."

She didn't, not until she'd managed to slip far away. Then she did a quick call, but only to say, "I've gone to find the boys."

The problem with walking eyes wide open into a trap was not knowing if she'd ever escape.

Chapter 4

WE SHOULD LEAVE.

His gator expressed his displeasure and had been doing so since they left Bitten Point. Wes couldn't blame him.

I wish I could go back in time. Change things so he wouldn't find himself here, in this place. Trapped in this nightmare.

Wes paced the room they'd given him at the new and supposedly improved Bittech Institute. Although calling it an institute sounded too nice. Try more like fucking torturous dungeon, only this time it sat above ground.

The new place wasn't even all that far from the original, but this new location had a hell of a lot more security, layers upon layers, and barracks for the employees working within.

No more wandering into town and flapping loose gums. No more curious residents asking questions.

Bye-bye, freedom.

Then again, Wes had lost his freedom the day he made his choice. *Do as we say, or else.*

The "or else" had made his decision a no-brainer. Still, though, the bitter pill proved hard to swallow.

A pack of smokes came out of his shirt pocket, and he tapped one out. He snagged the filtered tip with his lips as he yanked out a lighter. He paused as he caught a glimpse of a smoke detector on the wall and the sprinklers in the ceiling.

"Fuck." Stupid anti-smoking a-holes. Couldn't light a cigarette anywhere indoors these days without getting into trouble or causing thousands in water damage as automated fire systems engaged.

Stepping out of his room—if you could call the cell-like square a room with its double bed, desk, single chair and television—he headed along the bland gray corridor to the bright red Exit sign gleaming at the end. The hall on this third floor of the employee housing was quiet this time of the morning, unlike the previous eve when the guards and doctors, brought over to the new place, moved in.

The majority of the commotion died down around midnight, but Wes never did manage to fall asleep, not with the image of Melanie, betrayal shining in her eyes, reminding him of his douche-bag status.

I betrayed her.

His gator harrumphed. *You betrayed all of our own kind.*

And the worst part? He knew what people would say. *Not surprised at all he turned out to be a traitor. He is a Mercer after all.*

The stigma of his name followed him and, in this case, proved well deserved.

Stepping out of the compound, Wes noted in the distance the guards patrolling not only the entrance—which required identity cards and thumbprint swipes—but also those guarding the perimeter, not all of them human.

It seemed Bittech Institute wasn't trying very hard to hide anymore. Wes had to wonder how long before the outside world took note.

Hopefully it would take a while before an intrepid human drove the two miles down the long, winding drive to the new institute and noted the monsters roaming around. It didn't bear thinking what would happen if the world found out monsters lived among them.

The brisk dawn air hit him, and he inhaled deeply, filling his lungs, a man grasping at a freedom taunting him just out of reach.

The fresh, crisp air and wide-open sky teased Wes. It called him. *Leave this place. Swim free. Hunt for pleasure, not for others.*

Funny how that voice sounded an awful lot like his inner beast.

The freedom he'd lost chafed. The fresh air taunted him with—

The acrid smoke curled from the tip of the cigarette he lit, wiping away the torturous reminder of what he couldn't have. He pushed back against the insidious whispers telling him to escape.

If I leave, what will happen?

It didn't bear contemplating, and he wouldn't second-guess his choices now, not when he knew he'd make the same decision again.

Regret was for pussies. A real man made his bed, and he fucking slept in it, even if it was lined in nails, rusty ones.

Argh. He threw the cigarette, but its feathery weight worked against him. The lit butt caught in a gust of wind and flew back toward him.

Fucking hell. The discarded smoke hit the one rip in his jean-clad thigh and singed. He flicked it away, but the damage was done. A hint of red there and a dose of heat to sear the skin—*mmm, barbecue.*

Not funny, you sick bastard.

As Wes rebuked his inner gator, he slapped himself, only to hear a voice he never thought to hear again after last night.

"You're slapping the wrong part of your body. Why don't you stand up and I'll help you get the right spot?"

Melanie. *What is she doing here? I thought she escaped.*

He straightened, ignoring the taunting red cigarette glowing on the concrete patio that ran the perimeter of the building. "What the fuck are you doing here?"

"No hello for an old friend?" She arched a brow, the thin line of it truly evocative, especially when she angled a hip.

A petite five-foot-something, Melanie had curves, and a fiery attitude to match her wild, wavy hair. At times like these, when her irritation coursed unbound, Latina fire burned in her eyes and accented her words.

He shook his head. "How did they catch you?" And why wasn't he informed? Andrew kept him apprised of most of his moves, something Wes needed given his defined role as personal guard. He used to enjoy the position of head guard at Bittech until he'd been brought over to this new place. Over here, he'd hovered in limbo since some dick called Larry already seemed to be charged with keeping the place secure.

"What am I supposed to be doing?" he asked as Andrew handed him a box in his old office.

"Bringing this to my car."

"Not the box"—asshole—*"I mean at this new place. If that other dude is running shit, then what's my role?"*

"You'll do whatever I tell you or else."

Apparently do whatever Andrew said didn't include letting Wes in on his plans for his wife.

We could easily make her a widow, his sly gator reminded.

I'm thinking about it.

Melanie deserved better.

Like us.

No. Better as in someone who wasn't a dick.

As Melanie blasted him, most of it about him being a lying sack of shit that she wouldn't piss on if he caught fire, he caught words that froze him and made him interrupt her litany of his faults.

"Rewind. What do you mean Andrew kidnapped the boys?"

"Oh, please. Don't act so innocent," she snapped. "You guys made it pretty clear last night that you're chummy. Don't tell me you don't know."

He shook his head. "I haven't seen your boys. Are you sure Andrew has them?"

Brown eyes pinned him with disdain. "Know a lot of other guys with a flying lizard on staff?"

"Which lizard?"

"Does it matter?"

As a matter of fact, it did. "That bastard. I can't believe he'd stoop to scaring his kids like that."

"Then you don't know Andrew very well," she retorted.

"Are the boys all right?"

At this query, her angry composure wavered. Her eyes filled with moisture, and she bit her lip as soon as it began to tremble. "I don't know. I have no idea how they're doing. I spent most of the night awake getting driven in loops to lose anyone who might have followed."

"Who brought you?"

"I did, of course." From around the other side of the car, an older man appeared, dressed in a suit, hair impeccably cut.

Wes knew him. Most people did. His name was Parker, and he sat as a councilor on the SHC—crooked fucker if there ever was one—oh, and a Mercer. Parker's mother had married outside the family—contrary to popular belief in town that they'd interbred.

But a different last name couldn't dilute the fact that half of Parker's DNA remained pure, bad-to-the-bone Mercer.

"I wondered when I'd see you again, Uncle."

Melanie blinked. "Uncle? You're related? I thought I'd met all your uncles. At least those not doing time. This one is—"

"Respectable?" Wes sneered. "Only until you get to know him. Then you'll see he's just like the rest of our family."

Parker slapped a hand over his heart. "Such disdain. And for family, too. After everything I've done, I'd expect a little more gratitude."

"I'll show you gratitude. Anytime you like, you and me. No one else." The feral grin felt great.

Melanie frowned. "I'm beginning to feel like I'm in a soap opera."

"Isn't real life always a never-ending punch line?" Wes pushed away from the wall. "So where is she staying, Uncle?"

"What, aren't you going to automatically assume she'll be living with her husband?"

His lips tightened. Why did his uncle hold a taunting smirk on his lips? Had he guessed how he felt about Melanie? He'd tried very hard to hide it.

"Take me to my boys, this instant. They're the only reasons I caved to Andrew's blackmail. I want to see them now."

Distaste twisted Parker's lips. "Ah yes, the brats. I think I'll let Wes take you to them. I never could abide children. Noisy, messy things. Useless, too, until they're much older."

His uncle really deserved a smack, and Melanie seemed determined to deliver.

Wes grabbed a hold of Melanie's arms, holding her back lest she launch herself, claws extended, at Parker's face. Knowing his uncle, that wouldn't go over well.

As she snarled and thrashed, growling, "Let me at him," he asked, "Where are the twins?"

"Tell me now or I swear I will shred you to ribbons." Melanie just might, given she managed a curled lip and a snarl, a sound no human body should ever be able to make.

Parker seemed completely unruffled by the fact she'd eviscerate him in a heartbeat. "Top floor. The new nursery unit. They're the first ones to enjoy it. But we hope to change that very soon."

For a moment, Wes stood still as a rock, despite the fact that Melanie pulled and yanked, desperate to go find her kids. Wes couldn't move because Parker's ominous words hit him with the force of a sledgehammer.

The first...implying there would be more children, yet more innocents getting drawn into the sick game his uncle and the others played.

"You can't be serious," he finally managed to mutter.

"I am. And you will not question me. Now take the woman to her brats. I've other things to attend to." With that order, his uncle stalked away.

We should eat him, too.

Except his uncle, with his tough and stringy carcass, would probably give him indigestion.

"What are you waiting for?" Melanie said, snapping him out of his paralysis. "Take me to my boys."

"I'm waiting for you to not harp."

"I don't harp. I bitch. Loudly." She eyed him with tight lips. "So move or I'll take my ranting from mildly peeved to full-on she-bitch."

As he led the way to the building, a need to explain burned, trying to force its way past his lips. He clamped them tight. No, he wouldn't make excuses. Melanie deserved better than that.

Besides, real men didn't admit to making mistakes.

Neither did assholes.

The line between the two stretched very thin.

As they walked through the heavy metal reinforced doors that led into the research building, Melanie craned her head and let out a low whistle. "Look at the security in this place. Cameras, motion sensors, guards."

"Heat sensors, too. Also, all the doors and elevators in this place require not only a keycard but a thumbprint."

The interesting thing about the keycard was it remained clamped to a person at all times. They'd built it into the bracelets all the staff wore. Brandon, his brother, called them cuffs. But they were more than that. They were almost foolproof because they couldn't be passed along or copied. Cut the bracelet off, and as soon as it stopped touching living skin, it died—as did all that person's access.

Between that and the thumb scan, again from a living being, and the place proved impossible to navigate for any but approved personnel.

He explained that to her as they went through the security checkpoints.

"What if there's a fire or something and the electrical stops working? How would all these people get out?"

"They wouldn't."

Melanie wouldn't relent as he pressed his wrist against the

scanner and then his thumb. "Surely there's some kind of back door to escape. I mean you can't convince me that Andrew and the others would rather let everyone die than have an easy way to escape."

As he yanked her into a spot before the elevators, screened by a potted plant, he leaned down and hissed, "Stop being so fucking obvious that you're looking for escape. There are eyes and ears everywhere."

"I am just showing a healthy curiosity." Her guileless appearance didn't fool.

"If you're a cat burglar casing the joint," he retorted.

"You can't blame me for wanting to leave."

"No, I can't."

The ding let him know the elevator had arrived, and he stepped out of the blind pocket, face a rigid mask, bearing straight. Let no one see the turmoil inside him.

He stepped into the cab, Melanie at his side. The doors shut, and the swipe-press combination allowed him to choose the top floor, level nine. As he stepped out and noted the bright colors, and attempt at colorful murals, he wondered if they should just rename the floor "twisted nursery."

It truly was. He'd not actually visited this floor before, assuming more offices or labs graced this level. He rarely cared to visit those. He kept his interests in the lowers levels, where they housed the experiments.

The C-shaped desk proved the island of control for a matronly woman, late fifties, her face florid, with hair scraped back in a tight bun. She wore scrubs with happy, smiling elephants, probably to counteract the scowl on her face.

"You aren't authorized for this level," said the nurse.

"I am, and so is she. This is Mrs. Killinger, the boss's wife. We understand you've got her boys here."

The flat lips of the nurse disappeared entirely in disapproval. "Indeed they are. Absolute hellions. Nothing like their father. They must have gotten the wrong side of the DNA coin toss."

The snide remark hit Melanie, but to his surprise, she didn't fly into a rage. Maturity from the firecracker he knew?

Melanie kept her eyes demurely downcast. "My boys can be a handful. If you could take me to them, I'm sure they'll calm down once they see me."

The harrumph eloquently said that Nurse Bitch didn't think so.

Since Wes had yet to release his hold on Melanie, he found himself going along, each step more horrifying for the bright flowers painted on the walls, the glimpse in rooms with glass doors, the tiny beds, empty and waiting. Too many beds. The sight of the cribs made him stumble. Melanie pulled from his grasp, face stony as she followed the nurse. He trailed more slowly.

The nurse stopped before a solid partition that required a card slide, thumbprint, and a code.

"Don't bother memorizing it," Nurse Bitch snapped as Melanie showed too much interest. "It changes every shift."

With a click, the door opened, and the nurse stepped in. Several things happened at once. Something dropped from above the door onto the nurse, something lunged at her from the floor, and amidst the screaming—lots of it comparing the twins to satanic imps escaped from hell—Melanie laughed.

"There's my good boys. Come see Mama."

Chapter 5

ONLY WHEN MELANIE HUGGED THE TWINS' small, wiry bodies did the fluttery panic, barely held at bay, subside.

My babies are okay.

They were prisoners to a sick bastard, but unharmed in body and definitely not cowed by the rabid nurse practically foaming at the mouth as she screamed, "You rotten little bastards. I don't care who your father is. You're in my domain now."

The nurse lifted a hand, but before she could use it—or lose it because Melanie would tear it off if she tried to hit her boys—Wes caught it.

"I really wouldn't do that if I were you."

The nurse tightened her lips. "I know who you are. You're Mr. Killinger's pet gator. You don't scare me."

Wes leaned close until they were almost nose to nose before he nicely, too nicely, said, "I should, seeing as how I'm hungry, annoyed, and your antics are reminding me why being a vegetarian is overrated."

"Your kind don't eat humans." Despite her claim, the nurse pulled at the iron grip Wes had on her wrist.

"*My kind* eats whatever the fuck it wants, and we know how to not leave a trace behind. So, *human*"—amazing the amount of sneering he could infuse in a single word— "care to piss me off further? Go on. With the mood I'm in, it won't take much to make me snap." To emphasize his point, he noisily clacked his teeth.

The nurse wisely took a step back. A shame, because Melanie was also in a mood and wouldn't have minded seeing the bitch taken down a few more notches.

No one threatens my family. Rowr.

Head held at a haughty angle, the nurse practically spat, "Mr. Killinger and Mr. Parker will be hearing about your behavior."

"Go ahead. Do it. Tattle on me. We'll see who's more valuable to them." He winked. "I already know, so I'll bring the hot sauce for later."

"Arrrrgh." The screech of outrage lingered long after the sound of the nasty nurse's steps disappeared.

Tension eased out of Melanie, and she peeked at Wes over the heads of her boys. "Thank you."

He scowled. "Don't you dare thank me. If I hadn't put her in her place, you would have."

"And probably not as nicely." Years of trying to act the perfect mother and wife had taken their toll. Melanie could feel her Latin temper—and her inner feline—wanting to snap.

"That woman is vile and shouldn't be around people, let alone children."

Taking her gaze from Wes, despite the temptation to truly drink him in, she focused on her boys. She held them out at arm's length. "Let me see you. How are you both looking?"

She twisted them this way and that, relieved at their matching eye rolls and muttered, "We're fine, Mama."

"I'll be the judge of that," she muttered because she was most definitely not.

How had her boring, cookie-cutter life gone from wake up and feed the kids breakfast before school to trying to shoot her mad scientist asshat of a husband who'd kidnapped her boys and was keeping them prisoner in what amounted to a guinea pig lab?

Since she saw no signs of injury, she lightened the moment by tickling their underarms, netting shrill giggles and shrieks. When they gasped for breath, she hugged them close again, breathing in their little-boy scent.

"Mama," said Rory, his face tucked into her shoulder, "we wanna go home. We don't like it here."

"Daddy came and said we had to be good for the lady. But I don't like her." The huffy words were spoken with a glare aimed at the empty hall.

"Never fear, I will get us out of here." Too late she remembered Wes still stood watching. Her words didn't go unchallenged.

"Don't do anything foolish. The security is absolutely stupid around here. You can't go two steps without someone knowing."

"Doing nothing would be stupider. I won't let anyone touch my boys." Vehemently said. She'd die first.

"No one's touching them. Or you."

She blinked and almost asked Wes to repeat, except he was still talking.

"Just hang tight while I work some things out."

"You want me to wait while you work some things out?" She made a face. "As if I believe you. Two minutes ago, you said there were eyes and ears everywhere. Now you want me to believe you're colluding with me to escape?"

"I wasn't lying when I said that, but I think we're safe at the moment. Look."

At his pointed finger, she turned and peeked. Then laughed.

In one corner of the large playroom, the suspended camera sported a big ball of playdough around it while, at the other end, it hung from the ceiling in a dangling mess of wires.

"Did you guys do this?" she asked her twins in a mock-stern voice.

"Not me." The identical grins brought a giggle to her lips despite the dire situation.

"There's my smart boys."

"Very smart, just like their mom. So, let me say again, I will help you. Sit tight at least for a day or two and let me figure out a way for you to escape."

"With my boys."

"Yes, with your boys."

Wes left—with a swagger she forced herself to ignore.

Why ignore? her feline wondered. Her panther had a point. The man had a nice posterior. Very nibble worthy.

But the idea of leaving teeth marks on those sweet cheeks was distracting her from the true issue, which was, should she listen to Wes and see if he could help them? *I don't know if we can afford to wait a few days.*

It didn't take a genius to see this playroom contained elements out of the ordinary, starting with a large-framed mirror she'd wager was a one-way window. People observing the kids at play, creepy, but not as creepy as the restraining straps under the tiny seats situated around tables bolted to the floor. Bars covered the windows while vents that had nothing to do with air circulation projected from the floor, the lingering scent of gas, the same kind her dentist used to knock her out, showing they'd recently tested it. *Why on earth would they need to gas children?*

And why were her boys here?

It horrified her to realize Andrew, their bloody father, had sent their boys to a lab, one with toys and games, but still another place they were doing testing. On children.

On fucking children! Snarl.

It made her stomach ill. It made her inner feline pace with bristled fur. But she couldn't let her agitation show. Mustn't let the boys sense there was something amiss, even if they already suspected.

Melanie stroked Tatum's hair back from his forehead, listening to him as he recounted a story from a picture book he'd found. Much as it chilled her, she couldn't help but wonder if it was already too late. Did some strange chemical cocktail already run through their blood?

The afternoon passed quickly and quietly. The rude nurse she'd met never reappeared. As lunchtime rolled around, a slot opened in the wall and a shelf extended with three covered trays. Sandwiches, milk, and fruit.

She sniffed them thoroughly and tasted them first, too, before she'd let her boys take a bite. Starvation wouldn't keep them strong.

Sporadically, she attempted to open the door to the room, only to find it locked each and every time. It had swung shut after Wes left, and no amount of prying, slamming, or knocking opened it.

Dinnertime arrived, and once again, food appeared, this time a meat pie with mashed potatoes and veggies. It all smelled and tasted fine, but she barely managed more than a few bites, her knotted stomach making it almost impossible to eat.

She began to wonder how long they'd have to stay here. Alone.

No one came to see them. Not Andrew. Not Wes. Not anyone.

As night fell, the sky outside the barred window darkened. She began to wonder if they'd have to sleep on the chilly tile floor.

When the door suddenly opened, she startled, and her boys, sensing her sharp spike of adrenaline and fear, tensed.

"It is time for the boys to rest." A new nurse, prim and stoic in her blue scrubs, stood in the portal. She held out her hands. "Come with me, please."

Tatum and Rory clung tight to Melanie instead. "Not going."

"Staying with Mama."

Melanie did nothing to discourage their instinct, especially since she felt the same way. As their mother, she didn't mind the weight of them sitting on and wrapped around her. That weight meant they were with her and safe.

Just try and touch them, lady.

She glared at the woman who thought she'd separate Melanie from her babies. Bared some teeth when it looked as if the nurse might lunge and try to grab one.

"What's going on here? Where is Mrs. Killinger?"

Hope fluttered in her chest. It was Wes. He'd come back.

Attention turned away from inside the room, the nurse replied, "She's in here and refusing to cooperate. I know Mr. Killinger said to use whatever force I deemed necessary, but I don't want to hurt the boys' mother in front of them. I doubt they'd be cooperative after that."

"You think?" Wes couldn't hide his disdain. "Let me handle this."

"Go ahead. Just don't hurt the subjects. They've got tests to run in the morning."

Tests? The blood in Melanie's veins froze, and she wondered if her face appeared as stricken as she felt. The wide frame of Wes, still wearing his ripped jeans from the morning, filled the doorway.

She couldn't help but whisper, "Wes, what does she mean about tests?"

"We shouldn't talk in front of little ears."

"Why not?" asked Rory.

Tugging at his lobes, Tatum frowned. "My ears aren't little."

She hugged them tightly. "I'm not leaving them."

"You're going to have to for just a little while. They aren't going to get hurt. You heard the broad. They need them." Did she imagine the curl of his lips as he repeated the nurse's words?

She kept them close as she struggled to stand. The boys had gotten so big, their bodies sturdy, and heavy. A hand under her elbow helped her get to her feet.

"Let me have one."

"No." She squeezed them closer, but Rory leaned out, arms outstretched to Wes, and said, "Carry me. On your shoulders like Luke's daddy does."

She could only blink in surprise as her son willingly went to Wes. And she blinked again as her son sat atop his shoulders.

It looked so...right? She closed her eyes and gave herself a mental shake. *Don't be casting Wes into some pathetic hero mold. And don't even start thinking about using him as a new daddy.* Even if he'd just done more in that one second of grabbing her son than Andrew had, ever.

Andrew rarely touched their boys. Very rarely. In public was about the only time the boys got away with interacting with him at all, mostly because Andrew couldn't avoid it. He cared more about the appearance of being a good father than actually trying to be one. In light of his standoffish view on parenting, she'd found it surprising he'd been talking to her about trying for another child. Looking around this place, she really wondered at his motive.

Melanie tucked her son close as she followed Wes's long stride down the hall. During the day, bright recessed lighting in the ceiling made the trek light and colorful. In the dimmer evening illumination, the flowers loomed with shadows, ominous dark spaces that implied something more evil lurked.

Not such a friendly place now.

Tucking Tatum's head close, she quickened her pace to reach the open door spilling light onto the checkered tile. She followed Wes into the bedroom. If you could call a barrack-like space with six bunk beds a bedroom.

How regimented, almost military like.

There were a few subtle differences, though. The frames of the bunks appeared of modern cappuccino-colored wood. The sheets gleamed white while fluffy comforters sporting more cheerful colors and smiling animal visages kept the feel of prisoner at bay. Barely.

A room obviously made for children, and yet, as she twirled around, she couldn't help but realize this room was meant to keep the kids locked away from everyone, including parents.

Whose kids?

Looking at her boys scrambling onto a bunk bed sporting matching comforters with ravenous dinosaurs, her heart seized.

Dear God, that bastard truly is going to experiment on his own children.

She wished she could say she harbored some hope when it came to Andrew. Some remote hope he wasn't that sick of a bastard. A foolish hope. Fathers didn't, for any fucking reason, put their kids in barracks under lock and key.

"And you condone this," she whispered.

She couldn't help but look at Wes, pained anew by his handsomeness, which obviously hid a core of bad she'd never seen before.

Funny how Wes being capable of true evil bothered her more than Andrew.

It seemed to bother Wes, too. He stood still as granite, his face a stony mask as he looked around. "I would never condone this. Never anything with children. There are some lines even I won't cross." The last words uttered at a camera in the corner of the room, a red eye blinking showing it recorded.

How she wished she could believe what Wes said. Wished she could believe the anguish in his eyes.

He's already deceived me more than once. She'd need more than words and big gator eyes to sway her into trusting him again.

"I can't leave them here," Melanie murmured, trying hard to hold in her tears. She wanted to be strong, dammit. She usually was. Anyone who knew her described her as a bomb ready to go off.

That's me. TNT. She went off on everyone except Andrew, which would probably surprise most folks. People said you fought hardest with those you loved.

Did the fact that she'd never found it in her to lambast a man who just took it and said sorry mean she didn't love Andrew?

She'd fought often with Wes.

But she'd stayed with Andrew. She bit her lip instead of tearing Andrew a new one every time he pulled away from her and the boys, especially lately as his mood had begun to swing more erratically. She couldn't help but notice the differences in her husband.

The change in his smell...her inner kitty slyly added.

Ah, yes, his scent. An intrinsic part of any person. The bouquet Andrew once bore had changed, gone from an earthy musk mixed with damp fur and a feel of the woods to something slightly off kilter, and if truly pressed for an answer, she would have said alien.

He's not the man he once was. Hell, Andrew had never become the man she'd hope he'd be.

Perhaps she had an unrealistic ideal. *Maybe the man I want doesn't exist.* After all, Wes couldn't seem to handle her needs either. *Am I the problem here?*

Foolish thoughts that didn't detract from the fact that her husband was seriously whacked.

And her babies were threatened.

"Get into bed, boys. Mama will tuck you in, and then I have to pop out for a little bit."

"No. Stay with us." Tatum's lower lip trembled.

"It won't be long. You'll be safe here." The lie almost stuck to her tongue. "I'm going to talk to Daddy and find out some stuff. I'll be right back."

Do I ever want to talk to him? Wes was right about one thing. Running off half-cocked wouldn't achieve anything. It certainly wouldn't help her boys, and they were her number one priority.

Tucking the blanket just below the chins on her angels, she shivered with the righteous fury of a mother whose cubs were threatened.

If Andrew or anyone else hurts my babies, I will kill them.

Rowr.

Chapter 6

I'M GOING to have to kill Andrew.

Good. Crunch his bones. A great solution from his gator side that never liked the pompous prick.

Andrew never hid the fact he thought himself better than Wes. In his eyes, Wes was just a dumb, fucking Mercer.

A dumb, fucking Mercer that so wanted to slam his fist into the smug smirk on Andrew's face.

"Where are we going?" Melanie asked as he escorted her from the boys' room to the elevator.

"To Andrew. He asked to see you."

"Asked to see me?" She uttered a bitter laugh. "If he wanted to see me, then maybe he should have marched his lazy ass over to the prison block he's keeping our children in."

With a twitch of his finger, Wes brought her attention to the camera in the corner.

Melanie pivoted and, with a slow smile, raised not one but two middle fingers in a salute. "I hope Andrew is watching. I hope anybody watching knows what assholes they are to be working here."

"So much for the façade of genteel lady."

"You should know by now that I might fake it, but I'll be never a lady."

The door slid open, and they stepped forth, but he waited for the pair of white-coated doctors who were babbling as they passed into the open cab before he dipped his head to whisper, "You never faked it with me."

He didn't dare pause to see her expression. He walked away wondering if she'd retort.

No, but she did reply. Her sharp kick at the back of his knee caught him off guard. He stumbled.

A laugh rumbled from him. "Still playing dirty."

"Taking advantage of your weaknesses is not dirty. It's insightful. Don't forget I know a lot of your secrets, Wes Mercer, and I will use them against you."

Good thing she didn't know his biggest secret of all.

I never got over her. Probably never would. She was the one good thing in his life. The one thing not tainted by the Mercer name. And he'd let her go.

Because she deserved better than me. She still did, but had he known she'd settle for a shithead like Andrew, then maybe he would have stuck around because he certainly wouldn't have treated her so badly. And he would have loved any kids they had. *I'd certainly never let them be brought to a place like this*.

I wish things could have turned out different. He wished he'd made different choices.

Such as now, for example. Andrew had called him and said, "Bring me my wife," and Wes practically clicked his heels and ran to do his bidding.

He should note, however, that his haste owed less to the order and more to the anticipation of seeing Melanie again. It was bloody emasculating how a glimpse of her could brighten his day, even when she kept scowling at him.

A mate should have strength.

She's not our mate.

Yet.

Never. Because he didn't deserve her.

"How many buildings are in this compound?"

"About a half-dozen. Four of them are quarters for the staff. Another one, the two-story one, over there"—he pointed—"houses a gym facility, recreation rooms, and a variety store where you can also special order items."

"It's a prison," she observed.

"Yes." No point in denying it.

Noticing she didn't keep pace with him, he turned. She eyed him, her brow knit in question.

"You know this is a glorified prison, and yet, you seem content with it."

He rolled his shoulders. "Not so much content as resigned. I have to be here."

"Pays that good, does he?" The words daggered him with bitterness and a dose of repugnance.

"I'm not here for the money."

"Then why are you here? The guy I knew might sometimes skirt the edge of the law, but he would never be involved in something like this."

"I'm a Mercer. We're capable of anything."

"Don't you give me that line of bull. I know you and your brother Brandon at least were trying to change your reputation. To break the chain."

"Bad genes always win."

"Only if you give up."

He didn't reply. Instead, he swiped them into another building. "This is the C residence. Andrew has the entire top floor to himself." Unlike the hired lackeys, those in charge wanted for nothing.

"What about your uncle?"

"His penthouse suite is in the A building while Andrew's father is in B. The floors below them are designated to scientists, staff, and guards."

"Everyone in one place. How convenient."

More like inconvenient. Having that many people grouped meant eyes and ears everywhere on top of the cameras watching. Melanie didn't quite grasp just how under the microscope they were. She needed to stop airing her views aloud.

As soon as the elevator doors whooshed open, he yanked her in. Quick scans and a jab of his finger shut the doors, and as soon as they did, he said in a low voice. "There're no cameras in here. And before you ask, I have no idea why. I need you to listen. You can't keep ranting about Andrew and the others."

"Why not? I'm pissed, and I don't care who knows it."

"Well you should care, especially if you intend to be around for your boys."

"Is that a threat?" Her eyes sparked, and he could see the wild cat pacing behind her gaze.

"No, it's a warning. People who talk have a tendency of going missing."

"Like your brother?"

"Exactly like my brother. And others. How do you think they choose those they experiment on? Trust me when I say you don't want to become one of them."

Her lip curled. "So what are you suggesting? That I become the perfect Stepford wife?"

A snort escaped him. "As if Andrew would believe that. No, but I am saying you need to act cool. There is some strange shit going on, and when I say strange, I'm talking even more fucked up than usual. I want to help you escape. You and the boys. You don't deserve to be caught in this mess."

"No one deserves this."

The elevator jolted to a stop, but before the doors could open, he hit another floor, and it started moving again.

"I agree no one deserves the shit Bittech has put them through, but for some, it's too late."

"Is it too late for you? Are you one of their experiments?"

"Not yet, but only because they like their specimens healthy. Apparently a two-pack-a-day habit makes me ineligible. What a shame." His grin was a tad toothy, but it did bring a reluctant answering grin to her lips.

"I knew there had to be a reason for your nasty habit. So let's say I believe you when you say you're going to help me, what next?"

"You're going to have to pretend, probably for a few days—"

She interrupted. "We don't have a few days. You heard what that nurse said. They're starting on the boys tomorrow."

"Those are just the prelims. Height, weight, blood work, etc. We have time before they start."

"You've seen this before."

Wes couldn't reply as the elevator stopped. It opened and someone came on board. He and Melanie stood in silence as they went to a different floor. The stranger, with only a curious glance their way, exited.

Alone again, Wes pressed the button for the top floor. "I don't have time to explain everything. We can't stall any longer or Andrew will get suspicious. Remember what I said. Stay cool."

"I'll try."

And that was all he could truly ask for. With her cubs in danger, Melanie was a mother ready to do anything to protect. He just hoped it didn't land her locked up in the lower levels.

If it does, though, I'll find a way to bust her out.

Crunch some bones. His gator didn't mind indulging in a little violence for a good cause.

The elevator opened onto a square vestibule with a reinforced steel door facing them.

No one had access to it but Andrew. Wes put his hand on the scanner embedded in the wall, and when a female voice prompted, "Identify yourself," he said, "I brought your wife."

Not his! Snap. His inner gator couldn't help but crack its jaw at saying the word.

Andrew didn't deserve Melanie.

But neither do I.

There were clicks and the hiss of air as the door unsealed and slid sideways. Wes prodded Melanie in the back, sensing her trepidation. She straightened her shoulders as soon as she realized he'd noted her sign of weakness. Melanie always did have a strong spirit—and even stronger passion.

Remember how tight she used to hold us when we sank inside?

Nothing he did allowed him to forget. But he'd tried. Just ask his local liquor store.

Into her husband's lair Melanie stepped, the flip-flops on her feet a striking contrast to the beige Travertine stone floors. When it came to his suite, Andrew spared no luxury.

"About time you arrived, my lazy pet," Andrew called from farther inside. "I was about to send the hunters to look for you."

The hunters? A little extreme—and worrisome. Those savage creatures were more likely to rip apart their target than bring them back.

"I was tucking the boys into bed." Melanie spoke in his defense.

It irked. Wes could defend himself.

Really? Because you look like a lackey who takes shit.

And his gator looked like a pair of boots waiting to be made. The reminder of who he used to be didn't help him accept his situation, a form of slavery that involved gritting his teeth when Andrew said, "Good gator, fetching my wife. It's nice to see it's not just dogs that can learn tricks. And people said a Mercer couldn't be trained. Too dumb, they claimed. All that inbreeding, you know."

Out of habit, Wes clamped his lips tight. But Melanie didn't know Andrew did this on a regular basis, taunted him constantly in the hope of making him snap.

Hands planted on her hips, Melanie wouldn't let it slide. "Leave Wes and his family alone. He did what you asked. No need to insult him."

Andrew stood from his chair, and Wes recognized the glint in his eye, the mad one that appeared more and more frequently. "Are you defending him? Do you still have feelings for your high school sweetheart, dear wife?"

"Of course not. You should know me well enough by now to know I won't listen to you degrade someone. What surprises me is the fact I even have to say this to you. You never used to treat people this way."

"Perhaps I got tired of the so-called stronger predators treating me as if I was inferior." Andrew's lip curled in a sneer. "Now I am the one with all the power, and it's time to pay them back for some of their taunts."

Some people never got over the hierarchy from school. As a bit of a nerd, a rich one with a snooty attitude, Andrew tended to get shoved into a fair number of lockers. Wes knew he'd done it a time or two. Maybe more. Stolen Andrew's lunch, too, every Wednesday. That was roast beef sandwich day. Wes enjoyed every bite of that juicy meat on the fresh Kaiser layered with provolone cheese, a touch of mustard, and lettuce.

Wes leaned against the wall by the elevator, prepared to listen to Andrew's spiel about how mean people were.

"Don't bother getting comfortable, gator. The wife and I are going to have a chat. *Alone*. You may leave. I'll contact you when I need you again."

Bite his fucking face off.

His gator didn't like Andrew's attitude, and neither did he. But he also hated more the idea of leaving Melanie alone with the prick. His fists clenched at his sides. How he longed to lunge at the man —*bite his head off*. The crunch would sound so good. Yet, it would achieve nothing.

It would make me feel much better. His gator had no doubt.

We can't eat him. Not yet, not while Andrew and Uncle Parker held all the cards.

It irked another had that kind of power over him. Even worse, the guy with the power showed signs of madness, a side effect of the drugs he'd helped create and then imbibed.

Everything came at a cost. Andrew had gained great strength from the drugs he took, but he'd lost something else. All his marbles. Only a few seemed left rolling around. Anyone could see the growing madness in his eyes.

But Wes couldn't do anything about it yet.

We mustn't leave the female with him.

What if Andrew tried to hurt Melanie?

Chomp him if he dares!

And what of the others he had to also protect?

As if sensing his dilemma, she cast a glance over her shoulder. She didn't speak aloud, but her eyes said, "Go," and she mouthed, *I'll be fine.*

"Is there a problem?" Andrew asked.

Yeah. The fact that Andrew still breathed. He tamped down those words and instead forced out, "No problem, boss. I'm going to have a smoke, so if you need me, I won't be far."

A leer stretched Andrew's features. "Don't come running if you hear screams. The wife is a noisy thing."

I know, you fucking prick. He couldn't fucking forget. And the bastard poked at the memory wound.

Because he's a prick. Prick. Prick. The word repeated itself over and over as Wes stalked from Andrew's apartment and back into the elevator. His anger ran higher than usual after a session with his boss.

No denying the guy deserved an award for his extreme asshole persona, but Andrew deserved to die the most for having the legal right to be with Melanie every day.

I would give anything to be in his shoes and sleep beside her.

Sleep? his gator grunted. *A true bull does better things than just sleep beside his female.*

A smart male would do such dirty things to Melanie... Dirty, sweaty, fun things.

Things only Andrew could do! *Snap.*

But didn't. The loser.

Wes didn't understand it. How could Andrew have a woman like her, a freaking amazing spitfire of a woman, and not treat her like a queen? Andrew should worship her. Instead, he treated Melanie like shit.

We should go back for a chat. Just open our mouth and—

No eating him until I know I can get everyone out safe.

He wouldn't abandon anyone to this fate. And, no, that didn't make him a fucking hero. Perish the thought. Wes just didn't like assholes, which might explain why there were days he didn't like himself.

It killed him to leave her behind, killed him knowing that Melanie had to deal with Andrew alone, but he couldn't tip his hand too soon.

I need a cigarette. Instead of going down to the lobby, he jabbed a button to go one level down.

His keycard and thumb allowed him to open the door at the end of the hall and take the sturdy metal stairs two at a time. Then three.

Within him, a wildness burned and churned. Restlessness tore at him. Break out. Get free. Can't.

Fuck.

He slammed into the bar for the outer door and burst out onto the rooftop. He stopped dead in the crisp evening air, arms spread wide, head tilted. He sucked in a deep breath, trying to tame the wildness.

Need to find a quiet fucking place in my mind. He needed to calm himself. Concentrate on something else.

The dark sky greeted him, along with a roof deck that, while spotted with structures for venting, offered a lot of open space. In an attempt to remain green, they'd actually laid grass down, soft and downy. In an effort to save it from nasty smokers, at the far end, they'd built a gazebo, with benches bolted under it and ashtrays.

Best of all, it was far from cameras. Far from the door he wanted to barrel back through. He wanted to go back and take Melanie from Andrew. And kill the man if he stood in his way. Instead, a long stride brought him to the other end of the roof deck.

A hard jolt as he hit the bench made it creak. Nothing like some rude furniture to remind a guy he would never be a lightweight.

The cigarette emerged from his pocket, and in a moment, his lighter ignited with a dancing flame. He put the cigarette between his lips, clamping the fresh paper covering the filter. He sucked in, tugging air through the tip. A rush of warm smoke flowed into him, and his eyes closed as his head tilted back.

That's the rush I needed.

Non-smokers never understood the appeal. *All you're doing is inhaling smoke. Big deal*, they said. The health effects weren't worth it. All true, and yet, he'd admit to a certain guilty euphoria every time he lit one. He knew smoking was bad for him. Knew he shouldn't do it. But he did it anyway.

He sucked in that smoke, held it for a second, and exhaled. In and out, the relaxing mantra—a huge part of smoking relaxed him. Tension eased from his stiff frame, and for a moment, he didn't feel as if he'd explode.

Then his brother Brandon, who'd arrived with his usual stealth, spoke. "Tough day at the office?"

He cocked open an eye. "Aren't they all? This not smelling thing is really freaking me out. Are you wearing that damned cologne they're testing again?"

"Eau de nothing? Yeah. They've got it working, as you noticed, but it doesn't last more than a few hours. They're trying to extend it."

"That's not the only thing they're doing," Wes muttered. "Did you know they were moving on to testing with kids?"

Not a single twitch of surprise on his brother's face. "Did Uncle finally tell you?"

"He didn't have to. I saw it for myself. Why the fuck didn't you tell me?"

"This is the first chance we've had to talk since your arrival."

"Things have gotten so fucked up."

Brandon snorted. "As if they weren't already."

"Oh yeah, well, get this. Andrew's got his own kids living on the top floor of the lab in that weird freaking nursery he's got going. His kids, for fuck's sake."

"I'd hoped they would escape." Brandon sighed, and there was a leathery rustle as he shifted in the shadows. "Andrew is toppling into the abyss of madness. I think our uncle is, too."

Toppling? More like already ankle deep in shit in it. "How's your mind doing?" Wes asked.

A wry grin pulled at Brandon's face, crinkling it. "I'm mostly in control of it now, but it's a battle. There's a new voice in my head, and he's a cold fucking bastard. So don't forget your promise to me."

As if Wes could considering how Brandon had begged. *If I go mad, you have to kill me before I cause harm.*

The things a man had to promise family. Wes looked down rather than at his little brother, a prisoner of Bittech because of what they'd done to him.

"I remember what I said. No need to remind me." Because he hoped to never have to do it. "Unless you're trying to tell me something. Is this your way of saying you need a tail-whooping?"

"Anytime, big brother, anytime."

Neither of them moved, the ritual of words an old one. Wes ground out the cigarette in the mounted ashtray and immediately lit another.

"Those things aren't good for you," Brandon said.

"I know. The damned nicotine keeps showing in my urine tests, and I keep my job. Bernie, on the other hand, along with Judd, they weren't so lucky. None of the other shifter guards have had any luck recently. They're all gone. Is it me, or are the guards they're using all human mercenaries for hire now?"

"Saw that, too, did you? I didn't clue in until we got here. The missing shifter guards are being held in the new holding facility."

A polite term for they were the newest Bittech test subjects. "What floor are they keeping them on?" Wes asked, the smoke highlighting his words.

"Below ground. And highly secured. I thought for sure after what happened to Merrill I'd wake up in there."

"But?" Wes pushed, knowing the cameras didn't extend this far from the stairwell.

Brandon rolled his wide shoulders. "But what? I guess when they found me passed out on the ground they figured I was a victim. No one has said anything about suspecting I helped those others escape or that I turned on Merrill."

"So you're in the clear."

"I guess. For now."

"I think if they suspected, we wouldn't be talking now. And who's left to betray you?" No one, and it was hard for dead bodies to talk. See, Brandon had tried his best to aid some of the captives in fleeing their prison. Key word being tried.

All of the attempts had failed but for one. The only escapee who'd made it out successfully had been Aria, and as soon as she did speak, Bittech shut down and relocated.

"At least that prick Merrill is finally dead," Brandon announced with a bit of glee.

About time, too. He was another guy who'd taken the Bittech cocktail and found himself with a few loose screws.

"Way I heard it, Constantine got a little peeved when they took his girl from him." And snapped Merrill's neck like a twig.

I can't think of a more deserving punishment.

"The man is a beast."

No, Constantine was a python with a penchant for hugs. Constantine was also one of the good guys. "And off-limits. We're damned as it is. Let's not start adding the death of decent folk to it."

"I don't hurt my friends," Brandon hissed, in better control these days of his rolling S problem. "I'm not fucking crazy."

"Yet."

"Yet. So don't piss me off, or you'll be first on my shit list."

"What do you mean first, you prick? Shouldn't that slot be reserved for Andrew? Or our dear uncle?"

"They've only tortured me for a few years. You, on the other hand, started the day I was born." Brandon smiled, not the human smile he was born with.

"You needed it. I toughened you up. It's a fucked-up world out there. You gotta be strong to survive it."

"Some days I'd rather just say screw it."

"Never give up, brother. Never give up."

Because, if a man couldn't believe in redemption, then what was the point of living?

Chapter 7

WITH WES GONE, Melanie found herself alone with Andrew, suffering a trepidation she'd never felt before around her husband. She couldn't help but recall his new strength. Would he use it against her?

If he tries, we'll claw him good.

Except, she still couldn't seem to manage to draw out her cat.

A cat that now sulked at the reminder she was stuck.

"Alone at last," Andrew announced with all too much glee. His smile too wide. His teeth too many.

To distract herself from Andrew, and his oddly frightening expression, she glanced around the space. There was certainly a lot of it, and richly appointed, too.

Hardwood floors gleamed from one end to the other, covered in thick shag rugs in varying shades of gray. Strategically placed modern furniture with lots of glass, chrome, and odd art pieces defined the various areas.

A massive bed, which made her stomach roil, took up one entire corner. Across from it sat a matching leather couch and club seat arrangement in front of a huge television screen. Look at that. It sported a game console underneath, but she'd bet it wasn't there for the boys.

As she kept pivoting to take in details, she couldn't help but see her husband, a husband who looked markedly different. For one, his face appeared bare. Without his glasses, Andrew's eyes looked small. Sly. He held himself a tad straighter in his comfortable name-brand athletic pants and matching shirt. No off-the-rack bargain items for him. He was very finicky that way.

Realizing he was the center of her regard, Andrew swept an arm. "Welcome, dear wife, to your new home."

She shook her head. "I had a home. A nice one that I decorated myself. You know, the one with a room for the boys." Funny how she used to hate the cookie-cutter neighborhood with its bland sameness, but now missed it something terrible. That house represented normalcy. This place however? While large, it definitely was not designed to be kid, or even wife, friendly. For all intents and purpose, it appeared as a bachelor pad.

The realization worried. She got the impression Andrew had this place tailor-made. If that were the case, then the omissions for his family were intentional, and it meant Andrew no longer felt a need to maintain a pretense of being a family man. She didn't know what else to conclude because, otherwise, he would have included in the design quarters with an extra bedroom for the kids.

The fact that he never intended to have the boys live here bothered her, and it also brought another realization to the forefront.

If he's willing to abandon his children, then what will he do to me?

Tread carefully. This one is dangerous.

She didn't need her feline's warning to recognize the potential for ugliness in her current situation. She wasn't dealing with the man she'd married. This new pacing Andrew exuded a weird kind of energy. She could almost see it humming inside him, practically bursting to get out.

The cracked mirror on a far wall made her wonder if his control had slipped already.

He's going mad.

And Wes left her alone to deal with it.

Some might say give the guy some slack. He'd dropped her off to see her asshat of a husband. She said no way. Real men didn't deliver a woman to someone with a mad glint in their eye.

Then again, lily-kneed husbands didn't usually turn into borderline lunatics.

"What's going on, Andrew?" With no sure option, she chose the direct approach.

"What's going on? Why, the beginning of a new era, one where we can all be strong." Andrew flexed his arm, and the muscle in it did a sickly ripple.

"You experimented on yourself?" She couldn't help a horrified lilt to her query.

"It's not experimentation if it's proven beneficial."

But she cared less about what he'd done to himself than what he planned to do with their sons. "Why have you brought Rory and Tatum here?"

"Can't a father want to be with his family?" The toothy smile sent a shiver down her spine.

"You've never shown an interest before."

"Because before I never had a use for them. At the time, they were too young."

"Too young for what?"

The creepy grin widened. "You'll see."

Screw not saying anything and staying cool as Wes advised. Wes wasn't here, and someone threatened her boys.

"No, I don't see. I don't understand how you could think it was all right to experiment on children."

"When it comes to great scientific breakthroughs, risks must be taken."

"Some of those risks have proven deadly. Look at all those who've died."

"Unfortunate casualties."

She blinked as he continued to blow off all the things he'd done. The things he planned to do.

I made a mistake in coming here. I won't be able to reason with him. She should return to the boys and keep watch over them until she could fabricate a plan for them to escape. Despite Wes's reassurance, she couldn't wait. She didn't dare wait.

Turning on her heel, she headed back to the door, only to hear Andrew snap, "Where do you think you're going?"

"Away from you."

"You won't get far without this."

Whirling, she was just in time to catch the envelope he tossed at her.

"While you're acting very bitchy, I've been a wonderful husband preparing you this wondrous apartment, and look at the bracelet I got you. Go on. Pull it out."

Fingers trembling, she pulled the tab on the envelope, the rip of paper loud in the silence between them. She shook out a bracelet, heavy gold and metal, embedded with garish bling.

"I spent a fortune on it. Put it on."

She didn't want to. It reminded her too much of the shackles keeping her here, in this compound, with this lunatic.

But it might be the key to our escape.

Swallowing back the sour taste in her mouth, she clamped the cold bracelet around her wrist, trying not to wince as it clicked shut.

"Behave and you'll have free run of most of the compound."

"And if I don't?"

"I wouldn't recommend it. Now, aren't you going to come here and thank me for my generosity? Parker thought you'd be too difficult to deal with and wanted to put you in a cage."

Her eyes widened, and shock kept her from speaking.

Andrew's face hardened. "But I reminded him that you were my business. *Mine.* I decide what happens to you. Me!"

Given his vehement response, it probably wasn't a good time to declare she wanted a divorce.

Death would be faster.

And probably more satisfying, except she currently was at a disadvantage. No kitty popping out meant no chance against Andrew.

Thank for the reminder that I'm stuck. Her kitty went off to pout again.

It just added to the surreal moment. She needed to escape before the scream building within her unleashed.

"I have to go."

"So soon? Why?"

Would Andrew take offense if she said she needed to get away from him because he'd obviously gotten a bit of loon in whatever drugs he'd taken? "I have to go check on the boys."

"No need to leave. They're fine. See?" Andrew aimed a remote at the television, and it blinked from an aquarium scene to a room lit in bright green.

She took a step forward, jaw dropping at the sight. "You're spying on our kids?"

"I prefer to think of it as keeping an eye on the investment."

"They're not lab rats, you bastard. They're your children."

He arched a brow. "Are you sure of that?"

He did not. Oh yes he did.

"Are you implying I slept around? You know I was never unfaithful. Those babies might have come from a tube, but they're still a part of both of us."

Andrew shook his head. "That's where you're wrong, wife. They're not mine at all."

The roaring white noise in her ears didn't let her hear if he said anything more. What more could he say? He'd just taken her world and turned it upside down.

If Andrew spoke the truth, and the boys weren't his, then were they even hers? She should have stayed and asked, but she couldn't. Couldn't bear to hear more of his vile truths.

Blinded by his words, she somehow stumbled from Andrew's

presence and managed to make her way to the ground floor. She staggered from the elevator, ignoring the curious glances of those waiting to grab it.

Air. I need air. She bolted for the front doors, bursting out into the crisp evening. She sucked in a heavy lungful, but it didn't clear the taint from her lungs. All of her being was tainted with Andrew's revelation. As she leaned against the building outside, she reeled, and her breath came in short, panicked pants.

What if the boys aren't mine?

Furry slap. Her feline growled. *Those are our cubs.* The boys, no matter what DNA ran in their veins, were Melanie's in every way that counted. She'd carried them, birthed them, changed their poopy asses, and bandaged their cuts.

They are mine.

Her cat snorted and then took a big, exaggerated sniff. It hit Melanie.

Their scent. How could she forget the fact that her little tykes smelled feline and were the spitting image of Daryl at that age? How could she have doubted for even a second. *They are my flesh and blood.* No ifs, ands, or buts about it.

Yet, if Andrew told the truth and he hadn't contributed the other half, then who provided the male gene to her sons?

Who is their true daddy?

"You shouldn't be out here."

A scream got caught in Melanie's throat, and she pushed against the hard wall at her back. She blinked at the lizard man that drifted to the ground on leathery wings.

What a strange sight. Sure, she'd heard about the flying dinomen plaguing town, but to see one in person? Seeing one also made her wonder, *did I get the sane or crazy lizard?* An answer that would determine her chances for survival.

Because, according to sources, there were two—the one that wouldn't hesitate to tear a man to pieces and the one who seemed to want to be on their side.

Please don't let it be the killing lizard.

Wings pulled tight against its back, jutting in a tall peak over the shoulder. The man, with scaled skin and alien features, cocked his head. "You shouldn't be outside. There are monsters about."

You don't say. An urge to giggle clenched her teeth tight, and taking a deep breath, she managed to mutter, "Are you going to kill me?"

Very human eyes stared from the reptilian face. "Depends. Are you going to try and kill me?"

Given he towered over her and had big teeth and claws? "Probably not." She remembered enough to know a touch of his claws or tongue and he'd inject enough paralytic poison to incapacitate her.

"Then we both shall live another day. Pity."

He sounded quite put out about the whole surviving part. "Who are you?"

"Ace. I work here." As he explained, he tugged the collar around his neck. Ringed and seamless in appearance, she'd heard enough from Renny to know Bittech used them to command the shifters, using pain as their whip.

A crappy thing to do. And yet, despite that, it hadn't stopped one of those guys from trying to do the right thing.

"Are you the guy who helped Cynthia's friend, Aria?"

A slight flare of his nostrils and a smidgen of wider eyes. Melanie could see his lips mouth the word no, a word Ace orated aloud. "No. Not me. The bird flew the coop on her own."

He lied. But why? It took her only another second to remember the cameras. Shit.

I really need to remind myself I'm on a sick version of reality television where my every move and word is watched.

Not saying anything, though, would appear suspicious. Surely some basic discourse was allowed. She couldn't exactly nod and smile all the freaking time. She started with an obvious question.

"Were you always like this?" The query shamed her almost the moment it left her lips.

How rude of her to assume he suffered a deformity. Perhaps he enjoyed his hybrid shape. Half-man in shape, with two legs and arms. He wore clothing, pants and a shirt, which seemed at odds with other reports that claimed they wore nothing.

"And its balls and man thing are hidden," Renny confided.

"Then how could you know it's a male?" Melanie queried as she used nail polish remover on the marker on the wall.

"You can tell."

Renny proved correct. No mistaking Ace for anything less than male. And he seemed familiar somehow.

He also answered her question before she could recant it.

"Are you asking if I was born a monster?" The lips turned down on the reptilian face, a human mannerism that made him seen less alien. "It doesn't really matter now, does it? I know what people see when they look at me, and there is nothing I can do to change it."

Such sadness in those words. "Maybe doctors could..." Her sentence halted.

With a coil of his hind legs, Ace leaped into the air, unfurling mighty wings with a canvas snap. The wings caught an air stream. They filled and let him soar above. With a hard sweep, he shot higher before banking and flying out of sight.

The night returned to its normal silence. The playing of a radio from somewhere, the occasional sharp bark of laughter as some people went about their lives as if they weren't all fucked.

Like totally fucked.

How am I going to get myself and my babies out of here?

Climb. There wasn't a fence that existed she couldn't scale. Her cat had no doubt they could do it, yet what of her little ones? They couldn't move into their cat self yet. They were agile, and fearless. However, they would be limited by their age and their bodies.

But I can't leave without them.

The dilemma burned. *I'm their mother. I'm all they have. I have to fix this.* She wasn't so desperate, though, as to not realize she needed help.

Daryl would move heaven and earth for her in a second if she asked. Maybe she could get to a phone and call him.

And how will he know where to go?

Good question since she hadn't the slightest clue where they were. When she'd obeyed Andrew's instructions to come, she'd obeyed all too well. She'd been handed a hood, and worn it, trying not to panic under the material. She also tried to not blow a fuse until she found her boys. There was a time and place for anger. And when she did unleash her anger, it would leave a river of pain.

Leave no enemy breathing.

No enemy indeed, she silently promised from under that hood. Parker meant to take away her power but, instead, wound up making her stronger. Although he had achieved one thing. She'd gotten completely, utterly lost. The car appeared to turn and turn again during the ride to the new Bittech compound with Parker.

So what exactly would she say to Daryl if she did call him? *Hey, big bro, so I'm like in this place, a big place with like buildings and people, lots of people with guns, oh and a fence. A big fence. With like woods around it. Under a sky.*

Could she get any more freaking vague?

Don't waste a phone call until you have an actual pinpoint on your location. Thinking of pinpoint, she could have slapped herself. A cell phone could map her location.

Next question: who to get the cell phone from?

She heard the whoosh and click of a door opening then shutting. She remained leaning against the wall of the building.

"What are you doing out here?"

It didn't surprise her to see Wes appear. Everywhere she turned these days, she ran into him. "Funny you should ask because Ace just asked the same thing."

At the mention, he stiffened. "You met Ace? You talked to him?"

"Only for a moment." She turned and fixed her gaze on him. "You know him?"

"Yeah."

"He's not what I expected. He didn't kill me."

"That would be because Ace isn't like the others. He hasn't let the treatments drive him to madness. But that doesn't mean you should trust him."

"Then who am I to trust then? It seems I can't rely on you. Or have you forgotten you're the one who tried to bring me here in the first place? Let's also not forget the fact you're Andrew's lap pet."

He stiffened. "I'm not his bitch."

"Perception is everything, though, and from where I'm standing, you are just as dirty as him." She took a step away, aiming herself in the direction of the medical facility that housed her sons.

Wes kept pace. It shouldn't have pleased her.

"Go away," she snapped.

"I'm not leaving you. The monsters are off their leash tonight. It's not safe."

"You don't say, seeing as how I'm being escorted by a monster right now.

"They didn't experiment on me."

"Well la-di-da for you. What about everyone else?"

His lips tightened. "Who do you trust that you can call for help?"

"Are you asking for people who might look for me? Looking to grab them, too? Make some monsters out of the people you know?"

"I'm not the enemy. I want to help you." He tried to grab at her, but she danced out of reach.

"Don't you touch me," she snapped.

"I know you hate me right now, but you need to calm the fuck down."

"Or you'll what? What can you possibly do to me that would be worse than this hell I'm living already?"

"I don't want to make shit worse. I want to make it better. Which is why I am asking you to give me a name so I can get your ass out of here. Who should I call? Your brother, Daryl? What about that uncle you've got living in Tampa?"

She whirled, and her hands shot out at him, pushing at his hard chest, trying to shove him back. What she really wanted to do involved shoving all her frustration and anger somewhere the sun never shone.

"No. No. And no. I can't call anyone, dammit, not Daryl, not my uncle. No one. I can't risk their lives. I won't have them suffer because my husband is a madman."

This mess with Andrew is my problem. My responsibility.

But she couldn't say that out loud, and hitting Wes felt good. She even yelled a bit as she kept pummeling at him. And he let her, let her wail and scream and hit and cry until eventually she collapsed against him. Her breath came in stuttering hitches, and her eyes burned with hot tears she couldn't shed.

Don't cry. Crying is for pussies.

We are a pussy.

He wrapped his arms around her and held her tightly. He didn't say a word. The best thing he could have done because there were no words to make this better, no words to make things right.

Although he did find three that managed to warm her for a moment.

"I'll kill him."

Chapter 8

"I'LL KILL HIM."

Yes, he'd said those words. Out loud. While Andrew's wife—*the woman I want*—was listening.

Most women would have received his claim one of two ways. Exclamations of happiness and calling him their hero.

Others, knowing of the Mercer reputation for violent solutions, would have recoiled and screamed.

What did his sweet Latina do? Melanie laughed. And laughed. Snorted, too.

Absolutely adorable. But totally at his expense. "Why are you laughing?"

"Because that is a load of crap. I will kill him," she mocked in a low voice. "As if. You were the one who told me there are cameras outside. No way are you going to say something like that on live feed unless it's a ploy to get me to trust you. Not happening."

"This is not a ploy," he snapped. He'd noted the pair of crushed cameras on their walk over to the science lab building. One of them littered the ground in a pile of plastic and wires. The other had left only the mounting brackets behind.

Something hating technology had passed this way, meaning there was a blind spot in the system—and an angry predator loose.

Melanie evaded his grasp and sprinted to the door of the building. She ran her wrist on the scanner and then squashed her thumb.

"Andrew gave you security access?"

She held up her arm. "Yes. Gaudy, isn't it? Apparently he wants to try and make things work."

"And do you?"

"You only get one chance to fuck me over." She yanked the door shut, sealing it, and moved away, but he could still see her through the glass.

He should have turned around and walked away at that point. Just point his feet in the other direction and go.

Yeah, who was he fucking kidding? There was only one place he wanted to go. He swiped his wrist and pressed his thumb on the scanner. The door hissed open on its mechanical track.

He strode in and then through a second set of doors manned by a guard who only briefly looked up from behind his bulletproof glass.

Layers and layers of security. A place meant to ensure no escapes—at least none that were alive.

Wes caught up to Melanie at the elevators, where she waited with arms crossed. In the blind spot, in a low voice, he resumed their conversation from outdoors. "It won't happen again." All too aware of the cameras in the ceiling, he kept his words neutral and hoped she'd get the hint.

A sneer lifted her lip, but on this fiery Latina, it served only to heighten her appearance. The Melanie he remembered always showed her every emotion on her face.

And the emotion expressed right now was anger. She stomped into the elevator and opened her mouth. He punched the camera before she launched in on him.

"Aren't you a big, brave man now, hurting a poor, defenseless camera? Afraid management will find out what you say behind their back? And I mean say because, if you ask me, someone in this place took your balls or else you would have acted a long time ago."

Ouch. She knew how to hit a man with words. "I never condoned what they did."

"But you sat by and watched. Fuck, you even led the whole gang on about it. What was that about? Telling Daryl and Caleb and Constantine that you think something is whacky at Bittech; meanwhile, you know there is. Hell, you had access to it."

He should have realized she'd eventually remind him of his subterfuge with Caleb and the rest. She thought he'd done it to garner info. The reality was he'd started the rumors and then kept feeding them in the hope someone without their hands tied could act. Then again, though, if the SHC couldn't ride to the rescue of those caught by Bittech, then who could? One lone gator was no match for the perfidy he'd encountered.

I could have done more to lead them to the atrocities. But at what cost? If Wes got caught, he wasn't the one who would suffer most.

What he could do was apologize. It almost made his gator death roll in shame. "What I did was wrong. I won't deny that. Just like I won't deny I'd do it again. I wouldn't have a choice."

"We all have choices. I chose to marry a douchebag. You chose to work for him. One is easy to walk away from. The other is going to need a good divorce lawyer."

"I can't walk away. And I think you know by now you can't either."

The doors slid open for the top level, and he glanced through them to see the nurse behind her station eyeballing them with curiosity.

He slapped the door-close button. "For now, at least, I have to stay and do as I'm told."

"Waiting for a final paycheck before you run?"

Dammit, he was tired of her accusations. Tired of her thinking he was just like Andrew.

I'm nothing like that bastard. He had reasons for what he did. And perhaps it was time he stopped hiding them. "I can't run until I find out where Parker's hidden my baby sister."

Chapter 9

THERE WERE times in a person's life when you felt like a jerk. The time you borrowed your best friend's last tampon and didn't replace it and her period came early. When you shortchanged the waitress at a diner on her tip because you forgot your debit card and didn't have quite enough cash.

Then there was accusing a man of being a total douchebag, only to find out he acted as he did because of his little sister.

He did it to help his family.

Dammit. Melanie's back hit the wall of the elevator, and with it bracing her, she slid to the floor.

I'm such an awful bitch. She'd accused Wes of doing this because he wanted to, but like her, he had to. They both did for those they loved.

Wes balanced on the balls of his black boots as he crouched before her. "Are you okay?"

"No. I don't think I'll ever be okay," she said in a half-sob. "This is a freaking nightmare, and I just want to wake up." The bottom of her hand hit the floor in a fisted thump.

"Shit's pretty bad right now."

"Pretty bad?" She eyed him with a wry grimace. "We're being held prisoner by men who think nothing of holding children as hostages against us. How much worse can it get?" At the bleak expression he got in his eyes, she held up her hands. "Wait. Don't tell me. I don't think I want to know."

"Things are escalating. We need to escape."

"You have a plan?" She turned a hopeful gaze on him.

His lips pulled taut. "No. Not yet. A lot of this security was put in place without me. I don't have the same freedom of movement that I had previously. No one does."

"Are you saying you can't leave?"

He shook his head. "If I get anywhere near the fence, my bracelet jolts. If I keep going, a guard finds me and asks me what the fuck I'm doing."

"That's a little emasculating, don't you think? A human asking you to go back to your room and be a good boy?"

"Are you seriously mocking me?"

She shrugged. "Someone has to." *Because a true predator would eat any human that dared to cage them as a snack. Crunch.*

Oops, she might have said that out loud because Wes laughed.

"The problem with eating guards is those damned buttons on their shirts tend to get caught in the teeth"—he grinned wide as she gasped—"of my wood chipper."

She punched him. "You jerk. You tried to make me think you really are a man-eater."

"Not yet, but lately I've been tempted."

It reminded her why Wes was as much a prisoner as she was. "Which of your sisters did Parker take and hide?"

"The youngest. Sue-Ellen."

"And you haven't gotten her released yet?" Even though she didn't say it, the unspoken words hovered in the air between them. *And you expect me to believe you can help me?*

He explained. "The reason I haven't taken off is because only

Uncle Parker knows where she is, and he's not telling. She's his leverage to get me and Brandon to behave."

"Wait, Brandon's here, too? I thought he was missing. That's what everyone in Bitten Point said."

Wes sighed. "I've been saying lots of shit to keep their fucking secret. I was warned that, if I didn't, they'd do something to my family." He shrugged. "I'm their brother. I did what I had to."

"Oh, Wes."

"Don't give me that look, angel." The old nickname slipped from him and hung in the air.

She glanced to the side, breaking the eye contact. She had to find her equilibrium.

The futility of the situation made a tear slip and run hotly down her cheek. A rough thumb wiped at it.

"Don't cry. Don't you dare fucking cry. You know I hate it when you do."

The words served only to make more hot tears roll. Two. Three. He wiped each and every one, except for the one that made it to the corner of her mouth.

That one he kissed away. Awareness exploded at the gentle touch, and she inhaled sharply. She didn't move, couldn't as his hands cupped her cheeks and he continued to kiss her, exploring her mouth with slow sensuality.

Tasting her. Savoring her. Igniting the senses she thought dulled.

He reminded her what it felt to be alive. To be a woman. To...

"No." She pushed away from him, and he let her go, the ease of her escape a frustration to go with that of her burning lips and aching body.

She liked the touch of Wes against her. Her body wanted more.

Rub against him. Skin to skin.

"We can't do this," she whispered, her voice husky and low. "It's wrong."

"You're right. We shouldn't do this, but the problem is it's right. You know it feels right."

More right than anything other than her sons right now. But thinking of her sons reminded her she wasn't a free woman. Married women, even unhappy ones, did not make out with ex-boyfriends in elevators.

"Don't do that again." She rose to her feet and needed a hand against the wall of the elevator to steady herself.

Rising more slowly, Wes towered over her, but she wouldn't look at him. Instead, she reached around his broad bulk and jabbed the door-open button. She ducked under his arms as they swished apart. "Goodnight, Wes."

He didn't reply. He didn't follow.

Why doesn't he chase me?

Melanie itched to turn around and see what he felt. See if he cared.

The doors swished shut, and the elevator hummed as it left.

Wes had left. It hurt more than it should have, which meant she was in no mood for the nurse who tried to get in her way.

"This wing is for the children only."

Oh, hell no. You chose the wrong night to play dominant with me.

Melanie raised her gaze to pin the nurse with laser-hot eyes. "If you want to keep your throat intact, then you will not get between me and my sons."

The nurse might have a few pounds on Melanie, but she had enough wits to realize who would emerge the victor.

Just in case the other woman needed reminding that she dealt with a predator, as Melanie strode the length of the hall, she strained hard enough to pop some claws—finally some success!—and she dragged them along the wall. The sound proved exceptionally delightful, given the painted murals cleverly covered the metal-plated walls.

Screech. She hoped that sound haunted the nurse's dreams.

Chapter 10

AFTER A SLEEPLESS NIGHT, Wes found himself outside on the quad, leaning against a tree, a cigarette clamped between his lips.

For the first time in a long while, the acrid smoke did not calm him. Nothing could calm him, not while Melanie was here.

In danger.

Fuck.

Even worse? He didn't know what he could do to help her.

Double fuck.

But at least his visit the previous evening to his uncle's apartment had given him that hope.

Parker opened his door and arched a brow at seeing him. "A little late to be visiting, don't you think?"

Pushing past his uncle, Wes entered the richly appointed suite, noting that, like Andrew, his uncle had spared no expense when it came to his accommodations. Unlike Andrew's open loft concept, his uncle had gone with a more traditional layout, with the foyer opening onto the living area and the bedroom hidden from view.

"We need to talk about Andrew's plan to experiment on his kids."

"Andrew's plan?" His uncle shut the door and strode past him. "Is he taking the credit for my idea?"

Could a gator's blood run any colder? "You mean this is your doing? What the fuck is wrong with you? You're talking about screwing with kids."

"Think of them more as our bright future." Stopping before a sideboard sporting several glass decanters with amber-hued and other tinted booze, his uncle poured himself a drink in a snifter. He brought it to his nose and sniffed. "Ah, nothing like a good bourbon." He took a sip. "Perfection. But I should mention not all bourbons are made equal. Just like not all shifters are made the same. Some are strong. Some can fly. So many traits that, when separate, make us unequal. However, let's say you could blend some of those into everyone. What if we took away the barriers and gave everyone the ability to fly?"

Wes couldn't help a snort. "You are not doing this to be altruistic. As if you'd let anyone get that strong."

A grin twisted his uncle's thin lips. "How well you know me, nephew. You're right. I don't think everyone should have this power. This strength. But for the right sum, it can be done."

The fact that his uncle did it for money wasn't new to Wes. Parker didn't do anything for free. "Your money-making scheme isn't a reason to start experimenting on children."

"That's where you're wrong. See, the researchers believe that some of our epic failures are because our test subjects were too old. You might have noticed that only the most strong-willed retain their sanity. The most alpha, I guess you could say. Their theory for that is quite simple. The addition of more animal genes creates a schism in the mind. Too many thoughts in one place. So they devised a theory. What if those genes were blended into the DNA structure of a child before their beast emerges? What if we could stop the madness before it starts?"

"What if you're fucking wrong? You're talking about driving children, innocents, insane? Maybe even turning them into killers like some of your other epic failures."

The number of failures mounted, as did the death toll. Andrew, who was supposed to be a success, now showed signs of the madness, as did Wes's uncle. One had only to see the feral light in his eyes to recognize it.

"I have allowed you somewhat of a loose rein because you're family." The distaste in Parker's words shone through. "But need I remind you that insubordination will have consequences? I might be fond of Sue-Ellen, but I won't hesitate to wring her neck if you do anything to stand in the way of progress."

And there it was, the implicit threat to someone he loved more than himself. Much as it galled him, Wes couldn't help but plead. "Don't do this. Not to kids."

"Too late. The trials begin tomorrow. Andrew has graciously volunteered his progeny. And soon Fang will be on the hunt for more. We'll even be working on the women in our custody, impregnating them via test tube and, in some cases, by more natural methods. Interested in being a part of that group, nephew? I hear you have eyes for the woman I brought in."

The horror of his uncle's offer couldn't stop the hot rage. He hit his uncle! Crack. *A blow that should have knocked the old man on his ass.*

Rubbing his surely-made-of-granite jaw, Parker laughed. "You'll have to do better than that, nephew."

But it wasn't the realization that the modifications had made his uncle so strong that chilled him through and through. It was the peek of familiar eyes from behind a door.

A glimpse seen for a moment then gone.

She's here.

His sister was here. Within reach. At last.

Problem was how to get her out, along with Melanie and her boys.

What of the others also trapped here?

What of them? He cared nothing for the humans who came to work for Bittech. As to those inside the lower levels, those already tainted? Could he truly release monsters onto the world?

"Unleash the beasts!" Melanie's cheerful decree brought his head up. He noted her exiting the building, Rory and Tatum racing ahead of her, their excited squeals filling the quiet morning air.

He knew she saw him standing there. She had to, yet her gaze went right over him. Not welcoming, hell, not even acknowledging. Someone seemed determined to ignore him this morning.

Not today. Wes pushed away from the tree and strode toward her.

"Going somewhere, angel?"

"You know, I've only been here a day and I'm already getting tired of hearing that question every time I leave a room."

"You said it best. This is a prison."

"All prisons have a weakness."

Given the missing cameras had yet to be replaced, he didn't have to temper his words. "I'm looking for one."

"I hear a but."

"Because it's going to be tough. This place is nothing like the original Bittech. There is security everywhere. No one goes in or out without authorization."

"What about over the wall?"

"Electrified and eight feet with barbed wire at the top. So unless you're planning to look like that cat in that Chevy Chase Christmas movie, then don't even think of it."

Her lips pursed. Was it wrong to want to kiss them to soften them up? She'd probably slap him if he tried. Then Andrew would have him killed. *Fuck.*

Do it anyway.

His gator loved to live dangerously.

Melanie frowned. "Electrified? Shoot. I'll have to warn the boys not to touch."

"Speaking of your boys, I'm surprised the staff let you out with them."

A smirk tilted her lips. "I didn't give that nurse a choice. I told her they needed fresh air and a run or she'd never get them to cooperate for the tests they plan later."

"You're going to let them touch your kids?" He couldn't help a note of surprise in his tone.

A sly grin tugged at half her lip. "Like hell they are. You told me they only want healthy specimens, right?"

"Yeah."

Still wearing a smile, Melanie walked past the buildings to a part of the compound that, while mown, retained plenty of trees and foliage. A spot of nature amidst supposed progress.

Whooping, the boys ran into the sparse copse, their little bodies bolting and zipping among the trunks.

At the edge, Melanie flopped onto the grass and crossed her legs lotus style.

Her casual pose drew a frown from Wes. "What are you planning?"

Wide eyes with an innocently spoken, "Nothing," did not settle his unease.

Mischief brewed behind her guileless expression. He turned his attention to the boys, cute little buggers with their mother's tanned skin and dark hair. Yet their eyes, those looked nothing like Melanie's —or Andrew's for that matter. The twins seemed healthy and fit. Energetic, too. They played a game of tag, in and out of the trunks, not caring if they caught each other quick or slow. Their laughter rang out as if they didn't have a care in the world.

It left a bitter taste in his mouth as he wondered how much they would laugh once the testing began.

There has to be a way to stop it from happening. He just couldn't see it. Yet. *Because I won't stop until I find a way out for them.*

And I keep telling you it's time to crunch some bones.

Crunching bones won't get us past those gates.

Melanie plucked at the grass, gaze aimed downward as she addressed him. "Why are you following me anyhow? Doesn't

Andrew need you to do his bidding? I thought evil overlords liked to keep their henchmen close."

"This is his bidding. Apparently the nurse called him, freaking out about your decision to take the kids outside. He sent me along to keep an eye on you." Of course that had taken a little nudging of Andrew's paranoia.

"You need to keep them safe, or you'll appear weak," Wes warned Andrew.

"Guard them with your life!"

Melanie snorted. "Stuck babysitting me and my boys. How emasculating."

"Thanks for pointing that out," was his wry reply.

"Yeah, especially since you suck at it. You're going to be in a touch of trouble."

"Why?" His gaze immediately went to the boys, who returned with red-smeared lips, the remains of some wild cherries still clutched in their hands.

But more worrisome were the spots all over their skin.

"Guess I'm not getting the mother of the year award because I don't know how I missed spotting the fact you had cherries out here. My boys are highly allergic to them. They get head-to-toe hives and a serious case of the runs."

How awful and yet great because this meant that, until the allergen flushed from their system, no testing could be done.

He couldn't help but laugh because he doubted those boys had eaten those cherries by accident. Their smell permeated the air, which meant Melanie did it on purpose. "Angel, you're a fucking genius."

Now that she'd given him a little wiggle room to work on an escape plan, he'd better come through because he doubted they'd get a second chance.

Chapter 11

THE GLEE at foiling Andrew's plan to test her boys didn't last. Melanie knew Andrew wouldn't appreciate her not-so-subtle ploy. She also realized an opportunity like that wouldn't happen again. She had only to hear the chainsaws that afternoon and peek out the window to see the cherry trees, actually every tree in the place, taken down.

This meant she had less than a day before the plan to mess with her boys was back on track, and she was no closer to finding an escape.

As evening rolled around, and as she tucked her spotted boys into their beds, she felt Wes's presence. Funny how she never needed to see him to know he'd arrived. For some reason, he exuded a vibe that she couldn't help but pick up on.

It's because he's ours.

She wished her cat would stop with that certainty. She wanted nothing to do with him. "Back to playing guard? I'm surprised, given your failure of this morning." She taunted him as she exited the bedroom, shutting the door behind her.

"Yeah, apparently I didn't get any blame since Andrew didn't know of your boys' allergy to cherries."

No surprise there. She'd counted on Andrew not remembering. "Crazy thing to happen, especially to a shifter, huh?" Because most shifters healed rather rapidly and rarely got sick.

"Very crazy. So how long before they're well again?"

"Not long enough," she murmured as they strode the hall in the direction of the elevator.

The night nurse didn't spare them a glance as they got in the cab. The doors slid shut, and the crushed camera meant she could drop her shoulders and sigh. "I don't know how to get out." As Wes had said, security was just too damned tight.

"I might have a plan, but we're going to need some outside help."

Her gaze rose sharply to meet his. "You can get us out of here?"

"Maybe. But like I said, we're going to need someone on the outside to pick you and the boys up. I know you said you didn't want to call anyone, but the plan won't work without a bit of help."

"How dangerous is it?"

He shot her a look. "Stupid question. So I won't give you a stupid answer. Anyone you call is going to be in danger. They might end up killed. Or they might not. It all depends on how quietly they can sneak. We need them to get close enough to provide transportation once I get you and the kids out of the compound."

The gears in her mind whirred furiously. She knew Daryl would do it in a heartbeat. No question asked. Hell, Caleb and Constantine would, too. They weren't guys to let a thing like danger get in their way of helping.

The thing was, what if this plan failed? Or what if Wes lied to her and this was simply a ploy to draw those she trusted close so he could nab them for Andrew?

It's a risk I have to take. Because he offered her the only chance she had right now.

"Get me a phone and give me a time and place for Daryl to meet us."

"A phone won't do you any good. They're jammed from receiving or making outside calls."

"So how the hell are you planning to contact him?"

"He's going to get a phone call. It just won't be from me or you. I think I know someone who can get through the fence and call for us."

"How do you know you can trust that person?"

"It's my brother, Brandon."

Exiting from the building, she went silent, as did he, the outdoor cameras having been replaced sometime that day making any conversation they had public knowledge.

If Wes spoke the truth, then he had a plan, and in order for it to work, she had to lull Andrew into thinking she was resigned to her fate.

Speaking of Andrew, "Why does he want to see me?"

After the previous night, she'd thought they were done talking. What could she say to the man who boasted he'd fertilized her with the sperm of another man?

"I don't know what he wants. But I will say, watch yourself. He's not been himself today." Wes whispered those words as they went through the next checkpoint into C building.

The elevator ride, even though there was no camera, happened in silence. What could she say to Wes? *I wish I'd been smarter in my choice of guys. I wish that maybe I'd tried harder when you pushed me away. Hey, your ass looks mighty fine in those jeans tonight.*

Because hitting on the guy escorting her to her husband was such a fine plan.

At the door to Andrew's loft, Wes paused. His eyes were a storm cloud of emotions; she could read so many of them. Worry. Anger. But not at her. Toward her, she sensed frustration and perhaps even a hint of something warmer.

Taking a deep breath that he released in a loud sigh, Wes knocked on the door without saying a word.

Bzzzt. The electronic lock disengaged, and Wes opened the door. He went in first, not because he lacked manners, but because the predator in him must have sensed something amiss and wanted to scout first.

She understood his unease. Within her own mind, her feline prowled. Hackles raised. A low snarl filled her head as the negative vibe within the apartment touched her.

Just ahead of her, she could see Wes tensing. He sensed it, too, a pervasive sour smell of evil. And it came from Andrew.

If she'd thought he looked off kilter yesterday, then Andrew appeared ten times worse today.

Wearing only a loosely belted robe, her *husband*—said with a mental sneer—sat in a club chair, hair in disarray, legs slightly spread, almost enough to expose him.

The by now familiar wild glint in his eye went well with his curled lip.

"If it isn't my dear wife."

"What do you want from me?"

A brow arched. "I'd say that was obvious. A wife's place is by her husband. Serving him."

"I was taking care of my sons."

"You should be taking care of me!" Andrew sprang from the chair, every inch of him vibrating with repressed irritation. "I have needs, too, wife. Needs you've been neglecting for years."

His accusation riled. "Are you seriously going to blame me for the fact you were always too tired or too busy?"

"Maybe it's because you are just too boring."

"Enough," Wes said. He interjected himself between them, and for a moment, she slumped behind his broad back, thankful for the reprieve. Sticks and stones might break bones, but names and accusations cut more deeply.

I told you to stay away from him, her cat chided.

No one likes a smart-ass cat, she snapped back.

"This is none of your affair, gator. Leave." Andrew addressed his icy request at Wes.

"I am not leaving unless I know you won't hurt her."

"What I do with my wife is none of your business."

"You won't be doing anything," she muttered. Playing nice was one thing, allowing this travesty of a man to touch her another.

Andrew heard her denial. "I will do whatever I want to you. And none will dare to stop me."

"I will." Quietly spoken by Wes, yet the words hung quite clearly in the air.

Andrew didn't like them one bit. "What's this? Are you expressing an interest in my wife? Are you the reason she won't fuck me, her husband? If I'd known you were into slumming, dear Melanie, I wouldn't have been so nice."

Crack. The sound of a fist striking flesh brought her around Wes's body. Andrew sat on the ground, rubbing his jaw, but the maniacal smile remained.

"Not bad. And further proof of my so-called wife's perfidy."

"I never cheated on you," she declared hotly.

"And yet your sons are not mine."

"What's he talking about?" Wes growled.

"He's talking about the fact he impregnated me with someone else's sperm. Apparently, I was nothing more to him than an incubator so he could make babies to play god with."

A high-pitched laugh stuttered from Andrew. "I am doing more than playing. I. Am. God."

"No, you're insane. And I want nothing to do with you. I might not be able to escape this place"—*yet*—"but that doesn't mean I can't say no. So unless you're prepared to rape or kill me, I'm leaving," she announced.

"Go. Don't come back unless you're ready to crawl and beg for my forgiveness. But don't be surprised if, when you do, you have to share my bed. A man has needs."

"I won't be back."

"You say that now, but let me add that, if you're not going to be my wife in every way that counts, then you will serve the needs of the project. That is, your womb will. And maybe this time we won't use artificial insemination to get what I need."

Turning on her heel, she tugged blindly at the door, her throat tight and dry. Fear made her hands shake. Wes's smooth grip overtop hers lent some of his strength.

She fled the lair of the madman with only one thought—escape.

Run. Hide. Her cat, usually the bravest of predators, did not know how to handle this level of crazy.

Actually, that was untrue. Her feline did have a solution. A permanent one.

Andrew has to die.

Chapter 12

ENTERING THE ELEVATOR, Wes could sense her turmoil. Hell, he dealt with a whirlwind of it himself.

It took everything in him to not rip into Andrew.

Why do you let him live? He is just meat.

Because dead meat couldn't help him to escape. He needed to find a way to use his proximity to Andrew to execute an escape.

First, though, he had to calm Melanie, even though he felt nothing but stormy himself. He understood, however, she couldn't go back to her boys in this frazzled state.

He stopped the elevator one floor below and dragged her down the hall.

"Where are we going?"

"You'll see," was his reply as he tugged her through the door at the end of the hall and up the stairs. They spilled out onto the roof.

Melanie took a few steps then suddenly dropped to her knees and screamed. And screamed a little more. Her vocalization came with some choice swear words.

There was nothing gentle about her rage and fear. In that moment, she was a fierce mother, an angry wife. A scared woman.

Comfort her.

He didn't have that right. And he didn't think she would accept it. Not now. Not from him.

When the last echo of emotion faded, her shoulders slumped and her head bowed. Only then did he approach, wary in case she lashed out. She didn't move. He leaned over and grabbed her hand. He drew her to her feet and led her to the far side of the rooftop, away from electronic eyes.

Wait, those eyes were gone. He noted the ragged ends of the wires hanging out. More evidence of vandalism to the cameras. It seemed not everyone enjoyed being under Bittech's watchful gaze.

Wes dropped onto the bench and dragged Melanie onto his lap.

At first she struggled. "Let me go. Don't touch me."

Fuck that. He was done doing what he thought was the right thing for her. Done fighting the fact that he still cared too damned much about Melanie.

He wrapped his arms tightly around her, hugged her like he'd wanted to hug her for years. But he didn't completely lose his balls because he growled, "Calm the fuck down, angel," instead of kissing her.

Should have kissed her. More fun. His gator sulked.

"I won't calm the fuck down," she snarled, glaring at him with eyes that gleamed wildly. "Andrew's out of his fucking mind."

"Yeah." He couldn't disagree with that assessment.

"My choice is sleep with him or be raped by whomever he chooses."

Like fuck. "Not happening." He'd let his gator go on a rampage first.

"And how are you going to stop it?"

He shrugged. "I'm a Mercer. I'll find a way."

She laughed, a hysterical giggle that turned to wordless high-pitched noises. "I don't know what to do."

"Then do nothing. I'll take care of this."

"How and why? Why put yourself in danger?"

"Because."

"What of your sister? I thought she was the reason you turned to evil."

Wes sighed. "I love my sister. Don't get me wrong. But I can't let you and your boys come to harm." Because, if he did, something inside him would probably die.

"I'm scared, Wes." The softly spoken admission hurt him.

How could words make him ache so badly? *It's because I love her so fucking much still.* The thought of her coming to harm...

"I've got you, angel. I will not let anything happen to you." He palmed her cheeks, forcing her to meet his gaze. "I'd die first." He sealed his promise with a kiss, the salt of her tears flavoring it with bittersweet despair.

At first she remained still under his soft caress, but then, as if a dam within her burst, she came alive in his arms. Her lips pressed insistently against his. Her body turned and leaned into him, the plushness of her ass squirming against the hardness of his cock.

Fucking jeans confined him, but he wouldn't complain, not one word, not when with a simple embrace she ignited all his senses.

I'm on fire. On fire like he hadn't been since they'd broken up. He'd been with women since Melanie, more than his fair share, in an attempt to forget her. None, not a single goddamn one, ever made him feel like she did.

She's mine.

Her mouth parted at the insistent tease of his tongue. He truly got to taste her again, a sensuous slide of flesh, a nibble on her tongue.

His mouth wasn't the only thing busy. His hands roamed her shape, a little fuller than it used to be, a woman's shape, all curves and sexy plushness.

Rearranging her so she straddled him took only a little maneuvering. Melanie seemed as eager as him to get closer. With her facing him, the core of her sex rubbed fully onto his erect shaft.

It didn't matter that clothing separated them. They burned as if they were skin to skin.

Thinking of skin, he slid his hands under the hem of her shirt, stroking the smoothness of her back. His mouth left her swollen lips and nipped along her neck, sucking at her exposed column, her trust in him in that moment absolute.

He kissed the fluttery pulse at the base of her neck. Then went lower. His hands pushed the fabric of her shirt up, up and over the swell of her breasts, the peaks protruding with excitement through the cotton of her bra.

He dipped his head and caught a tip, sucking on it, even though fabric barred his way. She let out a breathy moan. He took more of her breast in his mouth, loving the fullness of it.

Since she had her fingers dug into the muscles of his shoulders, he allowed both his hands to cup and squeeze her ripe peaches. He buried his face between them, inhaling her scent.

Melanie squirmed against him, the heat of her core scorching. He needed to touch it. To touch her. To feel her moistness on his fingers.

Her molding athletic pants did not impede his exploration, but her position did.

"Turn around," he asked.

She quickly complied, turning so she still sat on his lap, facing outward. Leaning back against him, her head rested on his shoulder. He nuzzled her neck as he let his hand skim past the waistband of her pants. He encountered the edge of her panties and slid under those, too.

He cupped her and hissed at her scalding heat. Her sex practically pulsed against him. It certainly wet him with her honey.

With the tip of his fingers, he found her nub and rubbed it. She cried out. He rubbed again then froze as a sound drew his attention.

"Shhh," he whispered in her ear as someone came out on the roof deck.

He kept an eye on them as he continued to circle her clit. They didn't seem inclined to move far from the door, and he could hear the two men—intruders!—chatting in low murmurs as they smoked.

Another time, he might have rebuked them for not using the

designated section, but given he pleasured Melanie, he decided to let it pass.

When she squirmed as if meaning to get off his lap, he wrapped his free arm around her and whispered against her ear. "You're not going anywhere. I'm not done."

And by done, he meant with her. For too long he'd tortured himself with the memories of what they shared. Too many nights, as he stroked himself, he recalled her fiery passion, the sweet scent of her honey when she moaned at his touch.

He pinched her button, and she trembled as she whimpered. He murmured, "Remember to keep quiet, angel. We don't want to be discovered."

At his words, she shivered again. She always did so enjoy making love with a fear of discovery. It seemed that hadn't changed.

She relaxed against him and spread her legs wide so they draped on either side of his lap. She gave him complete access to her.

Sweet fucking glory.

Some men were selfish lovers, caring only about giving the woman enough pleasure in order to ensure they got a piece of action.

Not Wes, and never with Melanie. With her, he loved watching her as he stroked her. Loved the hot slickness of her pussy when he slid a finger between her soft folds. Nothing was more beautiful than Melanie with her eyes closed and her mouth parted as he inserted a finger into her tight channel.

He finger fucked her, adding a second and a third digit to his penetration. Her sex clung tight to him, the flesh hot and welcoming. Still so beautifully tight.

Her breath came in short pants as he stroked her faster and faster, the pad of his thumb rubbing against her pleasure button at the same time.

He whispered against her ear. "Come for me, angel. Come for me. Quietly. Now."

She uttered a tiny sob as she obeyed, the muscles of her sex suddenly spasming and undulating as her orgasm crashed through her.

He held her as bliss made her tremble, turned her head and kissed her to catch any sound she might make.

In that moment, he made her his again.

Yes, mine.

And, this time, he wasn't ever going to let her go.

Chapter 13

A PART of Melanie didn't want to leave the rooftop with its panoramic view of the stars. But it wasn't the view that gave her the biggest reason to stay.

Wes did.

Don't I mean Wes did me?

She, a married woman, had let another man touch her. More than touch her, he'd made her *feel*. Feel a sense of closeness and desirability she'd forgotten existed. He'd made her come. Hard. And, dammit, she'd loved it. Loved that sense of feeling alive again.

It was selfish. Wrong. Totally not what she should be doing or thinking, but she didn't regret it. *I refuse to regret it.* She'd spent too many years living as a shell of herself, trying to be someone she wasn't.

I am not a cookie-cutter trophy wife. She'd hated that life. The only good thing that had come out of it was her boys, and it turned out they didn't even belong to Andrew. Given his lies, his actions, and, she realized, her general dislike of the man, as far as she was concerned, she no longer belonged to him either.

Time to move on.

To those who might condemn her actions because she didn't wait for a divorce? To them she raised a middle finger. The marriage had ended the day Andrew inseminated her with someone else's sperm.

And he'd been a dead man living on borrowed time as far as she was concerned the moment he threatened her sons.

"I can hear the gears in your head churning," he muttered against her ear, the hotness of his breath against her lobe.

Since she didn't want to talk about their current situation, she asked him something she'd never really understood. "Why did you really dump me?"

A heavy sigh.

"Wes?"

"You that determined to hash this out now?"

"Yes."

"How about if we just left it at I was an asshole who thought he was doing the right thing."

She tilted her head back to look at him. "How was dumping me, after eating my cake, the right thing?"

"Well, because eating the cake after would have just been a total dick move."

She elbowed him, and yet he still laughed. "This isn't funny," she grumbled. "You broke my heart. And, now, here you are, acting as if you care, and I'm confused."

"It's not an act. I never stopped caring. I cared too much, which was why I had to let you go. You deserved better than a swamp gator like me with a reputation."

"You thought you weren't good enough for me?" She couldn't help a note of incredulity.

"Look at you. You're gorgeous. Smart. With me out of the way, you could marry a guy with a good name. No family baggage. You could have the life you deserved."

"Are you saying I deserved this?"

"Fuck. No. Of course not."

"Let me explain something to you, Wes Mercer. I settled for

Andrew. Settled for a man that did not ignite me with a single look. I settled for a guy who thought work was more important than family. I settled because I couldn't have you."

The words spilled out of her, shocking in their honesty. Spoken, she couldn't take them back. She waited for his reply.

"I can't turn back time."

"What of the future?"

"Until I get you out of here, there is no future."

Bleak outlook, and one she couldn't talk about because more people decided to emerge onto the roof deck, their steps taking them to the shadowy gazebo.

Wes didn't spare them a greeting or glance as he led her from their rooftop bower to the stairs. Only when they were alone in the elevator, free from nosy ears, did Wes mutter, "I'm getting you and the boys out tonight."

"How?"

"I have an idea, so be ready." He yanked her to him for one brief kiss before the elevator shuddered to a stop. "I will come for you."

Would he really?

She wanted to trust in him, especially after his revelation. Wanted to believe him when he said he cared.

But he'd hurt her once before...

Anticipation rendered sleep impossible. As she lay in that barrack room, listening to the soft sounds of her sons' snores, she waited, maybe even fantasized a little about the future.

When we get out of here, maybe we'll move away. Start somewhere new and fresh for both of us. It would be good not only for Wes to escape the Mercer taint, but also for her boys. The quicker they forgot their life with Andrew, the better.

It was time to let go of the mistakes they'd made and forge a new future. A future together.

Because Wes will come for me. The more times she repeated it, the more times she recalled his tender caress, the more she believed it.

In the wee hours of the morning, when the door whooshed opened, it didn't surprise her. Already awake, she sat up, ready to act.

Only the man standing in the doorway wasn't Wes. She could only gape in stunned disbelief at Andrew, especially since he held a gun in her direction.

Uh-oh.

Chapter 14

LEAVING Melanie took everything he had. A part of him wanted to grab her and run. Run fast and far. Now. While they had a chance.

Utter stupidity. Such a rash act would only get them killed or worse. He had to remain calm and steady. No acting until he knew he had a chance of success.

But you promised her an escape tonight.

How could he not when she so desperately needed hope? Thing was, he couldn't afford to make a mistake, just like he couldn't afford to wait any longer.

He had to get Melanie out of here. The sooner, the better. And only one person could help him do that.

He located Brandon perched atop the rooftop of the building their uncle inhabited. A dark gargoyle that could at any moment spread his wings and fly, but who, like Wes, remained chained.

Time to throw off the shackles.

Chances were his brother heard his approach, but just in case, Wes paused and lit a cigarette. The acrid smell of smoke and the click of his lighter provided enough of an announcement to not startle the predator his brother had become.

Let's not die now.

Don't mistake him. He loved his brother, but at the same time, Brandon was a gator, just like Wes, just like most of the Mercers. Their cold blood ran fierce when it came to keeping the family lines strong. But Brandon was more than that gator now, too. Something darker lived inside him, an entity that wanted to swallow his brother whole. This dark presence kept Brandon from resuming his human shape. Made him a monster, one determined to pick a fight.

"You need a shower," his brother observed. "Or are you intentionally trying to poke the bear by sleeping with his wife?"

"Maybe it's time someone did some poking. I'm tired of being Andrew's fucking patsy."

His brother peered at him over his shoulder. "Was the pussy so good that it completely devalued the life of our sister?"

"No. Of course not. I love Sue-Ellen. You know that. But I also fucking love Melanie. I never bloody stopped. And if I don't do something to help her, Andrew's going to end up hurting her."

"So you slept with her?"

"Not quite. And not the point. Even if I wasn't in love with her, I couldn't stand by and do nothing when I know Andrew's planning to hurt those boys."

"Ah yes. The children. They have such an interesting smell about them," Brandon whispered, turning his head away to again face the darkness.

It chilled Wes's blood to hear his brother speak that way. "When did you get a chance to sniff them?"

"Parker has had me playing bodyguard as he wanders around the compound. It seems our venerable uncle doesn't trust his new lackeys."

"Afraid his monsters might rip his throat out?" Wes surely found himself tempted.

"He should be afraid. If not for Sue-Ellen, he'd be dead already."

"She's here, you know."

His brother whirled from the parapet. "What?"

"I said she's here. I saw her, in Parker's apartment."

"I smelled nothing."

It surprised Wes to realize he didn't recall scenting her either. That stupid cologne. It took from shifters one of their main advantages. "I'm telling you I saw her."

"We must help her escape. Once she's gone..."

"Then the ties binding us are, too," Wes finished. "We also have to take Melanie and the twins."

"You ask much, brother. It will be hard enough for us three to slip the leash, but to add in others? We will be caught."

"I won't leave without her. I have a plan."

"Does it involve three magical wishes?" his brother retorted.

"No, but it does require one flying lizard."

Brandon hunched farther. "Then it's doomed to fail."

"What are you talking about?"

"I am going to assume you mean to have me transport everyone over the fence."

"Yes. Once we're out, we'll start running, and you can fly ahead and call someone for help."

"Except we can't get to the other side of the fence." Brandon hopped off the ledge and turned to face him. His fingers hooked under the collar circling his neck. The collar that controlled his actions. "There have been some new modifications to the collar. Starting with tracking devices in all of them and a trigger when we get within ten feet of the fence."

"So fly twenty feet over."

Brandon shook his head. "Lester tried that. Let's just say roasted psycho lizard smells like chicken when it hits a fence and fries. Whatever signal Bittech is emitting extends into the air. I'm just as penned as you are, landlubber."

"Well, that fucking blows my plan to shit."

"It's hopeless," Brandon said with a shrug of his shoulders. "Perhaps it's time we accepted it."

Accept being a prisoner? Accept the fact that Melanie would hate him and blame him if something happened to her kids?

There had to be a way out of this mess. A way for them all to escape.

Then again, did they all need to escape? What if a single person could slip away? What if they could get word to those in Bitten Point? Surely someone would come to their rescue.

"Follow me, but stay out of sight," Wes advised as he strode across the roof to the access door.

"What the fuck are you planning?"

A quick glance showed the cameras had suffered the same fate here as elsewhere.

"We are going to rescue Sue-Ellen, and then, she's going to rescue us."

"How? I thought you said she was with our uncle."

Wes, with one hand on the door, replied, "I am going to cause a distraction. Once I do, you grab her and fly as fast as you can to that fucking fence and toss her."

"You want me to chuck our sister like a football?"

"Yes."

"And what if she's got a bracelet or collar, too."

"Then we're fucked."

"More than fucked," announced Parker with a shove on the door that sent Wes reeling. "What naughty nephews, planning mutiny."

"Get out of here, Brandon," Wes yelled, lunging at his uncle.

But his brother didn't leave, and Parker hadn't come alone. Riddled with darts, Wes sank to his knees, blinking slowly. Sinking.

He whispered, "Melanie," and then a blow to the head sent him into darkness.

Chapter 15

WHERE IS WES? Melanie failed miserably at hiding her shock upon seeing Andrew in the doorway of the room.

"Expecting someone else, dear wife?"

"What are you doing here?" she asked, the beginning of fear trembling inside. "It's the middle of the night."

"I know, and yet I couldn't sleep. I got some bad news, you see, and since I was awake, I thought why not come over and take you to your new quarters."

"I'm not going anywhere."

Andrew arched a brow. "Really? Funny because the way I heard it, you're not happy with your current situation. Rumor has it you're thinking of running away."

"I don't know what you're talking about," she lied.

"Did you really think I wouldn't find out about your little plan with the gator to escape? He told me everything."

"You're lying."

"Maybe I am. Maybe I'm not. Doesn't really matter. You're still being moved. I have plans for you."

"You can take those plans and stuff them up your tight, repressed ass." Probably not the best idea to antagonize him, but she couldn't sit back and allow him to threaten her.

His eyes narrowed, cold and menacing. "If I were you, I'd really watch that tongue. You don't need it for what I have planned."

Red-hot anger mixed with icy fear wouldn't let her cower. "Touch me and I will kill you."

"Did you know your gator lover threatened the same thing not even an hour ago? I put him in his place."

The words chilled her. "What did you do to Wes?"

"You should be more worried about what I plan to do to you."

"Don't you touch my mama!" Rory yelled before launching himself from the top bunk.

He never hit his target. A rapid blur of movement resulted in a tall lizard dude catching her son mid-flight.

It wasn't Ace. Even more worrisome, there was nothing human in this reptile's gaze. "Smellsss good."

It flicked a tongue and licked her son, and it was only her prior knowledge that the saliva acted as a paralytic that kept her from freaking when Rory went limp. She didn't dare do anything, lest the sharp claws holding Rory puncture baby skin.

Tatum began to wail in his bunk. "You're a meanie!"

With a scowl of annoyance, Andrew barked. "Stop that noise at once."

"Make me!" Tatum launched himself at the man he thought was his father. Given he was on the lower bed, he had no problem scooting across the floor until he sank his teeth into Andrew's leg.

"You little bastard!" Andrew screamed.

Pussy.

With the distraction, Melanie knew she had to act and prayed that she didn't miscalculate. *They need the boys. The lizard thing won't hurt Rory.* She hoped.

She dove at Andrew, intent on getting her hands on the gun, but she'd not counted on the third person to enter the room.

Parker.

It took only his cold gaze and tersely uttered, "Stop your antics this instance, or both your children will die," for her to freeze in her tracks.

Andrew might not want to kill her babies—he needed them for his perverse plans—but this man... The evil within him didn't care who he harmed.

"Get this thing off me," Andrew snapped, shaking his leg but unable to dislodge Tatum.

Tossing a limp Rory onto the bed, the lizard thing went to his boss's aid and licked her poor son.

Gross, but they'd recover. She on the other hand? She was in a big heap of trouble.

"Do I need to have Fang get a taste of you, too, or are you going to be a good girl and behave?"

Since she needed to survive in order to escape, she bowed her head with a meekness she didn't feel. But she wouldn't promise. She just let her feet shuffle in the direction they pointed, and as she did, she gave a message to her boys. "Don't worry, babies. Why don't you play a game of manhunt while you're waiting for Mama to come back for you?"

"How optimistic of you, dear wife."

She shot Andrew a glare. "Not your wife for long because, first chance I get, I'm making myself a widow."

"Is this where I mention the fact our marriage was never valid?"

She blinked, thrown for a loop at his words. "What are you talking about? Of course we're married. We have the damned thing on video."

"My father managed to have it annulled when the brats were born."

Shoved into the elevator, she whirled and had to ask, "Why?"

"Because that was when my father drew me into his plans. I am destined for greatness. I deserve better than a swamp girl as my wife."

"You're a snob."

"Thank you." Andrew's leer stretched wide.

Parker didn't join them in the elevator, having stopped by the nurses' station on the nursery level to have a word.

Bracketed between Andrew and his lizard henchman, the elevator dropping levels—...three, two, one, sub level A, B...—she didn't get a chance to run.

Even if I did manage to slip them, where would I go? She still had no way over the fence, and she couldn't leave without her boys.

The elevator finally stopped moving, and the doors slid open. Given she could hear ominous music in her head, she kind of expected to emerge into the bowels of Hell. Instead, she noted they were in a large control room. Numerous screens hung on the wall, with a pair of human guards watching them.

She couldn't help but scan the images on the screen, images of cages for the most part lining an empty corridor. "What is that?"

"Welcome to our experimental levels. It's where we keep our test subjects as they go through their changes."

Changes? The very thought made her stomach clench. "How many people are you experimenting on?"

"Not as many as we'd like. We had to dispose of a few during the move. But never fear. We'll gather more."

"To do what?"

"Ah, there is that famous curiosity known in cats." Andrew's smile displayed too many teeth. "Do you want to see? Do you truly want to *see*?" he asked, his voice dropping a few octaves. Andrew achieved a darkness in his words and a coldness in his eyes that brought a shudder.

Smart people ran when they recognized the presence of true evil. Melanie angled her chin. She'd married this monster. She should bear the burden of seeing what he'd wrought under her nose. "Show me what you've done."

"With pleasure. Come and bask in the glory that is science." Andrew stepped to the sealed metal portal. "Open the doors."

The doors clanked, and air hissed as they slid open. A veritable bunker meant to keep things in and not get out.

Andrew stepped in. Nudged from behind, and worried about Fang who whispered, "Tasssty," Melanie followed.

The smell of wrongness hit Melanie as she crossed the threshold, and she froze.

I can't go in there. To go in there was to set eyes upon madness. To see her possible future.

She spun, ready to run, but there was nowhere to go. Clawed fingers grasped at her and whirled her forward. The reptilian henchman frog-marched her into Hell.

As soon as she entered, she couldn't help but utter a horrified sob as she saw the true purpose of Bittech.

The first few cages held a few people still seemingly normal. According to her nose, some were actually humans. Was he turning them into monsters, too?

These scared people in cages gripped the bars at their approach, turning pleading eyes toward them. "Help us."

"I will help, and soon. Then all of you will thank me for improving you," Andrew announced with the arrogance of a madman wearing a twisted crown of blood and insanity.

So far, not so bad, but the smell of wrongness lingered, and it didn't emanate from these people. They went farther into this hidden level, a cluster of empty cells giving her a reprieve. Still, nothing could have prepared her for the appearance of the monsters past those.

Their alien stench hit her hard, but not as hard as the frightening hunger in their inhuman gaze.

"You have more of the lizard things," she stupidly noted aloud.

"We refer to them as our hunter models."

"Your what?" Melanie drew her gaze from the raptor-like monstrosities with hooked beaks, whipping tails, and leathery wings, barbed on the tips. Scary Fang, who guided her steps, looked cute and cuddly compared to this bunch.

"You are looking at our aerial soldier models. Swift. Deadly. And—"

"Fucking nuts." She didn't mean Andrew and his pride in this twisted creation, but rather the deadly hunger in those monstrous eyes. "These are killing machines." Killing machines with no humanity left in them. Then again, given their captivity in cages barely big enough to stand in, was it any wonder?

"Killing machines." Andrew chuckled. "Indeed they are and in high demand from certain government factions. Once we fine-tune the command collars, they'll fetch a lovely penny."

"You're selling them?"

"Bittech is selling all kinds of things. Soldiers, upgrades, even the chance for the richer humans to become a shifter themselves, for the right price."

"The world will notice what you're doing. You can't blatantly unleash these things and not get caught. How can you risk all of our kind for money?"

"Perhaps it's time we stopped hiding. Parker says—"

"This is Parker's idea?"

"Parker has a vision. One where, instead of the wolves hiding from the sheep, the wolves rise and take their rightful place."

"The humans won't stand for it. They outnumber us. You'll kill us all if you out us."

"Not if we kill them first. And you will help us with that. We're going to need soldiers. Strong, able-bodied shifters loyal to us, born and raised under a new doctrine."

What a frightening vision. "I won't help you."

"You don't have a choice." Andrew stopped before an empty cell. "Say hello to your new home."

Panic clawed at her, but her inner panther scratched harder.

Run, her feline screamed. *Run before they cage us.*

Her sudden yank saw her slipping the grip of the lizard guard, and she sprinted, ran as quickly as she could, only to have a heavy body slam into her from behind.

It took only a slimy lick for her to slump. But it was the needle jabbed in her arm that dragged her eyelids down.

Chapter 16

"URGH." Wes sucked in a deep breath, similar to that of a man grabbing his first breath after drowning. A needle receded from him, the pinching pull of it sliding out not something a man ever forgot. The shot of adrenaline zinged through his body and yanked his consciousness from a dark abyss, shoving it rudely into bright fluorescent lights. The kind of lights that said, "Oh shit."

Oh shit number two came when Wes realized the restraints holding his wrists and ankles wouldn't budge.

A word of advice if this ever happened to anyone. Waking up to find yourself tied and spread-eagle in an operating theatre never boded well. For anyone! Seriously. It didn't, especially since he seemed to have lost most of his clothes. He wore only his form-fitting boxers. And before a wrong conclusion occurred that cheesy music would begin to play before some debaucheries, keep in mind, again, that real life did not suddenly turn into porn at the loss of his pants. At least by leaving his underpants, they left him a little dignity.

Not little, his gator slyly remarked. *Those puny cowards didn't wish to expose our impressive girth.*

In a gator's world, size did matter in a lot of things.

Turning his head, Wes noted Dr. Philips, whom he recognized from the old Bittech. The doctor, with no scruples, having been ousted by a pharmaceutical firm for unlawful experimentation, used to work in the secret installation. There wasn't a thing this doctor wouldn't do. Science had made him hard. Subjects dying due to failure didn't bother him in the least.

Seeing him made his gator wary, especially since Dr. Philips held a giant fucking needle.

"What the hell are you planning to do with that thing?" Because in no sane world did a needle that size do good things. Ever.

"Do?" Dr. Philips seemed surprised at the question. "Why, my job, of course." Not the most reassuring of words.

Washed-out blue eyes regarded him. It took Wes a moment to realize Dr. Philips no longer wore his glasses. He'd also misplaced his stooped shoulders. The thinning hair atop his head hung in lusher hanks. As a matter of fact, Dr. Philips looked like a taller, prouder, thicker version of himself.

"What the hell did you do to yourself?" Wes asked with a pitch of incredulity. It didn't take a reply, though, to figure it out. What he had to wonder was, what sane man would inject those dangerous cocktails into his own body after having seen firsthand the possible madness and deformities?

Not everyone would care about the risk, not when they saw so much to gain.

He sees the strength he can have.

Vanity. Greed. Want. His gator understood, wanting to be the biggest and baddest. The strongest males controlled. The strongest males survived. But what of when the lowest ones applied unnatural enhancements? Who became the alpha then?

"What have I done?" The doctor smiled. "What everyone will soon be clamoring to do. A new evolution is coming to mankind. We are about to embark on the next step, and as one of the creators, I am one of the first to enjoy the fruits of my labor."

"Are you already out of your fucking mind? Have you forgotten the raving lunatics that have emerged from some of these tests?"

The doctor made a dismissive noise. "Early mistakes that have since been corrected."

The needle still hovered, and Wes hated the trepidation he felt when he asked, "What's in that thing? It better not be one of your goddamned enhancements. I like myself just fine as is."

"As if we'd waste such an elixir on someone like you." Dr. Philips squirted some liquid into the air, the tiny droplets catching the light and Wes's attention. "The fluid in this needle is meant to prep you for the insemination phase."

What the fuck! Wes's mind processed the words. Rejected them. Tried again. Freaked the hell out. Freaked out even more when he could do nothing to stop the needle from plunging into his thigh. He bucked in his restraints. "What the hell did you just inject me with? What are going to do to me?"

"Let me explain it in words my stupid nephew will understand. Dr. Philips here is going to make sure your swimmers are ready to go because you're going to need them to fuck and impregnate a woman." The cold statement from his uncle saw Wes whipping to peek at the other side of him. The bastard had snuck up on him. How that peeved. But Wes could only blame himself and his cigarette habit.

Bloody smoking dulled his sense of smell. The nicotine clung and prevented him from deeply tasting of the scents.

If I get out of here, make that when, I'm quitting, cold fucking gator.

Seeing Parker's smug smile made Wes forget the restraints that bound him. He lunged, his body arcing off the table, yet for all his straining, he remained pinned.

"You fucking bastard. I'm going to bloody kill you."

Parker angled his head as he tsked. "What a futile threat given you're so helpless I could slit your throat right now and there isn't a damned thing you could do about it."

"Try it." Dying might be preferable to what they planned.

Dying is cowardly.

Fucking honor.

Parker neared and stared down at him. Wes's exposed bare skin pimpled at his perusal.

"Don't tempt me, nephew. I came close once I discovered your plotting. Lucky for you, you have excellent genes."

Snort. "Given they're Mercer genes, I'd beg to disagree," Wes stated.

A hand waved away his words. "You see only the reputation. A reputation that you idiots perpetrate. Move away from here and start fresh. Live the life you choose. The Mercers in Bitten Point are only restricted by themselves. They don't have to live under that stigma."

"Funny, you moved away, and yet you're probably the dirtiest Mercer of all."

"Dirty for wanting better for myself? Is it wrong to want greatness? Power?" His uncle's brows rose. "And this is the problem with the Mercers of Bitten Point. Always thinking small."

"Then why come back? Why use us to further your sick goals?"

"The reason is simple. The Mercer branch of Bitten Point has excellent genes. Healthy genes. Strong ones."

"If it's so strong, then why mess with it?"

"Because it's precisely that strength that we need. When you add some elements from other species, our strong DNA handles it better than most. It's why the Mercers are so valuable to this project. Our blood seems able to handle anything." Parker's eyes shone, but the frightening thing about his fervor? The madness Wes noticed before no longer inhabited his gaze.

He's not insane anymore. He's calm and convinced.

Somehow, that seemed more worrisome.

"Is that why you took Brandon? And now me? To test your cocktail on us?"

"Your brother ended up serving as the answer to why it didn't work. You will help create the next generation that will."

"What the hell are you talking about? I am not helping you do shit."

"Really?" The smile on his uncle's face took his cold blood and turned it to ice. "Then I guess you don't mind if we use someone else to fornicate and impregnate Melanie. Odd, because I would have thought you'd prefer to handle it yourself."

Snap. With a roar not meant for human lips, Wes surged from the bed, parts of him shifting and bulging. A gray deadly haze filtered his gaze while strength coursed through his limbs.

The puny restraints could not withstand his yank. Nothing could cage him. He would kill the thing before him that dared call itself family.

He swiped, and the male dodged his strike and then stopped him with words.

"Harm me and I will give Melanie to the less savory results of our experiments."

Despite the cold thoughts running through his head, Wes retained enough wits to know Parker meant it.

He wants to hurt my angel. He couldn't allow Melanie to come to harm, and yet his need to protect the female he considered his mate warred with his instinct to protect his sister. How to resolve it?

Kill him.

The simplest solution and the only way to ensure the man couldn't hurt anyone he cared for anymore. But an attempt now would never fly.

We have to bide our time, my cold friend. Do as I ask for now, and when the chance arises, we shall wreak our vengeance.

Crunch some bones? his gator self asked.

Crunch them with glee—after dousing them in hot sauce. His gator did so like things with a little bite.

Let's make him think he's won for now. He needed to glean more of the situation. Wes hung his head, unable to meet his uncle's gaze for fear the smirk of triumph Parker surely sported would make him snap again.

"I'll do as you ask." He almost choked on the words. He no longer wanted to listen. He was done being a pawn for his uncle and Andrew. But he had to be smart about this.

"Obeying won't be the horrible task you're worried about, nephew. You get to fuck your old girlfriend Melanie. You will do your best to impregnate her."

Was it possible to hate and want what Parker offered at the same time?

"I will." Because hopefully she would see his touch as the lesser of so many evils. He hoped. He also hoped to find a chance to escape.

And crunch some bones on the way. Snap.

"Stand still as Dr. Philips gives you the second shot."

More fucking needles. "What's the second one for?"

"It's to ensure you're up to the task. Can't have you limp for the next phase."

"I don't need help."

"Perhaps not, but just to be sure you don't balk, you will let the doctor administer it. Or else."

Again with the threats that made him impotent. What could he do? Nothing but let Dr. Philips approach with his second, smaller syringe. Wes leaned against the medical bed, and stared at his bare feet rather than the doctor. He had to look away because otherwise he might lose his shit completely and kill him. The rage simmered at his surface, an almost living, breathing thing.

A power he would use when the right time hit.

Not yet.

But soon. So soon.

The sharp prick of the needle didn't disturb. It was the thought of what they injected him with that did.

"If this is some kind of aphrodisiac, then what was in the first one you gave me?"

"That mixture was a serum to temporarily enhance your animal side and remove the block we placed on your ability to shift."

"You did what?" He forgot his own promise to not look and shot his uncle a glare.

"We give it to all shifters in our control to ensure compliance and because angry animals are hard on our human staff. You wouldn't believe the money it takes to cover up a death these days."

Give the guy credit. It took balls to complain about the hardship that came with being a murdering sociopath. "When the hell did you give that blocking shit to me? I haven't had any needles or blood work done in a while."

"It's in the food." His uncle grinned. "And you never even noticed."

"It also didn't work so good," Wes taunted right back, "given I managed to half shift a few minutes ago."

That brought a frown to Parker's face. "So I noted. Odd because the serum shouldn't have worked that quickly. The formula might require some adjustment."

Great. Wes and his big mouth had just ensured he'd get drugged harder the next time. "Why are you taking this blocker off anyhow? Aren't you afraid I'll snap and eat some guards?" Wes couldn't help a predatory, toothy grin.

"We've run into an interesting dilemma. Having the beast side repressed affects the sperm ejected during climax. In other words, you shoot. If we want to succeed, then we need your animal genes to fertilize."

"Why not just test tube the babies?" he asked, not because he didn't crave Melanie's body against his but because, to him, it made no sense. "You know interspecies mating is hard. The chances of me getting her pregnant are pretty small."

"Except for the fact her body's been conditioned with fertility treatments to accept implantation. And we've enhanced her eggs within her ovaries as opposed to after we've harvested them. For some reason, very few enhanced in-vitro specimens survive. They lack something in their conception that we think can be solved with true coital procreation."

"Does Melanie know you turned her body into some kind of genetic farm?"

Parker smiled. "Andrew wisely made her think all the treatments she received were to make her more fertile. Which isn't exactly untrue. It just wasn't making her fertile for his sperm. The man's balls are devoid of life, much like his personality," his uncle confided.

"Why are you telling me all this?"

"Why not? Who are you going to tell? And even if you did find someone to listen, so what? I think it's time the world knows who we are so I can share with them what I am doing."

The claim caught his attention. "What do you mean, the world? You sound as if you're planning to announce what you're doing and what we are."

"Because I am." Parker took on a calculated gaze. "It's time we came out of the shadows, nephew, and took our rightful place. As leaders."

"You can't fucking—"

"Reveal us to the humans? Why not?" Parker's grin said it all.

And Wes suddenly realized it wasn't just him and Melanie and everyone else held prisoner at Bittech that was in trouble, but all of shifter kind.

Fuck. *The Mercer reputation is about to get even worse.*

Chapter 17

SITTING UP ON A CONCRETE FLOOR—WHICH really lacked the comfort of her pillow top mattress at home—Melanie tried to not let fear control her first waking thought. Although she certainly had reason to shake in her boots, if her feet weren't bare.

Actually, most of her was kind of naked except for the paper gown covering her, a giant tissue with holes for her arms and a big gaping seam at the back. She certainly hadn't dressed herself in it, and the fact that she didn't remember anything past the point where the lizard thing had taken her down really freaked her out.

What happened while I was asleep? It didn't take a vivid imagination to think all kinds of awful things. She palpated herself, hands running over her limbs looking for sore spots, anything that might have indicted abuse or worse.

Stomach a tight knot, she stared at the pinprick hole in her arm. A needle mark. What had they injected her with?

She didn't feel any different. *Kitty, are you in there?*

Rowr. The discontented rumble of her cat relieved her, but that feeling was short-lived as she tried to shift and couldn't.

Not even a single hair.

Crap. Still blocked.

Meow. A sadder sound she'd never heard.

Don't worry, kitty. I'll find a way to get you out.

Since she couldn't unleash her beast and roar her displeasure, she perused her prison.

Her new bedroom sported the latest in jail cell décor. It featured a concrete wall at the back and bars on the other three sides. "He put me in one of those goddamned cages." She couldn't help but utter her disbelief aloud. Sure, Andrew had said he would, but a part of her truly hadn't believed it. Thought it was a ploy to get her to behave.

Wow, was she ever wrong. Again. She truly needed to stop underestimating this new version of Andrew. He seemed ready to do anything at all.

The entire situation wasn't good. Not good at all. First off, she really preferred comfortable cotton—less chafing on the skin. Second, people wearing paper gowns in cages didn't have a good prognosis. Especially when in the custody of Bittech and the mad men running it.

I don't want to be a monster.

She sat up and peeked around. Still the same set of bars and direness. *I need out of this cage.*

But how? She stood and walked to the bars, peeking through them to the one across from her. Whoever lived in that cage slept, a hump under a wool blanket. But she didn't care about the person in the cage. She peeked at the lock and could have cheered when she noted they'd gone old-style padlock. Thick ones that wouldn't break on a good pull. The kind that needed a key.

Sweet, old-fashioned tumbler lock. Electric panels, while sleek and cool, relied on electricity and ideal conditions. A little too much moisture, or dust, even a surge of power and the components fried.

The last thing they'd want was for a lock to fail and loose a monster.

I wonder if I can open it.

Now, most people knew Melanie as the respectable wife of

Andrew Killinger. She kept a nice home—in between the boys destroying it. She cooked lovely meals—often with a bit of spice because it was the only way her husband ever sweated. She also had a sex toy party—done to shock the ladies at the institute, only to end up shocked herself since most of them owned the implements of pussy torture already.

Sad to realize she was the prude of the group.

However, all that stuff wasn't really who Melanie was. Melanie had grown up on the same wrong side of the tracks as the Mercers of Bitten Point. Her family was just smaller and nicer to people.

Yet, being nice didn't mean she didn't have her share of vices. One of her interests in her teens ran to lock picking. It obsessed her. The idea people could hide secrets or, in her mother's case, the junk food that would rot her teeth.

Lithe fingers made for nimble fingers. And nails, especially long feline ones, could do more than scratch. Lock picking became an art.

But to make it work, I need to grow kitty nails. She'd just tried and had not been able to pull on her cat at all.

Try again.

She couldn't worry if she didn't even attempt.

Closing her eyes, she took a deep breath.

Here kitty, kitty.

Really? She could practically see the disdain in her feline's tilted head.

Wanna play with a lock? Because once they got out of this cage, her cat would probably have a lot of playtime. *Hope you're in the mood to spar and run.*

Always. Her cat practically purred in her head.

Okay, here goes nothing. She imagined her claw growing from the tip of her index finger.

Given her last failure, she almost expected it to not work. But she could have cried when the sharp tip pulled at her existing nail, reshaping into something long and more needle-like. She did it to the index finger on her other hand. Then she hugged her cage.

Her slim arms slid between the bars with ease. For a moment, she feared cameras watched. *They'll know what I'm doing.*

Then I'd better move quicker.

Face smooshed against the bars to give herself the most wiggle room with her arms, she went to work, poking at the lock, wishing she wasn't years out of practice.

A click sounded, a mechanical indicator a door had opened. Since playing opossum could provide valuable clues, she flattened herself on the floor, shutting her eyes, and feigning sleep.

Footsteps approached, and she heard the murmurs of two men talking in a low tone.

"Have you finished the preliminary workup on female patient PK1?"

"Yes. Her blood work matches that previously on file. Another dose of DRG4.1C was administered."

"She showed no adverse signs?"

"None."

"What of the two subjects being held in the nursery unit?"

Melanie bit her fist as she strove to not scream the question burning the tip of her tongue—*are they talking about my boys?*

"The initial blood work and measurements have been taken. The results are good. Some time later today or tomorrow, we will begin dosing subjects PK2 and PK3."

"Why later?"

The other man did not reply.

A huff of impatience filled the silence. "I said why later? Mr. Parker will want to know why there is yet another delay in getting that part of the project moving."

A heavy sigh was followed by a scuff of fidgeting feet. "The subjects seem to have disappeared."

"What do you mean disappeared?"

"Exactly that. The nurse on duty left them secured in the specially designed playroom. When she returned, they were gone."

"Gone? How the hell did they manage to lose both boys?"

If Melanie wondered before, she knew now. *They're talking about Rory and Tatum.* By the sounds of it, her boys had managed to hide themselves.

She wished she could fist pump in glee. Maybe they'd managed a way to escape or at least hide until the cavalry arrived, which should be any day, any hour, any second now. It was, after all, the plan, the one she'd concocted when she encased the second little GPS tracker in bubblegum and swallowed it before going on her road trip with Parker. She had to hope Daryl noted it was gone. There had been no time that night to leave a note, and she hadn't dared say anything aloud in case Andrew or his goons listened. Hell, she'd not even thought about the damned device making its way through her digestive tract since her capture. With the monsters Andrew created, who knew what he was capable of. What if flying wasn't the only ability he cultivated? What if he'd found a way to read minds?

Then he'd know how much I hated him.

Although, deciphering that didn't need a mind reader. She declared her dislike every time she spoke to or about Andrew.

Back to the tracking device. Daryl would have noticed it was gone and made the connection, which meant he would have been following her. She hoped. She wasn't too sure if the signal still worked once she ingested it.

If she miscalculated, then she was in a heap more trouble than expected. She'd not expected, once she got within the new Bittech complex, that she wouldn't get a chance to get in touch with anyone on the outside.

Everything rests on Daryl now.

What of Wes? Given Andrew's claim, she could only hope he still lived.

The guy outside her cell didn't sound too happy as he said, "I want those brats found. Stupid rotten felines. I hate working with them. Such sly, disgusting creatures.

Going to slyly rip your face off. Rowr.

Her cat took insults very personally.

"When are we beginning the next phase with the female?"

"She has already been added to the implantation roster. They want her starting as soon as possible.

"I thought the other feline subject was pregnant."

"There are complications."

It took all her self-control not to shudder at the reminder of the heap of fur with misshapen limbs, distended belly, and expressive eyes that had begged for death.

And now this psycho wanted to do the same to her!

"Which in-vitro treatment is she receiving?"

"No in-vitro for her. Misters Parker and Killinger are both insisting she be slated for actual implantation by another subject."

"Who's the lucky guy who gets a piece of her tail?"

"Whoever the boss says. Makes me kind of wish we were taking the mods. It could be us."

Did either of them see the shudder that shook her body?

"Get her room prepped. Once we're done here, I'll find out from the bosses who they want to use with her."

"I'll put her in implantation room number two. It's got viewing windows."

"Excellent plan. Do you have the needle ready? We need to get her injected with the serum to remove the block before she's transported."

"Locked and loaded."

The jangle of keys and the scrape of one against metal let her know they planned to get in the cage with her.

It took every ounce of will she possessed to keep still. All she wanted to do was jump to her feet and pound on the bars while elucidating the things she'd do to the pair of them when she got loose. They proved colorful and, in one instance, involved a certain hot spice shoved where no light shone.

The imaginative ways she thought of to hurt the men kept her from moving long enough that they opened the cage and came right in.

That's it. Get closer. Come here, you bastards, so I can give you a nice scratch.

She could feel them staring at her.

"She's a hot one. I still can't believe the boss put her down here. I thought they were married."

"It's not our place to speculate. Inject her."

"Are you sure she's sleeping?" he asked with a little trepidation.

"She should be for at least another hour. She's not one of the enhanced subjects, so the drugs still work well on her."

No, they didn't, but she wasn't about to correct them. Nor was she keen to let them stab her with the needle. But without her cat, could she really take on two men?

Jab.

The inner musings took too long. The plunger came down, and with a scream, she reared up.

In the second it took her to open her eyes, really open her eyes, she noted things with a crystal clarity that only seemed to come in times of great turmoil.

For one, the pair of guys in the cage with her were human. Puny. Scared. Humans.

And whatever was in that needle didn't put her to sleep, or hurt.

On the contrary, it ignited her senses, especially those of her hunter side. She rolled to her hands and knees, belly low, lip curled in a snarl. While she might still wear her human shape, they had enough sense to feel the menace radiating off her.

The older of the two guys went scrambling for the open cage door while the other pressed against the back. She went for the one trying to take away her freedom.

She tackled him, her lithe body springing and hitting his with enough force to send him falling to the floor. His head snapped back and hit the concrete, and his eyes shut as he went limp. And she made sure he stayed that way—permanently.

In the bayou, there was only one law when it came to surviving—kill or be killed.

One down. A blubbering one to go. She turned around, a short Latina in a blue paper gown, and yet, the other man shivered in the cell, his eyes wide.

"Don't hurt me."

She took a step toward him and was pleased when her fingers managed to pop claws.

"OHGODNO!"

He begged. He screamed. She showed him no mercy. She couldn't. He wouldn't have shown her any, and judging by what she'd seen, the pleas of all the prisoners went unheeded.

Suffer not the guilty. He paid for his crimes, noisily, and yet no one came running to his aid.

Once he died, silence fell in the massive containment level. The other cages around her were quiet, except for the occasional whimper. The despair in the air tried to cling. How long had it taken to break these people? She didn't intend to stay and find out.

She exited the cage and stooped to grab the keys the first man had in his possession.

"What are you doing?" a voice whispered.

"Getting out of here," she replied as she tugged the ID bracelet off the guy, too. It probably wouldn't work for her, but it didn't hurt to have.

"Those who try to escape are always punished."

Melanie let her gaze rove until she located the speaker two cells to her left. The young, rotund man clutched at his bars.

"They'll also punish me if I stay. I'll take my chances. You can escape, too." She shook the keys at him.

"No thanks. I'm not going to get punished. I like it here."

Like it? She couldn't help but gape at him. "Are you insane? How can you like it? They're planning to inject you with drugs to change you."

The man shrugged. "At first, I was kind of pissed, but the shots they give us aren't so bad. They're better sometimes than the drugs I used to take."

She narrowed her gaze at the guy. "They've been experimenting on you?"

"Yes." He sounded so happy, and she noted the shine of madness in his eyes. "The one they just tried on me almost lets me turn into a bear. At least my arms and legs."

"What were you before?"

"A nobody. I didn't even know people could change into animals before coming here."

She'd stepped closer as she spoke to him, close enough to smell his twisted essence. "You're human."

"Not anymore," he said with glee. "And neither will you be. If you survive, they might even let me have you. The next stage of the program is to see if we can cross breed." He leered between the bars. "I can't wait to start."

Not with her he wasn't. Any thought she'd had to let him out evaporated. Right now, she had to ensure her own escape, which meant getting her chubby ass out of there before she became crazy patient number one hundred and ninety-seven.

Ignoring the guy who now moaned and dry humped the bars, Melanie walked past his cage toward the other end of the massive containment level.

But the guy didn't let her leave unchallenged.

"What are you doing? Get back in your cage. Guards. Guards, she's escaping."

Melanie couldn't believe the guy was ratting her out. Even worse, the other prisoners began rattling their bars, too, and shouting.

Hell no. She couldn't get caught again. *I have to get out.* She bolted past the cages where people—and things—rose to their feet shouting.

"She's escaping."

"Don't leave me here."

"I feel like chicken tonight."

The variety of suggestions showed the different levels each prisoner had reached. Some were almost hunter ready.

They were scary, almost as scary as the fact that there was only one door out of here that she could see. For some reason, it made her think of the song "Hotel California" by The Eagles. Once checked in, could she escape? She had to. If she got caught, she might never get another chance.

The elevator door didn't yield at her shove. The video screen alongside it stated a simple, "Please tap your access card."

Unfortunately, prisoners didn't get the same perks as the doctors and henchmen did. She wanted to sob at the injustice. What kind of stupid building required special privilege to move floor to floor?

One designed to keep secrets in.

She tried slapping the access bracelet she'd stolen from the dead guy's wrist.

The screen turned red. Invalid Access. A siren began to whoop.

"Security teams to level three B."

Defeat cackled in the background, and her inner kitty slashed at it until it retreated. There must be another way out. Air shafts. Lock picking. Speaking of locks...

Didn't doors with electronic access always have a manual override? She eyed the panel, inset within a frame, which, in turn, sat flush within the wall. What was behind it?

Let's find out. She popped claws from the tips of her fingers. Using the tips, she pried at the panel, hooking the metal. It held firm. She yelled in frustration and punched it.

It continued to flash red as it mocked her.

So she hit it again. And again and again until the door opened. One glimpse of the lizard dude standing in the cab with Andrew and she turned on her heel to bolt, knowing full well there was no escape. Didn't matter. She wouldn't just stand there and let them take her.

"Fetch her."

She ran faster, but it proved futile. A hand grasped at her hair, and she found herself screaming in pain as she was lifted off her feet. Fingers scrabbled at the scaled fist holding her aloft. The pain proved excruciating, and yet the horror at what capture meant hurt more.

Setting her on her feet, Fang paid her no mind as he strode back to the open elevator. She had to stumble after him lest he drag her. Tears of defeat pricked at her eyes, but that didn't mean they'd broken her fighting spirit.

"I'm going to rip your cojones off and stuff them with rice and spices before I eat them!"

And she'd eat them with pleasure.

Now before anyone judged her, keep in mind that, while human sensibilities might find themselves offended at such a cannibalistic threat, shifters weren't human. Not completely. Most of them lived with a predator sharing their mind, one that liked to hunt its food, kill it, and eat it. Usually raw.

Ugh. What could a girl do when her feline side wanted to rip into someone and make them into chunks of meat? At least manage to cook them before they got eaten.

By eating the enemy, I take on his strength. An old belief of her mother's that liked to rear its sage head every so often.

But Melanie's inventive suggestions on various ways of cooking psycho Fang's body parts did not loosen his grip. On the contrary, he got even more stupid as the blood north of his waist drained.

Apparently, feisty women who wanted to kill him for food acted as an aphrodisiac.

Eew. Turned out the crazy hunters did have a penis. It flopped out of his body from wherever it hid and poked at her.

"What is it with you and reptiles?" Andrew stated with disgust. "I should have known to steer clear of you when you broke up with Wes. I deserve better than that gator's leftovers."

"I deserved better, too," she muttered. "You were always lousy in the sack."

Expecting the slap, she managed to move her face with it, lessening the impact, but it still stung.

"Whore," Andrew spat.

"Tiny dick."

Slap.

Nice to know she still had a knack for pushing people's buttons. Even nicer to know she'd finally stopped kowtowing to Andrew the a-hole. She smiled through the pain as she taunted, "I had better orgasms masturbating."

But she didn't get a third smack.

A sneer distorted his features. "I see your game. You think you can anger me enough to hurt you so you don't have to participate in the next phase. Guess again. I'm going to be watching as you get taken by one of the special projects. It might even be Fang here."

The grunt behind her made her clamp her lips tight. Horror stole her breath.

The elevator trip proved thankfully short. As the doors slid open, she noted a long corridor, one she was forced into as Fang prodded her from behind.

Please let that be a finger and not something else.

Only a few doors lined this blank level. Nothing indicated its purpose. No signage, no windows to peek in, nothing.

The hallway employed recessed lighting behind solid steel cages. A precaution to prevent broken lights? Only someone expecting to piss off its prisoners would worry about that. The few doors on this level sat in thick metal frames, with embedded keypads alongside them.

For some reason, this area frightened her more than the line of cages. What horrors hid behind these benign portals? What torture would she have to survive?

And I will survive. Of that, she refused to have any doubt.

No matter what they did to her now, she needed to live so she could save her boys—*and shred that bastard, Andrew.*

Stopping before a door labeled Observation C, Andrew poked at the scanner but didn't swipe his wrist.

"Identify yourself," said a man.

I recognize that voice, she realized.

Her cat knew exactly who it was and pictured a man in a lab coat with glasses.

Dr. Philips. The one giving her fertility treatments.

Oh shit.

"It's Killinger. I've got the female."

"Excellent. The male is already inside waiting."

"What do you mean you already have a male? Who chose him?" Andrew asked.

"Parker did. He wants his nephew to have first crack at impregnating her."

Melanie felt a surge of relief. They wanted to put her with Wes? She could handle that.

"Why him?"

"It is not my place to question," Dr. Philips announced. "If you have a problem with it, then take it up with your partner. Now, if you're done questioning, get the female inside."

Displeasure creased Andrew's features, but he didn't argue further. "Before I open the chamber, is the male contained? I don't want any incidents."

"Pussy," she taunted.

Andrew smirked at her. "Perhaps you should show a little more fear, given you're about to be locked in a room with him. Did I forget to mention the gator might not be acting like himself?"

"What do you mean?"

"You didn't think we'd just want normal babies, did you? Wes has been given something a little extra to make this moment special."

With that, a door opened, and a rough shove sent her reeling in. She took a few stumbling steps before she could stop herself. Behind her, the door shut, and she heard the click of a lock engaging.

Great. Just fucking great. Anxious, she hugged herself and peeked around. There wasn't much to see. Four walls, padded in a strange substance. She pressed her fingers against it.

It squished, but when she dragged her nails across it, didn't even scratch.

The floor appeared to employ the same substance. It added a bounce factor to walking.

Embedded within another wall, the one at her back, she noted dark glass. Reflective on her side, showing a disheveled woman in a partially torn paper gown, her hair a frazzled disaster. She kept staring, the realization dawning that the glass acted as a viewing window.

People watched. Andrew watched. Which meant they expected a show.

She gave them one. Two slowly rotated digits and a smirk. They might hold the upper hand for the moment, but she'd not given up yet.

At a metallic cranking sound behind her, she whirled to see a section of the wall pulling apart. As the opening widened, a scent hit her.

Musty. Reptilian. Male. Wes. Another sniff and she could pinpoint another scent—violence. Madness.

Predators knew that smell. *Stay still,* her feline hissed.

While remaining still, she did peruse the now much larger space. With the dividing wall gone, the room proved rectangular in shape, long and narrow. Also dim. Very dim.

So dim that, at first, she didn't see the shadow at the far end.

Knowing it was Wes didn't ease her trepidation, not with the hint of violence in the air.

"Wes?"

No reply. The shadow stepped closer, a dark, hulking shape that brought a shiver to her skin.

"You're scaring me." An admission she hated to make, and yet, there was something in his slow advance, the way he moved, that frightened her.

I don't think Wes is home.

The alien scent drew nearer, and she didn't realize she backed away until her back hit the smooth glass wall behind her.

Fear thumped, an irregular stutter of her heart as her breath drew short and ragged.

Inside her head, her feline yowled. She wanted out. She wanted to stand strong in the face of this threat.

But poor kitty was locked in. Melanie had tried so many times on the way over, and nothing other than a pop of a few claws worked.

It was only her, a paper gown, and whatever Wes had become.

Which, as it turned out, was a walking, talking dinosaur.

And he grabbed her by the throat!

Chapter 18

HE HELD the female off the floor, high enough that he could properly peruse her. His mate appeared uninjured, and yet he could smell the fear rolling off her. He brought his snout close, inhaling her aroma, rubbing himself on her skin to mark her with his scent. Wearing a bull's mark would reassure the female that he would protect her against danger.

At least now he would. His pinker self might have had problems accomplishing the task, but he was stronger now. In control, too.

Such strength flowed through him. *I am the strongest.* And to him came the rewards along with the irritations.

A fly buzzed in his head. *Put her down. She's fragile, you big, dumb gator.*

No talking. I am in control.

For now. And only because of those drugs.

I am strong. I shall eat our enemies.

Yeah, well, if you're going to do that, then you need to have a bit of patience because we're not getting out of this room until we do the deed.

The female requires insemination.

Let's try and not call it insemination. And you might want to let me drive for this part.

If I relinquish this part, you will let me have the hunt?

Yes.

We have a bargain. Snap.

The quick flash of thoughts between them took but a moment, as did the changes back to himself. Wes's more sane and human-looking self.

Along with his man skin came shame.

"Fuck." He couldn't help but curse as he released Melanie.

He waited for her to launch into him. He knew he would have with the roles reversed.

"Are you okay?" she asked.

The lack of freakout upset him more. "No." The single syllable a guttural grunt. No, he wasn't fucking okay. Neither was she. None of this was fucking okay.

He spun away from her, a few short strides removing him from the reminder of his failure.

I didn't save her, and now we're both stuck here.

"Argh!" He smacked the wall beside him with his fist, only to feel it sink and bounce back.

He leaned his head against the wall, breathing slowly, trying to come down from the fact that his colder side had taken over. Scarier, he'd had to cajole it into giving control back.

The injection, while not meant to change him—at least according to the doctor—did, however, grant more strength to his inner beast.

Not necessarily a good thing.

"Might I remind you that time is wasting and you've yet to fuck her?" Parker's sly words emerged muffled in this strange place. For a moment, as his gator retook control of his motions, he peered around, looking for an enemy to chomp.

No one appeared. Cowards. It was only him and Melanie here.

A pity. He had some pent-up energy that needed expending.

"Do I need to find another male to take your place?" Parker threatened.

"No." As he spat the word, he pushed from the wall and walked stiff-legged back to Melanie. He stood over her, looming as he stared down. His skin prickled with awareness. He knew the window she leaned against hid watchers.

Leaning down, he bent far enough that his forehead touched hers. He breathed her scent in and heard the rapid flutter of her heart.

Still frightened, but also oozing a sense of anticipation. Did she know what would happen? Would she hate him for it?

"You don't have to do this," she said softly.

"You would rather do another?" He couldn't help the jealous accusation. It came from a primal part of him.

"What? No. I don't want to do this at all. You know what they are attempting. If we do this, then we play right into their hands."

"And if we don't, then you'll be forced by another. We don't have a choice, angel. I'm so sorry." He truly was. He took all the blame. Things might have gone differently if he'd acted that night when Andrew went to fetch her. That was the night everything truly started to go to shit.

Or why not go back further? If I'd not set her free all those years ago, then she and I would be together. And she might have never entered his uncle's or Andrew's radar.

Maybe gators will fly, his beast snorted.

Wait, they did.

Fuck.

"I'm waiting. Tick. Toc. Should I come in there and show you how it's done?" His uncle's taunt drew a rumbling growl from him, and he glared at the smoky glass, seeing only the terribleness of his eyes. The darker side of him swam close to the surface.

Soft hands cupped his cheeks and turned his gaze to her gentler one. "Ignore him."

"I wish I could."

"But you're right. We can't. So let's do it. Right now."

A grin threatened to pull his lips. "Isn't that what you said right before the first time we screwed?"

She smiled. "You remember."

"Of course I do. I never forgot anything about you." Not the way she clutched at him and cried out his name. The way she shyly admitted she loved him.

"Blah blah blah. Get the show on the road, nephew."

"Argh." He punched the glass, feeling the slight vibration from the impact. Stupid tempered shit. He wanted to smash through it and kill those watching on the other side. Instead, he could only sigh. "Sorry it came to this."

"Not entirely your fault. I mean, you didn't marry the douchebag that got me involved."

"That douchebag is watching," Andrew announced.

"Keep watching. Then maybe you'll see where you kept going wrong," she snapped.

Wes almost laughed. "You know that is just pulling his stubby tail."

"I don't care. What else can the bastard do to me?"

"Don't ask and don't tempt. And never forget it's a Mercer running things."

"And this Mercer"—she poked him in the chest—"will find a way to fix it. I know you will." Her faith in him didn't warm as much as the soft brush of her lips on his. She caught his mouth and sucked at his lower lip. Nibbled it.

What is she doing?

He knew this wasn't what she really wanted to do. Hell, he certainly didn't want her under these circumstances, but...

At what point did a man stop fighting the inevitable? This would happen, and in front of an audience.

But he could do his best at least to make sure they saw as little as possible.

Wes clutched Melanie in his arms, tucking her tight against his chest. He moved them, down to the middle of the room, the farthest from both viewing panes framing the space, in the deepest of the shadows because they didn't dare use proper lighting in here. No light bulbs, not even caged ones, lest they get used as a weapon.

The soft, phosphorous glow that came from the very walls and floor itself bathed Melanie in an unearthly sheen. He ran a knuckle down her soft cheek, the contrast of his rough, working hands against her smooth, tanned flesh a reminder of their differences. She grabbed his finger and sucked the tip, reminding him of the fact that they were so perfect together.

He leaned into her, his lower body pinning hers, his thin briefs unable to hide his erection. No matter the circumstances, he couldn't help but desire Melanie. He could make this good for her. Good for them both. He owed it to her in case it was their last chance.

The thought spurred him to action. He caught her lips with his, sucking at that lower one, catching the soft pants of her breath.

His hands skimmed her curves from the indent of her waist, the wide flare of her hips, then the curve of her thighs. The edge of her paper gown crinkled as he raised it. The palms of his hands stroked the silky flesh as he bared her, but in such a way that none could truly see.

She caught onto his idea and, bracing her hands on his shoulders, lifted her legs to lock them around his waist.

Their kiss deepened, her mouth parting for his tongue. He tasted her, thrusting his tongue into her mouth for a sinuous slide against hers. The erotic nature of the kiss thrilled him. Aroused him. Aroused his primal side.

Bite her.

He pushed the impulse down. He would do this as a man, not a beast.

Silky skin met his touch as he skimmed over her body, titillating her all without truly exposing her. It proved a torturous form of fore-play. He so wanted to drop to his knees and taste her. Stab his tongue between her velvety folds and taste her sweet honey. But they were watched.

Was it wrong to find arousal in that concept?

He whispered to her, "I want you so bad, but I don't want to hurt you." A man his size needed to prepare the way.

She clasped his hand and brought it between her legs. "Touch me."

Slick honey met his fingers as he stroked her mound. So hot. So wet.

Irresistible. Fuck those watching. This might be his last chance, her last chance, for pleasure. He dropped to his knees and tucked his head under her gown.

She parted her thighs for him, and the full impact of her scent hit him. He could have shot his load right then and there. He didn't, though. He preferred to hold back, to feel the pain of abstaining as he let his tongue dart forward and taste of her sweetness.

Pure fucking bliss. He suckled happily of her nectar.

It seemed some weren't happy at his actions. He vaguely heard a complaint of, "I thought he was supposed to fuck her." And, "If you can't handle watching, leave."

He didn't care. He lost himself in the scent and heat that was Melanie. His. *Mine.*

His tongue stroked her velvety folds, spreading them that he might stab his tongue inside her, feeling the tightness of her channel. She lifted a leg over his shoulder, granting him better access, and he used it to stroke the tip of his tongue over her clit.

A shudder rocked her frame, and a small gasp of his name, "Wes," slipped past her lips.

He stroked her faster, alternating tugs against her button, feeling her body quivering at his touch while her pulse raced erratically.

When she neared her peak, he stood. His erection throbbed within the confines of his briefs. He lifted her first, anchoring her against the wall. She locked her legs around his waist. He freed himself, only to have her reach between them to clasp him.

Tight fingers gripped around his cock. The urge to thrust his hips and come was so strong. But he knew a better place to bury himself.

He lifted her gown, pushing the paper liner out of the way. With her legs wrapped around his hips, none could see the tip of his cock probing at the pinkness of her sex. He watched as her channel hungrily gobbled his length. He pushed in, and she took, the heat of her squeezing all around.

She grabbed his head and drew him to her for a kiss. Their bodies pulled together tight, and all of him ended up sheathed in her welcoming heat.

Pure bliss. He moaned against her mouth. This shouldn't have felt so good. They came together because they had to. How could he take such pleasure?

Take it. Because who knew if he'd ever feel pleasure again.

He rotated his hips, pushing into her, driving the very tip of his cock deeper. So deep.

Her flesh squeezed him, much like a tight fist gripping him as he pushed in and out of her, driving her with his need, raising their arousal to a point where they both panted and glistened.

"I love you," she whispered against his mouth just as her body tensed.

"You shouldn't," was his reply. And then he could speak no more as he came. She came, too, with a sharp cry and undulating waves, the sweet flesh of her sex shuddering around him and drawing out his pleasure to a bittersweet point.

He might not want to admit it aloud, but he could, here, in this moment, in his head.

I love you, too, angel. So much that it hurt.

Chapter 19

REALITY WANTED TO INTRUDE. Melanie didn't want to let it. She refused to think about the fact that they'd made love in front of an audience. Refused to think about what would happen next.

She hugged Wes tight, as if by holding on she could keep the ugliness away.

It didn't work. "The subjects will move to opposite ends of the room," a man's voice ordered.

"Dr. Philips can kiss my ass if he thinks I'm leaving you. I'm not letting you out of my sight." Wes set her on her feet and smoothed down her pathetic excuse for a dress.

The words warmed, and yet, she couldn't help but wonder how Wes would manage to keep his promise. "What are we going to do?"

"Bust out of this joint."

Great optimism, but for one teensy problem. "How? In case you hadn't noticed, we're locked in a room."

"Yup."

"And?" she prodded.

"And I will get us out."

A heavy sigh blasted past her lips. "How?"

"Dare me," he said with a grin that didn't quite match the cold glint in his eye.

"Dare you?" she repeated.

"Yes, challenge me to get us out. I'm a Mercer. It's part of my genetic makeup to have to attempt it, no matter how impossible seeming."

"And how is challenging you going to change facts?"

"Because I'm a Mercer. I'll find a way."

"Enough chattering. There is no escape. You are in a sealed room. You will separate and move to opposite ends. Comply or I will release gas into the chamber."

Wes pivoted to face the glass window—tall, straight, and bristling. Danger hummed under his skin. "Are you really stupid enough to think for one minute I'd believe you'll gas us? Like hell you will. I know you, Dr. Philips. I know how desperate you are for your little project to succeed. You won't do anything that might risk your breeding experiment. Because, if you do, my uncle will have your balls."

An imp made Melanie add, "For dinner."

Wes tossed her a look, his lips twitching in an almost smile. "With hot sauce."

"You are not leaving that chamber until you are separated and contained. The longer you refuse, the longer you stay locked in there." Dr. Philips put on his sternest voice for his threat.

It left Wes unimpressed. "You want to leave us here? Sounds good to me."

It did? She quickly saw his logic. In there, together, at least, she could pretend some hope.

"You're being stubborn."

Wes cocked his head. "Just being a Mercer. Now, if you're done, go inject yourself with some more stupid shit. With any luck, you'll think you're a dog and decide your time is better spent playing fetch."

This time, she laughed out loud. The situation was dire, her life in jeopardy, but still, Wes was with her.

With her. Loving her. He might not have said as much, but he had to. Why else fight for her like this?

Dr. Philips made a sound that came close to a growl. "You won't get any food, water, or any other amenities until you obey."

Tapping his chin, Wes smirked. "No food? Are you sure about that?" He sniffed. A big, long whiff with his eyes shut that culminated in a wide, tooth-filled grin. "I smell coward behind that glass. It's not my preferred meal of choice, but a gator's got to eat."

"You can't get to me. This is bullet-proof glass."

"Never did much like that word can't. And I never could say no to a challenge." Wes flexed his arms, his skin rippling. "Stand back, angel. I think it's time we blew this joint."

Past time. She might have asked how he planned to get them, except she noted Wes began to morph, his control over the changes in his body astonishing. His torso widened, and thick scales rose from his skin, their color dark and dull out of water. The skin she'd so recently touched and admired turned into something else. Wes made himself into an armor-plated beast, which then ran on powerful legs at the glass.

Bang. He hit it shoulder first, the window absorbing most of the impact. Most being the key word. The window vibrated at the shock, and she heard the slight crackle of things straining.

"You can't get through."

Surely Wes heard the waver of uncertainty in those words. She did, and she could have laughed. The room surely was impenetrable —to normal people. Even difficult for most shifters to escape from. She'd wager the walls were concrete. The doors reinforced steel. But in wanting that window to watch the action, they'd created a weak spot. A weak spot not meant for a big, bad gator in a pissed-off mood.

Wham. The vibration went on longer this time it seemed as the glass shuddered.

Wes retreated and ran again as it still quivered.

The doctor screamed, "Stop!"

As if Wes would listen. *Bang*. He hit the glass again, and this time, it did more than shudder. He left behind a hairline crack.

The doctor stopped yelling. Not a good sign.

Wes took a few steps away from the window, readying for another rush. In the silence, she heard the hiss of escaping gas. "They're going to drug us!" she warned, taking a deep lungful of oxygen before it became contaminated.

Wes didn't reply. This dark beast had no expression. He charged again, ramming hard against the window with his shoulder. The single split fractured into a spider web of lines.

An alarm went off. *Whoop. Whoop.* The strident sound pierced her ears. But she didn't mind it because it meant Dr. Philips was scared.

He should be scared. Very scared because they were coming for him.

With his next bull gator rush, Wes smashed through. The hard ridge of his scales prevented him from getting sliced to ribbons. His armor also meant the dart the doctor fired at him bounced off.

"Ffffucker." Wes hissed the word as he lunged through the opening.

"Don't touch me," screamed the doctor, and surprisingly, she aped his words.

"Don't kill him. We need him alive to use the elevator."

"I'll save him," Wes grumbled, "as a snack for later."

The use of her air to talk meant her lungs burned. The gas swirled around Melanie as she fought not to breathe. She ran at the opening in the wall, reaching it just as Wes finished knocking out the sharp shards remaining.

He vaulted through and then turned to offer her a hand. She grasped it and let him pull her into the control room. She ignored the slumped body on the floor, gasping for air, feeling the tinge of the tranquilizer gas, acrid on her tongue.

The gas oozed into the room, overtaking the fresh stuff.

"We need out," she wheezed.

The door wouldn't yield to Wes's tug. She tapped his wrist, and he growled, "Duh," before grabbing the unconscious doctor and tossing him over a shoulder. Melanie held the doctor's wristband and then thumb against the scanner.

The door clicked open, and they stumbled into the hall, the gas trying to follow. She quickly slammed the door shut then turned at the *rat-tat-tat* of feet.

A pair of human guards ran toward them.

A roar erupted from Wes.

The guards replied by dropping to their knees and firing.

Wes immediately threw himself in front of Melanie. The darts fired fell harmlessly to the floor. As Wes advanced on the men, Melanie realized she couldn't keep hiding behind Wes.

I'm not a coward. But she could use some help from a certain feline.

Here kitty, kitty. Can you come out and play?

Ever since that last shot in her cell, she'd noted her senses coming alive. Could feel a certain vibration in her body that let her know she was returning to normal. She'd managed to pop some claws, but was that all?

Time to see if she could shift.

Ready?

Meow! Her panther burst out in an exuberant rush of fur and fangs, scattering the remnants of her paper gown. Power coursed through her limbs. Strength as well. With a push of hind legs, she bounded down the hall, snarling at the humans with wide, white eyes. Eyes that stared blankly once she bowled into them.

Keep me prisoner will they?

Rawr!

She kept on running past the downed guards, the other half of her reminding the alarm would draw more of the humans with their weapons.

Squeaky toys. Yay.

Dangerous, her more logical self reminded.

Yes, dangerous, with their weapons that fired those things that made her want to sleep. At least they were firing darts and not bullets. But that might not last long once the enemy realized she and Wes were on the loose.

The elevator doors slid open just as they arrived. The guards sporting real guns never stood a chance. They didn't even have time to scream as she leaped on one and Wes thundered into the other. Between the two of them, she slashed her foe into silence while her mate crushed the weaker body.

We make a formidable pair. No wonder their enemy Parker wished to mate them. Their children would be stupendous.

As the elevator door closed, shutting them in the box that moved, her fur remained hackled. Anger made her twitch. Someone had tried to lock her away. That male, the one she'd had as mate, tried to do her harm.

And they took my cubs.

She planned to get them back.

The doors opened and surprised those standing outside. Wes tossed the body of the human he carried at the guards, sending most falling to the floor. As for the one that dodged to the side and dared to raise his weapon?

With a snarl, she leaped and took him down. It proved messy, another layer of grime on her lush fur, but she'd have to groom herself later. They hadn't escaped yet.

No escape until we locate the cubs.

Their last location put them at the top floor. However, she and the gator appeared stuck on the main level. The elevator doors had sealed shut and wouldn't open, no matter whose wrist and thumb Wes slapped against the scanner.

Let me back out.

Her cat relinquished control, and Melanie shifted back, welcoming the painful reshaping of her bones as a sign that at least part of her was back to normal.

Wes remained in his hybrid shape. She couldn't have said how. She'd heard that, while it was possible to maintain a half shift, only a few could manage it. The strength of will required too much for most.

"What should we do?" She truly was at a crossroads of dilemmas. She needed to locate her boys, and yet, if she stayed, she would run the high risk of getting captured again. Maybe killed.

On the other paw, if she escaped, she could go for help, but would she get back in time to save her boys?

Instead of replying, Wes's head lifted.

She heard it a moment later, too. The crack and pop of gunfire.

"What the hell?" she muttered, taking a few steps toward the windows at the front of the building.

An explosion rocked the floor under their feet. The whooping alarms trebled in reply.

A glance through the glass windows of the lobby for the research building showed people running and screaming, but more interesting, smoke billowed in the distance by the front gate.

"What's happening?" she asked.

A computer voice announced, "Perimeter breach. All personnel please lock down your workstations. Security forces to the gate. This is not a drill." *Whoop. Whoop.*

It would have proven fascinating—in a movie! Being a part of what sounded like guerilla warfare? Kind of freaky, especially when Wes exclaimed, "Stay here. I'll go look."

Wes charged through the glass, the more decorative windows on this floor easier to break than that several levels below.

She thought about following, and yet... She stared at the ceiling, wondering if her missing boys had left the building. Given how hard it was to get in and out, could they have taken her advice and hidden where no one could find them?

How could she go and look?

The elevator doors dinged open, but the cab appeared empty. She dove into the elevator and slapped at the console to shut them. *Move, do something*. But the screen flashed red and mocked her with the word, "Lockdown."

But there was more than one way to go up. She peeked at the ceiling. While hard to distinguish, it was there. Just like in every movie. A hatch. It took her jumping a few times, banging it, to push it to the side then another leap to grab the edges and haul herself through.

Once inside the shaft, she peeked up, way up. A metal-rung ladder embedded in the concrete provided a method to climb.

As she stared at the daunting climb, the whooping alarm cut out. In the new silence, her ears rang a bit with the echo of the strident call. Fingers gripping the metal, she climbed, trying to ignore the distant sound of gunfire. What happened outside? Was it the good guys, come to rescue?

Or had Bittech drawn the attention of enemies? Their kind long feared humanity's discovery. If they knew monsters walked among them, would they move to rid themselves of a perceived threat?

She didn't even want to contemplate a world where their kind might get hunted.

Never hunted. We are the dominant species. They are only prey.

A very simple animal reaction, an outdated one. Today's humans didn't keep things fair by fighting with only their body. They used knives, spears, and, most deadly of all, guns.

All the skill in the world couldn't help if someone shot a shifter long range.

Please let this be a rescue. Let this nightmare end. Let her find her babies.

Keeping her boys in mind, she clambered up the ladder, the adrenaline of doing something powering her movement. She only slowed at the top, stumped initially by the closed doors. Now what?

Open them. Put a little muscle into it.

Smart-ass cat. But her feline was right. *I can open these.* Before, she'd found herself unable to pry them open, the surface seamless with nothing to grip. But they'd not paid as close attention within the shaft.

The tips of her claws wedged in the seam, she took a few deeps breaths before straining. It took a bit of grunting, a few muttered choice words—including "open, you fucking piece of scrap metal." They finally opened when she talked about taking a blowtorch to them and melting them into a puddle. A gaping portal didn't mean she immediately dove through. Wanting to live meant acting smart.

Breath held, she stood to one side of the open doorway and listened.

"Who's there?" a female voice asked.

Could Melanie be so lucky? She couldn't help a feral grin as she stepped out and saw the human nurse she'd first met. The one she didn't like.

What must Nurse Bitch think as Melanie stalked naked from the elevator, body covered in blood. "Where are my children?"

The nurse's complexion paled as she backed away. "I don't know where those demon spawn are. They disappeared."

"Did you seriously call my children demon spawn?" Melanie arched a brow and smiled. "Thank you. But don't think compliments will save your life."

"Don't come near me." The nurse pulled out a needle. A wee one.

Melanie laughed. "Let's play cat and mouse. Guess which one I am?"

Even in her human guise, Melanie could move quickly. She also knew how to fight dirty. A quick jabbing left that hit a jaw. A grasp of a flailing arm. A twist of a wrist to get a certain needle dropped. More twisting to get the woman to drop to her knees.

"I am going to ask you one more time." She applied a little more pressure, even as the nurse whimpered. "Where are my children?"

"I told you. I don't know."

"Then you are of no use to me." At the moment. Melanie snagged the discarded needle and jabbed the nurse with it, sending her into instant sleep. Killing her wasn't an option yet. She might need the nurse's active wristband and thumb to get out. With her boys.

Once she found them.

Chapter 20

RUSHING out of the medical building, Wes found himself immersed in noise, out-of-place noise that took a moment to process.

Under the whooping wail of the siren, he could hear the crackle of gunfire as weapons were discharged. Smoke curled with wispy tendrils in the air at a distance. Yells, screams, and even the roars and snarls of animals filled the air. More surreal was the golf cart that went whipping past, a pair of guards holding on for dear life. On their tail? A galloping moose.

He blinked. Yeah, still a moose with a big fucking rack chasing the shrinking cart.

By the time he saw the polar bear and the caribou, nothing could surprise him.

Was he hallucinating from the drugs pumped into the observation room? It might explain the madness around him.

A guttural roar saw him looking to his left. He wasn't surprised to see a big brown bear taking on one of the scaled hunters. It seemed the creatures were loose. He noted more than one monstrosity diving and flapping in the sky.

What of his brother? Was Brandon among them? He'd not seen nor heard of his brother since his capture. What did that mean?

The vicious snarls of the Kodiak and the lizard snapped him back to the present. He really should help, even if the bear seemed as if he was doing a fine job. He danced away from the claws that might poison him. He kept clear of the slavering jaws. The Kodiak also had help in the form of a massive timber wolf nipping at the heels of the dinoman.

What should he do? He'd left Melanie inside, but he'd not had time to ensure it was secure. Wes had to trust Melanie could take care of herself while she awaited his return. A return that was delayed as a black panther leaped from the top of a careening SUV to land in front of him with a snarl.

Wes only knew of one family of cats in the neighborhood. Forcing himself to release his hybrid gatorman shape, he stood before Daryl, hands cupping his junk because it was never wise to dangle things in front of irate kitties.

For a moment, Daryl paced in front of him, peeling back his lip for an angry noise. He did that a few times before morphing into his human shape, a human shape resembling that of a very angry Latino male, who punched him in the face without warning.

"Asshole! Where the fuck is my sister?"

Hit him back, his gator advised as Wes rotated his jaw. Melanie's brother packed an impressive punch. But he wouldn't return it. Melanie wouldn't like it, and that mattered to him. "Melanie's still inside the building. I didn't want to bring her out until I knew what was happening."

"Retribution has arrived," Daryl replied with some pride.

"Those your friends?" he asked, jerking a thumb at the polar bear who cuffed a grizzly, who then proceeded to head-butt the furball until they both shifted shapes and stood glaring nose to nose. Only to laugh a second later.

The camaraderie of good friends. Other than Brandon, Wes had given up on that years ago, but he missed it.

"They're friends. Allies. Call them what you like. They're part of the rescue team."

"How did you know where to come?" It was possible someone from Bitten Point had followed them, yet unlikely. Andrew and Parker took many precautions, precautions that seemed unfounded, given their open flaunting of shifters in and around the compound. "Did my sister make it out to tell you?" Wes asked.

He'd not spoken to Brandon since his capture. For all he knew, his brother had made it out of here with their sibling.

"Your sister? She's here, too?" Daryl couldn't hide a genuine inflection of surprise.

Deflation sucked some of the hope out of him. "If Brandon and Sue-Ellen didn't get out to tell you, then how did you find us?"

"My idiot little sister swallowed a tracker before taking her stupid ass off."

"Melanie wanted to save her boys."

"She should have told me what she was planning and we could have better prepared," Daryl grumbled.

As if. Melanie was too stubborn and brave for that. "Took you long enough to come for her," Wes noted.

A scowl crossed the other man's face. "I would have been here sooner, but Caleb and the others made me wait for backup."

Gesturing at the caribou racing around with a screaming guard on his rack and the moose who stood watching with evident disgust, Wes said, "Interesting help."

"I know. Not my friends. Apparently, Caleb knew a couple guys, mostly army dudes, from Kodiak Point."

Wes couldn't help his surprise. "Up in Alaska? And they came down here?"

"Them plus all the able-bodied folk in our town. And a few others. Once they all heard what was happening, no one could ignore it."

Knowing Daryl had come with enough aid to truly shut this place down lightened Wes's heart, and yet, at the same time, something niggled. Wes had left Melanie alone for more than a few minutes. Who the hell knew what kind of trouble she'd get into?

"I gotta go find Melanie."

"I'll come with you."

At least that was the plan when Daryl began loping back with him to the building until the sound of a chopper overhead distracted.

The news logo on the side almost made him trip. Wes recovered and darted into the building, wondering if anyone on board filmed his naked butt sprinting.

What were they doing here? It hadn't been long enough since the attack started for anyone to have reported the smoke or movie-style shoot-'em-up action. Had someone tipped them off?

This could get ugly, as in ditch-everything-behind-and-start-over-somewhere-new ugly. Another thing to worry about.

I'll have to watch the news later. After he found Melanie, who, of course, hadn't stayed where he left her.

It didn't prove hard to follow her scent. It went straight into trouble. He stared up the long shaft of the elevator and sighed.

Why couldn't shit ever happen in the bayou? He could swim great in there. Scuttle across the marsh lightning quick. Sneak attack. But climbing? That was for the lighter limbed.

But it took only a hollered, "Don't touch my mama!" for him to get moving.

I'm coming. In a zillion, billion rungs. *Ugh*.

Chapter 21

THE NURSERY LEVEL muffled the sounds of battle coming from outside, but she still heard them. The temptation to find a window to peek out of proved strong, but not as strong as Melanie's mommy instinct to find her babies.

On bare feet, Melanie padded the empty halls, straining for any sound or clue as to their location. The stillness in the air felt unnatural.

Inside, her inner kitty paced, and the sense of danger bristled her fur. *Don't trust the quiet,* her feline advised.

No worries on that count. The whole floor held a quality, that certain something, that let her know all was not as peaceful as it seemed. It was more than a gut instinct. She could feel it because buildings, places, they absorbed things and then oozed them. Right now, this twisted nursery oozed the calm before shit happened.

The smart move would be to leave, now. Find Wes. Find help. Do something. This level appeared abandoned, not a peep from her boys or anything else living, nothing except for that pervasive sense of danger.

I can't leave. What if my boys are still around here? At their size, they could hide anywhere. She would know. She'd almost lost her fur entirely more than once when they seemingly just disappeared.

Such as the time one peeked at her from a shelf in the closet behind spare linen. That fright took one of her lives.

The naughty little demon that popped up from the linen basket from under dirty clothes made her scream—and she lost another.

High entertainment for her boys and now, with danger stalking them, a honed skill that hopefully helped keep them out of harmful hands.

How to find them? Melanie didn't have time for a thorough search. But how else to find them when, as she walked, she couldn't help but taste the bitter ammonia in the re-circulated air. Its stringent scent nullified all others.

Forget scent. If she couldn't see or touch the boys, what did that leave?

Let's see if you're listening, babies. "Ollie, Ollie, oxen free," she sang, the universal song from her childhood for when they played hide-and-seek. "Come out. Come out, wherever you are." *Come out because Mama is here and I will keep you safe.*

She yodeled again to let her children know she'd arrived in case they remained on this level.

Good plan, and we'll let any enemies know we're here, too, so we can take care of them. Rowr.

She didn't correct the bloodthirsty plan. Anyone who got between her and her boys was asking for it. However, she doubted she'd really see much action. During her previous stay on the nursery level, she'd not seen any regular guards floating around, just the one nurse, and that bitch currently snored at the front desk.

Past the nurses' station, she got to peek down the long hall lined with doors and windows. It seemed all the rooms were open. How strange. They'd always been locked before when she'd tried to get in them.

Given she figured her boys had either disappeared from the playroom or the barrack room with beds, she headed to the closest one first.

The playroom door teased with its wide opening. Easing along the wall, she halted for a moment to listen before she peeked in to see it looked like a tornado had gone through the room.

A tornado or a lizard? Even with the antiseptic smell in the air, traces of that psycho reptile lingered, as did his actions. Tables torn from the floor and overturned. Chairs thrown against walls, some smashed. Around the ventilation grills, the flooring and the plaster on the walls showed signs of damage. She wondered if the gaping holes were part of the search for Rory and Tatum? Just how crazy did Andrew and his people go looking? And how had her boys vanished?

Not seeing her sons in the room didn't mean she took off right away. She decided to look closer at the ripped openings just in case she found her babies tucked inside. Tatum had once made it into the attic and popped his legs through the vent in the bathroom.

Andrew had been less than impressed, seeing as how he was in the shower at the time and screamed like a girl. A scream Tatum kept, unfortunately, mimicking.

Sob. Please let my babies be okay. She missed them so much. She feared so hard for their safety. The best sign? There was no blood.

By the rip in the flooring, she dropped to her knees and peeked in the hollow and narrow space. No way had Rory or Tatum squeezed in there. Not only was the vent much too small, the area around the conduits was much too small to move through unless they were the size of a hamster.

Moving on, she noted the walls also didn't provide any clues, the steel plate underneath a solid barrier.

So where are they?

She stepped into the middle of the room and inhaled deeply. Once again, that stupid ammonia smell permeated, wiping all essences except the truly strong one of the lizard thing known as Fang. Had they unleashed that crazy bastard after her babies? Had he found and hurt them?

He better not have.

The reminder she wasn't there to protect them angered her. Claws popped from her fingers, and the hair all over her body prickled.

This is Andrew's fault. His and Parker's. They took my babies. She would kill them for that.

She stepped back out into the hall, first taking a peek to ensure it remained clear.

Outside the building, the crackle and pops of gunfire had pretty much ceased, and she no longer heard the vicious barks and roars of the animal kingdom gone to war. She did, however, hear the *whup-whup-whup* of an approaching helicopter.

I must move more quickly.

A few strides and she arrived at the gaping door to the sleeping room. Her heart stuttered at the sight of the mussed bunks. In here, she could smell her sons. Smell their little-boy scent.

None of the destruction of the playroom had made it to this place. A walk around the perimeter didn't reveal any clues or other exits. If her boys were here, she couldn't have said where. A peek under the bunks didn't reveal anyone.

"Where are you?" she muttered.

"Right here."

She whipped around at the words, a feral smile stretching her lips as she realized who stood in the doorway. "Andrew. Just the man I wanted to see." Wanted to see dead, but she didn't specify that. He'd learn first-paw soon enough.

"Looking for the brats?"

"Where did you put my sons?" A rumbly growl accented her query.

An irritated scowl crossed his face. "Nowhere. They disappeared. From a locked room no less."

"They escaped." She couldn't help a spurt of elation. Now if only she could be sure they'd escaped this place entirely because she couldn't wait to leave.

First, though, she needed to ensure the man before her didn't live long enough to ever harm her boys again.

"Are you gonna run and make this sporting for me?" she asked with a swing of her hips as she walked toward Andrew. She was done catering to his little ego—and she meant little. Her cat hovered, waiting for a chance to leap forth.

"We'll see who does the running. I'm a changed man now." As he spoke, his voice changed. It dipped deeper. He began to sprout hair, coarse brown and black strands, and yet he kept his human shape. He also kept his face, if hairier, but his eyes, they glinted a dark orange, and they glowed from within, alight with madness and violence. "I am so tired of people thinking they're bigger and better than me. Especially you. You always made me feel small."

"You never could grasp it wasn't about size. All you had to do, Andrew, was believe in yourself. To stand tall."

"I'm standing tall now." He certainly was, as his body pushed upward and thickened. How was he doing this? Animals were restricted by the size of the host. Big men turned into big creatures. They were also heavy men as humans. But still, certain laws applied.

They just didn't seem to apply to Andrew. He stood about eight feet tall. His body kept its human shape, despite his freakish size and fur.

She should also mention the honking huge claws. While over his shoulders peeked... She gasped. "Wings?"

But Andrew didn't seem too interested in answering her surprise. With a roar of primal rage, he charged at her. She leaped out of the way, changing mid-air, a skill she'd learned as a cub because of an older brother determined to teach her to protect herself. Daryl used to practice by tossing her in the pond behind their house. She quickly learned to flip in mid-air and land with four paws on the one rock projecting from the surface. She hated getting her feet wet.

She also hated things that wanted to eat her. As Andrew rushed past, she landed behind him and slashed with her paw, her own claws extended.

Score! The cuts oozed dark red. A victory she couldn't bask in because Andrew had already turned around. Snorting, much like a bull, his eyes seemed to get darker. He came at her again.

As her feline, Melanie could spring and dodge with ease, but Andrew possessed a long reach. The tip of a sharp nail caught her, and she screeched at the sudden bright flare of pain against her rear haunch.

It was then that a blanket flew off a bed, and from a hollowed-out spot in the mattress, a little body came flying out, arms and legs spreadeagle.

"Don't you touch my mama!" Rory yelled.

He hit the papa bear and clung like a monkey, his little fists pummeling. So heartbreakingly brave, so woefully small. Andrew immediately plucked her son and held him out, short limbs kicking and punching.

A low, menacing rumble oozed from her, the intent clear—*Don't hurt my baby.*

Andrew roared and shook Rory.

Oh, hell no. She wanted to leap at Andrew, tear him to shreds, but she had to tread carefully. The man held her cub's life in his paw.

She took slow, slinking steps toward them, her gaze unwavering. As center of attention, Andrew let a parody of a grin stretch his misshapen features. He pulled Rory close and inhaled deeply. Then licked his lips.

A horrifying threat that her son understood. He hung from Andrew's grasp like a scolded puppy. Limp. Head hanging.

My poor baby. Mama's here. I won't let him hurt you.

She caught a glimpse of her son's eyes through thick, dark hair. Mischief gleamed, and he winked.

What. The. Hell? She couldn't even scream, *Don't do it*. There was no time. Rory flipped from feigned terror to rabid kitty. He flipped in the air, using the hand holding him as a pivot point. He managed to lock his little legs around Andrew's neck while, at the same time, landing a bite.

A fantastic move on anyone else, not an eight-foot, mutant freak.

Andrew snapped a gasket, yanking her son away and shaking him, hard.

He shook her child. Shook. Him.

I will shake you. Once she clamped him in her jaws. She'd whip him around like a rag doll for daring.

Rowr. Her roar vibrated in the air, challenging the bear in front of her who dared threaten her cub.

"Don't move," grunted the Andrew-thing. "Or the brat dies."

At that threat, Tatum appeared, standing on the bed to Andrew's left. Rory lifted his head, his eyes still not cowed. In twin tandem, her babies replied to Andrew's threat. "But don't you love us, Daddy?"

The boys didn't know, and Melanie wasn't about to hide the truth from them. She shifted back to her human form. "Andrew is not your daddy."

"Then we don't have to be nice anymore," Tatum announced as he dove at Andrew's legs.

"Hate him," announced Rory, who swung suddenly, his two little feet connecting with Andrew's less-than- impressive family jewels.

Teetering on one leg, and thrown off balance, Andrew fell, and she could only watch in fascination as her darling twins, who should have been unable to shift yet being so young, turned into something feline, yet scaled.

Oh my.

Her twin terrors nipped at the monster, instinct controlling their actions.

But Andrew wasn't done with the surprises. With a massive roar, he flung their little bodies from him and stood. And he grew. Grew even bigger. His eyes turned a complete red, and he huffed. "Meat."

Um, no.

Time to get out of here.

Chapter 22

AS HE EMERGED from the elevator shaft, it took only a quick glance to see nobody was in sight. Wes immediately sprinted for the hall. How frustrating during the seemingly interminable climb to hear the signs of a fight and yet be so far.

But he'd arrived, and as he bolted toward the corridor past the nurses' station, he skidded to a halt as he spotted a naked and bloody Melanie racing up the hall, one scaled cub boy on her hip, the other loping on all four, his yellow eyes ablaze.

Behind them galloped a monster. Holy fuck, what was that?

Part bear, part bat, part insanity. Whoever and whatever it was, Wes had to stop it.

"Shoot it!" she screamed.

As if he had a gun hidden on his naked ass. "Get into the elevator shaft. I'll slow it down." Because killing a thing that size might prove a little challenging.

Challenge? His inner beast perked. *We are stronger than Andrew.*

This was Andrew? How did his beast know?

As Melanie raced past him, she confirmed it. "Andrew's taken some kind of drug. Whatever it is, it's made him hard to hurt. And huge."

Great. A really big challenge for this gator.

Ready?

Stupid question. His gator surged forth, pushing Wes out of the way, wanting this fight, wanting to test himself in this battle of will and strength.

At the sight of his gator, a gator that seemed larger than even Wes recalled, the charging monster slowed and halted. At the junction of hall and reception area, Andrew paced, head low to the floor as he circled slowly, his nose twitching as it tested the air. *Snuffle. Snort. Grunt.*

Wes didn't know what the monster did, but he also didn't want to spook it quite yet, so he didn't move from his spot in front of the elevator shaft. Melanie needed time to get down with her boys to safety. She was going to get that time.

And maybe a new fur rug.

His slitted eyes tracked the mutant bear as it crept closer. The reach on those paws was insane, the clawed tips rendering them even more deadly.

The leathery wings at its back fluttered, but given their stunted size, Wes doubted they provided any real use.

He heard excited yells from the shaft at his back. The echo moving upwards from some place low. Melanie and the boys made good time in their descent.

They're safe.

Time for him to deal with Andrew and then join them.

Wes opened his mouth wide in invitation. Then clacked it shut. Snap. The message was clear. *Come and get me, asshole.*

Andrew lunged, but Wes was ready for it. He scuttled to the side and whipped around, jaws chomping at a hairy hindquarter. A major roar erupted as he scored a bite.

Wes sidestepped as Andrew whirled and slammed a fist down. Smash. Smash. Left fist, right fist. Both cracking tile.

Before Andrew could pull upright, Wes darted in and grabbed hold of Andrew's wrist. He locked his teeth around it and tried not to gag on the hairball in his mouth. Ugh.

A normal creature would have freaked and tried to pull free. Normal being the key word. Andrew was way past that point, and he proved freakishly strong. The Andrew monster lifted his arm and dangled fucking Wes from it. Shook him, too.

You are not getting rid of me that easily. Wes held on tight, even when he got slammed into the wall alongside the elevator shaft.

That smarted.

So he bit harder, feeling sinew and flesh tearing, the acrid blood of his enemy coating his tongue. Revolting and definitely not the yummy flavor of something freshly hunted. The blood tasted wrong, and that was the reason why Wes finally relinquished his grip. He wanted to spit the foulness from his mouth. Needed to rid himself of the vile taint that numbed his tongue.

Andrew took it as a sign he won. The mutant freak pounded his chest and roared. Enamored of his supposed superiority, Andrew never looked down. Never saw Melanie as she reached from the elevator shaft and grabbed his leg for a yank.

She didn't have enough weight to make it work, and before Andrew could react, Wes propelled himself forward as fast as he could.

Smack. He plowed into Andrew's hairy legs, and the teeter turned into a totter, and then gravity gave them a hand.

Down the shaft Andrew fell, bellowing, his stunted wings flapping, arms and legs pedaling. None of it helped.

Thunk.

The sound of Andrew's body hitting the elevator roof made the whole shaft tremble.

Speaking of tremble, he could see Melanie's arms shook where she held on to the lip of the door. Quickly, Wes shifted shapes, determined to grab her. A quick roll on the floor and he snagged her wrists before she went elevator shaft diving.

Their eyes met.

"Hi," she said.

Happiness at her safety flooded him, but the only thing he could think of saying was, "You were supposed to escape with your boys."

"Daryl has them."

"And he let you come back?"

"In his defense, I didn't tell him I was. They were all kind of distracted by the helicopter outside filming them."

Shit. The news chopper. Not good. Not good at all. "We need to get out of here before that news clips hits the air."

"Then what are you waiting for?" She smirked.

"For you to move that sweet ass out of the way."

In the end, he helped her with that ass, her adrenaline finally having peaked during the battle. She clung to him, arms and legs wrapped around his body as he clambered down.

As he neared the bottom, they couldn't help but note the body atop the elevator, a body now shrunken and pink skinned again. The body also wasn't quite dead. The chest rose and fell, and a wheezing rattle whistled through Andrew's lips.

As Melanie and Wes hopped onto the roof of the elevator cab, Andrew opened bloodshot eyes. "Fucking bitch. I should have killed you when I had the chance."

"That would have taken balls." Melanie glanced at Andrew's groin. "And we both know how lacking you are in that department."

"My father will kill you for this."

"Your father hasn't been seen in days," Wes reminded. "He knew the end was coming and got out."

"Liar."

"Doesn't really matter, does it?" Wes crouched down on one knee. "You'll be dead in a matter of minutes. You lost."

A chuckle rattled from Andrew's broken body. "Did I really lose? My legacy will live on in my creations. Even you can't escape the taint, gator. It runs in your veins now and in that of your sons."

Wes assumed Andrew spoke to Melanie, and yet why did the man never break their stare?

"Stupid fucking gator. You still don't get it, do you?" Andrew's attempt at another chuckle turned into a wet cough. Blood filmed his lips. "The boys are yours. And you never even knew it."

With that final shocker, Andrew died, his eyes staring sightlessly above.

Wes might have died a little in that moment, too.

Holy fuck, I'm a dad.

Snap. His chin hit the top of the elevator as he slumped forward.

Chapter 23

WHAT'S WRONG WITH WES? A flutter of panic swept Melanie as Wes keeled forward moments after the news he was actually the father of the twins.

Mine and Wes's. How could I have not guessed? Then again, why would Melanie ever have thought them anything other than Andrew's, given the elaborate hoax her supposed husband perpetrated all those years.

If Andrew wasn't already dead, she'd kill him again.

Or maybe she should thank him. At least her sons wouldn't have to grow up thinking their dad was a psychotic murderer. Now they could have a dad who was just a psychotic gator.

The mind-blowing reality would have to wait, though. Something ailed Wes. He'd yet to move since he'd plunked face-first.

Please let him be okay. She sank beside him on her bare knees and turned him over to check him for signs of injury. She didn't see any obvious wounds, only a few bruises and scratches. Had someone poisoned him? Those crazy doctors were pretty liberal with their use of drugs and needles.

She cupped his cheeks, reassured that he at least breathed. "Wes! Wes!"

As she shouted his name, his eyes fluttered open, the ridiculously long lashes framing them so beautifully. "Angel? Is that really you? Am I in heaven?"

"No, you idiot. You're still on the elevator giving me a scare. What's wrong with you?" Please let it be something not fatal. She didn't think she could handle losing Wes again.

"I'm a daddy," he uttered with incredulity.

She blinked at his words. "Yeah. You're a daddy. To twins terrors, I might add. But I asked you what's wrong with you."

He repeated himself. "Fuck me, I'm a daddy." With that, he closed his eyes again.

He's freaking out because he's a father? She gaped at him. She also slapped him.

That got him wide-awake and glaring. "What did you do that for?"

"You're a daddy. Get over it. No need to go all fainting princess on me."

"I am not fainting. I am merely resting my eyes and processing events."

"Well, process them later. Weren't you the one saying we had to get out of here? I'm expecting the cops will show anytime now. I don't know about you, but I'd rather not explain why I'm naked and covered in blood."

"There's no way we're going to be able to keep this hidden," he said, scrambling to his feet. "If they even taped half of what happened, there are going to be questions. Lots of them."

She couldn't help but agree. "The kitty is out of the bag, and I don't think there's any hope of stuffing it back in. But that doesn't mean we should stick around and wait for shit to happen. I, for one, don't want to get stuffed back into another cage."

"Good point. Let's get out of here."

She could have snorted as he suddenly went from Mr. Limp

Noodle to Mr. Decisive. Wes shoved Andrew's body to the side, away from the opening. He leaped down first, took a peek, declared, "All clear," and then held up his arms for her.

Unnecessary. She could have jumped down on her own, but she did appreciate the gesture.

His callused hands caught her around the waist as she hopped down through the opening. He lowered her slowly, letting her body rub against his during the descent. She couldn't help a shiver of desire. Nothing like skin-to-skin touch to remind her she lived.

Wes clutched her close and buried his face in her messy hair. "Is it wrong to want to hold you forever and keep you safe?"

Not wrong, and it did all kinds of crazy things to her heart. She hugged him. "Let's plan on hugging like this again later. Naked. If you're good," she teased, and that was if they got out of here. Let her promise be the incentive he needed to get them to safety because, even with Andrew dead, they weren't out of the woods and safe in the bayou yet.

Emerging from the elevator, she noted a large sports utility vehicle out front. Her brother leaned against it, wearing only track pants while talking to another big guy, also only in pants. Being raised as a shifter meant she knew not to stare at all the bare flesh, and they extended the same courtesy. She exited and caught the T-shirt he tossed at her.

"Where are the boys?" she asked as she tugged the fabric over her head.

"Safe thanks to their most excellent uncle." Daryl growled. "What happened to stay put, don't move? I turned my back for one freaking second and you were gone."

"Wes needed me."

"Did not," Wes refuted. "I had things perfectly under control."

"Whatever."

Daryl clapped his hands. "Argue about it later and get in the truck. We're about to have company. Someone called in the media and the cops and anyone else who ever wanted to join a three-ring fucking circus."

"I can't leave without my sister or brother," Wes announced, yanking on a pair of gray track pants.

"Where are they?"

Just as Wes pointed to the building housing Parker, an explosion trembled the ground underfoot and the windows blew out. Smoke immediately followed, as did more explosions as, one by one, the buildings imploded.

"Move!" Daryl yelled, shoving her toward the truck.

She understood his haste. If someone had set off bombs to get rid of evidence, then the medical institute would probably go next.

Sliding into the backseat of the truck, she didn't make it far before little arms, poking from oversized shirts, grabbed at her.

"Mama!" the twins yelled, crushing her in their exuberance. She loved it and squished them right back.

My boys. They're safe. Tears pricked at her eyes.

"Move over, angel. Make room." Wes climbed into the back seat with them, and he'd no sooner shut the door when the SUV sped off, Daryl in the passenger seat, a stranger at the wheel. Just in time, too. The biggest explosion of all made the whole world vibrate, and something hit the top of the truck hard enough to leave a dent.

"Fuck me, that was close," Daryl exclaimed.

"Yup," said the fellow behind the wheel.

"Who are you?" Wes asked, grabbing the T-shirt Daryl handed him from the bag he pulled it from in the front.

"Our driver is Boris," said her brother. "Dude with the big rack." To which Boris grunted.

"Thanks for coming out."

Melanie could have screamed at the polite exchange. "Say thank you later. I want to know what's happening."

"What's happening is the end of shifter civilization as we know it," Daryl announced.

"What do you mean the end?" she asked, and Daryl hesitated as he shot Wes a look.

Her brother sighed. "You want to explain it, or shall I?"

"I'll do it." Wes angled his head to face her. "Remember, angel, how we talked in the elevator shaft about how the cat's out of the bag? When Daryl says it's the end, what he means is our old lives are gone. We can't go back to Bitten Point, angel. None of us. What just happened back there? It's not going to get swept under a rug or ignored. People filmed us. Hell, we're probably being followed right now."

The warning saw her hugging the twins tighter. "So, what do you think is going to happen? Are we going to get hunted down?" Treated like animals instead of people?

His expression bleak, Wes shrugged. "Maybe. Depends what kind of spin the press puts on our existence."

"Where are we supposed to go?"

It was her boys who answered, "On an adventure."

Their optimism put some things in perspective.

I'm alive. They're alive. They might not be one hundred percent normal, but they were her babies. *Mine and Wes's.*

In a day filled with danger and surprises and death, it turned out the boys hadn't lost a daddy. They might have gained a real one.

If a certain gator was up to the challenge.

She didn't get to talk to Wes until after the boys were tucked into a motel bed, exhausted by their ordeal. She slipped through the connecting door, shutting it softly, to find a freshly showered Wes watching the television. His face was grim.

"How bad is it?" she asked.

"Take a look." He gestured to the screen, and she couldn't help but wince at the footage being shown. Animals tearing into each other. Men shooting beasts. Men shifting into animals. Then back. She could only watch in stunned silence.

Even over the stutter of the helicopter blades, she could hear the sounds of screaming, guns firing, and animals snarling. It sounded like a full-on war. And, in a sense, it was. A war to free themselves from the tyranny of a few who thought they should change the status quo. But what would the humans see? Think?

They will see us as monsters. Shiver.

As if sensing her turmoil, Wes wrapped an arm around her and hugged her close. "No shoving it back into a closet now. For better or worse, shifters have been outed."

"Are we okay for tonight?"

"More than okay. I've yet to hear anyone make the connection to Bitten Point yet. Some of those who didn't budge from town say no one's come around. Whatever things Parker and Andrew did to set up the company didn't leave a trail, and your brother and the others made sure to obscure license plates before the invasion."

"Does this mean we can go back home?"

"Maybe. I'll know more in the morning. We can decide then."

She ran a finger down his chest. "We?"

He caught her finger and held it. "Angel, I—"

Stupid man thought he was going to talk, and not to say the right things, judging by the serious look on his face. She wasn't about to let him ruin what they had, not this time.

She put her finger against his lips. "Shh." She replaced that finger with her lips, brushing them against his.

He held himself stiff at first, but she knew his weak points. *I am his weak point.*

She murmured, "Kiss me. Make love to me. Touch me, Wes. I want to feel alive."

What man could resist that plea? Wes didn't even try. With a groan of surrender, he tumbled them back on the bed, his lips taking aggressive control of her mouth. Commanding her lips to open. Dueling with her tongue for dominance.

How she loved this side of him. All man. *All mine.*

It was past time she showed him he wasn't the only one with a need to taste things. She pushed him onto his back and straddled him.

His big hands spanned her waist, and his heavy-lidded eyes perused her. "You are so beautiful," he murmured.

"And you're obviously still under the influence of drugs. My hair is a mess, I'm wearing a man's T-shirt, and I haven't managed to shave any important bits in days."

His lips quirked. "And yet, you've never looked sexier."

He drew her down for a kiss, a slow, sensual teasing embrace that had her fingers digging into his chest and her sex heating. She squirmed atop him, feeling the hard ridge of his erection beneath the fabric of his pants.

Pushing away from him, she sat up and gripped the hem of her shirt. She yanked it over her head, baring herself to his view, wondering if he would care that her breasts hung a little heavier and that her curves were a little more pronounced.

"Fuck me, angel," he breathed, the reverence in his tone clear, but even more telling, in the thickening and pulsing of the cock underneath her.

He likes what he sees.

Nothing like a man's admiration to make a woman want to preen and purr. She arched her back. "Wanna taste?"

With one arm anchored around her waist, he sat up while, at the same time, leaning her back to give him the right angle to tug a nipple into his mouth.

Sweet heaven. The molten tug of his mouth against her nub made her pussy clench. It felt so damned good. He sucked her nipple into his mouth, swirling his tongue around it.

She might have whimpered when he let go, but then she moaned as he grasped the other nipple with his lips and gave it the same torturous attention.

Yes!

He spent a few minutes playing with her breasts, teasing them in turn until she panted and squirmed atop him.

But he wasn't the only one who wanted to play.

She shoved him back down and ordered him to, "Lace your hands behind your head." Her turn to lick something.

Getting to her knees, she crawled backwards, letting her lips tease the taut flesh of his chest, moving lower and lower until she reached the waistband of his pants. Her teeth grabbed the material and tugged. Tugged and got caught on his erect cock.

Grrr. Yeah, she growled with impatience as her fingers had to tug the fabric over his erect shaft. Freed, his dick bobbed upright, long, thick, and oh so yummy looking.

She gripped it, and he hissed. She shot him a warning stare. "Don't move those hands."

He growled back.

Her laughter vibrated his cock as she took him into her mouth. Mmm. The salty drop at the top flavored the big bite. How she loved the feel of him in her mouth. She worked her lips up and down the length of him, tasting every inch, loving how he pulsed at her sucking. How his breathing came harshly at her bobs up and down.

But as much as she wanted to taste all of him, she needed him inside her tonight. Needed that close connection she felt with Wes every time their bodies joined so intimately.

It took only a little maneuvering to position her over his cock. She lowered herself slowly onto it, head thrown back as she took him deep, deeper, until all of him was buried.

Slowly, she rotated her hips, grinding herself on him, pushing until the tip of him hit that sweet spot inside.

He helped her find that rhythm, his hands on her hips, the firm feel of them on her skin so nice. Together they rocked, her pleasure coiling tighter and tighter until, with a scream she had to muffle, with a bite to her lip, she came. The pleasure rolled through her, leaving her limp, so limp she collapsed on his chest.

But Wes held back. He didn't come. He rolled them until she was under him, flat on her stomach. He yanked her ass into the air, exposing her to his view. She clutched at the comforter as he entered her slowly from behind.

Inch. Another inch. A slow, torturous invasion. She could have screamed as her still pulsing flesh stretched to accommodate him once again. Only once he was fully seated did he stop being so damned gentle.

Withdraw. Slam. Over and over he thrust into her welcoming flesh, teasing the remnants of her orgasm and then bringing it to a peak again when he reached under and rubbed her clit as he thrust.

She buried her face in a pillow as he fucked her into a second orgasm, a stronger one that had her yelling into the fabric then almost whimpering as the pleasure proved to be almost too much.

Just when she thought she might die of a never-ending orgasm, which kept her sex quivering and pulsing, he came.

Came with her name on his lips. "Melanie." Came with a growled, "Mine."

Came and then collapsed on her, just like a man. Her man, a man she wrapped her limbs around for a cuddle. A short cuddle before the mommy gene kicked in.

"Put some clothes on."

"What?" he muttered.

"Pants at least," she admonished as she rolled off the bed. She yanked on her T-shirt and located her missing panties. When had those come off? And how had they ended up on the lamp?

She padded away from the bed to open the connecting door a few inches and peek in. Still sound asleep. Good. She left the door ajar as she returned to Wes sitting on the side of the bed wearing track pants and a bemused expression.

"Get back under those covers and scooch over," she ordered.

"What now?"

She smiled. "Cuddle time."

And sleep, because the events of the day finally caught up, and in the arms of the man she loved, she found peace.

Chapter 24

WAKE UP, dumbass. Someone's in the room.

He fought to keep his eyes closed, even though every nerve tingled as he heard the soft pad of feet, the shushed giggle, smelled the sweet scent of innocence. It was the boys. But why were they up? It was the middle of the night.

Before he could ask them why they were awake, he had to hold his breath and hope that the little hands and knees clambering over his body missed the important bits. It proved close, but his jewels survived a pair of warm bodies worming their way in between him and Melanie. The twins snuggled in, and a few minutes later, the soft whoosh of their breaths let him know they slept. Slept with absolute trust beside him.

The very concept froze him in shock. What did one do when a bed was invaded by little people?

Not just any people.

These are my sons.

His sons.

At least this time he didn't faint at the realization, but it did make him anxious. It also reminded him how woefully inadequate he proved as a father. He'd not only not been there for these kids—and, no, he didn't give himself a free pass on the subterfuge over their creation; he should have known—but add to that the fact he'd played a part in their capture, in Melanie's capture, and in all the shit that happened with Bittech—he was the last person they should be trusting to sleep with.

I've brought them nothing but trouble. And he would continue to do so because it was the Mercer way.

All the self-flagellation came back in an instant, despite Melanie's sweet words and sweeter caresses.

He didn't deserve the woman in this bed, and he most certainly didn't deserve these awesome little boys.

What should he do? What could he do?

I need a smoke.

Easing from the bed, he tugged on a shirt and, from the table by the door, grabbed the pack of cigarettes he'd scored. He headed outside, moving away from the motel itself into the darker shadows at the outer edges of the parking lot.

Boris had driven them for a few hours until he deemed them far enough to stop for the night, and as the grizzled moose stated, "Regroup and plan our next move in the morning." A move that would probably involve them all finding new identities and homes until they could know for sure what their exposure meant.

The question was, what should he do? The last time Wes had done the right thing, he'd hurt the one person he loved most in the world.

Flick. The tiny flame lit the darkness with orange before setting the tip of his cigarette on fire. The first drag of smoke abraded his lungs, and he coughed. And coughed. The stench of the nicotine repulsed him.

"Filthy goddamned thing." He tossed the offensive butt to the ground. But that wasn't enough. He threw the full pack after it and stomped it. Ground it into the fucking dirt.

"About time you quit."

His head jerked at the sound of his brother's voice. "Brandon?"

Screw his tattered mancard. Wes threw his arms around his brother and hugged him. Hugged him so fucking tight he might have cracked a rib or two.

"I take it you're glad to see me," his brother rumbled.

Releasing him, Wes took a moment to spit on the ground—damned ashtray taste in his mouth lingered—and nonchalantly admit, "Maybe a little."

Brandon laughed. "I'm glad to see you, too, big brother. Although, you weren't easy to follow."

"You followed us?"

"In the sky." His brother looked upward. "Which took some fancy flying considering those freaking helicopters toss around a lot of wind."

Wes reached out and tapped the collar around his brother's neck. "I thought this thing stopped you from going over the fence."

"Those folks that attacked the perimeter knocked the zapping mechanism offline."

"And they freed you."

Brandon shook his head. "I don't know who freed me or the others. I woke up in a cage to see other prisoners running for a secret exit. Turns out there was one hidden at the opposite end."

"What about Sue-Ellen? Did you manage to help her escape before they grabbed you?" *Please let her not have been in the building when it blew.*

"I don't know what happened to her." Brandon shook his head. "Like you, the fuckers darted me before I had a chance to get off the roof. Then, later, when I got out of the below-ground levels, I emerged into a warzone. Guns. And fighting. I took to the air to see what was going on, and that's when I spotted you getting into that. Then everything blew to hell. I figured it was best to follow you. Do you think Susu died in the blast?"

Fuck, he hoped not. It burned Wes to know he'd left without trying to find his sister. Then again, what choice did he have? If captured or detained, he'd do nobody any good. It didn't help the guilt.

"I should have stayed behind and looked for her."

Brandon shoved Wes hard enough he reeled into a tree.

"What the fuck was that for?" he snapped.

"Get off your fucking martyr trip. This isn't your fault. Sue-Ellen. Me. We're not your responsibility."

"You're my family," Wes uttered through gritted teeth.

"Yeah, we are, but that doesn't mean you have to give up everything for us."

Yet, didn't they understand he would? He loved them, goddammit. Stupid pollen in the air made his eyes water, and he ducked his head.

The rustle of wings made him look up sharply. "Where are you going?"

A sad smile curved his brother's lips as he hovered a few feet above ground. "Somewhere you won't be in danger."

"What are you talking about? We should stick together."

"In that you're wrong. The world knows monsters now exist. Humans know our secret. How safe do you think you'll be if you stick with me?" Brandon gestured to his body. "This is who I am now. I can't hide among the masses like you can. Therefore it's best I leave."

A part of Wes understood why Brandon did it, but it didn't mean he liked it.

Funny because weren't you thinking about doing the same thing? Leaving the people you care about because you think they're better off without you?

"How will I know if you're okay?" Wes asked.

"I'll use that trick Uncle Sammy did when he was smuggling contraband. I'll post ads in the classifieds. Single lizard male is looking to reassure his pussy of a brother he's fine."

Wes couldn't help but snort. "You're an asshole."

"Love you, too, big bro. Stay cool."

With a final salute of farewell, his brother ascended, big wings flapping, another shadow in the sky that Wes soon lost from sight.

Another person he couldn't help. But, then again, his little brother seemed bound and determined to make it on his own. It wouldn't be easy, just like life going forward wouldn't be easy for any of shifter kind. The secret was out. The thing they'd all grown up fearing had come to pass. Such a defining fucking moment in every shifter's life.

But not as defining as knowing Melanie's boys were his.

I'm a fucking father. And it scared the piss out of him.

What did he know of being a dad? What could he offer those kids? Wouldn't it be crueler to taint them with the Mercer name?

Melanie was single again. She could remarry, to a nice guy this time who would—

Oh, like fuck.

Who was he kidding? *I left her once. It almost killed me. I am not leaving her, or my sons, again.*

And anyone who dared to stand in his way would get a big ol' gator welcome.

Snap.

Chapter 25

STANDING AT THE MOTEL WINDOW, Melanie hugged the phone to her ear. "Why are you sighing again?" her mother asked.

Why not? Waking to find the boys in bed and Wes gone left her feeling empty.

He's gone. The thing she'd feared most when she let Wes back into her heart.

Melanie knew her mother wouldn't be sleeping, not with everything that happened, and so she called her, even though she could have just walked a few doors down. While some people might have stayed behind, Daryl ensured their mother hadn't.

"Can't a girl just sigh?" she finally replied to her mother's query.

"No!" her mother retorted.

"I think I'm entitled. I mean, my whole life just got dumped on its ass, and now I've got to figure out a few things."

"Like?"

"Like what to do now that Parker has outed us to the world? Do I take a chance and return to Bitten Point? Go somewhere else? If I do stay, what happens to the house now that Andrew is gone? I mean, according to him, we were no longer legally married, so who gets it now that he's dead?" Did she even want anything associated with that madman?

"Your Uncle Rodriguez will make arrangements. Don't worry about that," her mother declared. Her uncle had a knack for fixing the books. "Why don't you really say what you mean, which is, what should you do about the fact Wes is the boys' father?"

Ah yes, the shocking revelation by Andrew just before he did the world a favor and died. "What of it? I know what he's going to do." She could see it in his eyes. *He's left me again.*

"So don't let him. Your Wes, much like Caleb, has got this stubborn idea in his head that you're better off without him. Isn't that why he dumped you in the first place?" Her mother didn't mince words.

"He dumped me because he was a jerk." Who thought he wasn't good enough for her. Funny, because she'd always thought he was too good to be true.

Did he still believe she deserved better? Dammit, she did. She deserved better than the raw deal she got with Andrew. She deserved something from the guy who donated sperm to make her awesome twin terrors.

She deserved something from the man who made her feel alive again and then ran away the moment he could.

Like hell.

She let him run once, and look what happened.

Chase him down.

Yeah.

Pin him.

Yeah.

Pee on him to mark him as ours.

Um, she was thinking more of a love bite, but yeah!

Time to go stalk my man.

She flung open the motel room door, ready to hunt Wes down if he hadn't gone too far, only to stop dead.

Wes stood in front of the motel door, surprise etched on his face. "Where do you think you're going?"

She arched a brow. "I was coming to get you before you ran away again."

Wes opened his mouth, but before he could speak, she held up a hand. "Don't you dare say a word. I let you do all the talking years ago when you decided what was best for our relationship. And look what happened."

"You married a psychopath who used you in medical experiments."

"I did. And it's all your fault."

A smile tugged his lips at the accusation. "I guess it is. So what are you suggesting I do?"

"First off, you should beg forgiveness for being an ass."

He dropped to his knees, a supplicant before her. "Angel, losing you was the stupidest thing I've ever done."

Her turn to gape.

He winked. "And I'm still a dumb ol' gator, but if there's one thing I'm smart about it's knowing you are the best damned thing that ever happened to me. I know I've got lots of apologizing to do. And things won't be easy, not with what's happened and all. But I intend to stick by you, no matter what. I want a chance to love you. To protect you. You and our sons. I want to try and be the man you thought I could be."

"Oh, Wes." Tears brimmed in her eyes, and her throat felt tight. "You always were the man I wanted. The one I love." She threw herself into his arms, wrapping him tight. "Don't ever leave me again."

"Never," he said in a fervent promise.

But he froze when a little voice said, "Are you my daddy?"

This time, Wes didn't collapse on his face. He didn't even blanch. He stepped away from Melanie and turned to face the little boys standing side by side in the doorway. Their solemn gazes took in the man who provided half the genes in their body.

Wes sank to his knees. He held open his arms wide. "I am your daddy. And I swear no one"—his voice lowered—"no one will ever harm you or your mother again."

It took the boys only a half second to react. Her twin terrors threw themselves at Wes, and he didn't recoil or push them away. He gathered them in a hug to beat even that of their snake friend, Constantine. Wes held his sons, and dammit, she couldn't help but sob—tears of joy—as she noted the moisture in his eyes.

For better or worse, no matter what the future brought, they would face the challenge together. As a family. A Mercer family who would show the world what they were truly capable of.

Snap and rawr. Forever.

Epilogue

THE SHIFTER HIGH COUNCIL appointed a spokesperson to deal with the news of their existence. One guess on who was chosen for that role.

The bastard who purposely maneuvered them into revealing their secret took the stage with a great big smile. He wasn't alone. The where-is-Sue-Ellen question got answered. With eyes downcast and hands clasped in front of her was his little sister, still in the clutches of their mad uncle.

But the fact that she lived wasn't the most shocking thing about the news conference. Parker's words were played and replayed on all the news channels. People recited them on the street. Everyone was talking about the revelation.

"My name is Theodore Parker, and I am here to tell you that, yes, shapeshifters do live among you. But despite what you might have seen, or think, you needn't fear. We're just like everybody else."

What a crock of shit.

"Our kind is, with a few exceptions that my company was trying to help, peaceful."

Whopper of a lie.

"We"—Parker drew Sue-Ellen close with a benevolent smile —"look forward to letting you learn about us." Ha. The only thing Parker was interested in learning was what it would take to control those making the laws.

As one of his inner cadre, Brandon knew what Parker was really after. He'd made his intentions quite clear. Being the hidden leader of the SHC wasn't good enough for him. He wanted more power. Wanted a spot in the limelight. So he shoved all of his kind out of the fucking closet into the public eye.

Madman! Despite Parker's announcement, on a live broadcast no less, with a trusted television news anchor, people couldn't forget the other videos. The ones showing their more feral side. Those clips of the battle at Bittech brought a tidal wave of problems.

Humanity felt threatened. Humans felt deceived.

The different became hunted. Laws scrambled to accommodate this unexpected development. Accusation began. Innocents died as neighbor turned on neighbor.

All of Brandon's kind, family and friends, they had to move underground, fight extra hard to appear normal. To appear *human.*

Not everyone could fake it. Brandon certainly couldn't, not with what Bittech did to him.

The world changed, yet Brandon truly didn't care what happened next. The fact that he lived, unchained and able to roam the world, didn't help him.

It didn't make him normal again. When people saw him, they saw the monster.

They screamed.

He got annoyed.

Eat them.

Too often he told his inner self—a now much colder, more cynical dark self—to calm the fuck down. No eating humans.

But they did tempt him, especially when they smelled of chocolate. He still had a sweet tooth.

As he crouched on a rooftop, a living gargoyle observing this new city, yet another place he couldn't blend in, he wondered why he even bothered to try.

Perhaps he should give up on finding answers or help for his monstrous dilemma. He should forget trying to regain normalcy and accept that this new look would stay with him forever. If he melted into the wilderness and lived off the land, maybe he could stop the yearning. Perhaps, in time, he'd forget what it meant to be a man.

A whisper of sound from behind him alerted him he shared the rooftop. He whirled and couldn't help but stare.

Willowy shaped, with long hair the color of moonlight and eyes even stranger than his own, a woman stood. She canted her head to the side, perusing him.

Of most interest, she didn't run. She didn't scream. Inhaling deeply, she tilted her head back, revealing the smooth column of her throat.

Kill her now before she calls for help.

No. He wouldn't kill her, even if all his senses screamed she meant danger. Dangerous how? All he could see was her fragile beauty—

The impact slammed him to the ground. The air oomphed out of him as her lithe figure landed atop him with more force and weight than expected. A hand, a strong hand tipped in opalescent claws, dug into his throat. Her eyes stared down at him, the orbs slitted and burning with green fire. Her almost pure-white hair lifted and danced around her head.

"What's this roaming my city? A male, both unmarked and unclaimed," she whispered, dipping down low. "I should take you right now."

Perhaps she should. A certain part of him certainly thought so, and it didn't help she squirmed atop him.

The fingers around his throat squeezed, yet no panic infused him. If he was meant to die, then so be it. He tired of hiding.

Her lips hovered devastatingly close, the heat of her breath warming his skin. "How did you come here? Tell me your name."

A name? The one he started the world with no longer seemed to fit. He was more than just a simple Brandon and, at the same time, less than the naïve man he used to be.

"My name is..." Ace? No, he wouldn't use Ace either. That was Andrew's rude misnomer. So what did that leave?

"I am no one, and I come from..." *Don't spread your taint to a town already devastated.* "Nowhere. Who are you? What are you?" Because she smelled like him, but...different.

"What do you mean, what am I?" Her brow crinkled. "I am the same thing you are." Her shoulders drew back, her head tilted imperially, and for a moment, shadowy wings glistened silver at her back. "We are dragon."

TO FIND OUT WHAT HAPPENS WITH ACE/BRANDON, CHECK OUT DRAGON POINT.

THE END

Printed in the USA
CPSIA information can be obtained
at www.ICGtesting.com
LVHW090326220824
788963LV00007B/113